Dawn Wind

Dawn Wind

Christina Savage

A DELL BOOK

Published by
Dell Publishing Co., Inc.
1 Dag Hammarskjold Plaza
New York, New York 10017

Printed in the United States of America

Dawn Wind

Prologue

Jennifer Blackheath danced naked in a forest of towering evergreens. Around her, tiny multihued butterflies darted, spun, and floated in tremulous circles like all the flowers of the earth come to life. A thousand, ten thousand diaphanous, powdered wings brushed lightly against her flesh. Entranced, she opened her eyes, laughed, and said, "Oh! Pretty!"

And then nothing.

Sewal Blackheath placed his wife's slim, fragile hand beneath the sheet and brushed the tips of his index and middle fingers across her eyelids. When he straightened, the black horsehair upholstery pricked through his white shirt. Face bland, he ran still calloused fingers through his iron-gray hair.

"Goddamn it, Jenny," he said, trying to divest himself of the unavoidable guilt stemming from his relief that her six months' dying had at last ended. He was angry with himself and with her and with himself all the more, and repeated, "Goddamn it, Jennifer. Goddamn it!" The words helped alleviate the terrible ache in his throat, but not by much. He told himself that Blackheath men were not given to crying.

Guilt. Enough of guilt, he admonished himself. Unable to bring his lips to her thin, pale ones, he leaned forward and lightly kissed her forehead. Seventeen years and three months earlier he had kissed her for the first time. This would be the last. That she had not yet reached her thirty-fifth birthday—Jennifer had been so full of life and laughter—was a sorrow Sewal held at arm's length.

It would be morning soon. Hands clumsy, Sewal pulled the comforter up to Jennifer's neck, pushed the straight-backed chair away from the bed, and left the room. In the hall the shutters on the ocean side of the house vibrated in the gusting, wailing northeast wind, a sound like the death rattle that had drowned whatever last words Jennifer might have spoken. At least she had smiled at the end. Perhaps the pressure of his hand around hers had managed to penetrate the laudanum-induced dream state in which she lay. Hand on the smooth walnut balustrade, he paused at the head of the stairs. The guest room in which he'd been sleeping during the last month of Jenny's illness lay to the right, but he could not face it alone. Slowly, mindful of the creaking boards, he made his way down the stairs. There, in the quiet, he would await the morning and the time he would have to tell the children.

The fire in the living room was blazing and the dull chunk of metal poker on heavy logs sounded above the wind's noise. Perplexed, for the hearth should have been cold hours ago, he entered and found his three children gathered about the fireplace. Michael, the eldest at fifteen, was busily rearranging the logs. Justin, a year and a half his junior, was offering unasked-for advice on how to position them in order to achieve maximum heat. Eve, the youngest at twelve, and wrapped in a shawl given her a Christmas ago by her mother, slept soundly.

Michael and Justin looked up silently as they became aware of their father's presence. Sewal walked slowly across the room, gathered Eve in his arms, and carried her to a couch. When he lay her down and pulled the shawl around her shoulders, she stirred, opened her eyes briefly, and frowned much the same way as her mother used to frown when her sleep was disturbed.

"She's dead," Michael said, his boyish voice tinged with adult sobriety.

"Yes," Sewal replied, turning to face him. Michael, big and gangly, his clothes, however well made ill-fitted his rapidly growing frame, sat cross-legged in front of the fire. He looked quite serious and not a little frightened. He's a man now, Sewal thought. Fifteen years made a man in any captain's log. "You boys should be in bed," he continued aloud.

Pale-faced, Justin stood, raised a hand to flutter long, sticklike fingers about his tight, bloodless lips. The skin on his face was drawn tightly over prominent cheekbones. His jaw was sharp and fiercely jutting. Only his eyes, widely spaced and deep brown as chestnuts, reflected the softness of his mother. His were stern, almost predatory, intense and unforgiving features that harked back to nine generations of puritanical New Englanders. Anger born of pain and anguish had drawn all traces of childishness from his face. His eyes, red-rimmed and pouched from lack of sleep, were fixed on Sewal with a burning stare. "Congratulations, Father. You even look appropriately distressed. Well done."

Mounting fury overpowered the heavy, frustrating sorrow in Sewal's heart. Without warning even to himself, his arm swung out and the flat of his hand cracked against Justin's face. The force of the blow sent the child spinning to the floor. "No son . . . No son of mine . . . may show such disrespect!" Consumed with rage, he stepped forward and towered, legs spread and fists clenched, over his son.

Justin did not move. Did not flinch. He lay sprawled, body propped on one elbow. His cheek was turning red where it had been struck, but he did not cry. His eyes glowed like coals dredged from a fire and his lips curled with contempt beyond his ability to express in words.

Sewal stepped backward and retreated from the look on Justin's face. He had struck his sons before, but as punishment only and without malice. He was mortified by what he had done, stung by his son's reaction. And now confused, embarrassed, and shamed. "Justin," he began, holding out his hand, "I . . . I'm sorry."

"So am I," Justin answered hollowly. As if inviting another blow, he rose and stood trembling in front of his father. When Sewal did not move, Justin stalked from the room and, sobbing at last, ran up the stairs. The slamming of the door to his room echoed like a gunshot in the night-lonely house.

Fascinated and perplexed, frightened by his brother's words and his father's rage, Michael had watched silently. "Father?" he said at last, startled by the sound of his own voice.

Sewal shook his head. "Justin is upset. We all are. Of course, what he said was inexcusable."

"He didn't really mean it," Michael said, his voice still shaky.

Sewal managed a smile, and squeezed his son's shoulder. "I look to you for help in this hour, son. Eve will have to be told. . . ." He trailed off.

"I know," Michael said bravely, afraid he would cry. "There's time enough, sir, when she wakes."

"Yes." Sewal nodded. "I suppose there is. We'll let her sleep where she is. You get some rest too. Tomorrow will not be a pleasant or easy day."

"I think I'd rather stay up, if you don't mind."

"As you wish. I will be outside on the bluff. I, ah, need a moment alone."

"Yes, sir. I understand."

Sewal gazed at him. Here was a son of whom one could be proud. He would stand in the face of adversity, as Blackheaths had for generations. "Keep watch over your sister, then," he said gruffly and, moved, left the room before his emotions showed.

Hanson Pole, the family butler, emerged from the side hall. His heavily jowled face, drawn and pale from the lack of sleep, appeared ghostly in the light of the candle he held. Master and servant stopped five paces apart. The look on Sewal's face told Pole all he needed to know. He had respected—loved, really, but he never would have presumed to use the word—Jennifer Blackheath, and her passing affected him deeply. This too he would never willingly show, though his sorrow was evident to those who knew him. "Would you care for—" He was forced to clear his throat. "—care for anything, sir?" he asked stiffly.

"No, thank you, Pole. Nothing for now," Sewal said. He checked the hall clock. The sun would rise in two hours and forty-eight minutes. He made himself concentrate. "We'll let her wait until daybreak. She deserves that much. Time enough to start then." He inhaled deeply, as if each word was an effort. "Breakfast will be . . . at the usual time."

"Of course, sir," Pole said in a subdued tone, and disappeared.

The foyer was chilly. Sewal walked to the hall tree by the door, pulled on a thick, black wool sweater, and stepped into his rubber boots. A heavy slicker, yellow and lined with black cracks from years of hard use, followed. A sou'wester, the heavy waterproof hat with a flap in back to keep the water from his neck, completed his preparations against the cold, wet night. Hand on the doorknob, he paused, then turned and clumped back up the hallway to stand in the living room door. There he watched Michael squatting in front of the fireplace and staring into the flames. "You're a brave one, Michael," he said softly. "Courage. That's a rare quality in a man."

One half of his face in light, the other obscured by shadow, Michael looked at Sewal. "What will I do, Father?"

"You are the eldest son of a Blackheath. You'll do what needs to be done, as always," Sewal answered. Coat flapping, he headed for the front door.

The wind rushed into the foyer with the velocity of a locomotive. Once outside, Sewal automatically leaned into the stiff gusts that buffeted him from every side. A lubber would have stayed indoors, but Sewal Blackheath had ridden out tougher storms, first on board his father's whalers, and later when his father died and it was his turn to take over the family shipyards, in the unforgiving world of business. This storm would not dissuade him as he walked the fifty yards to the tip of the peninsula. A hundred feet below, gray-black breakers tipped with flat sheets of spindrift shattered on the rocks and exploded into the air in mighty plumes.

Dawn soon, Sewal muttered to himself. And with it, this day, high tide. The faces of his children passed before him. Eve was already as unfathomable as a full-grown woman. He could hardly hope to give her the advice and companionship her mother would have. Still, Eve would blossom and grow. By then I'll have her married, Sewal thought, and she'll be her husband's problem, as every girl must.

Justin appeared as a stranger. The boy was hurt and angry, and his face twisted all too often with youthful scorn. Sewal knew he should have been closer to his second born, but what was he to do? The lad had his own feelings. Only with time, and when he saw the world from a different perspective, would he understand how his father felt and why he acted as he had. Perhaps they would become friends then.

And Michael. Now there was a fine young man! A lad of whom a father could be proud and cherish. Upon this rock I shall build my—

"All right, Jenny. Our. Grant me this one sacriligious play on words."

But Jennifer Morgana Blackheath would grant nothing more, for she was lost in the timeless sleep of death. Sewal stood alone in the midst of the buffeting storm as it raged over the table-flat promontory that had been called Dawn Wind since the first Blackheath sailed into the bay below. Even on quiet summer days, when the sun hung heavily over the bright green treetops, soft breezes from the Atlantic coiled and curled about the wood-and-granite house erected almost a hundred years earlier. As he edged nearer the precipitous drop at the far eastern end of the jutting rock, Sewal Blackheath's back stiffened. He clenched his fists and dug them deeper into his pockets.

"Dawn Wind," he said. The dawn of a life without Jenny. A wind to bear away a soul. His mind strove to remember a passage she would have liked, for Jennifer had been a God-fearing woman as well as robust and desirable. If only he could remember she would be pleased. The wind made his eyes water, or so he told himself. His heart was weary, and so weighted he could scarcely move.

> The wind goeth toward the South and turneth about unto the North; it whirleth about continually, and the wind returneth again according to his circuits. All the rivers run into the sea; yet the sea is not full; unto the place from whence the rivers run, thither they return again.

The words from Ecclesiastes came haltingly at first, then with the strength of those who have known sorrow and taken heart and gone on to the next day. He spoke them, though the wind swept them away and scattered them over the cold and rain-drenched land where only the storm—and maybe Jenny—might hear.

Part I

December 1859

Chapter 1

"Are you ready, ladies and gentlemen? Please. Please!" J. Abner Frendlam, photographer, poised on the tips of his toes, perused the grouping he had arranged. His face was intent and he chewed violently on his right moustache, a habit that caused it perpetually to hang down, in contrast to his left, which swooped up with waxen splendor. "No, no, no," he grumbled, and ducked under the cloth draped over the rear of the camera. Immediately, his subjects shifted, trying to find more comfortable stances.

"No, no. Please!" came a muffled cry from under the cloth. Frendlam's head popped out and he stalked to the young lady seated by her fiancé. One hand darted into his apron pocket and emerged with a small cake of soap. The young lady jerked away nervously as he reached for her. J. Abner smiled reassuringly and pointed to her head. "Your jewelry sparkles. The sparkle will ruin the picture."

"But soap, sir? On my emeralds?"

"I assure you, madam, the soap is entirely harmless."

This was Rosamond's third portrait of the evening, and her patience was wearing thin. The first had been of both families in a group. The second of her and Michael with Admiral and Mrs. Cabell. This one was of her and Michael with Sewal, Justin, and Eve Blackheath. There was one yet to come: Michael and her together alone, officially enfianced. She smiled thinly. "Well, go ahead, Mr. Frendlam."

"Thank you, Miss Cabell." J. Abner was not fooled for a second. Five years as a photographer in Washington's social jungle had taught him to recognize venom when he heard it. The glare eliminated, he stepped back to check. Rosamond Cabell was beautiful, no doubt about that. Her long, soft, dark auburn hair was gathered in a chignon wrapped about with silver and emeralds and then tucked at the nape of her neck. Her high cheekbones complemented a long neck of classical proportions. Her nose was a little on the skimpy side, but its lines were good—straight and sharp, yet not harsh at all. Most remarkable were her eyes. Widely spaced, they were round with exquisitely shaped long lashes. As for their color—it was a shame the camera could not capture the uncommon dark violet that, in certain light, verged almost on green. He might have painted those eyes twenty years earlier, back when a man might still make a living with a brush and palette. He would have known what to do after each session too, for Rosamond Cabell's eyes were more than just dark violet: they were a smoldering invitation. J. Abner walked rapidly back to his camera, turned, and dove under the black cloth. The offending sparkle was gone. They could proceed.

"Very good, ladies and gentlemen. Just one moment, please, and we will begin." He opened his box, took out the covered plate prepared only moments earlier, and plunged it into the slot in the top of the camera. He checked the intensity of the light falling on the grouping and pulled out his watch. Watch in one hand, he gripped the knob on the shield plate, and as the minute hand reached the top of the dial, said, "Go!" and pulled out the shield.

The seconds ticked away against frozen smiles that would be caught and held for years. Michael in his midshipman's uniform, bright with shined brass, Rosamond at his side. Sewal stiffly formal, like a surprised Moses. A strangely solemn Justin, and an Eve so fragile she looked as if she might shatter. For one observer, who had eyes only for Eve, the effect was unnerving.

At the age of twenty-one, Clifford Sarandon was a young man who was destined to rise. Born and raised in opulence in King Louis Philippe's France, he had emigrated to America when he was seven years old with his father and mother, prior to the February Revolution. Neither handsome nor ugly, but a plain, fair-skinned, soft individual bordering on pudginess, his most substantive attribute, according to pattering parlor chatter, was his family's wealth.

Sarandon was, indeed, a name to be reckoned with. Hébert, his father, was a silver-haired, honorable gentleman with a survivor's instincts, the shrewd smile of a fox, and a European knack for intrigue. Carefully arranging for his money to precede him, he had prudently slipped out of Paris late one January evening in 1848 and, two months later, took up in America with barely a pause. Since that time he had established himself as a leading merchant in New York City. And because money and politics and society were keys to power in New York, as they had been in Paris, and because the Sarandons counted among their friends the most affluent and influential families of the day, the family fortune had continued to increase. Hébert and his wife Angelique, a lady of refined tastes and impeccable breeding, as well as the daughter of a count, took all this for granted with the practiced ease of the nobility.

As did Clifford. He carried elegance easily, but without seeming to be elegant. Grandiose gestures bored him, as did overt displays of wealth or power. He understood that his life was an extended education which would lead to the assumption of his father's place when that unhappy time should come.

Clifford and Eve had met almost exactly a year earlier, at a New Year's Eve ball. He had been twenty then, and a senior at Harvard. She was nineteen and had accompanied Sewal to New York on a business trip. After being introduced by a mutual friend, Clifford and Eve had spent virtually the entire evening together, dancing and talking and eating and strolling through the gardens. When the party ended, Clifford drove Eve through ice-glistening New York streets to the Park Avenue Hotel where she and Sewal were staying. Not until a half hour later, sitting in the lonely splendor of the Sarandon carriage as it approached the landscaped drive to his father's Gramercy Park house, did Clifford realize that he had fallen hopelessly, irrevocably, and head over heels in love. He spent the night on the conservatory balcony, and the next day was as fresh as if he had slept around the clock.

From that evening Clifford's life changed drastically. Although he continued his studies at Harvard, graduated magna cum laude, and entered his father's business, the pursuit of Eve was his sole concern. He alternated between euphoria and utter disenchantment. Eve liked Clifford and enjoyed being with him, but did not return his love. Dawn Wind was almost three hundred miles from New York, and he did not see her for weeks at a time. He wrote and Eve answered, but always in light, cool tones that often made him wish she were more like other girls, so he might simply have her and be done with it. Invariably, the next moment found him cursing his baser instincts, for he knew full well that he loved her most because she didn't fawn over him as other girls did. Most galling was his parents' attitude. The Sarandons looked upon Sewal Blackheath as little more than a craftsman, and suggested gently but insistently that a match between such mixed stations could not possibly prove successful. Hébert, in private, was more blunt. Sewal Blackheath and his family had been making wooden ships for generations, and wooden ships were rapidly becoming obsolete. Contracts he could have won easily were going to other yards because Blackheath was a hide-bound traditionalist who, as had become widely known in shipping circles, was stuck in the past. For whatever the reason, he refused to convert his yards to the construction of iron ships. Consequently, his trips to New York were those of a man grasping at straws; the Blackheath Shipyards were in a state of disarray, if not on the brink of foundering. He suggested that the daughter was acting on the father's instructions, and that her coolness was a clever ruse to insinuate herself into the Sarandon family. The very idea, though he did not believe it for a second, drove Clifford to distraction.

Michael and Rosamond's engagement party had been a godsend. Clifford had known a month in advance that he and his parents would be in Washington for Christmas and had begun planning early. An invitation to the Cabell's Christmas Eve ball had been easy to arrange. Convincing his father and mother that they should go had been more difficult, but constant badgering—the fact that Senator Seward would also be there helped immeasurably—had finally won the day. From what he had seen, his plan was working. At least his father hadn't begun to twirl his watch, invariably a sign that he was ready to leave. Only one hurdle remained, and that was Eve herself.

Troubled, Clifford slipped out of the room and headed for the wine table. He'd already had two glasses of champagne but poured himself a third and withdrew to one side, only to find himself looking at Eve again, this time in a mirror. There was no escape, it seemed. Nor did he seek escape, really. She was so beautiful. Golden hair was piled high on her head and crowned with a simple lace caplike affair. In her face was the best of the country his parents had adopted. Her eyes, alive with sparkling Yankee curiosity and intelligence, were the purest, lightest translucent blue. Her face was softer, more like her mother's, if the portraits he had seen could be believed. Soft lines predominated there, lines soft as a landscape shimmering in the heat. Her shoulders were the purest white, heightened by a touch of shadow on either side of the base of her neck. How he wished he could kiss her there!

"She is beautiful, isn't she?"

Clifford started, looking over his shoulder. Senator William Seward, a mutual friend of his father and Admiral Cabell, stood behind him. "Yes. She is," Clifford agreed.

"Your mother tells me you are enamored of her."

"That too," the young man said, his face reddening.

"Can't say I blame you. Sorry we haven't had a chance to talk recently. Hébert says you're going to help manage Morton Aston's campaign."

"I hope so. He's promised me a job as legislative assistant if he wins," Clifford said.

William Seward, one of the most powerful and prestigious men in the United States government, laughed. "Start at the bottom, eh? Good for you. You an Abolitionist?"

"I prefer to think of myself as a moderate, sir."

"Follow the Little Giant, eh?"

"No offense meant, sir, but Senator Douglas *does* seem—"

"I'll give you a free lesson, Clifford. Never apologize, not even to a ranking senator." Seward clapped the young Sarandon on the shoulder. "Your opinion is as good as any man's. If you agree with the Judge, say so. I'll not hold it against you. Stephen Douglas is a feisty gamecock. We may not think alike on all matters, but I respect him."

"Yes, sir. I'll remember that."

"Time!" J. Abner called from the next room. A chorus of relief followed.

"You'd better see to her," the Senator said, taking Clifford by the elbow and leading him toward the door. "Women are a great deal like constituents. You must give them your full attention or you'll lose them."

"Yes, sir. Thank you."

All five were moving about, stretching out the kinks. J. Abner was busy taking the plate out of the camera and hurrying to the temporary darkroom he'd set up in the pantry. "Ah, Mr. Sarandon. I trust you're enjoying yourself?" Clifford's hostess asked, intercepting him in the doorway.

Clifford forced himself to smile as he turned to her. Mrs. Cabell's voice was high and irritating, the more so because he was anxious to be with Eve. "But of course, Mrs. Cabell. You have a lovely place here. I swear, madam, you Washingtonians are going to put New York to shame."

Cornelia Cabell was inordinately pleased. "Mr. Sarandon! You *will* make a politician!" She went on but Clifford, wishing people would stop talking about politics, focused his attention on Eve, who was standing with her father.

"Damned infernal machines, if you ask me," Sewal said, stepping into the center of the room. "Unnatural."

Eve laughed. "You're such an old fogey, Father. Wait until you see how fine you look."

"I've seen how fine I look. Stiff as a board. Like I was laid out for my own funeral."

"Fie, Mr. Blackheath!" Mrs. Cabell exclaimed with a nervous titter. "Such talk."

"The truth, madam, the truth." Sewal chewed on the inside of his lip. Cornelia Cabell called to mind everything he despised in a woman. If her husband weren't due to rise to the top of the Department of the Navy, he'd have nothing to do with her; certainly, he would never allow his son to marry her daughter. How a man like Dayton Cabell managed to get along with her at all was a mystery. "Admiral? You were going to show me a drawing of a ship you had in mind, I believe."

"Ah, yes," Dayton Cabell laughed. "If we have time before dinner, dear?"

"You have a little less than an hour," Cornelia answered. "Dinner will be served at nine."

The older man moved toward the library. Eve edged toward the front parlor to be alone for a moment, and stood in silence in front of the fireplace.

"You are pensive."

Clifford's voice broke through the trance Eve had fallen into. She smiled wanly. "Just enjoying the fire, really," she said, turning back to the flames.

Clifford stood at her side. "You're quite impossible, you know," he said at last, with a chuckle.

"I never claimed to be perfect," Eve said, smiling.

"There was no need to, for I have thought of you as being so since the night we met." He took her hand and turned her toward him. "Eve, I—"

"Clifford, please."

"No. You've hardly spoken to me all evening. We have known

each other for nearly a year. In that time, my love for you has grown until—"

"I don't wish to hurt you, Clifford. You have been a dear friend, and when not smitten with my 'perfection,' a delightful companion."

"Then marry me. The companionship can become permanent as well as delightful."

"You flatter me, sir, but no."

The words were spoken gently, but to Clifford's ear crackled as sharply as the fire before them. In the instant of Eve's "no," he felt he hung suspended like a photograph miraculously brought to three dimensions. There were the rosewood chairs upholstered in thick, scarlet tapestry. There the book-lined walls, which soaked up light and let it out again in occasional flashes of gold-leaf lettering, empty cryptic messages. There the pile of glass-covered wax fruit set on a pedestal. And there too, Clifford Sarandon, stiffly erect, a pained smile on his face.

"Oh, dear. I hope I'm not interrupting."

Clifford released Eve's hand and turned to see Rosamond Cabell. "You aren't," he said. Feeling like an actor in the wrong scenario, he crossed the room and stepped past the admiral's daughter. "At least not anything that won't be resumed at a later date."

"Oh, dear," Rosamond said as Clifford exited. "I *did* intrude. I hope you will forgive me, sister."

Eve bridled at the familiarity. Rosamond Cabell was not her sister and never would be. "There is nothing to forgive," she replied graciously. "Clifford and I were merely chatting."

"Of course." Rosamond laughed easily and moved to join Eve in front of the fire. "He is a fine catch," she said conspiratorially. "Why, Clifford Sarandon would make a wonderful husband. I can't think of a better family. Will you have a glass of champagne? No? May I? You really ought to accept his proposal."

"You seem to have a great deal of knowledge about my private affairs," Eve said icily.

"Not at all, my dear," Rosamond disagreed with an ingratiating smile. "Only what Michael has told me, and that was very little. But I do think it a shame that you are so blithely immune to a man of Clifford Sarandon's wealth and social standing."

"I find it particularly unsettling you do not mention love," Eve snapped.

"Oh, but love can come later, Eve," Rosamond said, as if talking to a child.

"From which, I assume you are marrying Michael for his wealth and social standing."

Rosamond glared momentarily at Eve, as quickly glanced down at her champagne glass. Her eyes were hidden, making it impossible to tell her true thoughts. "I didn't say that," she whispered. "I love Michael first and foremost."

Eve might have believed that had she not already made up her mind to dislike Rosamond. "Then you are the exception to your own rule," she continued sarcastically. "How fortunate for Michael."

Rosamond's features froze as she spun about. Her skirt flared, then settled back down. The look of sweetness and innocence was completely gone. Her mouth opened and closed. At last, unable to invent a suitable retort, she swirled out of the room.

Eve sighed wearily. What was it that so disturbed her about Rosamond? Was she being jealous? Was she being overprotective, butting in where she shouldn't? She and Michael had always been close. Perhaps she should give Rosamond a chance. After all, they *would* soon be sisters, of a sort. And then she realized: That was precisely what did bother her.

"I'll sell my ships to whomever I damned well please, and be happy for the sale." Sewal's voice filled the library, where the conversation had taken a turn from the design of a specific ship to the nature of the shipping business in general.

"Even to inimicable Southern concerns?" Lieutenant Commander Kerstine, one of the Cabells' guests, shot back.

"Inimicable?" Sewal Blackheath's chest swelled and his scalp reddened. Ever since the bottom had dropped out of the California grain market and the demand for new ships had plummeted in fifty-seven, and with the ever-increasing, if misguided, popularity of iron ships, he'd been fighting to keep his head above water. He would have sold to the devil himself if it meant keeping the shipyard solvent. "I don't know the meaning of inimicable, sir. I know dollars. Hard cash." At his side, Hébert Sarandon nodded in agreement.

"Then I insist, sir, that you and others like you tread a dangerous path," Kerstine said. "One day those same goods, whether tools, food, or ships, may well be used to destroy the Union."

"That is unadulterated nonsense, young man, not to speak of the fact that you are impugning my name."

"Mr. Blackheath." Admiral Cabell lay a restraining hand on the Mainelander's arm. "It's John's job to prognosticate."

"It's not his job to be a damned fool," Sewal trumpeted. "I'm supporting a hundred men on my payroll. That's more than five hundred mouths to feed and backs to clothe. How do you think that happens, Mr. Kerstine? By default? No. By my getting orders however, whenever, and wherever I can."

"I understand that, Mr. Blackheath," Kerstine said, trying to be reasonable. "But that's not the point. I'm talking about a much larger picture, and many more souls than five hundred." He turned to the dour-faced Senator Seward. "In all candor, Senator, and never to be repeated, by me at least, are you completely sanguine about the future of the Union?"

A pained look crossed Seward's face. "I don't know," he finally answered. "I would like to say, 'Yes,' but the slave states are being very difficult these days, and there is talk . . ." He shrugged. "The danger *is* great, I admit."

"Which proves exactly nothing," Sewal said doggedly.

"On the contrary, sir. It proves my point. If an Abolitionist President is elected, your ships could well become enemy ships."

"To which end you suggest I go out of business?" Sewal asked pointedly. He turned to Hébert. "What about it Mr. Sarandon? What would *you* do?"

Hébert found himself more and more impressed with Blackheath's bluntness, and beginning to believe that Clifford's assurances that the man couldn't care less about the Sarandons' money just might be true. If the daughter were anything at all like the father—and every indication he'd had that night showed she was—a match between the two families might not be as onerous as he had feared. "I speak for commerce, Mr. Kerstine," he replied bluntly. "Without commerce the whole laboriously constructed system disintegrates. Indeed, you may sit in your office for months on end and postulate a half a hundred dire events, all of which are possible. Are businessmen then to plan their affairs accordingly? It is *possible* that New York will burn down tomorrow. Should we then all move out today? No, sir. If the world heeded every pessimistic prognostication, we should be paralyzed."

"Hear, hear!" Sewal said, raising his glass.

The door behind them opened and the Cabells' butler stepped into the room. "Dinner is served, gentlemen."

No one paid him the slightest bit of attention. Kerstine's face was turning red. "You simplify to the absurd, sir."

"Simplify? You're damned right. Because what could be *more* simple?" Sewal asked, his temper rising.

The butler tapped the admiral on the arm, and whispered in his ear.

"Nothing is *that* simple," Kerstine argued heatedly. "I am suggesting that because of certain complications in these matters, there are ramifications you haven't considered."

"Gentlemen, gentlemen!" the admiral broke in. "I'm told that dinner is served and that the ladies are waiting."

Cigars were left in ashtrays, drinks set on tables. "Bunch of poppycock!" Sewal grumbled to Senator Seward as they started out of the library together, but loud enough for everyone to hear.

"Please, gentlemen," Cabell interrupted, steering them toward the dining room. "The Union is not yet dissolved. And, if Senator Seward does become our next President, as I assume we all agree he shall, I have no doubt all our fears shall come to nought."

"Another prognostication, Admiral?" the Senator asked with a laugh that was quickly taken up by the others.

"Not at all." Cabell led the way into the dining room where the ladies, Michael, Justin, and Clifford waited. "My function is merely to see that you are all fed. My dear?" He winked reassuringly at Mrs. Cabell, who had heard the men's voices raised in anger, and looked alarmed. "I take it we may be seated? Let me see. Sewal, you are at Mrs. Cabell's right, of course. Eve, you're up here beside me. The rest will find their names . . ."

Gold-embossed vellum place cards at each setting determined the seating order. Everyone talked at once as, amid good-natured confusion, they found their places. The servants along the side of the room waited for the gentlemen to help the ladies, then moved forward to seat the gentlemen before pouring the first wine.

"Ladies and gentlemen!" The buzz of conversation ceased. All eyes turned toward the head of the table and Admiral Cabell. "Mrs. Cabell and I are pleased and honored to welcome you to share a most felicitous moment." He glanced at Rosamond, who smiled and demurely lowered her eyes.

"By now you have all met Michael Blackheath. The Blackheath

name is one long honored in our country's annals for its moral uprightness and the fine ships that bear it. Michael himself, firstborn of the tenth generation of American Blackheaths, and the repository of the traditions of excellence established by the preceding nine generations, is worthy of the name. I have spoken to him at length on various occasions and find him a young man of intelligence, breeding, and perspicacity. He will graduate from the United States Naval Academy in Annapolis next June and is destined, I believe, to rise to great heights in the service of his country."

He paused, looked around the table. A smile grew on his face. "Mrs. Cabell and I, therefore, are proud to formally announce the engagement of our daughter, Rosamond Elizabeth Cabell, to Michael Alexander Blackheath."

Rosamond beamed. Michael's face reddened as warmhearted applause filled the room. Toast followed toast, and Eve, no matter what her inner feelings, drank to the health of the newly betrothed. No sooner had the last toast been drunk than a procession of servants filed into the dining room. First came the Christmas turkey, a huge bird, brown as a nut on the outside and stuffed with wild rice, chestnuts, and spicy sausage. A ham as large as the turkey followed, accompanied by a dozen side dishes of creamed onions, potatoes, candied carrots, bowls of cranberry sauce, and more. Once again the admiral rose, this time to offer thanks. "Dear Heavenly Father . . ."

His voice droned on. Head lowered, Eve peeked across the table. Resplendent in his uniform, Michael sat stiffly. His head was bowed, but she could still see how handsome he was. At his side Rosamond sat quietly, her face, as earlier, unseen. Michael seemed happy enough, she admitted, and Rosamond sincere enough. Perhaps, Eve thought, she was indeed merely playing the part of the jealous sister. Was she judging Rosamond too harshly? "Lord," Eve silently prayed, "help me to be charitable, for if I am not aware of my own motives, how can I be certain of Rosamond's? Bless my brother, Michael, and—"

"—In the name of our Lord and Savior, Jesus Christ, amen," the Admiral finished, and with a flourish, began to carve the bird.

Margaret Benchmen was near-sighted, and a giggler. Justin snared a new cup of punch and retreated to the mantel while the music droned on. At another time, perhaps, he would have enjoyed the quartet, but in this place and at this time, the lively polkas and waltzes set his teeth on edge. His father's presence didn't help. Michael, his uniform beginning to look a little wilted and a distracted smile glued on his face, was steering Margaret back toward the fireplace. Justin pretended not to notice. Trying to look as if he'd suddenly remembered something important, he angled across the dance floor, out the door, and into the front parlor.

"Another fugitive?"

Justin turned to see Clifford Sarandon. "Oh. It's you. Thank God. I don't think I could have taken another polite word."

Sarandon laughed. "A matter of training. You get used to it."

"I doubt that."

"Inured, then. Calloused. With practice, you don't hear a word they're saying."

Justin winced. "I hope I don't have to practice that much. What are you drinking?"

"The Widow Clicquot, I believe. The punch is too sweet. Care for a glass?" Clifford turned and poured without waiting for an answer. Justin was a year his junior, yet acted as if he were much older. Serious, almost studious, he had a cold feeling about him sometimes that, when he thought about it, Eve too was capable of displaying. In addition, an air of detachment seemed to emanate from Justin, as though, unconnected to the world about him, he hovered over it and occasionally glanced down to see how the rest of humanity was faring. "Here you go. The perfect anaesthesia. So how is Bowdoin?"

"Worse, I think."

"I told you you should switch to Harvard." Clifford eased into a chair. He and Justin had met the summer before during one of Clifford's visits to Dawn Wind.

"Is there a difference? Justin asked. "I'm tired of drinking and partying, and can't imagine how staying another year could benefit me. You know that blank, staring look in the eyes of statues? That's the way I'm beginning to feel. Father, of course, doesn't understand that kind of talk."

Clifford nodded in sympathy. "Fathers seldom do. Still dabbling with photography?"

Justin laughed. "Is there anything else? I take it Eve has told you about my cameras."

"I'm afraid Eve doesn't tell me very much at all," Clifford sighed. "Your sister—" A pained look on his face, he let the sentence dangle unfinished.

The strains of a waltz floated into the parlor from the conservatory. Justin shifted uncomfortably from foot to foot as he realized for the first time that Eve had been less than honest with him. "Eve said . . . you were friends," he finally said, his wording sounding inept. "But it's more than that, isn't it?"

"Yes." Clifford smiled awkwardly. "I trust that doesn't offend you."

"Offend me?" Justin asked. "Not at all. My God, if you want to marry Eve, that's *your* problem. I'll even help you. All I have to do is tell her I think you're a cad and she'll fly to your arms. If *that* doesn't work—"

"There you are, you naughty boys!" Justin spilled his champagne. "It's midnight," their hostess said. "Christmas is almost here, and you're hiding away. Come along, now, quickly." Without waiting, Cornelia Cabell swept from the parlor.

Clifford rose wearily. "Well. Our hostess calls."

"Yes. Doesn't she." Justin put down his glass, looked around furtively and wiped the champagne he'd spilled on his hand on the edge of the tablecloth. "If Christmas is here, can peace be far behind?"

"Not more than an hour, I'd say," Clifford said dryly. "At which time, our carriages will be here." He bowed deferentially. "After you, my good sir. And remember to be of good cheer. Wouldn't want to disappoint our hostess and dampen everyone's spirits, don't you know."

In the parlor a waltz was in progress. Hébert and Angelique Sarandon, the Kerstines, and Michael and Rosamond were dancing. Michael's face was flushed from alcohol and exertion. The press of Rosamond's bosom against his chest, the warm sweet smell of her, the spinning candles overhead, and the promise of summer to come left him lightheaded. Rosamond's eyes glittered brightly. She was his, a perfect mate for the future owner of Dawn Wind, a virginal beauty no one else would ever own. Could she read his thoughts? Her gaze lowered, but her hand pressed more tightly against the back of his neck.

Barely audible over the music, the grandfather clock started chiming the hour. Cornelia Cabell appeared in the doorway and signaled to the musicians, who tacked a hurried ending onto the waltz. In the silence the final three bass gongs, chased by a soprano "Merry Christmas" from Mrs. Cabell, echoed through the house. Everyone had been warned to expect a surprise. As the quartet began a rousing version of "Deck the Halls," the dancers hurried from the floor and Cabell's servants wheeled in a half-size sleigh filled with gaily wrapped gifts. Hébert Sarandon led the applause. Cornelia, not yet finished, gestured again, and two more servants entered, carrying a table. Immediately, the air was filled with the cinnamon apple aroma of steaming wassail.

Sewal Blackheath held back as the other guests surrounded the sleigh and wassail bowl. "A perfect match," he mused, wishing Jennifer were there to share it all. She would be so proud of Michael. Proud and happy. He watched Eve, standing at the edge of the ring of guests waiting for their gifts. Her face was so like Jenny's—smiling yet private, unwilling to display her emotions. Michael's marriage was imminent. Eve's, to judge from the way young Sarandon had been mooning about her all evening, might not be too far in the future. The Sarandons were a better family than he'd hoped to be able to find for her, but not at all a bad idea now that he'd met them. In fact, young Sarandon was perfect, if Eve would have him. She was like Jenny that way too. He smiled, remembering how he used to tease her. Stubborn Jenny, he'd say. She'd laugh then, and toss her head. . . . Sternly, Sewal chided himself for remembering too much, and made his way through the tangle of chairs toward Eve as the quartet launched into a lilting "We Wish You a Merry Christmas."

Eve watched her father approach.

"Merry Christmas, Eve," he said, and kissed her hand.

Eve looked over the festive crowd gathered around the gift-filled sleigh, at the decorations crisscrossing the ceiling dangerously close to the candle-lit chandeliers, at Rosamond and Michael, arm in arm, laughing and smiling and singing, the very picture of love. Even Justin, booming out the harmony, looked as though he was having fun. Suddenly, the doubts and cares that had oppressed her all evening disappeared. Eve slipped her arm through her father's and hugged him, then raised herself on tiptoe and kissed him on the cheek. "To you too, Father," she said, kissing him again. "And a very happy New Year."

Chapter 2

His eyes were slate-gray, fathomless, like a morning mist that yields only vague, visionary glimpses of distance. At thirty years of age he had a long, angular face that was creased with cheek lines too deep to pass for dimples. Thick black hair was brushed back from his forehead in waves. Heavy dark eyebrows arched high over eyes often given to laughter but now somber and guarded. His chin was narrow and clean cut. His lips were even and usually smiled as he spoke in the soft, lilting Virginian accent of a gentleman. His nose was marred by a peculiar crook that gave his face a rugged though not unpleasant quality. Many women found him handsome. A few had told him so. His name was Lion McKenna.

McKenna did not want to be in New York City; he did not like the abnormally cold, wet, early June weather. There had been one hour of sunshine during his week in the city, and he had missed it because Duquesne, in his insatiable drive to sign contracts for more ships, had him closeted in yet another of what seemed to be a ceaseless string of meetings. Given his choice he would have returned to Virginia on the first train he could find, or on foot if need be. And if the South seceded en masse and prematurely the next day, so be it. The break they had all worked so hard for would be an improvement over Duquesne and his never-ending, sordid schemes, the most sordid of which involved Le Jacques' gambling parlor and the recently graduated Past-Midshipman Lion had been following since late that afternoon.

"Two," the Past-Midshipman said now, and Lion studied him as Michael Alexander Blackheath slid his discards across the green felt tabletop and took a pair from the dealer. He was looking for a third queen and missed, instead drew a pair of tens that fit, incredibly, with the ten he'd held in order not to give away the fact that all he had was a pair. The man to his left took two cards, the next player one. The fourth folded immediately and the dealer stayed pat and bet low, just to build the pot.

"Yours and a double eagle more," Michael said, placing a pair of coins in the center of the table. In the last hour he'd bluffed four times. He hoped everyone remembered and would play him for the bluff again, because the full house was the best hand he'd had since he'd joined the game. He turned to the man at his left, a Southerner with whom he'd struck up a conversation at the roulette table shortly after he arrived. "That's to you, Lion."

Lion glanced at his cards, patted them into a neat rectangle, and tossed them alongside the deck across the table. " 'Fraid not," he drawled. "Too rich for poor cards."

"I hadn't taken you for a cautious man," Michael laughed.

Lion shrugged and leaned back in his chair without comment.

Jaspar Starr, across the table from Michael, drummed stubby, sausage-shaped fingers on the tabletop. The room was warm, but he refused to acknowledge the heat or the trickle of sweat that ran down from his left armpit. He lay his cards face down and picked up a handful of coins. The boy across the table was acting a little too cocky. Starr knew he'd bluffed two hands that he'd lost, suspected he'd done the same with two or maybe three that he'd won. If the boy was going to bluff again, the time seemed right. Starr reached out, dropped two coins into the pot to match the prior bets, and added five more twenty-dollar double eagles. "And a hundred dollars more," he growled.

Interest around the table brightened at the prospect of a big hand. The dealer squinted. One hundred and twenty dollars to him. He decided to let the boy and the drayman butt heads alone. "Out," he said, and placed his cards on top of Lion's.

Michael tried to remain placid, wishing the other three hadn't dropped so quickly. Taking his time, he flipped open a sleek gold case and chose a slim cigar which he clipped and placed between his teeth. His broad shoulders bunched beneath his new uniform and he tried to flex the tightness out, hoping the nearly imperceptible movement would convince Starr he was nervous. "A hundred to me, eh?" He fingered his coins, picked up two-hundred-dollars worth, then hesitating, dropped a hundred and sixty into the pot. "And sixty more," he said, his voice brittle with excitement.

Starr decided he was bluffing. "Your sixty and another hundred," he said without hesitation.

Michael counted his opponent's money. "And another two hundred and twenty-five," he added quietly.

The game took on a new dimension. Everyone watching had been convinced, with Starr, that Michael was bluffing. No longer were they so sure. Starr picked up his cards and peeked at them. Including the ante, he had almost three hundred invested. Two hundred and twenty-five was all he had left. If he called and lost that would be it for the night. Suddenly, his hand didn't look so impressive. He stared at the boy across the table. A rich kid, he could tell, in a fancy new uniform his father had bought him. Didn't know what it meant to work and build a business. The hell with him. Nobody bluffed a Starr out of anything. Face reddening with anger, he shoved the last of his coins to the center of the table. "I call, damn you!" he said, at the same time fanning his cards for everyone to see. "I've a full house."

Michael saw the aces first and almost fainted. But there were only two of them, accompanying three nines. "Not enough, Mr. Starr," he said carefully, afraid he may have pushed the older man too far. Keeping his eye on Starr, he turned over his cards. "Tens full. I win."

Starr slammed his fist on the table and rose, knocking over his chair. "Damn you!" he shouted. "Damn you for an insolent, reeking pup of a—"

"That will be all, Mr. Starr," a quiet voice interrupted. A man stood at either side of him. The burly one to his left took him by the elbow while the dapper owner of Le Jacques' talked to him. "You know I run a quiet place. You're welcome to come again. Another night."

No one moved. Finally, Starr shook off the bouncer's hand and stalked out past the onlookers. Relieved, Michael watched as the dealer counted out the house's ten percent and pushed his winnings to him. The crowd stirred, drifted away to other tables. The action was over, soon forgotten in amiable chatter, refilled glasses, and newly lit cigars.

Lion McKenna watched the new hand being dealt. He had seen enough of Michael Blackheath to tell him everything he needed to know. Duquesne, damn him, had been right as usual. Blackheath ran a good bluff and was middling strong when he had a good hand. His strength came not from himself, though, but from the money on the table. There was a difference. Lion had seen his type before. The son of a strong and domineering father, he was expected to mirror that father's strengths without ever having to face a challenge, and had probably never had to fight for anything he wanted. The card game had shown it all. Especially the big hand with the drayman. Michael was a nervous and conciliatory—and yet secretly gloating—winner, a man who would play foolishly if he were a few hundred dollars up. Had he lost, Lion was sure, he would have been petulant and sulky, perhaps even more virulent than Starr had been.

Lion looked at his cards, glanced around the table. The new player was a sharp who had been waiting for someone just like Michael since early in the evening. Lion shook his head. Michael Blackheath was long past recognizing his own weaknesses and almost made himself a target. It was a shame, really. A pity. No one should be that easily deceived, by himself or anyone else.

"Two dollars to the third hand," the dealer prompted.

Lion smiled wryly. " 'Fraid I've gone stale, gentlemen," he said, tossing in his cards. "You'll excuse me?"

A new player took his place as Lion left the table. Curious, he mingled with the crowd, followed the flow, and spent his time listening. Most of what he heard was innocuous talk of business and women, but some conversations were chilling and intensified his and the Coalition's fears that New York City's politically murky mixture of pro- and anti-South sentiments would ultimately solidify against the South. He wished every planter and landowner south of Maryland could hear how intent the North was on driving the South to its knees, and how imperative it was to be prepared to fight for freedom and independence. Lion gripped his glass and scanned the room. "Don't be too sure of yourselves," he said to himself. "You may be mighty, but we are in the right. You haven't won yet."

Michael's luck had soured. Flush with success and the big pot won from Starr, he had begun to drink and bet recklessly. Three small pots came his way in quick succession, but then he started to lose, usually to the new player to his left. Not until he lost over a hundred dollars on one hand did he become sober and look at the diminishing pile in front of him. Realizing he'd better quit while he was still a few dollars up on the evening, he excused himself and left the table.

It was nearly three in the morning. Fog-wrapped gaslights flickered balefully along the waterfront. The dense mist rising from the East River swelled over wharves and sedentary ships at berth, then curled inland. Wheel deep along the narrow city streets of Manhattan Island, it muted the sounds of New York City's nightlife and transformed them into mysterious whispers. The few carriages, surreys, and coaches left on the streets seemed to float effortlessly over the fog as they carried the wealthy on their playful rounds. The cool June mist moistened the faces and muffled the rushed steps of those on foot.

Michael stumbled on a curb, caught himself, and reached out to a building for support. Some food was in order, but more important was the girl—damned if he could remember her name—who waited in his hotel room. "Soon I will be wed," he sang, a little drunkenly, his voice losing itself in the mist. "A week of freedom left, then less the chance to taste the pleasures of another's bed." He couldn't remember the rest of the rhyme, but it didn't matter.

"Sir?" a frail voice piped out of the fog. Another lost soul risen from the gutter, hand outstretched for a wayward coin, Michael thought. He dug a few coins from the purse at his belt.

"Sir?" A shuffling figure, a stooped, broken vagrant emerged from the shadows.

"Here, my man," Michael said, holding out three or four small coins.

The panhandler suddenly straightened and lashed out with a length of pipe. Ducking instinctively, Michael shielded himself with his walking stick, only to hear it snap in half from the force of the deflected blow.

"Now!" a voice called. Footsteps pounded on cobblestones and someone leaped onto Michael's back. He straightened and twisted. The attacker crashed into a wall.

Michael was turned around, disoriented. The mist made everything indistinct and he wasn't sure in which direction his hotel lay. A whistling sound warned him. He tried to jump to one side, but the pipe glanced off his shoulder. Pain raced down his arm, nearly immobilizing him. A third and fourth figure, ghostly in the fog, started closing in. Something behind him made a sound and he forced himself to forget the pain. Whirling, he struck out with the remaining half of his cane and felt it strike flesh. The man—the one with the pipe? Or the one who'd jumped on his back?—cried out.

At least he'd gained a few seconds. Michael groped in front of him, found a wall, and placed his back against the rough bricks. The figures, silent as the mist, converged and whispered. A second later they spread apart in a rough semicircle. Michael was surrounded.

The panic started somewhere deep inside him. He'd faced danger before, but always at the hands of nature. As a boy he'd scaled the most perilous cliffs around Dawn Wind. After his mother died he had gone to sea on one of his father's ships. There, in ice and driving snow and wind-driven rain that struck as hard as flying gravel, he'd climbed masts and worked a hundred feet above the plunging decks with no more than a half-inch line under his feet. Once he had been lost off the coast of Maine in a small boat during a nor'easter. Each of those times he had known fear, for his life was in danger.

But he had never panicked. Never encountered a situation in which man was the enemy. Therein lay the difference: weather and the ocean were mindless forces without malice. The men who faced him were thinking, sentient beings who obviously meant to rob and kill him. The panic grew. He was breathing heavily and could think only of escape. He had to run away.

They were closing in silently, their clawed hands clutching pipes. Michael howled, pushed himself away from the brick wall, and smashed into the assailant closest to his right. The robber clutched at his coat, but Michael pushed him aside and ran past him.

Where was the hotel? Where was someone to help? Blinded by fear and the mist, he darted around a corner, glimpsed a pool of light at the end of the street, and headed toward it and safety.

A brick wall loomed ahead of him. He was trapped in a boxed alley! The light that had looked so promising came from a window too high to reach. He turned to retrace his steps, but had run no more than a half-dozen paces before his pursuers blocked the alley's entrance. Sweat beaded on his forehead. His mouth tasted like gun metal. He tore open his cravat and collar, the better to breathe. "Who are you?" he rasped, backing away slowly.

One of them snickered. "He's big, all right. But he ain't that big, right, Tom?"

Tom didn't answer. Frantic, Michael tripped over a crate, grabbed it, and slung it against a wall. "Hey!" he shouted. There was no answer. "Hey, somebody!"

Still nothing. He found another slatted box and hurled it at the advancing men. One dodged aside easily. Another laughed. Michael turned. His boots slipped in the refuse-strewn mud and he fell, somehow managing to break his fall with his hands, but skinning his palms in the process. There was no time for pain. He sprang to his feet, leaped for the fence, and missed the top edge by inches. He spun, put his back to the wall. His heart felt as though it was about to burst through his rib cage.

Money! That had to be it, he thought, in the same instant tearing into the pouch at his belt. "Is that it?" he asked aloud. "I don't have much, but it's yours. See?" Outlined in the dim light of the window above him, he held out his hand. "It's yours. Just leave me alone."

They laughed. Michael threw the money at them. Bills and coins fell into the mud. "Take it, damn you. Take it!"

A scuffed, worn shoe covered one of the bills and pressed it into the mud. A grizzled face poked into the dreary light. "We'll have your money too, bucko, as soon as we've earned it."

Starr's men! They had to be. But for a few hundred dollars? "Your employer lost fair and square. He has no call to . . ." Michael stopped as a new figure detached itself from the shadows. It had to be Starr himself, the owner of the hauling company come in person to exact revenge for his loss. Visions of the drayman's calloused hands beating him were almost more than his heart could bear. All hope lost, Michael cringed against the wall.

"You don't mind if I join the fun, I hope?" a voice said. The figure advanced as he spoke and, without breaking stride, threw the grizzled leader of the attackers against one of the walls.

Michael's hopes soared. "Be careful! They have lead pipes!" he shouted.

"Outnumbered, looks like," the newcomer said, joining Michael before the others fully realized what had happened. "Lion McKenna, from the card game. Remember?"

"Of course," Michael said, "thank God someone . . ."

"Need help?"

"I'm afraid so," Michael answered. "They caught me on the— *watch out!*" He pushed Lion to one side, leaped away himself as a pipe whistled through the air and thudded against the wall. The man moaned once and fell as Lion's cane lashed down onto the back of his neck.

Michael struck at the one closest to him, ducked a pipe, and swung again. The leader charged him from one side and crashed into him, knocking him from his feet. Michael's shoulder, the same one hit by the pipe earlier, exploded in pain. The leader stood over him and aimed a kick at Michael's head. Just as his leg pulled back, Lion reached down, grabbed the man's foot and jerked up. The leader pitched forward awkwardly and fell onto Michael, who rolled out from under him and clubbed him in the small of the back with his doubled fists.

An elbow caught Lion in the face and blood spurted from his nose. Lion grabbed the man, pulled him close, and jammed a knee into his groin. Choking with pain, the man doubled over and staggered away.

"Damn you!" the last one cursed as a huge knife materialized in his hand. "You'll taste my Bowie."

Halfway to his feet, Michael froze, spellbound by the gleaming steel. He wanted to cry out, but his voice caught in his throat.

Lion grunted and stepped back as the man feinted and closed in. Lunging, he swept the long blade in an arc that barely missed tearing through Lion's shirt and into his abdomen. The Southerner spun, twisting away from the steel. In the same blurring motion his hand darted toward his belt and his arm extended. The cracking sound of a pistol echoed in the constricted alley and the knife blade disappeared, leaving only a harmless hilt in the attacker's hand. The assailant stared at his broken knife, then at the four lethal barrels of the pepperbox that were leveled at him. Cursing, he dropped the useless handle and ran. The fight was over.

Lion threw back his head and bellowed with laughter. Michael struggled to his feet. He didn't feel at all like laughing. His knees were weak and his stomach churned sourly. He'd had a damned close call. Without Lion's help—he shuddered.

"A first class party!" Lion said. "The first time tonight I enjoyed myself." The blood trickling down from his nose looked black in the dim light. "Good thing I had my gun. Wouldn't want to face a knife like that without one." He picked up the blade. It was fully a foot long. "It *is* a Bowie. Lucky they didn't decide they needed steel earlier."

Michael's shoulder throbbed painfully. Afraid of a break, he touched it gingerly, then grasped it and swiveled his arm back and forth. The pain was intense but not sharp. He decided the shoulder wasn't broken.

"Are you all right?" Lion asked.

"I think so," Michael replied, fighting back nausea. "They surrounded me in the street and took me by surprise. One of them got me in the shoulder with a pipe." He groaned.

"Sneaking thieves," Lion said, turning over the grizzled one. "Damn, look here." He straightened. A second knife, as long and dangerous-looking as the one his bullet had broken, gleamed evilly in his hand. Lion grinned and handed the Bowie knife to Michael. "Here. A keepsake."

Michael tucked his left hand in his belt in order to steady his shoulder and bent to retrieve some of his money. The heavy knife made it difficult, but he managed to pick up three or four gold pieces and a couple of the larger bills before giving up.

"Hungry?"

The question took Michael by surprise. Food was the last thing he wanted, but he could hardly admit that. "Why, yes. I suppose so," he said, more heartily than he felt. "Where to?" The Southerner named a hotel he was sure would be open and led the way.

The fog was still thick, but evidently hid no more assailants. Michael half listened to Lion's enthusiastic account of a similar episode in the back streets of Montmartre and hoped the color would return to his face by the time they reached brighter lights. He didn't want Lion to see him bloodless and pale from the brief ordeal. "Here's where they first struck," he said, interrupting Lion and pausing to peer into the gloom. "After my money, I expect."

"Lucky I was passing by and heard you call," Lion said. "Four against one is nasty odds."

The fear returned, and with it shame. Not for fearing, or for needing help, but for breaking and running like a coward. He knew he should have stood and faced them no matter what the odds. As Sewal himself would have done. But he couldn't admit that aloud. Not then or ever, especially to his father. "I might have handled two, but the third and fourth?" He chuckled, hoping his voice hadn't betrayed him. "I expect I owe you my life."

"I doubt that," Lion replied self-deprecatingly.

"Nevertheless, I insist on thanking you. At the very least by buying you the best food we can find."

"That sounds like an excellent idea." Lion shook Michael's hand, then stepped back and laughed. "If anyone will serve you."

Michael looked down at himself. His hands, coat, and trousers were muddy from where he'd fallen and rolled in the alley. Only then did he realize he was soaked clear through. Self-conscious, he tried to wipe his hands on his coat, but did little more than redistribute the filth caking him. "A wash and change would be in order," he admitted. "We can use my room. I think I've a spare clean shirt you can wear."

"No need of that," Lion answered cheerfully.

"Oh?" Michael asked. "You'll think differently when you see yourself in the mirror."

Lion touched his face and felt the wetness. "What the devil!" he exclaimed, pulling out his blood-spattered shirt front to inspect it. "I'll be damned. Didn't even feel it." He wiggled his nose with two fingers and winced. "Hope I haven't ruined my good looks."

"That, my friend, you'll have to ask the ladies," Michael said with a laugh. "Come on."

The last of the champagne trickled into the delicately stemmed glasses. "Gone. Just like what's-her-name," Michael said dolefully.

"Who's that?" Lion asked with a yawn.

Michael's voice slurred. "The girl in my room. And I paid her to wait. Funny thing. Do you know what?"

They'd drunk the night through. Confusing reflections of gaslights danced on the surface of two empty bottles. Lion tried to read the labels but they were written in an ostentatious script that baffled his eyes. The name didn't matter. The Peacock served only cheap champagne. "What?" he finally asked.

Michael placed the empty bottle to one side and leaned toward Lion. "The girl and the champagne cost the same. And that, my friend—" He hiccuped. "—Is a comment on humanity. One woman, one bottle of wine. Four dollars each. Of course, I gave her some extra. Money, that is. Not champagne." He raised his glass, finished off the wine. Lion had sat back and was staring at him. "I drink too much. That's what you're thinking, isn't it?"

Lion had never been one to call the kettle black. Too much wine early in the morning had moved more than one man to cheap philosophy. He wondered how cheap. Four dollars worth? But to say as much would be an insult. Mind buzzing, he leaned forward. "You are merely a victim," he said in all seriousness, "of an ailment, the easement of which can only be found in champagne." He thumped the bottle.

"Ailment?"

"Impending marriage."

Michael cocked his head and looked shrewdly at Lion. "How did you know I am to be married?" he asked suspiciously.

"You told me." Lion held up his right hand and extended three fingers. "Three times, but never to whom."

"Oh. Yes. My marriage." Michael shoved aside one of the booth's curtains. *"Garçon!* Another of the same," he called, placing both empty bottles on the floor. When the curtain fell closed he fumbled inside his coat pocket, produced the photograph taken the night of his betrothal to Rosamond Cabell and lay it on the table for Lion to see.

Lion sucked in his breath. An excited Duquesne had pointed out the tall, dark-haired son of Sewal Blackheath two days earlier in the lobby of their hotel. "Michael Blackheath," Duquesne had whispered. "His father, the one we talked about in Maine, is next on our list. We can use him for the clippers. If we get close to the son it will be just that much easier to sign a contract with the father. You'll have to meet him. As soon as possible."

At first it had all been ridiculously easy, and Lion had succeeded remarkably well. But for a brief second he wondered if he possessed the ability to continue the deception. A sidelong glance at Michael, deep in his cups, and the surety of Duquesne's scorn, gave him the assurance he needed. His eyebrows raised. "Your family?" he asked.

"Yes. And my betrothed, there . . . What's wrong?"

"Isn't that a coincidence?" Lion said, picking up the photograph and tilting it so the light was right. "I know her."

Michael took back the photograph, glanced at it, and stared at Lion. "You know her?" he asked, his eyes narrowing.

Lion shrugged, instantly on guard but careful not to show it. "Not well at all, really," he said. "Met her in Richmond, oh, maybe four years ago. Her father's an admiral, isn't he? What's her name again?"

"Rosamond Cabell," Michael said, accepting Lion's explanation. "As virginal as new fallen snow, she is. As delicate as fine Bruges lace. As my father says, I am a fortunate man. Of course, in all modesty, I must say she was mine the moment we met."

"In all modesty," Lion concurred. "And it doesn't hurt a young Past-Midshipman's chances to wed the daughter of an admiral."

"Exactly. An easy life in Washington. Rapid advancement, with luck. Of course, the boredom . . ." He paused, and abruptly brightened. "Say. Tonight was the most interesting time I've had in months. I have a marvelous idea."

The waiter opened the curtain, showed the bottle to Michael, who waved his hand imperiously and accepted it. "You say you have no plans," he went on, at the same time struggling with the cork. "Well, then I have one. Why don't you accompany me home as my guest?

Only hold you up a week. You can watch me become an old married man, and be on your way back to Virginia on the eleventh. What do you think of that?" The cork popped out with a loud noise and disappeared over the curtain. Michael began pouring without missing a beat. "You've never been to Maine. What better opportunity?"

Lion watched his glass fill. "I don't know," he said hesitantly. "I would think such an occasion should best be reserved for close friends."

"Which you are," Michael insisted. "You saved my life, after all." He set down the bottle. "I will accept no answer other than yes."

Suddenly, Lion was tired. His eyes burned. His throat was raw and his stomach was queasy from too little sleep and too much to drink. His head ached. The Shenandoah valley seemed farther and farther away. But Duquesne and the others were counting on him. Lion glanced down at the photograph on the table. Michael's father looked to be a shrewd, hard man. His sad-eyed younger brother seemed distant and uncomfortable, as if he wished himself somewhere else. The sister appeared—what? Angry? Perturbed? He couldn't tell. Only that, though her face was incredibly beautiful, she looked cold and formal, as if she were holding herself together with the utmost effort. And the bride-to-be? He finished his drink, for courage.

"Well?" Michael asked.

Lion grinned and raised his glass. The respectable life of a Virginia farmer would keep. "Done," he said. "When do we leave?"

Chapter 3

A distant piping cry of morning gulls. A whisper of dissipating mist rising from the shore. A silent golden light creeps through a corner window and touches a shirred bed canopy, slides down the bedpost, and illuminates a worn book lying open on a nightstand. Dazzling spring brilliance spreads across the bed. A silken sleeping gown clings skinlike to a sleeping woman's tapered waist, the rounded rise and fall of her breasts. Her slender neck and face are free of the lines of age and care. A tumble of curls golden enough to challenge the morning light casts delicate shadows in a frame about her face. The eyelids flutter open, squeeze closed, and open again.

The cock cardinal that had taken over the old maple tree whistled sharply and repetitively. With the sound Eve realized, as always, that the silence was nowhere near complete. The piping of ubiquitous gulls rose from the water's edge and from the rising currents of air that raced over the stony cliffs. Fainter, but there if one listened, the same air whispered through the maple tree and, nearer by, the slightly opened window. Underlying all was the deeper tone that never ceased, the unending, muted roar of breaking waves that were so much a part of her she was uncomfortable when absent from Dawn Wind.

Eve kicked off the covers and lay back in the sunshine, stretched, and yawned in a most unladylike and satisfying manner. Nothing in the world could be so luxurious as a lazy morning in bed, and nowhere in the world could one be so satisfyingly luxurious as at Dawn Wind. A breeze ruffled the priscilla curtains on the window and stirred the flowerlace shirred fringe on the canopy over her bed. Outside in the hall the grandfather clock sang its deep song, ending with seven evenly spaced gongs. The smaller Seth Thomas on her mantelpiece chimed a treble reply. Seven o'clock, up and about. Only a lazyhead lies abed at seven on a Monday morning.

Lazy, indeed. She deserved one late sleep, with all the work she'd been doing in preparation for Michael's wedding on the tenth, only six days away. Normally, of course, a wedding didn't take place at the groom's home, but Cornelia Cabell had been taken ill in the middle of April and had been ordered by her doctors to stay out of Washington's miasmic, marshlike atmosphere. Sea air was thought to be good for her, so she had been living in Newport, Rhode Island. Both parties had agreed, under the circumstances, the wedding should take place at Dawn Wind. Consequently, the house had been in an uproar of scrubbing and waxing and polishing and painting for the last month. Wednesday last, Eve and Sewal had taken the train to Baltimore to see Michael graduate from Annapolis. On Thursday they all went to New York, where Sewal met with Hébert Sarandon to discuss, Eve was surprised and irritated to learn two days later, a match between her and Clifford. They returned home Friday, leaving Michael behind in New York for a final bachelor fling. Sunday had been church and the Lilac Festival, followed by Justin's arrival on the evening train. Here it was Monday morning already, and Michael was due to arrive on the five o'clock train that evening.

Eve swung out of bed. Pulling on her robe, she hurried across the rug-strewn hardwood floor to the front window and raised the sash. A line of clouds far to the south made the horizon lumpy, but overhead the sky was absolutely clear. The sunlight sprinkled diamonds on the gray-green water, flat with distance. She knew better from the sound, though, for unseen below the edge of the cliff, high rolling breakers from the wild Atlantic were curling and cresting and dashing themselves against the broken granite.

The windows of Eve's room faced east and south. All four, in fact, looked onto some part of Waupinau Bay or the Atlantic proper, for Dawn Wind crowned the tip of a squash-shaped peninsula that was almost an island. The eastern edge was bare, with time-and-weather-cracked granite. To the north and south the drops were less precipitous and laced with long-established paths that led to the water. Stunted trees grew along these broken cliffs, down which adventurous boys, though not the very young, could pick daring new ways. A natural bridge, no more than twenty-five feet across at its narrowest point, connected estate and mainland. The grounds about the great house were spacious enough for gardens, shrub-lined walks, and even, along the northern rim, a dense stand of virgin white pine.

Jubb Peters, the grounds keeper, had told Eve years ago that if the sea ever cut the rib of rock, Dawn Wind, house, trees, Eve, and all would drift helplessly into the Atlantic and never be seen or heard of again. Eve chuckled softly. Often as a child she lay on her stomach on the cliff edge and peered down the broken wall to the waves below. To a child's eye each wave was a knife that cut into the living rock, a drill that bore into the base of the causeway. Each imagined lost pebble or grain of sand brought the dread separation closer. But of course Jubb, unaware that she took him so seriously, had been teasing. What had happened to those awful fears of youth? She could not remember. Perhaps they never really left, but were buried somewhere with other youthful fancies.

A knock on the door interrupted increasingly gloomy thoughts. Eve turned to see Maisie Duncan enter. All freckles and good cheer, the smiling maid carried a silver tray neatly arranged with a china teapot, cup, saucer, and plate of strawberry muffins.

"A beautiful day," she said. "The town is buzzing about Hattie and Clarence Tremain. You remember the row they got in December last? Well, they're at it again. Clarence got started on the rum—on the Sabbath too—and Hattie took a lobster pot to him. Broke the pot, and Doctor Cutcheon had to sew up Clarence's head. . . ." Chattering, gossiping Maisie deposited tea, china, and muffins on the table in front of the fireplace, crossed to the south windows, and threw back the shutters. The flood of light on the cream-and-brown-flowered wallpaper made the room seem especially happy. "There, miss. Isn't that lovely?"

"Yes, thank you." Eve dropped a lump of sugar in her tea. "Maisie?"

The maid turned in the doorway. "Ma'am?"

"Is my father up and about?"

"Yes, ma'am," Maisie answered brightly. "Took a horse from the stables, I believe. And his gun."

"Ask Hamlet to saddle Mirabell for me, would you? I'll be out as soon as I've bathed and dressed."

"Yes, ma'am."

Eve sipped her tea, broke apart a muffin, and nibbled at it. So Father was hunting. And he expected her to stay in the house and supervise? A determined look crossed her face. We'll see about that, she thought, and without consultation declared the morning a holiday.

Justin Hancock Blackheath poked his sharp-pointed features toward the cooling rack of freshly baked bread, inhaled deeply, and voiced an audible sigh of pleasure in the direction of Eustacia Peters. But the cook continued to maneuver around the kitchen with practiced ease, not even glancing up from her chores as she spoke. "Justin Hancock, you don't go pokin' your nose into food other folks'll be eatin', you hear?" Her round chocolate face was split by a broad, toothy grin. She wore a wide, gingham dress with small, bright flowers printed on it. The great bulk beneath jiggled and sloshed, yet not unappealingly, for she bore her weight merrily.

Brown eyes distinctly unrepentant under fogged spectacles, Justin stepped to one side. The kitchen was a summer/winter affair dug under the northeast corner of the house. In cold weather it could be closed up for maximum warmth. In the heat a passageway through the root cellar funneled cooling ocean air through the cooking area, then out a door and a set of wide windows that opened onto the lawn facing the stables. Justin liked the kitchen best in the winter, he thought, for then it was the warmest, coziest spot in the house with the huge hearth blazing with light and heat. After all, nowhere but in this one room could he stand with eyes shut and nose aquiver, assailed by a hundred swirling, combinant and conflicting mouth-watering aromas. He sniffed and, knowing precisely what he'd find, headed for the window. As predicted, a homecoming present of freshly made oatmeal cookies plump with raisins and grated carrots and brown sugar and cinnamon lay cooling on the sill. He reached for one and sniffed it closely in anticipation.

"You breathin' my cookies again, Mister Justin?" Eustacia laughed. "I swear, you is the only man I know breathes cookies. Here." She handed Justin a cup and picked up the cooling cookies. "Two, you can have with your coffee." Justin took pains to find the largest. "And see you eats 'em." She moved off, pleased with her little joke. "Don't nobody sniff cookies in Eustacia's kitchen. No, sir! Cookies is for eatin'!"

Justin poured a cup of the rich, black coffee and spooned in sugar. Only then did he taste the first cookie. It was good to be home. Nobody, he thought, but Eustacia made cookies so delicious nor a kitchen so comfortable.

"Mornin', Mister Justin." An age-bent figure angled across the room from the door. "She keep that coffee hot?" he asked, pouring himself a cup.

"You know it is, Jubb Peters." Eustacia plunked down the cookies and started transferring them to a heavy crock. "Ain't never a cold pot of coffee on my fire. But why you need coffee, I don't know. Already had two cups."

Jubb Peters moved as sprightly as a youngster despite his sixty-odd years. His eyes were like two pools of sulphur set in wrinkled pitch. In his youth he must have been handsome, Justin thought, but the years had been harsh and his face was seamed and wrinkled. Once slaves, he, Eustacia, and their infant son, Hamlet, had escaped to the North in 1836 when they learned Eustacia was going to be sold to another plantation. That had been before Justin was born, but he'd heard the story from his mother. Elkahan Waldrop, the Congregational minister in New Forest had arrived at Dawn Wind's front door one winter day and announced he had found the perfect replacements for the Blackheaths' recently departed house and grounds keepers. Sewal had doubts. There were laws concerning runaway slaves, but Elkahan pointed out that with Michael barely a year old and another child on the way, Jennifer needed help, and produced papers that showed Jubb and Eustacia had bought their freedom. Justin doubted they had, from the stories he heard later, but the papers were sufficient at the time, and the frightened blacks were taken in. Over the years they became as much a part of Dawn Wind as the house itself.

Jubb finished his coffee and ran his hands through the thatch of snowy hair that covered his skull like a fleece. He glanced through the side door to the separate room where he and Eustacia slept. "Well, about got them chairs done already," he said with a yawn.

"And more to do before the day's over, so don't go gettin' no ideas, Mister Peters," Eustacia warned, plunking the lid on the cookie jar. "You can sleep tonight, like ever'body else around here. Mr. Pole come in here and find you nappin' . . ."

"Hush up, woman," Jubb growled, then turned and winked at Justin. "Who said anything about nappin' anyway?"

"Ahem!" A chilly voice from the doorway ended further familiarities. Hanson Pole, the butler, could smell laxity, it was said. He also possessed an overdeveloped sense of place, which was displayed every time he entered a room. His presence fixed each person, whether he wished it or not, with a code of conduct that somehow demanded to be followed. Suddenly, Justin was the young master. Eustacia was cook. Jubb was handyman. And Pole was in command, as always.

Justin coughed uncomfortably and started for the open door. "Good morning, Master Justin," Pole said, his inflection no different than it had been the last morning he had greeted Justin two months earlier. The icy, proper greeting stopped Justin. "I did not see you come down."

Justin almost apologized, then realized how foolish that would sound. Here he was, a twenty-year-old college man, and still Pole could make him feel like a miscreant for moving about in his own house without explaining himself. But then people like the butler had the ability to make Justin feel that way. Not that Pole was unkind. The Englishman was merely doing his job.

"I looked for you in the back shed, Jubb," Pole went on, swiveling his gaze to fix the handyman. "You said you would be there staining the last of the dining room chairs. I do not find you there, but in here." He sniffed imperiously. "In here doing Lord knows what." The butler's sandy, close-cut hair was swept forward to conceal a receding hairline. Not a single strand was out of place. His eyebrows arched. His jowls were like twin bookends at either side of his pale, frowning, thin lips. His round abdomen, bulging under a starched white shirt and buttoned black coat, expanded and contracted with each breath. "I'm waiting for an explanation, Jubb," he said in the same tone with which he might have addressed a child.

The Negro shrugged. "Why, I'm stainin' my innards, Mister Pole," he replied, holding up his coffee cup. "Them chairs will be done by ten, like I said."

Eustacia glared at her husband. Pole rolled his eyes toward heaven. Justin held his amusement in check until he was safely out of the kitchen and into the bright outdoors. It wouldn't do to undermine Pole's authority by laughing.

The day was beautiful. The northern sky was clear, the Atlantic choppy and dotted with whitecaps. Ahead, the white pine grove protecting the stables waved slightly in the ever-present breeze. Justin stretched and inhaled deeply of the sea-perfumed morning air. No doubt about it. Being inland just didn't compare to the coast. Bowdoin was all well and good, but he'd had all he could stomach of academia. At least for a while. His father would be furious, of course. Telling him he wasn't going to return for his senior year would lead to an argument that would culminate, as usual, in harsh words. Trying not to think that far ahead, Justin ambled along the path leading from the kitchen entrance to the stables. Dogwood, red bud, and lilacs dotting the landscape with patches of white, magenta and lavender turned his mind to more pleasant thoughts. He stopped by the three lilacs that his mother had planted on the occasions of her children's births. Not too many years ago he could remember how their heights varied. Now, with Michael twenty-two, he twenty, and Eve nineteen, the shrubs' growth had evened out. All were of an equal height. As always he felt compelled to stop there the first few days after his arrival. And as always, especially when the fragrance lingered, sorrow and anger rose in his chest.

But the day wasn't for sorrow, he decided. Nor anger. Striking out briskly, he headed for the corner of the house and the path that cut across the long drive and led to his studio. He'd gone no more than a dozen paces when a noise from the stables attracted his attention. Turning, he saw the powerful ebony frame of Hamlet Peters throw open the stable doors. A second later Eve cantered into the sunshine, astride a gray mare. Justin watched her circle the prancing animal, then trot out of the fenced area in front of the stable and across the lawn.

"Off to your hermitage on such a lovely morning, Justin?"

"You don't know how I've missed that place." Justin smiled, held the halter, and stroked the mare's neck. Three of the men from the shipyards had built the single room that served as his studio and workshop under the mixed hardwood grove at the edge of the southern precipice overlooking the bay. Justin had used it first for his painting, but since discovering photography three summers earlier, he had packed it with photographic equipment. "Anyway, it's little enough privacy I'll be allowed once Michael and his guests arrive and the festivities begin."

"You worry too much about privacy."

"Do I now?" Justin laughed. "And who is it who goes off for long, solitary rides by the sea?"

"Not I." Eve shook her head. Her long, golden hair floated back to settle on her shoulders. She wore a simple cotton blouse and riding skirt with too few petticoats. "I have Mirabell."

The mare tossed her head at the sound of her name. Justin removed his round, silver-framed glasses and brushed a hand through prematurely thinning hair. "I hope you aren't thinking of riding into town like that."

Eve pretended shock. "Why, Justin Blackheath! To think you'd even suggest—"

"I heard," Justin interrupted. He wagged a finger. "The Misses Johnstones fainted in unison, I was told."

"Those spinsters!" Eve giggled maliciously. "They need a scandal now and again. It keeps the blood moving in their veins."

"At a rapid pace," Justin agreed, glancing up as a gunshot sounded in the distance. "Is Father hunting?" he asked, adding, "In a foul mood, no doubt."

Eve grimaced at the pun, turned serious. "He did want to talk to you last night."

Justin looked wary. "The journey was long and I was tired," he said shortly.

"Something was bothering him."

It was Justin's turn to frown. "Clipper ships and shipyards, I imagine."

"They have made us what we are," Eve said.

"In a manner of speaking, I suppose they have. And if Father has his way, what we will be for the next century or two." The anger growing in him, Justin walked away from Eve and the discussion that had turned sour.

Eve nudged Mirabell and caught up with him. "You shouldn't look down your nose at our ancestors, you know. Or Father, either." Justin stopped and stared at her. Eve's eyes flashed. "I mean, there's simply no excuse to be so obnoxiously holier-than-thou about—"

"I'm sorry if I offended you, Sister," Justin interrupted coldly. "Please accept my apologies. And now, if you'll excuse me, I would like to set my studio in order." Without waiting, he stalked off.

Eve swore under her breath. "You're angry with me now," she said, staying abreast of him.

"Not at all. Why should I be?"

"Because you think I take Papa's side."

"I don't really care whose side you take, Eve."

"You needn't snap at me."

"I didn't snap, damn it!" Justin stopped. He could tell Eve. Sketch the scene, the time, the circumstances of their father's iniquity. It would be simple enough, and utterly devastating. His face was red and he fought to control his anger. "Look, Eve," he finally said. "It's my first day home. I don't want to argue with you. But please. You don't know what you're getting involved in when you step between Father and me."

"I don't see—"

"And you won't. Ever. Let's leave it at that." Glad he had held his tongue, Justin smiled and reached up to lay a hand on Eve's forearm. "Did you know I can't help still thinking of you as my little sister? Silly, isn't it? Possessive. But I did miss you. There was no one with whom I could talk, or be comfortable. Let us at least stay close."

Eve hesitated. Her father and brother were different in temperament. An unstated antagonism between them had existed for years. When she was younger she accepted it as part of the way the family was. As she grew older she'd dismissed it. Now, suddenly, Justin was leading her to suspect a specific cause for the hard feelings, and the suspicion troubled her.

A gunshot echoed once again. Several gulls rose above the treetops, glided back down out of sight. "I'd like," Eve said in the ensuing hush, "to get involved. I mean, it's my family too."

Justin sighed deeply. "Go riding, Evie," he said. "I shouldn't have spoken as I did. I won't again." Lightly slapping Mirabell's rump, he turned and walked away.

Eve sat on the mare without moving. She *would* discover what caused the bitterness, she decided. If not that day, another. Nudging her heels against Mirabell's flanks, she set the mare at a trot. Justin turned as she passed him and noted the determined look on her face. A bitter smile twisted his lips. "You're wasting your time, little sister," he said under his breath. "He won't tell you either. Not in a thousand years."

Eve dismounted and peered down to the beach where her father had tethered his brown gelding. The trail down was a crumbled cascade of boulders and moss-carpeted stones. Carefully, Eve and Mirabell picked their way through the twisting, turning descent until they arrived on a broad, flat expanse of sand.

Sewal Blackheath was clad in broadcloth breeches, a heavy shirt over wide shoulders, a worn corduroy coat, and well-oiled boots. The patriarch of Dawn Wind remained motionless as his daughter rode up the beach, dismounted, and climbed the jagged face of the boulder to join him above the dashing water. A knit cap covered his head down to the closely trimmed white ruff of hair, the last of what had been black waves in his youth. His clean-shaven features revealed sun-browned flesh and a strong Roman nose. His eyes were the cold, cold blue of icy ocean depths. "Did you ever see anything like it?" he asked, as Eve approached.

Nothing stirred on the limitless expanse but the water itself. Eve hugged her father's arm and pressed her cheek against his shoulder. She loved to be with him when he was in one of these moods. He seemed dark and mysterious then, a man of granite as hard as the cliffs, of strength as great as the winds.

"Every time I go away, even for one day, I can't wait to get back here," Sewal went on. "Trains, cities, hordes of people. I don't understand. Never have, never will. How can a man live with all that noise and stench and press?" He shook his head.

"Some people thrive on it, I guess," Eve answered, huddling against him for warmth in the chilly breeze.

"I suppose so. Still and all, if we didn't need every contract I could lay my hands on, and if New York wasn't the best place to find them, I'd never leave Dawn Wind again." He noticed Mirabell, head down, standing at the base of the boulder. "You'll cripple her.

Oughtn't to ride a horse onto this sand," he remarked gruffly. "It's too shallow."

"Don't worry, Father. She knows this stretch of beach, and I check her hooves often. Anyway, it's too nice a day for you to be so grumpy."

Sewal relaxed, slipped one arm around Eve's shoulders. "Just like your mother. Couldn't tell her anything either," he said, tousling her hair.

Eve laughed. "That's because I'm as smart as she was."

"Vanity of vanities, saith the preacher," Sewal quoted, the faintest of smiles on his lips.

"Pride in achievement," Eve corrected.

"If marriage to Clifford Sarandon were at the top of your list of achievements, I would be much happier."

Eve tensed. At first Sewal had paid little attention to Clifford. His interest began to grow, however, when he'd met Hébert Sarandon at Michael and Rosamond's engagement party. From that time on, increasingly, as the shipyard continued to encounter difficulty in finding new contracts, he had pressured Eve to accept a proposal from Clifford. "You're just saying that because you want to get rid of me," Eve teased, hiding her nervousness.

A note of determination crept into Sewal's voice. "On the contrary. Clifford Sarandon is an excellent match."

A large wave broke and sprayed them both with fine droplets of icy water. Eve stepped back, shook her head. The subject of marriage had become more and more of an issue between them during the last two months, and had come to a head two nights earlier when she learned of Sewal's meeting with Hébert. They had argued at the time. Since then she had decided that her best defense was light-hearted banter. Perhaps if she didn't take the proposal seriously, Sewal would cease to. "I should think one marriage per year at Dawn Wind would be sufficient," she finally said, her cheerful tone forced.

"A second marriage would increase my joy twofold."

Eve made herself laugh. "Well, I am sorry, Father, but you shall just have to be content with one."

"I could order you," he warned, the look in his eyes hardening.

"Don't," Eve snapped, forgetting the tactic that had worked until then.

"Is that a challenge?"

"Yes. I won't be an object to be auctioned off to the highest bidder. Not even to save the shipyards."

Sewal's shoulders tightened. "There has been no bidding, no auction," he said, his voice low and ominous, "and I resent the implication that—"

"And I resent being forced to marry someone I don't love simply because his family has money. Please, Father . . ." She stopped, suddenly realizing she had gone too far. Tears of frustration welled in her eyes. "Please," she whispered. The anger drained from her. She lowered her gaze. "Would you treat me so cruelly?"

"Cruelly?" Sewal raised his eyes in astonishment. "Is it cruel for a father not to want his daughter to end up a prunish spinster? Am I a tyrant to place you in such a dire situation as a marriage to a handsome, wealthy young man of influence who, I might add, loves you very much? Ye gods, woman, but you try my patience."

"I'm sorry, Father," Eve said contritely.

"You are, eh? Sorry, eh? And what does that make me?" Sewal asked, softening.

She had won again. For the moment, at least. Eve smiled sweetly. "My distraught, but loving, father." Eve reached up on tiptoe and kissed Sewal on the cheek. "And I'm your ungrateful daughter." She jumped down from the boulder, climbed onto Mirabell, and rode off. Before her flustered father could reply she was galloping down the beach, safely out of earshot.

Shoulders hunched and head thrust forward, Sewal stared after her. Above, hovering gulls dipped and canted in the steady offshore breeze. What was wrong with the girl? Sewal wondered to the piping cries of the gulls. Waspish one moment, contrite the next. He couldn't keep up with her. As for Clifford Sarandon, she couldn't ask for a better husband. She'd have to marry sooner or later in any case. Why not Clifford? Hébert Sarandon was one man in a million, by God! And what if the shipyards were saved in the process? That was purely a fortuitous coincidence. Sewal thrust his hands deep into his pockets, turned to face the ocean, and looked to the future. Contracts through Cabell, capital, and credit through Sarandon: the Blackheath Shipyards would be secure. He could relax for the first time since the crash of fifty-seven.

The trail wound up a steep, pine-covered slope to the top of the Whale's Hump, the highest point of land within a day's ride of Dawn

Wind. Her shod hooves thudding dully on the soft, pine-needle-covered path, the mare needed no guidance; it was one of Eve's favorite routes and Mirabell knew the way. Eve rode in a trance, for spring was on the land. Maple, oak, and hickory were covered with a light green haze of newly sprouting leaves. Deep in the forest to either side, lone dogwoods glared white in the heavy shadows. Everywhere, ferns, myrtle, forget-me-nots, and wild skunk cabbage pushed up through last year's leaves. Even the moss was green with new life.

Mirabell surged ahead, crested the last sharp ridge and stopped, shaking her head and snorting. Absentmindedly, Eve dismounted and let the reins drop. Here was her favorite place, the spot she sought out whenever she felt the need for solitude. How many eons this mound of granite had stood against the Atlantic was impossible to tell. Many, many, though, enough for a thick layer of topsoil to form, inch by painful inch. Enough too for the mammoth white pine to take root and flourish and climb to impossible heights, there to form a cathedral of bole and branch and cone. These tall, straight conifers were among the very, very few remaining in the whole of the northeast, for white pine had been the most sought after for masts and spars. Generations of Blackheaths had had an eye for beauty and grandeur, however, so these had been spared the axe. As a result, the Whale's Hump was the most beautiful spot in the vicinity, as well as unique.

The path twisted through ribbed corridors of pine and opened onto a glade that overlooked the Atlantic. There, caught in the slatted sunlight and surrounded by a rim of violets and lilies of the valley, two score headstones faced the east and the ocean the Blackheaths so loved. Eve knew all the names and dates by heart. Gladstone Henry Blackheath, born in London in 1623, died in the New World in 1695. Ruell Terrence Blackheath, wife Rebecca, daughters Beth and Hope, killed by Indians in 1722. Nathaniel Peleg Blackheath, lost at sea during a battle in 1778. And more. Collectively, they recalled the history of not only the family, but the State of Maine and the nation as well.

Today, though, Eve had only one name in mind: Jennifer Morgana Blackheath, born 1818, died 1853. No other memoriam or endearment graced the pink granite slab for, as Sewal had often said, grief was not a public passion to be traipsed before the curious. Words of sorrow were best inscribed on the soul and heart. "Tradition again," Eve sighed, running the sleeve of her blouse across her eyes.

"I'm afraid I drive Father to distraction, Mama," she whispered. "He's so determined to have things his way. If I want just one little thing my way I'm no longer the dutiful child he thinks his daughter ought to be. I suppose I'm a disappointment. But do you really think it wrong not to marry a man I don't love? You loved Father, didn't you?"

The wind murmured disapproval, or so Eve imagined. Self-conscious in her solitude, Eve turned and left the silent graves, whistled to Mirabell, and continued on the path that circled the top of the Hump. Minutes later, she emerged in another open glade and stopped. As always the view caught her breath and held it like a lump in her throat. A pale strip of beach to the south and west led to the peninsula and magnificent white house that was Dawn Wind. A glimmering, cone-shaped lighthouse five miles across the bay kept watch, guiding ships away from treacherous shoals and submerged boulders. Broad and deep at its mouth and shaped like a warped and elongated horseshoe, Waupinau Bay stretched inland, there to peter out in shallow tidal pools and mud flats. The Blackheaths had first sailed up the bay to take fresh water from the river that flowed into it. Once there they stayed and built ships for the Crown, then for a revolution, later for a growing nation—and always for profit. They named their town New Forest, for it was indeed that: a new forest for lumber and ships, and a land for new lives.

As the family prospered so did the town, which stretched along a full half mile of shoreline and back into the low rising hills. Houses of granite or whitewashed oak led down to the Blackheath shipyard. There hulls of ships hunkered on the waves and waited for the ministering efforts of the shipwrights, the men who knew the grain and stress of oak and pine and hackmarack, the sea and what it did to wooden ships and frail, frail lives. As she watched, Eve noted the changes that had taken place in the yards. No more than four years ago there had been as many as ten or twelve hulls under various stages of construction, now there were only two to occupy the builders.

No wonder her father was so anxious for her to marry. The reasons were laid out on the beach with dreadful clarity. Two hulls destined to become clipper ships and to ride the windswept ocean, their vast array of cloudlike sails hinged to the water by deep, ingot-filled keels. "Only two," Eve said aloud, painfully aware for the first time that all their vast estate, all of Dawn Wind and the life she lived, was hinged to the shore not by a narrow stone bridge, but by something far more tenuous. Two hulls, where once there had been ten.

Chapter 4

The headlines of the New York *Herald* of June 3, carried an announcement of the arrival of overland mail from California, and on the same day a prize-fighter's victorious return from England. On another page the death of a colored man named Thomas Thomas, calling Eating Tom of Flip Penny Alley, who had consumed a large number of cucumbers two nights earlier, washed them down with prodigious quantities of ice water, then died of the colic. In another column, next to the results of a benefit for Garibaldi, advertisements: "Brandreth's pills to thin the blood." Further down the page, announcements of two new books: *Somnambulism and Cramp* by Dr. Madelle Thornborough and *Leaves of Grass* by Walt Whitman.

Michael Blackheath folded the newspaper and muttered, "What's the use?" beneath his breath and leaned back to try to rest. But he was too tense. Sitting up abruptly he glanced at Lion and saw he was still asleep. He tapped the paper against the Southerner's knee.

Lion stirred, opened one eye.

"I'm going forward to find a drink," Michael said, standing and stepping into the aisle. "Want to join me?"

"No," Lion mumbled, shifting position to try to get more comfortable.

Michael braced himself against the seat as the train took a curve. "Suit yourself," he said, walking forward with the help of the seats. The platform between the cars was empty. Michael leaned against the railing and stared dully at the countryside. The motion of the train was almost like that of a ship, he thought. Which is where I'd be if it weren't for my father. On a ship. The train lurched and Michael almost fell off the platform. "Damned rails. You'd think they'd be able to make a level bed," he shouted.

Ashen-faced, he pushed open the door and stumbled into the next car. A woman with her face painted heavily to hide the scars of a childhood bout with smallpox squeezed past without apology. Michael almost fell into the lap of an elderly gentleman, but caught himself in time and forged ahead to the club car. Luckily, the car was almost empty. Michael chose a narrow table with only one seat and ordered a double Scotch, then another when the waiter brought the first. He was drinking too much, he knew, and couldn't really grasp the reason why. Or didn't care to. But why not drink? He was getting married, wasn't he? A last bachelor fling. Too soon he'd be tied to a bride.

"Tied to a bride," he sang quietly into the Scotch. A bride who loved him. A partner in life. The problem lay in the unseen partner, her father, the admiral, whose retinue he would join.

He was trapped. The feeling of helplessness that had been building in him for the past month rose to choke him and he drained the first Scotch to wash the bad taste from his mouth. He loved Rosamond but a Blackheath was destined for the sea, damn it. The sea was where he belonged. The sea, and only *then,* when it was necessary, a desk. His father had said that all his life, and now he was going back on it.

The waiter picked up his empty glass, left him a full one. Michael stirred the drink with his finger. His throat burned. Bleary-eyed, he shook his head. His father had seen to it that he would get a desk job where he could help engineer contracts for the Blackheath Shipyards. But why him? Why was the responsibility his? Why was he alone expected to save the family business? Ever since he could remember it had been drummed into him. You. Michael Blackheath, the eldest. It's up to you, son. Nine generations of Blackheaths are counting on you. You may not permit them to have labored in vain.

Hell, let Justin get off his high horse, forget all that photography hogwash, and take some of the load. Let him spend *his* life running the yards from behind a damned desk. What did it matter who was the eldest? The hell with being the eldest. As soon as he and Rosamond were married he'd talk the admiral into seeing that he got out from behind a desk and onto a ship. That was the answer. Nothing but a ship would do. Especially if there was a war.

A vision of an alley where a frightened Michael Blackheath cringed and begged for mercy sullied the thought. That was different, though, he told himself for the hundredth time. Hell, everybody was entitled to a lapse or two. Everybody but you, a small voice in his brain said accusingly. Everybody but you, because you're supposed to be perfect. Nothing but perfection is allowed for Michael Black-heath.

"But what the devil," Michael slurred drunkenly. No one needed to know the secret thoughts the whiskey helped him hide where even he couldn't hear or feel them. "Safe safe safe safe," he muttered over and over again. The waiter brought him a third drink. He had not even needed to ask.

He noticed colors first. Soft, swirling pastels that whirled and streamed in graceful arcs. Suddenly, out of them, startlingly bright violet eyes, staring at him. Lion shifted, felt fingers at his throat. His own. Intent on those eyes, he was adjusting his tie. At last came sound. Music and bright chatter—the social type that doesn't require close attention—touched his consciousness to tell him where he was. A party, then. Why Lion was there he wasn't sure. To escape the boredom, perhaps, though there must have been a hundred better ways to do that. He floated through the room and came to a stop in front of the violet eyes. When a face took shape around them he knew where he was. "Hello," she said, her voice throaty above the background talk. "You're Lion McKenna. I asked. My name is Rosamond Cabell."

Tears of rain on a window. The scene, the surroundings had shifted. The chatter was gone, replaced by the soft hiss of lanterns. Outside, carriages bustled along a street. Miniature geysers erupted as iron-rimmed carriage wheels thumped through potholes. Anger and frustration rose like the steam from the backs of the horses as fuming drivers examined broken spokes and cursed other carriage owners who splashed them as they passed. Again, he knew where he was. Lion turned from the window to watch Rosamond, who appeared enchanted by the chaos outside, and caught his breath when her eyes met his. "I'm glad we're out of that," she said, catching him off guard.

He was in Richmond; it was spring of 1856. Raindrops pummeled the windowsill. Heady as the scent of violets and lavender, mystery made the air heavy, wrapped Lion like a moist blanket. Enticements. Unspoken promises. Lion could feel the tension in his bones, in the tendons that flexed his fingers, between his shoulder blades, in his groin. A tingling. Anticipation. Rosamond with the violet eyes was playing a game. But then so was he. He was fresh from a love affair gone sour. And she . . . was attracted to his dark and dangerous looks, and by the gossip that followed him through Richmond drawing rooms. He raced horses, gambled, was a dead shot, and had killed a man in a duel. It had been enough to provoke Rosamond's interest, and she had flirted and provided him the opportunity to escort her home.

She wore a pale green gown, soft and lustrous in the lantern light. Heads turned to watch as they had passed through the downstairs common room of the Bannister Tea House. The owner, who knew Lion well, was gracious enough not to wink. The private dining room upstairs in which they sat was intimate and quiet. A table for two was in front of the window. Behind them, arranged in front of the fireplace, were two heavy easy chairs and a large divan draped with a soft blanket. Beyond, the door, oak solid, was locked. They were alone. What had started as tea had become dinner. Burgundy, a soft, deep red that matched the color of the blanket on the divan, sparkled in crystal goblets. Rosamond's finger played along the rim of the crystal.

"Your father will be worrying about you," Lion said.

"Papa is at some silly meeting," she answered, tilting her head to one side. Rosamond looked at the divan and back, beneath thick black curls, to Lion. "We have time for dessert."

The swirling colors, now darker and somehow ominous, returned. Rosamond's lips were moist and tasted of burgundy. And of danger, Lion thought, as she melted into his arms. It didn't matter. Nothing mattered as they moved toward the divan . . .

Something bumped his leg. Lion woke, slitted one eye in time to see Michael drop into the seat opposite him, then watched as his companion leaned back and, almost instantly, fell asleep. Lion studied him closely for a second, considered the consequences should Michael ever learn of Rosamond's affairs, especially the one with Lion. Yet, a bride-to-be could hardly be expected to announce prior indiscretions. The possibility of trouble was remote. They would meet, exchange civil if awkward greetings, and nothing more. There was really nothing to worry about. Even if there was, the only alternative was to turn around and leave, and that he could not do. Not at this stage of the game.

They were approaching New Haven, Connecticut. Curious, Lion extricated himself from the cramped seat and headed for the observation platform at the end of the train. It looked like rain. Heavy clouds filled the sky and scudded along at right angles to the train's path. What direction that was he couldn't tell. The train pulled into the station and a gust of wind funneling through the narrow spaces filled the air with a cloud of dust and debris. His eyes stinging, Lion ducked back inside and headed for the club car.

Michael was still asleep. Lion kept moving, showed the conductor his ticket, finally reached the club car, and took a table alone to wait until the train started again before a waiter appeared.

The tea was strong and hot. The train speeded up as New Haven fell behind. Lion stared through the rain-streaked windows, followed individual drops as they raced horizontally along the glass, and considered the events of the last two days. Saturday night and Sunday morning's drinking had left him drained. Sunday evening he'd spent posting his trunks to Virginia, dining with Michael, and then, after the newly graduated Past-Midshipman had drunk too much again, pouring him into his bed. Later, he'd sat until the wee hours relaxing and catching up on the journal he had maintained since his travels had begun. He wished he were on his way home and told himself that he would be soon, for the first time in more than a year.

Lion's travels had started shortly after he joined the Coalition, a loose-knit organization of Southerners who anticipated the breakdown of the Union on the issues of States' Rights, slavery, and economics. Handsome and persuasive, his potential as spokesman was recognized rapidly, and he soon came to the attention of Ambrose Duquesne, one of the four men who ran the young but growing group. His first assignment had taken him throughout Virginia, from Richmond and Norfolk to a hundred scattered small towns to recruit new members. Later in the year, as the House of Representatives failed over and over to elect a speaker, and as the national conventions neared, it became obvious to even the most hidebound observer that deep differences divided the country. The Coalition believed the eventual emergence of the South as a separate nation was inevitable. That the North would react with force of arms was also conceded. To that end Lion and others like him had been dispatched to England, France, Russia, and the rest of Europe. Lion's job had been to point out to those in power in England that it would be to their advantage to deal with two American governments instead of one and to ascertain just what assistance they might be willing to render. Numerous meetings in London, in which lower cotton prices for

England's mills had been promised, had aroused various members of Parliament to voice private and unofficial support for the Coalition's goals. Flush with success Lion had returned to New York, where the talk he heard confirmed everything he'd believed for the past year. The South *would* be forced to fight, and like the lumbering locomotive ahead, no living man could single-handedly stop the coming conflict.

The train lurched and clattered. Its whistle sounded a shrill message across the green fields. To the right, patches of Long Island Sound could be seen between racing trees. Telegraph poles whipped past so close to the window that they blurred. Pensive, Lion extracted an envelope from his pocket. He knew the contents by heart, but read through them one last time before sealing tne envelope, as Duquesne had instructed.

> Harmon, Duquesne, and Leithe Shipping Company hereby authorizes Lion Burleson McKenna to act with full authority as their agent in the purchase of eight (8) sailing ships hereinafter described.

An irrepressible grin spread across his face. Whatever happened during the week ahead, the Blackheaths' reaction to that first sentence alone would be worth the trip.

Michael woke sometime after two o'clock. Ravenous, but otherwise little the worse for wear, he returned to the club car and ordered a prodigious meal for both himself and Lion. Outside, the difference in climate became more pronounced as Massachusetts gave way to New Hampshire and, scant miles later, Maine. The train passed still-bare trees, and budding flowers that Lion knew had bloomed more than a month earlier in Virginia. From time to time the sharp-eyed traveler could catch a glimpse of the massive boulders that formed a resolute barrier against the explosive Atlantic tides, and beyond, even more rarely, the ocean itself, slate-gray under the clouds that were following them north.

Michael and Lion returned to their car and spent the last two hours of their journey talking. Only then did Lion reveal the letters he carried authorizing him to buy ships, and held out to Michael the distinct possibility that the Blackheath facilities might supply them An awestruck Michael listened with increasing excitement. God!

How his father would be pleased. An order for eight clippers would insure a healthy profit for the next two years. At that rate Sewal could indulge his hatred for steam. Before he knew it the time had passed and the train was clattering over a long trestle. "Waupinau Bay," Michael explained, and pointed forward to a picturesque town nestled on the northern shore. "And that's New Forest. Looks like a stereoscopic picture from here. It's real enough, though, as you'll see." Far to the right a barque ran up-channel toward the train. "She'll dock over there." He pointed again, this time toward the Blackheath shipyards. "Plenty of time to miss the storm. Tide's on the way out, though, so she'll have to take care to miss Haden's Bar. We'd better get ready." Michael pulled down their carpet bags from the overhead rack, straightened his new uniform, threw back his shoulders, and assumed a heroic pose. "Past-Midshipman Michael Blackheath reporting to impress the home folks, sir," he barked mock-seriously. "Well?"

"Well what?" Lion asked, laughing.

"Do you think they'll be impressed?"

"Only if they're unmarried and female," Lion answered quickly. "And it's too late for that as far as you're concerned."

"Remember. I have almost a week left," Michael shot back, brushing the sleeve of his knee-length coat across the gleaming brass buttons arrayed in twin columns down his chest.

"New Forest!" the conductor called. "Station is New Forest!" The sound of the wheels on the rails changed as the train rumbled off the bridge and pulled into the station on the western edge of town. Brakes squealed and the engine sighed voluminous clouds of steam that ballooned and dissipated in frail wisps. Sunlight, sliced into amber rods by pine trees on a low ridge to the west, streamed horizontally across the tracks and flickered along the barely moving train, then stopped, lighting one window and leaving the next in deep shadow.

New Forest was a side stop on the way to Portland, so few people got off. Michael led the way down the aisle and out the door. Near the front of the train a half-dozen ragtag boys stared enviously at the engineer, who ignored them with regal pomposity. As soon as Lion left the steps the conductor folded them back and bawled, "All aboard" to the almost empty platform. The boys up the track jumped back as a huge cloud of smoke belched from the stack, the whistle shrieked, and the mighty pistons pushed the wheels into agonizingly slow motion.

"Michael!" The robust voice belonged to a stern-faced gentleman Lion recognized from the picture he'd seen two nights earlier. Sewa: Blackheath strode across the platform and grasped his son's hand. Behind him a woman dressed in a light-blue crinoline dress with white undersleeves gathered at her wrists stepped down from the shadows of the depot door. Hair the color of molten sunlight billowed out from beneath a gaily trimmed blue capote. Lion stared at her. This could only be Eve Blackheath, but unlike the rest of the family, the photograph had lied, for those chemically derived images were an anemic substitute for the spirited, intelligent-looking beauty who faced him.

"I should like you to meet Lion McKenna, Father," Michael said. "I took the liberty of inviting him to be our houseguest for the wedding." Sewal's eyes ranged over Lion's sporty brown coat, yellow vest, and brown bowler, so markedly different from Michael's formal Navy uniform. "We met in New York two days ago. Aside from a business proposition you'll be pleased to hear, I am more in his debt than many friends are to one another in an entire lifetime."

"A debt, you say?" Sewal growled, diverting Lion's attention from Eve.

"A gang of brigands attacked me on the street Saturday night. Lion joined with me in driving them off. Why, he saved my life."

The patriarch of Dawn Wind softened considerably. "Then I share that debt with my son," he said, vigorously shaking Lion's hand. "And happily, too."

Lion laughed easily. "Michael exaggerates, Mr. Blackheath."

"And Lion is modest," Michael insisted. "But wait until you hear. A dozen pipe- and knife-wielding men against us, our backs to the wall . . ."

"Only a dozen? Why not two dozen?" a bespectacled and bookish young man said, stepping forward. "I'm Justin. The black sheep of the Blackheaths. Have a Doctor Hubbard's?" Justin held out a small white box labeled DOCTOR HUBBARD'S CELEBRATED WILD CHERRY AND ICELAND MOSS COUGH CANDY.

"You remember my younger brother from the photograph," Michael said, his displeasure with Justin's flippancy barely disguised.

Eve approached and held out her hand. "Justin's non sequiturs hide a kind and generous heart," she said, at the same time boldly shaking Lion's hand. "I'm Eve. And now that you've met the family, it would do well to bring you to Dawn Wind."

"A curious name," Lion said, bowing graciously and not releasing Eve's hand until he had kissed it in cavalier fashion.

Eve laughed. "For the house, I trust you mean, sir," she said.

"I am certain you will find it an appropriate title," Sewal said. "Hamlet?"

A Negro approached. "Yes sir, Mister Blackheath. I pulled the carriage around to the side. Welcome home, Mister Michael."

"It's good to see you, Hamlet," Michael said, at last able to speak at a normal volume as the train, spewing charcoal black smoke from its stack and rending the tranquil New England air with a shrill whistle, disappeared around the bend. "This is Mr. McKenna. He will be staying with us for a few days. His wishes are my wishes."

"Yes, sir," the black man replied.

"From the South," Justin noted pointedly, with a sidelong glance at Hamlet. "Your accent gives you away, sir."

"My accent?" Lion asked. He had not noticed the angry glint in Hamlet's gaze. "Strange. I was under the impression that all of *y'all* had accents."

Laughing, they started for the carriage. Lion couldn't help noting the close physical resemblance between Sewal and Michael. The son was taller and stouter than the father, but both men shared the same eyes, square-cut features, and forceful stride. Justin and Eve were slim of face and with high cheekbones, and Lion could only assume they took more after their mother.

"We weren't expecting a visitor," Sewal said as they walked out of the station, "so I brought the carriage instead of the hansom. I hope you won't mind being crowded, Mr. McKenna."

Lion smiled good-naturedly and glanced surreptitiously at Eve. "I shan't mind in the slightest," he answered.

That they were indeed crowded detracted little from the ride. Lion took a deep breath. The mingling of pine scent and salt breeze was delightful. Lion's impressions of the North had been formed during stays in New York and Boston, where the air was filled with smoke and the stench of too many people packed in too small spaces. In contrast the clarity and brisk freshness of a Maine afternoon came as a startling surprise. The town itself, as Michael had said on the train, was real enough, and picturesque as the photographs of New England he had seen. White houses, simple box-shaped constructions with pleasant little lawns bordered by white picket fences, dotted the rolling landscape. Others of stone and clapboard appeared more rugged, but no less cozy. All seemed handsomely maintained and meticulously kept. Then, as the road climbed a low hill, dipped, and ran some yards below the ridge, Lion glimpsed larger, more stately homes buffered from neighbors by mixed hardwoods and fruits.

"New Forest's finest," Michael explained, pointing out one columned mansion. "Our mayor, Allan Castebury, lives there." Just down the road he pointed again, this time to a new-looking mansion of red brick with blazing white trim. "That's the Aldrins'. You'll meet him tomorrow or the next day, probably. One of New Forest's oldest families."

The carriage jolted into a new set of ruts, started downhill past the Congregational Church, and entered the town proper. Here the street was paved with cobblestones. Lion read the names on the signs as the carriage rattled past Miss Ellen's Millinery, the Bank of New Forest, Oxford's General Store, the post office, and the firehouse—all with their backs a scanty twenty feet from the western shore of the bay. At the end of the row a placard in intricate script read, NEW FOREST PRESS. Lion noted the village green with its central bandstand was no different than those found in any of a hundred sleepy, rural Southern towns. Nor, indeed, were they different from many he had seen in Europe, where beaux with their young ladies would stroll arm in arm along flower-lined walks under the watchful eye of a careful parent or aunt or uncle.

The business district continued with less ostentation on the far side of the green. A pair of competing eating establishments faced each other across the narrow street. Dressmakers, the New Forest schoolhouse, and a dozen other buildings Lion could only guess at disappeared, cut off from view by a covered bridge over a canal emptying into the bay.

Here, quiet at the end of the day, were the coopers' and ships' chandlers and blacksmiths' shops. Here, too, noisy with music and laughter, were a half-dozen scattered taverns where sailors and lumbermen and common laborers gathered to drink and carouse. A hundred yards down the road, Michael gestured toward the shadowed outlines of a large group of buildings. "The Blackheath Shipyards," he explained. "That's the rigging loft and there behind it the sail loft. The long one—" fully as long as any ten of the houses in town placed end to end "—is the rope walk."

The road branched as they passed the shipyard. "That way winds back around town to the lumber mill and then north to Portland, if you follow it far enough," Michael said, pointing to the left fork. "We call this Bayside Drive," he added as the two-horse team bore right and slowed. They climbed away from the water to the top of a bluff that paralleled the edge of the bay. Far ahead, visible through a wide lane of greening poplars, the land jutted dramatically up and out to form a craggy peninsula crowned by a magnificent granite and wood-trimmed mansion set about with towering pines.

That has to be Dawn Wind, Lion thought, as the stand of trees ended and the carriage sped over a stretch of bare granite.

The view was stunning. Lion had traveled far in the last thirty months, but few sights could compare to the vista laid before him. Waupinau Bay, restless in conflicting winds, spread west and south to the far hills and east to the ocean itself, which stretched to the limits of imagination. Above him the sky was still clear, but nearby to the south, the bank of towering cumulus clouds that had followed the train north, their tops still brilliantly lit by the setting sun, reared over the awesome panorama. In contrast, a feeble blinking light stretched like a finger from a tiny sliver of white on the opposite shore.

How puny are the works of man, Lion couldn't help thinking as he envisioned sailors tossed on the angry sea and staring at that guiding beacon. How grandly we perceive ourselves, and how vainly strive to twist nature to our own ends. And history, too, he reflected silently, thinking of the papers he carried and of how he had deceived Michael and hoped to manipulate Sewal Blackheath to his own ends. Quite suddenly he felt incredibly small and insignificant. He was, he thought, like the keeper of that frail light. One strove to soften the blows nature unleashed on mankind, the other sought to right the wrongs man perpetrated against his own kind. Both tried valiantly, but with no assurance of success. Lion didn't know about the light-house keeper, but could say this of himself, he could only try. No matter how insignificant his individual effort might be, therein lay his single hope for honor.

Chapter 5

"Well then, young man, what have you for me?"

Lion removed a thick envelope from his coat pocket and extended it across the desk to Sewal. "As Michael told you, sir, I represent a firm that wishes to buy Blackheath ships. Once you've read this, I'll be happy to answer any preliminary questions."

"Mmm. Harmon, Duquesne and Leithe. Of Charleston, you say?"

"Yes, sir."

Sewal hefted the envelope as if its weight and texture held a message of its own, then set it on the desk in front of him and stared openly at Lion. McKenna's slate-gray eyes revealed little of his thoughts. A long moment passed. "Very well. Sit down. Make yourself comfortable. Michael?"

Lion sat in the wing chair Sewal had indicated, crossed his legs, and lit a cigar. The old man's business may have been going through some rough times, but that would not make dealing with him any simpler, he decided. The Blackheaths hadn't gotten where they were, or lasted this long, by running scared. His eyes roved the room. Three walls were covered with bookshelves, of which only about a third were full; the rest of the space was given to models of ships and a wondrous assortment of seafaring mementos. The fourth wall was hung with portraits and paintings of ships. In one corner a huge family Bible lay open on a rack.

"Interesting," Sewal grunted, at the same time dipping a quill and writing a note. He waved the first sheet of paper from the envelope. "Here," he said, handing it to Michael before going on to the second sheet.

Meticulous, hard-headed, God-fearing, proud. Lion ran through the list of attributes he'd ascribed to Sewal. Dawn Wind itself reinforced his opinion. The furniture was sparse, but elegant. Clean, sharp lines predominated amid muted colors that set off a great deal of natural wood and sparkling white paint. Dress was simple and almost austere, reflecting, Lion thought, the austerity of the landscapes he had seen. The three men wore black suits and Eve, from whom Lion had hardly been able to keep his eyes, a simply cut, light-blue cotton gown. Even—or especially, he thought—this room conformed to the general atmosphere. The huge brassrail bed, a pair of ladder-back chairs, a small combination wardrobe and dresser, and a wash-stand all looked stiff and uncomfortable.

A rustle of paper distracted him. Lion looked up in time to see Sewal hand the last sheet to Michael, then busy himself with more notes. There had been an awkward situation, he reflected. Dinner was over, and Sewal had risen. "Tell Eustacia thank you, please, Mr. Pole. Mr. McKenna? Michael?" Without waiting, he had preceded them to the library, leaving Justin and Eve behind. The eldest son favored, Lion thought. Neither rare nor unlikely, but perhaps not overly wise, either, to judge by the look on Justin's face when Sewal so pointedly excluded him. Still, if Sewal Blackheath wanted to run his household and business like an Old Testament patriarch, it was not for Lion McKenna, an outsider, to comment.

"So. Eight ships," Sewal said, when Michael finished reading.

"Yes, sir. Eight fast clippers."

"For?"

"For commerce, of course. Cotton to England, sundry goods back to America."

"Yes." Sewal looked down at his notes. "Eight ships is a large order, Mr. McKenna. Nowhere in these documents—" he tapped the pages, "—did I see a price mentioned."

"We await your bid, sir, at which time we trust you are open to negotiation. My purpose, at the moment, is to ascertain whether or not you are interested, or if your company has the capacity to deliver these ships in the time stated."

"I see. Michael? What do you think?" Sewal asked.

"Eight months from signing is awfully soon."

"I agree."

"We don't, sir." Lion rose, paced once across the room, and stopped in front of the desk. "Especially not if all eight ships are identical."

"What do you know about shipbuilding, Mr. McKenna?"

"Not a great deal, sir. Not nearly as much as you, to be sure. But I do know that eight identical vessels in eight months in an established yard staffed by experienced workmen is not unreasonable."

"One hundred twenty tons of wooden masts and yards. Three

thousand feet of chain. Five tons of metal hoops for the masts and yards. Eleven thousand yards of canvas for *one* suit of sails. Twenty tons of copper for sheathing. Fifteen hundred tons of white oak—in very short supply, I might add. Three quarters of a million feet of pine, most of which has to be shipped in." Sewal stopped, reached his hand forward, and tapped the desktop with his forefinger for emphasis. "Times eight, sir. We are not speaking of a minor undertaking."

"We understand that, sir," Lion said firmly. "Which is why Harmon, Duquesne and Leithe is prepared, as you will note in paragraph twelve, to assist in obtaining supplies."

"And are likewise prepared to assist in alleviating a Maine winter?" Sewal asked.

"A great deal of the work is done inside to begin with." Lion leaned forward for emphasis. "And for the amount of money involved, you should be able to afford a shed large enough to continue work on the hulls."

Sewal rose, walked around the desk to a small side table, poured three snifters of brandy, and served Lion and Michael. "Please sit," he said, taking a seat in front of his desk. He swirled the brandy, gazed at the ceiling. "Late April, eh?"

"Yes, sir," Lion said.

"In time to ship the winter cotton crop?" Sewal asked drily.

Lion's hands tightened on the brandy snifter. He forced himself to relax and let the anger drain through a calculated smile. "Eight ships times approximately sixty thousand dollars equals something in the neighborhood of four hundred and eighty thousand dollars. Permit me to answer your question with another."

"By all means."

"When, Mr. Blackheath, were numbers of that magnitude last discussed in this room?"

Michael coughed nervously. He had never heard anyone except Justin speak that way to his father. I should have warned Lion, he thought. Father's rage will be monumental. To his surprise Sewal began to chuckle, then laugh openly.

"Plain words plainly spoken. You go to the heart of the matter, Mr. McKenna." Sewal's eyes were twinkling; he looked almost pleased to have been bested. "Michael?"

"Sir?" Michael asked, startled.

"Can you answer the gentleman's question?"

"I'm not sure." Michael was uncertain of how much Lion knew or of what Sewal wanted him to say. "Not too long ago, I'm sure."

"The last time was March of 1856," Sewal snapped. "The shipping depression of fifty-seven drove even David Makay, the nation's largest shipbuilder, bankrupt. And his resources were—and are—much greater than ours, as I'm sure Mr. McKenna knows full well."

It was Lion's turn to be embarrassed. "We did . . . delve into the situation in a small way. Discreetly, of course."

"Of course. Only damned fools wouldn't have." Sewal rose and set his brandy snifter on the desk. "Very well, then. My son and I will discuss your proposal, sir, and you will have an answer before Friday. In the meantime I suggest you inspect my yards and our New England spring scenery."

Lion was being dismissed. "A splendid idea," he said, rising. "It's been a hectic day, and I could use a little sleep. If you don't mind?"

"Not at all." Sewal let the way across the library. "You know the way to your room?"

"Top of the stairs, second door on the left." Lion held out his hand and shook Sewal's. The two men's eyes locked. "I hope we'll be doing business together, sir."

"We shall see, Mr. McKenna. We shall see," Sewal said, opening the door.

"Good night, sir. Michael."

"Yes. Good night . . ."

The door closed. Michael remained standing while his father circled the desk, sat, and picked up the proposal. "Well, Michael, what do you think?" he asked suddenly.

"We build the ships, of course. We need the business."

Sewal nodded. "Of course. Tell me. Do you know who Ambrose Duquesne is?"

Michael took a sip of brandy. "I assume he's one of the principals of Harmon, Duquesne and Leithe."

"Which, until two years ago, was Harmon and Leithe."

"Oh?" Michael shifted uncomfortably. Earlier, his father had pretended not to know the company and now he was clearly leaving out something. If Lion was in any way disreputable, and he had brought him to Dawn Wind . . . "I don't see what that has to do with it," he said a little lamely.

"I know my shipping firms, Michael. Large and small, North and South, and most of the European ones as well. Harmon is a good and decent man. So is Leithe. Duquesne is a rabble-rousing, virulent secessionist who forced his way into the company late in fifty-seven when they, too, were on the verge of bankruptcy. It smells, Michael. It smells to high heaven. And the very thought of a Blackheath ship being used in a war against the Union goes against everything this family has ever stood for."

Father and son sat without talking, each mulling over the problem from his own viewpoint. Michael leaned back in his chair, closed his eyes, and sighed. "How many bottoms on the ways do we have?" he finally asked.

"Two. Each less than a thousand tons," Sewal answered.

"And under contract?"

"One more."

A log fell in the fireplace. The grandfather clock in the hall struck eleven. A whisper of thunder seeped through the thick stone walls. "Do you really think the secessionists will have their way?" Michael finally asked.

"I don't know," Sewal said. "Clearly, they do."

"But it could be a legitimate proposal," Michael insisted heatedly. "They do have to ship their cotton."

"Yes, they do." For the first time, Sewal sounded hesitant. "I would like to know more about McKenna, though. Is he Duquesne's man? Or Harmon's and Leithe's?"

"He saved my life, Father. We can't let the business founder."

Sewal shuffled through the papers. At last he rose and moved to a large work table behind Michael's chair. "They want a quote," he said in a tight voice. "Under the circumstances, tonight is as good a time to start figuring one as any."

Lion's eyes glowed a ghostly pale gray as he stared at the ceiling. He still wore boots, trousers, and shirt, and he lay atop the comforter. His room was on the northern side of the house, and outside the storm had filled the sky. The only light that penetrated the room came from lightning, the only sound from the windswept thunder and the tumultuous waves crashing against the granite base of the Dawn Wind promontory. The dark interspersed with unpredictable blue-white light, the absence of any human sound, the strain of being among strangers for less than honorable reasons, had begun to take their toll. His body felt as though it was contracting with each flash of lightning, expanding again with the absolute darkness.

Enough. He had to get out. The bed creaked as he sat up, and the floor groaned as it accepted his weight. He groped for the door and pulled it open, then walked carefully to the railing surrounding the stairwell and peered over. Light still spilled from the library, and he could hear Sewal's and Michael's voices as they worked.

Relieved, Lion looked about. His was the only open upstairs door. Above him a dim light gleamed in the cupola. The Captain's Walk, as they called it in the North, had been pointed out to him earlier, but he had paid scant attention. Now, unable to sleep and excited by the promise of success, he determined to climb up there. Cotton shirt open to the waist and trousers tucked into soft deerskin boots weren't the proper attire for prowling around a strange house, but Sewal and Michael were busy, and no one else would be up. He placed his hand on the railing and, stepping close to the edges of the stairs to insure a minimum of noise, began to climb, pausing only when his head cleared the level of the floor, for another had preceded him to the glass-enclosed octagonal room.

Eve Blackheath stood alone, one hand resting regally on a magnificent brass compass case. Her face was turned to the south, away from Lion, and toward the center of the storm. She wore a floor-length silk nightdress, and a quilted overgown lay draped over a captain's chair at her side. Her golden hair was braided into a single, thick strand that ran almost to her hips.

Lion realized he was holding his breath and exhaled slowly. Outside, the sky shimmered with sheet lightning that outlined her naked form beneath the silk. Lion's throat tightened and his pulse raced. A gentleman would have turned away, but any thought of doing so faded with the lightning. Lion ventured three more steps.

Eve tensed. She had been staring into the night, and as the lightning vanished, a face materialized in the glass. At first she thought it was a hallucination, but the vision cleared and became the full figure of a man. Momentarily frightened, then angry, she spun. "Sir!"

"Your pardon, Miss Blackheath. I had no intention of disturbing you."

"Yet you make a rude appearance."

She was more beautiful than Lion thought possible. The warm lantern light softened the lines of her face and made the silk gown glow until she looked as though she were sheathed in amber light. Her legs against the gown were trim and molded, her breasts high and firm and hard against the soft silk. "I . . . I could not tell it was you," Lion said lamely.

"Did you think I was a ghost, then? Really, Mr. McKenna."

"Not a ghost," Lion interrupted, drawing close to her and looking directly into her eyes. "But an image crafted of dreams."

Eve could not move, felt frozen to the spot, like a tiny bird enthralled by the unblinking eyes of a cat. "Your excuse is a poor one, Mr. McKenna," she said, unable to understand why it should be so hard to speak. "Unless you are a somnambulist."

"Perhaps I am dreaming," Lion said slowly, his voice thick. He raised his hand and held it near her cheek. "If so, my fingers will pass through you as easily as a bird flies through the mist. If not—" His hand moved, and two fingers lightly touched her on the side of her face. "—Your skin will feel as soft . . . and smooth . . . and cool . . ."

Eve's eyes closed. His fingers felt cold as ice, warm as the sun. Nothing had ever prepared her for the sensations that coursed through her body. Blindly, her hands raised until her fingers touched the line of his jaw, then ran lightly over his hard, handsome face. When she opened her eyes, he was leaning closer to her. His black hair blended with the shadows. His eyes, she thought, changed from gray to quicksilver. Before she could protest his lips touched hers with a caress as soft as a feather.

Blue fire filled the cupola. Simultaneously, a hissing bolt of lightning split the air. Startled, Eve jumped backward and, her senses restored, looked around frightened.

"A close call," Lion said, his voice abnormally deep.

"Yes," Eve whispered, staring at him. Suddenly ashamed, she seized her overgown and held it protectively in front of her breasts. Her forehead creased and, fingers trembling, she touched her lips. "A very close call," she said faintly. "If you'll excuse me, please? . . ." Eyes lowered, shoulders rigid, she stepped around Lion and started down the stairs.

He heard her slippers on the steps, the creak of wood, finally a door open and close. She was gone. Lion looked around. A moment earlier the cupola had been a place where dreams were made. With Eve's passing he stood once more in the mundane world of wood and glass and metal objects. Sighing, he folded his hands behind his back and stared at his reflection in the glass. Every time the lightning flashed outside, it disappeared. He stood for a long time without moving while muddled thoughts of ships, and war, and Eve circled endlessly in his mind. Appear, disappear. Darkness, lightning. Eve. Slender legs, trim and molded. High breasts, firm and hard against soft silk. Hair the color of gold. Skin unbearably soft. Appear, disappear.

The lantern went out. Lion's reflection faded. Only the darkness, and the vision of Eve, was left.

Chapter 6

Lion didn't go to sleep until after three, but woke refreshed and buoyant before six. Standing in front of the mirror, he stretched and flexed his muscles. Not bad for thirty, he thought, and then dressed quickly and hurried downstairs. A half hour later he'd drunk coffee, decided to take a walk, and found himself whistling and striding briskly along the perimeter of Dawn Wind.

Later, unwilling to let Eve out of sight, he followed her and placed himself where she couldn't miss him. Each time he was certain they would meet and talk, Eve began to fidget uncomfortably and seek the most crowded room available. Shortly after noon, Lion realized he was acting like a fool and, embarrassed, set off again, this time to wander the northern beach and ponder what had happened to him.

Thirty years old. In love once, but never again, for that lesson had been learned. Infatuated? Numerous times. Why else did women exist? Fall in love as often as you like, he'd told himself. Just don't let it get in the way of common sense. It was good advice. Anyway, there was work to be done. First things first. He'd come to Maine to get ships, not a woman. Feeling better, he skimmed rocks along the waves for a few minutes and, whistling again, made his way back to the house.

The next few days passed quickly. That afternoon Sewal and Michael led Lion on a tour of the shipyards, explained each stage of the shipwright's art, and assiduously avoided mentioning the contract. Tuesday night was the last that any of the men would sleep in the house, which was to be reserved for the women until after the wedding. On Wednesday morning Lion helped erect the large pavilion-style tents brought to house the men, transforming the western lawn into a scene from medieval England. That afternoon they went to the train station early to meet Michael's best man, Jack Travis. Jack was from South Carolina and had gone to St. John's University in Annapolis, mainly because his father was an instructor in navigation and fencing at the Naval Academy. Through fencing, Michael and Jack had become close friends. That evening they were back at the train station to meet Aunt Millicent Neal, Sewal's mother's sister; John, her son, and Mimi, her granddaughter and Eve's second cousin. The pace at Dawn Wind was quickening. By the time everyone had been introduced, eaten a cold buffet supper, and exchanged the latest news of absent friends and acquaintances, the flimsy cot Lion had been assigned was a welcome relief.

Thursday was bedlam. Eve, Eustacia, Maisie, and Mimi Neal spent the morning converting the upstairs of the house into a dormitory. Hired help from town arrived with a wagonload of cots, another of tables, yet another of chairs. On the east lawn carpenters from the shipyard were busy building the dance floor and the pulpit where Michael and Rosamond would be married. Extra stable and kitchen helpers scurried about underfoot. The pace didn't slow until almost four in the afternoon, and by then it was time to rush down to the docks to watch the United States Navy sailing frigate, the *Congress,* bring the Cabells to New Forest.

Every line taut and in place, her brightwork sparkling, the *Congress* was an impressive sight as she drifted to a stop and let loose her anchor with a loud splash and a roar that rumbled across the water. Moments later, to the shrill wail of bosuns' pipes, the captain's gig was lowered over the side. Everyone held his breath as the captain, accompanied by Admiral and Mrs. Cabell and Rosamond, negotiated the narrow ladder from deck to gig, then set off across the water.

Michael's palms were sweating. He was convinced that Rosamond loved him but sometimes that love left him faintly surprised. God knew, there were other wealthier or more talented or better-looking men who had sought her hand. And yet she had chosen him. Sometimes, as during that moment when he reached out to help her onto the dock, his heart skipped a beat. If he ever lost her, if any other man ever won her away from him, he knew he would be destroyed.

"Michael!" she whispered, her voice low and rich as she came into his arms.

"I've missed you," Michael said in return, holding her to him.

"Well, Blackheath, we made it," the admiral's voice boomed. "Watch your step, my dear," he added over his shoulder to Mrs. Cabell as he stepped onto the dock and shook Sewal's hand.

The captain of the *Congress* and the Neals were introduced. Lion stayed in the background, putting off the inevitable meeting with Rosamond as long as possible. When the admiral noticed him and called out his name, he took a deep breath.

"McKenna! What're you doing here, lad? Good to see you again."

Lion made himself smile and shook the Admiral's hand. "Friend of Michael's, sir," he said. He could see Rosamond out of the corner of one eye. She was staring at him. "Good to see *you* again," he added lamely.

Six feet away, a shaken Rosamond tried to concentrate on something Sewal was saying and missed it entirely. For a moment she thought she would faint, but then, trembling, composed herself.

"Something the matter, dear?" Michael asked, turning from Mrs. Cabell and taking her arm.

"Matter?" Rosamond's smile was dazzling. She took Michael's arm as much for support as to be closer to him. "Just getting my land legs again. And a little too much excitement, I think. Michael?" She stood on tiptoe to whisper into his ear. "I love you."

"And I you," Michael whispered in return. "Come on. There's someone I want you to meet."

Admiral Cabell was introducing Lion to the captain of the *Congress* when Michael and Rosamond approached. "Lion?" Michael said, interrupting.

I shouldn't have come here, Lion thought, steeling himself. "Yes?" he said aloud, turning to see Rosamond and Michael at his side.

"You remember Rosamond, I believe."

"I do, indeed," Lion said heartily. He forced himself to breathe evenly, to smile naturally. "Hello, Rosamond."

Rosamond held out her hand for Lion to shake and paled slightly at his touch. "So we meet again, Mr. McKenna," she said, a little stiffly. "What a pleasant surprise!"

Michael was looking from one of them to the other. Unless his imagination was running away with him, something was going on between them. Had they been better friends than Lion had indicated?

Was Rosamond capable of—he made himself stop. Fantasies like that led down a path he refused to take. Things were as they seemed. They had to be, he thought, breaking the spell he'd cast upon himself.

"—What was her name?" Lion was saying.

"Stephanie Harris. Surely you remember her? Blonde hair and a little, turned-up nose? She's going to be my maid of honor."

"Michael? Rosamond?" Sewal called from across the dock. "Are you ready?"

"Yes." Michael beamed. "I guess it's time to get to the house. You'll have a chance to talk over old times later." He took Rosamond's arm. "Shall we?"

"By all means," Lion said, indicating with a sweep of his arm that they should precede him. The moment their backs were turned he heaved a silent sigh of relief. Rosamond had carried it off impeccably. The worst part was over. And as far as he could tell, Michael suspected nothing.

The rest of the more than a hundred guests due to arrive from Washington, Baltimore, New York, Boston, and points between and beyond began to arrive Friday morning. Stephanie Harris and her family came from Richmond. A brace of admirals accompanied by wives and aides from Washington. A half-dozen of Michael's classmates from Norfolk. Lucius Pemberton, a business associate of Sewal's, and his daughter, La Dana, a close friend of Eve's from New York. Assorted relatives of both families from as far west as Ithaca, New York, as far north as Quebec, and south as Atlanta. More friends who had done business with Sewal, along with their wives. More of the military, and a few politicians and bureaucrats who were associates of the admiral. By Friday afternoon the confusion was so great that Lion had almost forgotten Rosamond was even there, and managed to dismiss Eve so completely from his mind that he accepted without qualms a request to drive her and Justin to town and the train station. Clattering through the covered bridge and down Grant Street, he pulled to a halt in front of Knight's General Store. "You handle that pair like you know horses," Justin said, leaping to the ground.

"I do," Lion said, climbing down and offering a hand to Eve.

Eve's pink dress billowed like a cloud. For an instant, their eyes met. The touch of her hand and her weight, surprisingly light as he lifted her to the ground, kindled the fire he thought he'd extinguished. "Ever an honor," Lion drawled, wishing he'd been able to leave Justin behind. He let his hands linger on her waist for one fleeting second and then, with a private smile only she could see, released her.

"Are you two planning to stand in the street with the horses?" Justin asked, pulling a watch from his vest pocket. Lion bit his tongue to keep from answering, offered Eve his arm, and escorted her inside.

Eve always experienced a moment of bliss when she entered Knight's store. Eyes closed, she breathed in the rich aromatic blend of tobacco, apples, cloth, cedar, leather, and sweets. "Afternoon, Miss Blackheath," a thin, reedy-looking man called as he finished wrapping a parcel and handed it to Alice Johnstone.

"Good afternoon, Luke. Did that lace I asked about arrive?"

"Yup. Ain't unpacked yet, though," he said, pointing to the far side of the store. "Gentlemen."

"Afternoon, Luke," Justin said, peering into a case. "Business good?"

"Big wedding always helps. Be with you in a minute."

Alice Johnstone, who shared a large, cheerless manor with her sister Rose, turned from the counter. "Good afternoon, Miss Blackheath," she said, looking Eve up and down in an attempt to find something out of order. Black eyes snapping, mouth pursed into a tight smile of disapproval, she turned her attention to Lion. When he removed his hat and nodded in her direction, she looked away quickly, stalked past the three newcomers, and out of the store.

"Well, you made an impression," Justin grinned. "Too flashy," he added, indicating the light-gray coat and trousers and the pale-blue silk vest Lion wore. "A real gentleman would dress more conservatively. Our town spinsters will shred your reputation in no time."

"I doubt Mr. McKenna cares much about reputations," Eve said.

"On the contrary. I do. But not enough to throw away my entire wardrobe," Lion quipped.

Luke Knight emerged from behind the counter. His movements were all jerks, as if he had to think over each motion before he completed it. In this addled manner he picked his way through a jungle of boxes and crates. An apron covered his chest and hung down below his knees. The long sleeves of his white shirt were rolled up to reveal round, bony elbows that looked as if they'd burst through his flesh every time he moved his arms. Stopping in front of Lion he wheezed and wiped his bulbous nose with a blue-and-white-dotted handkerchief. "You're the feller from down South, aren't 'cha." Lion nodded and would have answered, but the storekeeper had already turned to Eve. "Won't be long now," he said, "only two more days. Gonna be a big crowd, eh?"

"Big enough," Eve concurred.

"And that ship! Been a long time since New Forest seen a forty-gun frigate. Longer since they seen a real admiral."

"Sailors ought to be good for business, too," Justin said, opening a box of chocolates from Holland.

"Well, you folks look around," Knight said, flapping his elbows preparatory to another proprietary dash through the store. "Come along, Miss Blackheath. I think I can lay my hands right on that lace." Darting off, he left Eve to follow as best she could.

Lion started after her then gave up, stopped, and looked around. Two glass-fronted counters ran the length of the main room. The left side was devoted to fabrics and notions. Netting, bolts of cloth, vestings, shawls, dress and sewing silks, edgings, embroideries, and parasols lay in neat stacks to be pawed through by housewives with a few precious cents to spare. Toiletries lay further to the rear. Ivory-handled toothbrushes, scrimshawed hairbrushes and pins, curling irons and scissors. Boxes of bath salts and bottles of cologne, perfume, and rosewater and glycerine for chapped hands were arranged artistically around a stack of Hyde and Sans Castile Soap, each cake attractively wrapped to protect the delicate scent it contained. Lion smiled knowingly at the wooden case behind the counter. Cryptically marked with numbers, it would hold feminine necessities to be dispensed in hushed whispers by Mrs. Knight.

To the right were foodstuffs. Boxes of chocolate lay next to others of washed figs, raisins, and candied lemon slices. Bottles of orange, lemon, peppermint, and Bergamet flavorings glowed in the dim light. Tins of Fell's Spices, ginger and mustard and dill and coriander fairly begged to be opened and fill the air with their own sweet pungency. Boxes of Charter Oak, Epicure, Autocrat, and Ponce de Leon coffee sat next to the grinder supplied for those few homeowners who didn't own their own. Tea packed in lead, jars of licorice, boxes of salt, biscuits, and cheeses filled shelf after shelf, and what room was left was given over to rows of canned goods. Barrels of wheat, corn, and barley sat behind the counter. In front, more apples had been left as an invitation for the customer to help himself. A tobacco tree, the doweling sunk into an upright chunk of oak log and festooned with figure-of-eight twists of chewing tobacco, stood next to a case of knives, watches, and chains. Here was the place where boys and men stood and indulged in their own secret fantasies while mothers and wives went about more serious business.

Lion stepped around the cast-iron stove that dominated the center of the store. The back room was devoted to large items, many one of a kind. Farm implements and cookware, washing tubs, irons, crocks for pickles and sausage and eggs, churns, and cradles lay strewn about the floor. Huge, dark, wooden barrels labeled "prime pork," "pickled mackerel," "sperm oil," "smoked herring," and "salt beef" lined the side walls. Stacked and hung on the rear wall were lobster pots and floats and nets and seines. The room looked like a monstrously complicated parlor game in which the participants are given one minute to view a table full of assorted articles in order to remember as many as possible.

"Chocolate?" Justin asked, holding the open box in front of Lion. "I suppose this doesn't look like much after Paris and New York."

Lion bit into what looked like a solid chunk of chocolate. The center was creamy maple. "On the contrary," he replied, swallowing rapidly. "This is all of New York and Paris rolled into one store. What could be more fascinating?" He grinned, picked up a leather harness, and held it to his nose. "Or smell better? It reminds me of home."

Justin shook his head, followed Lion to the front room where Mr. Knight had located the lace trim Eve had ordered and was adding the price of it, and Justin's chocolates, to the Blackheaths' bill. "Quite a store you have, Mr. Knight," Lion said, stopping at Eve's side.

"Been here twenty years. Had a little bit of almost everything in here since then. 'Spect we'll catch up on what we missed in the next twenty," he said proudly. "Anything I can help *you* with?"

"Oh, my goodness!" Eve exclaimed, grabbing her lace and running to the door.

A worried look on his face, Lion followed. "What's wrong?"

"What time is it?"

"Five in three minutes," Luke Knight called from behind the counter.

A train whistle blew in the distance. Eve lifted her skirts and ran toward the carriage, turning back to shout over her shoulder, "Hurry, Justin, Mr. McKenna! We're late already."

Lion and Justin ran after her. "Just who is this we're meeting?" Lion asked, helping her into the carriage.

"Why, Clifford Sarandon, of course. Didn't Justin tell you? You'd better drive again. Justin will point the way."

"Foiled again," Lion muttered as he vaulted into the seat, took the reins, and eased the team into a fast trot. "Who's Clifford Sarandon?" he asked Justin.

"Family friend. Right here and up the hill. Watch out—"

Lion sawed the reins and curved around a trio of ladies crossing the street. From the rear seat, Eve caught a glimpse of Alice Johnstone pointing at them, and groaned with the certainty that the Misses Johnstone had set another mark against her in their book. Lord only knew the stories they'd circulate. Thank goodness, Justin had been along or else they'd have her and Lion nearly married. She giggled. Married, indeed! And then she remembered Lion's face that night in the cupola, remembered the way his eyes had bored into her, and the restive dreams that had waked her during the five long nights since then. Frightened of her own feelings, she clutched the hand strap and rode the rest of the way in silence.

The train to Portland had already discharged its passengers and, exhaling billowing clouds of steam, was pulling out of the station. A portly young man surrounded by bags waited at the edge of the platform and waved as the carriage approached. "That's him!" Justin shouted over the din.

Lion had expected an older man. With sudden clarity he sensed whose particular friend Clifford Sarandon was and, in spite of himself, didn't like it. Irritated, he pulled up close enough to the edge of the platform to force Sarandon to jump backward.

Eve leaped from the carriage without assistance and walked toward Clifford, who doffed his hat and bowed to kiss her hand. A glance over her shoulder showed that Lion was watching closely. "You look very well, Clifford," she said, raising her voice so Lion could hear. "We've missed you. Justin? Will you help with Clifford's bags?" Placing her arm in his, she led Clifford back to the carriage. "You must meet a friend of Michael's, Clifford. He was kind enough to drive us today. Mr. McKenna? This is Clifford Sarandon. Clifford, Mr. McKenna. He comes from Virginia."

"Virginia? Pleased to meet you. My heavens, but you have come a long way." He paused, a little confused by Lion's age and silence.

"Are you . . . uh . . . from Annapolis also?" he asked, trying to be polite.

"No," Lion replied curtly. "I'm a farmer."

"Oh." Clifford smiled and coughed delicately. "I see." He looked around. "My bags? . . ."

"All aboard," Justin said, joining them. "Ready?"

Clifford helped Eve into the rear seat and climbed in next to her, leaving Lion and Justin standing in the street. Justin stole a glance at Eve. He could see she was doing her best to make Lion jealous, and loving every minute of it. Succeeding, too, from the look on Lion's face. Well, well, he thought, won't this be fun. "Coming?" he said aloud, stifling a laugh.

Not answering, Lion climbed into the front seat. "Any place special, ma'am?" he drawled, ignoring Sarandon and looking directly into Eve's eyes.

Eve jerked her hand away from Clifford's arm. "Why, Dawn Wind, I believe," she answered.

Lion winked at her. "Dawn Wind it is, then," he said, not missing the flush blooming on her cheeks, nor the fury in Clifford's eyes.

"Flan!" Aunt Millicent Neal pressed a hand to her cheek and closed her eyes. "Why, I haven't tasted flan in years," she gushed as the last of the men filed out of the room. "And a coffee made it? I've never known a coffee to cook flan before."

"Eustacia is remarkably competent," Eve said, wincing inwardly and hoping her great-aunt's cutting remark didn't get back to the kitchen.

"They're not generally good at it," Cornelia Cabell sniffed. "Too heavy-handed, to my way of thinking."

"I believe there's tea in the parlor," Eve said, cutting off that particular line of conversation. "Mimi, would you help me pour?"

They reassembled in the front parlor where, perched on the front edges of hard, straight-backed chairs, they gossiped of weddings past. Aunt Millicent, still going strong at eighty-seven, led the conversation. She recalled weddings—and births and funerals—from before the turn of the century. Mimi Neal, her granddaughter, had heard all the stories at least twice before. Bored to tears, she sat with a glazed expression on her face and wished, along with everyone else, for the return of the men.

A vastly different scene was being played in the library. There the men relaxed in after-dinner torpor. Dayton Cabell exchanged a few desultory remarks with Sewal, then leaned back and closed his eyes. Justin and Clifford sat with splayed legs on the sofa. Brandy snifters warming in their hands, they traded college stories. David Neal, Sewal's not-so-favorite cousin, sat alone with a bottle of brandy for company. Michael, Lion, and Jack Travis puffed on cigars and, two to one, disputed the legality of slavery in the territories.

The Constitution was ambiguous in reality, but not in the opinions of those who based arguments on it. That the subject had been expounded upon in pulpits, legislatures, country stores, and county fairs made little difference. Luckily, a heavy meal followed by quiet surroundings meant an atmosphere in which tempers remained dulled and pleas for reason were uninfected by passion. "I trust you've solved the world's problems," Sewal said, joining the three.

"Yes, sir," Jack said. "We've just decided the question of slavery in the territories, and—"

"Oh-ho!" Michael interrupted. "*They* have. I haven't."

"—And propose to settle the runaway problem once and for all."

Sewal laughed. "We'd all be better off if you'd work on the price of copper. Or the availability of decent oak."

"Can you wait fifteen minutes?" Michael asked, straight-faced.

"We're due to rejoin the ladies at ten," Sewal said, glancing at the clock.

"That's cutting it a little close, sir," Jack said seriously. "But we'll try. I have a few ideas, even if I don't know much about ships."

"Good. Mr. McKenna? Do you have a moment?"

"Certainly. Gentlemen?" Lion's pulse quickened. This was the first time Sewal Blackheath had asked to speak to him privately since their original discussions. It didn't seem possible to Lion that the old man could reject the proposal outright, but there was always the chance he could set impossible conditions. Carefully maintaining an air of confidence, Lion followed Sewal to his desk.

"I drew this up earlier today," Sewal said quietly, handing Lion two pieces of paper. "It's a letter of intent, if you'd like to read it."

"Of course." Lion read rapidly. Price, approximately sixty-five thousand per ship. Date of delivery, in stages, ending no later than May 30, 1861. Size of ships, approximately thirteen hundred tons. All prices, sizes, dates, and specifications to be agreed upon after more thorough negotiation between the parties involved. "It appears concise enough for the moment, sir. I can't think of anything you've left out," Lion said, handing back the document.

"Good. This is a draft. I'll have two copies drawn up tomorrow, and we can sign them then." He reached across the table, poured two glasses of brandy, and handed one to Lion. "A subdued ceremony, I'm afraid, but under the circumstances? . . . To your health, sir."

Lion touched his glass to Sewal's. "And yours," he said. "May we both prosper."

So that was that. Relief washed over Lion. He'd gotten what he came for, and come what may, the South would have eight more fast ships, each of which would be invaluable. The taste of success was sweet. Euphoric, he poured another brandy, toasted himself, and drank it down.

"Gentlemen, I believe it's time to join the ladies," Sewal said, at the same time opening the library doors. In no great hurry, Lion followed, stood just inside the parlor, and watched Mrs. Cabell commandeer Michael. Grasping each of them by an arm, Aunt Millicent started on Sewal and the admiral, regaling them with the embarrassing story of how little Sewal, at age five, had gone to sea alone in a dory to hunt whales, and got paddled for his trouble. Mimi Neal and Jack Travis were deep in conversation.

Suddenly, Lion realized how tense he had been and still was. It had been a long week, and he was incapable of any more niceties. All he wanted to do was drink until he could sleep and then fall into bed. Quietly, he walked back to the library, picked up his glass and the bottle of brandy and made his way outside to the porch.

The night was peaceful. Dark patches of clouds raced across a nearly full moon. Waves beat a dull, soporific roar on the rocks below. The breeze smelled sweet and salty, scrubbed clean by its three-thousand-mile journey across the open sea. Across the dark waters of Waupinau Bay, the lighthouse glimmered like the eye of a dragon.

"What are you thinking?"

Lion sipped his brandy and didn't answer immediately. "You surprised me," he finally said.

"Then it is lucky for you I am a friend," came the teasing retort from the shadows behind him.

"No. I didn't mean that. I knew someone was there." Lion turned, perched on the railing. Rosamond was sitting on the porch swing. He was sure she was smiling. "I just didn't expect it to be you."

"Oh?" Was she laughing? "And whom did you think I might be, then?"

"I don't know. If I'd been asked, though, I would have expected you to be inside, socializing."

"Ah. I didn't think you knew me that well."

"We both know each other that well."

"Knew," Rosamond corrected.

"Yes," Lion agreed.

"And now that you have found me again, you see I have blossomed into a profound as well as a beautiful woman, and you are once again hopelessly, tragically infatuated. Am I not right?"

Lion paused. She was beautiful—and Michael's, now. "I try not to live in the past," he said.

Rosamond's laughter was clear and musical. She rose from the swing and stood next to him. "Then there is someone else. Let me guess. Ah! Sweet sister Eve. Better keep it from Michael. He's very protective. How terribly amusing."

She smelled like wisteria. "I'm glad you have such a well-developed sense of humor," Lion said coldly.

Rosamond cocked her head to one side and tucked a wayward curl behind her ear. "Poor Lion. A lover of lost causes, driven to strive for that which you can never attain, to hold that which you can never own."

"I sound very tragic," Lion said half humorously. "Too bad you're mistaken."

Rosamond stared into the night, to the horizon where the stars swept down to the sea. "No," she said in a voice as soft as the scent she wore. "No, I'm not." Dark eyes luminous in the moonlight, she gazed at him. For a moment it seemed she would touch him, but her hand fell to the railing. "Men are such children. You dine in the company of women, then retire in privacy to smoke cigars and tell musty old jokes, or plot the ruinous course of the world. Sometimes I think women are the only ones who grow up—and old." Rosamond took the brandy snifter from Lion. She sipped daintily and handed it back, holding on to the glass as his fingers touched hers. "I remember the first time we shared a glass this way. I've been watching you since I arrived."

Lion glanced down at her hand, then back to her eyes. "I was under the impression you had eyes only for Michael."

Rosamond let go the glass. "Eve is going to marry Clifford, you know," she said mockingly, striking back with barely a pause. "Next spring, I suspect. Her father is determined, and whatever Sewal Blackheath wants, he gets, sooner or later."

It took a second for the news to sink in. "That's interesting," Lion said, careful to keep his voice neutral in order not to give away the unexpected hollow feeling in the pit of his stomach. "I wish them well."

"My, aren't we the noble one, though," Rosamond said. She stepped behind him and spoke quietly. "Why did you leave Richmond, Lion?"

"That was four years ago," Lion said. "It doesn't matter anymore."

"Oh? Are you so sure?" Her hand touched his shoulder. The contact was brief and quickly broken. "I loved you, Lion," she said, a hurt tone he had never heard before in her voice.

"No," Lion answered, more harshly than he meant to. "Not really loved. You were younger, then, and believed your own dreams. People like us are drawn together for a time, but we cannot love. After the bed has cooled we're too busy destroying one another to build a life. So I left, before things got out of hand."

Rosamond smiled sadly. "Always wise and considerate, aren't you?" she said. "And wrong."

Lion could sense her move away from him, could hear the rustle of her gown as she crossed the porch. "Rosamond," he said, saying her name for the first time. He could hear her stop and turn. "About yesterday. You handled yourself very well. It's a good thing you did. He's more fragile than he looks." He paused, decided that saying too much would be as bad as saying too little. "Don't stop being careful."

The door closed. Lion leaned back against the post, shook his head, and wondered why fate had to be so damn treacherous as to bring Rosamond Cabell back into his life. As for Eve marrying Clifford, the very idea was preposterous. Not that it mattered to him. Why should it? Eve's future was certainly none of his business. What she did mattered not in the least to him.

Rising, he drank off the last of the brandy. A cold fury had seized him. He lunged away from the post and hurled the snifter as far as he could. Shoulders hunched, he watched the glass sparkle in the moonlight and shatter into icelike slivers against a bare outcropping of shale. One action spurring another, he stalked off the porch.

To hell with the Blackheaths. If it weren't for the contract he'd leave right then. He'd had a belly full of politics and family squabbles, of Michael afraid of his father and Justin sniping at the old man, of Rosamond acting coy and catty, of Eve playing hide-and-seek. She wanted to marry Clifford Sarandon? Fine with him. Let her. He didn't care. Didn't care a bit. He'd almost told himself for the third time that he didn't care when, through the window, he saw Eve and Clifford standing together talking. About what, he wondered. A wedding next spring? Confused and irritated with himself for being so unaccountably angry, he turned away from the scene, headed for his tent, and then to the stables.

New Forest port was alive and bright with light and activity. A hundred yards offshore, the *Congress* lay at anchor. Half its crew had been given liberty and could be found weaving from one to the other of New Forest's four waterfront bars. Lion, not a little unsteady himself, shoved past a reeling lumberjack, pushed open the door of the Anchor and Chain. The churning anger that had driven him to ride at an insane gallop down the night-treacherous road from Dawn Wind had abated, leaving in its wake a dull ache and nasty temperament.

Shells crunched underfoot as he crossed the puddled, pot-holed street. Conflicting music mixed with drunken songs and shouts jangled his brains. Sullen, unable to get as drunk as he wanted, he climbed a set of steps and stared at the curlicued letters on a crescent slab of planking over the double doors. The Land Lock, it said. "Good enough," Lion mumbled, and shoved open the door.

Inside the air was thick with tobacco smoke and the reek of spirits and unwashed men. Sailors and lumberjacks clung to gambling tables. Women in various degrees of undress moved through the crowd, served drinks, and slapped away hands that groped beyond the point prescribed by enticement: anything further demanded cold cash. Their blood fired by rum, endearments, and caresses, a steady stream of men followed suddenly businesslike companions up the creaking stairs.

Lion took in the scene with a glance. A sailor with a pocket watch in his hand had fallen asleep at a table. The watch would be gone when he regained consciousness aboard the *Congress*. A lumberjack and a sailor were arm wrestling at another table. Saucers of live coals smoldered beside their elbows. The loser would be burned for more than the money he had bet on himself. A drunken lumberjack sat at a third table. Left hand splayed palm down, he held a hunting knife with a heavy, foot-long blade in his right. In time to the music, he jabbed the knife into the table between his fingers. Faster and faster flew his right hand until the blade was a blur in the lantern light. A half-dozen onlookers laughed uproariously as, with a howl, the lumberjack finally missed and tacked his ring finger to the table.

"Rum!" Lion shouted over the din when he finally got to the bar.

"What and how much?" the keep demanded.

"Rum. Jamaican if you have it. A bottle," Lion said, throwing a twenty-dollar gold piece on the bar.

A small hush spread out from both sides of Lion as a dozen pair of eyes stared greedily at the gold. The keep picked it up quickly and bit it. "That's not too smart, friend." He smirked, at the same time gave a high sign to someone across the room. "Men have been killed for less around here."

"I'm ready for the one who wants to try me," Lion said, looking up and down the bar and then to the keep. "You know any takers?"

The bartender slapped Lion's change, a bottle of Haitian rum, and a glass on the bar. "Not that are standin' in front of you," he said with a wicked grin. "I'd watch me back, though, if I was you, mate."

"I'll do that," Lion said, tossing a dollar tip on the bar and pocketing the rest of his change.

A table was hard to find. At last, spying one in a corner, Lion made his way toward it. He'd set down his bottle when two sailors claimed the same table. "Sorry, mate," one of them grinned. "This 'un's spoke for."

"By me," Lion growled, looking forward to a fight. "Go find another one, scum."

The first sailor winked broadly at the second. "Aye, and yer scum now, Jacky. You heared the man."

Jacky's eyes rolled comically and his hand inched toward his belt. "Do you remember, Arthur, what happened to the last gentleman called me scum?"

"Broke his legs, as I recall."

"No, yer wrong there. That was the one before. The *last* one I mashed in his face."

"Aye!" Arthur grinned at Lion. "A dandy, just like this one. Fancy gentleman, he was, with a pretty blue vest on. Oh, but the blood set it off nice, it did."

Too drunk to be wary, the sailors separated and started around the table. Lion backed a step for room, pushed a chair out of his way. When a knife flashed in Jacky's fist, Lion's hand snaked into his coat and emerged with the pepperbox pistol.

"Aw, he's got a gun, Jacky," Arthur said, slowing and pulling a knife of his own.

Jacky guffawed. "One shot is all you'll get, Mr. Dandy."

"That will be enough, gentlemen. Gun and knives away, please." The voice was high-pitched, almost a squeak. All three men looked around, then down to see a blocky dwarf dressed in black boots and trousers, white shirt and gold satin vest. A gold ring gleamed in his right ear.

"By the Jesus!" Arthur's eyes widened. "What the hell is it?"

The answer came almost too fast to see. Without warning the dwarf swept a lead sap from his rear pocket and slapped it across the unsuspecting sailor's knife hand, then back and down to catch his left knee. The sound of splintering bones preceded a howl of pain. Almost in the same motion, the dwarf spun and ducked Arthur's thrust. Before the sailor could recover, a steel-edged boot raked down his shin and a tiny fist slammed upward into his groin. Choking with pain, Arthur slumped to the floor.

As surprised as anyone, Lion stared in disbelief and, when the dwarf turned to face him, hurriedly tucked the pepperbox back in his coat pocket. "It's away. It's away," he said, showing his empty hands.

The dwarf stared at him. "Are you making fun of me?"

"Good God, no, man!" Lion answered hastily.

"Good." Ignoring the awed onlookers, the dwarf picked Lion's bottle of rum off the table. "Follow me," he said, stepping around Arthur, who still lay groaning on the floor.

A path opened through the crowd. Intrigued, Lion followed him to a side door and into a hall. "Wait," he said, stopping. "Who are you?"

The dwarf's black eyes glowed in the lantern light. His face was solemn, so much so it looked as if he had forgotten—if ever he had leaned—how to smile. "I am Demetrios," he said matter-of-factly. "You do not belong in there."

"Why not?" Lion asked.

"You are a gentleman."

"Oh? Who told you that?"

Demetrios jerked his head in the direction they had been going. "Madame Laurier said so. I will need your gun, please."

"Now, wait a—"

"Madame allows no weapons inside." Diminutive though he was, Lion had seen him at work, and recognized that same cold look in his eyes. Curious about what came next, and remembering how quickly Demetrios' hands and feet had done their work, he reached for the pepperbox and handed it, grip first, to the dwarf, who tucked it in his waistband. Then he threw open the door, bowed, and ushered Lion into a large sitting room. Large gilt-framed mirrors reflected lanterns and candlelight. A plush bar covered in red velvet took up one corner. Red lounging chairs and couches lined the room, facing a huge plush red ottoman in the center of the floor. Red-lacquered end tables held oil lamps whose globes were decorated with exotic red birds in flight or mating dances and gave off a subdued, rosy light.

It took a second for Lion's eyes to adjust. When they did he realized he was not alone. A girl with skin the color of honey lay on one of the couches. She wore only a light, skin-colored chemise that rode up nearly to her hips. A second girl, taller, more statuesque, and dressed in a long, sheathlike slit gown sat in a chair next to her.

"If I had known you were coming, Mr. McKenna, I would have sent Demetrios to guide you to the gentlemen's entrance at the rear." A door to Lion's left closed, and he looked up to see a woman approaching. She stopped by Demetrios, who showed her the rum Lion had bought. "Mr. McKenna can afford better than that," she said. "Bring us a bottle of the Mumm's. I believe there's some of the fifty-one left." She turned and fixed incredibly clear hazel eyes on Lion. "Welcome, Mr. McKenna. I am Marie Laurier. Won't you sit?"

Her accent was Southern, her voice throaty, almost gravelly, but softer by far. "Should I know you?" Lion asked, knowing he'd never seen her before.

"Of course not. But I know you. You are from Virginia, have been traveling overseas, and are the Blackheaths' houseguest. You came to buy ships."

Lion sat next to her. Plump but not fat, she was dressed in a black gown made of lace that caught at and surrounded her full bosom. Hair black as midnight was pinned in a tousled heap on her head.

Her face was hard, but not unpleasingly so. Once, he was sure, she had been beautiful. "Word seems to travel," he said at last.

"To those who will listen, yes. I listen." A soft pop sounded. Demetrios had entered silently and stood before them. He poured two glasses of champagne, wrapped the bottle in a white cloth in an ice bucket, and left. Marie Laurier picked up the glasses and handed one to Lion. "To your health," she said, so quietly he could barely hear.

"Thank you." Lion drank. The champagne was cold and bitter after all he'd drunk, and he had to make an effort not to grimace. "You're from the South yourself, from your accent," he finally said, making conversation.

Madame Laurier smiled. "I was once. New Orleans," she said. "I'm from New Forest now. A long, lonely way from home." Her eyes closed. The pale green painted on her lids looked almost white in contrast to her long, black eyelashes. Lion watched her raise the glass and drink. When she lowered it, a large red print of her lower lip was left on the rim. Ill at ease, he drank off the rest of his champagne and refilled his glass. "But that is not why we are here, no?" Madame Laurier snapped her fingers. "Molly . . ."

The girl in the chair rose slowly and walked to the ottoman. When she placed her right knee on it the long slit in the side of her dress spread open to reveal the whole of her left leg and hip. Slowly, she raised her arms, placed her hands under long, flowing auburn curls, and lifted it into a cloud around her face. When she let go her hair, her hands floated down her body, caressed her breasts, spread over her stomach and, fingers splayed, traveled down her thighs. As the dress opened even further, Lion realized he had not had a woman in over a month. His belly tightened with desire.

"Her name is Molly. I believe her father was German. Molly is a delightful girl who reserves herself for the strong and willful. Very few have enjoyed her favors, for though she is paid, she will not suffer the touch of a weak or timid man. If you choose her, be careful." She snapped her fingers. Molly uncoiled and left by a concealed door next to the bar.

"And the other one?" Lion asked, surrendering to the cumulative powers of rum and champagne.

"Do not be in too big a rush, Mr. McKenna," Madame Laurier said with an enigmatic smile. Again, her fingers snapped, and a veil descended over Lion's head from behind. Startled, he grabbed for it, only to feel it slide forward, whisk over his champagne glass, and be drawn to the center of the room.

He blinked. Tall as the first girl, this one stood barefooted on the ottoman. She was dressed entirely in veils which covered her from her head to just below her hips, leaving exposed what he thought must be the most spectacular legs he had ever seen. Breathless, Lion leaned forward.

"She is Salome. You may not see her face, Mr. McKenna, but I assure you she is more beautiful than you can imagine," the madame said. "Do you want her?"

"Has any man ever not wanted her?" Lion asked, spellbound as Salome pivoted slowly and the veils billowed out from her body. A lamp behind her made the thin material provocatively translucent, and revealed every line and curve of her body. As Salome spun faster, images shifted, blurred against his embattled senses. Transformed, they became the cupola and Eve, the provocative curves of her body outlined by flashing lightning, standing against the storm-strewn sky. Lion closed his eyes, tried to shut out the sight and the roaring sound that filled his ears. The room reeled so much he had to open them again to retain his balance. Eve. Salome. Heart racing, Lion emptied his glass. He wanted his hands to stop shaking, but they wouldn't. "Send her away!" he hissed. "Get her out of here!"

Madame Laurier waved. Salome stepped down from the ottoman and floated from the room. Lion leaned back, rested his head on the couch. Sweat beaded on his forehead and he felt queasy.

"Are you ill?" Madame Laurier asked. Lion shook his head no, closed his eyes again, then opened them when he heard ice clinking. The madame was wringing out the towel that had been wrapped around the champagne bottle. When she saw his eyes open, she smiled gently.

"Lean back again, my friend," she said, folding the towel and wiping his forehead.

Neither spoke for some time. The cold felt good, and Lion accepted Laurier's ministrations gratefully. "So it's more than ships, after all," she finally said dreamily.

Lion sat up, took the towel from her. "What?"

"You men," she sighed and shook her head. "You put on such a show of indifference, but when you're in love you turn to jelly as quickly as wine turns to vinegar. No woman is more ardent, more miserable, more consumed." She laughed gently. "Or more confused."

"I don't know what you're talking about," Lion said nervously, wadding up the towel and dropping it in the ice bucket.

"No, I don't expect you do." She stood, extended a hand to him. "I am not blind, Mr. McKenna, nor ignorant of the ways of men. I should have known better."

"I assure you . . ." Lion began angrily.

Laurier raised a hand to stop him. "New love is the sweetest flower when first in bloom. But like all flowers, it must fade. Return when the first bloom has worn off. I will have new girls then, for my garden buds the year round."

"I think I'd better leave," Lion said, rising abruptly and heading for the door he'd come in.

"The back door would be better," Laurier suggested.

"I'll go out the way I came in." Lion tried to open the door, and discovered it was locked.

"Your horse is out back," Demetrios said. He had entered from behind the bar. "The small bag tied to the saddle contains your gun."

Lion glared at the dwarf, at last started across the room. Demetrios stopped in front of him. "The champagne cost twenty dollars. Less four for the rum you didn't drink, you owe Madame Laurier sixteen."

Furious, Lion pulled a double eagle from his pocket and slapped it into Demetrios' hand. "Keep the change," he growled, stepping around him. "You earned it."

Waiting by the open door, Madame Laurier placed a hand on his arm to stop him. "Tell her, Mr. McKenna. Perhaps this flower of yours will not fade." Her voice was wistful, tinged with sadness. "It would be nice to be wrong about life for a change."

Lion looked down at his arm, back to her face. "You got your twenty dollars," he said coldly. "Will that be all?"

She didn't answer, merely stepped aside. His head pounding, Lion stalked past her. The horse was waiting, as he'd been told.

No dreams. Not without sleep. Eve stared at the ceiling, listened to Mimi's steady breathing, and envied her. She'd not slept well for . . . how long? No sense asking. Since the night in the cupola. Restless, she rolled out of bed and padded to the window, searched the grounds below, and asked herself a thousand questions. Why hadn't he returned to the parlor the night before? Had he simply left? But why? Had she angered him? Was he too jealous? Would he come back? Why did he . . . ?

Stop! she ordered, clamping a hand over her mouth. Stop it, now! He doesn't care. He'll be gone in a couple of days. I'll not see him again. Her breath caught and she strained to see in the slanting moonlight. Was that him? No. Only a tree waving in the wind.

Eve leaned forward, pressed her forehead against the cooling glass, and closed her eyes. She could see him that way. He wasn't handsome. Well, yes he was, in a way. There was a great deal of character in his face. His forehead was broad and free of lines. His eyes were clear, at once unrevealing and exciting, and at their corners the skin crinkled when he concentrated. His nose—remembering, Eve smiled to herself. His poor, bent nose. She wondered who had hurt him and wished she had been there to ease the pain.

Now what kind of talk is *that,* Miss Blackheath? For shame! Sighing, she opened her eyes for one last look and froze as a shadow detached itself from the trees. He's back! she thought wildly, and then frowned. It was only the shadow of a drifting cloud. The moon and her own emotions had combined to trick her again. Ghostlike behind the glass, she turned and slipped into bed. Not until much later did she drift off to sleep and troubled dreams.

Chapter 7

Something woke him. Confused and groggy, Michael raised himself on one elbow. The lantern that hung from the peak of the tent glowed dully. Outside, it was still dark. "What the hell? . . ."

"Relax. It's me." Jack Travis, who shared the tent with Michael, sat on the edge of the bed.

"What time is it?"

"Umph." Jack tugged a boot off, dropped it to the wooden floor, and started unbuttoning his shirt. "Four, four thirty."

"Good God!" Michael shook his head to clear the cobwebs. "Where the hell have you been?"

Jack grinned. "Out. You sailors aren't the only ones who can navigate by the stars."

"And I suppose you navigated yourself right into someone's bed."

"Not exactly. A bed, that is."

"A bush, then."

"That's closer." Jack chuckled, stripped off his shirt, and rubbed a red spot on his chest. "Why some bite and some don't is a mystery I'll never solve. But that's all right. I'm not complaining."

"Who?"

"La Dana Pemberton."

"My God, she's engaged to Samuel McNalen."

Jack looked aghast at Michael. "Dear heavens, Michael, have you acquired scruples on the eve of your marriage?"

Michael actually blushed. "Let's just say I've gained a certain clarity of vision. Or a different perspective. There's something to be said for chastity."

"That may be true, but not by La Dana. I wasn't the first, and I doubt I'll be the last."

"You mean she wasn't a virgin?" Michael asked, truly shocked.

"My God, no, man," Jack said, amused. "Another bear beat me to that honeyed hive. Still, there was enough left for me to enjoy myself."

"Sam McNalen will be the laughing stock of New York, and you'll be part of the reason why."

"Oh, come on. If a woman offers herself to a man and he refuses, think of the harm done to both parties. The lady loses her self-esteem—" Jack leered wickedly. "—And the gentleman his mind."

"I give up." Michael threw up his hands and lay back. "It'll be dawn soon. I trust you'll be able to wake up long enough to hand me my ring."

"Don't worry," Jack said, stepping out of his trousers. He slipped beneath the covers. The cot creaked as his weight settled. He was exhausted. Indeed, he hadn't the nerve to explain to Michael that before Miss Pemberton there'd been an equally torrid rendezvous with Stephanie Harris. Jack was too tired to endure his friend's newfound penchant for moralizing. Much too tired.

Michael watched his friend for a moment, then lay back himself. Four o'clock. Four thirty. Time to get up in a while. Maybe snooze a little. It was going to be a long day. A married man . . . His legs jerked violently as a dozing dream of tripping on a step woke him.

The sound of Jack's breathing was feather soft. Outside, a night bird called over the muted roar of waves on rock. The moon cast a dark, jagged shadow of a tree limb across the top of the tent. Darker fantasies followed, tendrillike. Try as he might, Michael could not stop them.

Hollow laughter floated through the tent. A woman's laugh. A man's too. Legs. Arms writhing, wrapping, nails clawing. A shaking bush, moved by the forms concealed underneath. ". . . Some bite and some don't . . ." And more laughter. Sniggers from hidden corners, from behind his back. "If a woman offers herself . . ."

No! She wouldn't. Couldn't! The night was alive now with hoots and howls of derision. Insane, choking laughter. Michael's temples throbbed against his palms. His whole body ached with undefined fury. Trembling, he stood and stared down at Jack. He'd kill him! Despoiler! Thief! Michael's fingers curved into talons as he bent over Jack, then suddenly straightened.

Good Christ! but he'd done the same thing. Another time, another woman, but the same thing. Shaken, he pulled on his trousers and stepped out of the tent. The grounds were still, bathed in fresh sea breeze that smelled sweetly of salt. Dawn Wind slept. Carefully picking his way on tender bare feet, Michael moved around to the front of the house and stretched out on the lawn. The grass was cool and soothing. Slowly, the rage passed and reason returned. Very well. He, too, was guilty. But it was different for a man. Different, too, once one approached marriage. Besides, a man could tell which women were that way. Something about them announced their availability. They gave off signals. A turn of the hand, a glance, a rising inflection. Not all of them, to be sure. Certainly not Rosamond. Frowning, he concentrated as he tried to remember. They had met at a party in Washington two years earlier. She was wearing white, and he had been fascinated by her eyes. Had there been signals? Not that he could recall. She had even flinched, he thought, when he first touched her.

And what of later meetings, before they became engaged? Rosamond had given no indication she was one bit less than she appeared. She was modest, she was chaste. Above all, she shared and returned his love. Michael couldn't imagine loving anyone else, couldn't imagine a more perfect wife, a more perfect mother for his children. Let Jack—himself, for that matter—have his flings with the La Dana Pembertons. Such women were for others, not worthy of a Blackheath, barely above despising. He did not need to worry, did not need to plague himself with senseless, black fantasies. His mind at rest, Michael returned to the tent, undressed, and lay down. Sleep, the predawn slumber that revitalizes the worn body and overworked mind, came swiftly and easily. Before the next day ended, Rosamond and he would be wed. No man alive could have been happier.

Sunday morning dawned bright and clear. Unable to sleep, Eve lay quietly in bed and watched the windows lighten. Michael's wedding day had arrived. The house was packed with relatives and friends. No one minded. The men, old and young, and for the most part married, enjoyed the brief respite of bachelorhood. They drank too much, regaled each other with bawdy lies of earlier halcyon days, and would have been shocked to learn of their wives' and daughters' equally ribald tales.

The house came awake slowly, and when the other girls in her room stirred, Eve rose and walked to the window and watched daylight brighten the bay. A desultory conversation started behind her but she paid little attention, for Lion had emerged from around the corner of the house and could be seen walking across the drive toward the bayside cliff. Confused and frightened by the emotions he aroused in her, she couldn't take her eyes off him.

"I don't care what you say. I think he's the most handsome thing I have ever seen," Mimi Neal said.

"You have got to be kidding!" Stephanie Harris exclaimed, eliciting nods of agreement from four of the maids-in-waiting who had been assigned to Eve's room. "Jack Travis is a much more beautiful man, and younger too!"

"Oh, Stephanie, you're such an innocent," Mimi insisted. "That's precisely what's wrong with Jack. He's too pretty."

"You think so?" Stephanie asked dreamily, recalling her rendezvous with Jack. "Well, if you ask me, Mr. McKenna looks like some old craggy rock."

Mimi wasn't to be dissuaded. "Looks are fine across the punch bowl, but believe me, it's a dawn I'd have close up, and Lion has a way about him. As for age, I'll choose a man with experience any day. I envy you, Eve, having him all to yourself until we arrived. Eve? Why, you aren't even listening."

Eve turned from the window. "What?" she asked.

Mimi tucked her sleeping gown between her legs and scooted

across the bed. "I said, lucky you having Michael's friend all to your-self. Stephanie here prefers pretty men, but I say a fine plumaged bird is not necessarily a gamecock. Don't you agree Lion is abso-lutely delicious?"

"I hadn't thought about him one way or the other," Eve said, hop-ing her face wasn't reddening.

Mimi leaned forward and patted Eve's arm. "We're simply going to have to have a long talk, dear." She lay back on the bed. "All I can say is I wish Michael were *my* brother. I'd be happy to entertain his friends."

"You probably have at one time or another," Stephanie tittered, her face split by a grin. Mimi rose to her knees and struck the girl with a pillow. The other girls broke into giggles, grabbed their own pillows, and gleefully joined the battle.

Only Eve refrained. She glanced out the window again but Lion had disappeared. Well, she thought, watching him would do no good anyway. He'd leave after the wedding, and that would be that. Mak-ing her way through a cloud of feathers, she slipped into the hall in time to see Rosamond standing in the doorway to Sewal's room, her auburn hair in wild disarray.

"Tell Jubb I don't care what he is doing," Rosamond was saying to a flustered Maisie, "I am the bride and won't be married unless I have that slipper fixed. I cannot wear it if the strap is broken. Now you said he could fix it. I must have it this morning in time for church. And see that Hamlet brings more hot water for mother's bath. That's a good girl, and do hurry, for I shall require your assist-ance while I dress."

Maisie curtsied and mumbled, "Yes, ma'am," and hurried down the hall, brushing past Eve with a muted, "Morning, Miss Eve." Eve scowled at Rosamond's retreating figure and stalked down the hall, her animosity preceding her like the bow wave of a ship. She entered her father's room without knocking. Rosamond and Cornelia Cabell were sitting on the edge of the bed, busily stitching hoops into a crinoline petticoat.

"Thank heavens!" Cornelia exclaimed. "I was wishing for an extra hand, and here you are. Be a good dear and help with these, won't you? Oh, this is such a trial." Eve sighed. What was the use? She couldn't explode with Mrs. Cabell present, and somehow the older woman had a way of defusing the energies of anyone who came in contact with her. Cornelia rose and offered Eve her place. "This is so sweet of you. There are so many things that need seeing to, and I just can't be in two places at once. At least now I can bathe." Assuming without question that Eve would help, she fled into the bathroom.

Lacking an excuse to leave, Eve sat and took up where Mrs. Cabell had left off. The two women worked in silence. Eve had been busy greeting new arrivals and, as hostess, making sure that all went according to schedule. Rosamond had been busy with her own friends, and with last-minute details. In consequence, the two had hardly spoken which, as far as Eve was concerned, was fine. They had little in common and less to say to each other.

The needles darted in and out, and before a few minutes had passed, it became evident to each girl that the other was trying to reach the panel seam first. Neither acknowledged the fact, only worked the faster until, with no more than twenty stitches to spare, Rosamond finished first. "There!" she said, snapping the thread.

"You've beat me," Eve laughed, slowing slightly and glancing to the side. Rosamond's stitches were small and evenly spaced. "You're very fast," she said.

Rosamond glowed. This was the first hint of comradeship, much less respect, her new sister-in-law had shown her. "I had a head start," she demurred.

"Nonsense." Eve bent over, bit off the thread. "It's your little finger. I've never seen anyone do that."

"I just pretend I'm knitting or crocheting," Rosamond said, shifting the petticoat in order to begin on a new hoop. Deftly, she wrapped the thread around her little finger which, once extended, kept the tension even. "There's much less chance of getting tangled up. See?"

"Mmm." Eve tried, failed miserably. "I think I'd better practice in private," she said, giving up. Again they worked silently, moving slowly away from each other. "You know," Eve finally said, "you needn't have waited until this morning to finish these. My goodness, there are a dozen relatives who could have helped."

Rosamond smiled almost shyly. "I didn't want to impose. Everyone was so busy."

"Oh, nonsense, Rosamond. You're so silly. They've been sitting around and gossiping. Come on. Race again? I'll beat you this time."

Their fingers flew. It was peaceful in the big bedroom. Little sound intruded save for the peal of laughter from one of the other girls or the splash of water from the bathroom where Cornelia was bathing.

The pace slowed only when it became necessary to put new thread in the needles. Eve actually felt relaxed and, for the first time, at ease in Rosamond's presence. How badly we misjudge others, she thought, through our own near-sightedness. Rosamond simply came from a different world and was uncomfortable around strangers. That was no reason for Eve to have decided so arbitrarily to dislike her. Of course Rosamond had been difficult to get to know. She'd never been given a chance. From now on, Eve decided, I shall be warmer and more patient.

She looked up in surprise. Rosamond's eyes were red. A tear rolled down her cheek. She was crying. Not loudly, but definitely crying. Eve's first reaction was one of skepticism, followed quickly by guilt and not a little shame. She had prejudged again, had immediately assumed an ulterior motive. Angry with herself, and embarrassed for Rosamond, she kept her eyes lowered and paid strict attention to the work at hand.

Crinoline, hoop, needle, and thread blurred into one foggy mist, but Rosamond kept to work, as much by feel as anything. God, how she wished the wedding was over and she and Michael were alone. If she could only get past this one day, everything would be all right. At first she had not loved Michael, but her father, seeing the Blackheaths as rescuers of a sort, had urged her to accept his hand. The scene between Rosamond and her father had been painful. Dayton Cabell was unmercifully blunt. Contrary to the expectations of others, he had risen as far in the Navy as he ever would. There would be no more promotions. Her mother was ill and needed care he could not provide. Rosamond was beautiful, but beauty was not security, for beauty was subject to time. Michael Blackheath loved her. Very well. The moment Rosamond and Michael were married, he, Dayton Cabell, would begin channeling Navy business to Sewal Blackheath. There were ways. And by the time Michael took over the family business, the Blackheath Shipyards would be as large and strong as any in the country.

Rosamond had met the real world, and though the meeting was a shock, she was intelligent enough to understand that her father was right. Alone that night, she wept for a carefree past, and at last, eyes red but shoulders set, accepted the future her father had given her. She was twenty, after all, and getting no younger. As the wife of a Blackheath she would be free of the economic constraints that came with an ill-paid father who, because of his position, was forced to live beyond his means. There were further advantages. How lovely it would be to buy a dress without having to create a scene! How delightful to invite friends to dinner, to give a tea or social without having to wait until Papa or Mama approved.

Of course, this all came dear. The most immediate cost was the knowledge that Sewal Blackheath was paying for the wedding. More taxing was Michael's attitude, for she was perceptive enough to understand that he entertained a number of dangerous illusions about himself. Groomed from childhood to take over a large and prestigious firm, he was outwardly self-assured. Underneath, however, he was brittle, a direct result of Sewal's demands for perfection. He had placed her on a pedestal that was as susceptible to shattering as his own shaky confidence. Whatever happened, Rosamond knew she could never allow Michael's faith in her to collapse. She had to be everything Michael, and his father, wanted her to be. All that remained on that score was to convince him that she was not to blame for the missing virginity she knew he prized so highly. Two children at play, she would explain, and she had been hurt, how badly she hadn't understood at the time. Beyond this she could only count on his love for her, and hope he never learned of Lion—thank God, he would remain discreet—and the others before and after him. Though a kernel of fear occasionally nagged her, she was confident of her ability to handle the crisis when it came.

As the weeks of their engagement passed, Rosamond's deceit became reality. No longer did she see Michael as a means to an end, rather came to believe that her love for him was no less than his for her. She became virginal, and dreamed of being a devoted wife and mother. She and Michael and their children—they'd name the first boy Sewal, the second Dayton—would live wonderfully happy lives and, after Michael took over the shipyards, have family reunions with lots of children and grandchildren running about and yelling and playing underfoot.

Fears, hopes, and fantasies. She had worked so hard for this marriage, fought for it every step of the way. The tension had been overwhelming. When Eve finally laughed and spoke kindly, Rosamond knew her victory was complete. The shell of equanimity she had erected around herself crumbled, and she wept.

Eve kept on for a moment. Unsure of how to react or what to do or say, she pretended she didn't notice. But she couldn't long ignore the tears and, at last, painful sobs. Gently, she took the petticoat and needle from Rosamond, laid them aside, and took her soon-to-be sister-in-law's hands in her own. "It's all right, Rosamond," she said, choking a little herself. "We're all your friends. You needn't cry."

"I know. It's just that . . . that . . ."

"Shh."

"I'm so frightened."

Eve pulled Rosamond close and held her while she sobbed. "There's no need to be, Rosamond," she said softly. "There's no need to be." And then, unaccountably, she too, was weeping.

A veritable battalion of shipwrights, most of them longtime employees of the Blackheaths, had set up rows of tables on the sweeping eastern lawn. At land's end a facsimile of a ship's bow had been transformed into the pulpit from which Elkahan Waldrop would marry Michael and Rosamond. It was noon of Michael's wedding day, and Hanson Pole's finest hour. No general commanded his troops better, no admiral his armada. Daughters and sons of the residents of New Forest, hired specifically for the occasion, raced back and forth, but always returned to Hanson Pole for further instructions. Woe betide the girl or boy who stuck a finger into a freshly baked pie or let a sleeve brush across one of the newly-iced cakes.

The butler had just issued a new stream of orders when Sewal Blackheath, back early from church, strode into the kitchen. The effect was as if a ranking general had just strolled into a military encampment. Everyone cried, "Good morning" in unison and sprang to attention. Sewal winced and answered with a wave of his hands as Pole, with an impatient gesture, hurried everyone on his way. The room cleared instantly, leaving the master servant, Eustacia, and Sewal alone. Pole brushed the remaining strands of his hair forward, cleared his throat, and stepped up to Sewal.

"Mr. Blackheath, I wanted to take this opportunity to wish you, from all of us in the household on this joyous occasion—"

"Them fellas from the shipyards have done tied into one of them roastin' pigs," Jubb interrupted, entering. "I told them they was eatin' weddin' food, but they weren't about to listen to this poor nigger, so I . . ."

He noticed Sewal at the same moment Pole, coattails flying and a cry of fury on his lips, raced through the door. Jubb grimaced, tried to smile. "Mornin', Mister Blackheath. I was just—"

"They really into that pork, husband?" Eustacia asked, hands on hips.

"Well—" Jubb looked embarrassed at having been caught in a practical joke. "They's lookin' mighty hard!" He could contain himself no longer, and in spite of his employer's presence, laughed aloud. "Anyway, things was sort of gettin' dull, what with everybody off to church and all. Good gosh a'mighty, woman, Mister Pole done been givin' so many orders he forgettin' what it feel like to do anything, and afore long he's gonna get rusty. This way I sort of give him somethin' to do. Kind of like a favor, see?" he asked, looking to Sewal for approval.

Sewal shook his head and chuckled. "Jubb, you do yourself a favor and stay out of sight until Pole calms down. Or face the consequences."

"Now that there is sage advice, Mister Blackheath. Yes sir, pure sage." Flashing a huge grin, Jubb sauntered out the door and disappeared around the side of the house.

Eustacia glared at the empty doorway, then at Sewal. "Mister Blackheath—"

"Now, now, Eustacia. Today's a day of celebration, remember," Sewal said.

"And that man will, too," Eustacia said, "seein' as those instructions come from you. And nothin' Mister Pole can say to him when he catches him."

"If he does. Jubb's an old manipulator," Sewal grunted good-naturedly. "Anyway, he's an old man and we've two dozen young ones to finish up and do the running back and forth. Is everything ready in here?"

"Yes, sir!" Eustacia crowed. "Just take a look around. I done cooked enough for a whole army."

That was an understatement. Sewal poked around the vast array of foodstuffs waiting for the afternoon hordes. To one side were tray upon tray of lemon molasses cupcakes. A rum-soaked cloth covered the Black Cake, a massive cousin to a fruit cake but reserved for weddings in the north country, which had taken Eustacia the better part of a morning to create from brown sugar and nutmeg, flour, currants, raisins, molasses, candied fruit, nuts, buttermilk, and at least a dozen eggs. The pint of brandy added at the last minute gave it a rich aroma that had clung to the kitchen for the last two days and still overpowered all the other aromas.

Another table held jars and plates and trays filled with tiny biscuits, condiments, and pickles contributed by the ladies from town.
Spiced apples and pears. Pickled cauliflower and onions and carrots.
Dill and sweet pickles, jellied hogs' feet and thin slices of tongue. A
dozen kinds of jam and preserves. Sewal peered closely into one jar
and shook his head. The Reverend Waldrop's wife, as usual, had sent
some of her never-ending supply of pickled carrots and raisins. As
far as Sewal was concerned, someone else could have his share. More
appreciative, he tasted one of Eustacia's giffles, pastry dough rolled
around homemade preserves, and rolled his eyes appreciatively.

There was more, of course. Checking the cellars, he found rack
upon rack of individual chicken pies created specifically to be served
cold on a summer day. Mincemeat, apple and pumpkin pies, fresh
out of the oven not an hour earlier, steamed in the chilled air. Outside, through the windows, he could see the pits where whole hogs
were roasting on a half dozen spits. Underneath them, tucked in the
coals, dozens of the best of last year's potatoes cooked under the
dripping meat.

Taking one of the chicken pies to hold him until it was time to eat,
Sewal returned to the kitchen in time to see Eustacia pull a rack of
bread out of the oven and set it to cool. With her left hand she
stirred first one and then another massive black iron pot. "Chowder,"
she said over her shoulder. "In case there's some room left in them
folks' stomachs. Something hot, something cold, please the young
and please the old."

Sewal polished off the rest of the pie, wiped his hands on a towel,
and patted his stomach. "If everything's as good as that pie I'll have
to set a close watch to make sure no one steals you."

"Now, Mister Blackheath!"

Sewal moved to her side, lightly touched her shoulder. "Can't
remember a better cook in all my days, Eustacia. Thank you."

Plainly embarrassed by the praise, Eustacia concentrated on the
chowder. "That's what you pay me for," she mumbled.

"Nobody can pay for loyalty. Or friendship."

"Pshaw, Mister Blackheath!" Her smile was radiant. "Here I am
listenin' to silliness, and bread to bake. Go on, now. Bunch of them
folks commence to starve, and you'll sing a different tune."

Sewal had to smile at himself. Pretty soon he'd be a sentimental
old fool, heaven forbid. Find a boat and set himself adrift before that
happened.

Eustacia watched him leave, watched the sunlight turn his hair an even more brilliant white. As he turned to round the corner of the house the same sun emphasized the deep lines and creases of his tanned face. "Can't believe that man be thankin' me!" she said, her voice husky with affection. "Just can't believe that." Fresh as if she'd just slept the night through, she turned back to work.

The yard was full of guests milling about, greeting old friends and being introduced to new. A stranger could tell at a glance which were townfolks and which were relatives come for the wedding. The relatives were the ones with confused looks on their faces as they tried to remember the names of aunts and uncles and cousins, and just exactly how they were related to whom. In the midst of them all, Justin moved about with his camera. Two friends from Bowdoin helped out, one busily preparing and processing plates, the other running back and forth between Justin and the studio.

The weather had held, as Sewal had known it would. Deftly picking his way through the throng, he slipped around the house and made his way to Michael's tent. Inside, Michael and Jack Travis had finished dressing. "Afternoon, Mr. Blackheath," Jack drawled in a deep southern accent. "Got your boy all ready for the slaughter."

Sewal laughed. "Good."

" 'Course, down South Carolina way, we'd sneak him a pint to make sure there was no pain."

"I could use a little of that right now," Sewal said, holding the tent flap open. "Michael, could I have a word with you?"

"Surely. Back in a minute, Jack." Laying down his top hat and gloves, Michael followed Sewal outside. "I think he's more nervous than I am," he said, jumping when the wind ruffled the tent and made a soft slapping sound like a sail luffing in the wind.

Sewal laughed softly. "You look like you haven't slept a wink since yesterday."

"So do you." Michael wiggled his neck, trying to get comfortable in the stiff, starched collar he wore. "At least I have an excuse. What about you?"

"It's not every day my oldest son gets married."

"That's for sure," Michael replied. "I thought it was bad luck for the groom to be seen in his wedding clothes."

"I think that's the bride. Let's talk a minute. You have forty-five of them left." Sewal took Michael by the arm and steered him away from the tent to the edge of the cliff overlooking the bay, then turned back to look at Dawn Wind. "Well. Now that you have a fine wife—"

"Soon will have," Michael interrupted, wondering what his father was leading up to.

"Yes. Not only can you look forward to a brilliant military career, but when the time comes, you will assume control of Dawn Wind and the yards."

"You are fit as a fiddle, Father."

"I was firstborn and Dawn Wind passed to me. So shall it pass to you someday. When I see the years slip away like grains of sand stolen from the shore, and my son once a wee boy with his first little boat and now a fine brave officer and husband to be . . . It makes a man think, Michael."

"You shouldn't think so hard," Michael tried to keep his voice light, but his father's words had moved him.

Sewal reached into his coat pocket and pulled out a gold pocket watch. "This is for you," he said gruffly.

Caught off guard by the gift, and not knowing what to say, Michael opened the case and read the simple inscription. "To Michael from his father. June 1860."

"The silver chain is deliberate," Sewal went on before Michael could thank him. "There is an identical gold chain on the watch in my room. It stopped the night your mother died and I have never rewound it. When you become master of Dawn Wind, you will replace this silver chain with my gold one."

"Father, I couldn't . . ."

"Don't argue with me. That's a tradition I won't have broken. The Blackheaths have passed that chain on from generation to generation. It was my father's and his father's and his father's. You'll be the fifth Blackheath to wear it. And when you become an old fool and can count the years ahead on the fingers of your hand, I expect you to repeat this little ritual with your first male child. The chain has seen many years, Michael, and not one link has been broken. Not one." He paused, looked out over the sea. "The watch is on my bedside table next to the portrait of your mother. I don't carry it anymore. Why carry a watch I won't wind? But it's there, nonetheless."

Michael's throat felt lumpy. Conflicts tumbled his brain, left him breathless. Of all the men in the world he loved none more than his father. Stern father, who placed trust and confidence in him, who expected no less from his son than from himself. No honor could be greater.

And yet . . .

Below, the sea crashed against the rocks that protected the cove and landing. Time broke apart like spindrift and Michael saw himself as he had been four years earlier. He remembered the day so vividly it made his heart ache. A tiny ship, a model he'd made of driftwood and canvas patches taken from the sail loft rested in his hands. He was at the edge of the sea, the end of a summer, no longer a boy to play with toy boats, but a man. That afternoon he would leave Dawn Wind for New York and then the Naval Academy at Annapolis. Childhood was over.

He stood upright and listened. Was it possible he had heard the train? Had it come so early? No. Only the wind and the sound of a bell buoy and the madness of gulls. The water receded from the toes of his boots. The wind quartered against his left cheek. Many an hour he'd played below these cliffs, a line in his hand so he might haul back the boat before it sailed too far away to be retrieved. He set the driftwood hull, smooth from the years, into the water. The wind filled the canvas, pulled taut the rigging that had taken him months to string properly. He held his breath, then relaxed as the ship righted itself and began riding the watery hills that swept past before leveling themselves on the strand.

More than anything else he wanted to go to sea. Not as an officer but as a deckhand bound for adventure; glorious, dangerous, irresponsible adventure. But he was firstborn and all of Dawn Wind would be his one day. He had to be prepared, though he did not want to be. Living for his father's dream left him hollow and a coward as well, not for the sake of his own skin, but the reputation of the Blackheaths.

. . . But what if . . . His mind filled with the uncompleted question. Finish it, fool, he chastised himself. What if he said, "No, Father, I don't want this. Curse me or bless me as you will, but I am not strong enough for this whole family, for all the Blackheaths living and dead. This is not what I want." It wasn't too late. He could still say it. Walk away. Become what he wanted, who he wanted. His *own* man in a world he chose for himself.

"Michael?"

His father sounded insistent, demanding as always. It was time to go. It was time to be Michael Blackheath. The thin line grew taut in his hands. The little ship at the end of its tether strained as its bow nosed into the waves.

"Michael?"

The hemp line slid through his fingers, splashed into the water. The ship bobbed, settled back, rode over a wave and dipped into the trough behind. Moments later it was a blotch of brown against the gray ocean. He made no effort to stop it. "One of us," he whispered. "One of us ought to be free."

"Michael? Are you all right?"

Michael blinked, brushed the back of his hand across his eyes. His father's hand was on his arm. A look of concern clouded his face. "Yes." Forcing a smile, he fumbled with the silver chain. "I, ah . . . can't seem to, ah, that is, my fingers . . ."

Sewal pushed the fob through the correct buttonhole, dropped the free end in one vest pocket, the watch in the other. "There. You'll have a wife to help with things like that before the day is out."

"Yes." The little ship had been gone for years. Perhaps it lived the dream Michael now only toyed with in idle moments. It didn't matter. Dreams died, to be replaced by new dreams. By Rosamond, whom he never would have met had he run from the responsibility his father had forced upon him. Grateful, he wanted to embrace Sewal, but instead pulled out the watch and flipped it open. "Three thirty. Just thirty minutes more. You coming?"

"In a minute," Sewal said. "You go on. Don't worry. I'll be there." He watched Michael turn and walk across the yard. "He's a proud-looking lad, Jenny," he said softly, and then softer still, "I wish you were here to see him."

Michael looked nervous, Rosamond composed. Their attendants were sober-faced and their parents and relatives solemn. Everything had proceeded smoothly and to the satisfaction of everyone concerned. From the dais in front of the ship's bow pulpit the Reverend Elkahan Waldrop's voice droned on, rising to invisibly underline each "God," and "Lord," and "matrimonial bonds," and "Rosamond and Michael."

Lion stood on the fringe of the crowd and watched the people around him. The New Foresters, craftsmen from the yards and shopkeepers alike, were mostly of solid, sturdy stock not unlike those he knew in Virginia. If he had to identify one differing characteristic he would have said only that they seemed more withdrawn and less open to strangers. Even that difference faded on further thought: few people were less clannish than Virginia country people.

"Do you, Rosamond Cabell . . ."

Almost over with, Lion mused, and smiled, remembering their talk on the porch. Rosamond Cabell might be slightly used, but Michael was getting one hell of a woman. He grinned, envying Michael the night ahead. If Rosamond wasn't as much as a man could handle in bed, Lion McKenna was a full-blooded Cherokee. And he wasn't.

Someone to his left sobbed. Rocking back on his heels, Lion could see the household servants lined up together at the rear of the crowd. Pole stood stiffly at attention. Eustacia wept openly, and blew her nose into a kerchief. Jubb, dignified in a threadbare hand-me-down frock coat, stood straight as the hard cider he'd been drinking would let him. Lion shook his head. With all the fine Abolitionist talk about freeing slaves the Northerners treated their colored little better than the Southerners did. If any further proof were needed all one had to do was compare Jubb and Eustacia to any of a million like them from Alabama to Virginia.

Lion stiffened, and squinted to be sure. Hamlet Peters was staring intently at the ceremony and holding Maisie's hand in his. Shocked, Lion almost moved to separate them, then remembered where he was and made himself stop. Aside from business, and Eve, what went on at Dawn Wind was none of his concern.

"Do you, Michael Blackheath . . ."

Lion shifted his weight, peered over the heads of the people in front of him. Michael looked as though he was holding up well. At least he'd not been drinking as heavily as he had in New York. I wonder how I'll react, Lion mused, craning to catch a glimpse of Eve and having to settle for a view of the top of her head. Probably be scared stiff, and . . . Wait a minute! Not you. Not Lion McKenna, a silent voice protested.

Quickly, as he had a hundred times since he and Eve had met in the cupola, Lion pushed that argument aside. Infatuation be damned. Madame Laurier had been right about one thing he'd been too dense or stubborn to see. He was in love with Eve Blackheath. Knowing that, neither Clifford Sarandon nor the threatening storm between North and South would stop him. He'd not had a chance to tell her yet, because she'd been so busy, but he would before the day was out. And if she demurred? He smiled grimly. Next spring was a long, long time away.

". . . Pronounce you husband and wife together. In the name of the Father, of the Son, and of the Holy Spirit. Those whom God has joined together, let no man put asunder. Amen."

A cry of excitement was followed by a lengthy round of applause as Michael lifted Rosamond's veil and the two kissed. Lion joined in as the applause swelled, but his thoughts were elsewhere, plotting a similar scene with a different bride and groom.

Everyone was smiling and congratulating each other as if they had all been responsible. Eve stood at the end of the receiving line and did her best to keep them moving toward the tables. Once this chore was over she would be able to relax until the cutting of the cake.

"I don't think I've ever seen a bride so beautiful . . ."

"So glad you could come . . ."

"More food than you can imagine . . ."

"So glad you could come . . ."

The phrases all ran together, became automatic responses. During lulls she checked first the head of the line, then the lines at the buffet tables. Everything was going smoothly. Rosamond was radiant and gracious, Michael beaming with pride. Fifty feet away the tables were beginning to fill up.

"I couldn't agree more . . ."

"My goodness, Aunt Agatha! Where have you *been?* . . ."

". . . Don't tell me you made it yourself! . . ."

"In Washington, Michael has an appointment . . ."

"*So* glad you could come . . ."

She was afraid her eyes were glazing. If she'd only slept a little later, she thought. Food too, might have helped, for she hadn't eaten since that morning. Barely able to concentrate, remember names, and pay attention to what everyone was saying all at once, she vowed to sleep the clock around twice as soon as the guests had all left.

"So glad you could come . . ."

"I don't envy you at all . . ."

"My, how you've grown, Emily! Why, the last time I saw you . . ."

"*So* glad you could come . . ."

"What!" Eve blinked. Lion was standing in front of her. "What?" she repeated faintly, not sure of what she'd heard.

He leaned forward and spoke quietly, his voice audible only to her. "I love you. Will you marry me?"

"I . . . I . . ." She couldn't think of what to say. Not a word came to mind. Stunned, she tried to pull herself together. "That's not very nice, Mr. . . . ah . . . Mr. . . ."

"McKenna, remember?" He glanced to his right, saw the line was held up. "Think about it."

He was gone. Eve's mind was hopelessly muddled. Had he really said that? The line moved on with the stream of polite chatter that quite suddenly had lost all meaning for her.

She couldn't marry Lion McKenna, of course. There was her father, and Clifford, to begin with. Anyway, she barely knew him.

"A little girl? How lovely! I'll come to visit as soon as . . ."

Imagine asking a question like that at a time like this! Why, how could I possibly marry him? I've only just met him, and couldn't fall in love that quickly, and with a man so brazen, so audacious, so . . .

". . . Glad you could come."

Oh dear! How am I ever going to tell Clifford? . . .

Sewal stood on his chair and raised his hands for quiet. Two or three of the nearest guests, noticing him, clanked their forks against their glasses. "Welcome to Dawn Wind," Sewal finally began once he had everyone's attention. "Now that you have had a bite—or a ton or two—" everyone laughed "—under your belts, I trust you feel up to a little dancing. But first, I'd like to propose a toast."

Men, women, and children filled their glasses. The men stood. Hanson Pole handed Sewal a chased gold goblet and stepped back. When Sewal turned to face his firstborn his eyes were bright. "I am a man of the sea," he began, his voice thick with rare emotion, "and as many seafarers are, sentimental beyond the current fashion. Because of this, I sometimes compare the love of a man and woman to the oceans. They are wide and deep, hold a myriad mysteries, delight beyond measure, and a challenge that never ends. It is my wish for Rosamond and Michael that their love grow until it is as wide and deep as the oceans themselves, and as eternal. Ladies and gentlemen, I drink to my son, Michael, and his lovely new wife, Rosamond. May God bless their union!"

The silence lasted a moment longer as all drank, then ended with a cheer as Michael and Rosamond embraced. On signal, the New Forest locals, augmented by strings imported from Boston, began to play a slow, sweet waltz. While the crowd applauded, Michael and Rosamond, arm in arm, left the head table and walked onto the especially laid out dance floor.

Deep blue and white, swirling giddily in time with the music. Rarely had New Forest seen a more graceful, handsome couple. Michael, straight and tall as royalty, wore a new, formal uniform bright with shined brass buttons and insignia. Rosamond's gown was of bone-white raw silk, high at the neck, long-sleeved, double skirted, and trimmed with snowy egret feathers. Above this floating cloud her long neck and classical features, set off by her auburn hair, were the perfect match for Michael's imperious features. As they danced the more emotional of the ladies were given a second chance to weep and remember the day they too had dressed in white and floated in the arms of men who now, more often than not, took them for granted.

The first dance ended and with it, the formal part of the wedding. The bride and groom were married, the preacher had spoken, everyone had eaten, and toasts had been drunk. Now came the festivities. Children ran about and shouted. Young men and women flirted, coalesced into small groups and broke apart again. Business at the punch bowls was brisk: even Aunt Millicent Neal had two cups, after which she danced with Michael.

Waltzes, two-steps, polkas, and reels—even a minuet for those who wanted to show off—spilled from the brass and strings. Eve, dressed in a pale green gown that set off the blue of her eyes and the gold of her hair, danced almost all of them, each with a different partner. Only Rosamond danced more. Once, during a brief respite for the orchestra, they met at one of the punch bowls and, misty-eyed, embraced warmly.

Dusk came early and unnoticed save by Justin who, disgusted, was forced to put away his camera. The hired boys rushed about hanging decorated lanterns. The girls ran back and forth carrying shawls for the older women. Pole looked harried, but pleased. Eustacia prowled the tables, making sure bowls and platters were kept full and worrying about Jubb, who had disappeared. Only Hamlet, assigned the job of keeping watch over the more than fifty horses tethered behind the stables, was left out. Whenever Maisie could find a spare minute and escape unseen, she brought him something to eat or drink.

Lion had danced, but not with Eve. A half-dozen times he'd watched her over the shoulder of his partner and tried to decipher what she was thinking. As many more times he was sure he felt her watching him. Twice, their eyes met briefly. Each time Eve had a quizzical, studious look on her face. His earlier admission of love and accompanying proposal had been an impetuous act, and as the evening wore on, he vacillated between self-approval and condemnation, and kept putting off a direct confrontation with her. At least she had only danced once with Sarandon.

The cutting of the wedding cake was scheduled for ten o'clock. At nine Michael's classmates and friends gathered in a knot and sent Jack Travis to fetch Michael. Lion was sitting out of the way drinking a cup of coffee when Travis, Michael, and Rosamond approached him. "I leave him to his own devices," Michael said, wagging his head sadly, "and he sits alone and drinks coffee."

"Nothing wrong with that," Lion pointed out. "I enjoy my own devices."

"But coffee? My God, man, this is a celebration!"

"I have a rule," Lion said. "Get drunk when everyone else is sober, stay sober when everyone else is drunk. Good rule."

"I don't know." Michael looked dubious. "At any rate, my friends from the Academy want to see me alone, and Mrs. Blackheath—" he wrapped a protective arm around Rosamond "—has broken a strap on her shoe. Could I impose on you to escort her to the house?"

Lion bowed and offered Rosamond his arm. "It is an honor, rather than an imposition."

"Watch him," Michael cautioned his new wife. "And no more punch. You've had enough. As for you, my fine Southern friend," he added, handing Rosamond over to Lion, "only one kiss. And *not* on the lips."

Rosamond giggled and pressed Lion's arm to her side, but didn't say anything as he led her off. They maintained an awkward silence all the way to the house, through the foyer, and up the stairs. Rosamond stopped outside her door, leaned against it, and raised heavy eyelids to look frankly at Lion. "I may need some help," she said, wetting her lips with her tongue.

Lion followed her into the room, watched her open her trunk, and remove a new pair of slippers. As she turned to him and smiled he decided he should leave, but her dark violet eyes and daring smile froze him in place. A little tipsy, she sank to the edge of the bed. "Oh, my, that punch is murderous!" she said, holding out the slippers.

Angry for allowing himself to be played for a fool, Lion took them and kneeled in front of her. "You have a terribly fierce face," Rosamond said, bemused.

"Stick out your foot." Lion pulled off the slipper with the broken strap. Rosamond pulled her gown halfway up her calf, slipped her left foot into the new shoe. "You know damned well this is foolish."

"Do I?" Her right foot ran up his left arm, touched his shoulder. "It's not foolish at all. You are just being a gentleman."

Lion fumbled with the buckle. "A few hours of marriage haven't changed you. You're still a desirable woman. What else is there to prove?"

Rosamond's foot rested on Lion's shoulder. She let her toe touch his ear. "You don't like me much, do you?" Her gown was up to her knees.

"We've been through this before, Rosamond," Lion said, grabbing her foot and putting the other slipper on it.

"Indeed? We've hardly talked."

He buckled the strap, dropped her foot, and stood. "We talked enough, under the circumstances."

Rosamond pushed away from the bed and grabbed his arm. "Michael gave you permission to kiss the bride," she said in a husky whisper.

Suddenly angry, Lion grabbed her by the shoulders and violently jerked her toward him. Rosamond whimpered, but the soft, pleading sound was cut off by his kiss. No sooner had she let her body find his and mold itself to him than she found herself held at arm's length. His fingers dug cruelly into her shoulders. "You were right," he said, his face twisted with contempt. "I *don't* like you. We'll leave now, before we're missed."

"Let go of me," she hissed, trying to pull away from him.

"I said, we'll leave now." His hand closed on her wrist. Rosamond tried to resist, but he dragged her to the door.

"All right!" She tore free of his grasp, stood panting in front of him. She struggled to focus. His rejection, even though she didn't really care that much, had stung. She wanted to slap him or cry or scream or throw something, but she didn't dare. "All right," she repeated sullenly. "You needn't create a scene." Stiffly, in control again, she straightened her dress and started down the stairs. When they reached the front door she let him take her arm. His touch meant nothing. If he didn't like her he had no idea of how much she despised him.

His mind in a turmoil, Lion handed over Rosamond to the first man who wanted to dance with her, then wandered away from the crowd and found a quiet spot where he could sit alone. He'd been crazy to go up there with her, insane to insult her. The kiss had been the act of a raving madman. What the hell was the matter with him? Granted Rosamond had forced the issue, but he didn't have to reciprocate. Not only had he angered her but, given her apparent instability, jeopardized his relationship with the Blackheaths. This marriage meant a lot to Sewal; there was no telling how he'd react if he heard that Lion had treated Rosamond badly. Most important, there was Eve. Lion shook his head in disbelief. He'd actually proposed to her, and in a manner that could be taken as a bad joke. And yet it hadn't been a joke, damn it. He was serious, did in fact love her. As for her father and the contract, the hell with them. Blackheath needed the contract in the first place. In the second, McKenna was as good a name as Sarandon, even if their bank accounts did differ by three or four decimal places.

He chuckled grimly to himself. What had started out as a relatively simple business trip to buy some ships had turned into a royal mess. There was nothing to be done for it, though, except keep on. One thing was certain: he wasn't going to let Eve get away from him. Not without a fight. Rising, he headed back toward the center of the festivities.

Most of the guests were still eating and dancing. The boys and girls from town were busy clearing tables and putting out clean plates and ever more food. The crowds around the punch bowls had attenuated slightly as the older guests switched to coffee, but there was still plenty of activity there. Lion heard a rustling in the shadows and looked the other way. New England might be noted for strict morals, but some things never changed.

He paused at the outer table and spotted Eve arm in arm with Clifford Sarandon. They were on the far side of the dance floor, threading their way through the tables. If they kept on they'd strike the path that went to the eastern edge of the peninsula. Determined to stop them, he looked around and found one of the hired boys. "You," he called, leaping one of the tables and blocking the lad's path.

The boy stopped and looked at the quarter Lion held in his hand. "Yes, sir?"

"You know Mr. Clifford Sarandon when you see him?"

"Yes, sir."

Lion flipped the quarter. "Would you be willing to give him a message?"

A quarter was a great deal of money. "Yes, sir!"

"Good." Lion pointed out Clifford and Eve, just barely visible at the edge of the light. "Tell him a gentleman needs to see him in his tent on a matter of the utmost urgency." He flipped the coin again, this time to the boy. "You don't know the gentleman's name. He must be one of the out-of-town guests, right?"

"Yes, sir!" The boy stuffed the quarter in his pocket, started to run off and then stopped. "A quarter to deliver the message," he said with a cagey look. "Worth another quarter to forget where I got it, wouldn't you think, Mr. McKenna?"

Lion tried to look stern, but couldn't. "What's your name, boy?"

"Aaron, sir."

"Aaron, I predict you'll go far in this world." Lion pulled a second quarter from his pocket and placed it in the boy's hand. "Just make sure you don't try that trick with the wrong person." He gestured with his head. "Run along, now."

"Yes, sir!"

The boy raced off. Lion skirted the tables and struck out across the lawn in order to intercept Eve without being seen by Clifford. A moment later he watched the boy talk to Clifford. Sarandon looked dubious, but Aaron was evidently persuasive, for he left Eve and hurried off. When Eve continued along the path Lion took a shortcut that brought him face to face with her.

"If it isn't Miss Blackheath," he said, looking startled. "And alone, too. How lucky."

Eve glanced at him, to the disappearing Clifford Sarandon, and back to Lion. "That was a despicable trick," she said.

Lion looked shocked. "Trick? Now who's being despicable?" He offered her his arm. "It was that evident, eh?" he asked as the lights fell further behind them.

"Yes."

Her hand was warm on his wrist. He thought she was smiling, but couldn't be sure. "No matter. I'll be gone before long, and Mr. Sarandon can have you all to himself."

"No man has me all to himself, Mr. McKenna."

"I see." They walked without talking. The path curved around the edge of the peninsula and ended at the bluffs above the stretch of sand where Sewal was wont to wander in thought. Far ahead, barely visible on the flank of the Whale's Hump, flickering torches pin-pointed the location of the elaborate tent erected for the newlyweds' wedding night. "But you continued to walk," Lion finally said.

"I beg your pardon?"

"You guessed, but continued to walk."

Eve let go his arm, shifted her weight away from him. "I think you presume too much, Mr. McKenna."

"I presume nothing," Lion said, taking her hand. "Unless I was completely wrong, and you simply wanted to be alone." She didn't answer, but neither did she withdraw her hand. "Did you?" he asked.

There was a long pause. "Yes," Eve whispered at last.

"This isn't a game, Eve. Tell me the truth. If you wish, I'll leave at once. Did you want to be alone? Do you now?"

"Yes." He started to leave, but Eve shook her head. "No." She raised his hand with hers and looked at it for a long moment. "I don't know."

They had avoided mentioning the reception line. Lion raised her hand further. When he kissed it their eyes met. "Then I may stay until you decide?"

"Yes," she finally said. "But . . . you mustn't . . . that is, you must refrain from . . . distressing me again." She lowered her eyes. "I'm not ready for surprises like that."

His declaration and proposal hovered over them. Lion reached out and touched her cheek as he had the night in the cupola. "I won't then," he promised.

Eve turned her head, pressed her lips against the palm of his hand. Every instinct told her to tell him that she loved him too, that she would marry him, but reason wouldn't let her. Not yet. It was too soon, and she needed more time. Needed time to think, to be alone, to say his name, roll it around on her tongue until she was used to it. She turned away from him, let her weight rest against his chest. His hands lightly gripped her shoulders. High overhead, scudding clouds raced across the sky. The ocean below shined like burnished onyx flecked with silver.

"So." His voice was deep and soothing. "If I am not allowed to speak of honest desire . . ."

"There are those who say there is no such thing," Eve said.

"I would have agreed until now," Lion said, his lips so close to her ear she could feel his breath.

"You promised," Eve warned.

"A difficult promise to keep with you so close." Eve stirred as if she would move away. Lion held her close to him. "But I will. See? I'll change the subject entirely." Eve relaxed and let the sound of his voice carry her away. "Shall I talk of Chartres and its cathedral, whose twin spires rise as prayers to heaven? I have walked there, alone. Its great vaulted ceilings catch the soul and pull it skyward. Stained-glass windows of incredible beauty filter the light and cause the sun's broken colors to mingle and flow like the blood of the saints.

"Perhaps I'll talk of Mexico with its monuments to gods whose names are unpronounceable and who exist only in the dim recesses of yesterday. I know, I'll speak of Virginia and the Shenandoah valley. My farm is there, set between lush green hills bordered by the Blue Ridge Mountains, whose loveliness can best be appreciated on a cool afternoon in the fall. If you walk there, you will swear that lanterns of blue flame adorn the tips of every tree and bathe the sky with a light seen nowhere else in the world."

Eve could feel his chest vibrate against her back as he talked. Her eyes were closed, but she imagined she could see his face. He was so vastly different from any man she had ever met. Her father and most of the other men she knew were of the sea. They had traveled the world, but what they had seen and experienced they concealed as hidden poetry in their hearts. Lion was not afraid to say what he felt, and if, as a result, he was sometimes rash . . . Suddenly, Eve wanted him to be rash, to be everything he was and more. She wanted him to sweep her into his arms and kiss her, to hold her close to him. But it was too soon for that too. No matter what she felt, she knew she had to resist her own impulses.

With a supreme effort she twisted out of his embrace and, with the same quizzical look he'd seen earlier, turned to face him. "They'll be cutting the cake," she said, sounding much more composed than she felt. "I'd better go back."

Lion stared at her, and understanding was in his eyes. The moonlight, wan and slanting, transformed her hair into a treasury of golden curls, her cheeks into living ivory. He was tempted to pull her to him, but refrained, instead slowly brought his lips to hers and thrilled as the spark of life and love passed between them. The kiss was not long, and after a moment Eve pressed close to him and wrapped her arms around him. Her cheek rested against his chest.

Silently, they stood without moving, feeling the wind rush against them.

"Lion?" She had said his name for the first time. It was a little thing, but the granite they stood on tipped.

"What?" His voice rumbled deep in his chest so that Eve felt rather than heard him.

"You spoke of games," she said. "Are you playing one now?"

"No." She could feel his head shaking. "I may be as frightened as you, my Eve, but no."

Soaring excitement alternated with a state of contented bliss. Whichever her mood she knew that her life was changed and that she was happier than she had ever been. No longer need she be at odds with herself, no longer did she need to contend with her father over Clifford. All she wanted was time to stand still, for Lion to kiss her again, and hold her forever. And if there was the slightest hazard there she refused to acknowledge it. She had found love, and though she would not act rashly, neither would she run from it and seek sanctuary.

She looked up at him and for a long moment gazed directly into his eyes. At last, satisfied, she smiled. By unspoken consent they turned and, arm in arm, followed the path back to the party.

The cake had been cut and eaten, save for those slivers saved and wrapped to be placed under hopeful girls' pillows. Rosamond had been taken to the house to change, Michael to his tent. With shouts and cheers and good-natured gibes, bride and groom had dashed through a shower of rice to their decorated surrey and ridden off into the night. Soon after, still talking about how lovely Rosamond was and what a handsome couple they made, the ladies from town gathered their husbands and called for their carriages. The younger folks kept on dancing for a while longer, but even they had had enough of partying, and arm in arm, called for Hamlet's help. By midnight the ladies staying at Dawn Wind were safely upstairs getting ready for bed, sleepily trading gossip, and discussing who had worn what and how so-and-so looked. The last carousers eventually gathered in one of the gaily colored tents on the west lawn where Michael's friends from the Academy sat up and drank and talked of escapades and conquests past and future.

Hanson Pole dismissed the last of the servants hired from town. A shy, dimpled girl, she curtsied and took the note signed by Sewal

Blackheath instructing the New Forest bank to pay her the very generous sum of a dollar for her services. She beamed with delight and ran to join the rest of the boys and girls in the carriage hired to take them home. "That's the last?" Eustacia asked, emerging from the storage cellar.

Pole nodded. "Yes, thank heaven." He sat at the long oak plank table. The sturdy high-backed chair creaked beneath his weight. Outside, coals glowed beneath a massive iron tub filled with soapy water, cooking utensils, plates, knives, forks, and an assortment of mugs and pitchers. Come morning and the fire would be built up and everything washed and either returned to its owners or put away for the next occasion.

"Then what's done is done," Eustacia sighed, sitting at the other end of the table.

"And well, I think." For a moment, Eustacia thought he'd lean back and kick off his shoes, but he settled for massaging the bridge of his nose and loosening his cravat. That alone was a telling gesture of his weariness, though, for he rarely relaxed in front of anyone. "It was a long day."

Eustacia nodded and looked up as Hamlet entered through the outside doors. "I asked them young men if they needed anything else, but they said I could go on," he reported.

Pole grunted. "They'll try to finish the last of the punch before they sleep. Lucky it isn't rum and they the King's Navy."

"I reckon you don't need me no more then." Hamlet yawned.

"No. We all worked hard enough for one day. Well done, Hamlet."

Hamlet peered at Pole in surprise. Seldom did the master servant praise anyone. "Yessuh." He looked around. "Where's Pa?" he asked Eustacia.

"He disappeared a long time ago," she said with a snort of disgust. "I looked for him, but I'm just too tired to look very far."

"Asleep, more'n likely," Hamlet said.

"Where? In the barn?" Eustacia shook her head. "I'll have that man's head tomorrow. If he dares show his face. "

"He didn't check with me, either," Pole sniffed.

"Jubb ain't the kind to ask someone if he can go to sleep when he's been in the cider," Eustacia said. "Man his age jus' do what come natural."

"Well, I'll check the stables," Hamlet said, starting for the door.

"No matter. He'll come draggin' in hang dog tomorrow mornin'," Eustacia replied, her eyes narrowing. "You let him sleep."

"I'll just check, then go on and sleep out there. Too hot in here, with all this cookin'." Avoiding Eustacia's eyes, Hamlet left the same way he'd come in.

Something was going on between mother and son, but Pole was too tired to worry about it. Yawning mightily, he stood and stretched. "I'll sleep well tonight," he said.

"Me too." Eustacia struggled to her feet. "Reckon I'll close up and go on to bed myself, if it's all right with you."

"Best leave the front door unlocked." Pole wagged his head to clear the fatigue enough to make it to his room. "Good night, Eustacia."

"Night, Mr. Pole," Eustacia said, heading for the stairs to close up. Pole waited until she was gone, then entered the cold cellar and emerged a moment later with one of the leftover chicken pies. Looking guiltily at his stomach, he listened at the stairs a moment, then tiptoed up to his room, breathing a sigh of relief when the door was safely closed behind him. Fatigue washing over him, he undressed, crawled into his nightshirt, and then into bed. He pulled a napkin, knife, fork, and spoon kept for burglaries of this nature from the bedside table drawer and pulled the pie toward him. "Well done," he sighed thoughtfully, and dug into his reward.

The house was quiet. Hamlet had watched his mother go from room to room, watched the lanterns wink out and the windows darken. The only ones awake were Michael's friends in the tent, and they wouldn't bother him. Treading softly, he entered the barn and at last found Jubb. He leaned forward and said, softly, "Pa?" One arm stretched out across piled straw, the other curled around a cider jug, Jubb continued to snore. Hamlet grinned and tiptoed to the ladder. The gray mare snorted. "You hush up, now," he whispered, glancing over his shoulder.

The loft was dark and smelled sweet with last year's hay. Hamlet made his way unerringly to the rear window where a little moonlight still snuck in. "He's asleep," he said, unbuttoning his shirt and kicking off his boots and trousers. His ebony skin glistened in the dim light. A pale hand emerged from the darkness and stroked his thigh. "Ma's closed up. You leave your window open so's you can get back in?"

"I don't like this sneakin' around," Maisie said, shifting her weight as he lay down beside her.

"Did you?"

"Of course. But I still don't like . . ."

"Ain't no other way." He pulled her to him, sighed as her breasts brushed against his chest, and the weight of her thigh settled on his groin. "You know I love you, woman."

"I know. I know." Tired though she was, her body came to life at his touch. "Show me, Hamlet. Now. Please," she said, then bit her lips to keep from crying out.

A more idyllic spot couldn't have been chosen. The specially made, opulently appointed tent that was reserved for Blackheath wedding nights sat in a cleared glade three quarters of the way up the Whale's Hump. To the south and below, New Forest was a scattering of dim lights. Further east stood Dawn Wind, regal on its promontory. Two hours earlier, when the newlyweds left in a shower of rice and gales of laughter and cheers, the grounds had danced with amber lantern light. Now, nearly one o'clock, it was a cold, bleak mass, one with the granite cliffs from which it sprang. Naked, Michael stood at the edge of the clearing and stared into the limitless sky. His rawboned form looked ghastly white. His eyes were shadows behind which reigned disillusionment and anguish. He had come to pluck a flower, and found instead a bed of thorns. And now he bled. Damn it, he bled.

"Michael?" Rosamond called from the bed of their uncompleted lovemaking. Naked, she rolled from under the covers. Her auburn hair, long and wavy, swept down her back like a cape. Her slim waist was accentuated by full breasts and rounded, low-slung hips. She stepped out of the tent, stopped behind her new husband, and put her hands on his flanks. "Michael?"

Michael swung around and shoved her away. "My innocent, my dove," he moaned. "A pretense. A hoax!"

Rosamond tried to reason with him. "If there is a hoax you have played it on yourself, Michael. I married you because I love you. Whether or not I was a virgin has nothing to do with our love, don't you see?"

"See?" Incredulous, he stared at her. "Be gentle, you said. Do not go too fast! Do not hurt me!" He pressed his fists to his temples as if the pain were too great to bear. "Of what were you afraid? That

I'd discover you had more experience than the most common street . . ."

"That's not true!" Rosamond insisted, frantically trying to think of a way to stop him before he ruined everything. "I love you, Michael. Everything I've done or said changed, disappeared in the past, the moment I said that the first time."

"And you played the part so well, didn't you," Michael said, not even hearing what she'd said. "My bride! My whore!"

The last, single loathsome word split what little poise Rosamond had been able to retain. "Bastard!" she hissed in return, unaware the word had been said before she heard it. Whiplike, her hand flew through the air and cracked against the side of Michael's head.

The sudden pain acted as an antidote for anguish. An icy, calm fury settled over Michael and he stared at Rosamond as if he'd never seen her before. Frightened, Rosamond backed away from him. Michael, in two strides, caught her wrist. Twisting her arm behind her, he forced her into the tent and threw her down. Rosamond cried out and tried to rise, but Michael dropped on top of her and shoved her forward, choking, into the pillows. "Who owns your maidenhood?" He grabbed a handful of hair and pulled her head back. "Who, damn it? Who?"

"A boy! I don't remember his name!" Rosamond gasped, barely able to breathe. "We were playing. I was only—"

"His name! You don't know his name?"

"No, damn you. We were children, don't you understand?" She struggled, but could not break his grip.

Michael tried to shake off the roaring sound that filled his ears. His worst fantasies were now reality. God only knew how many of those who would be his colleagues in Washington had lain with her, and would laugh behind his back. "And since that day you've enjoyed your rutting, haven't you." She didn't answer and he yanked viciously on her hair. "Haven't you!"

Tears rolled down Michael's face. Sweat beaded his brow. He thought his heart would explode. Wild-eyed, he struggled to his knees, plunged to the entranceway of the tent, and gulped in the cold air. When the great shuddering that coursed through his body at last subsided, he returned to Rosamond and kneeled at her side. "Listen to me." His face was blank, his voice flat and emotionless. "Because this is how it will be. Are you listening?"

Rosamond nodded, weakly. Her eyes were wide with pain and terror, her body weak and trembling.

"We are married, you and I, and that is how we shall stay. I will not endure the further humiliation of an annulment. We are married, and will play at appearing happily so. You are experienced at pretense, so it should not be difficult for you. Do you understand what I am saying?"

The dreams of happiness were demolished, lay in tatters, soiled by past mistakes and present anger. She had so wanted to love him, and be loved. So wanted security and happiness. She had tried so hard, and couldn't bear the thought of being denied everything. Damn the boy, the past, Lion McKenna, and the others. She shook her head from side to side. "No, Michael. Please. I love you. You can't . . ."

"Do you understand?" he shouted, raising his hand as if to strike her.

Rosamond closed her eyes, did not even try to stop the tears that rolled from beneath her lids. He would not listen. Slowly, all hope fading, she tilted her head up and down once, and then, her spirit crushed, lay without moving.

How long he crouched beside her Michael did not know. He had lost track of time, of himself and the world in which he lived. Eventually he rose, grabbed a bottle of champagne given them by Sewal, and walked into the night. He preferred something stronger, but the brandy was gone and champagne was all there was. Zombielike, he walked to a fallen log and sat down, ignoring how the bark pinched the bare flesh of his buttocks. He stared at the black landscape. Not a light could be seen. Nothing but darkness and the breeze. He began to shiver and, popping the cork on the champagne, gulped the cold, bubbly liquid. It was too damn weak, though. He couldn't understand why anyone ever drank champagne, couldn't understand why they even made it.

Naked in the dead stillness of the Maine night, he tried to put his life back together. He had always had to be perfect. The next heir of Dawn Wind . . . He had loved Rosamond Cabell as he had loved no one else, but she had proved unfaithful and soiled. Now he was married to her. Coldly analytical, he took stock. There had been those to rib him about marrying an admiral's daughter in order to gain favor and rapid promotion. He had scoffed at the idea at one time, even considered repudiating his berth in the admiral's office and asking for sea duty. But it didn't matter anymore. Nothing mattered very much.

He might as well get what he could as fast as he could, and damn the consequences. Silently, he raised the bottle in ironic salute to darkness. No, there would be no renunciation. The admiral's daughter could not give him what he wanted, so he would take what he could get and learn to be satisfied. The *Congress* sailed for Washington in the morning. He would be on it.

Chapter 8

"Hurry, Father!" Eve called from the front of the office.

Sewal rummaged through a stack of papers and diagrams blanketing the top of his desk. A clerk at the next desk glanced up from his work. "I have the construction reports right here, sir."

"Damn it, Eliot, why didn't you say so?" Sewal grabbed the reports and started toward the railing that divided the office into two.

"Sorry, Mr. Blackheath. Last Wednesday, September fifth, is on top. You'll note that . . ."

"Father!" Eve called again.

"Coming, coming." Sewal flipped through the pages. "What happened to this week's?"

Eliot blushed. "It will be finished late this afternoon, sir. Beckham lost the metal-casting reports and has to redo them. You know how he is about losing paperwork, sir."

"Damn!" Sewal grumbled. "If he wasn't such a good foundryman I'd see he lost his head."

The rear door slammed. "Ah, there you are, Blackheath," said a huge, blond-bearded Swede. Jon Naslund, Sewal's master carpenter and foreman, thrust his jutting chin in the door. "I think you call me, eh?"

"No, I didn't."

The Swede frowned, shook his head, "*Ja,* you call. Gunter tell me . . ."

"Oh yes, Mr. Blackheath?"

"Wait a minute!" Sewal roared. He turned away from the Swede. "Now what, Eliot?"

"You forgot to sign this draft, sir."

"Well, sign it yourself. My absence has never stopped you before."

Eliot sniffed. "Yes, sir," he said, ducking his head and forging Sewal's name.

"Now, Jon, what is it?"

"Them planks in loft three. They're no good." Jon anticipated his employer. "They was not cured right, and warp like snakes. I can use some of them, maybe, but the rest we'll have to—"

"I understand," Sewal said, cutting through the explanations. Damn oak, anyway. Hard to find, and cured wrong to boot. "Eliot!"

The clerk's head popped up. "Sir?"

"Write to Anderson at the mill. No, make it an official complaint describing that particular shipment of oak in loft three. Jon will tell you what you need to know. Can't trust anyone." He swiveled back to the Swede. "You deliver it in person this afternoon. No. Have that oldest boy of yours see to it."

"*Ja.*"

"And after he's read it, you have Gunter tell Anderson that unless he makes good with a new delivery by Wednesday, I'll by God send all six of you out there to settle accounts, and with axe handles instead of a contract. The pen may be mightier than the sword, but it swings a feeble second to a stout axe handle."

From long experience Naslund knew that Anderson might just welcome the arrival of an axe handle or two. It would give his loggers a diversion from eight weeks of solid work. Jon grinned in anticipation of a fight. He and his five strapping sons had been working hard too. A good brawl was just the tonic they needed. He slapped a plank-solid belly and tugged at his knit cap. "*Ja.* Me and all five boys go. We take care of it."

Sewal tossed the reports onto Eliot's desk. The Swede had a faraway look in his eyes that meant the rhetorical axe handles had been interpreted literally. "Now, wait a minute, Jon. I don't want you to start anything, damn it. Just get the wood. You get into it with those loggers and millworkers and I'll lose you for three days." Not waiting for a response, he kicked the swinging door in the partition and joined Eve. "Sorry," he said, lightly kissing her in greeting. "You heard. Something always comes up at the last minute."

The front door closed behind them. Sewal had to raise his voice to be heard over the din of a hundred men shaping wood and iron.

"That Anderson," he boomed. "Curse it all, if I hadn't sold my interest in that logging yard, I wouldn't have this trouble."

"No," Eve shouted back. "You'd be dead from overwork and wouldn't have any problems at all."

"Ha! Maybe so. But at least it wouldn't be from exasperation. Are we late?"

"Almost."

"It's curious, this sense of immediacy coming from a young lady who is always tardy." Eve scooted across the seat of the carriage and snatched her skirts out of the way so Sewal wouldn't sit on them. "The docks!" Sewal shouted up to the driver. "Well?" he asked as the carriage lurched into motion. The din of men sawing and hammering and shouting instructions increased as they passed the rising skeletons of three clippers.

"I can't hear a word you're saying with all this noise," Eve shouted back, changing the subject.

The piercing whistle of a steam donkey drowned out her words. "What?" Sewal leaned close to her ear. "I didn't hear you. Too much noise."

The carriage passed through the front gate of the Blackheath Shipyards and the noise diminished. "That's precisely the point," Eve said, taking her father's arm and hugging it. "All the noise. All the wonderful noise!"

Lion stood near the bow of the *Southern Star* as the foretopsail clipper fell off the wind and started her run into Waupinau Bay. To his right Dawn Wind looked like little more than another one of the huge boulders strewn along the coast. He had stayed there for three days after Michael's wedding, and spent most of his time in Eve's company. Both of them avoided mentioning his indiscretion in the receiving line. As a result theirs had not been the heady liaison of lovers, but the more tranquil, easygoing relationship of friends becoming more than friends. Only just before they parted did Eve's hand cling tightly to his. A moment later, as he shook hands with Sewal, he felt her eyes on him. When he chanced a look they were bright and flashing, as if daring him to stay, or offering promises scandalous and delightful.

He wrote her from New York, then from Philadelphia and Washington. By the time he arrived home there were two letters waiting for him. One had been written an hour after his train left New Forest, the other the next morning at dawn. The letters were warm and chatty, and tugged at Lion's heart. As he read his eagerness for home was dangerously compromised by an equally ardent desire to return to Maine. If his house hadn't filled rapidly with friends and neighbors who had come to greet him, he might have been tempted to turn right around and go back to her.

The responsibilities of his farm held him at home, however. The next day Lion was out and riding over the land at the first hint of dawn. The morning was bright and cool with fresh dew wetting the grass. Mockingbirds sang. The horse's easy gait felt good underneath him. The wisteria was bright green, the grass soft and succulent. Thirteen fine new colts ran in the east paddock. Laughing, Lion walked among them, as a bay filly with a curious white blaze on her forehead and one white ear wobbled off ahead of him. Mounting again, there was no doubt in his mind that he preferred horses over ships, and riding over sailing.

Sailors spoke longingly of the sea as a mistress, but the land was no less so. Lion had been gone for over a year, and this particular mistress demanded a great deal to make up for his absence. Fences and roofs needed mending, wells and ponds cleaning. Stock had to be cared for, fields weeded. Muscles groaning, his whole body reveling in the hard labor, Lion worked from sunup to sundown. Within a week he shed ten pounds of city indolence. In the evenings, weak with fatigue, he stripped and lay floating in the pond next to the house, surrounded by silence and the sweet smells of summer. Later, cooled and relaxed on the veranda, he took time to write Eve or fill page after page of his journal.

June slipped into July, July into August. Heat and mosquitoes filled the valley air, set everyone's nerves on edge, and triggered what quickly came to be called the Wainwright Incident. Four of Harold Wainwright's field hands beat him and ran off to the North. They had been worth at least a thousand dollars apiece. Lion, no less than anyone else, was incensed. Harold had clothed and fed them, built them houses to live in, carried the doctor to them when they were ill. And had a cracked skull to show for his troubles. A handsome reward had been offered, but no one held out any hope of their return. Once again, everyone in the valley agreed, the North had condoned insurrection and denied a man his property. In angry reaction Lion sold the last three field hands he owned and hired the next door neighbor's boys. They would require watching, but not as much as the blacks, about whom he would have to worry.

The August heat seemed to last forever. The farm was in reasonably good shape, though, and as Lion lay lonely and sweating at night, he began to manufacture reasons to accompany Ambrose Duquesne on a trip North to inspect the progress on the ships they had ordered. Before he knew it he was on his way to Portsmouth to embark on the *Southern Star*. Duquesne acted pleased but surprised to see him, for there had been no mention of Lion making the trip. When Lion recounted his many reasons the older man pursed his lips, thought of as many reasons why Lion was not telling the truth, but said nothing.

There were surprises for Lion too. The contract hadn't been signed until the middle of July, but due to a hefty earnest money payment, the Blackheaths had started work by the end of June. In addition a ninth and smaller clipper, already half-finished for another company that had gone bankrupt, had been added to the contract. Sewal had promised Duquesne that if he brought a skeleton crew with him, it could sail the new acquisition home at the end of September. Duquesne was in a fine mood. Things couldn't have gone better.

They left Portsmouth on Sunday, on September 2, in good spirits. On their first stop, in New York, those spirits fell. A yard there had contracted to build a frigate but repudiated the contract after a noisy local Abolitionist politician discovered the ship's destination and threatened the yard's board of directors with uncatalogued but dire consequences if work continued. The second stop, in Mystic, Connecticut, proved less disastrous. There, a pair of ships that could later be converted into blockade busters should the need arise to protect the clippers was well along. On September 13, on a good tide, the sleek two-masted foretopsail clipper reached out from Mystic, leaned into the wind, and boomed up the coast.

Each spin of the taffrail log took Lion another cable length closer to Eve. Finally, late the next morning, they rounded the lighthouse and started the five-mile run into Waupinau Bay. Lion's brown suit was soaked with spray, and the air hung sweet and salty. If it hadn't been for the hiss of water curling under the bow he would have thought they were standing still, for the wind directly behind them matched the speed of the ship and so left them in what amounted to a calm. Lion turned and walked aft to join Duquesne. The older man produced a flask and offered it to him.

"Thanks," Lion said, and downed several swallows of pure corn whiskey. "My God!" he gasped, suppressing a cough. The last time he had drunk from the flask it had held aged Scotch. "They have a name for stuff like this in the Valley." The gasp turned into a wheeze. "We call it Hell's Butter."

"I know," Duquesne chuckled. "Apt, isn't it?" He grabbed Lion by the elbow and led him to the starboard rail. "Look. You can see them from here. One on the water, and three on the ways. Good."

Lion breathed a sigh of relief. Sewal Blackheath was building their ships despite the country's increasing preoccupation with its differences and daily doses of anti-Southern diatribe in the Northern newspapers. Not that it was any different south of the Mason-Dixon line. If the newspapers there had their way, the country would be at war by Christmas.

It was ironic. Lion, as a member of the Coalition, was partially responsible for the fever pitch that ran through the South and threatened a premature and possibly unnecessary war that would make it impossible to buy the very ships so necessary to winning that war. Irony upon irony, the quest had led him to Eve, whom he would be in grave danger of losing should war come. There were no ready answers to the kind of questions that led to. When Cornwallis surrendered to Washington, the British musicians had marched off playing "And the World Turned Upside Down." The trumpets that played brash marching songs throughout the South could well find themselves retuned. "It could turn again," Lion muttered.

"What?" Duquesne asked.

Lion jerked, as if startled from a dream. "Nothing," he said. "Look, we're about to turn."

Forward, the jibsails collapsed, snaked down their lines. Aloft, a crew was busy reefing the foretopsail. Five hundred tons of ship barely slowed as they heeled to port, the first step of the twenty-minute process that would bring the large sailing vessel to a dock. The maneuvers were tricky and dangerous, and depended on an expert crew and a captain who could judge the exact moment to head the ship into the wind. It was all a matter of physics, an exquisite equation of mass and inertia and momentum that would bring the *Southern Star* to a gliding, nudging halt against the huge rope fenders hanging from the dock.

All the muscles in Lion's body tensed as the ship closed. It looked as if they would hit too hard, as if they should have let New Forest's single steamboat take them the last few feet. Lion forced himself to look up, saw a familiar carriage at the end of the quay, and then the trim, erect figure of Sewal Blackheath. Next to him, sunlight glinting on her golden hair, Eve stood with one arm raised in greeting. "Eve," Lion whispered. He felt a presence at his side. Duquesne was staring at him. His eyes were shrewd and evaluating, and Lion knew Ambrose Duquesne understood at last the real reason for Lion's eagerness to return to Maine.

Lines flew through the air. The *Southern Star* bumped gently against the fenders and, snubbed by thick hawsers, rocked to a dead stop. Seconds later sailors and dockworkers secured the gangplank, and Lion and Duquesne hurried ashore. "Mr. Sewal Blackheath, Mr. Ambrose Duquesne," Lion said formally as the two men shook hands. "Miss Eve Blackheath, Mr. Ambrose Duquesne."

Duquesne bowed in the European manner. "I am delighted," he said, stopping just short of kissing Eve's hand, "not only to make your acquaintances, but to see how far you have progressed on our ships."

Sewal, ready to dislike the man because of his reputation, found himself softening. "We've been hard at work. After you've settled in, I'll take you on a tour of the yards."

"Please, my friend!" Duquesne held up a hand. "I cannot wait. I'd be delighted to see them now, unless it is completely inconvenient for you."

Ever prepared to show off his pride and joy, Sewal glanced toward Eve. "I think it's an excellent idea," Eve said. "Mr. Duquesne, you'll find my father enjoys nothing more than an enthusiastic listener. Especially when he's talking tall ships and the building of them."

"Eve makes me sound garrulous, Mr. Duquesne. I assure you . . ."

"You know it's true, Father," Eve laughed. "You two go along. I'll show Mr. McKenna to the hotel. Just remember, dinner is at seven." Before Sewal could think of a reason why Eve should occupy herself in some different way, she had led Lion toward the carriage.

Sewal's mouth opened, then closed. Duquesne chuckled. "I have a daughter of my own, Mr. Blackheath. Amazing. It seems only a few weeks past I was teaching her how to walk. Now she treats *me* like a child." He shook his head. "They do grow up fast these days."

"Too fast, if you ask me," Sewal retorted.

"The young are impetuous. Especially two such as they, who feel so strongly about each other."

Sewal's eyebrows rose. "Really?" he asked in a tight voice. "I hadn't noticed anything out of the ordinary. My daughter places a great value on a cordial manner. Shall we start?"

"By all means," Duquesne agreed, dropping the subject and following his host across the quay to another carriage. He was sure there was more to Lion and Eve's relationship than met the eye, but he wasn't about to muddy the dark waters of Sewal Blackheath's ignorance. Picking his way through a low forest of hackmatack knees, which would later become corner braces in his ships, Duquesne made a mental note to warn Lion away from the girl. The South's interests could not be compromised. Sewal Blackheath had to be kept happy. And if Lion McKenna didn't like that, it was just too bad.

The Clipper was run by the Widow Mason, whose husband had been first mate and harpooner on one of Sewal's whaling trips years ago. Mason and three others had been crushed by the vast and terrible sweep of an old bull Blue Rorqual's flukes. The Blue measured out at over ninety feet when he was finally killed, but that was little consolation for a round-eyed girl who waited patiently over seven thousand miles away. When she did learn of his death, two years after the fact, the new widow donned the familiar black dress and appeared at the reckoning to claim her dead husband's percentage of the profits. A month later she bought the Clipper.

The hotel was set over Margaret Brighton's Dressmaking Salon and commanded a delightful view of the whole eastern end of Waupinau Bay. The rooms were identically furnished with a huge double bed, two highbacked chairs, a small writing table, a ponderous combination wardrobe and dresser, and a spindly, marble-covered washstand. An oval rag rug filled the center of the open space in front of the door, and smaller ones lay on either side of the bed and in front of the washstand. Only the curtains and quilt were permitted a color of their own. The light blue, in contrast to the stark white walls and old, deep-waxed brown of wood, seemed unnaturally vivid. Lion directed the men from the ship to place his luggage against the wall, then watched from the open door as Widow Mason led them to Duquesne's room. Inside, Eve pulled back the curtains and stared out the window. Her stomach felt tight and her flesh cold. They were alone at last.

"You've seen all that before." Lion's hands cupped her shoulders and slid down her arms. When his lips touched the right side of her neck she closed her eyes and tilted her head to the left. His hands slid upward to close over each breast. Eve caught her breath and, knowing he would stop if she protested, leaned against him and covered his hands with hers. "I have wanted to hold you," Lion whispered. "I have ached."

She turned in his arms, looked up into his eyes. "Do you remember the day Father and I took you to the train?" Lion nodded. "I have regretted, ever since then, that I did not do this." Eve's arms wrapped around his neck and her whole body pressed against him without reserve. Her kiss was long and warm, a kiss of abandonment and promise that took Lion by surprise.

Her eyes glinted with affection and amusement when she stepped away from him. "And what do you think of that, Mr. Lion McKenna?"

"I think it's a good thing Duquesne insisted on our staying here rather than at Dawn Wind. Being that close to you and under constant scrutiny would be excruciating."

The silence between them was as fragile as delicate crystals of ice found on a mountain pond on a fall morning. Neither wanted to break it, but the warm sun of joy could not be restrained. One began to laugh. The other joined in so quickly it was impossible to say who was first. They embraced again, this time as old friends, almost embarrassed by their passion.

"It is good to see you," Lion said, kissing the top of her head as her cheek touched his shoulder.

"What? No remorse for your beloved Shenandoah?"

"It is my home, and I have friends there. It is a land I love." She had washed her hair that morning and it smelled sweet. Lion thought of the morning mist rising from the stream that ran nearby his house and remembered how he had wished Eve had been with him to share the softness. "It wasn't the same this time, though. So much seemed hollow without you there."

"It was just the opposite for me," Eve said.

"There's a barb to pierce the heart. You did not miss me?"

"How could I?" Eve's head was warm against Lion's chest. Her voice was a caress. "When I walked the sandy beaches, weren't you there beside me to laugh when the ocean's breath caught my bonnet, when its fingers reached for my ankles in the changing tide? You must have been, for I saw you. I heard your voice whispering my name high in the trees above me as I sat beside my mother's grave and told her how brash and rude you were, and how I had tried not to like you. The sun glinting off the waves was the light in your eyes as I told her how my own heart betrayed me, and how glad I was that it did. The wind was your fingers running through my hair as I confessed that I wished we had had more time together. How could I miss you, dear Lion, when you never left my side?"

"Eve," Lion whispered, stepping close.

She raised her fingertips to his lips. "We are expected at Dawn Wind. If Father gets there first—" She left the sentence unfinished.

"You haven't mentioned . . . said anything about us to him?"

"No," Eve answered reluctantly. She stopped him as he was about to speak. "You don't know Father. He gets something in his head and believes that is the way things must be. Let him see us together and get used to the idea. Then I'll tell him."

"The longer we wait . . ."

"Trust me." She touched his cheek with her fingers. "Trust me?"

Lion smiled at last. "You trap me, tame me with a smile."

"No," Eve said. "I don't want us to be that way. Not ever."

"Then we won't be. Just let me get myself untrapped, and it'll never happen again."

"You're silly. A thirty-year-old man, who . . ."

"I am fourteen years old, and in love for the first time. Come on, before Widow Mason gets ideas." Exaggerating, he offered her his arm, and escorted her down the stairs.

Widow Mason leaned forward, elbows on the bottom half of the Dutch doors leading from her rooms to the front hallway. Her hair was tied back in a gray bun covered with a lace cap. She was a handsome, large-boned woman with a face full of memories that showed in a mask of wrinkles unnoticeable unless one was standing quite close. "Is the room satisfactory, Mr. McKenna?"

"More than, thank you, Mrs. Mason," Lion said, pausing in front of her door.

"Good. It's nice to have you back. I was at Michael's wedding. Best be warned, Eve. More than one pretty young thing cast an eye in the direction of your Mr. McKenna."

Eve laughed noncommittally and followed Lion out the door. The reference to "her" Mr. McKenna was disquieting. Were her feelings that obvious? "You need not smile so smugly, Mr. McKenna," she said as Lion led her to the carriage. "I'll have you remember I was not exactly wanting for a choice of partners either."

"Weren't you, now," Lion teased, climbing in beside her. "It just goes to prove one thing."

"Oh?" Eve asked.

"Yes." Surreptitiously, he let his knee press against hers. "We both chose wisely."

The mutton was delicious, the cake that followed even more so. Pole busied himself with coffee and small plates of chocolates. Duquesne leaned back in his chair like a sleepy cat. Sewal broke one of the chocolates and crumbled it into his coffee. "Reminds me of one voyage around the Horn," he said, chuckling. "Twenty-eight, I think it was. A good year. Took five sperm in less than two months."

"Ah, good." Justin raised his eyes in mock thanks. "Father is going to regale us with tales of high adventure under a cloud of sail."

The ensuing silence was quickly filled by the nervous sound of stirring spoons and clanking cups. Duquesne glanced to each side, mentally stored the fact that father and son didn't get along, and sipped at his coffee. Sewal stiffened, forced himself to relax. "We have guests, Justin. Why don't we declare a truce for tonight?"

"A truce? Indeed? Are we at war?"

Sewal ignored the remark, waved for Pole. "I think Mr. Duquesne and I will have our coffee on the front porch, Pole. Will you see to it? Bring the liqueur tray too, if you would." He rose, dropped his napkin, and rubbed his hands in anticipation. "About that chess game," he said, turning to Duquesne. "Still want to play?"

Duquesne smiled lazily. "By all means." He stood, took in the table at a glance. "If you will excuse me, Miss Blackheath? Gentlemen, I'll spare you the agony of seeing Mr. Blackheath soundly thrashed."

Eve glared at her brother, and the second the front door closed said, "Must you be so hateful?"

"Relax, Eve," Justin said. "I'm sorry. You weren't here. He issued an ultimatum this morning. Now that summer vacation is over, it's Bowdoin again or the yards." He shook his head and looked at Lion. "Why do fathers always have to have the last word?"

"I didn't have one long enough to be able to answer that," Lion said, a little put out with Justin's breach of etiquette. "Mine was killed when I was barely eleven."

Justin's face reddened. "I'm sorry. I didn't know . . ."

"It's all right. I'll tell you one thing, though. Many's the time I would have welcomed a word, final or otherwise, from him."

"I suppose you're right." Justin sighed, and made a fist. "But why is he so stubborn, damn it? Why?" His voice thickened, took on the tone of his father's. "I never yet saw a man who rose very high by making pictures of the *real* accomplishments of others."

"Ahem!" Pole stood in the doorway. Justin, caught in the act of imitating Sewal, concentrated on unwrapping a piece of chocolate. "There is fresh coffee and brandy in the parlor," Pole went on, pretending he hadn't heard Justin.

"That will be fine, Pole," Eve said, rising quickly. "Would you care to join us, Mr. McKenna?" Justin hadn't moved. Lion glanced at him, then back at Eve. "Don't worry about Justin," she said, sweeping past him on her way to the parlor. "He's in one of his moods."

None too sure of his ground in a family quarrel about which he was ignorant, Lion followed. The parlor was a visual feast. The walls were papered with a design of blue chrysanthemums on lifelike green vines against a pale cream background. The furniture was a hodgepodge of wildly varying styles and designs. The highbacked chairs had decorated a governor's suite in Lisbon. The center table sat on a pedestal carved into the shape of twisted serpents that held a tabletop inlaid with exotic woods and shells in swirls of rare birds and other fauna. A pair of end tables were decorated with brass oil lamps purchased in the marketplace in Tangier, and a massive tapestry of intriguing symbols carefully woven into a chaotic backdrop of geometric colors was of Moroccan origin.

"Is there anyplace your father hasn't been?" Lion asked.

"I'm sure somewhere," she said, sitting at the piano and beginning to play. "He went to sea when he was fifteen, and didn't really live ashore until Grandpa died and he took over the yards. He was almost forty then."

Justin handed Lion a brandy and sat down. "Tell me, Lion," he said, swirling his drink. "Do you approve of a father who is determined to plot the future of his offspring?"

Lion sat in a chair near the piano, listened quietly for a moment before answering. "It's not for me to approve or disapprove," he finally said.

"You have sidestepped the question."

"Have I? Don't we all choose in the long run? Even if someone else pushes us, we have to allow him to push, and agree to go in the direction he chooses."

Justin laughed thinly. "I'm not sure, but that doesn't sound very flattering. We are all responsible, et cetera et cetera."

"Possibly so."

"It's something to think about," Justin said sarcastically. "You might even broach the subject with Michael." Eve quit playing. "I'm sorry," Justin added sheepishly. "Still . . ."

"Is something the matter with Michael?" Lion asked, turning to Eve.

"You didn't tell him?" Justin asked. Eve shook her head no. "Perhaps it's best you see for yourself." Justin went on, "They'll be here tomorrow or the next day." Lion tensed at the news of Rosamond's arrival, but no one seemed to notice. Justin shrugged. "I say 'they.' Maybe only he."

"Justin!" Eve warned.

"Lion will be here, Eve. He might as well know now, so he won't be embarrassed later." Eve stared down at the keys. Justin took a sip of his drink. "Michael's marriage, arranged by my father, of course, if not—"

"That's not true, Justin," Eve broke in. "Michael married Rosamond because he loved her. Father—"

"Arranged it whether or not Michael knew it. He wouldn't have married her if Father hadn't wanted him to." Justin's voice was harsh and unrelenting. "At any rate, if you don't mind my saying so, the marriage hasn't been exactly blessed by the gods. More the Furies."

"Justin!"

"It's true, damn it, Eve. I don't like it, you don't like it, but there's no sense beating around the bush. He's changed. Drastically. Each visit is worse. This time he's been ordered to remain here until he achieves some sort of, and I quote, 'stable, constructive behavior befitting an officer.' I found the letter in the desk in the library."

"If Father knew," Eve gasped, rising from the piano bench. Brother and sister had forgotten Lion was with them. "Rummaging through his desk!"

"I'm a member of this family, and no matter what Father says, I have the right to know what's going on. And what's been going on is that he's been drinking and whoring and God knows what else."

Eve's eyes were flashing and her cheeks were pale with anger.

"That's enough!" she snapped, at the same time slamming her fist down on the piano. "I'll not hear another word of this . . . this slander. Michael is our brother!"

"I'm beginning to wonder," Justin said in an anguished tone. "He was never like that before, until Father—"

"I said, that's enough." She took two steps toward Justin. Lion thought for a moment she would slap him, but she stopped herself just in time. When she spoke, her voice was low and trembling with intensity. "We have a guest. I will not let you do this."

Justin's eyes closed and his head fell back as if he was asleep, then wagged from side to side. Sighing, he roused himself, stood, and set down his drink. "I have some work I want to do in my studio," he said hollowly. "If you don't mind? Eve? Lion?" Walking stiffly, he left without another word.

Eve stood motionless for a long moment after the front door closed. At last she turned toward Lion. "For Justin, the sun used to rise and set on Michael." She smiled wanly, tried and failed to inject some lightness into her voice. "You see what an idyllic family we have?"

She was near tears. Lion rose quickly, took her hands, and led her to the piano. "Play," he said, holding the bench for her. "Your family is no worse than a million others. Just play."

It took a moment for her fingers to remember. When they did they roamed through a melodic little tune that evoked sunshine and bright sky, the sound of summer birds and tranquility. Yes, he thought. It's what we all want. But a tune is only an abstraction of a desire. Wanting tranquility, we are faced with raucous disagreements. Wanting a pleasant sequence of happy events, we are forced onto disrythmic paths that lead us astray. Wanting generosity and peace, we are presented with avarice and the threat of war.

The song ended. "What was that?" Lion asked.

"A French folk song. I don't know the name. Mother taught it to me when I was little. She enjoyed the old songs."

"Did she teach you 'Willow Waly?' "

"I know it. A Scottish ballad. A lament, really. It's a sad song."

"Will you play it for me?" Lion asked.

Eve began to play and sing the lyrics. Her voice was clear and controlled, exquisitely pure. Lion leaned back and closed his eyes. It *was* a sad song. A song of love.

*   *   *

Sewal picked up his knight, removed Duquesne's pawn from the board, and replaced it with the knight. "Check and mate," he said, smiling broadly.

Duquesne shook his head. "I fear you've bested me. Lion warned me about you too."

"Yes. I gave him a lesson in tactics when he was here in June. A good game, chess. I taught all my children to play."

"Wisely so, I suspect," Duquesne said. "It teaches one to plan ahead, to be bold or cautious as the situation demands, and to respect one's opponents. Not to speak of a sense of competition." He drew a cigar case from his coat pocket. "You are no world champion, my friend, but an expert nonetheless."

"I think that could be said for both of us," Sewal said, rearranging the pieces.

"I like to think so," Duquesne replied, offering his opponent one of the cigars. "Virginia tobacco. The best." He handed Sewal his clip, took it back, and snipped off the end of his cigar. "So, Mr. Blackheath." Matches flared, the cigars were lit. Both men leaned back. "I know there's more to this than a game of chess between two old men sitting on a veranda."

Sewal blew a cloud of smoke into the air. The music had stopped for a while, but now a sweet, mournful tune drifted out from the parlor. It was one that Jennifer had liked to play, and brought back painful memories that he shrugged off with difficulty. "You've seen the ships," he began slowly. "You've seen my projections. Allowing for moderate delays due to the weather, we will complete them on schedule." Duquesne nodded. "Our arrangements, however, have skirted a most singular and complicated issue." He leaned forward and pointed with his cigar for emphasis. "War."

"War, Mr. Blackheath?" Duquesne asked, as if the word were new to him.

"You are aware that the Democratic Convention was a disaster, and that the party is hopelessly split and running two candidates. That makes four major presidential candidates, Mr. Duquesne, not to speak of a half-dozen minor ones who have sprung up. The electorate is fragmented as never before, and as far as I'm concerned it's a foregone conclusion that only the Republicans have a chance of winning. The inauguration of Lincoln, as you well know, will signal a mass exodus of the Southern states, which the North cannot allow. So, we come to my point."

"Which is," Duquesne began, "that if the times indeed become more unsettled—"

"Let's not evade the issue, Duquesne. If we go to *war*. Civil War."

"Uh—" Duquesne coughed. Such talk made him nervous, coming from Blackheath. "Yes. To put it bluntly."

"There's no other way," Sewal snapped. "Now. A question. If there is a war, will I—will I be *allowed*—to honor the contract between us?"

Duquesne inspected the ash on his cigar as if it held the answer. "Honor is a precious word, Mr. Blackheath," he said slowly, "yet one open to interpretation. For example, I suspect you are aware of, and do not think highly of, some of my past dealings. At another time, you might not have been able to assign a monetary value to honor. You have done that, however. Half a million dollars, if I remember correctly," he added drily.

Sewal ignored the sarcasm. "It is not a question of honor alone," he said. "You mustn't forget risk."

"To the contrary. I try to." Duquesne exhaled tobacco smoke from between round, full lips. "A man cannot overly concern himself with risk. If he does he never truly lives, but spends his time worrying."

"That is a basic difference between us then. Ask any man who makes his livelihood on the sea. The courses he charts involve risks, and every risk must be taken into account if he wishes to complete his voyage."

"Which is to say?"

"That there may come a time when risk makes honor assume a greater value. Say six hundred thousand dollars."

"Dear heavens," Duquesne quipped, the lightness forced. "I hope that time never comes."

"And if it does?"

Duquesne did some quick arithmetic, added and subtracted from secret accounts. "I imagine something can be arranged, Mr. Blackheath," he finally said. He hated to admit it but if Blackheath delivered in the face of the same pressures that had canceled the New York ship, a twenty-percent markup was most reasonable.

Sea breezes cooled the house and drove the tree limbs into an eerie, swaying dance. It was past midnight. Lion and Duquesne had returned to town hours ago, and Sewal was alone. He did not want it that way, but had grown accustomed to solitude. He folded his hands on his lap. It had been a long day and he was tired. The next day would be longer, with Michael's arrival. Michael. There was a sobering thought. What did the boy think he was doing? Drunk. Whoring. Conduct unbecoming an officer. That wasn't the Michael Blackheath he'd raised. He'd have to have a talk with him and straighten him out.

He poured a short brandy to help drain the tension and ready himself for sleep. The next day would be busy, as all the days had become. He would have to talk to Justin again, try to convince him he should finish at Bowdoin. Duquesne had mentioned something about Eve and McKenna, but had dropped the subject: he'd want to ask further about that too. It had gotten so a man didn't know what was going on in his own house, he thought sourly. If something was going on he'd have to nip it in the bud before the relationship with the Sarandons was threatened.

What else, he wondered, his eyes closing briefly. He had to draft a letter to Cabell and try to find out why the Navy contracts he'd promised hadn't come through. God knows the yards needed them. The Duquesne contract wouldn't last forever. It would catch them up and put Dawn Wind back on its feet, but that was about all. Whatever happened, Sewal couldn't afford another recession like the one in 1857. Not at his age. He was too old to struggle through all that again. With luck the Duquesne order would be the star that signaled the renaissance of Blackheath Shipyards.

He drank the brandy and tossed out the last few drops. Some renaissance. If the country was plunged into war before those ships were finished he'd have to do some fancy footwork to keep from being pilloried for delivering war materiel to the enemy. Some renaissance that made him put a price on his honor. But maybe it wouldn't come to that. If it did, that was the chance he had to take. Too many generations stood behind him, and he was damned if he'd let the estate crumble while he was in charge. Whatever needed to be done, at whatever cost, he'd do.

Yawning, he rose and headed inside. His mind continued to plan, to list. He needed more lumber from the mill. What was taking so long with the rigging? He would talk to Naslund and the other foremen first thing and see what they thought about putting on double shifts, possibly even triple if they could find the right people. With luck and a lot of push maybe they could finish before the worst happened. Maybe . . .

Chapter 9

September was glorious. Maple, elm, oak, and sumac blazed orange and red and yellow against the deep backdrop of bright pine green. The first fall storms held off, either out in the Atlantic or up in Canada. Nights were crisp and cool, and days were bright and virtually cloudless. It was as if time had split in two and left a gap around which the days flowed, leaving Eve and Lion to themselves.

Saturday was a day of reacquaintance, of walking along the northern beach and retelling the summer. Sunday was church and Sunday dinner and a lazy afternoon sitting in the gazebo and talking more, this time about Michael, who had arrived that morning, the lines of stress and tension modeling his face into an angry mask. Monday and Tuesday and Wednesday were working days for Lion. Forced to sit through interminable meetings, he fidgeted and half listened while Eve paced her room, pestered Eustacia and Jubb, and avoided Rosamond lest she forget her tongue and start asking embarrassing questions about Michael.

On Wednesday night Lion begged off Thursday's planned trip with Sewal, Michael, and Duquesne to Portland to inspect the iron-works and, if necessary, establish a direct line of credit with the factory. As soon as possible after the train left, Lion drove to Dawn Wind.

The day was bright and clear. Easterly winds from the Atlantic blew gently but steadily. The house was quiet. Rosamond still slept. Maisie was busy cleaning; Hamlet was occupied in the barn. Jubb had taken Eustacia to town to buy the week's supply of groceries, and Justin was hard at work in his studio. Laughing, Eve led Lion across the front lawn to the path down the southern cliff of Dawn Wind to the boat house. "I don't know about this," Lion said, looking down at the water more than twenty feet below.

"What?" Eve asked, leaning over the rail.

A pea pod hung from davits at eye level. Lion pointed at it, compared it to the expanse of gray, seaweed-littered Atlantic rolling onto the rocky beach. "It looks awfully tiny. You sure it's safe?"

"Landlubber," Eve teased, glancing above her to the cliff before giving him a peck on the cheek. "Here. Untie those two lines and let it down. I'm going in to change."

Still dubious, Lion loosed the knots and eased the boat down to the beach while Eve disappeared inside the boat house. A moment later she returned, barefooted and dressed in the scandalous attire of a man; a simple cotton shirt tucked into the waist of woolen trousers rolled up at the ankles. In comparison, Lion was overdressed in a lawn shirt, breeches, boots, cravat, and broad-brimmed hat. "You'd best leave the boots here," Eve said, as Lion stared at her in appreciation of the way the trousers clung to her hips. "Lion! Are you listening to me?"

He pointed at his boots. "Suppose we need to walk home?"

"Silly. Come on." Eve handed him the picnic basket and started down the stairs. "I know you Virginians consider yourselves exceptional, but I didn't think walking on water was one of your claims to greatness."

"All right, all right. No boots."

"Anyway, if we capsize, they might drag you under."

"Capsize?" Lion set down the picnic basket and started tugging at his boots.

"I'm not saying we will," she said, eyes twinkling. "Only that we might."

"That's most reassuring," Lion drawled, placing the boots on a high rock, out of the way of the spray.

"Michael, Justin and I used to sail from here all the time, and in the same boat. It's sturdy and handles well."

"I thought you said it held a maximum of two."

"Adults," she corrected. "More in a pinch, but it isn't a good idea."

They shoved the boat to the edge of the water and Eve, more hindered than helped by Lion, rigged the sail. Picnic basket and paddle aboard, they waded into the cold water until the boat floated free. "You want to take it?" Eve asked.

"Hell, no!" Lion said, blanching. "Your pardon," he added, apologizing for his language.

"Okay. Sit up there, then," she said, holding the pea pod steady while Lion climbed aboard. As soon as he was seated she sprang aboard herself, grabbed the tiller and sheet. Wind filled the small gaff-rigged sail and they were under way. "I thought you said you'd sailed before."

Lion turned a bleak expression toward her. "I have. In boats."

"What do you think this is?"

Lion glared at the small craft. It bobbed up and down, frail and lonely on the choppy expanse of Waupinau Bay. "Driftwood," he finally said.

The first few minutes were the worst. After that, finally convinced Eve knew what she was doing and that they wouldn't sink, Lion turned around and lay back, his feet on either side of the mast, his bottom and head resting on the low-slung seats. Before he knew it the steady slap slap of waves and the gentle hiss of the bow cutting through the water so relaxed him that he dozed off. When he woke they were almost to the other side of the bay. A few clouds had come up to dapple the still-blue sky. Eve was holding to a course a hundred yards offshore. Lion struggled up to his elbows to watch the coastline and marveled at its ruggedness. Maine challenged the sea, hurled boulders into the foam, and exploded incoming waves against its battered cliffs. The Blackheaths, at least Sewal, were a little like that too. Satisfied, he grinned. Eve carried Sewal's blood. Beauty might be skin deep, but underneath he sensed the toughness of generations who had battled unyielding land and rough waters.

"What are you thinking?" he asked, sitting up and turning around to face her. When she didn't say anything he followed her gaze toward the shore where the muted color of the water merged with the raw, primeval stone. Gray-brown broken spines and a great castle wall of granite swept up to a line of densely packed pines. And all around them a chorus of slate-gray and black gulls swirled and dipped.

"*Wabanake,*" Eve said, frowning slightly as the wind fell and the catboat slowed. "An Indian word. It means 'living at the sunrise.'" The pea pod, dead in the water, rose and fell on the Atlantic swell. Tiny wavelets slapped the hull in unpredictable rhythms. Waves and gulls; the only music, the only sound. Together, they linked time and space in silence.

The wind stayed down, and there was nothing to do but paddle to shore. "I thought you knew how to sail," Lion grumbled as he fought the paddle.

Eve shrugged. "I'm not in charge of the wind. We Mainelanders know our limitations."

"What's that supposed to mean?"

"It means we're both hot and tired of paddling. But since we're almost to shore, I suggest we forego an argument until we land."

"Let me back there," Lion said, half rising and making his way toward the stern.

"We're better off paddling. What wind we find will be unpredictable because we're in the lee of that cliff," Eve said. "You can't do anything I haven't done."

"I can try."

"Sit down."

"Let me back there," Lion repeated. His legs bent as he started around Eve.

"Sit down!" Eve exclaimed.

"You could at least . . ." A gust of wind filled the sail and tipped the boat just enough to throw Lion off balance and send him flying head over heels into the water. Seconds later he surfaced, sputtering. His black hair was plastered over his face.

"Well done, Mr. McKenna," Eve laughed. "I take back what I said. You did bring the wind. Only it's gone again. Perhaps you'd better come aboard and give another try."

"Just give me a hand," he sputtered, embarrassed and angry with himself.

Eve stretched out a hand. "Careful. Roll over the side or you'll tip us over."

Lion gripped her wrist and, with one leg over the gunwale, gave a hard yank and pulled Eve into the water. The boat lurched violently as he scrambled into it.

Arms and legs thrashing, Eve fought the water for a brief moment, then relaxed and let her natural buoyancy bring her to the surface. The bay, chilled by deep currents from the Atlantic, was icy cold. Her teeth began to chatter and she could feel her fingers turning numb. "Help me!" she gasped, at the same time reaching for the gunwale.

Lion caught her hand, dragged her halfway out of the water. "Sorry," he said grinning widely. "Just roll over the side so you don't tip us over."

Half an hour later they dragged the pea pod out of the water in a small natural cove surrounded on three sides by an overhanging cliff.

Eve dropped the rope and sagged to the ground. Her lips were blue and she was shivering violently. "You laughed," she said disgustedly. "I heard you laugh."

"I did no such thing," Lion protested, perching on the gunwale and beating his hands together in an attempt to warm them.

"Ha! Some gentleman you are. Look at me."

He did. The light fabric of her shirt, almost translucent when wet, clung to her breasts and outlined her nipples in sharp relief. The cove was small and no sun reached into it. Eve scooted over to sit against a rock, drew her knees up, and hugged her arms around them for warmth. "I . . . guess I'd better gather some wood," Lion said, clearing his throat. "Won't hurt to dry out."

There was plenty of aged driftwood. Lion dug a hole in the sand and lined it with dry sand from the back of the tiny beach. Using a knife from the picnic basket, he made a pile of shavings which he arranged over and around a flat piece of driftwood placed in the center of the hole. A few minutes' search turned up a bow-shaped piece of branch, to which he strung a length of rope from the boat. A second stick, sharpened and stuck in a starter hole drilled with the knife in the bottom piece, passed through a loop in the bowstring. Leaning over, he began to saw the bow back and forth. The pointed stick moved faster and faster. When a tiny wisp of smoke rose from the point Lion spun it a little longer, then bent close and blew gently. At last the tinder ignited and a tiny flame sprang up. Lion carefully added fuel and, minutes later, a pleasant campfire was adding its cheerful crackling melody to the rhythm of the waves.

"That's wonderful," Eve said, holding her hands over the fire.

"Old injun trick." Lion grinned, admiring his handiwork.

"Lion?"

He looked up at her, tried to avoid staring at her shirt, and almost succeeded. "What?"

"Our . . ." She couldn't bring herself to say it. Not immediately. Everything she'd ever learned screamed *no,* but she knew the time had come, and that she could no longer wait. Her lower lip hurt where she had been biting it. She sought his eyes with hers. Her voice was thick, barely audible. "Our clothes will dry quicker if we hang them over the fire."

Her straw-colored hair hung in thick, wet strands over her shoulders. Her eyes were bluer than he'd ever seen them. "Do you know what you're saying?" Lion asked quietly.

"Yes," she answered. "I know."

Lion stood, took her hand and helped her to her feet. He reached out and undid the top button of her shirt, then the next and the next. The fabric fell away from her breasts and left them open to the air. Slowly, Lion unbuttoned his own shirt, stripped it from him and tossed it aside. Breathless, Eve closed her eyes as he undid her trousers, pulled them down her legs and off her feet. When she opened them again he was stepping out of his own trousers. Eve thought she knew what a man would look like, but was unprepared for the reality of Lion's masculinity. Embarrassed, she pulled her eyes away from his sex.

He was beautiful. Roped muscles slatted his stomach. Thick black hair curled on his chest. A whitened streak of scar tissue creased his left shoulder, and his arms bulged with muscles that had always before been hidden by his clothes. Eve's breathing was shallow. Her breasts rose and fell quickly. Her whole being wanted him, yet she was fearful and uncertain. Lion's hands pressed lightly against the sides of her breasts. His thumbs touched her nipples. "You are magnificent," he said in a thick voice.

"Let's not talk," Eve whispered. "Not now. Just hold me, please." When their bodies met she knew she had said the right thing.

Flesh on flesh, dark against light. Hands touching softly, touching and touching again and again, unable to stop. It had hurt, no matter how gentle he had tried to be, but the pain had been overridden by the fierce demands of their lovemaking, and the explosive satisfaction that followed.

Content at last, Eve lolled on her side and rested her cheek against the thick layer of hair that covered Lion's chest. "I've heard women talk. I even discovered a book, once, in an old sea chest. It was from the Orient and described all the ways. I was appalled and frightened then. Now I want to do everything. With you."

"I hope not in one afternoon," Lion murmured, his eyes closed.

"So unromantic. Will you spoil these minutes for me?"

Lion opened one eye. "Not unromantic. Tired. And my back feels like a cat-o'-nine-tails has been taken to it."

Eve's eyes filled with sudden concern. "Did I hurt you? I thought you cried my name in passion."

"In agony," he said.

"Oh," Eve said, sitting up unhappily. "You've spoiled it." She put her hands over her face. Lion reached for her shoulders and pulled her back onto their sandy bed despite her efforts to resist. He kissed her hands and when they refused to open, leaned lower and kissed the pink crowns of her breasts. "Stop it," she said.

"Make me," he said. "Convince me you want me to stop." Her flesh grew taut between his lips. "I cried your name because I was falling from a mountain and only you could save me. I cried your name because I was alone on a blue-black sea with great waves towering over me. Suddenly you were by my side, and together we rushed down the other side of the tempest. I cried your name because you are Eve, first woman in Eden. All love, all beauty came from you. All life, all beginnings and endings, past and future. All here, all now, within my grasp, within my arms, within my heart. And so I cried your name."

Eve's hands left her face and cradled Lion's instead. Her eyes were wide and liquid soft with desire, her lips slack and moist, waiting for his kiss. "I do not want you to stop," she whispered. "I do not want you to stop, ever."

His eyes bore into her, met her unblinking gaze. Energy passed between them from her hands to his face, and from the tiny spot where their knees touched. Not a word needed to be said as Lion shifted his weight over her. Her hands still touched his face. When he entered her she wet her lips with her tongue, but did not speak. They did not move for a long time. At long last Eve's hips tilted up and closer to him. Lion's jaw clenched and his eyes closed briefly, as if the combined sensation of her touch and gaze was too much to bear.

Stars can be seen from the bottom of a well during the daytime. Languid, deceptive streaks of light, they sweep slowly across the narrow opening of black sky. Now, minutes, days, years, and centuries of light poured across Eve like fire-hot dots that pierced her skin. Sometime later, at the moment her body arched and the spasms threatened to shake her apart, the stars stopped and coalesced into a single blazing light that shone brighter than the sun. Eve moaned once, rose, spinning, into a light so intense it snapped the bonds of sensibility. Like Icarus, who flew too close to the sun, she floated down from the heights at last, into the luxurious depths of sleep.

An afternoon breeze playing over entangled arms and legs, the mischief of erotica, roused them. Half awake, they lay quietly, warmed by each other. Lion pulled his arm out from under Eve, flexed it to get the circulation going again. Eve stretched and yawned, and her stomach growled. "Mine, too," Lion said, patting his belly and then rising to tend the fire.

Neither made a move toward the dried clothes. Eve crossed to the boat, her feet leaving tiny craters in the sand. Their intimacy had negated all the old rules. Whatever restraints a straitlaced society had imposed upon her had disappeared. Lion watched with approval as, completely unembarrassed by her nakedness, she bent to retrieve the picnic basket. "*Voilà!*" she said, placing it next to him. "Wine, cheese curds, summer sausage. And—" she held it under his nose for him to smell, "—a fresh loaf of Eustacia's rye bread."

"A miracle," Lion exclaimed.

"No. Forethought," Eve answered, tossing the bread to him.

Feasting replaced conversation for the next quarter hour. Hunger assuaged, Eve leaned across the scattered remnants of their meal and kissed Lion, who managed to swallow a last bite of bread before kissing her in turn. A toying expression on her face, Eve straddled his ankles and, her fingers drawing random patterns on his legs, slowly slid up his outstretched legs. Lion lay back and watched her, raised his leg so his thigh was tight between her legs. "You're insatiable," he laughed. "A wanton. I hate to say it, but even though the spirit is willing, the flesh is weak. You'll have to give me a few more minutes." Eve pouted and sat back on his legs. "Have I disappointed you?" he asked, partly serious.

She smiled and leaned forward until the tips of her breasts brushed across his groin. "No," she said. "I'm just used to having my own way, is all."

"A mistake," Lion said, "with nature."

"Terrible."

"What? Nature?" He grinned. "I can't control nature. We Virginians know our own limitations."

"You spirit me away to a lonely place, seduce me, totally *ruin* my life, and then leave me to languish. You ought to be ashamed."

Lion pushed up on his elbows. "Do you mean that?"

"What?" Eve asked tickling him with her chin.

"Have I ruined your life?"

She paused, kissed his stomach, and sat up. Her face was serious. "No. I was afraid of it, but now that I've done it, I . . ." She looked troubled, suddenly moved away, and poured a glass of wine. "Tell me about your farm," she asked, poking a finger into the dark red liquid in order to extract a piece of ash. "Do you still have family there?"

Lion lay back and closed his eyes, pictured the sunwashed white house surrounded by emerald fields and bordered by blue mountains. "The McKennas and the Blackheaths have a lot in common. Four generations of McKennas have farmed the same three sections in the Shenandoah valley. A prosaic life, really. Tobacco, corn, horses—good horses. When my father was killed by a drunken Cherokee I became the man of the house. I had one good year before a rich family up the valley tried to buy me out. When that didn't work they tried to run me out. I didn't run, either."

His brows knotted. Eve caught a glimpse of something frightening; a flash of cruelty and violence she hadn't seen in him. "My mother, aunt and uncle live there now. A friend is watching over the farm when I'm gone. I have three sisters. The oldest married a neighbor down the road, the second a politician who lives in Richmond. The third hasn't been seen or heard from since she disappeared with a rambling lad who, it was said, was headed west. I think she is happy. My brother, Finian, was killed when a horse rolled on him. He was fifteen at the time, I was eighteen." He paused for a moment and a hard look came over his face. "Our home is not as grand as Dawn Wind, but what there is, I built. And what there was before that, I held."

He took the wine from her, drank it off, and set the glass aside. "Not very exciting, but solid. Everyday people in an everyday world."

"I don't think so," Eve said, shaking her head. "You have never been an everyday person in your whole life."

Lion shrugged. "Maybe, maybe not." He caught her arm and pulled her toward him. "But enough of the past. I have important decisions to make."

"Indeed. What could they be?" Eve said laughing, coming to him.

"Ah, let's see. First, whether to kiss you here—" he nibbled her neck and shoulder "—or here." His tongue etched circles around her breasts and his lips teased her nipples into hard buds. "The next, whether to kiss you here—" he traced a course across her stomach "—or here." He planted soft kisses down the inside of her thigh to the tender spot behind her knee, then back up the other thigh.

"Oh, Lion," she gasped.

They had waited long enough. Eve watched his tongue caress her, watched as his fingers parted her. She had wanted to experience everything. Everything. Her fingers clawed the sand, and her back arched as the spasms beginning in her loins spread throughout her body. "Lion!" Her voice echoed in the tiny cove, mingled with the shriek of screaming gulls. "Lion!"

He rose over her, and as she watched, entered her at last, filling her, plucking her nerves to a fever pitch that left her limp beneath him. Helpless, she wanted to match his urgency, but could only repeat his name, and weep, and at last wrap her arms around his neck and breathe, "Yes, yes, yes," while his fire filled her and the world spun away.

The pea pod slid from shore. Lion stumbled as the water caught at his legs. Quickly, he leaped aboard, splashing Eve in the process, then ducking as the boom cut the air over his head. The sail filled with wind and the boat careened to the left. Eve hung over the starboard gunwale to balance the craft and sent it skimming over the choppy surface of the bay.

They had stayed later than they should. Lion sat facing the bow, straining unconsciously to hurry them back to Dawn Wind. The wind ruffled his thick black hair. His mane, Eve thought, amused. He was a reckless, handsome man, and he was hers, as she was his. She looked over her shoulder at the cove—their cove—receding in the shadow-painted distance of the waning afternoon. Words slowly formed in her memory. Lyrics of the ballad Lion had asked her to sing, words full of melancholy and tender hopes.

Chapter 10

It was not an easy time to be in love at Dawn Wind. Sewal was becoming more and more aware of the attention Eve was paying Lion, and vice versa, and in his own determined way invented excuses to mention Clifford Sarandon whenever possible. Michael was obviously a troubled man. He had gained twenty pounds over the last few months. His face was puffy from too much drink and food, and his eyes were red and sullen. He was difficult to have around, alternately warm and expansive, or withdrawn and morose. No one was sure of his relationship with Rosamond. One moment he showered affection on her, much to her obvious discontent; the next he ignored her, or worse, treated her abominably. He ate either nothing or too much, but was never far from a wine bottle or flask of whiskey. Rosamond reacted with utter calm. Only in her eyes, which never smiled, could one see the toll she was being forced to pay. On top of everything, Justin was being difficult as only Justin could be. Eve and Lion anxiously awaited the rare moments they could be alone, confident their newfound love guarded them against disaster.

On Sunday Eve invited Lion to church and dinner. Reverend Waldrop chose as his text Revelations 18:14: "And the fruits that thy soul lusted after are departed from thee." The sermon, which dragged on until almost one o'clock, put everyone but Michael in a bad mood. By the time they got back to Dawn Wind it was after two, and Eustacia had put dinner back in the oven to keep warm.

Monday dawned gloomy and windy, with gusts caroming off the cliffs. Instead of waiting around the shipyards or the hotel, Lion rode to Dawn Wind to spend the morning. By the time he arrived Sewal had left and everyone else had adjourned to the parlor. Rosamond and Eve were busying themselves with needlepoint. Justin, still at odds with Sewal over whether or not he was going to work at the yards or return to Bowdoin, wandered down to his studio, but soon returned. Lion stared out the window, and Michael toyed with a snifter of French brandy and began to recount his experiences at Annapolis with forced joviality. When he began a tale about a prank played on Jack Travis's father, his fencing instructor, Lion, uneasy in Rosamond's presence, chimed in with an anecdote about the retired colonel who had taught at the Virginia Military Institute. Though Lion didn't fence often, he said, he loved the sport. Since there was nothing else to do, a match was quickly arranged.

The wind was relatively calm in the lee of the pines surrounding Justin's studio. Lion slipped the wire mesh mask over his head and waited while Michael made a last adjustment to the canvas jacket he was wearing. In addition each man wore a heavy leather glove, for the foils' bell guards offered scant protection from the blunted tips and dulled edges of the triangular foils. "Corsican steel," Michael said, bending his foil into a slight arc.

"An excellent balance," Lion acknowledged. He exercised his

wrist, going rapidly from parry four to six, to riposte and disengage. It had been a full year since he had fenced and he felt stiff.

Michael flexed his knees, bounced up and down a few times. The extra weight he'd added slowed him down. His legs would be screaming before they finished. What he needed was a little pick-me-up. Glancing at Justin and then Eve, as if daring either of them to speak, he pulled a silver flask from his hip pocket and drank from it. When he lowered the flask he saw that Lion was looking at him disapprovingly. His good mood disappeared in a flash. "Something the matter?" he asked.

"Why, no," Lion answered, taken aback.

"That's good." He tossed the silver flask aside and slipped the mask over his puffy, scowling features.

With Michael's mercurial changes Lion tensed as he realized that what had started out as a diversion could turn into something serious. Rolling his shoulders in an attempt to relax, he slipped into his own mask and assumed the fencer's stance.

"Cock your weapons, gentlemen," Justin said.

"If you're going to referee, referee," Michael snapped, glaring at him.

"Sorry," Justin said, bowing in mock deference. "Gentlemen, *en garde!*" Slender shafts of steel clicked together in a raised cross. "Fence!"

It wasn't like a formal match. The contestants were free to move sideways as well as forward and back. Their first lunges, parries, and ripostes were tentative. Knowing he was rusty, Lion bided his time and tried to catalogue Michael's strengths and weaknesses.

No more than a minute had passed before Michael attacked ferociously. Surprised, Lion gave ground, then grunted as Michael's blade slid past his guard and bent against his stomach. "Michael's point," Justin called. Conceding, Lion backed away and bowed.

"Well done, dear," Rosamond called, stepping into the clearing and joining Eve's applause.

Michael glanced at her and turned away. His voice was flat and tense. "Let's get on with it."

Once again Justin stepped forward. This time Lion was better prepared. Whoever had taught Michael to fence had done his job well, for he was good. But good wasn't going to be enough. Not this time.

"En garde!"

Eve watched, excited by the contest. Her brother's massive bulk appeared to give him an overpowering advantage, but she wasn't sure. "I hope he wins," Rosamond whispered in her ear.

"And I hope Lion wins," Eve replied.

Rosamond studied her a moment, then nodded, as if reading in Eve's eyes the events of the past week. "That's who I meant," she finally said, to Eve's puzzlement.

"Fence!" The blades touched, slid off each other. Singing steel thrust and parried, riposted and parried again. Lion stole the initiative at the outset with a wave of his hand that diverted Michael's attention for the briefest second and set him on the defensive. Retreating, he fought doggedly until he saw an opening and then went on the attack, forcing Lion backward.

Lion's face was set, a mask behind a mask. Michael was too serious, and growing a little wild. More and more he used his foil like a saber, and though that was dangerous, he was making it work. Lion ducked one swipe, lunged, and missed. Michael cursed, parried, twisted, and riposted from the other side with a lunge that passed between Lion's arm and side. Many more like that, Lion thought, and I'll be carried out of here, safety tip or no. Concerned, he pressed close to Michael in order to restrict his movements. A moment later, he faked a lunge, slipped under Michael's too wide parry, and lunged again for a hit just under Michael's mask.

"My point!" he called, not relaxing until he heard Justin echo the decision.

Michael stripped off his mask and wiped his face. He was breathing heavily, and his face was pale from exertion.

"Rest for a minute?" Lion asked, out of breath himself.

"Why?" Michael asked.

"You have ten years on me," Lion said. "We old men have to slow down from time to time."

"You old men are treacherous," Michael said. "That trick with the hand won't work again."

"Think so, eh?" Lion grinned, glad that Michael's anger had dissipated and that they were back to games. "Maybe something else, then. You never can tell about old men."

"I know," Michael said, his lips tightening and the color draining from his face. Quivering, he strode to the flask he had thrown on the ground, picked it up, and drank deeply from it. "Three hundred dollars on two out of three," he said in a flat tone.

"What?" Lion asked, wondering what had offended Michael this time.

"I said, three hundred dollars on the next point."

Everyone was holding his breath. Justin, approaching to start the third match, stopped, one foot ahead of the other. Rosamond and Eve sat poised and motionless. Lion's mouth was open in amazement at Michael's vehemence. He made a mental tally of his assets. A three-hundred-dollar loss would leave him sleeping in the street. "Agreed," he finally said, "but don't you think you're taking this contest too seriously?"

"Take it or leave it, McKenna," Michael said, punctuating the end of his sentence with an unexpected attack.

Lion jumped to the side, saw the blade pass by him. Taken by surprise, he tried to put his mask back on, but dropped it in order to use both hands to parry another lunge. Neither man was fighting with masks, and Lion had taken off his glove when they stopped to rest. Lion's parry jerked far to the side and his riposte was clumsy, but close enough to neutralize what would otherwise have been an over-powering offensive. "Now, look . . ." he began as, sword extended, his feet leaving the ground, Michael dove forward in a flèche.

Lion sidestepped, circled, and lunged, trying for Michael's exposed side as he was momentarily off balance. Somehow Michael twisted, caught Lion's blade, and pushed it upward. Straining, their breathing labored, they stood face to face, foils high in the air over their heads until, as if by agreement, they stepped backward and the blades slithered down each other's length, pinged off the bell guards, and came to rest again at *en garde*.

Sweat matted their shirts and streaked their faces. The fight had turned into a free-for-all, devoid of the niceties of a sport. Michael attacked with a *balastre,* front leg kicking out as he advanced in short hops. Lion retreated until he stumbled over an exposed tree root, then let himself fall to the left as Michael's blade bent on the tree itself. Circling, the two worked their way back to the clearing. Michael grew more and more frustrated. Four times he should have won, struck home, and ended the battle. Each time Lion managed to evade the point.

All pretense of finesse thrown to the winds, they circled each other like boxers. It wasn't talent thwarting him, Michael realized, but stubbornness. The Southerner simply refused defeat and manufac-tured, on reflex, whatever unorthodox movements were necessary to avoid losing the point. Still, Michael was convinced he had gained the upper hand, and that it was only a matter of time. His breath whistling in his lungs, he drove forward. His blade circled, attacked Lion's lower torso, then changed direction and went high to concentrate on the hand, in an attempt to wrench the weapon from Lion's grasp. Lion appeared to falter. This was the opening Michael had been waiting for. With a roar of triumph, he leaped forward.

Lion saw the flèche coming before Michael's feet left the ground. Twisting, he spun in a full circle and drove his shoulder into Michael's as the larger man stumbled past him. Michael, off balance, tripped and hit the ground, rolled and leaped to his feet and right into Lion's outstretched foil, which hit dead center on the heart stitched onto the front of his vest. His face white, Michael stared down at the steel arching upward from his chest.

"My point," Lion said softly, withdrawing his foil.

Michael whirled around and stalked off. Rosamond sighed, rose, and retrieved Michael's frock coat and flask. She looked at Lion, then at Justin and Eve. "If you'll excuse me," she said, dangling the flask. "He'll be needing this," and walked off slowly toward the house.

Eve crossed to Lion, slipped her arm through his. Together, they watched her brother disappear into the house and Rosamond walk across the wide lawn. Justin tapped an inch of ash from the end of his cigar. "Expensive stuff he carries in that flask. Three hundred dollars," he said dolefully, shaking his head.

Eve fixed him with an icy stare.

"All right." Justin held up his hands in surrender. "I promise not to be sarcastic for the rest of the day."

"How nice of you," Eve replied caustically, then tugged at Lion, who allowed her to lead him toward the house.

Justin dropped the cigar and ground it out with his foot. What Eve didn't realize was that the morning had ended as disastrously for him as it had for Michael. The disillusionment with his older brother had been growing steadily since Michael's wedding. Now it was total. And if that truth was painful he couldn't help it if he saw things as they really were.

Michael dipped his hands into a basin ringed with porcelain dragons and doused his face with cool water. When the door opened behind him he blinked the water-blurred image of Maisie into clarity.

"Oh, pardon me, sir," the maid said, starting to back out the door. "I didn't hear you on the stairs."

"That's all right," Michael said gruffly, then regretting his tone, waved her in.

Maisie dropped an armful of clean linen on the bed, crossed, and put away the sheets. When she turned back to the bed, Michael was staring at her. Hurrying, she picked up the pillow cases and started back to the dresser. "Won't be but a second, sir," she said, uncomfortable under his scrutiny. "I just . . . Oh!" Her foot caught on the corner of the throw rug and she stumbled. The pillow cases flew out of her arms and onto the floor. "Oh, dear me. If there isn't anyone clumsier . . ." she said, dropping to her knees to pick them up.

"I'll help," Michael said.

"You needn't, sir."

"I want to." Michael squatted across from her. His shirt was open to the waist and his flesh hung loose and pink on his frame. Her face red, Maisie concentrated on picking up the pillow cases, then froze as his hands caught her upper arms. "Maisie," he said.

"Please, sir." She tried to move backward, but he held her.

"Maisie." His voice was insistent as he pulled her toward him.

"Isn't this romantic," Rosamond said from the doorway. She entered, placed the flask on the dresser. Maisie gasped a plea of innocence, but Rosamond raised a hand to silence her. "Tut-tut, love. I don't blame you. Not in the least."

Rather than assume the role of a husband caught in an indiscretion, Michael stood and pulled Maisie to her feet. Not even looking at Rosamond he drew the maid closer and, lowering his head, kissed her on the mouth. Maisie struggled futilely in his arms, but his hand on her hip held her close. His lips bruised her. Only when she ceased to struggle did he release her.

Rosamond remained impassive. Maisie muttered something unintelligible then hurried, crying, from the room.

"You never cease to amaze me, Michael. Every time I think you have gone as far as you can, you find a new depth to sink to."

"Yes," Michael said. He started refilling his flask from a decanter of Scotch. "Soon I may even approach you."

Rosamond almost let herself go, almost gave in to the impulse to scream and attack him. Instead she bit her lip and forced herself to remain calm. "I'd like that, Michael," she finally said in a conciliatory tone. "I'd like that very much."

"Oh? Getting tired of the others?" Michael asked with a sneer.

"I have told you again and again, there are no others," she answered dully.

"Repetition does not make something true."

Rosamond told herself for the thousandth time in their two-month marriage that the lack of her virginity couldn't be the sole reason for Michael's attitude. Something else she didn't understand—she refused even to consider that he might know about Lion and her—was eating at him, and he was using her as an excuse to strike back. She had tried to humor him, to be the wife he wanted, in the hope he would change. Her efforts had been wasted, but she made herself try one more time. "I thought you might hear me, Michael. Just once, I thought you might hear me say I love you, and believe me."

He whirled on her. His face was white with fury. "I am the laughingstock of Washington," he hissed. "I ask myself, has this man—that man—or that man—been intimate with her? I see them lower their eyes or their heads or smirk—"

Rosamond's head was bowed. Tears squeezed from her closed eyes. "Michael, Michael, Michael, Michael," she said, slowly shaking her head.

"Stop it, damn you! Stop repeating my name like that!"

She looked up, looked him in the eye. "You manufacture belief from a dropped eyelid. You are convinced by the turn of a head. You convict me on the basis of a smile. My God, Michael. You believe those things, but not my tears? Not everything I say and do?"

"I believe our wedding night," he said flatly.

"I do not deny our wedding night!" Rosamond flared, beating her thigh with her fist.

"Because you cannot."

"All right," she sighed. "All right, Michael." She was tired, wanted only to stop arguing. "I'm sorry. I didn't know one little torn piece of flesh could mean so much to you."

"One little—!" Michael grabbed her arms, jerked her to her feet. "Don't you understand anything, woman?" His fingers dug into her arms as he shook her back and forth. "A man's pride, his honor—"

"Pride!" Rosamond jerked free. Anger flowed through her like muddied water through a broken dam. "Is that it? Pride?" Her voice rose to a screech. "Michael Blackheath cannot live outside the portrait he's painted of himself. But the portrait is a lie! It's distorted. It's himself as he desperately wants to be."

"Shut up," Michael growled.

She had struck home and she enjoyed the feeling. "No. I won't. Look at you. All pretense and make-believe. You're so convinced you're perfect, that everything will go your way, that you can't stand it when the real world intrudes and you find out the paint has cracked and chipped and faded, and that you're only the image of a man!"

Michael's hand lashed out and struck her cheek. Rosamond fell across the bed. Dazed, she struggled to sit up and touched her mouth. When she looked at her fingers they were smeared with blood from her cut lip. Calmly, she wiped her hand on the bedspread and, cold hate in her eyes, looked up at Michael. "You shouldn't have done that, Michael." He would pay. Oh! he would pay. *"Lion* wouldn't have."

He was trembling. "What do you mean by that?"

Rosamond smiled. "Are you going to hit me again?"

"Answer me, damn it. What about McKenna?"

He believed lies? She would twist the truth and manufacture a lie that would devastate him. "You once asked me, rather violently, I re-call, who had enjoyed my favors. Well?"

Michael staggered backward as if he had been slapped. "You're lying," he said.

Rosamond stood, walked to the wash basin and dabbed cold water on her lip. Michael's back was to her and she watched him in the mirror. Hands clenched into fists, she leaned on the washstand. "No, I'm not. A wife should be truthful, as you've so often pointed out. You didn't believe me before? Well then, believe this.

"As you know, I met Lion McKenna four years ago in Richmond. As we failed to mention, naturally enough, we had an affair. You can imagine our surprise when we saw each other here. It was as if a cold ember had burst once more into flame." She paused and tried to imagine Michael's reaction to what would follow. For a moment she feared for her own safety, but the satisfaction of seeing Michael devastated drove her on. "And then you sent us up here together. I was a little tipsy, and Lion had been drinking too. How it happened, I don't know, but the second the door closed behind us, we were in each other's arms. I . . . I couldn't wait, and neither could he." Her voice faltered, but she finished. "I didn't even take off my wedding dress."

Her knees unsteady Rosamond turned and walked to the door.

Michael hadn't moved. He stood with his shoulders hunched. Rosamond suppressed a shudder as she turned and looked at him. When
she spoke, she sounded as if she might be telling him about a new
dress she'd bought, or what she'd had for dinner the night before.
"We did it right there on your bed, Michael. And do you know? I've
never had better."

Michael straightened, jerked erect at the sound of the door closing.
For a moment, he swayed, then caught hold of himself. Carefully, as
if he was afraid he would shatter, he pulled on a shirt, then a sport-
ing coat of Lincoln green wool. Eyes glazed, he stood in front of the
mirror and tied an ascot at his throat. When he was dressed he stood
alone in the center of the room and stared at the bed. Slowly, his
head lolled back, his eyes squeezed shut and his mouth, lips tight and
stretched across his teeth, twisted open. "I don't believe you," he
whispered. "I don't believe you." But his face was the bleached color
of bone.

The rain had stopped a half hour earlier. Men scrambled over the
hulks of the three ships on the ways. The mammoth shed erected the
month before in anticipation of winter snows had kept the worst of
the rain off them, but the wind from the bay was bitterly cold. Inside
the hulls the sound of hammering beat a dull, thunderous tattoo.
Fifty yards away, moored in the chilly waters of Waupinau Bay, the
nearly complete ship rolled and pitched. Aloft, looking like spiders
scurrying over a complicated geometric webbing, a crew put the
finishing touches on the suit of sails they had just bent to the yards.
The new canvas, bright with occasional flashes of brass grommets
and wrapped with golden-colored hemp, was furled under the long
wooden spars.

Jon Naslund, the Swedish carpenter and Sewal's chief foreman,
joined his employer on the second-story landing outside the shipyard
office. Both men stared at a sight they had seen many times before
and hoped to see as many times again: the finishing off of a Blackheath ship. "She's prime, Captain. Prime for the sea."

"We've never turned out one that wasn't, Jon," Sewal replied, enjoying the camaraderie of the Swede. "By damn, man," he exclaimed. "What we're about is the only thing in the world worth a
man's time."

Naslund pulled at his earlobe, squinted at Sewal. "Next to the
sailing of them, Captain."

Sewal stared at him, then at the ship. "Yes. Next to the sailing of them."

Arvid, Jon's youngest and a carbon copy of his father, doffed a cloth cap in deference to Sewal as he approached. "The men are finished at the bow, Mr. Blackheath."

"Aye. Tell them to take their noon, then," Sewal instructed. "They've earned an extra half hour off."

"And a dram of spirits?" Jon asked with a grin.

"Sorry. Not on a Monday," Sewal said, smiling at a long ago jest that only he and a few men like Jon who had crewed with him might know.

Arvid nodded, brushed his long, unkempt, straw-colored hair away from his eyes. "I'll tell Gunter, then."

"And see that they do not tarry too long," Jon said. "I'll want that starboard rail on before the day is finished."

"Yes, Father," the youth said, and hurried off.

Sewal noticed his own son enter the front gate and canter his horse through a cluster of off-duty employees, who parted as Michael's horse splashed through their midst. "Be seeing you later in the shop, then, sir," Jon said.

"What? Oh, yes. Sorry. I was thinking," Sewal said.

The Swede waved aside the apology and clumped down the stairs. Sewal followed him in time to meet Michael as he swung down from his horse. "I'm glad you came," he said, taking the reins and looping them over the hitching rail.

Michael straightened his ascot and patted the sleeves of his riding coat. A black cloak clung to his shoulders and his high-topped boots were spattered with mud. "I received your note," Michael replied.

"Come and see the ships. The one is done but for a few finishing touches, and the next three ahead of schedule."

"So I've seen," Michael said, looking around. "But that isn't the reason you sent for me."

"Certainly it is." Their boots made squishing sounds as they climbed the waterlogged stairs and went to the telescope mounted on the railing. "Look at her," Sewal said, indicating the finished ship.

Michael swiveled the telescope, trained it on the rigging, white with rolls of new canvas. The glass swept down to the deck, then forward along the rail to the bow. Suddenly Michael inhaled violently. There, painted on the bow, was his name.

160   *Christina Savage*

"The *Michael Alexander*. Has a ring to it, eh? Do you like it?" Sewal asked proudly.

His face an angry red, Michael straightened. "No."

"What?"

"You heard me. I don't want my name on a ship built to run contraband."

"What do you mean?" Sewal asked.

"You know exactly what I mean. You've seen the papers. Abolitionists hanged in Texas and run out of Arkansas. South Carolina promises to secede if Lincoln is elected, and the rest of the slave states are merely hedging until the time is right for them to follow. You can build ships for them if you like, but don't put my name on one of them."

Sewal blanched. Color took its time returning to his face. "I'm building ships for a private firm, Michael."

"You know damned well that's not true. You knew it when that son of a bitch McKenna first gave you the proposal to read."

"Michael! Lion saved your life."

"Then he's the son of a bitch who saved my life."

Sewal's scalp was deep red in contrast to the fringe of white hair. "I don't understand this," he said, stunned. "What else except build ships do you think a shipyard does? My God, do you have any idea of how many yards like ours have closed down over the past few years? A ship is a ship—a job, food in people's mouths, a profit. Nine of them, in our case, is survival."

"And no matter what you say, how you rationalize it, I won't have my name on that ship's bow."

Sewal looked tired, depleted. He leaned on the railing, stared down at the mud-covered cobblestones below. "A ship is amoral and apolitical, Michael. It either sinks or sails. If the workmanship is true it is a creation of beauty, no matter who sails it or to what end. Wood and steel and hemp and canvas cannot be compromised." His hand beat slowly on the railing. His voice was sad but firm. "When the responsibility for this place falls to you, you'll understand that. On my oath, I promise you will understand. In the meantime, if questioning Blackheath prosperity is the cause of your problems, I suggest—"

"I haven't any problems," Michael interrupted.

Michael had spent most of Sunday drunk, and Sewal saw clearly how his eyes were fractured with a crimson mapwork of enlarged blood vessels. "Admiral Cabell's last letter preceded you, Michael," he said softly.

"So?" Michael asked. Sewal didn't answer. "Damn it to hell!" He spat and turned away.

"In addition, Pole said he heard what sounded like a shouting match coming from upstairs."

"Good old Pole," Michael said sarcastically. "How nice to know he's reporting back to you."

"He wasn't eavesdropping, mind you. He didn't know what was said, only that . . ." He stopped abruptly. Michael was his firstborn, the son who would carry on in his place. Saying what had to be said was painful, but he steeled himself and went on. "Drinking to excess. Conduct unbecoming an officer. Dereliction of duty. You've let yourself go physically. Gained weight. Dress sloppily half the time. And now this with Rosamond. I don't like it, son."

The list of his shortcomings rang in his ears. Michael laughed nervously. "Sorry to hear that, Father."

"I didn't mean it that way, Michael." Sewal groped for the words. "It's just that if there's anything I can do to help, any way I can—"

"What? Fix it?" Michael snapped. "I feel better already. Father will make everything all right."

"I don't deserve that, son. Not from you."

They stared at each other. Unaware of the drama taking place above them, the men who had been released early joked and laughed as they tromped past on their way home. "I . . ." Michael exhaled slowly. "I'm sorry," he apologized glumly. "Rosamond and I had an argument, is all. As for the other, I need time to myself to think and . . ." He faltered, looked about him as if he were trapped. "Listen, Father," Michael's eyes darted about and his movements were jerky, "there are some people I have to see, some friends."

"What friends?" Sewal asked, putting out a hand to stop Michael as he started for the stairs.

Michael shook him off, slipped on the top step and almost fell. "I won't be late," he called over his shoulder.

"Michael!"

"You'll just have to forgive me." He untied the reins, mounted quickly, and jerked the horse's head around. "Please understand."

Sewal's back was straight, but his soul felt crushed. Fists clenched helplessly, he watched Michael push the horse into a trot and disappear around the corner of the office building. "Forgive you," he muttered, staring into a twilight that was as gloomy as the future. "For what *has* happened? Or will?"

Chapter 11

Flesh on flesh, glorying in discovery, remembering, touching with hands and lips. Gentle motion silhouetted by a single candle, which is all the light love needs. A clock in the hall strikes a sonorous warning. Eight o'clock arrives and falls behind in the same unnoticed breath. Elsewhere children read by fires or, tucked into bed by loving parents, whisper to favorite toys and plot the next day's innocent adventures. Old men nod in rocking chairs set close to fires and dream of youth, strength, and quickness. Wives and grandmothers sigh and pluck the ivory eggs from the baskets in their laps, and continue darning the never-ending supply of holes.

Together in the tumbled warmth of his bed, Eve and Lion needed no dreams. Waking from half-sleep, Lion angled himself up on an elbow to better see the rise and fall of Eve's breasts. Her nipples were like small Oriental temples set side by side on moonlit hills of ivory. His kisses paid homage there.

Eve sighed, stirred, as his awakened desire pressed against the inside of her thigh. Her eyes were shadowed by his bulk, but he knew she was looking at him. When he whispered her name she pulled him atop her and moved beneath him, shifting to accommodate his weight and form. There was no urgency at first, only a whisper of motion. Then, as if they were a giant clock which, once started, ran faster and faster until the hands sped around its face, their movements became a blur that culminated in dizzy release. Spent, they subsided into grateful satisfaction and drowsy reverie. Outside in the hall the night clock sang a short, unchanging melody. Another half hour, as mankind measures time, had come and gone.

A knock at the door brought Lion fully awake. He glanced at Eve. Only her nose and eyes protruded from under the blanket. She shook her head. "Father thinks we're at the Waldrops' social," she whispered, frightened.

Lion thought for a moment it might be Duquesne, but then remembered the courtly gentleman had charmed his way into the Johnstone sisters' parlor. Quickly, he ran through the short list of people he knew in New Forest. None seemed a likely visitor. He shuddered a moment, wondering to his horror if it were Rosamond. He and Eve had entered The Clipper by the back stairs, a precaution necessary in a small town where gossip flowed as ceaselessly as a river. No one should have known Eve's whereabouts. Of that he was certain—almost.

The soft knock sounded again. Lion swung out of bed and padded to the door. "Who is it?" he asked.

"Demetrios," came the rasped reply.

Jesus, Lion thought. Sliding back the bolt, he opened the door a crack, enough to see Madame Laurier's henchman. "What the hell do you want?"

Demetrios hooked his thumbs into the blue satin sash at his waist. His frock coat hung open enough to reveal the polished grip of a small caliber pistol at his side. "Madame Laurier's compliments. You will come with me, please."

"The devil, you say."

"It is important, sir. You are a friend of Michael Blackheath?"

Lion felt Eve's hand tighten on his arm. She had stolen across the room to listen at his side. "What about him?" he asked.

Demetrios stared at the door, but didn't answer.

Could the little bastard see through solid oak, Lion wondered. "Well?"

"He is indisposed, and perhaps in danger. Should he be found at the Land Lock, it would bring embarrassment to his family. You will come with me now?"

The pressure on his arm increased. Eve was understandably worried. "All right. Go on. I'll be there in five minutes."

"I can wait." The dwarf smiled.

"I'll find my own way, damn it," Lion snapped. Demetrios shrugged, glanced at the center of the door again, and left. "Well, you heard him," Lion said, latching the door and turning to Eve.

"What are we going to do?" Eve whispered, shivering in the cold.

"Get dressed, and don't worry. I'll bring him home. What about you?"

Eve tugged on her dress, turned for Lion to help her with the fastenings on the back. "I'll take your horse and you can take the carriage. I'll run by the Waldrops' to make an appearance, and then go home. That way I'll be able to tell Father you came to the Waldrops' and told me you needed the carriage. If he asks."

"Good enough," Lion grunted, pulling on his boots. "I'll kill a few minutes at the Land Lock, then meet you at the land end of the bridge to Dawn Wind. Wait for me there."

Eve tied her bonnet, swirled her cloak around her. "By the way," she asked suspiciously. "Just how do you know your way to the Land Lock?"

"We haven't time for this," Lion said. He grabbed her arm and, after checking the hall, led her past the other rooms and down the back stairway. He lost a few moments saddling his horse and leading him out of the stable.

Once into the saddle Eve leaned over to kiss her lover. "Be careful," she said.

Lion patted her leg reassuringly. "You too," he said. "You sure you can handle that saddle?"

Eve hiked up her skirts. "You know I can," she said, and booted the mare in the side. Lion stepped back and watched her ride through the darkness and quivering pools of light cast by coal oil street lanterns. The second she disappeared he climbed into the carriage, circled tightly, and guided the team toward the less desirable alleys of New Forest's waterfront.

The night air was brisk. Lion shivered and wished he'd worn a heavier coat, a concern soon replaced by the overriding problem of Michael's predicament. If Blackheath was drunk and had lost his temper, as he had that morning, God only knew what a bunch of lumberjacks or sailors would do to him. Lion whipped the horses, then slowed as he skirted the main row of taverns, and turned into the narrow passageway that led to the rear of the Land Lock.

"Where you off to, bub?"

Lion looped the reins around an iron post. The voice had come from the shadows to his right, but he couldn't distinguish the man's form. Moving slowly, he ducked behind the horses. Why should anyone be waiting there in the cold? To waylay one of the Land Lock's more prestigious visitors? Michael Blackheath, for example? "Step into the light," he said, immediately changing position to the rear of the carriage, and pulling the pepperbox from his coat pocket.

"I like it just fine where I am," the disembodied voice said.

Lion fired in the direction of the voice. The pistol made a sharp cracking sound that was almost inaudible above the raucous laughter and shouts coming from the Land Lock. A heavy-gutted lumberjack in flannel shirt and woolen pants lurched into view. He held his hands before him as if to ward off another shot. "What'd you do that for?" he asked.

"I didn't like where you were."

"You got no cause—"

"My first shot missed because I aimed low," Lion said. "I won't the next time. Leave."

The man did not move. Lion thumbed back the hammer. He aimed the gun at the man's knee. "Can you fell trees with only one leg? Leave!" Lion grunted with satisfaction as the man waved away an imaginary second shot and scampered off. Tucking the pistol into his waistband, he turned to the door in time to see Demetrios poke out his head.

"I heard a shot," the dwarf said, glancing down the alley.

"I was practicing poker," Lion said.

"Sir?"

"Running a bluff. But never mind. Where's Blackheath?"

"Inside." Demetrios held the door as Lion entered, then led the way to the main sitting room.

"My dear, dear friend," Madame Laurier exclaimed, emerging from behind a curtain of beaded glass. She strode up to the Southerner and kissed his cheek. "You have been in town a week and not had time to see me. For shame!"

"You sent Demetrios to my room with a message," he said brusquely. "Am I to assume the message was a fabrication?"

The madame was not used to being rebuffed so cavalierly. "Assume what you will, my sweet, but do not presume," she answered icily. "He's upstairs. Demetrios will show you the way."

Demetrios bowed jerkily and led Lion up the stairs and down a long hall lit with flickering candles placed in tall columns of red crystal. Molly, one of the girls Lion had met on his initial visit, was waiting for them behind the fourth door. She wore the same sensual, slit dress she was wearing the first time Lion saw her. Michael, fully clothed, lay spread-eagled on her bed.

Lion sighed, crossed to Michael. "Did he pay you?"

Molly shook her head. "He didn't do anything. Just looked is all, and then passed out. He doesn't have to pay."

The lining of one of Michael's pockets was showing. Lion figured the prostitute's generosity had something to do with the empty pockets and a hidden safe box into which its contents had no doubt disappeared. He couldn't really blame her, and didn't begrudge her whatever she'd been able to steal from Michael. He had known whores to do a lot worse to a helpless trick. Besides, she had a pretty face. With a bit of luck she might have been one man's darling rather than courtesan to a flock of fools.

Demetrios helped hoist the unconscious Michael onto Lion's back, then preceded him out the door and past the other rooms, whose very stillness did more to convey an aura of carnality than a whole cacophony of impassioned cries. Madame Laurier watched the tiny procession from an alcove. She did not speak until after Lion had left, for his abruptness had injured her feelings. "All men are cruel," she sighed, at last. "Cruel."

Michael shivered. He had a right to. Water from the horse trough matted his hair and trickled down his chest and back. "You almost drowned me," he said, his arms wrapped protectively around his stomach. "Damn it. Damn you. Oh." He groaned, rocked forward on the seat. "Stop the carriage!"

Lion drove on.

"For the love of God, stop! I'm going to be sick. Don't you see . . ." Michael stumbled from the carriage before it stopped moving and fell to his hands and knees. The contents of his stomach steamed on the cool grass. Gagging, he crawled backward from the stench and retched violently until his stomach was empty. His ears were ringing and his mouth held an acidic, sweet taste. When he raised his head the sight of a wagon spoke startled him. He fought to bring it into focus, and gave up. What the hell had he been drinking? Maybe a little of everything. Certainly too much of something.

Lion was out of the carriage and trying to help him.

"Leave me alone." Michael spat, struggling to his feet. He tore free of Lion, almost fell again, and lurched into the carriage without assistance. Somewhere, in the great roaring distance, Lion took up the reins and whipped the horses into a gallop. Hold on. Hold on, Michael whimpered to himself. Hold on, hold on. Somewhere in the distance there were lights, and then darkness as he pitched headlong out of the carriage and landed in a crumpled heap on the gravel drive in front of Dawn Wind.

*   *   *

Shocked by his son's sodden, wretched state, Sewal retreated to the library and a glass of strong brandy while Pole and Lion maneuvered an unresisting but argumentative Michael to his room.

"Father?"

Sewal blinked. Feeling the weight of his years he raised his head and seemed to notice Eve for the first time since she'd arrived home from the social a half hour earlier. "Father," she said quietly, "Mr. McKenna is returning to New Forest."

Sewal's gnarled hands grasped the arms of the chair. He pushed himself to his feet. A conspiracy of lantern light and disillusionment made him look much older than he had only an hour earlier. "Yes," he said, working hard to keep his voice normal. The thought of a stranger being privy to his son's dissolution was almost too much for his pride to bear, but he would not be ungracious. "Thank you, Mr. McKenna, for all you have done."

Lion looked embarrassed too. "He'll be all right after a night's sleep, sir."

"I wonder. Still, that's our problem, not yours." He extended his hand to Lion. "Inhospitable of us to burden you." He looked around as if he had misplaced something. "If you don't mind . . ."

"I'll see him out," Eve said gently, taking Lion's arm.

"Yes, of course." Sewal rubbed his hand over his scalp. "I . . . Excuse me," he muttered, walking past them and out the door.

The hall was quiet. His mind blank, Sewal climbed the stairs to the upper floor. A sliver of amber glowed beneath the door to Michael and Rosamond's bedroom. He could hear Michael's muttered curses, and then the sound of vomiting. There should have been something to say or do, but he couldn't think what it might be. One hand touching the wall for support, he shuffled into his own bedroom and closed the door.

Michael pushed the chamber pot away from him and wiped his mouth on a wet towel. Her features twisted with contempt, Rosamond watched him. "Don't worry." Michael cleared his throat and spat into the pot. "You'll not have to witness this again."

"Oh?" Rosamond pulled her robe tight around her waist. "Have you suddenly discovered character?"

"No. I'm divorcing you."

Rosamond paled. She had not expected this. No one she had ever known had been divorced. Divorced, she would be a social outcast.

A second decent marriage would be virtually out of the question. Her mother would die of mortification. "You wouldn't dare," she gasped.

"I shall begin the proceedings tomorrow."

"You're mad!" Rosamond said, rising from the bed and towering over him.

Michael grinned up at her from his hands and knees. "What? Angry? I thought you would be delighted. Think, Rosamond. Soon you will be free to marry a real man. How about that, eh?"

"I don't want to marry another man!"

"Oh, come, come. Why not? Let's see. Whom shall we pick for you?"

Rosamond was near tears. "Stop it, Michael. Just stop it!"

"Ah, yes. McKenna! A logical choice. He's big, handsome, well enough off. You *are* acquainted, which should hurry things along."

"No."

"No?" His voice was mocking, insistent. "But I'll intercede for you. Dear Mr. McKenna, won't you please marry my wife?"

"Damn you, Michael Blackheath!" Rosamond hissed. "Damn you to hell . . ."

"Tut-tut, dear. Temper . . ."

He had baited her unmercifully, and now her turn had come. Rosamond turned her back to him, slipped into bed, and smiled, oh, so sweetly. "I'm afraid Mr. McKenna is out of the question, dear. You see, he's chosen another lamb." She leaned forward and pronounced the word very clearly. "Eve."

Michael came off the floor and reached the bed in two strides. "What are you talking about?" he asked, his fingers digging into her arm.

"Why, it's perfectly obvious." She chuckled self-consciously. "She's as much as admitted it. A glance, a touch. But you wouldn't recognize a woman in love, would you, Michael? That's your failing. Your sister and Lion McKenna are lovers, and you didn't even know it."

Michael let go her arm, staggered to the window, and pressed his forehead against the cool glass. Rosamond was telling the truth, he knew. Lion had been with Eve too often. Even Sewal had mentioned it in passing. Lion and Eve. Lion and Rosamond. The friend who had saved his life.

Friend? Michael sagged to the window seat and closed his eyes.

His gut ached. His head throbbed painfully. He was sinking into a pit from which there was no escape.

No escape.

Except for one. There was only one thing to do, he told himself. Only one thing. And he knew precisely what that would have to be.

Chapter 12

Sir:

In the manner in which you have been pleased to associate yourself with members of this family, I find your conduct contemptuous and worthy of a base and ill-bred scoundrel. I demand that satisfaction which is due to injured honor; and therefore insist upon your meeting me tomorrow morning with whatever friend you may think proper, in order to settle this business according to the laws of honor.

I am, sir, your humble servant,
Michael Blackheath
September 19, 1860

Lion crumbled the letter and threw it across the room. He had read the damned thing a dozen times since it had been delivered to The Clipper that morning by Hamlet, and with each reading the conviction grew. Rosamond must have told Michael about their affair. Four years had passed, damn it. Why had she brought it up now? "The manner in which you . . . associate yourself with members of this family." *Members.* Plural. Had Michael found out about Eve too? Even so, a duel? Just who the hell did Michael Blackheath think he was?

"Captain Jenkins will be ready to sail tomorrow afternoon." Duquesne's voice broke the stillness. The older man turned from watching the *Southern Star.* "Why don't you return to Richmond in my place? Stay in Virginia, man, for heaven's sake. Your home is there, and no doubt needs your attention."

"No," Lion said, striding across the room to pick up the note and read it again.

"You don't need to go through with this," Duquesne said. He saw the look in Lion's eyes. "You can't, damn it."

"I will."

"And jeopardize the entire venture? All the effort that went into arranging the contract? By heavens, man, think! All the planning and arranging. The attempt on Michael's life in New York, ingratiating yourself with the old man and his daughter—"

"I didn't—"

"It's the same thing! They're building ships for us, and I don't want them to stop. If that means you walk away from—" He paused. Lion wasn't paying attention to him, instead was looking at the door to the room. "What's wrong?" Duquesne asked in a hushed voice.

Lion pointed at the door. "Someone out there," he mouthed. "Keep talking."

"If that means you walk away from a duel," Duquesne went on hurriedly, watching Lion tiptoe toward the door, "you damned well walk away from a duel. We need those ships. Paid good money for . . ." His voice trailed off as Lion jerked open the door.

"Eve!"

She had heard enough. Enough to know that Lion had never loved her, only used her. Already she was fleeing down the hall. The stairs were narrow and dark, negotiated with difficulty, but Lion's voice and the overwhelming sense of betrayal gave her impetus. Unfortunately, in her haste she tripped on the door sill and her riding boot slid in a mud puddle. She fell to her knees. Scrambling desperately, she lost her hat and watched it blow away as she ran to the mare and swung into the saddle.

"Eve!"

His voice. The voice of betrayal! Eve whipped the animal, thundered out of town and along the Bay Road. A glance over her shoulder revealed the man she considered now a false lover in pursuit, and gaining rapidly. Dawn Wind was still more than two miles away. Eve reined her mare off the road and plunged the frantic animal into the woods. Branches tore at her dress, caught at her streaming, golden hair, whipped her cheeks until her eyes watered. Without warning, the mare suddenly leaped a hidden log. Eve lost her balance, skewered to one side, tried to hold on, and slammed into the ground. She lay on her back, staring up at the drifting autumn leaves. How much, she thought, they looked like the pattern of wallpaper her mother had designed. Strange, though, how they didn't move. Curious, how they hung in the air, frozen in space like a still print, then suddenly expanded to blot out the sky. . . .

Her face was wet. Cool water trickled down her temple and tickled her ear. Lion's voice brought her back. He was cradling her, dabbing at her cheeks with a moist kerchief. Vague features became the chiseled contours and planes of his face. She struggled free of him and sat up in defiance of the world spinning before her eyes. Her mare, ground-tethered and cropping the grass underfoot, stood nearby.

"Eve?"

"Leave me alone," she managed, shrinking away from him.

"You have to let me explain."

"What? Why you lied? Why you used me? Please, spare me the reasons. It is enough to know you lied."

"You can't believe that," Lion said flatly.

"I heard it from your lovely Mr. Duquesne's lips. You certainly didn't contradict him." Near tears, she started toward the mare.

Lion grabbed her arm and turned her around, then caught her wrist as she tried to slap him. "Listen to me, damn it, Eve."

Eve stared at his hands without speaking. When he released her she slapped him across the face. His head jerked slightly, but he did not flinch. She slapped him again. And again. And again. Blood trickled from his lip, but he did not move. Eve stepped back, unable to meet his gaze. Confused, she slumped to the ground. "Oh, Lion!" she wailed helplessly. "I didn't mean that. I didn't!"

He knelt in front of her without touching her. "Eve. I set Michael up. Those men were not to hurt him; they were to provide the opportunity for me to lend a helping hand. With the current state of affairs we couldn't be sure any reputable shipyard would take our contract, and we felt we had to have every advantage we could find or manufacture. I'm not proud of manipulating Michael. I had thought to see the papers signed and then leave quickly. We would have your ships, your father would make a good deal of money, and no one would be the wiser. But then I met you." Eve didn't dare look at him, instead stared at a tiny, moss-covered stone next to her knee. It was surprisingly soft to the touch.

"Look at me, Eve," Lion said gently. His fingers touched her chin, raised her head until their eyes met. "I love you."

She tried not to believe him. She tried with all her heart, but her heart was no longer hers.

"You have to believe that. No matter what you heard Duquesne say, no matter what I've told you, no matter what happens tomorrow, I love you."

Eve jerked her head back as if his fingers burned her chin. "Tomorrow?" she asked. "It's true, then, isn't it."

"About Michael? Yes. He sent me a letter—"

"I told him you wouldn't do it. I told him you wouldn't even consider such a challenge."

"And that's why you came to the hotel," Lion said. "To talk me out of it." His voice was curiously flat.

Eve shook her head. "Yes. To talk you out of murder."

"I can't just walk away from it. Not and live with myself, or face anyone who ever hears about it. He's a grown man, Eve, and he challenged me. A duel is not murder. It's an affair of honor."

"Words on a slip of paper."

"Maybe so," Lion admitted, "but men have died for less."

"Then men are fools!" Eve reddened. "I didn't mean . . . Yes, I did. They're fools."

Lion stood. His face was set. "If Michael retracts his challenge then the matter will be settled. That's my best offer, Eve. Which is more than considerate under the circumstances."

"But you know Michael won't!"

"It is his doing then," Lion said, refusing to budge.

Eve's shoulders slumped and she covered her face with her hands. She couldn't make him understand. The harder she tried, the more adamant he became. "No, it isn't," she finally said, near tears. "Don't you see? He doesn't know what he's doing. His grievances are figments of his imagination. It isn't a question of your honor. You don't *have* to meet him." She swallowed, took a deep breath. "I'm pleading with you, Lion," she whispered. "Don't do it. Please . . . don't . . . do it."

His face remained hard. He had searched for years for a woman like Eve. Now that he had found her he could sense she was slipping away from him. But he could not compromise his name, could not abandon all he stood for. Above all else he had to remain true to himself. If he did not, even having Eve would be a meaningless charade. "It's entirely up to Michael," he said. "He challenged me, I had no choice but to accept. I have to fight him, Eve."

Eve's face turned white. She rose slowly and stared at him as if she had never seen him before. "I came to you because I thought you loved me," she said.

She was giving him an ultimatum. "I do," he said, a great sadness descending on him. "I want you to be my wife."

"Words," she snapped. "Words!"

"Eve, my reputation is my bond."

"And love?"

"Binds me to you." He took her hands. They were cold, lifeless to the touch. "Look. The *Southern Star* leaves tomorrow. Be with me on it."

"Elope with my brother's murderer?" Eve asked, biting off the words. When he didn't answer she turned from him, caught up the mare, and mounted. "I love you, Lion," she said sadly.

"And I love you," he answered, hoping it wouldn't be the last time.

"That remains to be seen. Tomorrow." Eve backed the animal onto a game trail and kicked it into a trot. Within seconds the only evidence she had been there was the rapidly diminishing sound of hooves.

Lion watched her leave. Once she was completely out of sight, once he could no longer hear the mare's hooves, he sat wearily on a log and stared at the brown leaves on the brown earth.

A single ant, defying the coming cold, scurried up a dying blade of grass, reached the top, and realized it could go no further. Lion reached down and picked the blade of grass. "Perhaps men *are* fools," Lion said, watching the confused insect's antennae grope for the lost path. "But women make us so."

"Good Behavior for Gentlemen," Michael said, reading the title aloud of the book of etiquette from which, virtually verbatim, he had extracted the letter to Lion. "A marvelous work, really. Covers every contingency from announcements of births to letters of grief for the deceased. A whole lifetime of good behavior."

Sewal impatiently rapped the top of his desk. "You're evading the issue, Michael. Sit down."

"There are things I need to do," Michael said, starting to leave. "We can talk later."

"No," Sewal said, "We will talk now."

"Look, Father, I'm not in the mood . . ."

"Sit down!" Sewal's tone permitted nothing short of submission.

Michael glared at him a moment, but chose a seat across from the cluttered expanse of his father's desk. "I want answers, damn it. No excuses. Answers."

"My personal life is still my own, Father. I've told you what I've done. The reasons why are mine, and mine alone."

"And no insubordination!" Sewal barked, sounding like the captain of a ship. "My son has challenged a man to a duel. An extremely capable man, if I'm any judge of character. I have a right to know why. The honor of the Blackheath name is at stake."

"Very clever of you to put it that way," Michael finally said. He leaned back in his chair, closed his eyes, and rubbed the bridge of his nose with his fingertips. *"Good Behavior for Gentlemen,"* he repeated. He tossed the book onto his father's desk. "Unfortunately, for all his thoroughness, the author has forced me to improvise. You see, he failed to include in his thorough, if stilted, discourse, how a gentleman should act when confronted with his wife's adultery. It gives no clue as to how a gentleman should wear a cuckold's horns." Michael raised a stiff-fingered hand before Sewal could interrupt. "Nor does it advise a gentleman how to act when it is revealed to him that the man who stole his wife's virtue persists in his audacity by courting his sister."

Sewal paled. He folded his hands in his lap to keep them from shaking. "You are certain of this?" he asked weakly.

Michael stood. He stared at Sewal for a moment, then glanced out the window. The sky was overcast. He couldn't remember so dreary an autumn. There had been a time when, as a boy, he walked in orange-bright woods and led legion after legion of heroic leaves to gusty death in valiant charges. He wondered if the boy still played there in the silent forest, and if he would ever meet him again. "Yes," he said aloud. "Yes. I am certain," and turned and left the room.

Sewal didn't try to stop him. He was gripped with a paralysis of spirit that held him locked into the chair. The image of that universe he knew as Blackheath, normally so vivid in his mind, had become murky and ephemeral. Family, house, business—all had wavered under the threat of a name he didn't even dare say aloud for fear he would explode with anger. Over and over again the name ran through his mind. McKenna McKenna McKenna McKenna—until it too blurred into an amorphous mass of nonsense syllables that, monstrous in his imagination, threatened to destroy everything he held dear. He'd chase him out, by God. See him discredited, disgraced. He and Duquesne both, for the scoundrels they were. And then burn their cursed ships. Hurl the charred timbers into the bay and let them rot.

But even as he thought about it, he knew he couldn't. Too much was at stake. Every penny of the goodwill payments Duquesne had sent and every penny of reserve and credit he could muster had been committed to Duquesne's ships. If he repudiated the contract, the shipyards, Dawn Wind, and the family would be placed in an impossible situation. Slowly, he calmed his anger and tempered rash judgment with the necessity of survival. He hadn't spent twenty-five successful years at sea and almost twenty more in business by being rash and self-destructive. He'd learned as a young man that when danger or emotion threatened, that was precisely the time not to act hastily, the time to be deliberate and think a problem through. A deep calm settled over him, and Sewal leaned back in his chair.

McKenna had proved himself a villain. Duquesne was unsavory for all his charm, but unincriminated in the present instance. The ships were on the ways and the money was coming in. It would continue to do so. That Michael was a cuckold was unfortunate, but irremediable. The only recourse was to get rid of McKenna before he did any more damage. Sewal frowned. The duel was scheduled for the next morning. Michael was a good shot, but McKenna had the edge in age and experience. Only if Michael fired a bit early—which he could be counted on to do if Sewal hinted at the possibility . . . Sewal halted, pushed the unfinished thought away from him. Perturbed, he rose and paced the room. There had to be a better way, he thought, an honorable way to insure that Michael won. The books, the models, the scrimshaw did not hold the answer. Neither did the globe, nor the harpoons over the fireplace. Sewal stopped in front of the window and looked out onto the grounds. Only there did he find what he sought. Dawn Wind itself. The Blackheath family. The matter went beyond honor. It was a question of survival. Whatever else happened the line could not be allowed to die out. Michael had to live. A grim look spread over Sewal's face as, his conscience salved, the answer came to him. First, Doctor Cutcheon must officiate. He owed Sewal a great many favors. It was time to call in the doctor's debts.

Sure of his course, Sewal turned from the window. A short trip to town and a visit with Cutcheon first, then a talk with Michael. He'd

have to have a few words with Rosamond too. Put her on notice.
He'd see that Michael didn't divorce her this time, but if she slipped
again, he'd let her know she couldn't expect him to intercede.

Impatient to be gone, Sewal sent word for Hamlet to bring him a
horse, then paced the front porch and waited. When Eve rode up to
the house a few moments later, his blood boiled at the thought of
McKenna so much as looking at her, much less touching her.
"Where have you been?" he growled as she dismounted.

Eve recognized the danger signals. Her father's shoulders were
hunched, his fists held straight down and rigid at his sides. "Mirabell
saw something on the path and bolted," she said, immediately
launching into an explanation. "She got the bit in her teeth and went
into the woods before I could bring her under control, then fell when
she jumped a log." Eve brushed dried grass and leaves from her
dress. "I'm a mess," she said with a rueful smile. "I think I'll be
bruised for a week."

"You went to see McKenna," Sewal said.

It was not a question but an accusation. Before Eve could answer
Hamlet appeared, leading Sewal's gray gelding. Eve waited until he
tied the horse at the rail, took Mirabell from her, and left. She
couldn't remember seeing her father as angry since the time four
years earlier, when Justin had ridden a horse at full gallop along the
beach. With a broken leg the animal had had to be destroyed. "I
went to ask him not to fight Michael tomorrow morning," she said,
the minute Hamlet was out of sight.

"You lowered yourself!" Sewal's voice was harsh, grating with
anger. "What makes you think he would do as you ask?"

Eve's mind raced. What had set her father off, she didn't know.
Usually when he was angry he concealed it. Whatever had happened
there was no longer a right time to make her admission. "Because he
loves me," she said softly. "And I love him."

He took a step toward her. "I will not have it!"

"Father—"

"That is correct. I am your father, and you will do as I order. You
will not see this . . . vagrant again." He cut off her protest with a
pointing trembling finger. "Do not try me," he said, his voice mur-
derously soft. "Do not say another word."

Discretion is the better part of valor. Eve stood silently as Sewal
stalked past her, mounted the gray, and thundered down the drive-
way toward New Forest. To see Lion? To confront him for reasons

unknown to her? For a moment she contemplated riding after him then decided against it, for the simple reason that she had never seen or heard Sewal, even when he was angry, doing anything rash. Suddenly, she shivered. The wind off the Atlantic tugged at her skirt and curled her unbound hair around her shoulders. In that same moment the self-assurance and control that were the result of years of training fled her, and she stood alone, vulnerable and confused, torn between the duties of a daughter and the desires of a woman.

Chapter 13

The dawn rolled gray across the sky and vested earth, trees, and restless sea with a mantle of mist. Halfway down the cliff Eve stood on the deck outside the boat house. A breeze ruffled a single stray curl against her cheek. She wore a silk gown of varying yellow hues, overlaid and bordered with white ribbons. She glanced at the top of the cliff, then back down to the narrow stretch of beach where the duel would take place. Uncertainty marred her every gesture.

"Couldn't have picked a better day," Justin muttered, coming out of the boat house. He started up the stairs leading to the top of the cliff.

"You're leaving?" Eve asked incredulously.

"I don't intend to stay and watch my brother killed. That's a performance I'd just as soon miss."

"Lion won't come," Eve said confidently.

"Oh, no?" Justin asked, pointing upward.

Eve jerked around. There on the top of the cliff she could see the heads of two horses. A second later Lion and Duquesne appeared at the top of the steps. Eve clenched her fists to her side and fought for breath: a great weight crushed her chest. He had failed her! Failed her! Where was Rosamond? Hiding in her room? Why wasn't she here to run to her husband and plead with him not to fight?

Footsteps drummed on the stairs. Eve stiffened her back, held on to the rail for support, and stared straight out to sea. The footsteps stopped behind her. She knew Lion was standing there, but she couldn't turn to face him, couldn't stand the thought of looking into his eyes and seeing what waited there. After a moment the footsteps resumed.

Sewal and Michael and Dr. Cutcheon waited on the beach. When Lion reached the bottom of the steps he took off his black coat and hung it on the railing. Michael had already taken his off. Wind tugged at the lace on his shirt cuffs and on his shirt facing. Lion patted a wrinkle out of his blue brocade vest and, accompanied by Duquesne, started walking toward Sewal and Michael. Sand clung to the hem of his gray trousers and tarnished his black boots. No more than a dozen steps separated the contending parties. Those steps traversed, the men would talk civilly, like old acquaintances, act out the prescribed ritual, and then, on the count of ten, try to kill each other.

Brother and lover. Was she to care for one and not the other? This isn't real, Eve thought. Feeling utterly helpless, she waited on the boathouse deck, not out of some macabre inclination, but because she knew she couldn't even consider staying inside the house and hearing the shots without knowing who had lived and who had died.

"Mr. Duquesne. Mr. McKenna," Cutcheon said, beginning the ritual with an unnecessary introduction. "Mr. Sewal Blackheath. Mr. Michael Blackheath." Michael and Lion faced each other. The elder Blackheath and Duquesne bowed curtly. "You are ready to begin, gentlemen?"

Duquesne released the silver catch on the case he carried. The lid flipped open to reveal a brace of pistols nested side by side. Resisting the thought that the black walnut case with its silk lining looked disturbingly like a coffin, he thrust the case toward Michael.

"I have my own," Michael said. He gestured to his side and Sewal stepped forward with a brace of flintlocks converted to percussion weapons.

"Mine have a true aim," Lion said. "They are Kentucky-made by an excellent craftsman." A hint of a smile crossed his face. "I have never missed with them."

"I have my own," Michael insisted bluntly.

Lion shrugged. "Suit yourself."

Dr. Cutcheon, long-waisted and graying, stepped forward. His stovepipe hat was pulled tightly down across his brow to keep it from blowing away. "Gentlemen. You understand that dueling is illegal," he said. "Are you both then determined to resolve this affair with firearms?" Michael and Lion nodded. "Very well. You have both agreed to adopt and accept the following protocol, which I am required to repeat in order to assure myself that both parties understand fully what is expected of them." He paused, looked first at Michael, then at Lion. Neither so much as twitched an eyebrow. "Your weapons will be loaded with one shot each, said load to be inspected by me. When I give the signal, you will proceed to the stake I have driven into the sand. There you will stand back to back. If you both still wish to continue, you will step forward on my count. At ten, you will commit yourselves to God, turn, and fire. Is that understood?"

Both men nodded in agreement.

Cutcheon cleared his throat and held up a Colt revolver. This was the part he didn't like. "In the event that one of you shall turn and attempt to fire prior to the completion of my ten count, it is my unfortunate duty to shoot you down." He could feel Sewal looking at him. Embarrassed, he remembered how he had caved in to the shipbuilder's demand that he shoot only if McKenna turned prematurely, and hold his fire if Michael turned. It was unholy pact, but what else could he have done? He was an old man, and owed Blackheath more favors than he cared to recall. He suppressed a shudder. Shooting McKenna would be terrible, but not half so terrible as shooting Michael Blackheath. "Is *that* understood?"

Both men nodded again.

"Good." Neither McKenna nor Duquesne had indicated they were suspicious. The doctor breathed a little easier. "Once you have discharged your weapons, the duel is concluded, and you have agreed to concede that honor has indeed been satisfied."

Cutcheon then read a copy of the letter Hamlet had delivered to Lion. Completing that task he paused and asked, "Any comments, gentlemen?"

"You could stop this, Mr. Blackheath," Lion said quietly.

"Proceed," Sewal rasped in reply.

"Very well. Load your weapons, gentlemen," Cutcheon said.

Sewal and Duquesne held out the boxes to the duelists, removed the weapon each man indicated, and stepped aside to a table to load. "I have done my best to talk him out of this," Duquesne said, once they were out of earshot. "I hope—"

"You hope I will not burn those damned ships where they stand," Sewal interrupted. "I will not forget we have a contract."

Duquesne rammed shot and powder into the pistol, cocked it, and fitted a firing cap to the nipple. "In the event you do, there is the matter of a rather substantial advance that would have to be returned," he pointed out in an edged voice.

"Yes," Sewal agreed. He finished loading Michael's pistol. The money had been spent to satisfy old debts and build up his inventory. Returning the advance would ruin him. Anyway, his quarrel wasn't with Duquesne, but McKenna. "You need not fear on that regard," he said.

Lion and Michael waited face to face while Cutcheon inspected their weapons. Lion glanced up at the boathouse deck. Eve was still there, a small statue clinging to the railing. Her presence bothered him. He wished he'd said something to her. He wished his affair with Rosamond had never happened, wished he'd never met her at the party in Richmond. But he couldn't back down. Not now. The wind was cold and wet. The early morning light was gray and ominous. "You know I'm going to kill you," he said quietly.

Michael shuddered, stared at him. His mouth opened as if he wanted to say something, but then closed again when his father approached and put his pistol into his hand.

"Take your places, gentlemen!"

They stood back to back. The water was to Lion's right, to Michael's left. Ahead of each a short stretch of sand led to a jumble of granite boulders and a world in which there was room for both of them to live.

"One!"

Lion took a step, heard Michael do the same. Honor be damned. He wasn't about to be Michael's executioner. No dead men at this duel. He'd aim carefully and shoot only to wound. Perhaps, then, Eve would . . . He cleared his mind, and concentrated on each moment, each step, each tiny sound that might signal treachery.

"Two!"

Eve waited on the boat deck. Her hands were pale and bloodless where a length of ribbon was entwined around her fingers. The mist hid the cliff and lighthouse across the bay. Hid "their" cove, too, she thought bitterly. The shawl about her shoulders felt damp and clammy. Mist had collected on the wood and on the rocks, dripped from chips of granite and from the roof of the boat house. She could hear the sound as clearly as she heard her own heart beating, heard the gray waves nibbling at the shore, heard the sound of Dr. Cutcheon's voice counting.

"Three!"

Sewal's face was composed. The outcome of the duel was certain. All Michael had to do was remember to turn.

"Four!"

Duquesne swallowed. He hadn't come to New Forest to be a second in a duel. Damn the Blackheaths! But he needed ships.

"Five!"

Cutcheon raised the Colt and pointed it at the stake, ostensibly ready to swing to either direction should either man turn too soon. The first words of the oath he had taken so many years before niggled at the corner of his mind, but he shoved them aside and kept an eye on McKenna.

"Six!"

Michael felt the heel of his boot strike, then the sole roll forward. His toe dug in. His leg lifted and reached out. He'd never thought about walking before, about the actual effort . . .

"Seven!"

. . . Or about the .54 caliber load in the pistol he carried. McKenna's was the same, he knew. He'd seen how a bullet that size ravaged a man. And what a dead shot McKenna was. He'd never really thought about dying, either.

"Eight!"

He hadn't drunk since the night before. His head was clear for the first time in months. Suddenly, the possibility of death, the ultimate prospect of this confrontation, put his life in perspective. The conflicts generated by Rosamond's infidelity shrunk, became meaningless in a broader context.

"Nine."

Everything was crystal clear, seen and comprehended. The whitish halo of a hidden sun brightening ashen clouds. Sand crawlers and spiders, denizens of the beach scuttling underfoot. Seabirds frozen in midflight. Chopping waves solidified into a landscape of gulleys and ridges. The crackling mist. He could hear the spontaneous creation of individual droplets as they formed and floated and fell.

"Ten!"

Lion whirled to the right. The sleek dueling pistol rose and swept down on its intended victim with the perfection of a striking snake.

But Michael hadn't turned. Lion eased his finger off the trigger and glanced at Cutcheon, who stared with total disbelief at Michael.

"Ten!" he repeated loudly. Uneasy—he had never encountered

such a situation before—he looked at Sewal for direction. The older Blackheath's mouth was open and his face was white as chalk. "Ten!" he called again.

I hear you, Michael thought. I hear you. He took one step, then another. His spine tightened. Sweat beaded his forehead and his upper lip. It tasted as salty as the sea. To taste was to live. He wanted to live, desperately. His father's pistol dropped to the sand. His father had bought the bullet; his father had loaded it. He continued walking toward the rocks at the end of the beach. To his right a narrow path scored the face of the cliff. Michael had climbed there often as a boy. It was steep but easy enough if one knew the way. Never breaking stride he walked between two boulders and started up. The stares of the men below him were no less painful than had they been white-hot points of molten lead.

Sewal did not speak. Why hadn't Michael fired? He had challenged a man, been given the advantage, and acted the coward when the time came to fight. The ignominy was palpable. Cutcheon, Duquesne, soon everyone would know how the Blackheath name had been sullied.

"Mr. Blackheath," Duquesne said, searching for an appropriate remark.

Sewal shook his head, silencing the smaller man. "I want him gone from New Forest," he said, stabbing a finger toward Lion. "Do you understand me?" His voice was clipped and breathless. Each word sounded like a hammer blow and required as much effort.

Duquesne nodded. "The *Southern Star* sails on the afternoon tide. McKenna will be on it," he said.

"He'd better be." Sewal started up the stairs. When he reached the landing he stopped by Eve, but couldn't bring himself to speak. At last he shook his head helplessly and walked past her.

Eve's face was red with shame for Michael. Her legs felt like rubber, and she thought she might faint. She held on to the railing, breathed deeply through her mouth, and closed her eyes. When the world stopped spinning, she opened them in time to see Duquesne and Lion and Cutcheon coming up the steps toward her. She turned her head away from them, heard two sets of footsteps pass, the third stop by her side. Lion was standing by her, she knew.

"Eve?" His voice was soft, calling her.

"Why?" she asked, turning. Tears welled in her eyes.

Lion was frowning as if he'd just solved a problem, but was suspicious of the answer. "I had to, but I wouldn't have killed him."

"You said you loved me."

"Damn it, Eve, I—"

"I asked you, I pleaded with you. Did you have to humiliate him? All of us? Would it have been such a great thing to give him his pride?"

"Yes." The tension was draining out of him. Facing death was never easy, and once the adrenalin stopped flowing, a man felt empty and listless. He wanted to sit down, to drink some brandy. Wanted to rest and let weary bone and muscle catch up to the realization that he was still alive. "Too many people give Michael too many things," he said with brutal honesty. "Pride is something Michael has to give himself."

Eve's voice dripped with sarcasm. "Have you any more words of wisdom, or will that be all for today?"

"You simply refuse to understand, don't you?" Lion said, shaking his head.

"Yes. I simply refuse."

"And you don't think that's being just a little too perverse? Too contrary? Face it, Eve. Michael is a drunk who can't handle his own life. You are under no obligation to—"

"Michael is my *brother!*"

"So what?" Lion struggled to keep his voice down, to hold his temper. Had he so misjudged Eve? "Look, Eve. Michael challenged me. Why, I don't know. I gave him no cause."

"You came here. You held a gun. You stood back to back with him and walked ten paces. You—"

"Didn't shoot him. Michael is alive."

"Is he?" Eve asked.

"Yes. Why can't that be enough? Did you really expect me to stay away? Or expect me to back down like Michael did? You know me. I don't permit that kind of weakness in myself, and haven't since I was eleven years old. There's no room in my life for it."

"I wish you could hear how you sound," Eve whispered.

"I probably sound like a man who's just been damn near killed. But you wouldn't understand that."

"No. I wouldn't, would I?"

"Eve!" Both of them looked up. Sewal stood at the top of the stairs. "Get into the house immediately," he said, just before disappearing again.

"Him or me, Eve," Lion said softly. His hand touched her arm.

"I love you, but I can't cave in to you. Not on this. The choice is yours, and you have to make it now. Him or me."

Eve glanced at Lion, to the top of the cliff, and back again to Lion. Her face was set in hard lines, but her eyes were soft with pain. "I never thought I could be so wrong," she whispered sadly. "I never thought." Bracing her shoulders, she turned and started slowly up the stairs.

"I'm sailing at three," Lion said to her back. "I want you to come with me."

Eve paused. For a moment, he thought she might answer, but then she continued.

"I'll wait, Eve. Until three . . ."

Lion's voice was a distant echo tugging at her back, trying to turn her to him. "I'll wait . . ." She wanted to go, but his obduracy and the image of a broken Michael climbing the cliff shackled her. She had been wrong. Hurrying, she reached the top of the steps and rushed across the lawn to the house. The front door stood wide open. The hall was empty. Rosamond sat weeping in the parlor. Not wanting to talk to her or to anyone else, Eve stalked up the stairs and let herself into her room.

Her door slammed shut. Down the hall, Sewal jerked his head around at the noise. "Michael?" he asked. "Michael?"

There was no answer. Pole had seen him enter, had not noticed him leave. He wasn't in his room, nor in Justin's room, nor downstairs. "Michael?" he called to the cupola. Gray light dulled the stairs as he climbed. The cupola too, was empty. "Michael!" he roared in frustration. "Damn it, Michael!" The veins in his temples hammered. Fists clenched, he circled the inside of the cupola. The grounds outside were empty.

Slowly, carefully holding onto the railing, Sewal descended the steep stairway to the second floor and the deserted hallway. He knew in his bones what had happened, what Michael had done. The damned fool, he thought, staring about him. Dawn Wind, the shipyards, a career in Washington, all thrown to the winds. "And I tried so hard," he said in a painful whisper, not knowing that he had tried too hard.

Wearily, he entered his room, passed the portrait of Jennifer, and stood at the side of the four poster. There, on the embroidered quilt, its casing open, lay a gold watch and silver chain. He did not need to examine it to know the inscription read: "To Michael, on his wedding day."

Drained, Sewal slumped on to the bed, picked up the watch and stared dully as the large hand crept through one black dot, then another and another.

"Mister Blackheath?"

Sewal looked up. Hamlet was standing in the doorway. His hat was in his hand and one foot moved nervously. "What is it, Hamlet?"

"It's Mister Michael, sir. He just saddled himself a horse and rode out. He didn't say good-bye or nothin'." Hamlet looked apologetic, as if he were somehow to blame. "He's up and gone, Mister Blackheath."

Sewal raised the watch to his ear. It was ticking loudly. Deliberately, he closed the case and placed it alongside the one he had not disturbed for seven years. "Thank you, Hamlet," he said. "I know."

Noon. One o'clock. Eve, silent in a silent house, paced from parlor to dining room and back again. Her face was set, her lips pursed. Her arms were folded under her breasts as if she were cold. She had given herself to him! Given? No. Lowered. Her father had been right. Thank God he didn't know how far. She was a Blackheath, and didn't deserve this. Yet, she could see him still as he stood on the steps in front of her. Black boots wet with sand, gray trousers, a sky-blue brocade vest, and a white shirt. Oh, how his hair curled when he took off his hat! How strong his arm felt when she placed her hand on it! And he knew too. "I sail at three," he'd said. "I want you to come with me," he'd said. "I'll wait." Her only defense was steely control. Ah, yes, he had loved her enough to bed her, but not enough to honor her request not to fight Michael.

The house was depressing. Bric-a-brac surrounded her. Frustrated, she fled the dining room and walked onto the porch. Bright sunlight flooded the grounds. The wind had carried the morning mists away like spirits of the dead.

Rigid, one hand against the porch post, she stared across the empty lawn. Michael wasn't dead. Yes, he had taken a horse and left without a trace, but he wasn't dead. Lion's argument chaffed her conscience. She knew her father was upstairs in his room. Rosamond was in Michael's room. She could face neither of them.

"Ah, there's someone, at least."

Eve jumped, turned to see Justin coming out of the front door. "Don't do that," she snapped.

"Sorry." He tore a huge bite out of a sandwich, washed it down with a swallow of wine. His shirt and vest were stained with chemicals.

"You've been taking photographs?" Eve said, accusingly.

"Good for the soul," Justin mumbled around another bite. Eve turned her back to him. "Sorry." He threw one leg over the railing and perched there eating, without, it seemed, a care in the world. Eve continued to ignore him. "It wasn't his fault, you know," he finally said.

"I have no idea of what you're talking about," Eve said icily.

"I have no idea," Justin mimicked. He took another bite, another swallow of wine. "It wasn't Lion's fault and you know it. Michael chose his own path. Father had something to do with it, I suspect, but exactly what, I'm not certain." Wearied by his chatter and angered by his flippancy, Eve glared at him. "All right," Justin said, throwing away the last of the crust. "I'll say no more."

"I thought you weren't going to watch," Eve said.

"So did I." He frowned. "People are funny. What perverseness draws them to bloodshed I can't imagine, but there I was, watching and waiting to see what happened."

"Must you be so flippant all the time, Justin?"

"Who says I'm being flippant?" Suddenly looking drained, Justin leaned back against the nearest porch column. His eyes closed and his voice softened. "I've talked to Father, believe it or not. He looks as though he's in shock. I started to tell him he had no right to be disappointed in Michael because Michael has never had a chance to be himself. Only what Father wanted him to be. But I couldn't. Just couldn't." Justin opened his eyes, stared without seeing down the drive to the land bridge and the forest beyond. "He's taking it hard, Evie. Awfully hard. It's not a pretty thing to watch. All of a sudden he's human, and hurt. I've never seen him that way."

Eve leaned forward intently. "Then why in God's name don't you go after Michael? Bring him back? He'll listen to you."

Justin slowly shook his head. "No. Not that. I don't think he would. He's gone, Evie. Wanted to go and wouldn't come back if three of me went after him. Where doesn't matter. He probably doesn't know himself. There's not a thing in the world we can do about it. About Father, either." The old Justin smile returned. "Me,

I just amble along, good old eccentric Justin. But you? Now there's a lady to think about twice." His voice lowered and a bittersweet look played across his face. "He's still in New Forest. It's not too late, Eve. Not if you hurry."

Eve looked down at Justin's hand on her arm. Lion had touched her there, only hours earlier. The spot still felt cold. "You've made me hungry," she said in an icily calm voice. "I think I'll go see if Eustacia can fix a sandwich for me. A sandwich and a bowl of soup."

For once Justin lost his poise. "For God's sake, Eve. We're not discussing food!"

"Oh?" She plucked his hand from her arm, dropped it and turned away to go inside. "I am."

"Mr. McKenna?"

Lion turned. The first mate nodded in deference to the Southerner's authority. "The captain's regards, sir. There's a fair wind and a strong current. There won't be a better time."

Lion took off his hat, and ran his hand through his hair. The dock was empty, and had remained that way for the whole hour he had stood there.

"Sir?" the sailor called from the deck. He was ready to cast off. Two more of the *Southern Star's* crew were standing by the gangplank. Ambrose Duquesne would reappear if Lion remained on the wharf any longer, and he did not want to say good-bye to the man again. His pocket watch read three thirty. He had waited as long as he could. Grim-faced, he boarded. His feet thudded dully on the gangplank and the wooden decking. Behind him the mate shouted orders. The gangplank was hauled aboard, the last line cast off. Lion stared at the empty wharf, then turned abruptly and went below to his cabin.

Eve trudged the final steps to the tip of the peninsula. The wind was brisk, quartering from the northeast, and chilly. When she reached the top she turned to look out over a vast expanse of the bay and the ocean beyond. What she saw riveted her in place. Reaching out from New Forest, a foretopsail schooner cut across the bay. The cold wind forgotten, she watched the vessel as it approached the cove where she and Lion had first made love, then come about and head directly for her. A half hour later, almost directly below her, the *Southern Star* came about again and headed southeast on a tack that would take it past land's end and the lighthouse, and into the Atlantic proper.

"Go, then," she finally said. Her voice sounded pitifully small, and her wind-driven tears left pasty streaks on her cheeks. While she watched, the sturdy ship that carried Lion away from her became a toy boat, a cloud on the water, a fleck of white, and finally disappeared altogether in the vast, shimmering distance.

Part II

Chapter 14

SUNDAY, November 11, 1860. Home.

Lincoln has won the election. Just as he once split rails, he will now split the Union. Not everyone agrees with me, but I do fear the worst, and am saddened and exhilarated at the same moment. Great things, as they say, are afoot.

The Valley is quiet now, with winter coming. The fields are brown, the trees are shedding their leaves. Many of the horses are already shaggy in their winter coats. It is a peaceful time of year when the world rests after summer fecundity. It is a time for hunting pheasant, for tramping the woods, and contemplation. Maggie, Strider, and I wandered the western ridges the last three nights. Their night tracking songs are some of the sweetest music a man can hear. But oh, what a lonely sound that baying can be. Still, the woods cleanse me of the pain of loss. Why is it some men seem destined to wander alone?

But enough. I swore I would not be morose. I tell myself that we shall probably be at war within the year. Perhaps it is best Eve did not come with me.

Mother has taken a turn for the worse. Her vision continues to deteriorate and the circulation in her legs is bad. Dr. Shaffer says he now fears gangrene in her left foot. She slips into a coma from time to time. The conservatory has become a miniature hospital. Either Essie or Willie are with her at all times now. If Mother passes away Aunt Mary will be the last McKenna of her generation. Uncle Jiggs tries to keep her spirits up, but it is a difficult task. As for me, I can only hope that Mother departs peacefully rather than linger on and suffer at length.

Duquesne has written, and wants me to travel to Richmond. I haven't the faintest idea what scheme he has in mind. The farm is in *good hands with the Whitus boys, but for now all depends on Mother's condition.*

Rec'd papers today from Mr. Holcomb. Blue Rob is now mine. I'll have him at stud this next season. The white-eared filly, three brood mares, and the first issue of Blue Rob and Morning Sun is a stiff, but fair, price. God, but he's a handsome fellow!

FRIDAY, January 18, 1861. Home.

Mother is gone. God rest her soul. We laid her next to Father this afternoon. The sun was shining and the sky was as blue as the air was brisk. Aunt Mary says she and Father would have been married forty-one years today. Their first anniversary together in nineteen years.

I have decided to join Duquesne in Richmond within the next two weeks, or as soon as Mother's affairs are concluded.

The whole of the South continues in a fervor. Georgia and Louisiana vote soon, and I have no doubt they will choose to follow South Carolina, Mississippi, Florida, and Alabama. As for Virginia, a shock is needed. What exactly I don't know yet, but suspect that will be the substance of my meeting with Duquesne. I had thought I might be sent to Europe again, but Mother's condition delayed me, and my place has been taken by others. It's just as well.

Strange, but when Mother died there was no one here I could talk to. Not even this journal, the closest friend I have, filled the void in my heart left by Mother's passing. That night, all I could think of was Eve, and how much I wished she were with me. I wanted to tell her about Mother, what a strong woman she had been, how, through everything, she never lost her faith. How she died with dignity in spite of incalculable pain and agony. I wanted to spill out my heart to her, and share Mother's life and death. My need for her was so great that I actually found myself writing to her. I finished at three in the morning—almost eleven pages filled with Mother's life, with her courage and gentle pride and honest beauty. Only then did I remember the look in Eve's eyes after the duel. I tore up the letter. Still, the effect was cathartic, and I felt better for the writing.

"'Charleston, April 13, 1861. 10:00 A.M. The cannonading is going on fiercely from all points—from the vessels outside and all along our coast. Fort Sumter is on fire.'"

Eve Blackheath Sarandon lowered the New York *Herald* and

looked across at her husband. Clifford's elbows brushed across the yellow silk upholstery as he locked his fingers behind his head. Eyes closed, he leaned back on the Grecian couch. "We all knew it had to happen sometime," he said lazily. He stretched his legs and left them straight on the hassock. "Do continue."

"It appears to be a moment-to-moment account," Eve warned. "Almost the whole front page."

"Just the high points, then," Clifford said.

" 'Ten thirty,' " Eve resumed. " 'Major Anderson had ceased fire last evening. All night and into today he was engaged in repairing damages and protecting the barbette guns on the top of the fort. Dense smoke is pouring out of Fort Sumter. Now, thirty hours after the bombardment began, the federal flag is at half mast, signaling distress.' "

"The correspondent has a gift for understatement," Clifford chuckled.

"Yes." Eve scanned down the column, picked up the thread of events. " 'Twelve noon. Shells from Fort Moultrie are bursting in and over Fort Sumter in quick succession. Every shot . . .' "

"*Monsieur* Sarandon?" Winnie, the French servant, called discreetly from the door of the sitting room. "You still want the cloth?"

"Yes, by all means," Clifford replied, draping his right hand over the edge of the couch. Winnie entered quickly and handed him a steaming, moistened cloth that he placed immediately over his eyes. "Thank you, Winnie."

"*Oui, monsieur.*"

"I'm looking forward to supper," he added, waving her away. Every Monday Winnie created a marvelous cheese and mushroom soup that, along with loaves of piping hot bread and fresh butter, served with distinction as a light supper. Clifford pressed the cloth against his eyelids. "Damn that purchasing committee and Representative Carmichael with his perfidious cigars. By the time the Capitol building is complete, I shall be blind from peering through the noxious clouds he expels. I'm sorry, Eve. Read on."

" 'Every shot now seems to tell heavily. The greatest excitement prevails. The wharves, steeples, and every available place, as they were all day yesterday, are packed with people.' " Eve paused, ran a finger down the copy. "Let me see . . . Yes, here. 'Twelve thirty. Every building in Fort Sumter is burning. Major Anderson's flag has been shot away and now waves from a pole nailed to the ramparts.

Great havoc is created among the poor fellows.'" She folded the paper, held it to one side, and rested her right hand on her stomach. When she continued, her voice was hushed. "'Two thirty. Fort Sumter is surrendered. No terms offered other than complete evacuation of the defenses.'"

Clifford sighed. "The fools. The utter fools." He refolded the cloth. "Well then, it's begun. I must say the *Herald* gives a better account than yesterday's *Intelligencer*. Speaking of which, check it and see if *Flowers of the Forest* is still playing at the Washington, will you?"

"Must you be so blasé, Clifford?" Eve asked with a sigh.

"Blasé? On the contrary. It is very important to me, actually. They say Mr. Sothern is marvelously amusing. I missed him when he was last in New York, and don't intend to repeat the oversight here in Washington. We've already let *Who Poisoned Susan?* get by us. This is his last appearance on our stages for God knows how long."

"You know what I mean." Eve pushed herself up in the chair in an attempt to find a more comfortable position. "You listen to an account of war breaking out, and respond in the next breath with . . . Oh!"

Clifford removed the cloth and dropped it on the end table. "Eve. Dear Eve. Don't get so upset." He rose and crossed to her chair. "Look at you. Working yourself into a state."

"The country is at war, Clifford!"

"But such a tiny war!" he exclaimed impatiently. "Really, dear . . ." A look of concern clouded his face and he knelt at her side as Eve winced and placed a hand over her swollen stomach. "Are you all right?"

Eve took a deep breath. "Yes. He kicked, is all."

Clifford nodded, smiled. He placed his hand over hers. "There, you see? I warned you."

"I can't help it. I'm worried."

"Over a trifling military incident."

"The destruction of a fort is a trifling incident?" Eve asked indignantly. "Seventy-five thousand troops of state militia to be assembled, trifling?"

"And there," Clifford said with a chuckle, "is why men run the country and women stay home and bear the children. You are an alarmist, my dear, who in the first place hasn't read far enough, and in the second, jumps to erroneous conclusions based on warped perspective. The troops have been summoned for ninety days of duty. Three months. A rabble, any rabble—even a tiny, tiny minority of the populace, which is what we are talking about—makes a lot of noise."

Clifford had the ability to make a parlor serve as a stage. His voice took on a dramatic, thespian quality. "These Confederate States are all bluster. They're full of sound and fury signifying nothing. And that is precisely what this Sumter incident will give us a chance to prove." His hand raised, and wagging back and forth as if he were giving a lecture, Clifford stopped in the orator's pose he'd perfected as the president of the debating team at Harvard. "Believe me! We've held back. Now they have provoked us, and we shall respond with the only argument the rabble understands. Force! At the first sign of President Lincoln's seventy-five thousand our irate and quarrelsome Southern children will take a far more subdued approach, or suffer a paddling. Frankly, I hope they put up a bit of resistance. Our army is in a horrid state of disrepair and our navy almost nonexistent. Force us to give some thought to that, eh? Besides, a show of strength on the battlefield would benefit our foreign relations. Europeans respect a show of strength now and then. Make 'em sit up and take notice, I say. Cannon crashing, muskets popping. The forces of right triumphant, by God! Yes, one good battle—"

He trailed off. Eve was looking at him as she always did when he became pompous. "Now, don't worry, Eve," he said a little too heartily. "You'll see. And if it makes you feel better, I'll only wish for one battle. No more. To clear the air, you know. And be great fun, to boot."

Eve still didn't look convinced. Clifford smiled wanly, changed the subject. "I hope you've noticed the improvement," he said, patting his stomach. "Come to think of it, perhaps you've gained the weight I've lost, eh?"

Thunder rattled the windows and promised a spring rain. "Farmers predict we'll have a wet spring," he added lamely. Eve wasn't even looking at him, rather sat with her eyes closed and head leaning against the back of the chair. Clifford rubbed his eyes. His mouth opened, then closed. He cleared his throat. "I'll be down in a minute," he finally said, and escaped from her silence.

Alone, Eve kicked free of her slippers and rested her feet on the padded stool in front of her chair. The stool was embroidered with a red, gold, blue, and green peacock. Two of the stitches in the eye had pulled free to form raised loops. Half listening for Winnie's possible return, she threaded her little toe through the larger loop and tugged until it came free and hung like a golden tear down the peacock's face.

The wind was picking up. Raindrops began to spatter against the window and obscure the newly budding oak trees that lined Benbrook Drive. Eve watched the tree limbs quiver and shake, watched the wind send slanting gray curtains rippling across the Rock Creek vista of the nation's capital. East in the distance the lights of the city were vague apparitions of warmth in the gathering darkness. Eve imagined one cluster to be the White House, another, some distance beyond, the Capitol building with its scaffolding and cranes. As she watched, the lights delineating a territory of sin and corruption called Murder Bay, halfway between the presidential mansion and the unfinished Capitol, were lit one by one. Nice girls—certainly no ladies —never ventured into Murder Bay. Even so Eve had once expressed a desire to see what it looked like, during daylight hours, of course. Clifford had been horrified by the suggestion and refused even to consider the idea.

Eve sighed, pulled her shawl about her. "But such a tiny war!" Clifford had said. He didn't understand. Tiny or not, men would be killed, women and children left bereft of husbands and fathers. A painful, poignant contrast came to mind. War and all its glory: flags flying, horses galloping to the charge, heroic deeds on the battlefields, and winners' laurels. War in all its misery: devastated homes, naked, hungry children, and looting, rape, and bloody death. How many men throughout history prepared for war—tiny wars, included—with glory in mind, totally ignoring the misery that would inevitably accompany and follow it? Could they be so irremediably blind? Evidently. A thousand past and present illustrations existed to prove the point. Washington itself was a prime example. Seen by those in power as the seat of government, the center of authority and one of the gathering places of society, the city was in reality a haphazard conglomeration of the rich and the impoverished. Elegant townhouses like the one she lived in and imposing public buildings stood cheek to jowl with primitive hovels made of flimsy scrap lumber. In the winter the wealthy toasted and the poor froze. In the spring . . . In the spring some poor child—a harlot, perhaps, at the unmentionable age of twelve—shivered and wrung the rainwater from her cheap paper shoes, while Eve Blackheath Sarandon rested her naked feet on embroidered peacocks.

Not that Eve wished to change places. She was not so immature. She had tasted reality and found it bitter to the tongue. Her appetite required no further appeasement. Still, especially when the weather was gloomy and the child she bore weighed heavily, she tended toward despondency. At these times too, she was beset with the realization that, though she was content to be with Clifford, she desperately missed the soaring passion she had felt when Lion was at her side, and mourned his loss.

The direction of her thoughts guided her glance to the window facing south where the rain-dappled, muddy Potomac River separated Washington from Virginia. Awkwardly, she pushed her unaccustomed bulk away from the chair and waddled, as she defined her walk when she was in a sour mood, across the room. Windblown rain running down the window distorted the view. She bent closer to see better, then leaned back and, with a forefinger, wrote "Lion" in tiny letters in the condensation left on the glass. As she pondered the word and the emptiness it left in her heart, the child in her womb stirred. Eyes closed, smiling secretly, Eve placed her hand on her belly. The child kicked again as if it too could see beyond that rising shoreline to the hills, and past the hills to where the Blue Ridge Mountains cast their shadow over the valley carved by the Shenandoah River. Eve could, though her eyes remained closed. There, in her imagination, his gray eyes flashing and his black hair swept back by the wind, Lion McKenna rode through the twilight.

Hébert Sarandon arrived unannounced in the middle of supper. What had started as a relaxed and quiet evening at home became a tense chore which, as soon as decency allowed, Eve escaped. Later, after Winnie had been dismissed for the night, Eve lay stock still, rigid under the covers, and listened to the muted voices of Clifford and his father drift up the stairway. Though neither spoke sharply—in truth, Hébert seldom raised his voice in either ire or gaiety—Eve knew they were arguing. Furthermore, she knew why: The marriage Hébert Sarandon once had wholeheartedly blessed had become personally offensive to him, and he could not conceal his displeasure. The keen, Gallic nose that had sniffed out many a fishy deal during a long and lucrative life in business had smelled, as long ago as November, an ulterior motive, and the makings of a scandal.

He wasn't, of course, wrong, as he learned during a heated argument with Clifford one night a month after the wedding when, trapped by a sequence of lies designed to protect Eve, Clifford let slip the truth.

A week and a half after Lion left and a month before the election, Clifford had taken four days out of a busy schedule in order to visit Dawn Wind, only to be virtually ignored. Justin, soberly trying to please Sewal for once in his life after the shock of Michael's disappearance, spent most of his time at the yards, and the rest in his studio. Rosamond had rejoined her mother and father in Washington, and Sewal's every hour was occupied with the ships. Most important, Eve was preoccupied and distant, even, Clifford had thought, distraught. If he could have seen her studying the calendar she kept hidden in her drawer, he might have had some idea why.

Eve, for her part, tried to be sociable even though she was going through the tortures of the damned. Bleakly, pitting hope against hope, she counted the days since her last period. Every time she counted it came out the same: She should have started on the sixth, the seventh at the latest. Each day that passed saw her grow more panic-stricken. On the eighth she kept to her room and stared blankly at the walls, as if that would do any good. "What will I do?" she asked herself over and over again. "What will I do?"

Clifford's arrival on the ninth didn't help. He had been promoted to manage Ashton's campaign, and had run up, he said, for a quick visit. He had to be back in New York by Friday. All during dinner he kept up a commentary on the state of the campaign, Ashton's chances of winning and the satisfaction, for the first time in his life, of starting at the bottom and working his way up. He answered Sewal's serious questions seriously, and—out of character, for he had never been a raconteur—tried to cheer up an obviously despondent Eve with anecdotes. Nothing seemed to work, and no sooner had coffee been served than Eve excused herself and fled to her room. When Clifford looked to Sewal for an explanation, the elder Blackheath shrugged his shoulders helplessly, and steered the subject back to politics. On Thursday morning Clifford left Dawn Wind no more enlightened than when he'd arrived.

The next weeks were, for Eve, a single, extended nightmare. She couldn't think and didn't dare verbalize what she so dreaded. She rose in the morning, bathed, and secretly inspected herself in the mirror. She spent the day wandering about the house and getting in the way. Eustacia fretted, and concocted special dishes for her, which went untouched. Near the end of the month, she woke up nauseated one morning. Only then, in her horror, did she dare confront the truth. She was pregnant.

Nice girls didn't get pregnant outside of marriage. She envisioned Sewal's mortification and New Forest abuzz with gossip and cruel jokes at her expense. She imagined the scandal spreading to Boston and New York, there to flourish among Sewal's business associates while her "friends" watched her slowly swelling testimony to their poisonous tales. Shunned, rejected, girls in her situation were often sent away, exiled to dreary towns and given stories of dead husbands, which everyone knew to be lies. God only knew what became of their children.

One fantasy leading to another, Eve grasped at straws. Lion was returning. Or she wasn't really pregnant. Everybody missed periods once in a while. The body wasn't a perfect clock. Sometimes it malfunctioned. The weather, something she had eaten, the shock of losing both Michael and Lion on the same day. There was a logical reason. All she had to do was wait until her time came again. Frantic, she wrote letter after letter to Lion, then terrified by the thought of his distant scorn, tore up and burned each one of them.

The next days were excruciating. She wished desperately for someone to talk to, but knew there was no one. Not even Eustacia. That the cook would know soon enough never entered her mind. She simply didn't have the courage to speak, and under any circumstances couldn't have made her mouth and tongue form the phrases. The election on November 6, passed unnoticed, for Eve was more concerned with the events taking place in her own body. By November 8, the papers were bannering Lincoln's victory. There was jubilation in the North. The South too, cheered his election with a fatalistic obstinacy. Eve put another mark on her calendar. Two months. Two periods. Now she knew without a doubt: she bore the fruit of Lion McKenna's seed in her womb.

Clifford's plans crumbled when, his New York district curiously sympathetic to the South, Morton Ashton had lost his election. Another man might have brooded, but Clifford had been well trained by his father. Losses were to be taken, learned from, and put aside. Denied a post as legislative assistant in the House, he would simply find another route to power. By the time the final returns were counted, he and his father had set the wheels in motion with discreet inquiries and gentle reminders of favors owed. Within a week he had been promised a position on Senator Seward's staff as an assistant. His confidence in himself bolstered, his thoughts turned again to Eve. If ever there was a time to press his suit it was then. Not one to hesitate once a decision had been made, he took the Saturday morning train from New York to New Forest.

His initial reaction to Eve was shock. She looked pale and drawn, and had added weight. Normally spirited, she acted distant and distraught. At first confused, Clifford decided it was up to him to lift her from the malaise into which she had sunk. He tried for two days to get her to smile. On the morning of the third he virtually forced her to bundle up and walk outside. It had rained the night before and everything had frozen. Trees and rocks alike were covered with a thin film of ice that shone diamond bright when the sun finally broke through the lowering clouds.

They walked the slippery path to the sea end of Dawn Wind, and stood gazing out over the murky gray Atlantic. Clifford could hardly believe the Eve he accompanied. Gone was the aura of haughtiness, of icy control, and of unblemished beauty to which he had grown so accustomed. In her place was a more human Eve, one who needed tenderness and understanding and perhaps even protection. Huddled in a Hudson Bay company coat, she looked tiny and vulnerable. Her nose was red with the cold, her eyes tearing. The change was overwhelming, and exposed a facet of the woman he had never seen before, an added dimension that made Eve all the more precious to Clifford. "I don't understand, Eve," he finally said, careful not to touch her. "Whatever it is, do you want to tell me?"

Eve didn't answer, instead seemed to shrink inside the fur-lined hood.

"You have to talk to someone." Again, she didn't answer. "Do you like me at all, Eve?" he asked.

"Yes. Of course," Eve whispered. Her tears were not from the cold, then. "You are the only true friend I have, I think," she added, stepping forward toward the edge of the precipice.

Clifford spoke, gazing out at the sea. "I love you, Eve. More than you can imagine, I love you." He faltered, wished he could see her face. Taking a deep breath, he turned her to him, placed one finger under her chin and lifted it so she would have to look at him. "Marry me, Eve," he said huskily. "I've wanted you to since the night we met. You know that."

Eve stared into his eyes a moment, then stepped forward into his arms and let him hold her. Her head spun, and the sea roar in her ears was painful. She could say yes, she knew. The child would have a name. Clifford, with luck, might never know. Premature babies were common. And if he did guess the child wasn't his, he was too much of a gentleman to ever voice his doubts aloud. In that moment she almost agreed, but the words stuck in her throat, and she knew she had to tell him. If he still wanted to marry her after he knew the worst, well and good. At least their relationship would be grounded in the truth.

But she didn't dare look into his face. "I am pregnant, Clifford, with Lion McKenna's child." She felt him stiffen, but there was no way to drape the reality with grace. "You see, it was more than infatuation."

The worst part was over, and she dared look up. Clifford's eyes were closed and his forehead was furrowed. Gently, Eve slipped from his arms and moved back a pace. "You understand my situation here," she said, hating the clinical tone her voice had taken. "It won't be easy, yet I am prepared to face anything I need to face."

"Did he . . . force himself on you?" Clifford's voice came from very far away.

"No," Eve said, gently.

Clifford's eyes opened and he stared wildly at her. "He had to! He must have!"

"I'm sorry, Clifford," Eve broke in. "Nothing but the truth, between friends. He didn't force me." Clifford's mouth opened, but no sound came out. "I simply didn't think of the consequences when I . . . I wouldn't have this happen again for a thousand years," Eve said, her heart aching. A flood of tenderness washed through her. Clifford had told her he loved her many times before. He had asked her to marry him many times before. Only now did Eve realize how much he did love her, and how much that love meant to her. "If you ask me again I will accept, Clifford," she heard herself saying. "Should you not, you are still a friend, of whose affection I find myself unworthy."

Silence. A gust of wind. Cracking sounds, like a hundred tiny firecrackers exploding as the ice on the trees broke and tinkled to the crusted snow below. His father had taught him that, if a man wanted something badly enough, he often had to ignore the peripheral issues and keep his eyes on the ultimate goal. The successful man had a sense of what, though perhaps onerous in the short run, was acceptable in the final analysis. Never before had that advice seemed so hollow, and yet so apt. Clifford stared at his hands, or rather, through his hands, to the brittle ice on the path. He then glanced at Dawn Wind, framed by ice-crystal branches. At last he looked at Eve, and if his face seemed touched by apprehension, his voice was resolute.

"I love you, Eve," he said. "Will you marry me?"

"Eve?" Clifford's hand touched her shoulder. The past dissipated, floated away on the fading tendrils of dreams. Eve opened her eyes and watched as Clifford shrugged out of his coat and slipped off his suspenders.

He's never wavered, she thought sleepily. Never reproached me, tried to blackmail me, even hinted of disappointment or regret. Eyes half closed, warm under the covers, she watched him throw a log on the fire and fix it for the night. "Some spring," he grumbled.

"The rain will stop before morning," Eve said. "It will be warm tomorrow."

"I hope so," Clifford said, stretching.

Eve folded back the covers and patted the place beside her. "Come to bed. You look tired."

"I am."

"I shouldn't have left you alone with him," Eve said apologetically. "But I wasn't pretending. I truly felt out of sorts."

Clifford busied himself with the buttons on his shirt. "It's all right. I know it upsets you when Father pops in like that. I didn't expect him for another week."

"You quarreled?"

"You might say so," Clifford said drily. He bent, readjusted the logs to his satisfaction. A spark popped onto the hearth and he crushed it with his boot heel. "Seems to be a standard scenario, these days." He chuckled. "Father and I. Makes me think of Justin and your father, though we're hardly as vituperative."

"I never did know what came between Father and Justin," Eve said, the old question rising to nag her. "But I regret coming between you and your father."

Clifford grunted, walked over to sit on the edge of the bed and take Eve's hand. "I regret nothing," he said softly. "Father just doesn't understand how much you mean to me. He will one day."

Eve propped herself on one elbow, leaned over and kissed Clifford on the cheek. "I love you, Clifford," she said. "I love you very much."

Their eyes met for a moment. Brusquely, Clifford wrapped his arm around Eve's neck and held her to him. "Tomorrow's a big day," he said, after a long silence. "There's a cabinet meeting, and whither goest Secretary of State Seward, there goes his first assistant. I'd better get some sleep."

A day's end. Familiar rituals and small talk. Eve lay back, drowsy and content. Clifford rose and slipped out of his shirt and, forgetting as always that Eve had asked him a hundred times not to, tossed it across the chair in the corner. "You write to Justin yet?" he asked.

"Not yet," Eve answered. Justin had written again from Dawn Wind, where his patience with Sewal was wearing thin. He chafed to be away from home and going about becoming a full-fledged photographer. Indeed, he reiterated for the second time, photography had consumed him, and become his full-time dream to the detriment of whatever labor he was assigned at the shipyards. More to the point, he hinted that he might not be welcome at Dawn Wind much longer, and broached the subject of joining Eve and Clifford in Washington. Clifford and Eve had talked it over and decided he could come if he wished, at least until he found a place of his own. "Tomorrow," Eve added sleepily.

Clifford fought his boots and won. "Michael?" he grunted.

"No word," Eve said, shuddering at the thought of the wanted poster that declared her brother a deserter with a price on his head. "May be just as well."

"I'll talk to the Navy again tomorrow. See what I can do," Clifford said, tossing his boots under the chair with the shirt. His socks followed, and he padded into the bathroom to clean his teeth. "What'd you do with my brush?" he called.

"I put it away where it belongs."

A splash of water, and the sound of vigorous brushing.

"Clifford? Did Hébert say anything about my father?"

No answer, save a throaty gargle, and the sound of more water. Clifford emerged from the bathroom drying his face. He stopped in front of his mirror, dropped the towel on the dresser, and started brushing his hair. "Clifford!"

"Sorry." He picked up the towel and tossed it into the bathroom. "Just that the last ship left Dawn Wind for Charleston on Friday afternoon." Clifford thanked his lucky stars that Sewal Blackheath wasn't given to writing, other than to sign the papers his staff prepared. All things considered, it was best that Eve remain in the dark about the sanctions against the Blackheaths and three other ship-building firms that certain members of the House had proposed. Fortunately, Congress wasn't in session, and with any luck, such talk would fade before it even hit the *Intelligencer*. A word to Secretary Seward before the cabinet meeting in the morning, backed up by a note from his father, would undoubtedly help, since Hébert had always been Seward's richest backer. Besides, now that the ships had been delivered, and Fort Sumter had been fired upon, there was no doubt Sewal Blackheath would become a model patriot. "Supposed to arrive in Portsmouth Wednesday at the latest," he said, tossing down the hairbrushes and pulling a nightshirt from the drawer. "If Virginia doesn't secede before then."

"You think it will?" Eve asked apprehensively.

"I know so." Clifford pulled the nightshirt over his head and removed his trousers. Dimming the gaslights, he climbed into bed and lay next to Eve. She felt warm and soft through flannel and silk. "Are you worried about him?" he asked.

"Who?" Eve asked, her throat tightening.

Clifford turned onto his side. Eve's face was barely discernible in the wan light. He wanted to touch her, to rest his hand on the bulging covers, to hold her tightly. "McKenna," he said, careful to keep his voice even.

"I'm worried for us all," she said quietly. Then: "Please, Clifford?" In spite of her growing affection for Clifford, she knew she would go to Lion if he called. The thought filled her with guilt, the same guilt she had lived with for months. Her hand touched Clifford's arm. "Let's not talk about him, please?"

"It's just that, sometimes I wonder . . ." He trailed off, uncertain.

"I know. But I'm with *you* now. Don't you understand?"

The lump in his throat hurt. Clifford swallowed, swallowed again before it would go away. "Good night, my darling," he said. Gently, he reached over and kissed her, first on one eye, then the other. "Sleep tight."

"Good night, Clifford. I love you," she answered, as much to convince herself as to reassure him.

He listened as her breathing mingled with the music of the rain. Was she asleep or pretending? Stealthily, almost apologetically, he placed the palm of his hand on her abdomen. Rest easy, little one, he thought. I shall be your father, and you will be none the wiser. And before too much longer, you shall have brothers and sisters.

Clifford rolled onto his back. Summer soon, he mused, and the world would be warm and beautiful despite the petty squabbles of men. Did she still love McKenna? Perhaps. It didn't matter, though. Not really. You'll forget him, Eve, he promised her silently. I'll make you forget him, and our life will be long and full. You'll see. I have plans. He yawned. The rain had lulled him. I have . . . such . . . plans . . .

The last thing he remembered was her final words before she slept. "I love you." The simple phrase carried him into peaceful sleep, and the dreams of sunnier days and plans fulfilled.

Chapter 15

MONDAY, April 15, 1861. Home.
We are at war! This will be my last night at home for some time. Have been very busy recruiting a company of volunteers. Leave for Richmond tomorrow morning. God bless us all.

The country brooded, and lurched, like a drunken man, toward war. The reduction of Fort Sumter galvanized the North, and Lincoln's request for militia was quickly oversubscribed. The very idea of troops being called to invade her united the South as nothing else had. On Wednesday, April 17, Virginia seceded, making a total of eight states in the new Confederacy.

The South moved more quickly than the North. Within three days after Sumter's fall the gleam of Confederate troop campfires could be seen across the Potomac from a virtually surrounded Washington. The city, undefended, panicked. Civilians fled by the hundreds until the capital was virtually deserted. Public buildings were sandbagged and set about with gun emplacements. Clifford pleaded with Eve to go to New York or Dawn Wind, but she refused. If his job as Seward's assistant required that he stay, she would too. At last green troops from Pennsylvania and then Massachusetts arrived. Quartered in the empty House of Representatives, they helped bring some measure of calm to the city.

So far the war had been talk and skirmishes as if, the opening shots having been fired, both parties pulled back to figure out exactly what they wanted to do and how. In the North business, smelling profits the way a buzzard smells death, rallied behind Lincoln. The South, realizing its industrial limitations but retaining a belief in the superiority of the Southern soldier, was convinced of a quick victory. On both sides the first waves of expectant heroes blew occasional alarms of battle. Still, as April turned into May and the enervating heat of summer settled over the country, nothing spectacular had happened.

In the South the new Confederacy moved its capital to Richmond, Virginia, less than a hundred miles away from Washington. Diplomats hurried back and forth across the Atlantic in an attempt to align European states with their cause. Businessmen prospered as North and South gathered materiel for the conflict to come. Army and Navy budgets, earlier virtually nonexistent, swelled. New ships were outfitted, old ships refurbished. Country lads learned the formal intricacies of military drill, and the highly informal complexities of survival in the midst of smallpox, chicken pox, a dozen unspecified fevers, and the ubiquitous diarrhea brought on by polluted water, malnutrition, and crowded, unsanitary living conditions.

Civilian life underwent its own changes. From every corner of the country young men left home to join Lincoln's or Davis's troops. The difference between fighting zealous slaveholders or diabolical Yankees and seeking adventure hadn't yet been clearly defined, especially as far away as Vermont and New Hampshire or Texas and Mississippi. In truth most of the Northern lads who left home had never so much as seen a "darkey." Most of the Southern young men were too poor to own slaves or to be a meaningful part of the system they pledged themselves to save. Still, they were all given heroes' sendoffs and marched proudly down country lanes that would lead, eventually, to as yet unnamed battlefields and unmarked graves.

In May Arkansas and North Carolina seceded and joined the Confederacy. War fever increased. Washington was no different than anywhere else. Despite the fevered activities of politicians and generals, housewives and tradesmen and craftsmen slowly returned to the beleaguered city and went quietly about their business. Loaves of bread were baked and sold. Work on the Capitol building and the new Washington Monument crept along to the steady rhythm of stonecutters' chisels, masons' trowels, and carpenters' hammers.

Clothes and kitchen goods and harnesses and wine and a thousand other sundry items were sold from shelves that were still easily refilled.

Nothing was different on Benbrook Drive. Clifford's eyes still smarted from too much cigar smoke and too many hours in his office. Eve kept her minor worries to herself and, as her confinement neared, calmly made the necessary arrangements for a midwife and wet nurse. More and more her thoughts turned to the child. She occupied herself with sewing clothes and thinking of names. An occasional letter from Justin, who had decided not to visit after all, railed against his father's intransigence. From Sewal she heard almost nothing, for their relationship was at best awkward and strained. Like Hébert Sarandon, he too had assumed the worst, and though he was pleased she had married in time to save her name, he was uneasy with the thought that his daughter had behaved so indiscreetly.

June began pleasantly enough. The war was young, a feint here, a skirmish there. Lincoln's seventy-five thousand brought a greater measure of calm to Washington as they fanned out from the city and chased the threatening Rebel troops out of sight. To the west there was a victory of sorts as the North's first hero, Major General McClellan, drove across the Ohio River, soundly thrashed four thousand Rebels, and made western Virginia safe for the Union.

Eve's time was rapidly approaching. Tired of her unwieldy pregnancy, she counted the days, an exercise that plunged from optimistic expectancy to pessimistic gloom when Clifford's secretary's wife gave birth to a baby girl who died within twenty-four hours. Clifford tried to keep the news from Eve, but she found out anyway, and her own lying-in suddenly took on fearsome aspects. Clifford, normally a phlegmatic man, worried. Every hour he spent at work meant that he was that long away from Eve. To ease his mind he bought another saddle horse and hired an extra man whose duty was to be sober and available to ride immediately to fetch the midwife and doctor, then summon Clifford as rapidly as possible. In addition he sent a long telegram to Sewal, in which he noted that Eve was nervous and tense, and that he thought Eustacia's presence would calm her considerably. Five days later the black woman arrived.

If it hadn't been for Eve, Eustacia would have skedaddled home on the next train. Washington was a confusing and frightening place. Everywhere she looked there were soldiers. She hadn't seen so many black people at one time in the last twenty-five years. Accustomed to the seclusion of a country estate and the quiet of a New England town, the hundreds of carriages, horses, buildings, and pedestrians assaulted her senses. Worst of all she feared, irrationally as it turned out, that being so far south her former owner would find her and somehow take her back. Her fears dissolved when the carriage Clifford had sent for her rolled up the drive in front of the George-town house and she saw Eve waiting on the porch. Seconds later, the carriage still bobbing up and down from her hasty exit, she embraced her "baby," while both dissolved in tears.

"God!"

The physician dozed, indifferent. Beth Gilbert, the midwife, shot him a sour look as she slipped an arm behind Eve. "It's all right, dearie. Press down against my hand. That's a good girl."

"God!" Eve yelled.

A worried Eustacia pushed open the door with one hip, quickly closed it against Clifford. Moving carefully she deposited a basin of hot water on the bedside table. "Here it is," she said worriedly. "She all right?"

"It's starting out," the midwife said. She wiped her forehead with the back of her hand. However many hundred women she'd helped, she still sweated when the baby started. "Take a hold of your ankles, dearie. That's a good girl. Now push."

"Oh, oh, oh, oh . . ."

"Now just relax. Everything's fine . . ."

"What? What?"

"Just your water breaking, dearie. Don't you fret . . ." Leaning across the bed to take a wet towel from Eustacia, she winced as Eve screamed into her ear. "That's good. Scream, dearie. Scream the pain away. Helps, don't it?"

"Noooo!" The tearing spasms stopped. Exhausted, Eve lay back, nearly spent. Each time the contractions came they were worse. Each time they faded her exhaustion was more complete. They'd be back again. Too soon. Dazed, she felt her mind wander back to a figure that rose over her. Eyes closed, she could see Lion vividly, even to the flecks of silver in his eyes. She had cried out then too. In love? In pain? Was there a difference?

"Push now, dearie. Push. Don't fight it. Just push."

Men fight, Eve thought. They fight wars. Lion was a man. Was he fighting? Dear God, don't let him hurt like this, dear God. "Lion? Lion?"

Eve was suddenly aware of Eustacia's warm, brown eyes. Her cool hand was stroking Eve's brow. "What is it, baby?"

Eve's eyes opened wide with the realization of what she'd said. "Clifford," she corrected herself, panting. "Clifford?"

"He's in the hall, honey. Waitin'. You be finished soon."

"Push again, dearie. One more time." The midwife looked at the doctor with disgust. "Head's showing," she said calmly. "You sure you don't want to take over?"

The doctor ignored her sarcasm, as he had the whole proceeding. Bored, he glanced at Eve and laconically waved his head.

"Hold her shoulders," Beth ordered Eustacia. She slipped her hands under Eve's arms, grasped the tops of her shoulders from behind. "Like this. So she can push against you."

Eve felt herself tear apart. Her mouth opened but no sound came out. "Dear God," she prayed through the pain, "I can't take anymore. I can't . . ." Incredibly, the pain lessened.

"The head is out," she heard someone say. "Just a little rest, dearie. And push again. Not too fast . . ."

Jaws taut, Eve's breath rasped in her throat like a hard wind in a dry tunnel. Her hands were claws dug into the sheets and mattress. A brilliant summer sun streamed through the window and bathed the room in amber. Dust motes, tiny dancing diamonds, twinkled through the dulling pain that she already had trouble recalling with exactitude.

Like Lion. A numb memory, blurred but never forgotten. A part of her, always, like Lion McKenna, no matter how hard she tried to drive him from her mind and heart, no matter how many times she had told herself she loved Clifford.

There was activity all around her. Eustacia let her go, was handing rags to Mrs. Gilbert. Something squawled. A high-pitched, lusty cry. Too exhausted to look, Eve lay back on the pillows. ". . . Fine . . ." she heard. "Tell him."

Tell Clifford, that had to mean him—Cliff she thought drowsily. But what about Lion? It was his child. His and hers. And Clifford's too. She blinked, felt a weight on her stomach. The weight kicked. She smiled. Kicked outside of her. Her child. It was her last thought before, exhausted, she drifted into sleep.

The cry woke her. Eve opened her eyes a crack, enough to see dark brown hands gently slip her gown away from her breast. She'd dozed. Clifford's face hovered above hers. He was smiling. Out of the corner of her eye she saw Beth Gilbert. The midwife had a bundle in her arms, which she placed at Eve's breast. So tired she could barely move, Eve looked down as something warm and soft butted against her nipple, then caught it in a wet embrace. Her throat felt tight and her heart swelled with love. Slowly, her arms raised to hold the child, hold and gently rock as it suckled voraciously.

"A son, my darling," Clifford said, bending to kiss her forehead. "We have a fine, healthy, strapping son."

Chapter 16

James Ruell Sarandon had no use for patriotism. He was far more interested in eating and sleeping. Five days earlier, muted by some hundreds of yards of trees and a park that secluded the Sarandon townhouse from the rest of the world, the tramp of booted feet and the cacophony of drums and fifes and regimental brass, punctuated by the indiscriminate discharge of rifled muskets, had kept the baby wailing his displeasure. On that fated afternoon troop after troop of mostly ill-equipped and untrained Union soldiers under the command of Brigadier General Irvin McDowell had filed along Pennsylvania Avenue and taken the ragged cheers of the crowd that wished their army "Godspeed" and "On to Richmond!"

Now, the last of the troops was gone and life had returned to normal. Eve closed her blouse, hugged her baby close, and laid him in his crib. "Good-bye, little Doozie," she whispered, calling him by the nickname Eustacia had given him. James Ruell gurgled pleasantly, discovered his toe, and tried to stick it in his mouth. Barely touching him, Eve brushed a silklike wisp of hair from his forehead. "Mama will be back soon."

Eve tiptoed out of the baby's room and into her own. She stripped out of blouse and skirt, turned sideways to the mirror. James was five weeks old, and not a day since his birth had passed that she hadn't wished her stomach would flatten more quickly. But it was not a time to be glum. Today was to be her first outing, and she was determined to have fun. As Clifford had pointed out, James would have the best of care. Winnie was completely devoted to him and the wet nurse was the best that money could buy. If that wasn't enough Eustacia was still there, and God knew she alone was worth a whole regiment of nurses and servants. Eve ran a sponge across her breasts and the rest of her torso. Clifford was right, as usual, she decided, and hurriedly stepped into the traveling gown Eustacia had laid out for her.

Downstairs, preparations for the outing Eve and Clifford, along with half of Washington society, had been planning for the last few days were almost complete. The air of excitement that rippled across the city was occasioned by the imminence of the first major battle of the war. The generals had said it would take place near Manassas Junction, barely twenty-five miles southwest of Washington in Virginia. The generals also said that a Union victory was assured. The Rebels would be soundly whipped and sent, with their tails between their legs, back to where they came from. The war would be over, the Union preserved. And those who were privileged to watch would see the most exciting battle ever to take place in America.

The city throbbed with anticipation. Carriages were put in order, horses groomed. A victory ball was arranged. Stores were emptied of every available pair of binoculars. Trunks were filled with fresh clothes, blankets, and cushions so the ladies wouldn't have to sit on the grass. Picnic luncheons were prepared and packed.

The activity at the Sarandons' townhouse mirrored that all over the city as Clifford noisily oversaw the loading of his carriage. Winnie handed him a basket of food which he lashed atop a small trunk that rode unsteadily on a decking above the rear wheels. David Maxwell, a friend in the Navy Department, and his wife, Gretchen, a plump, ebullient woman older than her husband by seven years, waited in their carriage for Clifford to finish. Thaddeus Unger, a junior Congressman who had known Clifford at Harvard, helped tie the last of the straps.

"Now hurry, will you?" he said peevishly, brushing back his thick, brown hair and sauntering to the chestnut mare he was riding. "If we wait much longer we'll miss the whole affair."

"I'm doing the best I can," Clifford replied, understanding his friends' impatience. He was as excited as they. He hurried to the front door. "Eve? Are you ready?"

Eve poked a stray curl beneath her bonnet, tiptoed back into the nursery for one last kiss. The wet nurse waited in the doorway. Eve motioned her into the next room. "No matter what my husband has told you, I shall be gone no longer than two days. You can expect me Monday afternoon at the latest."

"Yes, ma'am," the black woman said. "Don't you worry none. Just you and Mr. Clifford have a nice time. You come back, he be just as fat an' sassy as he is now. Sleepin' too, likely."

"I hope so," Eve answered nervously, telling herself for the hundredth time that other women left their children with no ill effects. Quickly, while she still had the nerve to leave, she hurried from the room and down the main stairs.

"Eve!" Clifford opened the front door. "Come on. Everybody's waiting for you."

"I'll be right there." Eve grasped Eustacia's hand. "Take care of him, Eustacia. Remember . . ."

"Honey, I remember more about taking care of babes than you forgot. You think Eustacia's gonna let anything happen to her little Doozie?"

"No." Eve bit her lip, resisted the urge to run back upstairs for one last look. "No. I guess not."

"Then run along, girl." Eustacia pushed Eve toward the door. "An' have a good time."

Clifford was standing by the gig making a last minute examination of the luggage. He turned when David, Gretchen, and Thaddeus began to applaud. Eve, playing along with the fun at her expense, curtsied in acknowledgment. "Here I am," she called gaily, shading her eyes against the morning glare. "My goodness. It's already hot."

"Did you remember something for the ball?" Gretchen asked.

"Ball?" Eve asked in return, with a sidelong glance at Clifford.

Gretchen looked stricken. "You didn't tell her?" she accused Clifford. "You men! I told him to tell you. Senator Ely's wife has arranged a victory ball at the Fairfax courthouse. As soon as the Rebels have received their thrashing we're all to repair there. It will be just wonderful. But my goodness, if you haven't anything suitable to wear . . ."

"We are not unpacking that trunk," Clifford growled under his breath as he helped Eve into the gig.

"I'm certain I have something that will do," Eve said. "If it's at a courthouse it can't be too fancy."

Clifford jumped up beside her. "Time to worry about the ball to-morrow," he called to everyone. "Let's go!"

"We're on our way," David Maxwell cheered as he laid the whip to the rumps of his team and led the way down the drive.

Thaddeus's horse reared, then thundered past them in a cloud of dust. "See you there, slow folks!" he called, waving his hat over his head.

"Not too fast," Eve warned as Clifford urged their team into a quick gait behind the Maxwells' carriage. Still worried, she twisted on the seat, returned Eustacia's parting wave and turned away quickly, lest the premonition of something dreadful strike her, as it had during a dream the night before. "It's the baby," Eustacia had said in her calming way. "Good mamas always fearful the first time they leave their babies. You a good mama, honey. I'm tellin' you, ain't nothin' gonna happen to this child."

"There's no way anybody can go fast enough to suit Thaddeus," Clifford muttered now.

"He should be a soldier," Eve commented, hugging Clifford's arm to her side and trying to banish the gloomy atmosphere she had created for herself.

"He'd like to be," Clifford grinned. "I half suspect he'll resign from Congress and take a commission."

"God help the Union, then," Eve laughed.

"He does put on a show." Clifford slowed for the turn onto the road. "Well, we're off."

"You're excited, aren't you."

"Of course. Aren't you? I only hope the main battle hasn't started yet. Monday would be perfect. Give us a chance to get settled and find our way about."

Eve stiffened. "I told Eustacia we'd be home no later than Mon-day afternoon," she said pointedly.

"What?"

"I won't leave James Ruell for any longer than that."

"But a day—"

"Two."

"Eve. We have a chance to witness history in the making," Clifford said heatedly. He dug a kerchief from his coat pocket and tucked it in his collar. The day looked as if it was going to be as hot as the preceding three days. "Beside, even a passive role in this could do wonders for my career."

"I don't care about history," Eve said, her voice taking on a hard edge. She let go of Clifford's arm and withdrew to the edge of the seat. "I do care about my son."

"Our son," Clifford corrected, laying the whip to the horses in an attempt to catch up with the Maxwells.

Eve did not reply.

The temperature rose with each passing mile, and what had begun as a pleasant ride through the Virginia countryside became a gruelling journey. Buggies, gigs, and carriages bound in the general direction of Manassas Junction and the coming battle thronged the Warrenton Turnpike. Horsemen trotted their mounts to the side of the road in order to avoid the wheeled vehicles. The constant activity produced clouds of choking dust that transformed expensive silks and crinolines into rust-colored rags. Hot gritty air clung to horse and carriage and coated the throats and nostrils of the travelers. Washington's society, on its way to what was rapidly becoming the social event of the decade—how many times in one's life, after all, did one get to watch an enemy trounced on the battlefield?— was transformed into a huge, ambling, gagging throng. Luckily, Clifford and Eve had brought a jug of water. Eve wetted a cloth for what seemed the millionth time and held it over her nose and mouth.

"Dear God!" Clifford fumed as he maneuvered the team around a stopped carriage. "This will take forever."

It didn't of course. Only all afternoon. They entered Centerville at a quarter after five. Parched, hungry, sweaty, and tired as they were, the picturesque old village at the junction of the road leading to Manassas was a welcome sight. The streets were packed with a vast number of visitors mingling with colorfully uniformed soldiers. The Second Ohio wore gold embroidery down the sides of their dark blue trousers and sported the peculiar flapped caps called havelocks, a style associated with the French Foreign Legion. Blenker's Eighth and Ninth wore dusty gray coats and trousers. "Garibaldi Guards," Clifford said, pointing to a pair of passing soldiers. Their brown cuffs were stitched with gold-and-red thread, and their flat-brimmed hats, cocked to one side, were adorned with pheasant feathers that swept backward from the brim.

A familiar figure on horseback galloped dangerously through the throng. "Some sight, eh?" Thaddeus Unger said, appearing at their side. "Best follow me."

"Should we?" Eve whispered apprehensively as a cannon and caisson rumbled past, raising a billow of dust that left them all choking.

"Not much choice," Clifford shouted in her ear. "Hang on."

Centerville looked to be a huge holiday. The native Virginians were easily distinguished from the visitors. Women and children eager to exploit the influx circulated through the streets with baskets laden with food, as soldiers and civilians alike bartered for home-cooked delectables. The aroma of blackberry cobbler, sugar-cured ham, fresh bread, and sweet potato pie cut through the dust and set mouths watering. On one corner a youth juggled a set of horseshoes. On another an old black man with a one-string fiddle played a squeaky, indecipherable tune and collected coins in an old tin can. A trio of boys vying to see who was the most courageous stole rides on the backs of caissons, then dropped, rolling, into the dusty streets. Eve pointed excitedly to an alley where an enterprising soul had set up a temporary ring in which stout young farm lads, for the price of a two-bit piece, could wrestle with a trained bear. The atmosphere was so much like that of a country fair that, for a brief moment, Eve forgot they had come to see a battle.

The traffic thinned, but not by much. All along the street wooden-floored tents had been hastily erected to accommodate the inundation of newcomers. Thaddeus Unger led them to the northwest edge of town and a handsome inn built of stone and hand-hewn pine. Eve recognized the Maxwells' carriage among those at the hitching rail. A wooden sign suspended over the door read, NEWGATE TAVERN.

"Lucky I got here early," Thaddeus said while he hitched the Sarandons' team. "The management was about to give our rooms to another party, but I managed to persuade them not to."

"Good," Clifford said, helping Eve down. "Lord knows what would have happened if we'd been forced to look for other lodgings. Thad, the silver-tongued, saves the day again."

"Silver tongue, hah!" Eve whispered. "He promised the landlord four times his normal rate, is what he did."

"Shh," Clifford cautioned. "Would you rather have slept in a tent? Humor him. Thaddeus likes to feel important. I'm going to take Eve on in," he went on to the junior congressman. "She's pretty tired."

"Right with you," Thaddeus called, busy loosening the saddle on his horse.

The Newgate was pleasantly crowded with civilians and officers and a loud buzz of conversation filled the air. No sooner had Eve and Clifford entered than a bold, buxom Irish matron forced her way through the throng of guests. "Sorry, me friends," she said. "We're as full as a leprechaun's pockets."

"I wish to speak to the master of the tavern," Clifford said in his most impressive tone.

"Mistress, love. I'm Ellen Flanagan, and what I say goes." The woman dug her knuckles into her big-boned hips. A saucy smile lit her freckled face. Her carrot-red hair, gathered atop her head, was in complete disarray. Eve liked her immediately.

"This is Mr. and Mrs. Sarandon," Thaddeus said, entering late and catching the end of the conversation.

The Irishwoman brightened. "Ah, sure. The Mr. Sarandon for whom I'm holdin' Room 12. Welcome, sir, and Mrs. You're the last to arrive."

She showed them to the stairs. On the way across the large common room Eve noticed several familiar faces from Washington, older power wielders, already established in government and younger men very much like Clifford who had yet to secure their positions, but whose wealth and backgrounds assured that someday they would join the chosen ranks. Unable to free herself from the fatherly attentions of a medal-bedecked Union general, Gretchen Maxwell waved hello from the other side of the room, where she stood next to a young man dressed in a flamboyant uniform, complete with a white turban and scarlet trousers that ballooned from waist to ankle where the material was gathered by bands of canvas and thrust inside hightop leather boots. "What in heaven's name is *that?*" Eve asked, digging her elbow in Clifford's ribs and nodding her head in the soldier's direction.

"Fire Zouave," Clifford answered. "A New York regiment. Some damned European uniform they chose. Looks silly, if you ask me."

It did to Eve too. This isn't a war, she thought as they started up the stairs, her apprehension about being so far away from her son renewed. It's a costume ball. And everyone has come as a fool.

The trip had been simply too much for her first time out since James's birth. Bone tired, Eve had fled to the coolness of the upstairs bedroom after supper, and changed into a light dressing gown. That had been two hours earlier. Now, as dusk darkened into night, she sat before a vanity next to the four poster and brushed her long, golden hair. The room was comfortable enough. The walls were papered a pale blue with dark fleur-de-lis patterns. Wainscot chairs and a sofa were arranged in front of a soot-darkened hearth. An oil lamp burned on the mantel, another on the table to the left of the bed. The noise of celebration downstairs carried to every corner of the inn, but was thankfully muted by thick walls and floors.

"Mrs. Sarandon?" a voice called, followed by a knock on the door.

Startled, Eve jumped, then relaxed when she recognized the innkeeper's accent. "It's unlatched, Miss Flanagan."

The Irishwoman bumped the door open with an amply rounded hip. She carried a large covered pewter tray as easily as if it were a child's plate. "It's Missus," she announced.

Eve blushed. "I'm terribly sorry. I didn't . . ."

"It's all right. He wasn't much good for anything else other than givin' me a name. Still, folks around here appreciate a title." She set the tray on a small table beneath the corner window overlooking the street. "Even one so lowly as missus," she added with a wry grin.

"I know what you mean," Eve said sniffing the aroma of hot tea and cinnamon cakes. "For me?" she asked.

Mrs. Flanagan beamed. "Your husband said you were feelin' puny, and told me why. Thought I'd bring ye a little somethin' to cheer you up."

"That was very nice of you."

"Ah, tweren't nothing." She actually blushed. "Had to get out of that madhouse for a bit in any case." She glanced out the window, fanned herself with her hand. "You ever see anything like it? They'll be going until the break of day, like as not."

"It won't make any difference to me," Eve laughed softly. "I think I'm tired enough to sleep through double the noise."

Ellen Flanagan's voice was musical with the lilting rhythm of her forebears. "Two weeks ago there was nothing but the fireflies for entertainment," she said. Absentmindedly, she picked up one of the cinnamon cakes and plopped it in her mouth. "Well, back to the mines, as me father used to say."

"Please. Sit down," Eve said. "Have some tea. You've brought two cups."

The innkeeper grinned widely. "Actually, I was hopin' you'd ask. A bit of a breather is just what I need," she said, pouring a cup for Eve and another for herself.

A little self-conscious, Eve added honey to her tea and looked at the bobbing torchlights that illuminated Centerville. "This is very strange, really," she finally said.

"Oh? Why is that, dear?"

"Well, here we are invading, that is, the Union army is invading the South, and you don't seem at all perturbed."

"Perturbed?" The Irishwoman laughed aloud. "Dear heavens, child. Your husband has paid me thrice what this room is worth, and I've boosted the rates in similar fashion for every voice you hear below. Faith, I'm fifty years old and never seen the like. I only wish there was a war like this every week. I'd save enough in a summer to buy a cottage and farm in County Kerry and live my life there with nary a care but which blushing farm lad to take into me bed."

Eve joined her in laughter, then grew thoughtful. "How on earth did you come to Virginia, if you miss the—" she paused, took on an exaggerated Irish accent. "—old sod of Mother Ireland so much?"

Flanagan slapped her thigh. "By the hem of Saint Patrick's robe, but it was that man. Mark me words. Ask any woman how she has come to be where she doesn't want to be, and she'll tell you no less. A man."

"Oh, you exaggerate," Eve replied, nibbling at a teacake.

"You think so?" Flanagan leaned halfway across the table and tapped her nose with a pudgy forefinger. "I can tell you have no smell for battles, lass, so tell me why you're here."

"My husband," Eve admitted. "You are too wise."

"Wise?" Flanagan smiled. "Child, if something that obvious is wisdom, the merest child who can count his toes is as learned as the famed Aristotle. Ah, listen to me prattle on." She slid her chair back from the table. "I must be getting back. Can't leave those thieves who work for me untended for too long or I'll see not a silver penny in my cashbox, come morning."

"I enjoyed your company," Eve said, not ready to be left alone so soon. "And you've a lovely place. Maybe after this is settled, my husband and I will be able to visit again. With our boy, I think he'd take to you."

"And I to him. I've a soft spot for the wee ones, never having had one. And kind people too." A ragged cheer funneled up the stairway and through the open door. "Try to get some sleep."

"I will," Eve said. "Mrs. Flanagan?" Unaccountably, she found herself blushing. "You wouldn't by any chance know a family by the name of McKenna, would you?"

Mrs. Flanagan scratched the side of her nose. "Virginians?" she asked.

"Yes. That is, he said . . . Well, a man, actually. About thirty? He has a farm where he raises tobacco and horses. His name is Lion McKenna."

"McKenna. McKenna." Ellen Flanagan rolled the name around on her tongue. "A strong name," she muttered. "One I'd remember, if I'd heard it." She shook her head. "But I haven't. Friend of yours?"

"Not really," Eve said, hiding her disappointment. "An acquaintance, is all. Someone I knew. Once."

Flanagan touched Eve's arm. "Aye," she said softly. "We've all had acquaintances, someone we've known, once upon a time. But if there's one thing I've learned, they're best forgotten."

Eve recognized the tone of sadness in the older woman's voice. "Have you followed your own advice?" she asked.

The innkeeper's smile was wistful, and she shook her head slowly. "No, lass, I haven't. As they say, a fool listens to her own advice last of all."

"I don't think you're a fool at all," Eve said huskily. "Or ever have been."

"Hah! To bed with you, girl," Flanagan said brusquely, patting Eve's hand. "And have a pretty dream."

"I will," Eve said. "Thank you, Mrs. Flanagan."

The door closed softly. Alone, Eve crossed to the hearth and extinguished the lantern. The remaining light cast large shadows, as though, Eve thought, the room was populated with the ghosts of her past. She could feel Lion standing there watching her. From another corner her father cast a disapproving eye at her. Michael was there too. Dimly, she thought she could hear James Ruell crying. It was all so unreal, so unnerving. She stood in the center of the floor and, shivering, wrapped her arms around herself. The room's stillness pressed down on her, and she could feel death in the air.

"Marcy? Marcy!" Someone was tapping on the door. "Can I come in? It's me."

The ghosts whipped away into the night. Eve strode quickly to the door and locked it. "Go away," she said angrily.

"Aw, come on, Marcy." The speaker was obviously drunk. "Tonight may be our last chance, honey."

Eve had almost forgotten the reason everyone was in Centerville.

"Are you in the army?" she asked.

"You know I am, Marcy. Come on, let . . ."

"What's your name?"

"It's Jamie, honey. You just . . ."

Eve closed her eyes, leaned tiredly against the door. "Go away, Jamie whoever-you-are. You have the wrong room."

Silence. And then, plaintively, "You mean you aren't Marcy?"

"No. I'm not Marcy. Go away, please." One ear to the door, she listened as stumbling footsteps receded down the hall. "I hope you find her," Eve whispered to the unseen young officer. "Wherever she is, I hope you find her."

The key clicked in the lock and the door swung open, then closed again. Moving silently, Clifford walked to the bed and stared down at his sleeping wife. The windows in the room were all closed, and the air was hot and stuffy. Eve had taken off her gown, no doubt to be cool, and lay naked, save for her shoulders which were draped with a mantle of golden hair.

He stood for a long time without moving, transfixed by her beauty. He had refrained from making love to her when she was pregnant with Lion's child, and since that painful birth, Eve had claimed soreness and need for respite. To combat his need for her Clifford had thrown himself into his work and denied himself even the pleasure of the consummation of their marriage. Now, though, a little heady from drink, tired, and painfully aware of her body, he could not stop the images that flooded through his brain.

Her breasts rose and fell. A tiny dribble of milk ran down her left side. It was all he could do not to kiss it away. Her legs were parted slightly, her sex soft and beckoning. The desire to lie between her thighs, to plunge to the depths of her and rush his seed into her warmth was nearly overpowering. His boots slid off easily. Trembling, he undid his shirt, fumbled at his trousers and removed them. He leaned over and blew out the lantern.

"Clifford? Is that you?" Eve mumbled, half asleep.

The breath caught in his throat. "Yes," he said, kneeling on the edge of the bed.

"Would you get my gown, please?"

He paused, hand extended, almost touching her breast. I can, he thought. She will accept me. All I have to do is touch her, let her see and feel my need. . . .

But Clifford was not a rutting beast. More than anything in the world, he loved her, and had resolved to wait until Eve made the first move. He wanted her to want him: only then would she be totally his. Moving quietly, he picked up Eve's gown from the chair and handed it to her, then climbed into his own nightshirt while, still half asleep, Eve dressed and lay down again.

Slowly, painfully, the hardness drained from him. Clifford lay down beside Eve, folded his hands behind his head and stared at the ceiling in an attempt to forget the grinding, dull ache in his groin. It was hot. Groaning, unable to relax, he got up again and opened the windows. The air was cooler now, refreshing. One o'clock? Two? He couldn't remember. She was so beautiful, and he wanted her so badly.

"No," he growled to himself, clenching his fists. "Think of something else."

Brain muddled, Clifford lay down again. Eve stirred, mumbled sleep talk, and rolled over. Careful not to wake her, Clifford shifted so his knee touched the back of her thigh. Her skin was soft and felt cool, like silk. "I love you, Eve," he whispered. "I love you very, very much."

Eve shifted, poked her bottom closer to him so the front of his thigh lay along the back of hers. "Eve?" She didn't answer. Her breathing was even and soft. Clifford leaned forward and brushed his lips across her shoulder. "One day soon, my love. One day soon."

Chapter 17

Thunder in an empty room, rumbling through a hollow dream. For safety's sake, corridors of memory closed one by one. Thunder . . .

Eve sat upright and reached instinctively for her sleeping gown, only to discover she was already wearing it. Only then did she vaguely remember half waking during the night. "Clifford?" she said, groping for him.

The place next to her was empty, though clearly slept in. Her eyes adjusted easily to the half light of dawn creeping through the open windows. Alone with the thunder, she stretched and yawned deliciously. Rain would be a blessing after yesterday's stifling heat and choking dust, she thought, until the sudden realization that the sky was totally clear stripped away the last remnants of sleep. Eve stiffened, listened, as the sound cast a pall over the town's tranquility. Alarmed, she leaped from the bed and ran to the window. Across the street others could be seen at their own windows. Below, half-dressed men struggling with suspenders and shirttails stumbled into the street. There were no soldiers to be seen. Not one.

Residents of Centerville and early rising members of the invading army of visitors began to congregate along the street. Eve could imagine what they were talking about, what their excited gestures meant. Surely the same thing that burned in her mind. "It's started," she whispered. And in the distance, its increasing ferocity underscoring her most primitive forebodings, cannonfire rolled across the hills like a deadly storm. The battle they had come to see was underway.

In the stable Clifford calmed the mares, finished buckling their harness in place, and rewarded each animal with a carrot. Thaddeus Unger kicked at the dried droppings littering the floor. "Damn it," he growled.

"You're always hurrying me. I'm tired of it," Clifford said.

"It's not you," Unger explained. "If only I hadn't drunk so much. I could have been there to watch them ford the creek. General Heintzelman invited me. With luck, I could have witnessed the first volley."

"There'll be plenty enough shots before the day is over," Clifford sympathized. "Where are the Maxwells?"

"They left before dawn. Mrs. Ely asked Gretchen to come by early and help with the decorations at the courthouse. She intends the result to be quite splendid, or so I hear. But, of course, that sort of thing is for later."

The firing was growing heavier by the moment, and now seemed to come from everywhere to the south of them. "My God," Clifford said. "It sounds bigger than I thought it would be."

"That's a ruse," Unger explained importantly. "Heintzelman told me. They've put most of the cannon at the stone bridge and at the fords across Bull Run, south of the bridge. Mostly noise, really, to cover the real attack from the north, across Sudley Springs."

"Too complicated for me," Clifford said, strapping the picnic basket Ellen Flanagan's cooks had prepared for him. "Why don't you go ahead. I don't want to get Eve too close, anyway."

Unger wiped a silk kerchief across his forehead. "It was cool in the springtime," he said, ignoring Clifford. "Why couldn't they have done all this then?"

"Indecent of them really," Clifford agreed, amused by his companion's petulance. "What's that?"

Unger glanced down sheepishly at his coat pocket, tucked a pistol he was carrying back in place. "Singleshot Navy percussion," he said defensively. "Never can tell. I might get to wing a Reb with it."

"You're not a soldier," Clifford reminded him.

"Doesn't mean I can't do my duty as a citizen."

Clifford sighed. "Well, I have wine, cheese, sausage, and fresh bread. More than enough reasons to let McDowell and Heintzelman take care of the fighting. I'd better see about Eve. You waiting?"

The roar to the south swelled, subsided momentarily, then swelled again. Thaddeus's nose twitched, as if he was smelling the air. The mare at his side pawed the ground impatiently. "Going," he finally said. "See you later." Unable to restrain himself any longer, he jumped onto his horse and rode out toward the battle.

Clifford led the team outside and tethered it to the rail. The courtyard was a kaleidoscope of activity. Boys hired to help the inn's clientele rushed about on errands. Harried husbands tried to collect slow-moving wives. Excited by the confusion, horses reared and plunged, or balked and refused to move. Clifford made his way to the rear door and up the stairs, announced himself, and barged into the room. "You ready?" he asked.

Eve tied the last of her ribbons into place and adjusted her bonnet. "Just about. Except for the trunk."

"It'll be all right. I've booked the room for the next two days. Let's . . ."

"Clifford! . . ."

"Just as a precaution, Eve. Now, can we go?"

"I told Eustacia—"

"I know, I know. I told you just as a precaution. Meanwhile, we're missing the show. Could we *please*—"

"You needn't be so waspish, Clifford."

Clifford clenched his fists helplessly. Eve glanced one last time around the room and, unable to think of anything else she might need, reluctantly allowed herself to be led out the door and down into the main room. Ellen Flanagan entered from the kitchen. "Now, don't you two be worryin' about a thing. Not a soul shall approach your room, save for the maid. I'll see to that meself." Reddened hands planted on her hips, she grinned at Eve. "I'll never know what men see in war. There'd be nary a one if mothers ruled the world."

"And what would happen to business then?" Eve asked, remembering their conversation the night before.

"Ladies," Clifford said in an anguished tone. "Please? Some other time." Grabbing Eve by the wrist, he pulled her out the back door.

Half the inn's guests had left. Clifford hurried Eve into their gig, jumped in himself, and drove out of the courtyard. The street, normally an ordered thoroughfare, was a chaotic jumble of gigs and buggies and carriages. Complicating matters, a line of caissons and team-hauled twelve-pound rifled Parrot guns carved a path through the throng. Seizing the opportunity, Clifford steered his team into the rear of the line and called for Eve to hold tight.

The dust was horrible, worse than anything they had encountered the day before. "I thought the battle had started," Eve shouted in Clifford's ear.

"So did I," Clifford answered over the din. "Replacements or reserves, I guess."

"Perhaps we ought to turn back," Eve said, thoroughly frightened.

"No." Clifford looked more determined than ever. "We must keep on."

They did, as much because they had to as because Clifford wanted to. The army that had traveled the road during the night on the way to its positions had churned the clay into a fine dust that filled the air. Units that found themselves far behind schedule struggled to catch up. It took well over an hour to reach their first objective, the suspension bridge over Cub Run, and well over another hour to get past that bottleneck. At last, a hundred yards farther along, most of the military turned to the right down the narrow and winding road that led to the ford over Sudley Springs, where the Union Army was pouring into the Confederate left flank.

Relieved to be free of the press of the crowd, Clifford, Eve, and a dozen other civilian parties continued farther down the road. With so few soldiers to block their way the team went at a trot until, at a large post set in the ditch, they turned right and followed a weed-lined, seldom-traveled ribbon of dirt into the painfully green hills. "This is the road to Sharp's Hill," Clifford explained. "An officer told Thad, and he gave me directions. We ought to have a splendid view."

Except for the distant sound of firing it would have been impossible to imagine that a battle was being fought nearby. The air was clear, not yet too hot. Blackberry bushes dotted the empty land around them. Ahead, a covey of quail exploded from cover as the first team passed. Lush green grasses fringed the wheel ruts cut in the dry clay. At last they crested a slope. The drag on the gig eased, and it rolled to one side and stopped. Sharp's Hill was a rounded, grassy knoll without a speck of shade that overlooked the battlefield. Thankfully, a constant breeze stirred the long and undisturbed grass. "As long as the breeze holds, it shouldn't be too bad," Clifford said, sounding disappointed.

Almost every hillside within sight was populated with excited civilians who had come to watch. All around them people were getting out of carriages, tethering horses and teams, and spreading blankets. "It's a delightful place," Eve said. "Or would be, if men weren't dying over there."

Clifford, ignoring Eve's dark mood, stood in the gig and looked through the field glasses he'd brought along. "Not a bad view after all," he exclaimed. "Look."

Eve took the spare set of glasses and focused them slowly, as Clifford explained, to the best of his ability, what she saw. Immediately ahead Sharp's Hill swept down to a broad meadow that sunk, at its end, into the creek named Bull Run. Almost due west, nearly a mile ahead over a sharp bend in Bull Run, a horde of Union soldiers was crossing what Thaddeus had called Sudley's Ford. The glasses swung slowly to the south over more meadows on the other side of Bull Run. Beyond were gentle hills covered with thick stands of trees. Two or three farmhouses gave the scene a pastoral effect. The glasses moved on. Almost due south of them they could make out a bit of the Warrenton Turnpike and a stone bridge that crossed Bull Run. Just on the other side of the bridge an occasional soldier could be seen: it was their first glimpse of the enemy. As they watched, a distant shot sounded. A few seconds later a puff of dust on the other side of the bridge drove the soldiers to cover.

"Federal artillery," Clifford said, nudging Eve's glasses. "See by that big maple?" Eve focused her glasses just in time to see a puff of smoke, and seconds later heard the following report.

"My God," she murmured, swinging her glasses with morbid fascination. "But I don't see where it went."

"Off into the trees somewhere, undoubtedly," Clifford said laconically. "Well, not much going on yet. You hungry?"

"Mmm. I guess so."

"Me too," Clifford said, jumping down from the gig and hurrying around to help her.

Eve watched him as he ducked under the horse's neck. In the distance small puffs of smoke drifted among the trees. Where men were dying, she repeated to herself, suppressing a shudder. Where men were surely dying. Suddenly, Eve realized that Lion would never return. That part of her life was ended. What was past was past and now she must look to her—and Clifford's—future without pangs of remorse or hope for what would never be. The love she felt for Clifford did not match the secret, intense love for Lion. It was not a fiery love, not a blind love, but love nonetheless. Quiet, deep, affectionate. Warm and comfortable. A pleasant, cheerful love with which she could live and raise her child. She looked down at Clifford, his hands raised to help her out of the gig.

"Eve?" he asked. "Are you all right?"

"Yes," she said, letting him take her weight. His eyes were serious, intent. Slowly, even as she leaned toward him, he pulled her close and kissed her on the mouth. Eve found herself responding as she hadn't before, and let her mouth open under the pressure of his lips and exploring tongue.

After a moment she pulled away from him. "We can't . . . There are others . . ."

Clifford pulled her to him again and held her in his arms. "I don't care about others, Eve. I care about you."

"I know," she whispered. She looked up at him and, as if she were blind and was trying to memorize his features, traced her fingertips over his cheek and jaw and lips. "About last night?" she went on. He tensed. "I'm sorry. I was asleep."

"It's all right," he said softly.

She shook her head. "No. It isn't. The next time . . . I won't ask for my gown."

Clifford's eyes closed momentarily. When he opened them they shone brightly. "Is that a promise?" he asked huskily.

She was intensely aware of his body, of how his every curve fit hers, of the pressure of his manhood against her. "I love you, Clifford. That is a promise."

He was grinning. Wildly grinning. Exuberant, he held her at arm's length and whirled her around. Twirling crazily, head back and hair flying out straight, Eve laughed and, eyes wide open, watched the spinning sky reflect her heart.

The battle went on, faraway and virtually unnoticed. They picked blackberries and ate, passed the morning in pleasant conversation with the other spectators gathered on Sharp's Hill. Somewhere around ten one of the younger congressmen noted activity in the field across Bull Run. Everyone stood and gazed through his field glasses as part of the Union Army emerged from the line of trees and pushed back what must have been Confederate soldiers across the open ground. Shortly thereafter, the action came closer. No more than four hundred yards away, directly below them and to the south, two large detachments of Union forces could be seen. As they watched, the men crossed Bull Run at a ford no one had noticed before and moved to join the growing battle.

Questions were shouted back and forth from one carriage to another but no one knew or could figure out exactly what was happening. The soldiers at Sudley's Ford had all crossed, and that portion of the field was empty. The soldiers at the ford to the left of the hill had joined what appeared to be a formless melee that slowly moved from right to left until only Union forces could be seen in the brief clear spots where erratic winds blew away the gun smoke. Always, cannon belched and roared. Once, a roaring sound passed high over their heads and someone shouted that they were being bombarded. The spectators jumped to the ground and cowered next to their vehicles.

Inexplicably, the firing came to a halt. Slowly, the watching civilians rose one by one, brushed themselves off, and tried to overcome their fear and embarrassment with too loud jokes. Across Bull Run, as the wind blew away the smoke, crumpled bodies lay in the open. Stretcher bearers could be seen carrying their burdens to wagons, which headed immediately for the stone bridge over the turnpike. The spectators' fear gradually dissipated when nothing new happened for almost half an hour and talk turned to lunch. Soon blankets were rearranged and baskets opened. Clifford sliced a helping of summer sausage, made a sandwich of it, and refilled his glass. "This is a damned fine burgundy," he remarked.

Thaddeus Unger lay stretched out flat on his back. He had arrived an hour earlier, after having been chased away from Sudley's Ford by an officious lieutenant. A crumb of cheese clung to his moustache. "Lunch break," he said, waving one arm toward the quiet battlefield.

"A hell of a way to fight a battle." He ran his tongue over his teeth. "What time is it, anyway?"

"A few minutes after two," Eve said, without looking up.

"Aren't you going to check your watch?" Thad asked.

"Not against my mariner wife," Clifford said, grinning when Eve made a face by way of retort.

"What are you reading?" Unger asked, and rolled onto his side.

"Henry IV, Part I."

"I've read that." When Eve glanced at him, he said, "Does it surprise you? After all, I'm not illiterate." He brushed the cheese crumb away. "One thing is for sure. Shakespeare's battle scenes are far more exciting than what we've seen today. Or haven't seen."

He waved a hand toward the horizon. As if on cue cannon from both armies let loose a thunderous roar. Before the suddenly excited spectators could get to their feet and focus their glasses, a soot-gray haze hung over the whole southern and western horizon. The battle was underway again.

Within range of their glasses men made invisible by smoke and dust fought and died. Because they were invisible, like tiny toy soldiers, it was difficult to imagine that they bled or screamed or died. The battle ceased to have meaning for many. Some of the spectators gave up and left for Centerville to prepare for the ball that night. Eve found herself wishing more than ever that she had not left Washington, that she had never allowed herself to be a witness to the obscene, macabre drama that was being played out before her. She wanted only to leave. Suddenly, Thaddeus stood and started toward his horse.

"Where are you going?" Clifford asked.

Thad tightened the horse's cinch, cocked his bowler at a jaunty angle, and mounted. "Across the ford. I want to watch us win. I certainly can't see anything from here."

"Don't be a fool," Clifford said.

"I'll be back. From the sound of it, we've taken the day. Probably just a rearguard action. I suspect the Rebs are pretty well whipped," he said. Not to be dissuaded, he spurred his horse down the slope and plunged recklessly across the field into the trees. They caught only a glimpse of him before he crossed the ford and disappeared into the haze.

A horse whinnied. Startled, Eve woke, rubbed her arm where the book had left an indentation in her flesh. Clifford was standing, watching a mounted officer who had emerged from the blackberry bushes. The officer did not move. "Hello," Clifford finally called, "won't you join us?"

Eve looked around. They were alone on the hill. An almost preternatural silence had settled over the afternoon, and she felt goose bumps on her arms, as if something dire had happened. The officer's horse was wet with sweat and near exhaustion. Eve noticed the cavalryman's right trouser leg had been torn away to the thigh, revealing the baby pinkness of his leg. His right foot was bootless as it fitted the stirrup. Other than that, his uniform was impeccable, and he did not appear to be wounded.

"Will you . . . uh . . . have some sausage?" Clifford asked, trying to sound friendly in case the rider thought them an enemy. There was no answer. Disconcerted, he glanced at Eve, who started past him toward the officer. "Don't, Eve," he snapped.

"He might be wounded where we can't see."

"And he might be mad," Clifford whispered, more than a little awed.

Eve took a few more tentative steps. The officer looked to be in his midtwenties. He sported a closely trimmed moustache that flowed into long, luxurious sideburns that were now bedraggled and scorched. His hair looked to be a smoky-brown. The horse lifted his head as Eve, then Clifford, neared. The man blinked his eyes but continued to stare straight ahead. At least he isn't dead, Eve thought thankfully, reaching for the horse's bridle. "We have water," she said aloud. "Would you like some water?"

"I'm Clifford Sarandon of the Department of State," Clifford added in a soothing tone. "This is my . . ."

The officer, as if in a trance, slowly turned his horse. Not knowing what to do, Eve let go the bridle. The animal sauntered through the underbrush.

". . . wife." Clifford finished lamely as officer and horse disappeared. "Well. What do you make of that?" he finally asked, turning to Eve.

Eve didn't answer. She walked to the edge of the hill and looked down across the meadow to Bull Run. The cloud of hazy smoke that had long since obscured their view of the battle had expanded until it blotted out the entire southern landscape. Pressed on by a brisk breeze from the southeast, it billowed and rolled toward them. As she watched, the gray, amorphous mass covered the meadow below her, lapped at the base of the hill, and, as if seeking her, started upward. "Clifford!" Eve said, frightened.

His hand gripped her arm. "I'm right here," he said, transfixed by the phenomenon.

"I want to leave."

The cloud swelled before them and engulfed the summit. Eve began to cough as her lungs rebelled against the acrid smell of gunsmoke, the stench of dead flesh that had been lying in the sun for almost a whole day, and the salt-sweet aroma of fear.

"Let's get out of here," Clifford said, leading her back to the carriage. "Forget the food. Just get in."

Made skittish by the blinding smoke and strange, unsettling odors, the animals fought the reins. Eve's eyes began to water, but she forced them to remain open as Clifford attempted to guide the frightened team down the slope and along the narrow path, made treacherous now by the lack of visibility. The carriage lurched to one side. Eve grabbed Clifford's arm. "Easy," he said. "Just a little farther. Can you see the path?"

"I think so."

"It gets worse the lower we go. Wet a kerchief and hold it over your nose."

"I can't. The water is with the picnic basket."

"Damn!"

Snorting with fear, the horses plunged and tried to escape. Clifford was sweating heavily as he tried to keep them to the double ruts that he knew would lead them to the turnpike and safety. Suddenly, a new and undefinable sound coiled on the air, a sound like a dull, insistent drumroll.

"What's that?" Eve asked, fighting for control.

"God, I don't know. Hold on." They had reached the bottom of the hill and now had only a few hundred yards to go to the turnpike. Clifford whipped the horses, but the thick smoke still slowed them. Trees appeared out of the milky substance and as quickly receded. As they neared the turnpike the noise became louder. Gradually the mist thinned, but the smell remained. "Only a few more yards, and we'll . . ." Clifford began, then suddenly fell silent.

Three Zouaves had appeared out of the underbrush and were running toward the carriage. "Hold there. For God's sake, hold!" Soot-blackened hands caught at the team. "Make room, sir. Please." The man's eyes were wide as saucers. His two companions looked to be equally terrified. "My 'listment's up today. I don't fancy gettin' killed."

"Release your hold, man!" Clifford shouted, as terrified of them as they were of whatever they had run from.

"Hurry up, you two bastards. This here gig's our ticket," the Zouave shouted to his companions.

The horses tried to rear. Clifford leaned forward precariously and struck with his whip, slashing the forked tip across the man's face. The soldier howled and fell back; the gig charged forward. Eve screamed. Clifford lashed the animals' rumps. The Zouave's companions leaped to either side of the path. Dead ahead the turnpike swung into view, and the source of the ominous sound they had been hearing became obvious. A thousand and more pounding hooves, a thousand and more tramping feet. A thousand and more carriages and caissons and ambulances and wagons moved along the turnpike, northeast, away from the battle. Somehow, the battle the Federals were supposed to win was going the other way. The Union forces were retreating.

The chest-binding fear of the civilians trying to make their way through the retreating soldiers was contagious. Past thought, incapable of speech, Eve clung to the seat as if mesmerized. Clifford, cursing and battling the horses, swung the gig onto the roadway and narrowly missed a team hauling a caisson, to which clung a full dozen or more soldiers. Men on foot gave way only enough to barely miss being run over. A carriage pulled by a team of four matched grays sped past them. Eve recognized Senator Fry and his wife clinging to each other as their driver, with no thought for anyone else, forced his way through the mass of men and vehicles.

It was as if they had plunged into a seething, flooded river of men and animals and vehicles. The current raced on, oblivious to everything but the fear that impelled it. The only noise, and that filling the air almost as palpably as the dust, was the dull tread of feet and hooves, and the insane squeaking and creaking of wooden wheels.

And then a new sound intruded. Just as they had heard earlier on Sharp's Hill, a low humming passed overhead, followed by an explosion to their left. The fleeing mass seemed to sigh and move a little faster. "My God, we're being shelled!" a voice screamed.

Another shell exploded, this time overhead. Whirring fragments of iron sliced through the air and the canopy of the gig. Off to one side a horse screamed and went down, partially blocking the road. Clifford was trying to whip the team into greater speed, but the road ahead was clogged. Eve glanced behind them. Now even the soldiers had panicked. A dense mass of shouting, fleeing men and wagons covered the ground as far as the eye could see in the dust. The soldiers who still had weapons began to fire over their shoulders, as if the entire army of the South was at their backs. Mindless in their fear, they loaded and shot again and again as they walked or ran. The deadly hail cut down their own friends and comrades.

Another explosion, this one from far in front of them, revealed the strategy of the Rebel batteries. Ahead was the suspension bridge that crossed Cub Run. If that bridge were destroyed the pandemonium as men and horses and wagons attempted to traverse the muddy creek bottom would be incredible.

"We've got to get across!" Clifford shouted, more to himself than Eve. "We've got to make the bridge. Come on, damn it!" he screamed, laying his whip to the team.

They passed Senator Fry's carriage. They wove between a pair of caissons and swerved to barely miss a disabled cannon lying on its side. A shell exploded to their left. The horses shied and the gig tipped onto two wheels. Eve screamed and threw herself toward Clifford. The action threw more weight on the left side of the gig, which righted itself and careened onto the suspension bridge over Cub Run. Little blocked their way now. A pair of officers, riding low on the necks of their horses, passed them. Whipping the mares, Clifford stood and roared in triumph. Eve realized that she was yelling jubilantly.

Suddenly, the world exploded before her eyes. Dust blinded her. Hot metal screamed through the air. One piece passed through her skirts which, being thick, saved her from injury. More quickly than it took to think, they were through the flying dirt and across the bridge. Eve looked back in time to witness a second, and then a third, explosion bracket the bridge. To her horror the Senator's carriage was blown into the creek and a trio of cavalrymen was obliterated. A caisson overturned, another crashed into it. A wagon loaded with Washington's elite piled into the mess, spilling its occupants. Incredibly, no one seemed to notice. Men, horses, and vehicles kept coming on, swerving at the last moment and plunging down the bank and into the creek, there to be caught by the exploding Confederate shells.

Eve couldn't bear to watch. Her right hand clutching the seat, the back of her left hand caught painfully between her teeth, she stared, transfixed, straight ahead.

"They beat us," Clifford groaned, slowing the horses. "Dear heaven. What's to stop them from taking Washington?"

Eve shuddered. She didn't know. The panic would be even worse there. Already, she felt it building. The premonition she'd had two days earlier was now a stark reality. James was alone with Eustacia and Winnie and the wet nurse. No matter what happened she had to reach home, had to find her child and get him away to safety. The turnpike seemed empty in comparision to that morning. Clifford steered around wrecked carriages and through the vanguard of dispirited soldiers that had started the catastrophic flight from the battlefield. But something was wrong. Each motion, each expenditure of energy, elicited a moan. Sweat beaded his forehead. His face contorted in pain despite his efforts to hide the fact. "Clifford?" Eve asked, noticing at last.

"It's nothing," he grimaced. "Crossing the bridge. A fragment from one of those damned shells got me in the thigh, is all. I'll be all right." He whipped the reins in an effort to bring the tiring horses back to a gallop. "I never should have brought you."

"It's James I'm worried about," Eve said.

"I know." Clifford gritted his teeth as he swerved to miss a dead horse in the middle of the road.

"And you, now. Maybe we'd better stop and check . . ."

"I said I'd be all right," Clifford snapped. "We'll keep on. To Washington, you hear?"

Centerville loomed ahead. Eve thought Clifford would turn toward the Newgate Inn, but he steered instead into the first stable they came to. "Two fresh horses and be quick," he called as the stablekeeper looked up from his seat by the doorway.

The man was painfully slow. He inspected the mares, finally came around to Clifford's side of the gig. "If you mean to trade, them two of yours is about blowed. Hell, it'd take a week to rest 'em."

Clifford peeled two hundred dollars from the roll of bills in his coat pocket and tucked them into the man's shirt pocket. "Any two that can run," he said, holding another hundred in plain view.

Three hundred dollars was enough to galvanize the stablekeeper. Whistling for his helper he undid the harness, led the mares off, and replaced them with a pair of sturdy chestnut geldings. As soon as the last buckle was fastened, Clifford handed him the final hundred and put his whip to the new team.

Minutes, beat to the pounding rhythm of the horses' hooves, became years. By evening the heat that had been nearly intolerable became even more enervating as clouds moved in and the humidity rose. Their clothes stuck to them in a grimy mixture of sweat and dust. Clifford's face was pale and sweat streamed from his forehead. Gradually his movements slowed, became sluggish and clumsy. "Eve," he said at last, slumping exhausted against her. "Oh, Eve. I'm sorry."

"Give me the reins," Eve said, taking them before they fell from his hands. Dusk and dust combined to make the turnpike barely visible. Fearful of the scattered travelers who cluttered the roadway, Eve slowed the animals' pace to a mile-eating trot instead of the tiring full gallop.

"Don't care 'bout others," Clifford mumbled almost incoherently. "Just 'bout you." He was burning with fever, and his leg felt swollen and throbbed dully. The light was strange. Diffused by the heavy clouds, it emanated from everywhere and clarified the world with a bright yellow-orange glow that only gradually faded.

They were nearing Washington. Eve brushed a strand of limp curl from her eyes and concentrated on the road ahead. Clifford was a dead weight against her, now, and dreadfully pale in the waning light. Eve drove with one arm around him, the other handling the reins. "Stay well, Clifford," she whispered through gritted teeth. "I'll give you a child. A child of your own."

More minutes, punctuated by cries demanding that she stop. Hours, creeping slower than dreams that never seem to end. Shapes rose up from a squat patch of heavy shadow. "Stop!" they called. "Who goes there?"

It had begun to drizzle. Eve's arms felt as though they were hung with heavy weights. She felt drained and wanted to collapse, but Clifford needed help, and her baby waited. Even if the Confederates did take Washington the next day, she was determined to get husband and child to safety. At last the lights of a frightened capital appeared through the mist. Heads popped out of windows. Men stopped and stared. Children ran alongside. Ahead, the Long Street Bridge crossing the Potomac beckoned. They were close. At last, close.

Creaking wheels, the jingle of harness, the clip-clop, clip-clop of slowing horses, tired and blown and sweaty.

"Who goes there?" Two sentries lunged from either side of the entrance to the bridge and caught the traces.

Eve tried to speak, but she was too tired. No words came. She tried to lift her hand to indicate Clifford. Her hand fell limply to her lap.

"I'll be damned. It's a woman. Must be one of them from the battle."

"Course she is, you idiot." A face leaned close. It was a handsome face, for all its whiskered, meanish look. It smiled. "Ma'am?"

"My husband . . . Wounded . . . Needs help . . ."

"Is he a soldier?" a young sentry asked, leaving the horses' heads and going to Clifford.

Eve managed to shake her head no. "Clifford Sarandon." The words came slow as winter molasses and required infinite effort. "State Department . . . Needs doctor . . . Please? . . ."

"It's all right, miss," the soldier said. His voice was strangely gentle. "Don't you fret. We'll see you both to a doctor. You're among friends . . ." Clumsily, he dropped his rifle and caught Eve as she pitched head first into his arms. "Why, she's fainted on me. Here, now, miss." He slapped her face, but she didn't respond. "Now ain't that somethin'. Fainted dead away."

"Just as well," the young sentry said. He pulled his hand away from Clifford's chest and stepped back from the gig.

"An' what's that supposed to mean?" the other one asked as he eased Eve to the ground.

The eighteen-year-old pulled off his cap. The increasing rain beat on his bared head. His face looked older than its years. "Jest as well in her condition," he said, his face white in the deepening dusk. "Her friend here's dead."

Chapter 18

Ashes from a nearby field drifted incongruously like snowflakes in the warm summer sun. Someone was burning underbrush. Eve watched the flakes sift through the air and fall one by one, now on the green grass, now in the dark hole, now on the warm earth piled to one side. The ashes of labor quietly mingled with the ceremony honoring the dead. The irony of ashes and dust seemed to be lost on the mourners.

Do the dead grieve? Can they ever?

Eve brushed a curl from her cheek, tucked it under the severe black scarf. Let the dead bury the dead, she thought. Let great men suffer eulogies. Rest, Clifford. Rest.

". . . Thy kingdom come," the pastor intoned. "Thy will be done . . ."

Done. Eve glanced at Hébert. Head bowed, chin jutting down against his rumpled gray ascot, his eyes closed as tightly as clenched fists. How could things have become so . . . so utterly botched? Life had caught them laughing and killed their joy aborning. So much had been promised that had not been fulfilled. And I am widowed twice, Eve thought. Once atop the cliffs of Dawn Wind where I stood and watched Lion sail away into the distance, and now by death's greater distance. I'm so very sorry, Clifford. Almost his last words to her. So very, very sorry.

"Amen." The pastor's voice rang confidently on the bright air. The echoing chorus from Hébert, Sewal, and Justin was more tentative, as if they, more worldly than the man who had taken the cloth, did not view their mortality as such a small matter.

Eve, who had not been paying attention, felt Justin's arm tighten on hers. "Amen," she added hastily, wondering how much else she had missed. Was it over so quickly? A few words, a prayer, a scattering of awkward amens? She wanted to make them stop, to tell them there had to be more. Life ended too abruptly to be so easily dismissed and packed away underground. The dead somehow had to be told that those they left behind cared more than the perfunctory rituals played out over their bodies would lead them to believe.

Too late she tried to step forward and speak up. As Justin's arm restrained her the minister nodded grimly, and four young farm workers stepped around the mound of dirt, seized the ropes passed under the coffin, and lowered it into the rectangular wound in the earth. When they finished the ropes whispered out from under the coffin, snaked into coils around two of the young men's arms, and disappeared.

"Now," Justin whispered in her ear.

"I can't," Eve breathed. "I can't, Justin."

"Yes, you can. You have to," he hissed, propelling her forward.

Eve's feet felt like lead, her legs like brittle stalks of corn dried too long in the sun. In a daze she forced herself to walk the three steps to the gravesite. Her mouth was dry and her eyes burned. She glanced around. They were all watching her, waiting for her. Not a shred of emotion showed on their faces. How can you stand there like that? she wanted to scream. Is it forbidden to cry?

Slowly, her head bowed. She herself had not cried. Not cried for Clifford. Not yet, anyway. Someday, though, when she was alone. Her face stiff, masklike, she grasped a single clod of earth and held it over the open grave, the ultimate symbol of finality. When her fingers let go, it fell slowly. A hollow, dull thud was all the sound it made.

Justin helped her to her feet. "We can make room for you in the carriage," he said, steering her away from the gravesite.

"I'd better ride back with his father," Eve answered. Her voice sounded hollow and far away.

"Are you sure?"

"Yes."

"You'll be all right?"

"Yes."

"I'll see you at the hotel, then."

"Yes."

Justin nodded and left her to speak his brief condolences to Hébert. Nearby, Sewal waited awkwardly, still expecting Eve to walk with him. When she shook her head and smiled bleakly he turned and followed Justin to their carriage.

Hébert stood alone at the side of the grave. Eve's black gown rustled on the grass as she crossed to his side and touched his arm. Hébert jerked as if burned, looked up from his son's coffin, and stared at Eve for a long, dispassionate moment. Behind her the rolling hills were alive with yellow-and-white wild flowers that lined the newly graded road to Tarrytown, the picturesque upstate New York town Hébert had chosen for the family's country home.

"You never know," he said dully. His arms bent at the elbows, he held out his hands in a gesture that might have been either supplication or despair. "One hundred sixty acres, where a gentleman farmer might escape the pressures of the city. Where someday he can watch his grandchildren grow. Where he can, once the years have narrowed the natural schisms between generations, sit and share the hours with his . . ."

He faltered, cleared his throat. His hands dropped to his sides. "I've always liked apple trees. That's why I laid out this plot here, among them. I thought the first marker would bear my name, never . . ." He cleared his throat again. "Never . . . Clifford's. When word reaches Angelique . . ." He stopped, calculating the time it took a clipper ship to reach Normandy, where his wife was visiting her family. She would have need of their solace and comfort.

"Well!" He blinked, exhaled mightily, and drew himself up. His brief moment of weakness had passed and, embarrassed by it, he glowered at Eve. "I suppose you've decided what you'll do?" he asked gruffly.

"Why, go home, of course," Eve answered.

"But which home?" Hébert pressed. "Washington? New York?"

Eve had tried to bury the animosity between them since Hébert had learned that James Ruell was not Clifford's son, but his tone grated against her. "We both know I have only one home, Mr. Sarandon," she answered coldly.

"Then Maine." Hébert nodded. "And the child?"

"Will be raised there."

One eyebrow raised. "Do you think that's wise?"

"Dawn Wind will be a good place for my son," she answered quietly. She wanted to say more, but held her tongue.

Hébert looked as if he might offer a comment by way of rebuttal, but decided against it. Still, he couldn't hide a grimace.

"You disapprove?" Eve asked, the anger growing. "I thought you'd be delighted. It's perfectly obvious that any familial affections you might have toward us begin and end there," she snapped, pointing into the grave.

Hébert flinched as if he had been struck. "Isn't that a bit callous?"

he said, his face white. "I know I have been harsh with you, but—"

"You are a man who loved his son very much," Eve interrupted. "Your son married a woman pregnant with another man's child. You cannot forgive that."

"You are very frank," Hébert said, his voice kept under stony control.

"As I was with Clifford. And whatever you may think, I did love him. But I hid nothing from him. I did not bewitch him, I did not trick him. I tried to drive him off, refused his affections, at first, and pleaded with him to find someone else."

"That is nice to know." Hébert's voice was mocking, sarcastic.

"Your attitude does not become you," Eve said frostily. "Nor him." Unable to face her father-in-law a moment longer, she kneeled abruptly. Her stomach was churning violently. She felt ill. Mindlessly, she scooped a handful of dirt and let it trickle through her fingers. A light breeze blew some of the sandy soil into the grave.

"Exsanguination." Hébert's voice was hollow, infinitely sad. "What an ungodly, unholy word." His head shook slowly. "Such a little wound to bleed away my son's life. Dollars, companies, property. All of them I would have given. Even myself. So if I seem too angry . . . I like to think of myself as a gentleman. I do not . . . ah . . ." His voice trailed off and he stood motionless. Finally, he reached out a hand as if to touch Eve, then withdrew it and rubbed his palm over his eyes. At last he donned his hat and started toward the waiting carriage.

Eve felt him leave, reached out, and placed her hand on the warm earth that would soon cover Clifford. Not too many yards away the four farmhands leaned on their shovels and waited for her to leave. Eve closed her eyes. "Oh, Clifford, Clifford," she whispered softly enough for only him to hear. "Don't worry. Your father is upset. I understand. He thinks me to blame." She sighed, remembered the tiny, almost invisible hole in Clifford's blood-engorged thigh, and how his life might have been saved, had she but known. "Maybe I am."

The journey back to New York was a quiet, somber drive with the Blackheath carriage in the lead. Curtains pulled aside to let in the country air, Eve and Hébert rode silently in the trailing Sarandon coach. Hébert's driver, a sallow, lank individual named Guffrey, kept the team moving at a steady pace.

Eve's exhaustion was nearly total. The last three days, starting with the flight from the hill overlooking the battle, had been one ceaseless emotional drain. Heat, dust, and fear had left her limp. Clifford's death put her in a state of shock that the unending arrangements and hurried travel to New York had not alleviated. With Clifford's burial and the realization that he was gone forever, what little strength she had left fled, and she fell into a deep sleep before the carriage left Tarrytown. She slept without moving for the first hour, until the initial exhaustion was dulled and the dreams began. Once again, cannon roared. Men shrieked and lifted bloody stumps where limbs had been. Animals reeled in wide-eyed terror. She and Clifford drove through the thick cloud of dust, careened between disabled vehicles. The black road down which they raced stretched out before her. Clifford was slumped at her side. No matter how she called, how she shook him, he did not respond. As the weary, panic-stricken miles passed, he weighed more and more, until she thought he would crush her. Ahead, bright lights waited, shone into her eyes. "Help!" she screamed. "Help me!"

"Eve! Wake up. Wake up!"

Her eyes flew open. She was leaning against Hébert. The sun streamed through the carriage window and bathed her face. Embarrassed, sluggish with sleep, she pushed herself erect and sat stiffly, hands to either side of her on the seat.

"You were dreaming," Hébert said, concern in his voice.

"Yes," Eve answered.

"Will you be all right?"

"Yes, thank you."

"Here." He slid open a panel on the front wall of the coach and pulled a bottle of brandy and a snifter out of a concealed cabinet. "Drink some of this. You'll feel better."

The brandy burned. Eve relaxed, leaned back, and gazed out the window. The afternoon was getting on. Dazed, not thinking of anything, she watched the sun slant through the trees along the side of the road, watched occasional birds appear and disappear in the woods. How long she sat that way she didn't know, but at last the trees gave way and they were approaching New York.

The ferry docked. The trip was nearly ended. The rush of wind and the chatter of water birds gave way to the creak of axles and the incessant, madly rushing voices of New York City. Country colors were replaced by the drab browns and dingy grays of streets and buildings and soot-streaked windows. They were surrounded by a symphony of voices. Exotic languages and accents spilled around one another, coiled and rippled in robust themes and counterthemes, stuttered with staccato briskness from window to window, slurred melodiously along alleys, dabbled in the cultured pianissimo of the fortunate wealthy, and roared in the angry fortissimo of the strident poor.

The screams and shouts of brawling, tumbling children. The cries of fishmongers, ragpickers, and peddlers. The gab of hackney drivers and deliverymen and clerks and factory workers and policemen and housewives. A man can't buy a decent horse for love nor money. My heavens, cotton is ridiculous, but that's to be expected, have you seen the new melodrama at Nell's? And the cost of bread is skyrocketing. What about them new posters? Think of it! Regiments being formed all over the place. A two-hundred-dollar bonus for a six-month enlistment, and a dollar a day from then on in. Better than a man can do in this godforsaken place. Give me back my hoop, Charlie, and out of the way with you and your wagon, bud, 'fore I bust your spokes and cave in your bloody head.

The slate-colored stone façade of the Fifth Avenue Hotel was unadorned by recruitment posters. Any of the lower classes, the boisterous riffraff who chanced that way were scooted along with a prod from the patrolman on duty or the liveried doorman. Here the voices were muted. There was talk of the war, of who was to blame for the disaster at Bull Run and of when Washington would fall. Arguments couched in civil tones rose and fell over coffee and liqueurs. Some wanted revenge for the Union embarrassment and concocted ways to bring the Rebels to their knees. Others stated emphatically that the upstart Confederacy should be allowed to go its own way. A few, those who had been schooled in death, sat silently and wondered. The majority speculated on profit and loss, but mostly profit with armaments to be forged, uniforms to be cut and dyed and sewn, shoes to be stitched, food to be purchased from the ripe full granaries of the midwest, and fortunes to be made for the daring and quick, yes, fortunes, do you hear?

Guffrey reined the team to a halt behind the Blackheath carriage. Immediately, the door opened and a white-haired porter dressed in the hotel's livery helped Eve from the coach.

"Will I see you before you leave for France, Mr. Sarandon?" Eve asked through the open door.

"I . . . I don't know." He seemed surprised by the question, as if his mind had been far away. "Today is Wednesday, my ship leaves Friday. I shall be very busy."

"I see," Eve said, "I suppose, then . . ." She trailed off. It was obvious that he was barely aware of her presence, or the fact that she was leaving. "Good-bye, Mr. Sarandon," she said softly, at the same time turning to enter the hotel.

"Eve!" Hébert called her back, and then, too embarrassed to look at her directly, stared at the floor of the cab. "I am not . . . that is, I am not putting you off. I *will* be busy. And I am worried about Angelique. I should never have sent word. Perhaps I am a coward and could not bring myself to share her initial distress. I was very thoughtless." He sat back. Shadows obscured his face. "Perhaps in more ways than one," he said in a voice that was barely audible. "Will you accept my apology, Eve?"

And so it is left to me to show compassion, Eve thought, hating the bitterness and rancor she still felt. "Clifford thought of James Ruell as his own son, Mr. Sarandon. I hope someday you will be able to accept him as your grandson."

Hébert nodded, and his hand lifted in the briefest gesture of farewell. Eve closed the door. The last she saw of him was his hand, white in the dark interior of the carriage, as he rapped on the roof with the cane. When Eve stepped back Guffrey laid his whip to the rump of the lead horse, and the carriage pulled away from the curb and disappeared in the flow of coaches, hansom cabs, and trolleys that clogged Fifth Avenue.

People stood aside for Sewal Blackheath. The imperial aura retained from his years as a captain at sea clung to him and parted crowds. He was brusque and certain. When other residents of the Fifth Avenue Hotel were soft spoken, Sewal tended to bellow, especially if service was slack or uncaring. The staff might have hated him were he not so generous when pleased. Following her father at a discreet distance, Eve passed through a crowd of chattering guests exchanging recently acquired news beneath the ostentatious chandeliers that dominated the lobby. A single staircase broad enough to accommodate a dozen men standing abreast carved a gracious arc from the vast, ornate lobby to the quiet mezzanine where the Blackheath suite was located.

Justin had already disappeared, probably to prowl the streets of the city he loved so much. Sewal hurried into the seclusion of his room. Sighing, Eve entered her own room, only to be greeted by Eustacia holding her finger to her lips. She tiptoed to the bassinet where her son slept and, for the first time that day, felt at peace and happy.

"Happy birthday, Doozie," she whispered. His tiny chest appeared not to move. As always when he slept Eve held her hand in front of his face to reassure herself. A faint, barely discernible breath caressed her finger. His face was as serious as a politician's. And old-looking. Or wise, Eve thought. The wisdom of innocence. "Oh, James, James," she crooned. He would never be as sure of himself as he was at that very moment. Each day, each month, each year would compound the uncertainties of life. Nothing would ever be as simple as youth, when life was as smooth and unblemished as his skin. "Six weeks, baby. Six weeks old. Do you feel like an old man?"

Still, he slept. James Ruell was going to have dark hair. The blond wisps with which he had entered the world were already changing. Eve leaned over and puffed gently. His hair moved like down. His tiny fingers stretched and clenched in a pink fist and his eyes half opened, then closed again. Eve wondered if they would become gray like his father's, but that train of thought was rife with danger. Disconcerted, she pulled the light sheet over him and moved away from his cradle to Eustacia. "Did he eat well?" she asked.

Eustacia grinned. "Don't he always? Les' see. You left at six, the wet nurse come at ten, like you said to. I give him some of that bottle stuff at noon, an' the wet nurse come again around three." She glanced at the grandfather clock next to the door. It was almost five thirty. "I suspect he's gonna be ready for his mama any minute now."

"I *know* his mama's going to be ready for him," Eve said, sighing with fatigue. She sagged in a chair. "Oh, it's been a long day."

"Mr. Clifford?" Eustacia asked, standing behind the chair and massaging Eve's neck.

"All over with." Eve shook her head. "I still can't believe it, Eustacia. One thing goes wrong, and the world falls apart. Just when you think you've put things back together again . . . I just can't believe it." She sighed. "That feels good."

"You'll feel better when you get back home."

"Um. A little to the left." Luxuriating in Eustacia's soothing massage, she let her head loll forward. "I don't know, Eustacia. So much has happened. Lion and the baby and Clifford—and now this. I feel so different. I don't know if I can go home again."

"Pshaw, girl!" Eustacia gently shook Eve's shoulders. "That big old house, an' the breeze. Them cool Maine mornin's with the sun comin' up over the ocean. The smell of pine an' all. Curtains billowin' out of the windows. *And* my cookin'. Honey, three months an' this'll all be like a dream that never happened, 'ceptin' for little Doozie, of course." She paused, and her voice turned a little wistful. "Speakin' of which, when are we goin'?"

"Friday, I think."

"Good. I been gone too long. It don't do that man of mine no good to be on his own. I reckon he's got poor Mr. Pole—Oh, oh. There he goes."

A squawl had erupted from the cradle. Eustacia left Eve and hurried to check on James Ruell. "Um, um, honey," she said, picking him up and rocking him back and forth. With the baby in her arms she reverted to the old rhythms and sounds of the South. "I swear, I don' know if you be wetter or hongrier," she crooned. James let out a howl. "Hongrier? Well, you tell your mama to get ready, an' I'll get you ready. Get some food in this chile's belly . . ."

The stream of soothing words went on as Eustacia undressed, bathed, and redressed him. Across the room Eve removed her blouse and chemise. By the time her son was ready she was waiting with a shawl over her shoulders.

Dried but still hungry, James Ruell was a kicking, squirming bundle of life. Eustacia handed him to Eve, waited until he found a nipple, then, smiling, slipped from the room.

The door closed. At last Eve was alone, or as alone as she wanted to be. Sounds drifted up from the street, but so muddled and muted as to mimic the roar of the sea. Eve leaned back and closed her eyes, let the weariness and tension drain out of her. Lion was gone. Clifford was gone. Now there was only her and James Ruell. Images swam into focus, shimmered, and disappeared: the only thing she was aware of was the steady, pleasant pressure at her breast as her son nursed. And then that too, disappeared, and Eve slept.

Chapter 19

The human heart can sustain only so much grief. The dank, dark reaches of the heart and mind are inhabitable only for a short time for those who are strong. Rejuvenation is an automatic reflex: life asserts itself and banishes, if not the grief itself, the despondency generated by grief. For life does, after all, go on. Eve cradled James, let him search for and find her breast, and then let herself enjoy the sensation of watching and feeling him eat. By the time he had his fill, Eustacia had drawn her bath. The water felt good, and refreshing. If she hadn't been so hungry herself she would have lingered.

A full night's sleep had done wonders. The emptiness was still there, lurking, but to it had been added a strength and a desire to get on with the world. Laying plans for the day, Eve dressed quickly. The first order of business was her father. The breach that had grown between them needed to be healed. By the time she was ready to go out it was nine thirty. The baby was asleep again, and Eustacia was busy watching to make sure the hotel maid didn't wake him up. "I'm going, Eustacia. Do I look all right?"

Eustacia looked askance at the cut of Eve's gown. "I suppose so," she said half-heartedly. "When you comin' back?"

"I don't know. But if I don't get out and do something, I think I'll scream. Will the wet nurse be available if I'm not back in time?"

"She said she would be," Eustacia said a little grumpily.

"Good. I'll try to let you know if I'm delayed," she said, slipping out the door and unexpectedly colliding with Justin. "Oh, Justin! You startled me."

"Sorry." He grinned. "You look great. Feeling better, I take it?" His eyebrows raised. "You don't think that is going too far?"

Eve glanced down at the black gown she wore. "It's black."

"But hardly widow's weeds."

"Oh, my God, Justin, you sound just like Eustacia. Or the Misses Johnstone." She laid a hand on his arm. "It will be hard enough to put up with the others. Please. Don't you try to make me feel guilty too. Come on. I'm going to ask Father if he wants some breakfast. Why don't you come with us?"

Justin scowled. "You're joking, of course."

"Whatever do you mean?" Eve asked, a bit taken aback.

"I've had breakfast with him every morning for the last ten months. It's your turn. I'm on vacation."

Eve shook her head. "You haven't changed, have you? Still the witty, caustic, Justin. It couldn't have been that bad."

"Really?" Once again Justin toyed with the idea of telling Eve the secret only he and his father shared. The temptation was great, but he held back, telling himself it was for Eve's sake. Still, he could not totally hide his bitterness. "You don't know, not having been there. I tried, but nothing would do except that I become another Michael. If I worked in the office, my figures were wrong. If I worked on the walk, the ropes grew lumpy. If I tried my hand at the sailmaking loft, each seam I sewed had to be resewn. He was miserable, I was miserable."

"Perhaps it would have been better if you had left," Eve said icily.

"Perhaps, but there was no one else there." A rueful grin made Justin look boyish. "Do you know what? I actually felt sorry for him."

"If Father knew that—"

"At first, that is," Justin went on, cutting her off. "But he knocked that out of me. For the last six months I've just been waiting. Experimenting. Doing my photography when I could, and saving my money." He stopped, avoided Eve's questioning look. His fingers drummed nervously on the bannister. "You, ah, you'll be going home with him?"

Eve shrugged. "Where else is there to go?"

"I don't know." With Eve at Dawn Wind he was free, in good conscience, to leave. He tried and failed to hide the look of relief that flickered in his eyes. "He'll like that, in spite of . . ." Embarrassed, Justin cleared his throat. "That is, ah . . ."

"Blunt Justin at a loss for words."

Caught for once on the receiving end, Justin turned beet red. Barely able to keep from laughing, Eve embraced him with a quick little hug, then held him at arm's length. "Don't be embarrassed, Justin. I'm not. Whatever else has happened, however it happened, I'm proud of James. Father will be too. You'll see. Are you sure you don't want to come with us? At least try?"

"Can't. Really," he added quickly as disappointment clouded Eve's look. "There's a gent named Trullion who's giving a lecture on emulsions and exposure at Brady's studio. Perhaps I'll see you at dinner."

"All right," Eve said, kissing her brother on the cheek. "I tried. Take care of yourself."

"Of course." His bony, loose-jointed frame birdlike in motion, his waistcoat flapping as he trotted down the hall, a relieved Justin hurried off.

Eve watched him go, then knocked on her father's door and entered with a bright greeting.

Sewal glanced at her without answering, and clamped a bowler on his head. "Damned things look idiotic," he grumbled, scowling into the mirror. Throwing it aside, he replaced it with a high-crowned beaverskin top hat. The scraggly fringe of hair over his ears jutted out like a patch of silver thorns. Sewal nodded his head forward and to the side. The hat stayed on. "Well?" he asked, glowering at Eve.

"You look fine." Eve paused, kissed him on the cheek. "I'm glad you're here, Father."

"Did you expect me to stay away?" He patted her awkwardly on her shoulder. "You're still my daughter, after all."

"I know. But I did disappoint you."

"I don't want to discuss the past. It's a worthless expenditure of time," Sewal interrupted. He stepped away from her, checked in the mirror again, and discovered his cravat was awry. "Damn!" he fumed, fumbling at it.

"Here," Eve said. "Let me." Deftly, she adjusted his cravat and smoothed his collar. New furrows of concern had plowed across her father's features since she had left home. Eve wondered which ones stemmed from Michael, which came from Justin's obstinance, and which her own conduct had wrought. "There," she said, stepping back to admire her handiwork. "You look perfect. How about having breakfast with me? I'm famished."

"Breakfast? At ten o'clock?" Sewal's eyebrows raised. Ten o'clock was more near lunchtime than anything else. "I have an appointment with Sarandon at ten thirty."

"Hébert?" Eve asked, a sinking feeling growing in the pit of her stomach. "Why?"

"He's leaving Friday, and there are certain affairs that need to be discussed."

"I'd rather you didn't—"

"Namely, James Ruell Sarandon. Clifford died intestate."

"Father! You can't!"

"These matters must at least be sounded out and reflected upon."

Eve's face was reddened with embarrassment. "I make no claim upon the Sarandons."

"But the child does, through me." He glared at her. "He is due a portion of his father's estate. And you needn't cast those accusatory daggers in my direction. Someone has to look out for the boy's future." Sewal plucked a walking stick from the stand by the door. Then, on the verge of leaving, he turned back to her. "Remember how Jubb used to frighten you with tales of how the waves would one day eat through the rocks and leave Dawn Wind to drift out to sea?" he asked gently.

Eve nodded.

"The contract for the clippers alleviated most of our debts," Sewal went on, "but the last few months—since you left—haven't been easy. I don't mean to burden you, but I suspect Cabell has been keeping contracts from the Blackheath yards. Do you understand what I am saying? Dawn Wind is being destroyed, piecemeal, by nagging expenses. The sea is eating away at us, and if I'm to keep a child's fable from becoming reality, I must thrust whatever I can before the raging waters."

"And whomever," Eve amended, her voice trembling with anger.

"That's right," Sewal replied coldly, and left before anything else could be said.

Eve stood without moving for a long moment after the door closed. Finally, she stepped to the window and gazed blankly down at the sidewalk. The morning was bright and clear, a rare day for New York. As she watched, Sewal emerged from under the hotel's front awning and joined the hurrying crowd of city dwellers. Their faces set and determined, men in stuffy black attire strode purposefully to and from their business meetings despite the heat of the day. Fastidiously dressed children imprisoned in grown-up suits and gowns and without so much as a hoop or a top or a leopard stick to play with, chafed under nannies' strict observance. Gowned, jewelled, and coiffed ladies strolled the avenue looking neither to left nor right, as if they owned the street. And as elsewhere in America, in those days of turmoil, men in crisp military uniforms accoutred with epaulettes, gleaming brass buttons, and insignia stepped out briskly with a devil-may-care look.

Eve's stomach began to growl. She thought of asking for something from the hotel kitchen, but the recent encounter with her father had unnerved her. She felt hemmed in and terribly vulnerable. She had to escape, get out before the chilling loneliness that had oppressed her since Clifford's death sent her reeling into despondency again. Keep moving, wisdom said. Don't stop. In lethargy is madness. Don't think. Pausing only to collect her gloves and parasol, Eve bolted from her father's room and out of the hotel.

Fresh air helped. The city was vibrant, alive, and Eve soaked up its energy as she walked the three blocks to her favorite restaurant. *Pomme de Terre,* "fruit of the earth" to its American patrons, was set back from the street in a handsome courtyard surrounded by a wrought-iron picket fence. The maitre d', a white-haired, stuffy, diminutive gentleman of purported French ancestry, gazed across the round marble-topped tables and cushioned wrought-iron chairs, and at last shook his head. "It is hopeless, you see, madam. There is simply no room."

Eve's spirits flagged. The maitre d', eager to find something for an expensively dressed and beautiful widow, reexamined the crowded tables attended by a half-dozen white-jacketed waiters. "Ah! There is a table. Right this way . . . *Non.* I am sorry, madam, the gentlemen are returning to it. And over there, you see, they are waiting for dessert. I am desolate, madam. Perhaps you could wait inside. I am sure—"

"May I request the pleasure of having you join me, Mrs. Sarandon?"

Eve and the maitre d' turned simultaneously. A young man in uniform stood behind them. "Jack Travis!" Eve exclaimed. She had seen Michael's best man only once since the wedding, and then at a crowded ball in Washington some months before. "What a pleasant surprise!"

"Now I *am* flattered," Jack said, giving her his arm and leading her toward his table "I always feel fortunate when a beautiful woman remembers my name Here." He seated her, motioned for a waiter, and sat himself. "I am told, on good authority, that they have fresh strawberries, if you want them."

"But you've already finished," Eve protested.

Jack shook his head. "Not at all. I was having croissants and coffee. I'll order more."

Within minutes the waiter reappeared with a platter of the hot pastry, a dipper and clay pot of honey, an earthen bowl of cold butter, and a silver pot of coffee. Eve watched Jack while the waiter worked, and remembered how the girls at Michael's wedding had been so divided in their opinion, some seduced by Lion McKenna's rugged charm and others enamored by Jack Travis's patrician handsomeness. A year hadn't changed him, only placed him in uniform.

"You're staring," Jack said. He fingered the flat brim of his hat and the embossed brass emblem on the crown where two sabers crossed under the letters, u.s. "You're surprised?"

"I admit it," Eve said. "I didn't think you'd be wearing this particular color. Your home is—"

"South Carolina. The very first state to secede. Shall I tell you the day?" His voice was low, filled with bitterness. "January twentieth. My father was there." He shrugged. "Obviously, I didn't approve. I just couldn't see myself firing on the stars and stripes. I knew that. So here I am."

"And your father?"

"President Davis has put him in charge of building their navy, I hear. It's not just brother against brother. Not in this war."

"I'm sorry," Eve said. "It was none of my business, really." She dipped a strawberry into a saucer of cream, then bit into it. "These are delicious. I could eat a dozen of them."

"Be my guest." Jack held up one hand in mock protest. "No. No. No arguments. It's my last day of freedom. I insist on a splurge." He leaned forward and twirled his moustache. "Sure I can't tempt you with a strawberry tart as well, my dear?" he asked with an exaggerated leer.

"Heavens no," Eve laughed. "I'd blow up." She paused, her hand halfway to her mouth. "Oh, dear. I hope I'm not keeping you from something—or someone," she said.

"Please do." Jack's smile faded and he grew serious again. "I read about your husband. May I extend my sympathies?"

"Thank you," Eve said. "It all seems so incredible, so much of a shock. Father came to the funeral. I suppose I'll be returning to Maine and Dawn Wind."

"Good. At least I'll know where one friend is."

Eve blushed. "You exaggerate."

"Do I? Everyone I know in the North has congratulated me for turning my back on my family and half my old friends, and yet, the minute I open my mouth, my accent reminds them of where I'm from and I can see the doubt and suspicion in their eyes. 'Is he telling the truth?' they ask themselves. 'Can we really trust him? Better not be too quick. Let him prove himself first.' Suspicion. I'm sick of it. Sometimes I think Michael did the right thing." He stopped, embarrassed. "I'm sorry. I didn't mean that the way it sounded. But he is out of the war. I guess."

"And paying the price," Eve replied bitterly. "Wanted for desertion, and labeled a coward."

"And Rosamond?"

"I don't know. The last I heard, the admiral moved her and her mother here to New York when war broke out and Washington was endangered. Clifford says that . . ." She paused, made herself continue. "Clifford *said* that . . . she . . ." Unable to go on, she shook her head, and started to get up from the table.

"I'm sorry," Jack said, placing his hand over Eve's. The gesture caught Eve unawares, and she sat down again. Jack laughed ruefully. "We're spending a lot of time saying how sorry we are. Look. Here we sit made rigid by gloomy thoughts. It's a warm summer day and life is rushing all around us." He pushed back his chair and stood. "Come on. Let's walk together. I'll show you some of the cheerier aspects of the city."

"I can't . . ."

"But the day is young. Not yet noon."

"I shouldn't . . ."

"Aha! See? 'Shouldn't' is better than 'can't'." He put on his hat, held out his hand to Eve. "I have the afternoon free. My last one. Please, Eve."

The alternative was to spend the day alone, and there was a look of appeal in his eyes before he averted his glance. "Only the cheery sights?" she said.

"My word—" He stuffed a bill into the waiter's hand. "—As an officer and a gentleman."

"Yes, then," Eve said, relaxing and laughing easily for the first time in a long time. Arm in arm, the two of them entered the flow of the city that had been passing them by all during their conversation.

Justin squinted at the street signs in an attempt to read what appeared to be so many chicken scratches. At last he sighed, reached inside his pocket, and pulled out his wire rim spectacles. "Vanity, thy name is man," he sighed, and, as the signs swam into focus, leaped from his seat.

The trolley was passing Fifty-second Street. Charging up the packed aisle, he squeezed out the door and dashed into the street, narrowly avoiding being run down in the process. Twisting dextrously, he ducked a charging carriage, stubbed his toe on the curb, and barely managed to grab hold of a lightpost to keep himself from falling flat on the sidewalk in front of a gentleman and his lady friend. Justin recovered his dignity by bowing slightly and returning their amused glances with a look that said, That's the way I get off trolleys all the time.

At least he was where he wanted to be. Above him, painted in extraordinarily large letters on a two-story building, was the name Brady. STUDIO AND GALLERY had been added almost as an afterthought. There was no denying the man's ego. Justin stepped through the front door into a single large room, the walls of which were virtually covered with photographs. Portraits predominated, interspersed with scenes from around the world. A bewhiskered judge and his puritanical wife posed stiffly, captured on paper for eternity. The Sphinx, in all its inscrutable authority, slumbered against a sea of sand. A girl, all ribbons and curls, sat on a swing that had been held, Justin was sure, in its impossible angle by hidden wires. Next to her, in contrast, a wizened matriarch in a black silk gown stared sourly into the lens. A boy played with his lead soldiers. A grand duke appeared invulnerable. An Indian warrior with a spear stared trancelike. A castle hovered on a hill above the Rhine. Abraham Lincoln, legs crossed and wrists showing past the ends of his sleeves, appeared to be napping. Roses budded in an ornate vase on a Grecian pedestal. Corpses littered the mud near a shattered bridge at Bull Run. Those photographs not labeled M.B., for Matthew Brady, bore the sprawled signature of Menschell Trullion.

"Can I help you?"

Justin spun around. A middle-aged woman in a blowsy, soiled dress stood behind him. "Sorry. I didn't hear you," Justin said. "I'm here for Mr. Trullion's lecture. I believe Mr. Brady is hosting him."

"He is. Mr. Trullion's upstairs working. But there ain't goin' to be no lecture. Mr. Trullion put a notice in the *Herald* that it's been canceled."

"What? But he couldn't have!" Justin said, unable to hide his disappointment.

"Ain't my fault," the woman said phlegmatically. "I just clean up."

"Darn!" Justin had counted on meeting Trullion. The man was fascinating. An engineer, he had become interested in photography when he was fifty years old. Unable to learn as much or as fast as he'd wanted to in America, he had forsaken his native New York for Paris, then London. His keen, inquisitive, searching mind had led him to a rapid mastery of photography. Most important, his vision of the world differed strikingly from that of other photographers. If Justin didn't see him before he returned to Europe the chances were he would never see him. He sagged into a chair set by an easel on which perched a photograph of a beautiful young woman. When he looked up the cleaning woman was still there, leaning on her mop.

"I'm a student of photography," Justin explained. "I wanted to visit with Mr. Trullion before he returned to Europe. Of course, if he isn't here . . . Do you think Mr. Brady would mind if I just looked around a little longer?"

"Mr. Brady ain't here, and I don't care," the cleaning woman said. A sly look came over her face, and she extended one hand suggestively. "Of course," she said, lowering her voice, "if I was to be busy straightenin' up out back, I might never hear if someone was to come in and just sort of explore up those stairs. Wouldn't be my fault if that someone just sort of happened on Mr. Trullion workin' in the big studio up there."

A wide grin replaced Justin's look of dejection. He leaped to his feet and fumbled in his pocket for a coin. "I won't tell anyone," he said, slipping a silver piece into her hand and starting for the stairs.

"Wait a minute," the cleaning woman said, plucking at Justin's sleeve.

Startled, Justin turned. "But you said . . ."

"I ain't in the back room yet."

"Oh." He waited until the woman disappeared and the door closed and then, with a glance over his shoulder to reassure himself no one was watching, headed up the stairs.

The stairs were dark and narrow, the hallway dimly lit by gaslight. Two doors opposed each other halfway down the hall. He tried one, found it opened into a broad, spacious, and empty loft. Tiptoeing, he crossed the hall, opened the other door, and entered another loft as large as the first, but incredibly cluttered. The sweet smell of opium hung in the air, and the sound of a hacking cough came from behind a partition made of curtains and screens. Walking quietly, Justin made his way past piles of studio scenery and a hodgepodge of familiar photographic equipment, then stopped behind a collection of flats and stared slack-jawed at the scene he had stumbled upon.

"The hip, the hip! There to the side. A little more, damn it! A little—there. Hold it!" a muted voice rasped from underneath the cloth covering the back of a large camera set on a tripod.

Justin gawked, spellbound. Against a northern wall of windows and deluged in natural light, a naked woman reclined on a chaise. Her back was to the camera. A gown that covered the lower part of her legs was bunched at the end of the couch. She seemed incredibly small, yet was exquisitely proportioned. Her head was turned and she was looking into the camera. Justin was sure he had never seen anyone more beautiful. Of Oceanic or Oriental ancestry, her skin was of the lightest brown hue. Jet black hair spilled in thick coils past her left shoulder and hung all the way to the chaise, where it lay in a tangled pile that caught the light and glowed with a life its own. Her forehead was high, as were her cheekbones. Wideset, deep brown eyes gave the impression of innocence coupled with a sensuality so intense as to be almost overpowering. Her mouth was small, her lips moist and slightly parted as she breathed. Her back looked silken smooth. A pair of dimples marked her waist where it flared into rounded, muscular hips. Her legs tapered down to the gown that hid her knees and calves and feet. The room was warm, but Justin felt as if his breath must have clouded the air as it would on an icy winter day.

"Time," the voice rasped again.

The woman laughed at something, then kicked free of the gown. Utterly at ease with her nakedness, she stood, caught up a silk tunic embroidered with Oriental fish and mermen, and slipped into it in a single motion that allowed but a glimpse of small pointed breasts, a slightly rounded belly, and thighs that melted into a triangle of dark brown, tight curls. She couldn't have been more than five feet tall. She was not a girl, though. No. Had never been, Justin thought. A nymph, born woman. She laughed again in a dusky, mellow voice like poured syrup. Justin realized she was staring at him, even as he stared at her.

"Who is it? Matthew?" the rasping voice queried. An old man

peeked around a flat six feet away. Daylight cast a nimbus around the white wisps of hair that sprouted from his skull, thickened into sideburns and flowed into an unevenly trimmed snowy beard. "Who the hell are you?" the old man demanded.

Justin couldn't tear his eyes from the model. "Hrumph," the photographer grunted. He sniffed, sneezed, blew his nose on a filthy rag. "I'm afraid you've struck our young spy dumb," he snorted to the girl. "If this photograph has a similar effect on the Count, I shall have enough money to build a whole damned studio. And pay your way to California, to boot."

He approached Justin. The model walked across the room to join him. As short as Justin was, it was a novel experience for him to tower over someone his own age. The girl peered up at him. Her nipples, burnt-sienna petals that all but covered her breasts, pressed against the light silk wrap.

"Her name is Kendra," the old man said. He coughed. "Damn summer cold. My dear, I would suggest you find your clothes and put them on before our visitor here asphyxiates."

Puzzled over the word "asphyxiate," Kendra glanced at the photographer. "Runs out of air. Smothers. You know. You've not only stolen his voice, he isn't even breathing."

The girl nodded and laughed again, then ran across the room and vanished through a doorway.

"She's . . . she's . . ." Justin stammered.

"And more," the old man chuckled. "Damned good thing I'm well past the age where such charms can elicit more than a shortness of breath, or else I'd be standing as moon-eyed as you instead of going about my work. And now, it seems I must repeat myself. Who the hell are you?"

"You are Menschell Trullion," Justin said haltingly, looking at the older man for the first time.

"I *know* who *I* am, by God," the old man thundered. He sneezed again and wiped the rag across his beaked nose. "Now think, my witless friend. *Who—are—you?*"

"Oh! Justin Blackheath, sir."

Trullion stared, rubbed his bent back, buttoned the bottom three buttons of his vest, and squinted at Justin again. "Bravo!" he finally said, and shuffled back to his camera, where he busied himself by removing the recently exposed plate of Kendra.

"I came to attend your lecture," Justin said, confused by Trullion's sudden indifference. "But I heard it was canceled."

"It was."

"I read you would be working in the city, sharing Matthew Brady's studio."

"I am." Trullion coughed. "As any damn fool can see."

Justin followed him to a work table. "Are you still experimenting with the zinc emulsion bath and its effect on treated paper plates exposed to natural light?"

"Yes." The old man opened a black box, placed the plate inside, and closed the box again. "I'm changing the source of light, though, and recording the results. Adding considerable back light and trying to balance the resulting irregularities with multiple flashes. With that . . ." Trullion stopped, stared at Justin. "Now wait a minute, young man. I told you the lecture had been canceled."

"I want to learn. All I can," Justin insisted. "I'm at the Fifth Avenue Hotel now, but I could easily get a place around here in order to work with you."

Trullion thrust his arms into two black sleeves fitted into the side of the box, closed his eyes, and set to work on the plate. It had to be developed before more minutes passed. "Impossible," he grunted.

"Surely you could use help."

"If I took on an assistant, it would be someone able to keep his mind on his work," he said, nodding toward the door where Kendra had disappeared.

"I said I wanted to be your assistant." Justin's initial unease had faded. "That hardly entails my giving up being human."

Trullion almost smiled, managed to twist his face into a frown at the last moment. "The streets are full of men to carry my equipment. I hire strong backs as I need them. Yours looks none too promising for such drudgery. You've a brittle quality to you." He grunted again, pulled his arms out of the sleeves, and glanced at the clock. "Brittle backs break."

Justin reached into his coat pocket, pulled out a packet of photographic prints, and placed them face up on the work table. Trullion glowered, lifted one, inspected it, shrugged, and dropped it into a wastebasket. He glanced at Justin out of the corner of his eye, lifted another photograph and repeated the process. A third suffered a similar fate.

What verbal insults hadn't accomplished utter disdain for his work did. Flushed with embarrassment, Justin swung around and walked blindly into a flat that toppled into another flat that dominoed into several screens. A frightful ripping sound added to his confusion. Looking down, Justin saw his right foot had stepped through a painting of Niagara Falls. Completely flustered, he wallowed out of the torn canvas, nearly tripped over a disassembled tripod, fell through the open door, and ended up leaning against the opposite wall. At the same time a door at the end of the hall opened, and Kendra stepped out. A tight bodice lifted her breasts and lent them a false abundance. A cotton skirt over several petticoats hung to the floor. With a bonnet hiding her luxurious hair she looked almost common; nothing at all like the sensuous creature he had seen only five minutes earlier.

A wheezing, hacking curse floated out of the studio. Justin realized he had been staring at the girl again, as she was at him. Humiliated, he removed his spectacles and wiped his eyes, then replaced the wire rims for fear of stumbling down the stairs and making even more of a fool of himself. The girl started to walk toward him. Incredibly enough, Justin felt a peculiar empathy reach out from her to him. And then he remembered her earlier laughter. Resolved not to allow his pride to be further wounded, he turned away and descended the stairs, ran past the cleaning woman and out of the gallery. Nor did he lessen his stride until he was several blocks away.

It shouldn't have happened. Never the first time, and not again. They had walked until weary legs had screamed for rest. Jack had kept his word. Gardens rioting with blooms. Children playing in gushes of water from summer hydrants. A stroll through the still unfinished walks of Central Park. Gradually, sunlight and quiet conversation had stilled sorrow and subdued confusion and, though neither was aware of it, intensified the feeling of loneliness that had drawn them together for the afternoon. Eve had meant nothing else to happen, had accepted Jack's offer of a cooling drink at his hotel, then followed him to his room and waited while he rummaged through his bags and handed her a daguerreotype of him and Michael taken three years earlier when the two of them had posed with foolish grins before an unknown photographer. It was a memento of a far happier brother than the tormented one who had fled home and duty.

What followed could not have been anticipated. Somehow with a rush of horror and shame that wasn't powerful enough to check the desperate loneliness or negate the need for someone to touch and hold her, Eve found herself in Jack's bed. Guilt-ridden, she was still and tense, unable to give herself completely even as she was unable to stop, or leave. Only later, when she had dozed and wakened, did she realize her need, and begin to absolve herself of guilt.

Eyes closed, lazy, floating in limbo, she felt Jack stir. She opened her eyes to see him next to her, propped on one elbow and looking down at her. "Hello," he said smiling.

"Hello."

"You all right?"

"Mmm."

His smile disappeared, replaced by a serious, almost quizzical look. "I didn't start out with this in mind," he said.

"I know."

"It's just that—"

"Shh." Eve's finger touched his lips. "No explanations, Jack."

His lips touched her neck, her cheek, found her mouth. Suddenly voracious, Eve returned his kiss. Her palm brushed across his thigh; her hand tightened on his leg. His handsome, almost beautiful features were masked with masculine passion as he rolled atop her. Their faces, inches apart, searched each other's for guilt and found none. Only need: urgent, vibrant, desperate need.

Eve held him in her. She closed her eyes, saw Lion, saw Clifford, Lion and Clifford. Sucking in her breath, she jerked her eyes open again. Jack was staring at her, thrusting deeper into her, moving in ways she had forgotten. Eve felt herself responding, letting herself go, accepting him. Suddenly, he threw back his head and arched his back, held his climax and then resumed his efforts.

It had been so long. How many days? How many nights? She had had no man since Lion. Oh, Clifford, Clifford. I'm so sorry. Make me forget, she pleaded silently. Make me forget . . .

She was sobbing now. Almost there. She tried to call Jack's name, but her voice tightened in her throat. Her hair splayed across the pillow like a meadow of gold in the summer sun. The pale honey color of her flesh blushed where his hands touched her. The rhythmic filling and emptying fired her blood, provoked the madness of the body unfulfilled and crying for release. At last, Eve wrapped her arms around Jack's neck and sobbed unashamedly as the incredible spasms tore through and demolished all memory and guilt, held her poised and shuddering against him, and only then, slowly, eased her into the relaxed peace of satiety.

Jack Travis buckled his belt, tucked his gloves against his waistband. Eve's fingers flashed as she braided her hair to match the way it had been that morning, and pinned it to the top of her head. "Are you certain I can't join you for dinner?" he asked, his hands on her shoulders.

Eve brushed her cheek against the back of his hand. "Father won't admit it, but Michael hurt him deeply. Your presence would only aggravate an open wound. Please understand."

"I do." He smiled at her in the mirror. "At least let me escort you back to your hotel."

"It's only a few blocks," Eve said. "I can manage. Really. It's best if I leave and arrive alone."

"So," Jack said. "I must do as you say. An officer must be as adept at following orders as giving them." He turned her around, held her at arm's length, and looked at her as if he was trying to memorize her. "A gift I never expected," he said, shaking his head in wonder. "I leave for the West to join General Grant tomorrow. Without you, I would have departed a lonely man. For one afternoon, this was home, and I have something to lock away in my heart and carry with me."

Eve took his hand and pressed it to her cheek. "Dear Jack," she said, kissing his fingers. Her eyes shone with unnatural brightness. She was alive. She was a woman again, and desirable. The guilt and sadness and loneliness that had warped her last few days had been washed away. For a few hours she had touched and been touched. There had been closeness, but without the demeaning, awful lies of love. "I'm glad we met again."

"No regrets?" Jack asked gently.

"No." Eve shook her head. "No regrets." She embraced him, held him close. "Take care of yourself, Jack Travis," she whispered, and hurriedly left before he could notice the tears that gleamed in the corners of her eyes.

Their brief stay in New York was almost over. Eve and Sewal and Justin dined alone. The meal was not a success. Sewal pointedly refrained from mentioning his meeting with Hébert. Eve did not press him, knowing he would reveal as much as he felt necessary in his own good time. Justin barely spoke, and exhibited a rare passiveness toward Sewal that wasn't at all like him. His unusually glum expression managed to put Eve in a peevish mood, no small chore considering how buoyant she had felt earlier.

A night's rest didn't improve matters. The train bound for Portland hissed and steamed at the Friday morning passengers crowding the platform. Collectively out of sorts, the Blackheaths threaded their way through the dense throng. Eustacia, not trusting anyone as thin as Eve to keep from being knocked over, carried James Ruell and tagged along, huffing and puffing as she climbed into their car and settled uncomfortably in a seat next to Eve.

Sewal disappeared immediately into the smoking car. Justin slouched in the seat across the aisle from Eve. He could feel her staring at him, silently demanding an explanation, but what could he say? That he had made a fool of himself? That Sewal had been right, and that he had no future as a photographer? That he had been living a pretense? Images of Kendra quickened his pulse, yet even desire was an insult. A woman like her would never have anything to do with a bony, bookish clown like him.

"Mr. Justin Blackheath!" A boy entered the front of the car and hurried down the aisle. "Mr. Justin Blackheath!"

"Here," Justin said, standing.

"You're hard to find," the boy said, with a grin of obvious relief. "I had to run all the way from the hotel."

"Well?" Justin snapped. "Get on with it."

The boy held out an envelope. "A man gave me a quarter to deliver this. Said you'd give me another."

Justin fished in his pocket and handed the boy a coin. When he opened the envelope a photograph he had taken in Maine slid out. The photograph had been taken from a distance on a gray, overcast day, and showed a large house set on a high cliff. It was Dawn Wind, wreathed in a halo of fog, majestic in the mist. Puzzled, Justin fumbled with the envelope. A slip of paper fluttered to the floor. He retrieved it and, hand shaking, read the single, scribbled word written there. "Come." And underneath, the initials, M.T.

Part III

Chapter 20

In the short dark days of February, in the winter of 1862, the factions had yet to fully flex their strength, had yet to immolate themselves on the altar of uninhibited civil war. To be sure, more men had died since those fateful days in July at Bull Run. They died in minor forays, individually or in small commands. They died at Darren's Gap, Sawwood Ridge, and Otter Creek. They died at bends in rivers, on tree-shaded knolls of no consequence, on farms, and in sleepy villages ringed with supposedly protective mountains. Their deaths failed to fire the collective imagination of the artists at *Harper's Weekly,* the *Herald, The New York Times,* or the populace they served. People talked, but less excitedly. Issues that once burned lay as a furnace stoked for the night. Little attention was paid to the gaps, ridges, bends, hills, bayous, and glens, save for the men who had visited them and never left, and the bereaved and disillusioned families they would never again see.

The war was little more than distant thunder in Maine, no nearer than the day-late newspapers that arrived from Boston and New York and Washington. Very few of New Forest's young men had marched away to war. Those who did left silently, and with little fanfare. Not one of them had died, either on land or at sea. The war, not having touched New Forest in a personal way—Eve Blackheath's husband didn't count, in the town's considered opinion, because he was an outsider—had left it unscathed and forgotten. New Forest returned the favor, for the most part. Such comment as was necessary could be handled by the New Forest *Free Speaker* and, when a suitable theological occasion arose, by Reverend Waldrop.

Hanson Pole dawdled over a second cup of coffee. He sipped, held his lips flat against his teeth to keep the coffee from dribbling out, sloshed it from one cheek into the other. Every few minutes his Adam's apple bobbed until at last his mouth was empty and ready for another sip. While he drank, his eyes, squinting to read the small type, ranged back and forth, devouring the latest war news. He alone among the residents of New Forest in general and Dawn Wind in particular had taken an immediate and intense interest in the conflict, and even went so far as to clip all the important accounts from the paper and paste them in a scrapbook he kept by his bed.

"Swaller!"

Pole glanced up, startled. Jubb, his charcoal features knotted in frustration, sat across the table from him. The black man's eyes were wide, his teeth gritted together. "Lookee here, Mr. Pole," he said in a strangled tone. He grabbed his mug of coffee and drank the contents down, then slammed the cup on the tabletop and wiped his mouth on his sleeve.

"Yes?" Pole sniffed imperiously.

"The Lord's food was meant to be et, His drink to be drunk."

"Yes?" At a loss, the butler squinted first at Jubb, then at Eustacia. "I don't understand . . ."

"Dadgumit, but how in blazes you gonna drink if you don't never swaller? I never seen the like. You washin' yore tongue or somethin'? Lord have mercy, but it drives a man to perdition!"

Eustacia leaned over and refilled her husband's mug. Hanson Pole continued to stare aghast at his accuser. "It never ceases to amaze me, Jubb," he finally said. "Must I continually remind you of your place?"

"Place? My place?" Jubb was halfway out of his seat. "I know my place. Right here in this kitchen, where I eats." He plopped a gingerbread cookie in his mouth. "And drinks. And *swallers!*" To demonstrate he slugged the coffee down his throat. Immediately, his eyes grew wide. His face contorted and he spewed the coffee onto the floor. "God Almighty, woman!" he gasped. "Why didn't you tell me that was hot?"

"I figured you could see the steam, same as anybody else," Eustacia replied shortly.

"It appears I am not the only one who doesn't 'swaller,'" Pole said pointedly, peering over the table to the mess on the floor.

Jubb pushed his chair back and, quivering with anger, left the table. "You clean up that mess, now, Jubb Peters," Eustacia said.

"Wasn't me who poured hot coffee for an unsuspectin' man," her husband charged, drawing himself up to his full height. "You clean it up. I'm goin' out!"

"You'll catch your death."

Jubb stalked to the coatrack, shrugged into a heavy woolen coat. "Don't you turn agin' me too, woman," he said, jerking the door open. A cold gust of wind sliced through the kitchen's warmth. Narrowly avoiding the icicles that hung like jagged dragon's teeth from the overhang, Jubb ducked outside.

"What on earth is the matter with him?" Pole asked, wincing as the door slammed. "Most peculiar, really."

Eustacia groaned as she leaned over to clean up the coffee on the floor. "Same time every year he blows up like that," she said. "Same time every year you ask why, and same time every year I tell you the same thing." Rubbing her back she crossed to the window and cleared a spot in order to see the white, frozen world outside. "Cabin fever," she said with a sigh. "I think I got it too."

"His hair's already so dark. Getting darker still," Maisie said. She pinched the gurgling infant's plump calf, shook his leg back and forth playfully. "Doozie," she said. "You are a regular little doozie too." She picked up a stuffed rabbit and held it in front of the child's face. "What's this? What's this? A toy? Santa brought you a toy rabbit? Yes. Yes. Is this your toy? Is this your toy?"

James Ruell laughed, pleased with the attention, and grabbed for the toy. No sooner did Maisie let it go than he had one of the rabbit's floppy ears in his mouth and was chewing vigorously.

"You're going to spoil him," Eve laughed, laying aside her knitting. She was bored, bored, bored. The window rattled as a gray gust of icy sea breeze tried to gain entry. Enough filtered beneath the sill to set Eve shivering, and she moved away from the light to the welcome warmth of the fireplace. "Lord, but I'll be glad when spring comes," she said, sitting in the thickly cushioned chair that Justin had brought her from New York for Christmas. The light blue brocade nicely complemented the lavender velvet gown she wore. Across the room Maisie finished stacking the linen and was starting to leave. "Maisie?"

"Yes, ma'am."

"Sit a minute, why don't you," Eve said, gesturing to the chair across from her.

Maisie nodded. Back erect, knees together, she sat stiffly as she had been taught a lady should. She never would have considered taking the liberty of sitting crossways, back against one arm, legs dangling over the other, and feet held to catch the fire's warmth, as Eve did. Self-conscious, unsure why she had been asked to depart from the normal routine, she waited uncomfortably.

Suddenly, Eve chuckled. "Do you remember when we were both children, Maisie?"

"Yes, ma'am," Maisie said, wondering what Eve was getting at.

"And Father brought me to the shipyards and we played in the rope walk?"

"Until Papa ran us off," Maisie said. Her eyes misted at the memory, for Coryl Duncan had died the past fall, leaving Maisie and her sister the sole support of her ailing mother who lived in town.

"I was very uppity to your father," Eve said, her eyes closed as she pictured that long ago afternoon. "When I reminded him of just who I was, he took me over his knee and gave me a paddling."

Maisie couldn't help it. She giggled. "And then you ran to tell Mr. Blackheath."

"Yes. Father laughed and laughed. And I was furious." She smiled at the memory. "Furious. But it was the last time I tried to play Blackheath's daughter to the shipbuilders."

"Papa did the same thing when I sassed *your* father and he spanked me," Maisie said ruefully. "My bottom burned for a week. I never tried *that* again."

Eve winced. "Father has a way about him—always has. I talked back to him once. Once only." Boredom dispelled for the moment, Eve swung her legs off the arm of the chair and sat leaning forward toward Maisie. "What about the time when we found the carriage?"

Maisie forgot she was supposed to be proper, and rocked back and forth with laughter. "That day we both received spankings?"

"Lucky for us the horse was gentle," Eve said.

"And tired."

"Where on earth did we think we were going?"

"Have you forgotten?" Maisie asked. "I never will. Minnesota."

"You've named it. That's right. We'd heard the name somewhere, and . . . How in heaven's name did we ever think we'd get there?"

"I don't remember," Maisie said. "I suppose we thought that old tired nag would find the way somehow."

"Poor horse," Eve said. She sat back, obviously lost in thought.

Maisie shifted uncomfortably. She and Eve weren't children anymore, but maid and mistress. For a fleeting second she wondered how life would be if their positions were reversed. But they weren't, and nothing to be done about it. "Well," she said, rising. "I guess I better get back to work. Mr. Pole comes all a tither when things aren't set to right on time. He's not unkind, mind you," she added quickly, "but he can look awful mean."

"I understand," Eve said. She lowered her eyes, appeared embarrassed. "You know, Maisie," she said in a low voice, "if you or your mother need anything . . ."

"We're making do," the maid said, suddenly defensive.

"I'm sorry. I just thought . . ." She trailed off, realizing it was better to allow the woman her pride than to interfere, however well meaning the offer.

"It's all right," Maisie said, chagrined. She wondered if Eve knew about the pension her mother received from Mr. Blackheath, decided not to mention it. "We really are fine." Embarrassed herself, she started toward the door, then paused. A blush tinged her freckled cheeks. "Miss Eve?"

"Yes?"

"Can I ask you a question? Of a personal nature?"

Eve brightened. "Of course," she said.

Maisie wrung her hands, glanced around a room she already knew to be empty except for herself and Eve and the baby. The fire crackled in the silence. "If a girl was to be in love with a person—a man, that is—that *some* folks might not, well, approve of, but she saw the goodness and gentleness in him and everything . . ." She wet her lips nervously, searched for the right words. "I mean, should she love him anyway? No matter what folks said?"

Eve stood and walked to the window. It had begun to snow again, fat fluffy flakes that threatened to overburden already sadly drooping tree branches. The ocean was a gray smear in the obscure distance. Eve looked at the bedtable, the growing pile of letters from Jack Travis. Some were friendly, others implied much more than friendship. Next to them, in a lacquered box kept under lock and key, lay two clippings from the New York *Herald,* that mentioned the exploits of Captain Lion McKenna. She looked at her son, asleep in the crib, then out the window again. Out there, in her mind's eye, she could see a headstrong girl brimming with romantic notions watch her love sail from her life. More than her love, she thought wistfully. Warm summer afternoons, gathered flowers, physical discovery, whispered entreaties and vows, laughter and passion. Yesterday, for all the lingering pain it represented, was draped nonetheless in beauty.

"Miss Eve?"

Brought back to the present, Eve leaned against the windowsill. Flakes swirled, danced, died in leaden light. She shook her head. "There are a hundred clever answers, but not a one of them will dry a tear or replace what is lost. If I were to say yes or no, would it change what is in your heart?"

The fire crackled. "No. I suppose not," Maisie replied at last, her voice subdued and serious.

"Then you have the only answer I can give you," Eve said quietly. In the silence that followed she thought she could hear the snowflakes hitting against the windowpane.

"Thank you, Miss Eve."

Eve shook her head. "Don't—" she began. But the door clicked closed. Eve left the window, looked around for something to do. At last she sat on the edge of her bed. Her hand rested between the lacquered box and the stacked letters from Jack. "You have your answer," she repeated to the empty room. "If only I had mine."

A weimaraner bitch wrestled with its pups for possession of a deer rib Arvid Naslund had tossed onto the sawdust-covered floor. "Now, Valky. Share and share alike," the youth chuckled. Valky grabbed the bone and bounded across a lattice-work pattern of sunlight streaming through the framework of a framing jig. The pups tumbled after her. Arvid sighed, wiped his hands, and decided he'd better get back to work. The jig, a mold around which planks of pine and strips of cedar would be shaped to form the transom of a Crotch Island pinky to be sold to a wealthy Portland lobstering family, needed another half-day's work before it would be finished. The soft sound of a wood plane peeling away curling strips of pine melded into the general noise of the workshop.

A cloud of pups bumbling around the bitch's feet roiled past Sewal Blackheath, who deftly sidestepped to avoid a collision. "Here now, Valky!" Sewal commanded as the dogs disappeared around a workbench and yapped into the keelmold section. The workshop was a large, two-story frame and shingle structure that lent a false sense of prosperity to the yards. One needed only glance out one of the frost-encrusted windows and witness the dull snowy quiet of the outer yards to better gauge the bitter truth.

Sewal closed his eyes. The air was rich with the smell of resin, heady with the aroma of pine and cedar and oak and strong tobacco.

Voices harsh and lyrical, pounding hammers, the guttural rasp of crosscut saws cutting keelstock, the chunk of adzes biting into oak, were music to Sewal's ears. A seafaring man who no longer went to sea, Sewal always found release from gloomy projections and the dire consequences of the waning activity in the yards here in the workshop. Around him were the silent members of a seaman's family; *bateaux,* Captain's gigs, skiffs, pinkies, and dories. To one side, a Matinicus Island peapod waited for its mast. Behind it, a Muscongus Bay sloop, tool of fishermen and river dwellers for the past hundred years, was being planked. The craft, each one fashioned to stand the test of a lifetime's work, were Sewal's children, and in truth, though he would never put this feeling in words, he loved them no less than those of his own flesh. They were his life, his work. His name and reputation rested on them.

"Blackheath," Sewal whispered, affirming the identity his father and grandfather had left him. It was a good name. One a man could be proud of. Lost in his work, he bent to the half model he was completing. Already, he could see the imagined cutter slipping through the choppy waters of the North Atlantic coast.

One of the men left his workbench to stoke the black iron stove nearest him. An identical one stood against the opposite wall. Built for New England winters and fired to a cherry red, the stoves did little but create pools of warmth around them. Arvid, his sons, and twenty-three others glanced up as the stove door clanged shut. The rest of the hundred or so men who had found gainful employment in the Blackheath Shipyards less than a year ago had taken jobs up at the mill, or had become loggers. Some had enlisted, a few had found jobs in town. The last few waited, and eked out what living they could chopping and carrying wood.

It cut Sewal to the core to have to let good men go. But the yard was on the verge of bankruptcy as it was, only holding on by taking small jobs no other shipbuilder would touch. Every other Union shipyard, from Baltimore to Boston, was busy with Navy contracts. All but Blackheath's. Admiral Cabell had put the blame for his daughter's failed marriage on the deserter, Michael Blackheath, and clung tenaciously to his injured pride. Even before the onslaught of war and his decision to ship Rosamond and his wife to the safety of New York City, the Admiral had embarked on a course of retaliation against the Blackheaths in the only way he could, by using his influence to channel the flow of contracts away from the yards on

Waupinau Bay. For once in his life Sewal was powerless. With hard work and luck, he told himself, he would weather this storm as he had others.

The door behind him opened and a cloud of snow billowed in. Sewal turned to scold the guilty party. Eliot, his clerk, winced as if to avoid a blow. "Sorry, Mr. Blackheath," he said, shaking the snow off his collar. "But Mayor Castebury and Mr. Aldrin are in your office."

"Oh?" Sewal put down his carving knife and wiped his hands. "What do they want?"

"They didn't say, Mr. Blackheath."

"No, I suppose not." Sewal's fair humor was dampened by a rising squall of dissatisfaction. He braced himself, breathed one last healthy breath of worked wood and common men, then plunged into the icy February air.

The outer office was warm. "Coffee," Sewal ordered, rubbing his hands over the fire before stepping out of his overcoat.

"Yes, sir, Mr. Blackheath," Eliot said. He took the overcoat and hung it on the rack by the door. "Oh, yes. We got a telegram from Mr. White. He says go ahead."

"Go ahead, eh?" Sewal smiled grimly. "Pair of Newfoundland Bank trawlers, right? Well, well. Keep the wolf from the door for another couple of months." He started for his inner office.

Allan Castebury and Emerson Aldrin had made themselves at home. The mayor had the corner chair by the fireplace, and was tamping his pipe. "Can't keep the damn thing lit more than five minutes," he muttered to Aldrin, who didn't bother to acknowledge the comment. The Aldrins tended to ignore people. Emerson brushed a wisp of ash from his sleeve and grimaced. The Aldrins grimaced often; for it was their fate to envision the world as it should be, impeccable and without minor annoyances like ashes.

Castebury held a match over the bowl of his pipe. His cheeks swelled and shrank as he puffed. The lawyer decided the corpulent mayor looked like a cod. Still, he admitted that Castebury had his good points: his malleability, for example. He was clay waiting for the appropriate sculptor, which was precisely how Aldrin pictured himself. His father had taught him the art, and he had perfected it in the courtroom and in private life. There were few men he acknowledged as his equal. He stood as the swinging door banged shut and Sewal Blackheath approached. "Still snowing?" he asked.

"No." Sewal shook hands. "Just the wind kicking up a bit and lifting what there is. Sit down, Mayor. Make yourself at home. Coffee will be here in a minute."

Sewal settled in the chair behind his desk. Aldrin took the seat across from him. Castebury perched on his chair by the fire, worked on his pipe, and silently watched the sparring begin. His bones told him this would be an interesting match. The Aldrins and the Blackheaths had known each other well for four generations and had been, over the years, rivals, competitors, and associates, according to the way of the wind at the time. Aldrin's ancestors had invested in a wide range of commercial ventures that provided the family with a constant source of income and power. The Blackheaths' fortunes, linked to the sea as they were, crested to spectacular heights, but also suffered periods of ebb.

"Your grandson over his cold?" the lawyer asked.

Sewal stared at him a moment. Was there an innuendo there? He wondered if Aldrin suspected about Eve and James Ruell, and for the thousandth time admonished himself. Gossip was rife in a small town, but as long as people only thought they knew, there was no danger. "My grandson is in good health, thank you, Emerson," he said, waving Eliot into the office. "Thank you, Eliot. That will be all for now."

"Yes, sir."

Sewal poured coffee all around, added a healthy dollop of brandy to his, and offered the decanter to Aldrin, who refused politely, and to the mayor, who accepted. "To McClellan," the mayor said, raising his cup. "May he lead our men to victory."

Sewal shrugged and raised his cup.

"And to prosperity, no matter who leads whom," Aldrin added, setting his cup on Sewal's desk without drinking.

"Yes," the mayor agreed. "Which is precisely why we're here, Sewal."

Aldrin grimaced. "Never let it be said that you hold back, Allan."

Sewal chuckled. "You ruined Emerson's opening," he said. "Never mind, Emerson. I figured it was something of the sort. It had to be to budge you outdoors in this weather."

"I just finished arguing a case," Aldrin sniffed. "But I must say—" He leaned forward to emphasize the point. "—The yards at Bath have never been busier."

"Yards?" Sewal scoffed. "Foundries, say. They build foundries that float. Great buoyant—" He waved a hand as he searched for the right word. "*—Stoves*. Cast-iron stoves without form or beauty. I am a shipbuilder, not a boilermaker."

"Bath has never seen better days," Aldrin insisted.

"I visited there too," Castebury broke in. "Sewal, the change in the town is unbelievable. Everyone is working. Prosperous."

"I don't doubt it," Sewal replied glumly. "But as I said, I am a builder of *real* ships."

"Who is doing precious little building," Aldrin snapped.

Sewal sipped his coffee, appeared lost in thought. When he spoke his eyes focused directly on Aldrin, and his voice was low and menacing. "Save your venom for those who are susceptible to your sting, my friend."

Aldrin brushed a manicured finger across his graying eyebrows. "I speak the truth."

"A half truth."

"And the other half?"

Sewal decided Aldrin didn't need to know about the Newfoundland Bank trawlers. Not yet. "Remains to be seen," was all he said.

"It isn't fair that the citizens of New Forest must suffer," Castebury complained. "Iron ships are the future. Anyone who has an eye can see that."

"What can I do beyond what I am doing, Allan?" Sewal asked rhetorically. "I'm weathering the storm as best I can."

"One nautical allusion deserves another, does it not?" Aldrin said. "Let me see. 'A sinking ship' would serve best."

"Perhaps you're right, Emerson," Sewal said, his hands flat on the table. "Perhaps the ship is foundering. In which case, since you have been my lawyer for all these years, you no doubt have a solution." He stood, added a log to the fireplace. By the time he returned to his desk Aldrin had leaned forward and placed an envelope on the blotter. Sewal looked down at the letter, and actually smiled. "Well, well," he said, picking it up. "You *do* have a solution. Let me see." He weighed the envelope in his hand. His smile disappeared. "My old friend," he said sarcastically.

"Now see here, Blackheath—"

"Shut up, Emerson." He sat, stared at the envelope as if reading its contents. "Enclosed is a contract offering a substantial amount in return for ownership of the Blackheath Shipyards in toto. Lock, stock, and barrel. Not nearly what it's worth, of course, but quite a tidy sum. And under the circumstances. . . ."

Castebury stared at Aldrin. He hadn't expected this, had thought the two of them had come to discuss options with Sewal.

"I was caught in a storm once, rounding the Horn," Sewal said, still staring at the envelope. "Frightful experience. Lost the foremast and half of the mainmast. We were taking water and the pumps weren't keeping up. I thought we'd go down for sure, but we didn't. Do you know why? Because we wouldn't give up. We jettisoned our cargo. Provisions, tackle, even drinking water went over the side. Everything that wasn't *absolutely necessary*." Sewal held the envelope by one corner, scaled it across his desk, and into the fireplace. "I don't think I'll be needing a lawyer for a while, Emerson. I hope you understand. Not *absolutely necessary*. It's painful. I hate to have to let good men go."

Aldrin rose, stood stiffly in front of Sewal's desk. "I see," he said, buttoning his great coat. He put on his top hat, started tugging on his gloves. "You won't have another offer. It's a pity. It really is." Not waiting for a reply, he slammed open the gate that separated Sewal's office from the outer office and stormed out the front door.

Allan Castebury, open-mouthed, watched him leave, then turned to Sewal. "I . . . I had no idea . . ."

"Of course you didn't, Allan. Here. There's more coffee, and we've a jot of brandy left." He poured more of both for himself and the mayor, pulled the chair Aldrin had been sitting in to the fire, and sat down. "Don't worry, Allan," he said, holding the cup under his nose and inhaling deeply. To Castebury's surprise he appeared to be enjoying himself. "The game isn't over yet."

Chapter 21

Sewal had Eliot help the mayor to his gig, then waited at the door while Hamlet ascended the ice-slick outer stairs to the office. The black man was bundled in a knit hat and woolen coat that were covered with a light layer of blown snow. He knocked his boots off against the side of the door. "Got it," he said, handing a large package to Sewal.

"Come in and warm up. When did it get in?"

Hamlet pulled off his coat and hat, hung them on the peg by the door. "Mister Odam said the train left it off this morning."

"Good. Good. Let's take a look." Sewal led the way through the swinging door into his office, immediately began to rip the paper from the package. Within seconds the floor was littered with balls of wadded up newspaper, and a brightly painted cast-iron train—locomotive, six cars, and a caboose—was strung across his desk. "By God, look at it, would you?" Imagining how the train would look on the shelf under an already extensive collection of sailing ship models, Sewal rubbed his hands in delight. "Think he'll like it?"

As entranced as his employer, Hamlet stared in wonder at the train. "He sure will, Mister Blackheath. 'Course, he might have to grow some first."

Sewal looked wounded. "Pick up this mess and put it back in the box," he said gruffly. "I'll straighten out some papers, and we'll be on our way."

"Yes, sir, Mister Blackheath."

Sewal set about filing work orders and memoranda into their respective slots in the box on his desk. He tapped the tobacco from the pipe Castebury had left behind and lay the pipe next to the nearly empty decanter of brandy. His stomach felt warm. His feet lifted a bit too easily with each step. He did not remember putting on his overcoat, but suddenly it was on, along with his beaver top hat.

Hamlet led the way to the sleigh, placed the repacked present for James Ruell under the seat, and climbed onto the bench seat. Sewal joined his driver. "You get the afternoon mail?"

"No, sir. Wasn't sorted yet. Should be by now."

"We'll drive into town and pick it up then."

Hamlet flicked the reins and the mare stepped out gingerly across the icy yard and onto the drift-filled road. Sewal shrank into his heavy coat and wrapped the woolen blanket Hamlet carried for him around his legs. The late afternoon wind curled off the bay and through the trees. By the time they passed the dockyards and New Forest's barely condoned red-light district, the gentle motion of the horse and sleigh had lulled him into a light doze.

"Shall I stop, Mister Blackheath?"

Sewal jerked awake. Ahead of them a second carriage was

stranded in a drift that had concealed an enormous rut. Sewal peered through the gloom, recognized Madame Laurier's driver. "Stop," he said. "See what you can do."

Hamlet pulled the mare to a halt, tied the reins, and jumped down. Sewal leaned back and assumed an aloof stance. It was all very well and good for one of New Forest's leading citizens to help even a Madame Laurier if she were in distress, but he didn't have to communicate with her in the process.

A diminutive figure plowed through the snow toward them. Demetrios removed his bowler and bowed. "My compliments, Mister Blackheath." The dwarf's slitted smile revealed a row of even, bone-white teeth. "If I might presume upon your Nubian servant and your generosity for a moment, I think the carriage can be extricated."

"Ah'm here," Hamlet said, ambling over to Laurier's carriage.

"The right front wheel is stuck in a rut. You come at an opportune moment, my friend," the dwarf said, helping Madame Laurier to the ground before climbing into the driver's seat.

Hamlet ducked under the gray's head and kicked a path through the drift. "Ought to have put runners on it," he said, shaking his head.

The gold ring in Demetrios's right ear shone in the light of the lantern hanging at his side. "The sleigh is broken, unfortunately," he lamented, raising his hands in an exaggerated gesture. "What was one to do?"

"Fix it, I 'spect," Hamlet grunted, kicking the wheel in disgust. "Let me dig out some in front of it an' we'll be ready."

Madame Laurier waited near Sewal's carriage. She had no illusions. He would be reluctant to have anyone see him in friendly conversation with the town's leading prostitute. She couldn't expect him to invite her into his sleigh. All she could expect was a civil greeting. "This is very kind of you, Monsieur Blackheath," she purred, pulling her scarf tight around her neck. "Brrr! A chill, disquieting day. Still, I do not begrudge it. Maine winters are good for business. My business, I mean, of course. Is it so with you and your ships, *monsieur?*"

Sewal made no reply. Madame Laurier laughed sarcastically. "Ah, perhaps it is too cold for an answer. Or maybe my beauty has affected you. After all, it is written that a beautiful woman can often freeze a man's tongue."

"Git ready!" Hamlet called, saving Sewal from having to answer. Sewal watched as Hamlet put his back to the wheel, stooped, and grabbed two of the spokes. "When I lift you get that horse to movin'," he commanded. His back and leg muscles strained and he grunted. "Now!"

"Hey! Hey! Heya!" Demetrios flicked the whip against the horse's rump. The horse dug in, broke the three wheels on the ground out of the snow, and pulled forward. Grunting with exertion, Hamlet side-stepped alongside until he reached the hard-packed road, where he let down the gig with a thump, and jumped clear.

"Whoa! Whoa!" Demetrios applied the brake. "Most impressive," he said, jumping down and shaking Hamlet's hand. "An amazing feat of strength, my friend."

"I cannot thank you enough," Madame Laurier said to Sewal. She ran a violet-painted fingernail beneath her crimson lips. One eyebrow raised suggestively. "If there is *any* way I can repay you . . ."

"Don't mention it," Sewal muttered, cutting her off before she could finish.

The madam adjusted her hat, smiled coquettishly, and crossed to her carriage, where Demetrios helped her up.

Hamlet took his seat again and waited while the gig preceded them down the road. "You all right, Mister Blackheath?" he asked.

"Of course," Sewal grumbled. "Why?"

"You lookin' kinda feverish, is all."

"Well, I'm not," his employer snapped. "And you may drive on."

Hamlet shrugged. "Yes, sir," he said, clamping his mouth shut. He had learned the signs long ago: When the master of Dawn Wind was out of sorts, it was best to keep silent and move quickly.

Eve sat at one end of the table, Sewal at the other. Between them, a silver candelabra set aglow a beautifully proportioned bone-white china tureen molded in the shape of a nesting hen. Arrayed in front of each place setting of matching china were smaller chick-shaped bowls for vegetables, and individual Japanese wicker baskets. Crystal goblets gleamed in the light reflected off the heavy sterling imported years and generations ago from the far side of the Atlantic.

Eve dipped a chunk of corn bread in the juice of the red beans on her plate. "I love it," she laughed, pressing down with her fork to pick up the final grains of rice laced with tiny, tender cubes of pork. "Even if it is rustic."

"Eustacia, now and then, must exercise her Southern origins. Thank heavens, in an appetizing way." Sewal grunted with satisfaction. He peered down the table at the bowl of rice Eve had emptied just moments before. As he watched she finished a small saucer full of pickled cucumbers and tomatoes that had been canned in Eustacia's kitchen. "Not difficult to tell where James Ruell gets his appetite."

"You just wait," Eve said. "Another few years and he'll be eating more than both of us put together."

Sewal nodded at Pole for tea and sat back to contemplate his daughter. Radiant in a white silk gown whose bodice seemed molded to the swelling contours of her breasts, Eve had grown into a woman every bit as beautiful as her mother had been. But there was more than beauty in Eve. Grief and disappointment and confusion had left their marks on her. Sewal could see them in the corners of her eyes and the set of her shoulders. More important, at least to Sewal, was the resolve that had allowed her to transcend pain and loss, and the inner, defiant toughness that was the mark of all Blackheaths.

And there lay the root of his discontent. The walls of the dining room were heavy with oil paintings that traced, in stark visages, the line of Blackheath firstborn sons, from the soldier captain who had emigrated from Wales and founded New Forest. His son had built Dawn Wind, and his son carried on the tradition and passed it to the current master, Sewal himself. Sewal glanced at the space next to his own likeness. There the next heir would stare with sightless eyes at countless meals, listen with two dimensional ears to unnumbered conversations in the family dining room.

Sewal grimaced and his eyes filled. He rubbed the mist away. The next heir! Michael was gone, heaven only knew where. Justin, obstinate in his so-called career, was lost to him. Photography, indeed! They were thoughts to sour any supper.

"We have an apple cobbler, sir," Hanson Pole said, taking away Sewal's empty plates and replacing them with a new setting.

"Not for me. I'll take coffee and a liqueur in the library. Eve?"

"Not another bite," Eve said. "But I'll join you as long as Doozie is asleep."

"Doozie!" Sewal snorted, pushing back from the table. "Call a ship a ship, I say. And a man a man. Doozie, by my oath. You women assign pet names to everything and everyone."

"Like Silky?" Eve asked.

Sewal's eyebrows arched. "And just where did you hear that?"

"When I was little." Pole pulled back Eve's chair as she rose. "I remember hearing you call mother 'Silky.' I asked her, and she said it was a name you made up for her when the two of you were first married. A *pet* name, she said."

"Very clever, aren't you," Sewal said, his cheeks reddening as he escorted his daughter to the library.

The fire was bright and warmed the room. Sewal unbuttoned his coat and settled into an easy chair to one side of the hearth. He was more comfortable in the library than in any other room in the house. Here, with the memorabilia of a lifetime of work associated with the sea, he could let the cares of business drain away. Here too, were the treasures he and his forebears had accumulated. The carved and brightly painted torso of a South Sea Island woman, the figurehead from the first whaler he had captained, hung above the fireplace. Beneath her hung a pair of crossed harpoons, their crescent iron barbs still shiny, their shafts still oiled and ready for use. On a nearby shelf a sextant and a chronometer rested side by side with rare and priceless pieces of jade from the Orient. A glass case built into another shelf housed a collection of delicate scrimshaw carved into baleen, walrus tusks, and whalebone. Next to him a brace of notched and battered pistols—he had put down a mutiny with them once, and another time killed the crazed mate of a rival whaler—rested at the base of a flamboyant Chinese vase decorated with overglazed waterfalls that plunged through swirling mists to a peacock blue sea. Books, models, reams of charts filled the rest of the wall space. It was an environment that might have offended the sensibilities of the proper rich whose tastes ran more to stolid uniformity, but Sewal found it both relaxing and comforting.

Pole entered, placed a peach brandy at Sewal's side, and left again. Sewal sipped the liqueur and stared into the fire. Restless, he turned to Eve, but she was already engrossed in a book. He craned his neck to see what she was reading, and cursed silently. Flaubert's *Madame Bovary*. Sounded like a cow. He'd tried to read some of it when it was published four years earlier and found the heroine, Emma Bovary, a thoroughly boring character. Damn romantic claptrap. Just what you'd expect from a Frenchman. If Eve had to read foreigners the least she could do was pick Englishmen and their solidly crafted works. Dickens would have been fine. Or Thackeray. Or Bulwer-Lytton. Grumbling his anger, Sewal retreated to *The Last Days of Pompeii* and opened the leather-bound volume to the place he'd marked.

Outside, the wind howled. Somewhere in the house a door slammed. The logs in the fireplace settled with a shower of sparks that burst against the screen. Eve closed her novel and sighed. Moods came upon her suddenly these days. Abruptly, she rose and crossed to the globe, ran a finger across North America, and then turned and left the room.

Sewal observed her restless motions from the corner of his eye. As the door closed he tried to concentrate again on Pompeii only to realize a moment later that he had read the last line three times and hadn't the slightest idea what he'd read. It wasn't like Eve to leave a room without saying something. Cabin fever? Not likely. Not Eve. Sewal's brows beetled. The globe. Was she thinking about that damn McKenna again? Or Clifford, poor chap? More impossible notions from that idiot French author? He noticed a peculiar bookmark in the novel she had left on the table between their chairs. Sewal looked around the room and then, with guilty haste, retrieved the envelope. "Jack Travis," he said to himself, his fingers drumming on the arm of the chair as he read the return address. There had been other letters from Travis, he knew, but he had refrained from prying. Eve's shifting moods bothered him, though, more so each day. The letter lay in his lap, tempting him. Surely, he thought, a daughter's welfare was a father's concern. He looked around the room, listened closely to make sure he was alone and, bolstered by the knowledge that his intentions were good, opened the envelope and began to read.

My Dearest Eve,

We have come at last to Kentucky. And what a surprise! Instead of rabble-rousing Confederate sympathizers, the Kentuckians have welcomed us as deliverers. General Grant is determined to push us South, though no one knows our destination.

There. You have my gossip. As you insisted, and I promised, I refrained from beginning with thoughts of romance. I have kept my word which, though an officer and gentleman is supposed to be able to accomplish with the greatest of ease, I find difficult in the extreme. My heart simply has other ideas, and defies my orders like a poor soldier. I cry forward: it lingers with the days gone by.

And one day in particular. Do you remember, my dearest? I cannot forget.

The dispatch rider is saddling his horse, and the sergeant announcing his imminent departure. If I hurry, this will accompany him.

Eve, there is so much more I want to say. Someday, God willing, I will. Until then, I am

Yr. Respectful Servant and Admirer,

"Jack Travis," Sewal muttered, refolding the letter and tapping it against his thumbnail. "One day in particular." Just what was *that* supposed to mean? Well, she could do worse. God knew a widow with a child needed a husband. "Jack Travis," he repeated. "Mrs. Jack Travis. Maybe." Contemplative, he replaced letter in its envelope and stared into the fire. Not until ten, an hour later, did he finally stir, and take himself off to bed.

The morning sky was an inverted lake of high, thin mackerel clouds that robbed the low southern sun of what little heat it gave to frozen Maine. The clear air hung moist in the lungs of a black man and a white girl darting among the pines on the mainland out of sight of Dawn Wind. Hamlet did not duck quickly enough. A snowball caught him and covered his head with a snowy beret. Maisie laughed aloud and ran for the safety of the trees, but her long skirt dragged in the snow. Hamlet's boots crunched through ice-covered fallen twigs as he gave chase. She laughed harder, sabotaging her own escape. When Hamlet's hand caught her shoulder she twisted and collided with him, sending them both tumbling into the snow.

Gasping for breath, Maisie rolled onto Hamlet's chest. "Now I've got you," she said, shaking her head vigorously and sending a cascade of loose snow into his face.

"It's cold under here, woman," Hamlet protested, enjoying every moment of it. "This ain't sand I'm layin' on."

Maisie kissed him full on the mouth. "I'm warm," she said.

"Which is 'cause you ain't in the snow."

She kissed him again. "Let's do it right here. Spread a blanket."

"You crazy!"

Maisie giggled. "Mr. Peters, I won't be seeing you for another whole week, what with my sister having a baby and me left with Ma. I thought that would matter to you."

"It does. And so does freezin' my be-hind."

"You won't." She pushed away from him and stood. "Not with a blanket. I'll—"

"I said, stop it," Hamlet snapped, jumping to his feet and grabbing her wrist.

"What—"

"Shush up!" Hamlet studied the surrounding woods. A fish crow lighted on a branch overhead and sent a shower of powdery snow sifting to the ground. The bird had found a crab, and croaked in guttural delight over its good fortune. Hamlet tried to listen past the crow, but could hear nothing else.

"What is it?" Maisie asked, near tears.

"Thought I heard somethin', is all. Hey!" He took her in his arms, held her closely. "No point in cryin'."

"You don't want me anymore."

"Woman, I want you more'n anything else in this whole wide world. I lie on that pallet all alone at night and think about nothin' but you." His eyes were sad, his voice soft. "Goin' crazy wantin' you, woman. You don't know how much. But it can't be that way."

Her eyes brimming, Maisie looked up at him. "Yes, it can, Hamlet. I'm tired of hiding in barns. I'm tired of sneaking off to be alone."

"And I'm not?" His temper rising, Hamlet let her go. His fists clenched with the slow, dull frustration and anger he had always known. "Where you livin', anyhow? Can't be anywhere I know, else you'd see. Oh, there ain't no leg irons here, or no whips. Folks even talk 'bout bein' free. But talk don't change the color of my black skin, which is what white folks see first off, north or south." He paused, let the anger drain from him. "That's the way it is, honey," he said, dully. "A man like me is free, and he ain't. Both at once."

"Then we'll go away together."

"Where?"

"We'll find somewhere."

"Ain't no place."

"We'll make one."

Hamlet stiffened, glanced around, but saw nothing but the silent trees. He dared to cup her face in his work-hardened hands. "You almost make me believe, woman."

"We can, Hamlet," she whispered insistently. "We—"

"Shush!" He spun around, let his eyes linger briefly on a grove of birches, and ended up facing Maisie again. "Don't look. Just come on." Pulling her with him he forced himself to walk slowly and as naturally as possible to the sleigh. The woods behind them remained silent. Telling himself he mustn't panic, Hamlet lifted Maisie onto the bench seat and leaped up beside her. The sleigh cut through a drift and onto the road. Only when they were halfway to town, and Hamlet could see nothing on the road behind them, did he slow the mare to a trot. Her cheeks washed pale and bloodless, Maisie continued to stare at him. "Someone was watchin' us," Hamlet explained shortly. "Can't put a finger to it."

Maisie looked back. The woods seemed as empty as the road.

"Someone was watchin'," Hamlet repeated, his voice low with worry. "I couldn't see 'em, but they was there."

The rising sun finally burned away the mackerel clouds and left the sky the color of fresh water ice. High above Dawn Wind bridal veils of ice crystals clinging to the windows caught the sun and scattered diamond-white light through the cupola. Outside, Sewal Blackheath braved the treacherously slick Captain's Walk. The sun had drawn him forth as, years earlier, it had pulled him from the darkness of his ship's cabin into the light on the deck. Pacing gingerly, he clutched a heavy wool coat about him and shielded his eyes until they grew accustomed to the dancing pinpricks of fire playing across the snow and the trees below. Now and then a cutting gust set snow devils dancing across the peninsula. Seen from the surface of the bay, the entire mansion would have appeared to be floating on a sea of turbulent clouds.

Sewal circled the cupola, paused to stare at the bleak shore stretching north from Dawn Wind, then continued around to face the soaring infinity where the Atlantic reached to the horizon and joined the sky. Another eight steps took him to the south side, where the sun was the strongest. From there he overlooked the bay—his bay—from whence sailed the finest ships a man could make. Eight steps further took him to the western view where the causeway joined the estate to the mainland. Barely visible beyond the leafless trees, the town—his town—lay light-bright and fresh in the distance. His father had once compared the Blackheaths to feudal lords, and though feudalism existed only in history books, still the fortunes of New Forest depended to a great extent on the fortunes of the Blackheaths. The responsibility was more bracing than an Arctic wind, and the challenge as great as that of rounding the Horn when the westerly trades were blowing strong. Responsibility and challenge together were the source of Sewal's joy, and at times, though he seldom admitted it, his anguish. Without his sons he was forced to shoulder the burden alone. Not that he couldn't, of course. But the world rested heavily on his conscience. Alone.

Why was it that he of all men should be forced to take this road? For what sin was he paying? He had known no woman since Jennifer's death. He had no passion other than sealing the gate, securing the walls of Dawn Wind for those who followed him. It was his job to strengthen the bedrock and fortify the breaches made by men without the direction of a dream. *I will endure,* he cried silently. *I will.* Head back, his eyes closed to an inner vision, Sewal stood motionless against the storm from within, and from without. At last, the vision fading, he opened his eyes to the swirling, gusting clouds of snow—and a man that walked ghostlike among them. Knuckles white, Sewal gripped the railing and leaned forward to see better. The stranger carried a rifle and looked like a *voyageur,* the men of the north country who plied the many lakes and rivers in *bateaux* and sleek, birchbark canoes.

As the man advanced Sewal could see that he wore snowshoes and what appeared to be a beaver pelt cap. His huge frame was encased in a coat cut from a Hudson Bay blanket, the coarse white wool blending with the snow, the deep wide bands of color showing red, gold, black, and green. Snow lay crusted on his shoulders and frost dusted his beard with a veil of white. Sewal squinted, rubbed icy palms down his thighs to warm them, and stop the uncontrollable and inexplicable trembling. The man below plowed through the snow and dancing mists of ice crystals like some Moses parting the Red Sea. Closer now, his rifle and pack—a cumbersome, rawhide rucksack that might have buckled the knees of a lesser man—could be seen plainly. He walked with purpose, his pace confident, as though he were immune to the winter wind and cold.

Sewal's uneasiness increased. Suddenly, forgetting the ice he walked on, Sewal turned and groped for the door to the cupola. His heart was pounding. Slowly, almost painfully, he descended the stairs one at a time, balancing himself with a sweaty palm on the bannister. Eve was standing on the second-story landing but, his face bloodless, he brushed past her. More quickly now, heedless of disaster, he took the main staircase three at a time.

Eve was calling his name, but he didn't hear her. Panting, Sewal rushed to the front doors and flung them wide. A gust of snow whooshed into the hall, invaded the house like a knife thrust. Sewal stumbled onto the porch, grabbed the post by the steps for support, and watched as the *voyageur* rounded the corner of the house and came to a stop in front of him.

He wore eye protectors, carved wooden half-spheres with slits across them to keep him from snow blindness. His shoulders were wide, dipping over his collarbones where the straps holding the heavy knapsack cut into his coat. The wind gusted, moved his beard, cracked the ice encrusted there. Sewal stared, almost afraid to speak, not daring to believe what he wanted to believe, lest he wake in his bed to another unfulfilled dream. Neither man spoke for a long moment. A heavily mittened hand rose slowly to the man's face, grasped the eye protectors, and pushed them onto his forehead. His eyes were deep-set, the skin around them crinkled and whiter than his face that was browned from the sun and bright snow. Sewal waited, speechless.

At last the *voyageur* spoke. His voice was dry and husky, unused to all but necessary speech.

"Father."

Chapter 22

"Michael!" Eve rushed past Sewal and down the front steps. Michael caught her with his free right arm and held her to him. "Oh, my God! Look at you!" Eve exclaimed. "Look at you. *Look* at you!"

Michael hadn't taken his eyes from his father's. Gently, he disengaged himself from Eve's embrace, pulled off one mitten, and bent to untie his snowshoes. When he stood up and kicked free of them Sewal still hadn't moved. Slowly, he walked up the steps. "I'm back, Father," he said.

Sewal wanted to grab his son, wrap his arms around him, and hold him. His eyes misted. He blinked back the tears. At last, when he was fully in control of himself, he raised his hand and caught Michael's in a tight grip, through which poured all the love he couldn't bring himself to express in words. "Welcome home, Michael," he said, his voice strong and resonant. "Welcome."

Two arms engulfed him. He felt himself pulled to the snow-covered Hudson Company blanket coat. He could feel the length of the rifle, the cold steel through the back of his coat. He had never been hugged by any man, not even his grown son. He stood stock-still, confused, at last pushed Michael away from him. His face was beet red. "Here, now," he coughed, embarrassed, yet secretly filled with more joy than he thought possible.

"Mister Michael!" Eustacia ran out the front door, slipped, and almost fell.

Michael's hand shot out and grabbed her as she skidded past him. "Whoa!" he roared, laughing. "Here." He handed Sewal his rifle, got a better hold on Eustacia, and hauled her to her feet. "Where do you think you're going?"

"Oh, lawsy, lawsy, Mister Michael." She grabbed him around the waist and held him. "Lissen to me. Seein' you like that done took thirty years off me. Land sakes alive!" She stepped back and looked him up and down. "You must be near froze. You get inside this minute, 'fore you catch your death!"

Suddenly, everyone was laughing. Michael helped Eve up the steps and, with her on one arm and Eustacia on the other, entered the house. Sewal followed and, once inside, stood by the door and watched while Pole and Jubb greeted Michael and then helped him out of his pack and coat.

"Isn't it wonderful, Father?" Eve stood at his side, took his arm.

Sewal set the rifle in the corner. Michael had filled out impressively. Dressed in wool shirt and trousers, he was a bear of a man. His chest was bigger. So were his arms. His beard gave him the look of a logger. Whatever, he was no longer the broken man who had walked away so precipitously a year and a half earlier. It didn't matter. Nothing did, except that his son had come home.

"Yes," he finally said, his voice low and soft. "It *is* . . . wonderful."

There didn't seem to be enough words. Eve told him about Clifford and James Ruell, showed him the sleeping baby and, when he woke, let Michael hold his nephew for the first time. Leaving out the bad news and exaggerating the good, Sewal reviewed the activity at the shipyards. Michael spun tale after tale of living alone and discovering the beauty of the woods and the vast spaces between Maine and the Hudson Straits. He told of trapping for beaver and mink and fox, of living from gun to campfire to mouth, of surviving cold and snow and torrential rainfalls and maddening clouds of insects. He told of sunrises and sunsets, of full moons and dark, cloud-covered nights. He told of encounters with bears and wolves, with still-wild Indians, and that special breed of men who trapped and hunted the lonely wastes. He told of treks through empty forests, of drenching dashes down foaming rivers and of dangerous journeys over treacherous ice. Never once did he allude to the anguish and shame that had driven him from Dawn Wind.

Eve could not tear her eyes from him. He looked so different, sounded like a completely new person. The changes fascinated and baffled her, left her feeling as if someone had taken away the old Michael and replaced him with a strange, new Michael. Only occasionally, beneath a sometimes brusque, offhand remark or a moment of brooding silence or a bellowing laugh that rose from his chest and filled the library, did she recognize the brother she had known.

The sun was far in the west when Michael rose and stretched. "I've talked more in the last four hours than I have in the entire year and a half since I left," he laughed. "And drunk more good coffee, come to think of it. What's for dinner? I could eat a horse." He grinned. "You don't suppose Eustacia would care if I snooped, do you?"

"She'll love it," Eve laughed. "Go on down. We'll meet you in the dining room."

Michael peeked out the library door, tiptoed down the stairs to the kitchen. Eustacia was alone, fussing over the stove. Stealthily, Michael crossed the floor and came up behind her. "Fooood," he moaned. "Fooood!"

Eustacia jumped and, hand on mouth to stifle a scream, whirled around. Her eyes were wide with fear, which quickly turned to exasperation when she saw who it was.

"Lan' sakes, child!" she scolded. "What you mean, comin' in here an'. . . an'. . ."

Michael laughed. "Fooood!" he repeated. He leaned forward, sniffed appreciatively. "What is it?"

It was impossible to remain angry, but Eustacia tried to keep up the appearance. "Now looky here, Mister Michael," she said, "just because you been gone, don't mean you don't remember the rules. Nobody messes with my kitchen when I'm cookin'. Not even prodigal sons."

"I'm not a prodigal son," Michael said, stepping past her and peering into a steaming pot. "Beef. I smell beef. And turnips." He reached for the oven handle. "Let's see . . ."

Eustacia interposed herself between Michael and her stove. "Whatever it is," she said, firmly removing his hand from the handle, "is keepin' warm with the cake that is bakin'. An' if my cake falls—" She let the threat dangle, unfinished.

"I give up," Michael said. He stepped back quickly. "But I warn you. If I die of hunger—" He pointed an accusing finger. "—The responsibility is yours."

"You die of anything, it'll be impatience. Anyway, it's almost ready." Her face was stern, but inside she was laughing. "Now get along with you. 'Nother half hour an' you'll have all you can hold."

She was true to her word. Sewal, Michael, and Eve gathered in the dining room. In honor of the occasion Pole had set the table with the Wedgwood and the formal gold-and-ivory cutlery. The room glowed with more candles than necessary. Sewal had dressed in his best suit, and Eve was gowned in white and blue that matched the Wedgwood. Nobody cared that Michael, who had filled out to such an extent that none of his old clothes would fit, wore the same woollen wear in which he had appeared late that morning.

The meal, when it arrived, was sumptuous. Pole led the way with a wheeled table full of side dishes and condiments. Eustacia followed with a huge platter which she refused to entrust to anyone else, if for no other reason than it had taken her a full five hours to prepare. She had thawed two beef hearts and trimmed away the tubes and fat, stuffed the cavities with a mixture of fried salt pork and onions and spices and chestnuts, and then roasted it slowly. By the time it was served the meat had fallen away and lay in great steaming chunks amid the carrots and turnips she had added.

"I'm not the only one eating, Eustacia," Michael laughed, inhaling deeply. "But the way this smells, woe to him who tries to rob me of my fair share."

"An' there's an apple sauce custard pie an' a layer cake when this is finished," Jubb said, entering with a tray and setting it on the side table. "We sure are happy to have you back, Mister Michael."

With the exception of Maisie the whole staff was there—Eustacia at Michael's side, Jubb by the sideboard, and a silent Hamlet standing in the doorway. Embarrassed, Pole stared straight ahead and cleared his throat. "This is terribly out of line," he muttered.

"You jus' hush up, Mister Pole. You know you is as glad as any of us to see this boy back home," Eustacia said.

"Of course I am delighted," Pole stuttered, on the defensive. He looked to his employer for assistance, but even Sewal was smiling at his discomfort. "Because," he went on quickly, "I am delighted; that is, I should like to demonstrate that the, uh, staff, uh, has remained unchanged. Exemplary. Beyond reproach. Ah . . ."

"Don't worry, Pole." Michael was laughing outright. "I appreciate your concern. Everything is exactly as I remember." He winked at Jubb. "Except Jubb looks like he's getting a little soft around the middle."

"Now see here." Jubb sucked in his stomach and stood as tall as he could. "I can still split a cord a wood a day."

"And snore while he's dreamin' about it," Eustacia broke in, at the same time grabbing her husband's arm and steering him toward the door. "You come along, now."

Pole's face was beet red. "I beg your pardon, all of you," he said, the moment the door closed. "Peters is simply impossible to control."

"It's a special day, Mister Pole," Sewal said. "For all of us. You've done magnificently." Pole managed a weak smile. "Now, leave us, please. We'll serve ourselves."

"Certainly, sir."

"And you," Sewal added, nodding toward his eldest son as the door closed behind Pole. "No more talking. Eat."

James Ruell Sarandon cried until his face was blue. He cried until his throat hurt and his eyes were dry. Eve had decided it was just going to be one of those nights when Michael entered behind her and took the baby from her arms. Placing him belly down on the palm of his hand, Michael lifted him toward the ceiling and bobbed him up and down. James Ruell decided this was wonderful, and began to laugh.

"Bravo! Where did you learn that?" Eve asked, delighted and a trifle uneasy at the same time.

"A man named Poulette. I hunted with him for a month or so east of Hudson Bay. He had an Indian wife. An Ottawa woman he bought in his later years. He was a powerful old bear. Sired two cubs, both boys. Hoisted them aloft, one in each hand, every time they started to cry. Worked like a charm."

"Did he ever drop one?"

"Often," Michael said, straight-faced.

"I think James is ready for his crib," Eve said quickly.

Michael grinned, bounced his nephew once or twice more for effect.

"Michael!" Eve repeated stridently. "Please!"

Michael lowered the infant into Eve's arms, watched while she tucked him beneath his covers, and gave him a pewter nursing bottle. "I'm sorry. I didn't mean to tease you."

Eve smiled up at him. "It's all right. Shh." James was sucking voraciously at the bottle. At the same time his eyelids drooped and finally closed. "He'll sleep now," she whispered, tiptoeing away from the crib toward the hall.

Michael followed and closed the door behind him. When Eve realized he wasn't accompanying her she turned to see him standing in the doorway of his own room, reappointed in the past to accommodate him and his wife, and not changed since the day he'd left.

Eve walked to his side, put a hand on his arm. "I didn't mean to raise my voice," she said nervously. The hall was cold, and she pulled her dressing gown tight around her. "Silly me. I've always trusted you, Michael. Even when I didn't understand you."

"And believed in me," Michael said. "Even when there was little reason to." He walked into the room, touched the bureau, the bedside table. He sat on the side of the bed, testing it in his memory. "You can't imagine how often I thought of this room—and that day I walked away from it. For months, I've packed it up every morning, unpacked it with my blanket every night. How is she, Eve?"

"I . . . haven't heard."

"Don't lie to me, for heaven's sake. I could always tell when you lied. How is Rosamond?"

"Well, I am told."

Michael nodded. "Well. Well enough? Alive? Surviving? Where is she?"

Eve hesitated. "New York," she said, offering no more.

"I see." He walked to the window, stared down at the pale blue patches the moonlight made on the snow, and the blackness of the sea.

Eve walked to his side, shared the silent view with him. "Why did you do it, Michael?" she finally asked, her voice strained.

Michael didn't answer for a long time. At last he turned, wrapped his arms around his sister, and held her close. "I'm sorry about Clifford," he said, avoiding her question.

"It's all right. He was . . ."

Michael coughed, interrupting her. Eve was surprised to see that, though he hid them quickly, his hands were trembling. "Look—" Michael cleared his throat. "I don't mean to be . . . That is, I . . ." His face was twisted with anguish and his voice was low, little more than a whisper. "I think I need to be alone for a minute or two."

"Of course." Eve hesitated, reluctant to leave him.

"I'll be fine." Michael smiled bleakly, nodded reassuringly. "Really."

The door closed. Michael sat without moving, then abruptly lay back on the bed. The house he was born in, brought up in. His room, his bed. *Their* bed. He felt the tears roll down his temples and pool in his ears. "Oh, God!" he thought. "Running was so easy compared to coming back."

The north woods had been what he needed. Calming quiet and physical danger, the sort he'd never minded, had broken the web of introspection that had ensnared him. Rosamond and Lion McKenna and Sewal had been distant from him there. He had felt far enough away that their accusing eyes could not reach him—most of the time.

Then, one day a snowshoe rabbit he was about to shoot for his dinner panicked and ran smack into a tree. Stunned, the frightened animal sat back on its haunches and shook his head and blinked its eyes. The sight was so ludicrous that Michael, unable to aim for the laughter that shook his body, lowered the rifle and let the confused rabbit run off. A moment later the realization that he was laughing hit him and, a little stunned himself, he knew the wounds that had driven him from home and wife were healing.

The woods and his life in the open became a never-ending marvel, took the place of the oceans his father loved so much. Here everything lived in a harmony that, although sometimes brutal and unforgiving, was complete. The largest tree stood side by side with the most delicate, short-lived flower. Great lakes accepted tiny streams. Predators, winged, finned, or footed, capped the pyramid of meek, timid creatures that supported them and yet, far from being ruled by the eaters of flesh, existed with them. It was a mutual relationship that could truly be understood only by a man who had lived in the woods.

The weeks and months passed. Winter gave way to spring, spring to summer, summer to fall. When the first skim of ice showed on the rivers flowing toward Hudson Bay, Michael knew it was time to return home, there to say: I am a healed man, whole again.

But he wasn't. Michael sensed it first as he looked on James Ruell. The eyes, the cut of the face were familiar, and in the familiarity lurked pain that, though disguised, twisted his gut and kindled a fever in his brain. As if that were not enough, he had then stepped into the room where he and Rosamond—and Lion McKenna . . .

"Whore! Bastard thief!"

The words were acid oozing from his soul as he sat and stared around him. His hidden wounds dripped fresh blood. He could feel the wild hatred creeping through him, taste the bitter gall that had fed him, see the very act that poisoned his life consummated in the heavy, lumpy shadows. His heart raced. His stomach churned. His breathing became rapid. A cold sweat drenched him and his fingers, hands, and forearms tingled. His wife! His life! They had stolen from him, maimed him, made him a cuckold, driven him away. . . .

When Michael regained consciousness he was cold and lying on the floor. Slowly, he stood and made his way to the washstand. The basin and pitcher were dry, so he leaned his fists on the stand and stared into the mirror, into himself. Dark eyes stared back: he met them without shame or fear. The woods had given him that much, he thought, even if they had also given him an illusion of peace where no peace existed. The surface was healed, but the depths still festered. Greater damage than he imagined had been done. He saw it all with sudden clarity. Himself, Dawn Wind, the life he had been prepared to live. Everything was changed, nothing was the same. In that moment he knew he would have to leave again. And in that moment too, he knew where he had to go, and what he had to do.

The clock had long ago struck two. The house was quiet. Only Sewal and Michael were still awake, sitting in the library and talking quietly, as they hadn't been able to do during the last, troubled months they had been together. Michael tamped fresh tobacco into his pipe, passed a match over the briar bowl. Gray-white smoke hung in planes on the air as the leaf caught and burned smoothly. Sewal propped his feet on a hassock. The excitement of his son's return had not worn off, but had been tempered by far later hours than he was accustomed to.

"So Justin is an artist." Michael waved a snifter of Courvoisier under his nose and inhaled deeply. "God, this is a civil drink," he said. "If you could taste the poison they drink in the Territory, you'd think 'Jersey lightning' as mild and gentle as mother's milk by comparison."

"I've dipped a bucket in the devil's well in my time," Sewal replied, fondly recalling some of the appalling brews he'd tasted.

Michael sighed, heaved himself out of the chair, and crossed to the window to stare at the flashing beacon across the bay. He puffed in silence, enjoying the flavor of tobacco and good French brandy. "Funny," he said, contemplative. "A man doesn't realize how much a place means to him until he has left. There's a feeling of warmth and safety here. I like it."

Sewal let himself relax another notch. "It does take time," he agreed, at last letting himself believe that Michael would stay.

"The child is McKenna's," Michael said, totally in control of himself.

Every muscle in Sewal's body tensed. "I beg your pardon?" he said.

"His eyes, his hair, the cut of his chin. James Ruell Sarandon is Lion McKenna's child, isn't he?"

Sewal started to deny it, but some inner quality in Michael compelled him to speak the truth. "Yes," he answered quietly.

"Does the town know?"

"There is talk, but then there will always be talk. Gossip clings to the Johnstone sisters like sailors to storm rigging."

Michael lowered his head, rubbed the bridge of his nose. He tapped blackened ashes into a nearby Persian urn, then turned to the window.

Sewal chuckled in an attempt to lighten the atmosphere. "And I thought I was the only one to commit that sacrilege. Pole never says anything, but I can see it—"

"I am my father's son," Michael interrupted bluntly. He pressed his face against the glass. The frozen pane burned his cheek, but he did not mind the discomfort. "I'll be leaving in the morning."

"So soon?" Sewal could feel the disappointment in the pit of his stomach. "I had hoped . . ." His voice trailed off.

"What? That the prodigal son has come home? I'm sorry, but the story is a myth. It doesn't work out that way. Not in real life." There was no trace of anger, or sarcasm, in his voice. "They shoot deserters, Father."

"Please, Michael. Don't say that."

Michael's voice was flat and uncompromising. "You know it's true."

"I can't believe there isn't a way," Sewal insisted heatedly, struggling for a solution. His stomach was tied in knots, tighter than the clenched fists he pressed against his thighs. "There has to be. All of this: the shipyards, Dawn Wind. It's yours."

"No."

"It *is*. As firstborn son—"

"That son is dead, Father! Don't you understand?"

Sewal stared at him. "I did not hear that," he whispered hoarsely.

"I wish you had," Michael said. He started from the room, then changed his mind and crossed to Sewal's chair. His hand, more used to hewing wood or setting traps than to gentleness, rested awkwardly on his father's shoulder. "I failed you, Father. I failed Dawn Wind. Most of all, I failed myself. On the day McKenna and I dueled—it took me months to even admit that day had ever existed—I came back to the house. I stopped in the hall and looked in the mirror and realized I hated the frightened coward that I saw looking back at me. Being alone was the only answer." He paused. His knuckles were white against the black of his father's coat. He willed his hand to relax. "Well, I've been alone and had time to think. And today I looked in a mirror for the first time in eighteen months. I'm not frightened any more, Father."

"Where are you going?" Sewal asked dully.

"Some unfinished business, and then off to war. After that?" He shrugged noncommittally. "I don't know. Maybe I'll head out to California."

Sewal shook his head. "Madness, Michael. Madness."

Michael's laugh was harsh, almost sardonic. "These are mad times. Hadn't you noticed, Father?" He crossed to the door, opened it. "I'll sleep in the guest room, if it's all right with you."

"Of course—" Sewal began. The latch clicked, cutting off his words. He was alone. Stillness boxed the room. One by one, Sewal straightened his fingers. His lips moved in silent conversation. No choice, Jenny. His eyes shut against the pain. He's a man, and I have to let him go. But did you see those shoulders and arms? God damn, but he's grown . . .

A dreary mist blew up from the south, engulfed the sunrise and clogged the bay. It clung to the walls of the house like a second skin. The penetrating dampness kept Eustacia close to the stove, where she mixed pancake batter and brewed steaming pots of strong coffee. Behind her a sleepy-eyed Pole poked his head in the door, saw that everything was in order, and climbed back up the stairs, buttoning his vest on the way. The coffee began to boil in its brown enamel pot. The batter cooled in its heavy clay bowl. Eustacia frowned at the day. Times like this she longed for cypress trees and lazy summer nights. One good memory in a briar patch of bad ones, she thought, with a shake of her head.

"I'll take some of that coffee."

Eustacia turned to see Michael in the doorway. "Lord, gosh a'mighty. I didn't 'spect anyone be up but me an' the crows. You set yourself, child, and I'll fix you a whole mess a pancakes," she said, turning back to the stove and pulling a griddle from the shelf overhead.

"Might be better if you could fix me something to carry."

"Carry? Land sakes, Mister Michael . . ." Realization came late. Eustacia threw some bacon grease on the griddle, swished it around evenly. Michael was wearing his outdoor clothes. His boots were laced, and he carried his coat over his arm. Still silent, she filled a cup of coffee and carried it to him. "I guess you ain't aimin' to set long, after all."

"Coffee's good. Just like I like it." Michael looked up at Eustacia and smiled apologetically. "I've a long ride if I want to catch the train at Portland."

"Portland? Why, the trains all stop here. You know that. War has mebbe messed up the schedulin' once in a while, but not that much."

"But the Johnstone sisters won't be in Portland to see who's boarding the train." Michael rose and shrugged into his coat. "And that's all the difference in the world. Twenty minutes?"

"Yes, sir."

"Good. I'll be back down for it then." Michael drank the last of his coffee, patted Eustacia on the arm, and opened the door leading to the outside.

"Mister Michael?"

Michael stopped, glanced around. Eustacia's hands were white with flour. Her face was impassive, but her eyes glittered. "Case there's others about—gonna miss you, child."

Made larger by his coat, Michael filled the doorway like a great, shaggy bear. At last he nodded. "Me too, Eustacia," he said, and ducked out the door.

The fresh air smelled good, after a night in a house. Body arched forward, feet sloshing a path through the melting snow, Michael strode toward the stable. Inside, it was dark and warm with the musty, rich aroma of animals and hay. He stopped in the entrance to let his eyes grow accustomed to the light, and then, graceful for all his bulk, walked to the rearmost stall. "Hello, Debbie," he crooned, deliberately choosing the least of his father's stock. The lanky, mud-colored mare snorted and shied away from him, but let him lead her out of the stall and stood quietly while he slung a saddle over her back and cinched it in place.

Straw crunched behind and off to Michael's left. "You avoiding me, Hamlet?" Michael said, starting on the bridle. "Haven't seen but two shakes of you since I got here."

A shadow moved, became a man. "Once in the dining room," Hamlet replied.

"That's right."

"Which means it was you in the woods yesterday, wasn't it?"

"That's right too."

"What you gonna do?"

Michael buckled the last strap, checked the bridle for tightness. Out of the corner of his eye he saw Hamlet step from the shadows. He carried a pitchfork. "What I set out to do in the first place," Michael answered easily. "None of it concerns Hamlet Peters or Maisie Duncan." He walked to the oat bin, scooped a few pounds of grain into a burlap sack, and twisted a piece of twine around the neck. "I'm taking some oats. I'll leave Debbie at Northrup's Stable on Front Street in Portland. You know where it is?"

"I'll find it." Hamlet hadn't moved.

"Good." Michael looped the bag to the saddle, started for the door, and stopped in front of Hamlet, "I'll be gone shortly. Good-bye, Hamlet." He held out his hand.

Hamlet stared at it, then into the face of the heavily bearded man he once had known, but was now a stranger. Still, a likable stranger. One he might even have called a friend, he realized, which was something the old Mister Michael could never have been. A slow, cautious smile spread across his face. "I'll tell Maisie it's all right," he said, grasping, for the first time in his life, a white man's hand.

"I envy you both," Michael said. Without looking back, he headed for the house.

The mist was still thick. Michael tested it and found it to his liking. The more miserable the day was, the fewer people he'd meet on the road, and the happier he'd be. He tethered the mare on the porch railing and entered the house. His father was standing in front of the fire in the library. Michael's pack and gun were where he had left them the night before, leaning against the wall next to the fireplace.

"I'm borrowing Debbie," he said, not looking at Sewal. Sewal nodded, didn't say anything. "Told Hamlet where to find her, if it's all right with you."

It had been a long, sleepless night. Sewal's eyelids felt rough as sandpaper each time he blinked. He nodded again.

"You're going to let him leave?" Eve asked from the doorway. She glanced from father to brother and back again.

"He has no choice," Michael said, cutting off Sewal before he could say anything. "Neither do I."

"We could try. All of us together," Eve pleaded.

"Michael—" Sewal cleared his throat. There was still Justin, he told himself, his mind racing wildly in an attempt to balance the awful sense of impending loss. Sooner or later Justin had to come back. Or Michael, even. Justin. Michael. A litany of sons. A lament, wailing at the fringe of his hammering thoughts. "Michael has made his decision," he said hollowly.

"Did you try to argue him out of it?" Eve asked. She turned to Michael. "He let you go once, and said nothing."

"This does not concern you," her father said.

"You can't just sit by and—"

"This does not concern you!" He did not dare to look at either of them. Shoulders hunched, Sewal stared into the fire.

Eve took a step into the room. "I was silent before. Not now."

"Michael will come back."

"After he has redeemed his honor? Is that it?" She whirled to face

Michael. "You're going to war, aren't you? I thought about it last night and realized what you were going to do."

"I have to prove something to myself, Eve," Michael said. "Is that really so terrible?"

"Yes! It's nonsense. What is there to prove? That you are vulnerable? That you can be maimed? That you can be killed?"

Michael didn't answer. Instead, he shouldered his pack, took up the Hawken rifle, looked once at his father, then at Eve, and started out the door.

"Michael!" Was he catching cold? Sewal's voice sounded hoarse. He drew himself up. His legs were spread slightly for balance, as they had been long ago when he stood on the quarterdeck and watched the sea slide past. "Take care of yourself, son."

Michael's mouth opened, then closed as his face twisted into a wry grin. He nodded once, turned, and left without speaking.

"Michael, listen to me!" Eve called, following him down the hall and racing in front of him.

Michael stopped and placed a finger against her lips. He kissed her forehead, and stepped around her. Then he was gone.

The mare trotted gingerly across the ice-covered land bridge. Michael reined her around, dismounted, and only then remembered he'd forgotten the food Eustacia was going to pack for him. There was nothing to be done for it, though, unless he wanted to repeat those painful good-byes. He'd traveled on an empty stomach often enough before. Once more wouldn't kill him. Working swiftly, he pulled the pack from his back and tied it behind the saddle. When he remounted he sat in quiet reverie for a moment, memorizing the noble old house so muted by the mist, so aloof and grand above the relentless ocean. Once his childhood, family home. But no longer. He had spent the night in the guest room. Now the guest was leaving. It was as simple as that.

Chapter 23

SUNDAY, February 9, 1862. Hiding outside Virgie, Kentucky.

We have found a hole and are resting. Plenty of food for once, enough to last a week at least, and a fresh water spring flowing a hundred yards away from camp. The men and I need this respite. Besides, there is snow on the ground, and we can be tracked too easily. He who does not move cannot be followed.

Lost Grand and Neuler last week during an attack on a munitions train. Damned fine men, and I will miss them sorely. We blew up two cars of something—a hell of a bang—but I sometimes wonder if the bookkeeping balances. A man—not to speak of our five wounded—per carload of ammunition is a grisly price to pay.

We hear very little of the course of the war. Most of the action in Kentucky is in the west, where, from the secondhand, word-of-mouth reports we receive, things are going badly for our side. I fear the Federals will completely win Kentucky, in which case we shall be even more sorely needed. I will say one thing for us: We may be ill-fed, dirty, ragged, and short of arms and ammunition, but we are lean and dangerous. We have a tenacity that I believe will win the day when wiser Northern heads prevail in Washington to end the conflict and agree that our two nations should exist in peace, to the mutual benefit of both.

I do wish I knew more of what was happening at home. The last letter I received was long before Christmas, and that by the sheerest stroke of luck after having been posted in early September. All was well at the time. If I were with Jackson—they've taken to calling him "Stonewall"—I could keep a closer watch.

I have not yet become fully accustomed to living on the run. Oh, physically, I have, but not mentally. My personal effects are reduced to a razor and mirror and my guns and ammunition, and this journal and a stub of pencil. As for food, we take what we can when we find it, and for clothes, much the same. My fine uniform is a thing of the past. Boots that fit and keep out the weather are a luxury, and dry socks without holes are a dim memory. The Valley—and Europe and New York and Richmond and Maine—are so far away they might as well not exist.

Except for Eve, of course. I am torn. When I left Dawn Wind, I wanted nothing more in this world than for her to come with me. Now, I cannot be sure. Whatever else that is said about this war, they are not fighting in New Forest, and she is safe. Still, the thought nags. If she were only here by my side . . .

We are not without merriment. Our present larder was gained amid much laughter. Yesterday, Private Forbes, a lanky, slow-spoken boy from Texas, was riding point when he fell back and, with much waving of arms, stopped us dead in our tracks. At first we thought he had found Federals, but the news turned out to be much better. The enemy was three grown pigs accompanied by, of all things, a goose. Never have tactics been more discussed or better planned. Half of the boys split to the right, a quarter to the left. The boys to the right split again, and on their signal we knew we had our prey surrounded. Since we dared not fire our guns, the operation was to take place in complete silence. Forty-eight men fanned out through the woods and advanced a step at a time. The attack, when it finally came, was brutal—and comical. One man dove for the goose and missed. Another landed in the dirt by his side. A third managed to get a hand on a leg. A fourth came away with a fistful of feathers. At last the bird was subdued. The Battle of the Pigs was no less a farce. Pigs running every which way and men flying through the air at them, thumping to the ground, getting up, and trying again. And all the while squealing and honking and grunting and hissing and, from the men, curses and oaths such as these woods have seldom heard. The result, though, was full bellies, and a quiet evening followed by deep sleep, which we all needed.

> "Goin' down South,
> Goin' down South,
> Marchin' off to war.
> Off to fight
> To do what's right,
> Marchin' off to war."

The blind singer clapped his hands in time to the music. His partner fiddled. His bow raked the strings as he deftly fingered notes from the chipped neck and tired strings. Both men stomped their feet in a crude dance. Their faces were grizzled enough to defy any computation of age, and their dusky features blended with the drab, colorless, patchwork trousers and coats they wore.

Justin Blackheath stepped forward and dropped a coin in the tin cup the two street musicians kept on a small portable stand in front of them. The blind singer turned milky eyes toward his unseen benefactor. "Thankee, sir," he croaked, in a tone designed to elicit donations from other, more hesitant observers. "Mighty cold and mighty grateful."

"What are your names?" Justin asked.

"Folks call me Bugler, sir, an' that there's Artemus." The fiddler nodded and kept on playing. Both men continued stomping the ice-crusted walk.

"Well, Mister Bugler, how would you and Artemus like to make a dollar each?"

Artemus quit playing. They both stood stock still. Bugler's head turned from side to side as if he had antennae. "Not nice to tweak to a poor man's nose, sir," he warned in a whiny voice.

Justin laughed. "I'm not. You have my word. Do you know where Niblo's Theater is?"

"Yes, sir!"

"Good. Wednesday morning bright and early. That's five days from now. I'll need the whole day at least, and if it takes two, I will pay you another dollar apiece. What do you say?"

Bugler licked his lips, turned his head in his companion's direction. Artemus bobbed his head in agreement. How the blind singer knew how his partner had responded, Justin never did find out, but he turned back toward Justin and stuck out a grimy hand. "We'll be there. Mighty cold and mighty grateful."

"Just who are you?" Artemus said, speaking for the first time, and scratching his cheek with the tip of his bow.

"My name is Justin Blackheath. I am a photographer."

Artemus shrugged his bony shoulders, lifted the violin, and started to play. Bugler began to clap his hands again, and leap into the air. How he managed to keep from slipping and breaking his neck was anyone's guess.

"Goin' down South,
Goin' down South,
Marchin' off to war . . ."

Justin grinned. The only song they knew, likely enough. Leaving
Cooper Union behind, he dug his hands into his pockets, hunched his
shoulders against the cold, and headed uptown. A fierce wind blew
up The Bowery from the East River. Justin wished he had the pair of
gloves which, along with a warm winter suit, he'd let go to the pawn-
broker when the money he'd saved while working at the shipyards
ran out. Another two dollars a week added to the meager income
Menschell Trullion paid him—or a change in his father's attitude with
an accompanying allowance—would make all the difference. Just that
morning Justin had reminded Trullion that he could qualify anywhere for a position as a pack mule at a better salary, and that the
only reason he stayed was because he was lucky enough to work with
one of the world's foremost masters of photography. Trullion had
seen through the flattery and snorted. For the first time ever he
disparaged his own abilities and countered with the proposition that
Justin, rank amateur that he was, earned far more than he was worth
for part-time help. Only a munificent fool, he wheezed, could be so
generous. Still, his eyes had twinkled, and he had given Justin the
rest of the day off to spend as he pleased.

Justin was gaining confidence. During the eight months of his ap-
prenticeship with Trullion, he had watched and listened closely. Each
day new ideas and techniques sprang to mind. At least once every
fortnight he managed to slip away long enough to visit the Lewis firm
on Chatham Street, where a sympathetic member of the company
was letting him buy one of the finest new bellows cameras and pay
for it a dollar at a time. Justin mixed a batch of high-quality albumin
paper as fast as any man in the business. He was a budding genius
when it came to posing children: for some reason they responded to
him as they never did to Menschell Trullion, whom they seemed to
distrust. Each day, when he rose, he looked in the mirror and told
himself, "I am a photographer." The dream was so overpowering
that he endowed the term with far more significance than most individuals would have.

A storm had moved in the night before and left the streets covered
with a half foot of packed snow. The Bowery was almost deserted.
What life showed itself was limited to the homeless, who clustered

about flame-capped piles of blazing debris. The luck of the innocent seemed to protect Justin from these hard cases, or perhaps his own increasingly shabby attire lent him a degree of immunity. There was no doubt that he was rapidly becoming one of them, at least in appearance. Unless things changed soon he would have to give up the one good suit he had saved to wear when he assisted Trullion on commissioned portraits of New York's nouveau riche. He did sense a coming change. He had attended, in an official capacity, of course, galas hosted by the wartorn nation's newest entrepreneurs. He had posed Cyrus West Field, chatted with Edwin Forrest, and dined with the Erastus Cornings.

Thankful to be out of the worst of the wind, Justin turned down Houston Street and headed for Broadway. In another five minutes he stood at the corner of Broadway and Houston. Two and a half more blocks and he'd be safely inside the new studio Trullion had rented on Greene Street between Houston and Bleecker, when he and Brady had come to a parting of the ways. The snow had done little to stop the traffic. Drays and private carriages, pulled by steaming horses, wheeled by. The Broadway Line had taken its wheeled carriages off the street and substituted great, gaily painted sleighs. His mind made up before he was even aware of the thought, Justin darted across the street, dug a warmed nickel out of his pocket, and caught the next sleigh uptown. Only when he was aboard, sandwiched between a pair of portly merchants, did he admit that he knew precisely where he was going, and why.

The ice skating pond in Central Park was a scene of gaiety and restrained but exuberant pandemonium. Debonair rakes and their ladies, elderly gentlemen with grandsons and granddaughters, yipping dogs, and matriarchs riding in skate-fitted chairs propelled by liveried attendants slid effortlessly across the ice. Top hats bobbed, skirts ballooned, fingers hid in fur muffs, bonnets tipped askew, cheeks flushed, and bright colors flashed in combinations of rainbows irresistible to the eye.

Justin chose a vacant bench as his vantage point, from which he could watch the river of faces flowing past. His photographer's eye roved about, picking out details. Two plain-looking girls skated arm in arm and cast bouquets of shy smiles at every unattached male. An old man in a beret and a flowing crimson scarf, arms folded behind his back and pipe firmly clenched in his teeth, slipped deftly through the throng. To one side a vendor sold hot chestnuts from a wheeled brazier topped by a cloud of steam. A little girl no more than three sat alone in the middle of the ice, her head turning back and forth as she followed first one person and then another. A young man who skated backward leaped and spun and darted from side to side. Subtle badges of wealth abounded: Aberdeen wool capes, soft and smooth; millinery direct from Paris; intricately tooled calfskin boots; sable and mink and Russian fox furs. Here old wealth and new mingled and played, while in the melting pot tenements the huddled poor were too busy surviving the cold to play in it.

He heard her laugh before he saw her, just as he knew he would. She was at the pond every Saturday. This month she was Tiara. Last month she had been Salome, and months before that, Kendra. No one knew when she would tire of one name, nor what she would assume as her new one, for she invented names on the spur of the moment and as her mood dictated. Wise in the ways of New York from her youth, she survived and flourished by dancing, by daring, by charm, and her unique, mysterious beauty. Seeing her, hearing her, knowing she existed but not being able to touch or hold or possess her was like taking a fever or illness of the heart, for which there was no known remedy.

When he saw her his heart leaped, and then sank: She was with another man. Tall and handsome in a blond, Nordic way, dressed impeccably in an umber-checkered suit, he skated with the grace of years of practice. Arm in arm, they moved as one until Tiara saw Justin. Abruptly, she waved, disengaged herself from her partner, and skated toward him. The blond youth shouted in German and skated after her.

"My shadow," Tiara laughed, sending up a spray of ice as she braked. Her cheeks were red with the cold, her eyes black and dancing.

Justin rose, cleaned his glasses on a kerchief. "You . . . skate beautifully," he said with a shy smile.

Her laughter was as bright as the sun on the snow. "You can speak, after all!" She cocked her head to one side. "Would you like to skate with me?"

Justin paled. "I . . . uh . . ."

The German slid to a halt at her side. "You are coming?" he asked.

"This is Hrolf. He is very rich. He comes to see me dance. He wants me to dance some night only for him." Tiara glanced at the man. "Go away, Hrolf. I no longer want to be with you."

Hrolf's face darkened. He glared at Justin, then at the Oceanic girl and, obviously furious, skated off into the throng.

Tiara brushed a wisp of hair back from her eye. "You have made an enemy," she announced matter-of-factly.

"Me?" Justin asked, incredulous. "I didn't *do* anything."

"Hrolf thinks he can control me by intimidating anyone I look at or talk to. He's insanely jealous, even though I've given him no cause. I think he's a little crazy, *n'est-ce pas?*"

Justin shook his head. "Anybody who looks at you probably— *n'est-ce pas?*"

Tiara stood easily, hands on hips, proud of herself. "It is French."

"I know. I know."

"A friend taught it to me. When I say it Hrolf gets very angry. Now you will skate with me?" she asked, going from one subject to the next without so much as a pause.

"I haven't skated since I was a kid," Justin said. "I don't think I remember how. About Hrolf . . ."

But as far as Tiara was concerned, Hrolf didn't exist anymore. She shook off his name with a shrug. "Come. The owner of those skates has left them for you. Sit down." She stomped through the snow, pushed him to the bench, and kneeled in front of him. "I will help," she said.

Justin's fingers were numb with cold as they fumbled with the straps. He couldn't take his eyes off Tiara. She was beautiful. She was also a puzzle. She had ignored him for months, and then suddenly paying him more attention than, Hrolf considered, might be good for him. She was a cool, self-possessed woman of the world, and yet abruptly childlike. When she posed she was serious and completely unemotional. Now he saw the playful side of her. She looked completely incapable of doing anything, but her fingers on the straps as she buckled the skate to his right foot were sure and competent.

"There!" Tiara stood, took Justin's hand and pulled him to his feet. "I can tell. You will skate beautifully."

The only thing supporting his ankles was the snow he walked in. "I can tell I'll be sorry," he muttered, pausing at the edge of the pond.

He was. Two steps later his feet flew out from under him and he landed painfully on his rump.

Tiara giggled and helped him stand. "Push away," she instructed. "And slide. Push and slide. You see, I am wearing all these petticoats and find it simple. There! You are doing it! You are . . . Oh!"

Justin, flat on his back on the ice, winced. A child—Justin had a fleeting urge to trip up the little beggar—zipped by and laughed. Justin groaned and sat up, readjusted a loose strap, and slowly got to his feet. "You have any idea of how ridiculous I feel?" he said.

"Nonsense. Everyone must learn, *n'est-ce pas?*" Justin glowered in reply. Tiara's eyes went wide with innocence. "You do not like '*n'est-ce pas*' either? I am sorry. Come. Hold my arm."

It worked. Justin pushed, slid, pushed, and slid. Before long they were gliding along almost as fast as most of the other skaters. "There, you see how much you enjoy it?" Tiara asked, delighted with his progress.

He didn't really. Not ice skating. Her closeness was a different matter. Justin felt intensely alive. To be arm in arm with her, to feel her hip touch his, and to smell the freshness of her. "You are lovely," he blurted.

Had she heard? Tiara gave no indication, merely sped up. Justin gained confidence as his body remembered. When he was a child, before his mother had died, the whole family had gone skating nearly every Sunday afternoon on the canal that ran through New Forest. There had been races, then, and games galore. Usually there was a steaming cauldron of hot chocolate and, later on in the year, fresh maple syrup candy made in the snow. Both Michael and Eve had been better skaters than he was, but Justin hadn't cared. It was enough to be happy with everyone and laugh and have fun. His mother's death had changed all that.

A large man in a checkered, umber coat skated dangerously close in front of them. His heart beating wildly, Justin faltered and glanced sideways at Tiara. She was looking at him, hadn't even noticed Hrolf. Justin could feel the grin spread across his face. The hell with Hrolf, he thought, and stepped up the pace. Tiara shifted her hand so it was locked in his, and kept up.

"I thought you couldn't skate," she said, panting a little.

Pale-cheeked ladies glanced jealously at Tiara's olive complexion and flashing eyes. Young men glared enviously at Justin, who laughed for the sheer joy of being alive. His feet felt as light as birds' wings. He was slightly crazed, delirious. Suddenly, Tiara let go his hand and pulled free of him. "Hey!" Justin yelled. He was alone, rushing forward toward the bank with the awful, sinking realization that he couldn't remember how to stop. "Hey!"

The other skaters dodged out of his way. Justin grabbed at the air and fought for balance. His body whipped forward and back like a stalk of wheat in a whirlwind. He tried to turn, but he was going too fast. Time crawled to a stop, and powerless, he watched the shore rush at him. At last the tips of his runners struck the edge of the frozen shoreline, dug in, and flipped him. Justin flew through the air and dove head first into a massive snowbank, burying himself up to his waist. His legs kicked futilely. He thought he'd smother. Pushing frantically, he finally managed to free himself and, embarrassed and out of breath, collapsed on the snow. There was snow on his face and up his sleeves and down his collar. Red with cold and dull anger, he wiped his face and dug as much of the melting snow as he could out of his clothes. By the time he finished Tiara was standing in front of him. She was laughing. "Why the hell did you let go?" Justin demanded angrily.

"You are angry."

"You're damned right I'm angry. I might have been killed." He kicked off the skates, stood, held his arms out from his sides, and shook them to get rid of the last of the snow.

"You looked very funny. Do not step on your spectacles."

Justin reached down and retrieved his bent wire rims. When he put them on they rested somewhat askew on the bridge of his nose. Maddeningly, Tiara found that amusing too, and started laughing again.

"It isn't funny."

"I'm sorry," she said, suppressing a final giggle, and then becoming contrite.

"Why the hell did you let go?" he asked again.

Tiara shrugged. "If a man tells me I am lovely, and expects me to listen, he must be able to stand alone, *n'est-ce pas?*"

"Don't *say* that!"

Without warning, Tiara turned and skated off. Justin hobbled toward the ice. "Now wait a— Kendra! I mean Tiara! Come— Ah . . ." Dejected, Justin trudged away from the scene of his humiliation, through a stand of barren maples whose ice-encrusted branches looked like reindeer antlers, to the bridge across the narrow end of the pond. He stopped at the center of the bridge to look for Tiara, but could not find her. As he watched, though, Hrolf skated out of the crowd, slowly approached the bridge, and stopped almost directly beneath him. Justin stared at him with a combination of curiosity and fear while Hrolf, his eyes small and unblinking, stared back.

Abruptly, Justin wheeled and stalked away. "If it's that important, you can have her," he muttered angrily, wishing he meant what he was saying.

Kendra, Salome, Tiara. Who would she be tomorrow? Limping slightly, Justin reached Broadway and swung aboard the Broadway Line sleigh as it passed. As far as he knew Tiara was well paid for posing exclusively for Menschell Trullion. Every time she appeared at the studio her presence set Justin's pulse hammering. He had not been a mixer at college, but had remained aloof from what he considered his colleagues' empty-headed behavior. His free moments had been filled with invention and experimentation instead of drinking and skirt-chasing. He had finally been bewitched by Tiara, though, and had spent yet another afternoon tracking her down. And found her, as usual, in the company of another man.

"Damn it!" he said, loud enough to startle the elderly gentleman riding at his side. "She's no more than a—" He stopped, unable to bring himself to complete the sentence. If he could only be as objective as old Trullion. For him the girl was no different from a bouquet of flowers to be arranged. Flowers! The very idea.

The sleigh stopped at Houston Street and Justin hopped down to the sidewalk, stalked the three blocks to the studio, and stormed into the lower gallery.

Trullion looked up as the door slammed. "Glad you could make it back," he said, his voice dripping with sarcasm. "The light is almost gone."

"Flowers, indeed!" Justin said, slamming down his hat. "She's flesh and blood. You gave me the day off, remember?"

"So I did." Menschell nodded. "Nonetheless, a remarkable outburst." He ran a knobby, arthritic assortment of fingers through the halo of static-filled hair sprouting from his skull. "You make as much sense now as the first time I saw you. Ach! The confusion! You will watch the shop, no?" he finished, starting up the stairs, then stopping halfway up as a spasm of coughing bent him double.

Justin pulled off his coat and flung it into a corner. "If you'd forget the opium and take your medicine you'd get over that!" he called angrily.

"That syrupy, puerile poison? I drink it and moments later up it comes, along with dinner. I shall cure the grippe and starve to death in the process. Oh, yes. A man was here to see you. He left, but will return."

"A man?"

"I believe that is what I said." A note of weariness tinged the disembodied voice drifting down from the left. "Don't forget. Tonight we photograph Colonel and Mrs. Cademon's deceased infant."

"What man?"

"I did not ask his name, he did not offer it. But he was a big man. Very big. I should like to make a plate of him."

The Cademons' baby looked depressingly similar to all the other dead children they had photographed. The child was dressed in a black velvet dress and bonnet. His face was a pale blue, with heavily tinged lips. Extra lamps had been brought into the parlor and, with the aid of large lenses, brightened the tiny casket. Hovering over their month-old child, the colonel and his young wife fought to control their grief over the little boy's death. The artificially brightened lights made the whole scene macabre and, for Justin, profoundly depressing. At last the final pose had been committed to film. No sooner had Menschell murmured his condolences, than the colonel's wife broke down and fled the room. No one could ever say that Colonel Cademon was less than brave, but putting his own life or those of his men in jeopardy was nothing compared to the loss of that tiny soul that had sprung from his loins. His own eyes swimming, he shook Menschell's hand, told him a check would be sent in the morning and, shoulder stiff, marched out of the parlor. Only after the servant showed them the door did Menschell and Justin realize that neither had any money with them: They were stranded more than a mile away from the studio and would have to walk.

Photographing the dead always left Justin—Trullion too, though he would never admit it—unnerved. The wind had died down and the night was clear, with stars and moon to aid the gaslights. Though brightly lit, the city was mysterious and eerie, for the crackling cold had emptied the streets and left them as lifeless as the pale blue child who lay behind them. As helper, Justin was required to carry the equipment. They had brought the light Lewis bellows cameras and the even lighter tripod Justin had adapted from a surveyor's tripod, but the box of chemicals and plates and lenses was heavy enough to make an excruciating load. Worse, it creaked and clanked, always behind him, giving rise to the overpowering suspicion that they were followed. Justin shifted the load and glanced nervously down the empty, hollow streets while Trullion grumbled, coughed spasmodically, and threatened to find another assistant on the morrow. One who, he wheezed, could carry a miserable light load and not keep an old man freezing in the street.

At last they reached Houston Street, crossed Broadway, and staggered the final two blocks to Greene. The side street was darker and filled with ominous shadows, but at least they were nearly home. With a half block to go Justin was forced to stop one last time. "You think you could handle the tripod?" he asked, panting. "It's only four more doors."

"You think you could find a new job tomorrow?" Trullion asked in return, beating his hands against his sides to keep them warm.

"I sure as hell could," Justin answered. "Easily. And leave you without anyone to hold down the fort while you run off to Washington next week." Trullion stood still, hands tucked in his armpits, and shoulders hunched against the cold. He peered up at Justin and shook his head sadly. Justin stared back angrily, then suddenly broke into almost uncontrollable laughter.

"What's so funny?"

He couldn't stop laughing. Trullion was an irascible old gnome, and Justin liked him immensely. And, he realized, cold, load, aches, fatigue and all, he wouldn't have traded the life he was living for all the money in the world. "Nothing," he finally managed, picking up the chemical box once again and tipping the tripod onto his shoulder. "I just thought if I left, who'd see to it you got your medicine? Someone has to look after you."

Trullion cocked his head, stared quizzically at Justin's back. "Wait one moment," he called, rushing to catch up, then walking backward in front of Justin. "I don't need—"

"Get the door, Menschell," Justin interrupted, "or I'm liable to drop this in the street." Trullion dug into his pocket, pulled out the key, and opened the door. Justin stumbled into the showroom and let down the chemical box with a sigh of relief. "Thank Heav——" He stopped in midword, stared into the darkness. Across the room a red dot glowed brightly, then arced downward. He could feel Trullion tense next to him and sniff the air.

Someone was in the room with them. Justin could sense a presence almost as easily as he could smell the cigar smoke. His mind raced, stopped at a scene that afternoon in the park. The German? What was his name? Hrolf? Tiara had said he was insanely jealous, but would he go as far as to— "Who's there?" Trullion rasped, startling Justin half out of his skin.

A match flared, illuminating a bearded giant dressed in a Hudson Bay coat.

"Hello, Justin."

Justin stared, dumbstruck.

"That's him!" Trullion said, a clawed hand grasping Justin's arm. "The one who came by earlier."

Justin didn't know whether to laugh or cry. "You . . ." he stammered. "You . . ."

"Surprised?" A low chuckle followed the match as it moved to a lantern. Light spread through the room.

"My God! Michael!" Justin grabbed Michael's hand while Trullion dissolved in a fit of coughing. "He's my brother, Menschell. The one I told you about."

"Brother? What kind of a brother is that, to frighten an old man out of his wits?" The cough returned, more severe this time, wracking his body. Trullion hacked and spat, then turned and, obviously disgusted, stalked out of the room.

Michael shook his head in amazement. "Who the hell is he?" he asked.

"A friend," Justin answered with a laugh. He pushed the gear to one side and locked the door. "Don't worry. He'll calm down. Come on." He grabbed the lantern and led the way up the stairs. "There's food and wine, and almost two years to talk about."

Chapter 24

One empty and another half-empty bottle of wine sat on the packing case that served as a table between them. For makeshift chairs they used the cots; for added warmth, the blankets wrapped around them. The firelight glowed on their faces and highlighted Michael's shaggy head and beard with orange daggers of brilliance. Demonic shadows created by photographic flats and set pieces stretched against the dim reaches of the loft.

"It all sounds very exciting," Justin said, his hands folded behind his head as he stared at the ceiling and tried to imagine the scenes Michael had described. He grinned, propped himself up on an elbow, and reached for the wine bottle. "Whatever, it changed you. You look as if you've turned into the devil himself." He raised the bottle in salute.

Michael laughed, returned the toast, and drank. "Whew! What'd this stuff cost you, anyway?"

Justin winced. "A quarter a bottle."

Michael grimaced, took a last swallow, and set the bottle back on the table. "No wonder. But tasty!" Chuckling to himself, he lay back and stretched. "You know?" he asked, lazily. "I wonder how long it's been since we've talked like this?"

"Years, I guess," Justin said softly. "Years and years. Kind of sad, when you think about it. Michael?"

"Yeah."

"When you were small, did you ever think about what you wanted to be when you grew up?"

"Not really." There was a long pause. "Father had decided that before I ever got a chance."

"Yeah. I know what you mean." The fire popped. Somewhere in the darkness a rat made small, scurrying sounds as it searched for food.

"But that's all in the past," Michael said, ready to change the subject. "I've bored you with the north woods, now it's your turn." He took in the loft with a glance. The only heat was from the fire. A broken east window let in the wind. The nearest water was downstairs. Justin's clothes hung from pegs on a nearby wall that served as his closet and chiffonier. "It's a far cry from Dawn Wind, little brother."

Justin shrugged. "I have a bed, and clothes on my back. The great and sovereign state of Maine hasn't tried to conscript me. As long as I can keep on doing what I want to do—always wanted to do—and keep food in me, I'm happy."

"And Father sends you nothing?"

"Now who's being naive? Father hopes to wear me down. His faith in me—or should I say lack of faith—is positively stimulating. Because, you see, I'm not giving in. For the first time in my life I am my own responsibility, learning my craft and art—you wait, photography will be an art sooner than you think—in the only way possible."

Michael snorted. "If you ask me, I think the old rascal downstairs is taking advantage of you."

Justin wagged his head, no. "I understand him. To tell the truth, working with him has been a tremendous advantage. Trullion commands respect in many influential circles, and my name is more often than not spoken in association with his."

"See? A flunky."

Two years earlier Justin would have torn into Michael for such a remark. Now he just smiled. "Next week he's going to Washington to photograph Seward and the rest of the cabinet. While he's gone I'll be in charge of the studio." He turned his head, looked at Michael. "Which includes, by the way, photographing a party at the Astors' honoring Governor Seymour." His voice was tinged with pride. "Not to mention certain other commissions I've gotten on my own, which isn't easy, given the number of photographers in New York. He may not look like it at the moment, but your little brother has Peacock Alley in his pocket."

"Peacock Alley," Michael said, enjoying Justin's obvious pride in his accomplishments, and the camaraderie that had blossomed between them. They had not been this close since they were children. The tension that had grown between them as the years had passed was absent. "The crème de la crème. I guess you've met them all, eh?"

"I hate to brag."

"Let's see now. You've met the Astors?"

"Once."

"The Roosevelts and the Vanderbilts?"

"Yes and yes."

"Generals and admirals?"

"Indeed."

"The Cabells?"

"Yes." Justin's expression altered. He propped himself back on his elbow and stared at his brother. "You baited me, damn it, Michael." An uneasy silence enveloped the loft. Michael was staring intently at Justin. "Look," Justin finally said, "just why are you here?"

Michael shrugged, lay back. "I'm heading west. On the way, I thought I'd drop in and see my brother."

"An innocent act," Justin said.

"It's true."

"But not completely true."

Michael sat on the edge of the bed, picked up the bottle of wine, then set it down without drinking. "I want to find Rosamond. She is still my wife."

"Not so's you'd notice," Justin said, cursing his indiscretion in the same breath.

"You know where she is and what she's doing." His voice was low and intense. "I want to know, Justin."

"Our paths have crossed, is all. A month ago Menschell and I were photographing a reception for the English ambassador. Rosamond was there with a broker by the name of Sanger Stanford. He carries enormous influence in the business community, I hear." He shrugged. "She did not see me and I left before she could."

"There's more. I can read it in your eyes."

"Look, Michael . . ."

"I want to know, damn it!"

Images of the old Michael, made the more vivid by his stridency, flashed through Justin's mind. "Okay, okay," he said, relenting. "I asked around. Rosamond and her mother moved to New York when the war broke out and everyone was afraid the Confederate Army was going to take Washington. For some reason they haven't moved back. The doorman where they live, he's a gossipy old German with nothing to do but pass the day with anyone who has a question, says the admiral's only been to see them twice. And also that the old lady is weird, touched in the head. You can talk to him if you want all the sordid details.

"At any rate, I dropped it at that. Then, about a week ago, I saw Rosamond and this same Stanford fellow together at Christy's Opera House on Broadway, above Grand, and followed them. I suppose out of curiosity. Mr. Stanford keeps an apartment at the Stoneleigh on Forty-third. They went in together, he came out alone. I assume she lives there. Look—" He paused, afraid he'd said too much. "It's over. You left, so did she. Why in heaven's name do you want to see her again, anyway?"

Michael stood, wrapped the blanket around himself, and paced back and forth in front of the fire. "She's my wife. I want to talk to her before I leave, if that's all right with you?"

The closeness between them had vanished, but Justin wasn't about to give up. "That's fine except for one thing," he said with blunt honesty. "You're wanted for desertion. If you're recognized and caught you'll be thrown in jail and probably hanged."

Michael waved his hand in dismissal. "Nobody here knows me well enough," he said.

"Rosamond does. And I wouldn't put it past her. You have better things to do, Michael."

"Oh?" Shoulders hunched, his whole body tense, Michael stood in front of Justin. "Like what, for instance?"

"Like staying alive, for Christ's sake," Justin snapped, and then, as if drained, lay back and pulled off his glasses. He was tired of anger, of contention. Tired of Michael and himself, of bickering and fighting. "Ah, hell," he sighed. "I don't know, Michael. It just seems that you're better off forgetting her. Rosamond is Rosamond, and all she'll do is bring you grief."

The tiredness hit Michael too. Laughing softly to himself he sat heavily on the edge of the bed and ran one hand across his eyes. "Ah, little brother, little brother. You always were a pessimist where women were concerned."

"I guess so," Justin said. Sobered by the charge, he rose clumsily, poured himself a dash of wine, and drank it off. "Too bad I haven't met one to change my mind."

Michael pointed to the wall next to the fireplace, where a provocative photograph of a half-naked girl reclining on a Grecian couch hung. "Even her?" he asked with a lecherous grin.

"More than anyone else," Justin said ruefully. "Especially her."

A bath, shampoo, haircut, and beard trim had cost a dollar. A new suit, shirt, and shoes a speck over fifteen. Michael looked at himself in the mirror and waited while the clerk inspected the five-dollar gold piece lying on the counter, and tried to decide just how open he should be. "Well, sir—" The coin disappeared into his pocket and the clerk leaned forward conspiratorially. "Actually, Miss Cabell does keep an apartment here, but she doesn't *live* here, if, uh, you grasp my meaning."

Michael's eyes narrowed. "What number?"

The clerk glanced around to make sure no one was listening. "You're sure you're a friend of hers?"

"Yes." Michael winked, set a gaily wrapped package next to the five dollars. "An intimate friend, if you grasp *my* meaning, who wants to leave a little gift for her."

The clerk reached for the package and the gold coin. "Of course, sir. I'll just . . ."

Michael's hand covered the money. "In her room. Where she'll be sure to find it."

The clerk wet his lips nervously. "I don't know . . ." The gold winked at him. "I'd have to go with you," he whispered hurriedly. "To make sure nothing . . ." He trailed off lamely. "You know . . ." Michael's hand lifted. Fast as a lizard's tongue, the clerk's fingers flicked out and retrieved the coin. "Mr. Harvey?" he called officiously. His assistant looked up. "Watch the desk a moment. I'll be right down."

The stairway was dim, even at eleven in the morning. Michael, gift in hand, allowed himself to be led to the third floor and down a sparsely but tastefully appointed hallway to Room 316. Still apprehensive, the clerk opened the door and followed Michael inside. The room was furnished with two overstuffed easy chairs, a large-canopied bed covered with a thick, pink feather quilt fringed with white lace. Its polished surface mirroring the intruders, a massive mahogany dresser rested against the wall. A vanity with hinged beveled mirrors and an assortment of lady's beauty aids sat between the windows that opened onto Forty-third Street. A curtain emblazoned with a floral design hid the entrance to the private bath. Thick throw rugs woven in the same design as the curtain were strewn about the floor. The design was repeated in reduced size on the wallpaper.

"There. That will surprise her," Michael said, placing the package in the middle of the bed.

"Yes, sir." The clerk was clearly agitated. His hands made little fluttering motions designed to hurry Michael out of the room. "If you don't mind, sir . . ."

"Of course." Michael paused in the doorway, turned for a last look. "A really nice hotel you have here. Very nice."

The clerk hurried through the door, let Michael close it, and then twisted the key in the lock. Not wasting a moment for small talk, he led the way back downstairs and gratefully saw Michael out the front door.

Michael wasted no time either. Pulling his top hat low across his forehead, he made his way to the alley, cut through it to a side entrance, and slipped inside the hotel. A moment later he was taking the rear stairway two steps at a time. The third floor hall was empty. Striding confidently, as if he was supposed to be there, he made his way to three-sixteen and pushed open the door. He stepped inside, dug out the wad of tobacco with which he had surreptitiously plugged the bolt hole while the clerk was making a final check of the room, and closed and latched the door. He shoved the package under the bed and, satisfied, took a seat in one of the easy chairs. All he had to do was wait.

A woman in the hall laughed. The door rattled. Wide awake immediately, Michael rose from the chair where he had been dozing and slipped behind the curtain masking the bathroom. The clock on the dresser read a little after three. Prepared to wait much longer if necessary, Michael had been lucky.

The door opened. "So you liked it, eh?" an unknown voice said.

"Of course." It was Rosamond. "I like everything you give me. You know that."

"Then a gift for a gift, eh? Namely the delightful flesh of the most beautiful woman on the Eastern seaboard?"

"Sanger, really," Rosamond protested. Giggling, followed by a rustling sound and more giggling, and a long, drawn out sigh.

"I love your coyness. It arouses me."

"And I," came a suitably husky reply, "love you aroused."

"Mmm. Do that again," Stanford said, his voice muffled as his lips buried themselves against her neck.

The bed creaked. Michael stole a look through the curtain. Rosamond and her lover were lying back on the covers. Stanford was a short, trim, prosperous-looking fifty. Rosamond's long, pale fingers were ruffling his close-cropped hair. She made little cooing sounds of pleasure as Stanford hurriedly undid her bodice and his lips found her nipples. Michael's eyes closed and his fists clenched against his sides. That was his wife: He had been right all along. "Damn her, damn her, damn her," he said over and over again to himself.

Rosamond's voice was as seductive as he remembered. "When is Lillian expecting you home?" he heard her ask.

Michael's hands were trembling. Barely able to control himself, he looked out again. Rosamond was naked to the waist, and in the process of removing petticoats from under her skirt.

Stanford loosened his tie, began to unbutton his shirt. "You make me sound like. a child. Lillian is my wife, not my master," he said shortly, bending to untie his shoes.

Rosamond thrust her breasts forward, rubbed them sensuously

against his head. "She is, unlike some I know, a slab-chested old hag."

"Perhaps." Stanford stepped out of one shoe, then the other. "But well endowed in other areas. A seat on the Exchange doesn't come cheap, you know. Nor does this room." He kissed first one breast, then the other. "Ah, such sweet breasts . . ."

"That tickles!" Laughing, Rosamond sat on the edge of the bed. "Come here."

Stanford stood in front of her, watched as she pulled his shirt out of his trousers, and ran her hands over his chest. A sigh turned into a groan as she unhooked his belt and began to unbutton him. "And what do you think she'd say about this?" Rosamond teased, stroking him into hardness.

"Don't be absurd. She'd . . . Oh, my God. Don't stop now."

"My shoes," Rosamond said, pushing him away from her. "Besides," she giggled, "you look quite silly, half dressed like that." Ignoring him, she crossed her legs and started unlacing one shoe.

Resigned, Stanford watched her while he finished untying his tie. "You do that just to tease, don't you?" he said petulantly. "You know it makes me nervous to talk about husbands and wives, but you insist. I wish you wouldn't."

"I don't know why," Michael said, stepping through the curtains. "Seems like a perfectly natural subject, under the circumstances."

Rosamond gasped and covered herself. Stanford, his coat half off, almost fell over backward. "What the hell?" he said, staring in disbelief.

"Oh, my God. Michael!" Rosamond grabbed a pillow, held it over her breasts.

Stanford was terrified. "Now wait a minute! Now wait a minute!" he pleaded, one hand held in front of him to fend off Michael, the other fumbling at his fly. "I didn't know . . ."

"Good-bye," Michael said, taking a step forward.

"You'd better not . . ."

"Good-bye."

Stanford backed into the wall, found his cane, and raised it as if to strike Michael. "Don't come any closer, do you hear. I'll use this if I . . ."

Michael's forearm slashed down like a club. The cane broke into two pieces. Stupefied, Stanford sucked in his breath. "Now, let's not, uh, lose our, uh, tempers," he stammered, feeling to his side for the door.

"Good-bye," Michael repeated, and raised his hand again.

"But my shoes. You can't . . . See here!" Tie undone, shirt unbuttoned, trousers gaping open, and still shoeless, the broker spun, twisted the doorknob, and fled.

Michael slowly closed the door, turned, and leaned against it. Rosamond hadn't moved, sat frozen, stunned. Michael stared at her, at the body he had known. She seemed gross to him, an evil, despicable thing. Not even thinking, he started toward her. When he did, her mouth opened and her tongue glistened across her lower lip. Memories engulfed him. Once upon a time he had succumbed to those purple eyes that now peered into his. Her hand touched his thigh, burned through the fabric. Her throat was soft and warm to his encircling hand.

"Michael?" she whispered.

His hand tightened around her throat, forced her back to the pillows. Realization came slowly at first, then blossomed in a surge of fear. His face was inches from hers. She could feel his breath on her cheek. She tried to swallow, but couldn't. Her flesh tightened, her heart throbbed. Breathing was impossible. Frantic, Rosamond tried to push him away, but his weight was relentless. She reached for him, but his hand first batted hers away, then caught and clamped her wrists over her head. Her mouth moved silently in a desperate plea, but the look on his face was implacable. At last, senses reeling, no longer able to bear looking at him, she shut her eyes as if, no longer seen, the awful presence and pressure might disappear.

Strangely, it did. Air poured into her lungs. Cold air from the room in which she had not had time to light a fire. She let her eyes open, concentrated on the marvel of breathing and seeing. Gingerly, feeling each bone and muscle, she sat up. Her throat hurt. Her wrists, where his grip had ground them together, ached terribly. A purple splotch spread across her thigh where Michael's knee had gouged her. Sanger's shoes lay where he had left them. His cane, broken, lay in two pieces in the middle of the floor. And the massive, brooding figure of Michael slumped in the easy chair in front of the cold hearth. Her whole body shaking, Rosamond managed to stand. "You tried to kill me," she said, wincing at the pain in her throat.

He had. He had loved her as he had loved no other person. But she had failed him. Soiled him. Made him walk away from his birth-

right. She had tortured him, turned bliss into unholy jealousy, can-
cerous and debilitating. Most damning of all, he had let her. A terrible sadness weighted Michael's mind. Sadness for himself, sadness
for Rosamond. "Get dressed," he said, his eyes as bleak as ashes.

Rosamond limped to the bathroom, emerged a moment later in a
flowered dressing gown. She held a wet cloth to her throat, as much
to stop the spreading bruises there as to ease the pain. "Why did you
stop?" she asked.

"After what I just saw? . . ." He trailed off, ran a hand across his
eyes. "I wish I knew."

"He has money, Michael."

"And you play tart to his lust?"

"I survive. What do you expect?" Rosamond sat weakly in the
chair facing Michael. "I have no means of support, other than what
Father sends."

"Plenty of people live on less," Michael said scornfully.

Anger replaced fear. Rosamond's eyes flashed. "I'm not plenty of
people!"

"You *are* a married woman, though."

"You'll pardon me for paying little attention," came the sarcastic
reply. "You see, my husband deserted me—*and* his country. Or have
you forgotten?"

Michael's shoulders hunched and his hands clenched into fists. "I
remember a wife who—"

"I remember too!" Rosamond's voice cracked, but she went on. "I
remember everything, exactly as it happened. And now you come
back to pass judgment on me. Well, pass it on yourself, Michael. The
only use I have for you or your family is what's coming to me the
second I can legally have you pronounced dead."

"You'll not get one cent from me or my family."

"Really?" Rosamond asked sweetly. She stood, kicked Stanford's
shoes under the bed. "*Our* family, dear husband, according to the
lawyer I've talked to. As long as we are married, I have a legitimate
claim. And we shall remain married, unless you wish to declare yourself and face a court-martial and a firing squad."

Michael watched her pace, watched the length of her legs as they
pushed through the partially open dressing gown. "You are corrupt,"
he finally said in a low voice. "Totally, utterly corrupt."

"No! Not corrupt, Michael. Alone. Left alone by you." She turned
and sat on the bed, wrapped her arms around the post. "Mother lives

alone in her own dream world and squanders whatever Father manages to send us. When he's gone there'll be nothing but a pension." She wiped the moisture from her cheek. "I won't accept that, Michael. I am a desirable woman. I can have the man I want. Between Sanger and the Blackheaths—" She stopped, looked down at her hands. "I should do nicely, Michael. Yes. Nicely."

Michael shook his head. "You have it all planned, don't you?" he said.

Rosamond shrugged. "Things might have been different, but in a world ruled by men, it's catch as catch can. So there you are."

"Yes. Here I am," Michael agreed mirthlessly. He stood, looked down at her. When she didn't move he tilted her face up toward him. "You'll have bruises on your neck."

"I know."

"Pretty neck." His fingers brushed against her cheek, still moist with the paths of tears.

Suddenly, Rosamond reached up and took his hand, drew it down to her breast and kissed his wrist.

"Sometimes I make believe it's you," she whispered, her voice dreamy.

"Sometimes?" Quite without warning, the sadness returned. He had come to kill Rosamond, to exact revenge, only to find that it was too late for revenge. But the slate was not yet clean; the labor begun the day he walked away from Dawn Wind the second time was but half over. He was free, now, to continue his odyssey of redemption. He was certain he would succeed.

Michael's hand slipped from Rosamond's grasp. Caution returning, he checked the hall. Rosamond started to say his name, to call him to her, and hesitated. In that second, she lost him forever.

It had been a long, hard day. The Staten Island Ferry had been crowded, and conditions were impossible. Great cakes of ice from the Hudson had crashed against the boat. Fog and a freezing drizzle had slowed it to a crawl. Twice the ferry had barely missed collisions with merchant vessels. Once ashore the journey had barely begun, though, for it was still a three-hour trip to Newark and the trains west to Ohio. Not until four in the afternoon did they enter the great barn of a station.

Michael eased his pack to the ground, rested on it, and tried to relax while he waited for his brother to buy a ticket. The crowd ignored him, for which he was thankful. At Justin's insistence—"an ounce of caution is worth ten fatal seconds on the end of a gallow's rope," he had quipped—Michael had shaved off his beard but kept the long, bushy sideburns. Nervous, feeling a little naked, he fingered his chin.

Justin edged sideways through the crowd, almost bumped into Michael because he had been looking over his head. "Tired?" he asked.

"No, not really. Depressed is more like it. Setting out is the hardest part." He stood and grinned to show he was all right. "I'll feel better once I get started."

"Right." Justin pulled an envelope out of his coat pocket. "Here are the tickets. You leave on track eight, and go all the way through to Columbus. From there, you transfer to Louisville."

Michael inspected the tickets and tucked them in his pocket. "Good."

"I wish you'd explain why you're so determined to go to Kentucky, though," Justin said, helping his brother shoulder his pack again. "It doesn't make sense. If I were you and San Francisco-bound, I'd take a boat."

"And miss a whole continent? Not me. Always did want to see—" Michael gripped Justin's arm, nodded imperceptibly. A half-dozen soldiers were in the process of filtering through the crowd. Each carried a pamphlet to which he continually compared the faces he passed. "Well, well," Michael said.

"I warned you about Rosamond," Justin whispered.

"No, she has nothing to gain if I'm apprehended. It was probably Stanford, her friend. I wasn't very nice to him. Of course, they could be looking for someone else. I'm not the only—"

"You want to take that chance?"

"I guess not." Michael grabbed his brother's hand. "Thanks for everything, Justin. Take care of yourself. I'll write you from the goldfields." Before Justin could speak Michael was weaving through the crowd in the direction of track eight.

Justin looked around apprehensively. One of the soldiers pushed past him, staring at the train and the passengers climbing aboard. Justin glanced down at the crudely sketched picture of his brother. "Excuse me, sir," he said, thinking quickly and pointing at the picture. "Are you looking for that individual?"

His expression betraying disapproval of able-bodied men not in uniform the soldier stared at Justin.

"I saw him, I think." Justin didn't have to pretend to be nervous. "I'm sure it was him. He was hurrying across—" he pointed away from track eight "—those tracks toward that line of boxcars. I thought it odd behavior, but didn't know until noticing your poster that the chap was a criminal."

"Damn." The soldier glanced at the boxcars, peered closely at Justin. "You're sure?" he asked skeptically.

"Yes, sir. Beard just like that. And shifty eyes. That's what drew my attention to him in the first place. I can tell, you know. It's in the eyes . . ." He trailed off, sighed with relief. The soldier was fighting his way through the crowd and, with a shout, taking his companions with him. Justin chanced a look and glimpsed Michael waving at him through a passenger car window as the train slowly started to pull out of the station. Quickly, he doffed his cap in return and beat a hasty retreat. He'd come as close as he wanted to the army, and it wouldn't do to have the soldiers suspect him of mischief. The journey back to Manhattan promised to be a cold, lonely trip.

Trains and dragons, Michael thought, for some reason remembering the lighthouse with its single dragon eye across the bay from Dawn Wind. Leave one, leave on the other. Justin was gone, out of sight, the station disappearing behind a line of tenements. Pensive, he swung his pack onto the overhead rack, then sat abruptly as the train lurched forward. An elderly gentleman, likewise caught off balance, stumbled forward. Michael reached out an arm, caught him before he hit the floor, and helped him to his feet. A child cried out in alarm, a young boy whooped with delight. The train gathered momentum, settled down to a smooth pace measured by the clicking rails and telegraph poles flashing by.

Columbus, Ohio. And then Kentucky. Michael dug a scrap of yellowed paper from his coat pocket. Wrinkled and stained, he had cut it from a one-month-old edition of the New York *Herald* that Michael had discovered while passing through Quebec on his way home in January. The clipping was a dispatch from the Western arena of the war. Kentucky, once neutral, now by choice under Union control, was a state that was being subjected to a vicious guerrilla campaign waged with singular ferocity by a handful of Southern cavalrymen. One of the notorious leaders was a Captain John Mosby. Another, responsible for plundering badly needed Union shipments to the West, was the elusive Captain Lion McKenna.

Michael refolded the scrap of paper, then on a whim lowered the window. The tired paper fluttered and flapped, tore along a well-worn fold. Michael watched it closely. One tiny square flew away, ripped from the rest by the wind. His fingers got colder, but he paid them little attention. At long last he let go, allowed the icy air rushing past to whisk away what was left. He didn't need it anymore.

Chapter 25

Justin, huddled in front of the cheerful blaze, every now and then reached out to stir the contents of the kettle hanging over the fire. The stew was an old recipe of Eustacia's that had accompanied a half-dozen pages of the latest gossip and news of New Forest in Eve's latest letter. The tone was bright and chatty, but Justin was not fooled. He could sense between every line the loneliness from which it sprang. Eve's brother was more than grateful that he wasn't in the same predicament. Quite the opposite, as a matter-of-fact, for with Trullion stuck in Washington for another week, and possibly the whole of the next month, Justin was in exactly the situation he wanted. There was time to be alone, time to work, and more time than ever to experiment at leisure. Taking care not to gloat, he continued his answer to Eve, in which he described Michael's departure the week before and then plunged into an enthusiastic jumble of technical descriptions of his latest self-teaching venture, stereographs. For good measure he included a half-dozen of his most successful attempts. Virtually identical photographs fixed side by side on a heavy piece of paper, they portrayed some of his favorite New York scenes in full three-dimensional quality when viewed through the stereoscope he had sent her some months earlier.

It was almost dark when he finished his letter, gave the stew another stir, and rose to stretch his legs. The brief warm spell that had melted last week's heavy snowfall had been replaced for the last three days by a freezing drizzle that drenched good spirits and drowned health. Now a brisk and biting February wind sweeping down the Hudson and knifing across Manhattan Island had cleared the streets of evening traffic. Justin fiddled with the cotton wadding he'd stuffed in the broken window, fixed it so a little less air poured through, and retreated to the hearth to warm his hands.

The stew was ready. Slow bubbles rose and popped, sending tiny sprays of broth and grease into the fire. Justin wiped out his bowl, rubbed it with a clove of garlic, as Eustacia had suggested. His mouth was watering. "Just like home," he said, talking to the empty loft, then added, with a self-satisfied grin, "Only better."

He straightened suddenly, cocked his head. A hammering sound coming from downstairs was much too insistent to be attributed to nature. Now who could that be, he wondered. Another bereaved parent wanting a dead child photographed? Not unlikely, considering the weather. Or Trullion? No. Impossible. Soldiers? Had Rosamond discovered his deception and sent them to his place? Quickly pulling the pot away from the fire, he grabbed the coal oil lantern and hurried across the loft, into the hall, and down the stairs.

"Justin! Justin!" It was Tiara's voice, pleading, frantic. Justin ran to the door and threw it open. Tiara's long hair was soaked and plastered to her half-naked torso. An ugly bruise marred her cheek and formed a dark, ugly smudge beneath her left eye. Dried blood trailed from the corner of her mouth. Near collapse, she tried to come forward, but staggered backward into the street instead.

"My God! Tiara, what—"

"Please . . ." She could barely talk, clutched the tattered remnants of her dress to her against the bone-numbing cold. "Help me. He is—"

Justin ran to her and caught her around the waist before she fell. Her flesh was ice cold and she clung to him weakly. "Don't talk," Justin said. "Let's get inside where it's warm. Come on."

"Very touching. The tart knew where to run."

Justin's head jerked to the side. "Hrolf!"

"Thank you." A heavy overcoat and the half-light made him appear even more massive than he was. His boots scraped across the ice-covered street as he stepped closer and held out his hand. "I'll take her back now."

"No!" Tiara moaned and slid to her knees, unconscious.

Justin braced himself, turned as best he could to face the German.

"That's far enough," he said, fighting his voice to keep the fear from being too obvious.

"Really?" Hrolf smirked. He was enjoying his little game, and wanted Justin to know it. "She's been entertaining me for the past couple of days. You see, I'm leaving for Europe tomorrow, and I wanted something to remember your lovely country by. Oh, she struggled at first, but soon gave up, and quite happily did everything I commanded." He held his palms out and advanced slowly. His voice was low and taunting. "So perhaps you don't want her, I think. How ungrateful she is. I went upstairs to bid her farewell, only to find she had escaped. Now, how can I leave without a final farewell?"

Justin didn't bother to try to answer. Fury replacing fear, his arm swung in a wide arc over his shoulder as he hurled the lantern he'd carried downstairs. Hrolf tried to dodge, but wasn't quick enough. The lamp hit the pavement between the German's feet and exploded. Flames engulfed his trousers. Hrolf shrieked, danced madly as the fire singed, then feasted on his flesh. Howling, he raced first this way then that, batting at his trousers.

"Come on," Justin pleaded, grabbing Tiara under the arms and pulling her toward the door. He was sweating despite the cold, panting for breath. The door had swung shut. Awkwardly, one arm supporting Tiara and the other groping for the knob, he dragged Tiara inside and lay her down on the floor. When he rushed back to close and lock the door, he heard a loud splash. Looking cautiously outside, he saw Hrolf desperately splashing water on his still smoldering clothes.

Tiara's eyes were wide with fear; her teeth were chattering. Justin knelt at her side. "Can you stand up?" he asked gently. She shrank away from him until the wall stopped her. Justin pulled off the heavy sweater he was wearing over his shirt and draped it over her. "There's a fire upstairs and hot food. Don't be afraid. I won't hurt you." Once again he reached out to help her stand, once again she tried to pull away. "If you are afraid of me, then why did you seek me out?"

Her fingers and lips were blue. She couldn't stop shivering. A few feet away, kneeling patiently, Justin waited.

"Because I knew you would help me," she finally said in a voice as frail and soft as doves' wings.

"Then let me," Justin said. "Can you walk?"

"I think so." She let him take her hand, then gasped and shrank away as the front door rattled.

"Only the wind," Justin said, looking over his shoulder. "No need to worry. Come on." He helped her up, half carried her toward the stairs. "Anyway, Hrolf won't be back tonight. Or any other time, I suspect."

"I will kill him one day," Tiara spat. "If I had my knife, he would never . . ." She was on the verge of tears, trembling now with mingled rage and fear and fatigue. The fury in her, combined with the realization that she was safe, drained the last of her strength, and she lost consciousness again.

Justin grunted, scooped her into his arms, and carried her up the stairs to the loft. Small as she was, her body was solid and muscular, and surprisingly heavy. Panting, he maneuvered his way through the jumbled flats and set pieces to the fireplace, and placed her on his mattress. Her skin was pale and tinged with blue. Working quickly, Justin cut away the remains of her clothes and briskly toweled her from head to foot.

She still hadn't moved. Justin tried to remember what to do for someone so chilled. He couldn't feed her anything until she regained consciousness. Feeling helpless, he tore one of the blankets from the pallet Michael had used. He had to warm her, restore the circulation. Damn Hrolf, anyway. Why were there always those who felt their money and position gave them free rein to abuse the helpless?

He stopped, stood over her, mesmerized. He had seen her naked before, of course, but except for the first time, when he had been so surprised, the nakedness had seemed almost matter-of-fact, and Tiara distant and unassailable. Now she was tiny and fragile and vulnerable. Moved almost to the point of tears, unable to resist, Justin let his eyes rove over her body. Her breasts were petite, still rounded though she was lying flat on her back. Her chest rose and fell with the barest hint of motion. Her stomach was flat, her navel a soft indentation. The dark, triangular nest of her womanhood was a downy mystery that pointed to velvet smooth coffee-colored thighs and dimpled knees.

Justin swallowed with difficulty. Cursing the baser part of his nature, he realized he was aroused, almost painfully so. Unable to stop himself, he knelt by the side of the bed. Tiara's thighs were slightly open, her intimacy unguarded. He touched her there, then bent forward and brushed his lips against her thigh, drew back, and kissed the mound of love and let another kiss linger on her stomach. She was soft, softer than light or music or snowflakes. Whispering her name, he lightly kissed her bruised mouth, each closed eyelid and her forehead, then leaned forward until the center of his forehead barely touched her right nipple. For a long time, he did not move; rather, he let all the sadness and loneliness pour through that one, tenuous contact, from him to her.

Still, she didn't move. Her breathing was shallow and even. Gradually, the world returned and Justin sat back on his haunches and looked around. The fire crackled, the wind moaned through the broken, cotton-stuffed window. How long he had knelt there he did not know. Not long, though, for the pot of water he had put on had not yet come to a boil. And yet too long, he realized guiltily. Working quickly, he stood and covered her with the blanket, then wrung out a cloth and gently bathed away the caked blood from her face. As he ministered to her, he formed pictures of her in his mind. "I wish someday you would pose for me," he whispered. "The play of light and shadow on you, the depth of your eyes. Trullion captures the beauty that lies on the surface, but I could capture the vision."

"Then I will," Tiara said, a faint smile playing across her face.

Aghast, Justin stared at her. "How . . . how long have you, I mean . . ." He was blushing furiously. "When did you—"

"In time," she giggled, opened her eyes and turned her head to look at him. "When you finished drying me."

"Oh, God," Justin groaned. Utterly embarrassed, he hunkered down in front of the fire with his back to her.

"I will pose for you, Justin," she said, snuggling into the blankets. Her lips hurt, but she was warm, and felt safe. "As long as you like. I have no other place to go. I may stay?"

Silence, followed by a muffled, "Yes."

Tiara was patient if nothing else. She nibbled on a biscuit and clutched Justin's robe about her waist. From time to time she touched the bruise on her cheek, or dabbed her lips with the sweet oil Justin had bought for her. She had never met anyone quite like Justin. He had been embarrassed in her presence ever since the first night when he had thought she was unconscious. He was manly, yet more tender than any man she had ever known. Morning, noon, and night for three days, he had brought her hot tea and bowl after bowl of the nourishing stew that never seemed to run out. Tiara responded by rapidly regaining strength and putting, so far as she was able, the whole sordid episode with Hrolf out of her mind.

The loft was warm, almost cozy. The shifting shadows had become old friends. Earlier in the afternoon Tiara had volunteered to sit for him, and Justin had spent the rest of the day arranging a space he had cleared at the far end of the loft. Whatever he wanted to do had to be special: never before had she seen so much time spent in preparation. At last, with everything in place, he cleaned an eighteen-by-twenty-two-inch piece of glass with a compound of alcohol and decomposed limestone and dried the surface with a flannel cloth.

"Are you ready?" he asked, the earlier embarrassment forgotten as he worked. He coated the plate with collodion, blew on it gently to set it, and immersed it in a bath of silver nitrate. "Ten minutes, now," he said, checking his watch.

Tiara shrugged free of the robe, kicked it aside, and stood on the spot Justin had marked on the floor. All business now, Justin extinguished all but a pair of coal oil lamps, and adjusted the masking flats and reflectors he had set by them. He even masked the hearth with a flat. "You're sure you'll be able to hold still for nine minutes?" he asked.

"Positive."

"Good. Let's see." Tiara lifted her arms over her head, twisted her torso slightly. Justin stepped behind the camera, checked the image on the ground glass back plate, and nodded with satisfaction. "Good. Good," he said, slipping the lens cap up. "You can relax."

The plate was ready. He slipped it into the camera, checked everything again. "Okay. Let's try it." Tiara assumed her pose again. Justin inspected her, made a minute adjustment to a piece of masking. "Perfect," he chuckled. "The line of shadow is perfect. Now—" He removed the metal plate from the camera, waited for the second hand of his watch to hit the twelve, and removed the lens cap. "Don't move. Shallow breaths . . ."

The nine minutes made necessary by the dim light crept past. At last Justin called, "Time," replaced the lens cover, and slipped the metal plate back into the camera. Tiara dressed and returned to the fire while he disappeared under the dark tent to remove the plate and coat it with developing solution. Fifteen minutes later silver deposits had grouped where light had penetrated the film. Justin rinsed both sides of the plate and fixed the image by immersing the glass in a solvent of silver iodide. At last he lit a lamp, washed the plate in clear water, and dried it over a naked flame. As a final step he flowed varnish over the surface to preserve the image. The next morning he would print the photograph on paper.

"Well?" Tiara asked as he joined her at the fire.

Justin shook his head, sat heavily on the pallet across from hers. "The shading is wrong, damn it." He pulled the cork out of a bottle of wine, drank, and lay back with the bottle perched on his chest. "I didn't compensate enough for the earth tones of your skin."

Tiara shrugged. "I don't see why you had to have it so dark. Mr. Trullion always has me in the light."

"I am not Menschell Trullion. Nor am I making bawdy prints for some decadent count who can't—" He stopped, angry with her questions and with himself for letting her upset him.

Stung by his attitude, Tiara pouted by the hearth. She had posed for him, stood stock still for nine minutes while he took his silly picture. The more she thought about it, the angrier she became, and the less she wanted to be around him. Seething, she dressed in the clothes she had found in one of Menschell's costume trunks, then stalked out of the loft into the studio across the hall. "Photographs!" she fumed. "Art! Visions! Talk. All talk. See if I care!"

She sounded childish, even to herself. It was silly, really. More than silly, she decided, wrapping her arms around herself against the cold and staring out the window. The night had turned clear. A half moon lit Manhattan with a pale light that filtered through the dust-caked windows. Below, an occasional figure hurried along the street toward home and loved ones. And unpaid bills and responsibilities as well, she reminded herself. "Not me," she said to the darkness. "Not Tiara." Tiara was free, didn't want to owe anything to or be responsible for anybody. Not even a name.

"Tiara?" Justin called from the doorway.

Petulant, determined not to forgive him too readily, Tiara ducked behind a flat. He hadn't needed to talk to her like that. He was like all the rest. Suddenly remembering how he had saved her from Hrolf, she winced and, embarrassed now herself, stayed out of sight until he closed the door and she was alone again.

Justin stalked across the hall and slammed the loft door. "Let her sulk," he grumbled as he ladled out a bowl of stew. "Can't say anything." He made a face, dumped the stew back in the pot. "Damned stuff tastes like wood." Restless, he retrieved the negative of the picture he'd taken of Tiara and set it on a stand near the fire where he could inspect it more closely. It wasn't that bad, really. Tiara, like the moon, half-shadowed mystery, half-radiance; alluring, provocative. It was an uncommon photograph, totally unique. He may not have caught her exactly as he wanted, but he was on the right track. His camera had captured the essence of her and, by extension, all women.

The longer he looked the more pleased he was. He could not tear his eyes from it. The lines were vague enough to lend the impression that she was materializing out of the fabric of dreams, bold enough to suggest reality, ambiguous enough to meld the two into one. Reserving final judgment for the next day, he slid out of his trousers and shirt, tugged his long johns around his waist, and slid beneath the covers. He was tired. The day had been long and demanding. Slowly relaxing, he snared the bottle of wine he'd pilfered from Menschell's private cabinet. Let the old man holler. Justin grinned to himself, and took a healthy swallow. His empty stomach growled. He tilted the bottle again, drank, and lay back. As for Tiara, she could pout all she wanted. He was too tired to care, and his eyes burned from the chemical fumes inside the developing tent. He blinked, stared at the negative. It was worth it. "Get it perfect tomorrow," he told himself. "Way I want it."

His eyes still hurt. Sleep seemed unattainable. Justin eased out of the bed and crossed to the wash table he'd set up when he moved into the loft. The water in the basin was cold. Holding his breath, he bathed his face over and over, submerging his entire head.

"Your eyes?" Tiara asked behind him.

Justin toweled his head, turned to look at her. Looking boyish in the rolled cuff trousers and baggy shirt, Tiara was standing in front of the negative. Justin padded back to his cot and slid beneath the covers. "Well?" he asked.

"It is a negative," Tiara said, procrastinating.

"You've seen enough negatives to know how it will look," Justin said, refusing to accept that as an answer. "Do you like it?"

Tiara cocked her head, studied the photograph. She had never thought of or imagined herself as any more than an uncommonly pretty girl. But Justin had seen more, and had created more. A poem, perhaps, something more related to a song than an image. "Yes," she whispered in a soft and wondering voice. She left the photograph, stood over Justin, and looked down at him as if trying to make a decision. Her long, dark hair spilled over her face. "So many men see only what is before their noses. True vision is a gift. To see not what is, but can be. I like it very much."

Justin grinned self-consciously. "I'll get it better tomorrow," he said.

"No," she said, going to her own pallet.

"No?" he asked, surprised.

"No." She brushed the hair out of her eyes, tucked it behind her ear. "The trouble with men who seek perfection is that they never know when they have found it."

"What's that supposed to mean?"

Tiara smiled enigmatically and didn't answer. Instead, she carried a small bag to the hearth and took out a pipe with a long, carved stem decorated with coiling serpents. She applied a yellowish-brown paste to the bowl and, holding it near a glowing coal, ignited the substance. When it was burning to her satisfaction, she inhaled deeply and held it out in a gesture of invitation.

"No," Justin said. He had watched Trullion smoke before, but had never dared to try the drug himself.

"It will make the hurt go away."

"A little hurt is good for the soul. I prefer to hurt."

"I don't think so," Tiara giggled. She crawled over to him, knelt by his side, and once again extended the pipe on open palms. "You gave to Tiara," she said in a husky voice. "Will you not take from her too?"

Her eyes were sleepy and warm, the lids raised ever so slightly in expectation. Trapped by her question and the look in her eyes, Justin reached for the pipe and inhaled, coughing on the bitter smoke. Tiara's laugh was like the trilling of a wren, a far-off calling that led him on. He inhaled again, more deeply, and a marked feeling of euphoria washed over him. His eyes didn't hurt anymore. The ache in his skull was fading. He felt a delightful feather-soft pressure on his forehead: it was Tiara's breath, as she kissed him there.

Tiara took the pipe, inhaled again and, holding the smoke inside her, placed the stem in Justin's hand. Justin realized he was staring at the firelit beauty of her hair. He reached out and ran his fingers through velvet, watched with amazed delight as each strand slipped away and fell into place. Not even thinking, he inhaled again. The taste of the opium was less bitter, even desirable. He could hear his heart beating—or was it hers?

Time was slowing. Taking forever, Tiara stood, stretched upward toward the ceiling miles above him. The trousers she had appropriated floated to her ankles, then magically away from her feet. Her shirt hung to midthigh. She knelt again and took the pipe. Inhaling, she bent forward and kissed him on the lips, forcing his mouth open with her tongue, and exhaling so they shared the bittersweet smoke that joined them like some vaporous soul.

Tiara straightened, pulled aside the covers. Her hands tugged at Justin's underclothes, slipped his long johns down his legs and completely off. Her torso twisting away from him, the shirt rode above her hips, and then was gone. Justin placed his hand on her thigh and slid it up to cup the soft flesh between her legs. When she reciprocated, he closed his eyes and arched his back.

He was floating, the two of them floating on a magic carpet from dim Araby. Tiara's kisses started at his ankles, worked slowly up his legs. She brought one leg over his, explored the length of his body, pausing at the emblem of his masculinity. Justin's fingers tightened on her thigh: even in his drugged state he was shocked by her wantonness. "This . . . is wrong . . ." he moaned, ecstasy vying with a puritanical upbringing.

"Nothing we do is wrong," Tiara hissed. The tips of her breasts traced electric fires up his groin, along the hardness that rose between them. "No thing. No thing . . ."

Her kisses were flowers erupting into bloom. Her lips touched his nipples, his neck, his ears and eyes and mouth. Suddenly, breathing heavily, she sat up and slid back to sit on his knees. A bead of sweat that had formed between her swollen breasts ran down her stomach. Justin reached for her. His hands slid up her thighs until his fingers met in warmth. Tiara pressed his hands to her and stared at his blood engorged flesh. Slowly, almost sleepily, she slid forward, rose imperceptibly and guided him to the moistened gate shrouded in thick black curls. She groaned as she fitted him into her, paused, and then inched forward until she contained him wholly, until her legs were wrapped around his waist and her head nestled in the crook of his neck.

Overwhelmed, Justin gasped her name. Tiara pressed two fingers against his lips, then wrapped her arms around his neck. His hands pressed against her hips, forcing him deeper until she whimpered. "Did I hurt you?"

She shook her head no, and clung to him. Justin stroked her hair.

His breathing became more shallow. She kissed his throat. The flesh on his face was drawn.

"Tiara?"

"Yes."

"Tiara?"

"I am here. I am . . . here!"

It was starting. Uncontrollably, she felt herself tighten around him. An animal sound, a long, rasping moan began deep inside her, escaped between clenched teeth. Her body was a wild thing, every muscle straining, every nerve screaming. Insatiable, beyond pain, she pressed down.

Justin shuddered. His body was rigid, his face bunched in silent agony. His whole being centered in her; he fought for breath. And then he was plummeting from underneath her, through pallet and floor, the meager crust of earth, plunging to the star-core furnace, the boiling fire-full chasm of creation, then jetting upward again like molten elements bursting from the depths of the planet. At long last, languid images dissolved into reality, and brought him back to the room and the woman, to sleep and completeness and peace.

When Justin woke up it took a long second to remember where he was and what had happened. For another second he doubted, but the soft breathing and the knee pressed into his thigh was proof positive. Filled with wonder, he carefully rolled to the side. Her right hand cradling her face, Tiara slept soundly. She didn't stir when he brushed a lock of hair away from her eyes. Lying back, he grinned at the darkness hiding the ceiling. His body was tired in a pleasant sort of way; he felt drained, but more relaxed than he could ever remember. More than anything else, he was famished. Moving slowly, he rolled out of the warmth of the covers, filled his bowl with still warm stew and, crouched in front of the fire, ate ravenously. The negative stood on the stand next to him. Careful not to leave a print, he touched it and discovered the varnish was too warm. A fine treatment for a work of genius, he chided himself, and carried it to the far end of the loft where he would work on it in the morning. Suddenly sleepy again, he hurried back to the pallet and crawled beneath the blankets.

Tiara made a funny little cooing sound as she climbed out of sleep and snuggled up to him again. "Your legs are like ice."

"Sorry."

She slid her head into the crook made by his elbow, lay her own legs over his. Her thigh was soft against his hip, and her hand held him comfortably, as if they had been lovers for a long time.

"Tiara?" He kissed her on the shoulder. "I had a feeling." Her fingers moved, stirred him into life, but what he wanted to say was important. "I have such dreams, such plans. I want to be known and respected and sought after. I want to be greater than Brady or Trullion or anyone. I want to record it all, the beauty and the pain, for the generations to come so they can see who we were and what we thought, and maybe laugh at us, or feel comforted by us, or weep for us. I want to photograph the whole world, Tiara. Our world. And I want you with me."

Tiara pulled him to her, became one with him again. It was not an answer. But it was a beginning.

Chapter 26

A hot, late spring sun baked the blue grass and the pennyroyal. Mares about to foal searched for safe places among vines lush with grapes. The forest was thriving with the pulse of bear and wild turkey. The last drops of dew slowly evaporated from low-slung magnolia leaves and beaded the purple-shadowed petals of mountain laurel. Soft breezes played in dells and secluded valleys, bounded over knobs and bright limestone outcroppings, fell into hollows and rose again, brisk with new life. Assorted warblings and caws floated through cracks in the silence left behind by the wind.

The land was Kentucky, once a dark ground bloodied by internecine Indian warfare, then acquired by a nation expanding westward along the banks of the Licking and Ohio and Cumberland rivers, high along the lonely reaches of narrow-crested ridges, and deep in the heavy virgin timberland of the never-ending forest. Piece by piece, the land was explored by men like Simon Kenton, George Rogers Clark, Blue Jacket, and the flamboyant mountain man turned politician, Dan'l Boone.

The word spread to the land-hungry east, and slowly led by the bravest or most desperate, the trickle that would turn into a flood began. Feeling the constricting crush of civilization, the frontiersmen and explorers pulled up their stakes and moved west to test their skill and endurance against the varmint, or simply to see the other side of the mountain. Behind them the heart of a nation—farmers, builders, teachers, and merchants—moved in to till the fields and build the towns. Under their sometimes misguided stewardship the land yielded crops in abundance, the forests and rivers provided sustenance and shelter. The dream was fulfilled: Kentucky rewarded the earnest and diligent with prosperity. Slowly, the blood seeped into the ground until it was forgotten, and the land became accustomed to peace. Until the new war came.

Paint Lick was a meandering stream that split the community of Maddenburg in two. A railroad depot and a half-score businesses flourished on the south bank, and cottages and columned mansions dotted the north. Downriver, but still in view of the town, which had yet to reach a consensus of opinion on their presence, two companies of Union cavalry were bivouacked in the emerald shadow of Pine Mountain. No one knew when they would move out, only that they had arrived one night almost two weeks earlier, and were on detached orders to locate and neutralize the raiders who had been harassing Union forces and supply lines in that part of the state.

The camp itself was drab, and temporary. Officers' tents rose in a cluster of canvas pyramids near the center of a double row of smaller, patched, gray tents for the enlisted men. In front of them a small wooden structure, the only one of its kind in the immediate area, served as company headquarters and the officers' mess. Next to it on the east, facing a tramped rectangle that had been designated a parade ground, the commanding officer's tent enjoyed a singularly unwarlike view of a peaceful valley that ran between arrow-straight limestone ridges covered with spring green maple, elm, and hickory. Through this valley a column of seven riders dressed in blue rode toward the encampment. By the time they arrived in front of the company headquarters building a welcoming party was waiting. The officer in command, Colonel Jesse Stibbs, late of Washington, D.C., and the War Department, received his salutes, dismounted, handed the reins of his horse to an orderly, and hurried up the steps to be greeted by the major he had come to visit.

"Colonel Stibbs. You made good time," Major Jack Travis exclaimed, saluting and then shaking the hand of the man he hoped would be a more able commanding officer than the politician who had preceded him.

"Too fast." Stibbs, a stocky man of twenty-eight years, pulled off his campaign hat and loosened his coat. "The sergeant saw a deer, but we were making so much noise it ran off before we could get close enough for a shot. Nice place you have here."

"Thank you, sir." Travis grinned. "About that deer? It must have been the last one left in three counties. My best men haven't so much as seen sign of one for the last week."

"Hunted off, eh? Same everywhere else I've been for the last month and a half. Damned shame. Well—" Without warning he tossed his hat to an aide, turned, and entered the cabin. "Let's take a look at what you've got here."

The cabin held a table, six chairs, a black iron cook stove, and a work table—all amenities that made being an officer a good deal more pleasant than being a private. A map and the corner of a desk could be seen through an open door that led to the back room where official business was conducted. The table in the front room was set with real china plates and civilian utensils. In the center a sugar-cured ham lay surrounded by freshly buttered, steaming yams. A pie cooled on the windowsill and a pot of coffee steamed on the back of the stove. "By damn! This was worth a hard ride," Stibbs said, eyes aglow with anticipation.

"Thank you, sir." Jack took a brown bottle of aged whiskey and two glasses out of a cupboard. "Join me, sir?"

"Of course. Of course."

"A widow from town prepares my meals." He opened the bottle, poured a bit in each glass. "For a small remuneration, of course."

Stibbs took his glass, sniffed appreciatively. "Beware she doesn't poison you, Major. This state may declare its neutrality to the heavens, but a closer look will reveal a wasp nest of Rebel partisans."

"Her husband was killed by partisans, sir."

"Really?" A slow smile crossed the colonel's face and he raised his glass. "To your health, then, sir."

"And yours, Colonel."

"Ah," Stibbs sighed. "Very good. But down to business, eh?"

"May I suggest we sit outside?" Jack asked. "It's much more pleasant, and I can have the maps brought out."

"Good idea." The colonel waited a moment while Travis ordered an aide to bring the maps and whiskey, then accompanied his host to the tent next door where chairs and a table waited under a canvas fly that shielded them from the sun. "So," he began, taking a seat. "I'm making the rounds of my command to introduce myself. You can't judge how men will perform until you've sat across from them and looked them in the eye. You're from the South, aren't you?"

Major Travis colored. Not that again, he thought. "I was born in South Carolina. But I don't see what that . . ."

"At ease, Major," Stibbs chuckled. "We'll get along fine, you and I. You see, my ancestral home is Biloxi, Mississippi. Since Kentucky is so closely akin to the other Southern states, and because so many houses are divided in their loyalty, the War Department thinks it good strategy to put as many of us here as possible. Not only are we a highly visible symbol for those who do remain loyal to the flag, but we lend further credence to our claim that the Army isn't here as an occupation force, but as a sympathetic protector." Stibbs drained and refilled his glass. "But enough of philosophy. It's the day-to-day matters that concern us now. Any problems?"

Travis sipped from his glass. "Not really. We've plenty of food, enough ammunition. Boots are getting on the thin side, but your predecessor assured me there would be new ones coming within a month or two."

"I think I remember reading," Stibbs remarked drily, "a note or two of your concern on that matter."

"Some of the men are nearly barefoot, sir. I can't . . ."

"Don't you think you're being just a little too insistent, Major?" Stibbs asked in suddenly clipped tones.

"No, I don't, sir," Travis said, holding his temper. "I asked for those boots three months ago."

"After all, it's a minor matter, really, in comparison with—"

"Begging the Colonel's pardon, *sir,* but my men are all I have. If I take care of them, they'll fight well."

"I think that will be enough, Major," Stibbs barked, cutting Travis off. He rubbed his eyes and sighed in resignation. "No need for this sort of dissension. I concede your concern. We'd probably be a hell of a lot better off if more of our officers paid more attention to what their men need. At any rate, I'll check into it," he said, nodding to an aide, who made a note. "Anything else I need to know?"

"Not really," Travis said, relieved to have come through the altercation unscathed. "The men are still a little green, but I'm drilling them. Lot of colds and diarrhea this winter, but I think we're about over that now. Only three sick this month so far. Of course, being out here we get more fresh vegetables and not so much salt pork and dried peas. I'd be happy to show you around some if you'd like."

"Let's talk about this raider you're supposed to catch, instead. I've read the reports. They lack a certain, shall we say, finality."

Travis tried not to wince. "I've been tracking him for the last four months. Got over into Virginia and almost caught him in Red Ash back in March, then followed him west to Glasgow and south of Bowling Green. Now we're back here. He's slippery, sir," he finished lamely.

"You outnumber him, don't you? As far as I can see, you should have caught him by now."

"Yes, sir, but numbers have nothing to do with it. My men are mostly city boys, while his were born to horses. They strike out of nowhere and disappear like ghosts. He has men who know the terrain and is free to choose his objectives. Meanwhile, I have to divide my command, attention, and time between food depots, shipments, and rail lines. The opportunities for surprise and mischief in the area I cover are too numerous to mention."

Stibbs rose, stood in front of the map that one of Jack's orderlies had set up. As he talked his right forefinger stabbed at widely scattered locations throughout southeastern Kentucky. "Two train wrecks. Twenty head of horses stolen. The supply depot at Murphy's Gap plundered and eight soldiers killed. An ammunition shipment intercepted and five soldiers killed. This is hardly 'mischief,' Major."

"No, sir."

"So what do you propose to do about it? When are you going to bring me McKenna?"

Jack Travis sipped at his whiskey, mentally counted to ten before answering. "In answer to your first question, I intend to find him. In answer to your second, soon."

"Soon." Stibbs stared into his drink, dunked a finger into the liquid, and removed a gnat. "But first you must find him."

"That's right, Colonel," Travis said, gritting his teeth.

Colonel Stibbs sighed, sat wearily, and stared at the view. "Which is where this Black fellow comes in, I presume," he finally said.

"You know about him?" Travis asked, hoping the worry in his voice wasn't too apparent.

"Major Gruehwold in Liberty voiced a complaint. Hearsay, really, of irregular practices on your part. Just who is this James Black?"

Travis filled his glass, sat next to the colonel. "Someone I knew a long time ago. He's . . ." He paused, remembering the first astonished moment in late February when Michael Blackheath had presented himself at a winter camp on the Virginia border. ". . . A trapper and tracker. A Canadian. Not subject to conscription. However, our paths crossed while he was on his way west to try his luck in the goldfields, and he agreed to do a little hunting for me. Being a civilian and alone, he moves freely through places we can't pass unnoticed."

The colonel considered that, slowly shook his head. "Very well, Major. It's all right with me. Irregular is hardly the word, but wars are often won by unorthodox means." He grinned slyly and held up his glass. "And who will argue if your plan is successful?" He set down his glass and removed a pocket watch from the sash around his waist. The timepiece was as polished as his brass buttons. "Damn. I'll never make Liberty tonight."

Jack relaxed, decided that Stibbs would be outspoken and demanding, but fair. "May I offer the Colonel the use of my quarters?" Travis asked, happy to change the subject from the mysterious James Black. "You and your staff are, of course, invited for dinner."

Stibbs beamed. "By damn, but that's a fine idea. One of your men will see about quarters for my party?"

"Of course."

"Good. Which leaves one last but most important issue."

"Which is?" Travis asked cautiously.

"Why, that pie," Stibbs said, pointing to the windowsill in the headquarters building. "For an appetizer. It'll never go around, eh? Besides, Major," he clapped Travis familiarly on the shoulder, "it's high time you learned to take care of yourself as well as you do your men. Privileges of command, man. Privileges of command."

WEDNESDAY, May 7, 1862. Hiding.

A quiet, beautiful spring day. No rain for the last week, which means the ground is dry. Perfect weather for raiding. Abraham Northrup, the farmer whose boy's life we saved last week, found us four days ago and delivered news of a payroll wagon. After checking it—Corporal Benton with his Dutch accent is invaluable for these things—I have decided to ambush it tomorrow when it goes through the little valley where we found the peach trees. Once we have the payroll, I think we'll leave here. The land is about hunted out, and the men need meat.

Have finally heard reasonably substantial word about Shiloh. A Frederick Ransom, a straggler and (probably) deserter from the Thirty-eighth Tennessee, was captured while wandering down the creek yesterday. The Federals' victory was more complete than I thought possible. Johnston is definitely dead. Island Number Ten was taken. With these two losses, western Kentucky is gone for us, as is a good portion of the Mississippi River. What this means is altogether too clear. The Confederacy's western flank is exposed, and the Federal Navy is free to make the river its own.

No word yet about my promotion. Once we capture and deliver this payroll, I hope to find a major's commission waiting for me. And a new assignment. I would dearly love to be assigned to Stonewall Jackson in Virginia. Among other reasons, I'm becoming weary of this Major Travis. It's bad enough being chased, but worse to have one man after you for too long: After a while he learns how you think, and then things get dangerous. The main problem is that Travis is, no matter how tenuously, a link to the past. I don't remember very much about him other than that he was Michael's best man, but his very presence in this area stirs the memories of Eve, which have haunted me for all these months. June 4, 1860. Not quite two years ago. The date is indelibly recorded in my mind. I will never forget Eve in the cupola, never forget Eve the night of the wedding, never forget Eve that September day I returned to Dawn Wind, never forget Eve with me in the cove, and most of all, never forget Eve the day I left and she did not leave with me.

Two-day-old coffee brewed from hickory nuts was no way for a man to start the day. Or end it, Lion McKenna thought, watching the sun balance on the tips of the pine trees, then gradually enmesh itself in the uppermost branches before slowly dipping like a monstrous, melting ornament below the far green ridge. Coffee still on his mind, he tossed out the dregs of the bitter brew in his cup and, hoping that they'd find some of the real stuff that night, walked back into the cave. The anteroom, as he and his men called it, was an immense vaulted chamber whose ceiling arched overhead a hundred feet or more. The floor gouged a full fifty yards deep into the mountain. Smoke from a half-dozen dying cook fires explored the stalactites dripping from the roof, and a cool natural breeze welled from an opening that led to deeper chambers at the rear of the cave. Bedrolls for the men lay in a long, neat row at the far right side, with more for noncoms and Lion himself on the left. The raiders had been in the vicinity long enough to set up a tack stand, now empty of saddles and harness, as the men readied themselves for the night's ride.

"Beans, sir?" Sergeant Webster asked, offering a plate. "Some left over."

"No thanks, Andy," Lion answered, waving the man away.

"Forbes found some meat for the pot."

"I'll eat later. We leave in fifteen minutes. Get my horse up here and check the men's gear. Make sure everything is tied down and quiet. Food and water for twenty-four hours. We'll be coming back here before we break this camp."

"Yes, sir."

As he headed for his bedroll the sudden realization of what the sergeant had said hit Lion. If Forbes had done what Lion suspected . . . "Rags?" he called, hurrying toward the back of the cave. Apprehension growing, he called again. "Rags?"

A shape dislodged itself from a patch of sand underneath a low overhanging rock and, rear end wagging, ran toward him. Lion had found the stunned animal lying next to a wrecked wagon a month earlier and had carried it with him when his raiders moved back east and found the cave. Rest and leftover scraps had healed the pup and the two had become fast friends. Relieved to see the dog had escaped the stewpot, Lion knelt to pet the small wire-haired mongrel, who immediately rolled onto its back for a stomach scratch. "Attaboy," Lion said, grinning and complying. "C'mon. Let's go."

It was almost too dark to see. Lion paused in front of the piece of warped board that held what remained of his toilet gear and looked at himself in the shard of mirror that had accompanied him for more miles on horseback than he ever thought he'd ride. Raiding took a lot out of a man, he thought, rubbing his hand across the dark stubble that roughened his jaw. His black hair was matted and his eyes were deep set, almost hollow-looking under brows that never lost their seriousness even when he smiled. "Someone has to do it," he mumbled, strapping on a gun belt stamped "U.S." on the brass buckle. "Might as well be me."

"Five minutes!" Sergeant Webster's voice filtered through the opening of the cave. Lion checked the Colt revolver and returned it to its flapped holster. A second and third weapon he thrust into the black sash at his waist, to which he tied a small leather pouch filled with a half-dozen preloaded cartridge cylinders. His gray uniform was wrinkled and needed washing, a luxury for which he had no time. He tucked his trousers into high-top black boots, and from a rock shelf took a broad-brimmed hat trimmed with a black plume that had become his mark. If there was a bit of the dandy in his dress it was what his men expected of a Confederate officer: outfit and plume invited Yankee bullets in combat and denoted a man to be respected.

Everyone was ready. The cave was unnaturally quiet, save for the whisper of bats leaving for a night of hunting and the gurgle of an unseen underground stream that fed the creek in the valley below. It was time. Lion looked around, could spot nothing amiss. He took a bit of the bricklike biscuit that was the soldiers' staple from his saddlebag and tossed it to Rags. "You stay, now," he said. "Stay. I'll be back." The dog wagged his tail, sniffed the hardtack, and looked up at Lion as if to ask if that was the best he could expect. "Stay," Lion repeated, knowing exactly how that animal felt. He could use a good meal himself, but the Davis government in Richmond had forbidden the raiders to alienate the citizens by plundering homesteads or towns. McKenna's raiders were forced to hunt and trap the woods and raid Yankee larders for sustenance. Since both were notoriously barren, the pickings had been slim.

"Ready, sir," Webster called.

Lion took a deep breath, walked out into the dusk, mounted, and rode down the slope. "All right, men," he said, reining in before them. He took a second to look at each one, establish eye contact for perhaps the last time. They were a hardy lot, tough as razor-backs and every bit as mean. "Quiet as cotton and stay close together until Sergeant Webster passes the word. Tonight's raid will be the same as any other. With one difference: We're going after gold." He paused. No one moved. Even the horses stood silently.

"Now, just in case there's any question, our orders remain in effect, and I intend to carry them out. We're going to take that gold, get back to camp, and rest, then ship it to Tennessee and General Bragg, or whoever is commanding the Tennessee Army now, just as we've done with all the food and ammunition and supplies we've taken. And as much as I hate to have to say it—I know that all of you are loyal to the cause and good soldiers—I just want it known that if any man here finds himself tempted, he'd better think twice about it right now. Understood?" Not a word, not even a nod. "Good. Sergeant, mount them and let's move."

"All right, lads, mount up and look lively. Forbes, you've a jangle. Pad it. You, too, Mulhanna. Let's go. Double file."

Lion trotted his barrel-chested roan to the path leading into the valley, paused, and waited for Webster to finish and catch up. There wasn't a cloud in the sky; the moon would make it easy for unfriendly eyes to spot them, but they'd be able to position themselves better for the ambush. He tried to visualize all the farms and homesteads to be stealthily skirted on the long ridge ahead. It was a hell of a way to fight a war.

"All set, sir," Webster said in a low voice, reining in beside him. "It's a fine bunch we ride with."

Lion turned in the saddle and looked over the forty-three rough-and-tumble, haggard Rebel raiders strung out behind him. "Looks more like the tail end of hard times, Andy," he said, putting aside protocol and grinning as he kneed the roan into motion. "But they'll do. Let's ride."

Michael had been restless for the past week. He sensed something in the air, knew there was going to be action. Most probably the pay-roll for Stibbs' troops at Liberty. Where exactly it was coming from, and what route it was taking, he hadn't the slightest idea. But there was a good chance McKenna knew. If he did, it was sure as tomorrow morning that he'd attack it. Silently, not telling anyone he was leaving or where he was going, he slipped out of camp and rode southeast. Somewhere in that direction, somewhere in the hundreds of square miles of hills that lay before him, he would find the man he sought.

There had been nothing to go on except a general knowledge of the lay of the land. That alone left certain areas impossible and others highly improbable. Beating back the frustration that had gnawed at him for so long, he tried to outwit the Army. The best route would be discarded as too obvious. The second best for the same reason. Still hoping, but resigned to failure once again, Michael picked the third and rode slowly along the ridge overlooking a tortu-ous valley that eventually led, he knew, to Shiner Creek and Stibbs' headquarters. When nightfall came he dismounted, made a cold camp and, with his horse grazing close by, fell asleep.

He woke in the middle of the night. His horse was standing stock still, ears pricked forward. Silently, Michael saddled up and led the animal along the ridge. At last his patience was rewarded. Below, in the valley, their hooves muffled, a file of cavalry guarding three caissons rode stealthily through the night. Moments later, hidden behind a fallen pine tree where he was safe from ricocheting bullets and out of sight of the attacking Rebels, he watched the night explode in a fiery ambush. He might have tried to warn the Yankee troops, but a yell would have brought the Rebels down on his own head.

The fight, more a massacre than a battle, was over in seconds. Forty-four revolvers and carbines had fired as one, continued to fire until fifteen Union soldiers lay dead. Michael watched the Rebels ride out, replace the fallen horses on the caissons with new ones, and promptly drive off. A half hour later, deeming it was safe to begin following, he rose from his hiding place, only to duck down again immediately. A Rebel soldier had returned to the destruction.

Fistfuls of diamonds lay scattered across an onyx sky. In the valley, bathed in the ruby glow of burning caissons and an overturned wagon, the lone figure garbed in homespun butternut shirt and trousers rifled the pockets of dead Union soldiers and stuffed packets of food into a pair of oversized saddlebags.

Michael sighted down the length of the breech-loaded octagonal barrel. The range was a mere hundred and fifty yards, child's play for the Sharps' .50 caliber double load. His finger tightened on the trigger.

The Reb in the firelight must have sensed something, for suddenly he straightened from the half-dressed, contorted figure he'd been searching and pulled a pistol from his waistband. Good sense at last taking hold, Michael eased his finger off the trigger. The Rebel youth was a tempting target, but of more value as a guide. McKenna was cagey. This time he wouldn't get away: Michael would at last have the confrontation he had sought for so long. Easing back into the inky shadows, he studied the wreckage. Another example of the wisdom of the Army, he thought sarcastically. Travis had offered to guard the shipment, but some damned fool staff officer had decided that secrecy was the best protection against raiders and night riders and refused to divulge the route. Now fifteen men lay needlessly dead. Well enough, Michael thought grimly, quietly shifting his weight so his legs wouldn't cramp. The price for finding McKenna was high. At least he hadn't had to do the paying.

At long last the youth holstered his revolver and returned to stripping the dead of their belongings. An hour later the job was finished. Failing to notice the brooding shadowy shape that detached itself from the forest and followed him, the Confederate raider rode off after his companions.

The Rebel took no chances, went by a different way than the main body of his fellow raiders. Michael followed him all the night and through the morning. He drank from the same creeks as did the Reb, kept his horse to the same, slow walk. The trail meandered east, further into the hills, climbing and ever climbing until it leveled briefly about thirty feet below a ridge and twice as far above a deep gully. Michael had let himself fall the better part of a mile behind his quarry by then. As the trees thinned he slowed to study the incline ahead of him. Sharpened by danger, his senses reached out. Somewhere ahead there was a trap. Had the Reb spotted him? he wondered. Possibly. If so he would be waiting.

Two mammoth slabs of limestone jutted from the face of the ridge just above where the trail leveled. Michael patted the dust from his coat, nudged his horse into a slow walk. The closer he came to the limestone slabs the more he felt the tightness in his neck and shoulders. His eyes were riveted to the stone. He held his breath.

Suddenly, the trap sprang.

The Rebel leaped from the rocks, a wicked-looking knife held out to his side. Michael reacted instantaneously and nearly automatically, falling to the right and disappearing except for his left hand on the pommel as he clung to the side of the gelding. At the same time a blurred shape sailed over him, hit the edge of the trail with a thud, and toppled over the side. The gelding shied and reared. Michael hung on, fought the animal to a standstill. To his right the man he'd been tracking was pinwheeling down the steep slope, shrieking as his own knife drove into the front of his leg. His fingers tore loose shrubs and snapped branches too fragile to break his fall as he rolled head over heels, unable to stop the spinning, tumbling nightmare in which he found himself. At last his head glanced off the trunk of a tree. The blow knocked him unconscious. A second tree broke his fall, but unfortunately did the same for his neck.

How long? Five seconds? Ten? Death had been that close. Michael stared at the lifeless body of the Reb, stroked the trembling gelding in an attempt to calm him. When his own knees stopped shaking he dug into the saddlebag, pulled out a bottle secreted there, and drank deeply. The whiskey took hold, calmed him down, and helped him think. That the Reb had been taking a different trail from the rest of the raiders was evident from the lack of any other tracks in the vicinity. There was only one chance now.

The Rebel's horse, a red mare with a shredded left ear, was tethered further down the trail where the ridge angled gently down into a valley. Michael turned her loose, spooked her into a run, and then followed, hanging as close to cover as possible. Before long she slowed to a walk, then stopped to graze and drink. Michael let her eat, then tossed a pine cone at her, spooking her again. When she splashed along the middle of the shallow stream he stayed close behind, hoping that the valley didn't run out, and that the horse knew where home was. He had yet to see tracks, but that didn't matter: McKenna could have taken another route entirely. There surely had to be more than one way to his hideout.

The land seemed to close in, the mare moved more confidently. Cautiously, Michael pulled a pair of binoculars from his saddlebag and inspected the banks of the stream. Two hundred yards ahead, where the valley began a dogleg turn to the left, the bank had been churned to mud by many horses. Quickly, Michael caught up the little mare, reined in, and listened. There was no way to tell what lay beyond the turn, but he could feel in his bones the presence of men. Quietly, he rode into the woods, tethered the mare and his gelding in a stand of maples, then slowly crept forward toward a huge old chestnut tree that had been blown halfway over by a spring storm. Careful not to make a sound, he crawled up the massive bole until he reached a spot where he could see through a gap in the branches.

The valley was boxed. Steep sides covered with hardwoods sloped down to a quarter section of cropped-grass meadow through which the crystal clear stream he'd been following meandered. Daisies and black-eyed susans dotted the green grass. The back quarter of the meadow had been crudely fenced, and held what looked to be a half-hundred or more horses. Michael swept the glasses along the rear slope until they caught movement. Focusing carefully, he found what he had been looking for. There, camouflaged by trees, was the yawning mouth of a cave. Below it spilled a small waterfall that fed the stream. Suddenly apprehensive, he looked around. If the raiders were hiding out in the cave surely there would be sentries posted somewhere near the mouth of the valley. But no one had challenged him, and no alarm had been given. McKenna must feel awfully sure of himself.

A sudden shout echoed through the valley. Michael plastered himself against the tree trunk. When, after a moment had passed and nothing had happened, he dared raise the binoculars to look again. Everything looked the same, with one exception: a half-dozen men had gathered in full view at the mouth of the cave. Among them, dressed in gray, with a black plume jutting from his hat, was the man Michael Blackheath had sought for the last three months. "At last," Michael whispered. The flesh on his face tightened to form a mirthless smile.

Chapter 27

My Dear Major Travis:

Major, indeed! And I am certain you deserved the promotion, my gallant friend, for I imagine that leadership becomes you. Can there be any doubt that before another year passes you will be a full-fledged colonel? I think not.

Thankfully, little news reaches us concerning the West. The talk is all of Richmond, and will Europe interfere, and what will Lincoln do next. The newspapers are full of horrid accounts of battles and skirmishes and political moves complex enough to confuse a Borgia or a Machiavelli. For my part, I skim the headlines and pretend that all is at peace where you are, and that you are safe.

I wish I could report that circumstances here are prospering, more for Father's sake than mine. The many government contracts that have passed us in favor of other shipyards have left *Dawn Wind* in a precarious state. Father has traveled to Washington again, the third time in four months, to see what could be done, but has accomplished nothing. The frustration has grated away at his health and nerves, and as a consequence we all tiptoe about like ropewalkers.

But how inconsiderate of me to burden you with problems that pale to insignificance in comparison to the terrible ordeals you must be undergoing! I must remind myself that we are luckier by far than many.

James's first birthday—June 14—is still six weeks away, and plans for his party are already complete. His grandfather will present him with a train he's been saving for I don't know how long. Jubb is whittling an entire farmyard of tiny cows, horses, sheep, geese—at least I *think* they are geese—and a span of yoked oxen pulling a plow. Eustacia will bake him a mammoth cake in which we will no doubt be able to hide him, and a good deal of which will end up all over his hands and face. Everyone, even Hamlet, who has seemed morose lately and has kept rather distant, is enjoying himself immensely.

The New Forest Women's Committee for the Preservation of the Union, Alice and Rose Johnstone presiding, held a benefit last Saturday night. Much to their chagrin, I attended. And enjoyed myself. Father was my escort, and actually danced once, though I think it pained him. Everyone was there, including Maisie Duncan, who was in the company of Arvid Naslund. Maisie, if you remember, was our maid, whom we have reluctantly let go in order to be with her ailing mother. Father is relieved to have one less employee, but I was sorry to see her leave after so many years with us. She was a link to earlier, happy times.

Of my brothers, we hear little. Justin is still in New York where he has opened a studio of photography. Father is mortified. A number of Justin's pieces—some quite scandalous, I am told; I've only seen his landscapes—were shown recently in Boston. We have heard nothing of Michael. I can only pray he is well. This awful, awesome war touches us in more ways than is always obvious. Whether or not he lives—I have to believe that he does—Michael is our casualty, our unhappy contribution. I cannot conceive of losing more, as many have.

Father's ship's clock chimes eight bells. Another hour is gone. I shall send this to town with Hamlet in the hope it will leave on this afternoon's train.

Be careful.

Be well.

I am, with deepest affection,
Most sincerely yours,
Eve

"You should write her," Jack Travis said, handing Michael a cup of black coffee strong as sin and thick as bayou water.

Michael returned the letter. "When I get to California."

"You could leave now."

"And miss the fun?"

"None of this is fun," Travis snapped, folding the letter and tucking it inside his coat. He refastened the shiny brass buttons with meticulous care. "I have no business allowing you to come with us anyway."

"You'd have a hard time stopping me."

"Short of locking you up, I suppose so," Travis sighed. When Michael paused, midsip, he continued, "Don't worry. The thought may have crossed my mind, but that's all. Look—" He leaned forward intently. "You sure you don't want to tell me—"

"The answer is the same as the last time you asked, Jack," Michael said flatly. "Personal reasons, which is all you need to know."

"I still think he seemed like a nice enough fellow the one time I met him," Travis said. "All right, all right," he went on, holding up a hand, at Michael's derisive gesture, "forget I said it. Leave out what you want. It's your business, your mystery. I guess you're entitled. I can't leave you behind anyway. If we choose the wrong place to ambush McKenna and he escapes into Tennessee with Stibbs' payroll, I'll need you to help pick up his trail. At least that's what I'll tell anyone who asks."

"He won't escape if we leave now," Michael said, propping his boots on the tabletop and a map of the southeastern corner of Kentucky.

"I can't leave without Stibbs' approval," Travis said defensively. "You read his latest orders, same as I did. Move your feet," he added, tapping a pointer against Michael's boot. His view of the map unobstructed, he reviewed the situation for at least the fifth time since Michael had ridden in earlier that morning. The raid had taken place some twenty-five miles to their southeast three nights earlier. The boxed valley and cave was another half-day's ride due east from there. The ambush on the payroll train and the ride back to the Rebel hideout would have been wearing on men and horses alike.

McKenna would have to let the horses, at least, rest for a minimum of two days before he moved again. Jack hadn't a chance of catching them if he rode directly to the cave. They would be gone by the time he got there. All he could do was try to second guess McKenna. The Rebel's easiest and most direct route to Tennessee and the friendly Confederate forces there was southwest from the cave and through Printer's Gap. On the map his own position, McKenna's hideout cave, and Printer's Gap made an almost perfect equilateral triangle. Assuming McKenna would go that way, Jack and his men could ride due south, reach the gap before McKenna, and cut him off. "We can reach it tomorrow if we leave this morning," he muttered.

"If, if, if," Michael droned sarcastically. "If good intentions got the job done, you and I wouldn't have to be here."

Travis paid no attention. "We'll know immediately if McKenna's preceded us. If he hasn't, you go up the valley to keep tabs on him while I wait for Providence to deliver him into our arms," he said. Then, at a knock on the door, "Yes. Come in."

His adjutant entered. Lieutenant Schuler was barely twenty, had been a third-year man at West Point when the war broke out. He snapped to attention, his shoulders back in a West Point brace. "Sir!" he barked.

Travis shook his head. Schuler had been with him two months and his insistence on parade ground manners was depressing. "Would you *please* relax, Lieutenant? What is it?"

Schuler's brace softened, but only for an instant. "Colonel Stibbs sends his regards, and apologizes for the delay," he intoned, handing a piece of paper to his commanding officer. "Sorry, sir. I took the message while the telegraph operator was relieving himself."

"That's all right," Travis said, reading his orders. He stood abruptly, slapped the paper with the back of his fingers. "Approved!" he told Michael before turning back to Schuler. "Have the sergeants tell the men to cinch up and look lively, Lieutenant. I want this command ready to ride in ten minutes."

"Yes, sir!" Schuler barked, saluting and marching out of the room.

Michael smiled broadly and heaved himself to his feet. "One thing, Michael," Travis said, stopping him.

"Yes?"

"This is my command. If you ride with me, then you will conduct yourself accordingly. We'll outnumber McKenna. I hope we'll have him trapped as well. If I can talk him into surrendering, I will." A shadow flitted across Michael's face. He said nothing. "I'm going to spare every drop of blood I can, Michael. You *will* act on my orders," Travis said again. "Is that understood?"

The silence between them was punctuated by a flurry of commands from outside the headquarters building where the men were maneuvering their horses into double files. "Certainly, Major," Michael finally said. His voice was even.

Travis nodded, buckled his gun belt around his waist. "Good," he said shortly, and stepped outside into the compound.

Michael watched his friend leave. "Of course I understand," he said in a soft voice to the empty doorway. "Problem is, Jack, you don't."

Dusk found the long blue column snaking tiredly across a fallow field toward a rundown collection of buildings. The scene, for all the finery of a sunset rich with reds and oranges, was dreary and depressing. A gray, slat-board house, with rough-cut cedar shakes covered with dried moss and fronted by a rickety porch, tilted precariously at an angle that defied gravity. A barn made of quarry stone that had once been white but had long since turned to the same muddy-gray as the house sat forlornly in a sea of hardened mud that raised noxious puffs of dust when walked on. To one side hurriedly cut posts had been tied together with rusted wire and chocked with random stones to form what could have served as a pigsty. A ring of rock, covered with a roof, indicated a well, next to which a stooped man was busy casting a handful of grain to a small flock of scrawny chickens. The old man watched the Union soldiers approach with neither animosity nor approval.

Jack Travis held up a hand to stop the men behind him, motioned Michael to accompany him, and walked his mount into the farmyard. The chickens flapped their wings and scurried out of his way. A cow with swollen udders twitched an ear. The old man leaned against the wall and stared at Travis with hollow, unemotional eyes. "Good evening," Travis said, riding toward the old man. "My name is—"

"That's far enough, mister."

Travis stopped, held his hands away from his sides. "I mean you no harm," he said slowly and clearly. "Why don't you put that thing down?"

"Why don't you two just ride over here real slow so I can look at you."

Travis and Michael kneed their horses away from the old man, held them to a slow walk across the dusty barnyard, and stopped in front of the porch, where a young girl stood. No more than fourteen or fifteen, she wore a faded sack dress that barely covered her knees. Long, dull flaxen hair framed a work-smudged face that, with better food and a gentler life, might have been truly pretty. She held a double-barreled heavy-gauge shotgun leveled at Jack. "My name is Major Jack Travis," Jack said, trying to put the girl at ease. "If you'd put that thing down, maybe we—"

"Shut up." She took a step forward. The end of the barrel was no more than eight feet from Jack's stomach. She had a finger on each trigger and could not miss. "What do you want?" The tone of her voice meant business. So did the shotgun.

"A place to rest for the night and water for our horses," Jack said, gesturing to the trough next to the well.

"Git," the girl said. "Now."

"Now Laurie Ellen—" the old man began.

"We already done give soldiers all we got to give!" Laurie Ellen's eyes flashed with anger. "Two brothers gone, one to blue, one to gray. Ma dead from worry and a broke heart. Pa stove up and foundered from havin' to work the place by hisself with a bad back. The swine lost last month to Yanks, and then the corn to Reb deserters. No, sir. You rest yourselves somewheres else. We're through with bein' took from."

"Set yourself. You're welcome to the water," the farmer said in a tired voice. "Laurie Ellen, you put down that gun, you hear? And git back inside. You know what the last bunch took when they seen you paradin' yourself around."

The girl blushed for a second and rubbed her eyes. "That's 'cause I didn't have this," she said defiantly, and then, before running inside and bolting the door, "You just better watch out, mister. You and your men."

Travis relaxed, glanced at Michael. The crisis over, he rode back toward the well. The man standing there had been big and hearty at one time, but work and hardship had taken their toll. Almost six feet tall, his elbows were bony and his forearms thin where they stuck out from the sleeves of a cut-off shirt. His face was pale, nearing the color of the house and barn, and a meager diet had shrunk much of the meat off him, leaving his cheeks sunken and hollow and his ears and nose severely out of proportion to the rest of him.

"We're obliged, mister—" Travis began.

"Wixom. Barrett Wixom. You boys make yourself to home. I ain't got no coloreds. I don't give a hoot whether there's one flag or two. All's I want is to farm my land, and the sooner I get back to it without a bunch of bumbledickin' soldiers tramplin' my crops and stealin' my stock, the better. I'll be milkin' Bess if you need me."

Travis touched the brim of his hat. "Like I say, we're obliged, Mister Wixom."

The old man waved him into silence. "An' if'n any of your boys makes a move towards my chickens, I'll have Laurie Ellen shoot the britches off'n the son of a bitch. And some hide too," he added, by way of a parting comment as he led the cow away.

"Bring 'em on in," Travis called to Lieutenant Schuler, who was waiting stiffly at the head of the troops. At his side Michael had dismounted and was drinking from the trough. Travis joined him, dunked his head, then threw it back and let the water run down the back of his neck. "Nice family," he finally said, sighing.

Michael stood, spat into the dust. "Yeah," he said, the weariness coming through his voice. "What's left of it."

Campfires dotted the eastern edge of the fallow field. The clank of canteens and iron pots of beans hung over flames and stirred with heavy metal spoons blended with the soft snorts of picketed horses and a chorus of crickets. Muted voices, punctuated with good-natured curses and laughter, rose and fell as the men settled down for a few hours' sleep before the sergeants roused them in the dark hours before dawn. Michael scrubbed out his plate and packed it away in his mess kit. Travis looked as though he wanted to talk, but there wasn't any point to words. Michael didn't feel a need for friends. Coffee and silence suited him better.

The coffee was hot, but bitter. Stirring in a piece of hard candy to sweeten it, Michael drifted away from the fires and the men, trudged to the top of a knoll near the house, and settled down on a stump. Wixom's farm, for all its shabbiness, was a peaceful place. A valley. Plenty of water and wood. Good soil, if a man took care of it, treated it right. A wife, a couple of sons to help out . . .

A wedge of light expanded as the back door opened, contracted as it closed. Michael squinted, picked out the slender figure of Laurie Ellen, bucket in hand, as she walked down a wooded slope toward the creek that ran behind the house. Smiling, he thought of Eve.

Funny how traits duplicated themselves. Once physically pretty, Laurie Ellen was as feisty and spirited as Eve. Probably as stubborn too. Given the Blackheaths' money and position, fed and dressed properly, she might have rivaled Eve. Try as hard as he might, he could see no logical reason why one should be so blessed, another so deprived. But that line of thought led to unanswerable questions. Giving up, he set aside the empty coffee cup and lay back on the grass.

The hills around him seemed like mammoth waves frozen in time. The darkness hid the fact that they were made of earth, and thick with pine, hickory, and elm. Waves. Stars. The same he'd seen when looking up from Dawn Wind. Images of the sea intruded. And if he closed his eyes and stretched his imagination, the listless breeze that barely moved the branches of a nearby oak and fluttered the leaves of a milkweed near his leg could be magnified into the turbulent ocean breezes that climbed and leaped and swirled about the high cliff edges of Dawn Wind. There too, almost painful to look upon the gallery of his mind's eye, were the faces of Sewal and Eve and Justin. More so was the image of himself. Outwardly confident and dashing, the scion of Dawn Wind stood with bare head and exposed heart, and exchanged vows of love and fidelity with Rosamond.

But the dream went awry, became confused and jangled. Unable to stop the wild vision, Michael watched as the fabrication faded, transmogrified into the image of Lion McKenna holding Rosamond in his arms. Rushing, madly swirling through the mists, Rosamond became Eve, changed back into a laughing Rosamond who became McKenna, who, dueling pistol raised and cocked, faced him across an eternity of sand.

Breathing heavily, fists clenched, Michael sat up and shook his head violently to dispel the vision. But the face remained, the face he had sought down the flaming avenues of war. Always he had missed him, sometimes narrowly. Tomorrow or the next day the chase must end, though, and McKenna would be dead. After that the rest of the country could go about its suicide, for all Michael cared. It was the West for him, and a new life. A life without nagging guilt.

The noise of a struggle drifted up the slope and broke his introspective spell. "Damn," he cursed, knowing immediately what was happening. Jumping to his feet, he broke into a run toward the line of trees and the hidden creek. A voice shouted. He heard footsteps. Suddenly, Laurie Ellen appeared between the trees and ran full tilt into him. Panting and sobbing, she clawed at him until he lifted her and plopped her onto the ground, then turned to face a pair of soldiers who were chasing her.

"Hey, Black, we seen her first," one of them said, approaching confidently. "You can dibs third."

Michael's fist caught the side of the soldier's jaw. The man dropped soundlessly. His partner paused to consider, thought the better of it, and scampered back the way he had come. Michael turned to the girl, who was trying to fasten her dress. Eyes blazing with a mixture of anger and fear, she backed away from him on all fours. "What you gonna do?" she asked, brushing a twig from her hair.

"See you safe to the house." He held out a hand, helped her up. "Come on. I won't hurt you."

Laurie Ellen sniffed, tossed her hair. "I can take care of myself."

"Sure. Why are you down here at night by yourself?"

"For water."

"Why didn't you use the well?"

"Soldiers came by and salted it," she lied. Her hands smoothed the faded dress across her belly, stretching it tight over young breasts.

"Not true, Laurie Ellen. We all drank from it this afternoon. You came down here for a reason." The bravado faded and Laurie Ellen stared down at her knotted fists. "Maybe you wanted something to happen," Michael went on mercilessly.

"You don't know. You ain't got no right."

Michael shook his head, took her by the elbow, and steered her toward the house. "Didn't anyone ever tell you the night air is dangerous, Laurie Ellen?" he asked roughly. "I'll see you inside. You go to bed."

"You got no right," she repeated, stumbling along at his side.

Michael stopped, turned her so she faced him and looked searchingly into her eyes. "No right," he finally said, his voice gentler, almost sad. "I guess maybe I don't."

Laurie Ellen was confused. She wiped the moisture from her eyes. Her voice was tiny, that of the child she had had to leave behind too early in order to survive. "Sometimes . . . Sometimes, they pay. And, well, Pa ain't up to whole and hearty . . ." She turned, took a tentative step toward the house, and stopped. "I guess maybe I'll go on in now."

"Yeah." He waved her away from him. "Good night, Laurie Ellen."

Her footsteps were whispers in the dust that faded and disappeared. Some time later Michael heard the back door of the house squeak open, then close. Infinitely weary, he retraced his steps to the fallen soldier, slung him over his shoulder, and started back to camp.

The sun wasn't up yet, wouldn't be for another hour. Only a suggestion of light tinged the eastern ridges as Barrett Wixom, a scraggly hound, eight scratching chickens, and a sleepy, unconcerned cow reviewed the double file of soldiers riding away to the south. Jack Travis, still fighting off sleep, offered the farmer an unreturned salute of farewell and urged his horse into a trot. Michael, bringing up the rear, cantered over to Wixom and flipped a ten-dollar gold piece that landed at the homesteader's feet. "Don't let your chickens eat that, old man," he said and, skirting the dust churned by the column, galloped ahead to ride point. The day promised to be as long, hot, and tiring as the one before, and he had no intention of supplementing his diet with the grit billowing from the dry earth. When he crested the next hill Michael took the opportunity to glance back. The farm appeared pastoral from a distance. Wixom was in the yard still, with the diminutive figure of Laurie Ellen at his side. Michael hoped he was showing her the gold coin.

Printer's Gap had been named for Doctor Malcolm Printer of New York City who, due to a misunderstanding regarding the favors of a wife of a colleague, coupled with a natural bent for danger and adventure, decided to follow the movement west. Once there another similar but infinitely more dangerous misunderstanding, this time with a man who thought no more of killing another man than he did of filleting a trout, sent the doctor off in a new direction. In the process, necessity being the mother of invention, he discovered his own route through to the heartland of Tennessee.

The gap was a narrow valley that broadened the closer it came to Tennessee and was split by a sluggish stream whose high silt content lent a brown cast to the waters. The stream was bordered by wide, gently sloping muddy banks that required a definite commitment by the man or beast who sought to drink from the shallows. The meadow itself was in the shape of an hourglass, with the wide ends lying roughly north and south. Lush, thigh-deep grass stretched from the muddy banks on either side of the stream, then rose with the sides of the valley, gradually giving way to forest.

The ride, extended by a wrong turn up a valley that led to nowhere, lasted longer than expected. Consequently, the two companies hadn't arrived until after three in the afternoon. Jack had been furious, beside himself with a rage that didn't begin to ease until Michael, riding ahead, brought back word that the raiders had yet to come through. By the time the troops were bivouacked and pickets had been set, the sun was on its way down. After a hurried conference Travis decided to let the men and horses rest for the night. If McKenna hadn't shown up by the next morning, they would send out a reconnaissance party, followed by a sweep up the valley.

An evening breeze stirred the birches, sent the birds to bed, and woke the owls and foxes. The moon, nearly full, peeked over a ridge. Campfires, those still lit, twinkled in the dense stand of trees halfway up the slope from the meadow. Jack Travis, accompanied by Lieutenant Schuler, made the rounds of his command, acknowledged salutes and calls of respect from his troops. They were an assortment of shoe salesmen, coopers, masons, farmers, lawyers, ex-students, and draymen—men from every walk of life the North had to offer, who shared only two things in common: the flag of the Union and a distrust of horses. Assured that all was well, he allowed himself to relax a little, and headed back for his own fire.

"Get some sleep, Schuler," he said, flopping down by his bedroll. "Midnight will come sooner than you expect."

"Yes, sir. Sleep well, sir."

"Thank you."

Quiet at last. Grunting, Travis pulled off one boot, then the other, stripped off his hot, sweaty socks. He lay back, wriggled his toes, and luxuriated in the fresh coolness of the breeze. Almost worth it, he thought sleepily. A long hard ride left a man sore and tired, but once he quit and lay down . . .

Scowling, he sat up. There wasn't time for talk of quitting yet, no time for rest with McKenna still loose. Michael's intelligence indicated that the Union forces should outnumber the raiders by at least two to one. That was good. Corps intelligence indicated that the raiders were all rural lads and superior horsemen. Which was bad. All he could do was make sure the balance tipped in his favor. With the advantage of surprise and mobility—his men weren't loaded down with loot—he could box in the Rebels from front and rear before anyone knew what was happening. He had only one regret: the lack of a reporter. Every officer who was anybody and who wished advancement needed a reporter, someone to expound and enlarge upon that officer's bravery, tactical feats, and accomplishments. Here he was about to apprehend a notorious band of Confederate raiders, and there was no one to wire back stories of his exploits. There had been a reporter from the New York *Herald* in Lincoln, but Jack had been unable to budge him from the company of the General, who would undoubtedly end up receiving all the credit.

"Case you want to know, everything's quiet."

Travis looked up. "Michael. Sit down. You missed hot coffee."

"Yeah. Well . . ." Michael said, stretching his shoulders before sitting on a campstool. "I thought a little prowl would be more to the point."

"A double check never hurts," Jack said tactfully, in spite of the implication that he had been slack. He couldn't be sure, but thought he smelled alcohol on Michael's breath. "Nervous?" he asked.

"A little," Michael admitted. "You?"

Travis rolled onto his side, rummaged in his saddlebag, and found pipe and tobacco. "Funny," he said, sitting up and filling the pipe. "All the things we're supposed to be. Gentleman killers. Courageous beyond thought of personal safety. I remember the first time. A skirmish just over the line in Virginia. Both sides were riding along minding their own business. Neither of us expected anything. Suddenly, three men were dead, another dozen wounded. I remember being excited, that's all. It was a heady experience, especially when it was all over and I realized I hadn't run or held back. That was something I'd always wondered about."

He paused, lit his pipe with the glowing end of a stick. "Now?" He puffed, puffed again. The tobacco smelled sweet on the clean night air. "The more I know and the more I've seen, the less I want of the whole mess. And the more coldly professional I become. It's the only way."

"Maybe," Michael admitted, standing and walking beyond the fire to regain his night vision.

A horse snorted. Somewhere off to the left a soldier called out in his sleep. "Wasn't me, Pa," he said, quite distinctly. Jack's pipe made a sucking sound. Michael came back to the fire, started to unroll his blanket.

"You know," Travis said quietly, "the men are anxious enough without you acting like some brooding man of mystery."

"That's their problem," Michael answered shortly.

"No, it's mine," Travis corrected. "They're young and edgy. They don't like being in McKenna's backyard."

"You want me to give them a lecture in confidence?"

"I want you to help me, damn it."

Michael stood, wrapped in his blanket. His eyes bored into Jack's. "How?"

"Oh, hell," Travis sighed. He knocked out his pipe against his thigh. "I don't know. Why don't you get some sleep?"

Michael lay down, groped for and threw away a pebble that had been digging into his hip. "What about you?"

"In a minute," Travis answered. Quiet again. Jack sat crosslegged in front of the fire, stirred it with a twig that flared and then went out again. "Michael?"

"Yeah."

"You, ah, know I'm in love with Eve?" he asked hesitantly.

Michael chuckled. "I'd have to be blind, deaf, and dumb not to know that. Why?"

Travis was grateful for the darkness. "I think she shares my sentiments," he said, clearing his throat.

"So?"

"Once this war is over and all, you know . . . that is, I'd like your blessing."

"Blessing?" Michael laughed sarcastically. "You don't need any blessing I can give."

"I should like it nonetheless. If for no other reason than because we are friends."

"That has nothing to do with it, Jack."

The muffled voice that came out of the darkness behind him sounded strangely detached. "Close friends, Michael," Jack said quietly. "It would mean a lot to me."

Michael sat up, wrapped his arms around his knees. "I don't know." He could almost see Lion, and Clifford, too. "You may be a trifle too pretty for my sister's taste," he said, a trace of scorn creeping into his voice. "You might attract too many ladies. My sister can be most possessive." Travis's shoulders tightened, but he didn't say anything. Michael stared at his back, started to speak, but then lay down and stared up through the trees. "I'm sorry," he finally said.

"It's been a long day. I get that way sometimes. You have my blessing, Jack. And encouragement."

To say thank you seemed inappropriate. Still, Jack felt relieved, and suddenly tired enough to sleep. He turned, saw that Michael's eyes were closed, and heard his slow, even breathing. Sighing, he kicked dirt over the remains of the fire, pulled his own blanket around him, and lay back. The moon shining through the trees cast bramble-like shadows across his face. A long time later, sometime just before the watch woke Michael, he fell asleep.

Chapter 28

Michael rose when the watch changed at two, saddled his horse, and led it past the sentries into the dappled, waning moonlight. Still afoot, horse and man kept to the edge of the woods paralleling the stream, slipped from shadow to shadow, and worked their way north and east through the valley. Sunrise was still an hour away when he tethered his horse in a concealed hollow and crept forward to the edge of a spur that overlooked the path he and Travis counted on McKenna taking. This was the dangerous time, for the moon had just sunk, leaving the valley a pool of impenetrable inky blackness. Michael chewed on a piece of beef and drank from his canteen. By the time he finished the eastern sky was a dull, metallic gray, and there was enough light to see movement along the valley floor.

And movement there was. A self-satisfied grin spreading over his face, Michael lay the octagonal barrel on a flat stone. Shooting downhill could be tricky, which was why, the afternoon before, he had chosen a light gray boulder at the bottom of the slope as his hundred-yard marker. Further upstream a bright white V where a tree trunk split the water was his two-hundred-yard marker. Three hundred was a clump of isolated sumac. An ancient willow marked four hundred. As the leading raider rode past the willow Michael thumbed back the hammer to cock the Sharps. The sights steadied on a dark spot on the boulder, moved to the tree trunk. All he had to do was wait. The rest was simple.

Downslope and three hundred yards away, recognizable by the black plume on his hat, Lion McKenna led a closely drawn column of Rebel cavalrymen. Michael sucked in his breath. He and Travis had guessed correctly: the raiders' course would take them face to face with the Union ambush in a couple of hours. McKenna's horse was nearing the white V in the water. Two hundred yards would be a simple shot. His finger curled around the trigger. One shot: one only, and then California.

Slowly, almost painfully, reason overcame temptation. Michael released the trigger, eased the hammer down. That one shot would botch Jack's plans, as well as his chances for advancement. But there was something else. The stigma Michael carried would never be erased until he faced McKenna as closely as he had that lifetime ago on the beach at Dawn Wind. Unconcerned about being spotted from the valley floor, he stood and started back for his horse.

"Holy bee-Jesus!"

The sound of another voice stopped Michael in his tracks, as surprised as the grizzled, middle-aged Rebel corporal scout who stood a scant half-dozen paces away from him. The two men stared at one another for several ridiculously long seconds until, as if waking from a trance, the corporal groped for the single-shot pistol tucked in his belt. The movement startled Michael. Still frozen, incapable of motion, he stared in fascination as the gunsight caught on the scout's belt. He had to do something before the Rebel fired and warned the rest of them. His mind raced, spun uselessly until suddenly, almost unconsciously, he lunged forward and lashed out with the Sharps. The muzzle of the rifle struck the man's hand. Bone crunched. The corporal's scream of pain was cut short by Michael's fist slamming into his jaw. His hands circling the corporal's throat, Michael fell upon him like an animal. The corporal clawed at his attacker's face, squirmed, fell to his knees. The muscles in Michael's arms and hands contracted so violently they cramped. His thumbs ached. His face was a mask of hatred, of the darker, malevolent side of himself always before suppressed. He spoke a single word, repeated it over and over in a hoarse whisper, as he bent over the kneeling Rebel.

"Coward!" Michael said.

The Rebel pawed futilely at the bearded face that stared into his, reached with trembling fingers that had no strength.

"Coward!"

Senselessly, the Rebel's legs twitched as he tried to run. His arms flailed helplessly.

"Coward!" Michael's weight pushed the dying man backward until his knees cracked under the strain.

Fingers crushed flesh, veins, cartilage, the larynx itself. The corporal's eyes glazed, his tongue bulged from between his lips. At last he ceased struggling, and lay limp and lifeless.

How long it was before his muscles relaxed, before the madness drained from him, Michael did not know. Panting, head held back until he could breathe normally, he rested over the corpse. When he found the strength to rise, he wiped the sweat from his forehead and stumbled forward until he had the valley in sight again. The last horse had passed the light gray boulder; the column was well on its way out of range. Walking stealthily, Michael picked up his rifle, threaded his way through the trees to his horse, and rode off quietly. There was no time to lose. Not if he wanted to meet Lion McKenna.

Lion shifted uncomfortably in the saddle, guided the roan out of the lead, and motioned for the men to keep moving. The sun was barely over the hills, but it was already hot. The men rode listlessly through the baking dust that clung to their legs and shoulders and clogged their throats. Riding in dust beat riding in the mud, though, for they made better time on solid ground. Dust took the starch out of him too, Lion conceded grimly. He was thirty-two, old compared to the age of the average man under his command. Ancient, even, especially after a long, debilitating ride. Once he hadn't felt that way, but six months of raiding and living off the land had taken its toll.

Sergeant Webster reined up beside his captain. "You worried about Corporal Wayne, sir?" he asked, his eyes ranging the hills to their right where the scout was supposed to be paralleling their line of march.

Lion wiped the sweat from his eyes, realized he'd been daydreaming. "We're near the meadows," he said, pulling himself back to the present. "If he hasn't joined us by then, I'll send a couple of men looking."

"He's an old hand, sir, who'd find a way to let us know if there was trouble. We ain't heard nothin', he ain't got nothin' to report."

"Maybe. Maybe not."

"Not to worry, Captain." Webster shrugged. "I knowed him for a long time. Billy ain't about to lose hisself."

"I hope not," Lion said. His horse shied, backed away from the tarpaulin-covered buckboard that carried the Union greenbacks and an iron box of gold coins.

"A little grease would help, sir," Webster said, nodding his head toward the creaking wagon. "That thing sure is noisy."

"It does the job. Guns from England, Sergeant. Every penny counts."

Webster rubbed the light brown stubble on his chin. He was no slouch in a fight, but strategic considerations were beyond him. At last he saw the connection between the buckboard and guns and England. "Yes, sir," he agreed, rolling a half-smoked cigar between his teeth. "Better give 'em a rest soon," he went on, more concerned with immediate problems.

Lion smiled secretly. Webster had been a good choice for sergeant. Like many of his companions he was untutored, but intensely pragmatic. Which was, Lion thought, for the best. When all was said and done, the money they carried wouldn't buy a single gun if the men and the horses they rode were incapacitated by exhaustion and so failed in their mission. "We'll keep on for another half hour, and take a break where we shot that deer the last time we came through. It'll be cooler there."

"Yes, sir," Webster said, touching his cap and starting to ride off.

"One moment, Sergeant." Webster reined in, followed Lion's gaze as he searched the ridges. "Just in case, ride the buckboard until Wayne reports."

"Well, now, Captain . . ."

"That's an order, Webster," Lion said tersely.

"I ain't sayin' no, Captain." Webster glanced uneasily at the buckboard. "It's just that them powder kegs you stuck in there makes me a mite reluctant, is all."

"They ought to. Just make sure you keep an eye on me. And keep that damn cigar lit too. If there's trouble and I wave, touch off the fuse and jump. At least Grant's boys will go without pay."

Webster shook his head in disbelief. A pained expression crossed his face. "You really think," he asked, "that you got to *tell* me to jump, Captain?"

Major Jack Travis mounted and checked the alignment of his men. All those in sight sat astride their skittish horses among the pines. Pleased, he rode to the center of the line. "All accounted for and in line of battle, sir," his first sergeant reported. "We just received a wave from Lieutenant Schuler. He's in place and ready for your signal."

"Excellent," Travis said, returning the sergeant's salute. He studied the valley floor and the slowly approaching column of riders.

"A pity they aren't on our side of the creek, sir."

"Yes," Travis agreed absent-mindedly. He hadn't dared send a contingent of men across the creek for fear an advance scout might find the tracks and warn the Rebels. Instead, he had ordered a single line of battle minutes after Michael had ridden in, and sent forty men under Lieutenant Schuler upstream with orders to stay hidden until after the Rebels passed him and Travis made contact with them. All in all, Travis was optimistic. Once the raiders were too close to retreat, he would advance downslope and give McKenna an opportunity to surrender. Michael hadn't approved, but Jack had been adamant: no man in his command would die needlessly.

"I still say we ought to cut them down, Jack," Michael said, riding up. "They'll never surrender. You know that."

"On the contrary," Travis snapped. "I don't know that. I have issued an order, and expect you to follow it or get back up the slope."

Michael patted the saber hilt jutting from his saddle sheath. "I'll stay," he finally said.

The major's misgivings were overridden by the nearness of the enemy.

Whatever benefits they'd gained from the rest had been wiped out by the sun. Lion wiped his palms, considered for the hundredth time their location. Another twenty miles, he thought, mentally counting landmarks. By nightfall they'd be in Tennessee and would rest for a full day. A movement caught his eye. Hand raised, he stopped, felt the column behind him follow his lead. A crow swooping down to land in the pines across the creek and meadow had changed its course and flapped away from the slope. The concentration of the men behind Lion bore into his back. The crow cawed in alarm. When the last, distant echo faded, all the valley lay quiet and baking in the glaring sunlight.

Why did McKenna stop? Travis asked himself. He stared at the men in gray, at the buckboard heavy with gold, back to the Rebel raiders. The tension along his own line was palpable. The hour, the minute, the second was at hand. I have McKenna, Travis exulted. The next step was to capture him. Without bloodshed, if at all possible.

Michael tried to swallow, but his throat was constricted. Like the time on the beach when he had walked away, he thought feverishly. If Lion surrendered Michael would never be free. It wouldn't be the same. His skin felt tight. A rush of blood, a surge of madness swept over him. Not the same. Not the same. The words swirled through his brain. Travis raised his hand to start the men forward. Michael kept a tight rein on his horse, let the line pass him, then pulled his saber and slashed the flat of it across his horse's buttocks. The horse reared, and bolted from cover.

"Charge!" Michael screamed, as he raced between two unsuspecting troopers.

They did. Taken by surprise, the two privates leaned forward in their saddles as their horses followed Michael's. Like dominoes falling, the movement spread sideways until the whole Union line was sweeping forward at a dead run. Travis shouted for his men to hold, but the thunder of more than two hundred pounding hooves overpowered his voice. Though he was choking with rage at Michael's flagrant insubordination there was little left for him to do but draw his revolver and spur his horse forward: his only hope was to regain control of his command and save the day.

"Gawd damn!"

Whoever had said it spoke for them all, Lion thought, in a second of realization that seemed never-ending. At least fifty men were bearing down on them from their right front quarter. He whirled to face his men and was the first to see a second fifty break from the woods behind them. They were boxed, ambushed, trapped. "Them first!" he yelled, gesturing toward the frontal attack. The pincer movement coming from the rear had a good four-hundred-yard run. By the time they arrived their horses would be partially winded. If he smashed the frontal attack before the second fifty arrived, he'd have a chance.

Fuse in one hand, cigar in the other, Webster crouched in the buckboard. "Not yet!" Lion yelled, reining in violently alongside the gold shipment. The driver was fighting to keep control of the team. "Head for those trees up there if you can," Lion told him, and turned back to his sergeant. "See what happens before you touch it off," he shouted over the noise of gunfire and shouts. "If they're green, we have a chance. If not, blow it!"

The distance between the two lines closed rapidly as each side charged across the meadows. A chorus of Rebel yells mixed with sporadic gunfire filled the air. Lion raced his horse toward the creek and caught up with the rest of his men as they reached the sloping, treacherous mud flats. A surge of wild elation spurred him on. No detail escaped his eye. The water on the far side was deeper and slowed the Union horses, whose riders fought to keep their balance. His own men rode with their reins in their teeth and a cap and ball revolver in each hand as their horses charged through the shallows. He dared a glance over his shoulder. The Union cavalry coming from the rear was still over two hundred yards away. When they reached the action they'd have to take the long, slippery slope at a dangerous angle, or come to a virtual stop before hitting it head on.

Any semblance of order disappeared the second the leading riders met in the middle of the stream. Horses fought for purchase in the muck, slipped, and spilled their riders to be trampled in the churning morass of mud and blood. Revolvers fired pointblank, as dangerous to friend as to foe. Whirling sabers slashed men and horses indiscriminately. The blue line intermingled with the gray in violent, mad confusion.

Well rested, the awkward Union troopers somehow managed to hold against the exhausted Confederates until their reinforcements arrived. Lion fought like a madman, but his men were outnumbered, and even though some of the Union cavalrymen lost control of their mounts and made easy targets, there were simply too many of them.

Before the battle was three minutes old, it had broken up into small knots of men.

Michael kicked away the tumbling corpse of a Union private and, as a Rebel raider raised a revolver to fire at him, severed the hand that held the gun. The raider shrieked and was shot from behind by another Union soldier, who emptied his gun into the dying man and then continued to go through the motions. The hammer of his revolver clicked on the empty cylinders until a lead slug struck his spine, lifted him completely out of the saddle, and threw him head over heels into the water. Riderless horses plunged madly in all directions: three lay screaming and thrashing convulsively in the mud.

Jack Travis emptied his revolver, switched to his saber, and charged into a dense knot of horses and men. Four of his own troopers and three Rebels were flailing at each other with emptied guns, trying to knock each other off their horses. Grunting, cursing, howling, none of them saw Travis until he burst among them. One of the raiders fell in the initial charge, another screamed as Jack's saber ripped a foot-long strip of flesh from his forearm. The third escaped injury when his horse stumbled and Jack's saber whistled over his head. Travis grabbed one of his own men by the arm, shouted at the others to follow him. Kicking his boot heels into his horse and urging the animal to greater efforts, he weaved through the chaos and started after the heavily loaded wagon.

Behind him, the chaos had turned into a rout. The Rebels were broken and individuals were beginning to run. Lion tried to think, to make sense out of the reeling confusion. Desperately trying to rally his men, he spurred his horse up the slippery Union bank of the creek, only to find himself flanked by three nearly berserk youths. He grabbed the pommel of his saddle with his left hand and, right foot holding most of his weight, dropped off the right side of the horse in the same instant that all three soldiers opened fire. Black clouds of smoke billowed from three revolvers. Two of the soldiers fired into each other. One stiffened and rode off, his right arm dangling uselessly. The other's horse sat abruptly and then rolled over, shot between the eyes. Lion reached under his own horse's neck and fired. The third soldier slumped forward, tried to hold onto his saddle, but couldn't. The terrified horse raced off across the meadow, dragging the dying youth behind him. Lion swung his left leg back over the saddle, ducked as a bullet burned his ear. The man whose horse had been killed leveled his revolver for another try. Lion fired first. The private jerked once, then slowly tipped to the side and dug his shoulder into the mud.

Travis hadn't wanted bloodshed. He moved as in a dream. The men in gray were beaten, but still they fought. A half-dozen separated from the fight and rode to protect the wagon. The air filled with smoke, black smoke to sting the eyes and clog the throat. Men pointed guns at him. Tongues of flame darted at him like striking serpents' tongues. Acrid, caustic gunsmoke burned his nostrils. Men tumbled from colliding horses. Choking, pummeling one another with knotted fists and gun butts and saber hilts, men clawed at throats and eyes as they tumbled, writhing, to the ground. Carnage and confusion. Dust and death. His horse reared and screamed with pain as a bullet punctured its muzzle. Blood sprayed everywhere. But suddenly Travis was through, and his horse, crazed with pain, was running full out toward the wagon. He chanced a shot, was surprised to see the driver stand, dramatically spread his arms, and topple forward onto the wagon tongue. At the same time another Rebel emerged from under the tarpaulin covering the stolen Union gold, and jumped out of the buckboard.

Travis's horse was out of control in mindless, headlong flight. Hauling viciously on the reins, he maneuvered the wounded gelding next to the runaway team and leaped onto the back of the lead mare. The mare stumbled, swerved, caught her balance. Travis grabbed the dragging reins and leaned back with all his weight. At last the pace slowed from wild flight to a gallop and then a trot. He'd done it! By damn, he'd done it. Panting, trembling with fatigue, he swung around to ascertain the course of the battle at the creek. Triumph lighted his face.

And with a blinding flash, the world exploded.

Jack Travis heard men scream. All around him, men were screaming. He didn't recognize his own voice, but he was screaming with them.

For what had seemed an eternity, an orgy of war and death had erupted in the stream bed at Printer's Gap. Yet less than five minutes separated the Union charge and the explosion of the buckboard. Sensing the battle lost, the Rebel survivors scattered. Pursuit by the weary Union troops was haphazard. Lion evaded a man in blue, felt his roan's hooves strike solid ground, and headed for the trees. The nearest two Federals gave chase. The first, a freckle-faced youth, clubbed at Lion's skull with a breech-loading carbine. Lion ducked. The youth lost his grip on the barrel, and the rifle flew from his grasp. Blanching at his suddenly defenseless state, the soldier decided that if he continued the chase he just might catch the Rebel captain, and then what would he do? Unarmed, he swerved his horse and broke contact.

The second Yankee, a bearded man dressed in civilian clothes, was not so easily deterred. The civilian bore down on him. Lion raised his saber in time to block a killing strike and parried with a swing of his own. His attacker's horse shied and a narrow gap opened up between them. At full gallop the two men cut and slashed while their horses carried them up from the valley floor and into the wooded slopes. Lion did not recognize his adversary for the broad, flat planes of Michael's face were hidden beneath his beard and masked by a macabre mixture of mud and blood. But he knew the man could handle a sword, and he was hard pressed to stay alive. Suddenly, his roan stumbled and literally fell out from under him. Lion hit the ground shoulder first, heard a loud snap and felt a searing pain in his side as he rolled across his saber. When his outstretched arms and legs stopped his momentum, the trees and sky were whirling crazily overhead. Fighting the dizziness, he crawled toward his saber and stared in disbelief. The blade had snapped six inches about the hilt! A jagged strip of steel was all there was between him and death.

Horse and rider—terrible, towering figure in black—sat frozen in emerald shadow. Nothing was said. Wind sounding like a distant train rushed through the pines. The sound diminished, leaving a still void bathed in green light, as if the forest itself was waiting for one last act, one final moment of violence. Sweat stung an abrasion on Lion's cheek. The side of his shirt clung to the bleeding flesh under it. For the first time, he was frightened. There was more to the confrontation than he yet understood. Some secret he did not comprehend. Something left unsaid, unpronounced. Something undecipherable beyond the moment. He never took his eyes from the bearded man.

The horse reared, pawed the air. The enemy's saber rose into the air as he drove with irresistible momentum toward his foe. Where another man might have fled, Lion waited, loose and ready. He had one chance. It would have to be enough.

He waited until he could smell foam-streaked horse flesh and see the mad gleam in eyes that were suddenly familiar. He leaped, almost too late, and in the same instant, stabbed upward with the broken blade.

Horse and rider slammed into him like an avalanche. The descending blade carved his back. Once again he was in the air, watching the spinning ground rise up to slam the breath from his lungs.

His vision cleared slowly. Lion managed to prop himself on his hands and knees. He was breathing. He was alive. He looked up.

Horse and rider—terrible, towering figure in black—in emerald shadow. The animal's sides expanded, contracted, heaved laboriously for air.

Michael tried to swallow, but his throat was filled with phlegm. He spat. Blood flecked his lips. He glanced down at Lion's saber hilt protruding from his stomach. His mind refused to accept the pain of six inches of jagged steel lodged in his vitals. Refused. Not until McKenna was dead. With single-minded concentration, he reached for the Sharps, slowly drew it from his saddle scabbard. But the damn gun was so heavy, and growing heavier.

The rifle dropped from his grasp, floated to the ground. Michael blinked, squinted at the dissolving image of the man who had haunted him. He heard wind. Not the easy, peaceful rush of air through the valley, but real wind, sea breezes churning and gusting. Afraid but exhilarated, he clung to the face of the cliff. He was climbing, climbing, and the taste of the sea was on his tongue and the song of the birds filled the air and always the wind in turmoil, surrounding the cliffs for all eternity. The wind, the sea, the cliffs. Eve was there. And his father too. Sweet sister, stern father—fearful, watching, stretching out their hands. All he had to do was take them. All he had to do—"Father!" But the sea breeze tugged, whispered to him. All he had to do was let go, let go and soar free. . . .

He did, and fell. And the pain of loss was cruel and cutting. The hands and the faces and the promise were lost in his final plummet to the sea. I'm sorry. Sorry . . .

"Eve!" Michael's voice filled the glade, the strident cry punctuated by the hollow sound of his body striking the earth.

Lion paled as Michael's cry returned from the far side of the valley. Each reverberation cut through him more painfully than the sharpest saber, cut through to reopen the wound he still carried in his heart. As if drugged, he stumbled toward the man he had killed. The horse took a tentative step backward, but finding no threat in Lion, began to crop the trampled grass.

Every atom of his being warned him, but Lion had to see. Kneeling, pain forgotten, he held his hand over the dead man's face. As gently as if it were a babe, he wiped away the mud. And saw Michael Blackheath, at peace at last, in death.

His wounds nothing compared to the recognition, the realization, the horror, Lion shut his eyes. "Oh, no," he breathed. His head fell forward and his clenched fist beat the blood-stained ground. "Oh, my God! No!"

Chapter 29

Saturday dawned hot and sweet, as if all the lazy day were baking in Eustacia's kitchen. New Forest stirred and woke, yawned and bounced out of bed. September 6, 1862. The day of the big picnic. For weeks the New Forest Women's Committee for the Preservation of the Union had been cajoling and browbeating, arranging and deciding. Bigger than the Fourth of July, they said. For our boys, they reminded all. Patriotic duty, they pointed out with wagging fingers.

Nothing was left to chance. The cooking began Thursday night. Early Friday morning the decorations committee was out in full force. By ten Saturday morning the village green had been transformed. The bandstand was decorated with bunting. Over it a huge American flag with thirty-three stars—the correct number, by Northern standards—flapped ponderously in a light breeze. Other, smaller flags hung from poles set at each corner of the green. The whole eastern side was covered with chairs and tables garnered from all three churches, as well as the school, and the town hall.

The south side of the green was dominated by a rectangle of tables that, by noon, resembled a fortress with battlements constructed of mounds of food. Four standing rib roasts, three whole young roasted pigs, three stacks of baked chickens, and the hindquarters of two deer were surrounded by moats of scalloped potatoes and baked beans and succotash and cole slaw. By one o'clock, as each arriving family placed its fair share onto the already dangerously overladen tables, it was deemed necessary to enlarge the rectangle by adding an extra table to each side.

The west side of the green was reserved for the young ones. Hope Oxford of Oxford's General Store had donated two kegs—one sweet, one sour—of pickles, all free for the taking. Not to be outdone by his only competition, Luke Knight had arrived with a wagonload of new apples and a cider press. Running, jumping, hopping, squealing children with stomachs of cast iron ran from kegs to press in a contest to see who could hold the most.

New Forest was taking the day off. Emerson Aldrin spoke somberly of the war and the patriotic—nay, religious—duty of all Americans to protect the glorious heritage bequeathed them by their forefathers. Mayor Castebury, looking ahead to the election coming up in only a month and a half, trumpeted his and New Forest's accomplishments and importance to the war effort, and concluded with a stirring peroration in which he exhorted all those within earshot to support the Union and "all the fine boys who are the hope of our country, whose blood and youth are even now being spent on the field of battle."

The music began before the applause died down.

Mine eyes have seen the glory of the coming of the Lord,
He is trampling out the vineyards where the grapes of wrath are
stored.
He has loosed the fateful lightning of his terrible, swift sword,
His truth goes marching on.

Julia Ward Howe had written the words earlier that year, and they had taken the country by storm. Now the citizenry of New Forest sang them with fervor, for the "Battle Hymn of the Republic" was more than a hymn. It was a rallying cry, one which all could join to echo the speeches of countless Mayor Casteburys and other politicians spread across the free states. The song connected them, made them one, part of a shining ideal that was greater than any individual. Eyes were raised, hands clasped. The hymn swelled to fill the hearts and souls of all who sang:

Glory, glory, halleluyah,
Glory, glory, halleluyah,
Glory, glory, halleluyah,
His truth goes marching on!

And the festivities began. The band switched to more congenial tunes: "Comin' Through the Garden, Maud"; "When Johnnie Comes Marching Home Again"; "Darling Nellie Gray." Those who didn't head immediately for the tables gravitated to the plank flooring laid out at the north end of the green. Young and old alike, they danced polkas, waltzes, New Hampshire Highsteps, and ironically enough, Virginia Reels. People laughed, and when they weren't laughing they were singing. When they weren't singing, they were telling tales or arguing. And no matter what they were doing, they were having a rousing good time. The slowdown at the shipyards was forgotten. Personal tragedies were set aside. Gloom was forbidden. Above all, any reference to the more morbid aspects of the divisive war that wracked the country was banned in a common outburst of national pride.

No money was collected. Not a cent. A young man in the wilds of the Mississippi expedition or tramping across the battlefields toward Richmond or Nashville or a dozen less famous sites did not need money. The price of admission was clothing, whole boxes of which had been collected and lay in the shade of a specially erected canopy next to the bandstand. Socks—homespun, warm, soft socks—for soldiers far away with winter coming on. Undergarments, of a higher quality than the army could ever afford to issue, purchased wholesale from a factory in Portland. Soap—for cleanliness was still next to Godliness, even on the march. Small pouches of tobacco, smaller yet of coffee; luxuries to sustain a homesick lad through another week or month of loneliness. All would be distributed to Maine boys far from home, and who knew? one could very well be a son or brother or friend or loved one. New Forest understood that very well by the last quarter of 1862: the names of three of her own were already engraved on the stone column set at the southeast corner of the green.

The band had played and rested and played again. Two of the rib roasts were down to bare bones, half the venison was gone, as were two of the pigs. Now and then, over laughter and raised voices, the steady clunk of the cider press sounded an invitation to the thirsty. Sewal Blackheath folded his arms and shifted his stance. Perspiration trickled down his spine beneath the much too heavy frock coat he wore. He prayed, more fervently than for the salvation of his shipyards, that Hope Oxford would not notice him standing alone and ask him to dance again. The buxom woman had a cold and calculating eye that, he had been told, was set for him. Face grim and averted, he hobbled to the table set aside for Eustacia and her pies.

Eustacia looked up as he approached. "You hurt yourself, Mister Blackheath?"

"No," he answered shortly, edging closer and drumming his fingers on the tabletop.

"Well, what you limpin' for, then?" she asked.

"For the Widow Oxford. Don't look at me."

Eustacia busied herself cutting an apple pie, glanced out of the corner of her eye and spoke in a hoarse whisper. "I don't think it worked, Mister Blackheath, 'cause here she comes."

Sewal bent over as if to inspect a lemon meringue. "Damn!" he said, immediately embarrassed. He never cursed, not even in front of Eustacia. "Sorry," he mumbled. "She still coming?"

Eustacia laughed. "You is saved, Mister Blackheath. But you done looked at that pie so long, the meringue done caved in. You got to buy it now."

Eustacia's pies had been the only food item requiring purchase, the price being an extra contribution to the boxes of clothes. She had done her part for the government that was opposed to the slavery of her people. That the sentiment was only shared in part by Lincoln's cabinet in no way diminished her enthusiasm. Sewal glared at her. "I paid for the ingredients," he said gruffly. "I ought to get one free."

"Now, Mister Blackheath, you know . . ."

"Nevermind, nevermind." He picked up his pie. "I'll have Eve throw in another pair of socks later," Sewal said, grinning as he stalked off, minus all traces of a limp. A glance at the fate that had almost been his made him feel even better: the Widow Oxford had cornered Emerson Aldrin. The lawyer was no longer trying to buy the shipyards. He was waiting for Blackheath to go bankrupt so he could move in and pick up the pieces. A Hampshire Highstep in the arms of Hope Oxford would cool his ambitions, Sewal mused, and for a brief few minutes the awful responsibilities of the faltering yards and the nagging pain of absent sons slipped away as if no more than a bad dream. Glancing around slyly, he pinched off a piece of meringue and popped it in his mouth.

Gunter Naslund, Jon's oldest boy, a strapping man of twenty-eight, was escorting a flushed and breathless Eve back to the Blackheath table. Awkward in an ill-fitting frock coat and dress trousers, he thanked Eve for the dance, nodded to Sewal, and wandered back to the food tables.

Eve's hair was done in curls and ringlets. Its color matched the dress she wore.

"You dance well for an old lady of twenty-two," Sewal said, setting the pie on the table.

"And you, poor gentleman, not at all," Eve countered, craning her head to see what Sewal was looking at. "Perhaps we ought to see an end to this solitude. I am sure Hope Oxford would agree with me."

"No," Sewal said a little too quickly. A wry smile on his face, he sat down. "That is, my knees could never withstand her enthusiasm."

"In case you're wondering," Eve laughed, "Mr. Aldrin is now limping toward his carriage. I think he's had enough," she whispered conspiratorially.

"Good. He deserves everything he gets." Sewal pulled out his kerchief and wiped his brow. He'd overeaten. Looking at the pie was almost too much to bear. "I hate to say it, but the damned lawyer had an excellent idea. It is getting on. Almost five, I'd say, and we've been here since noon."

"Almost five? *Only* five." Eve leaned forward, put her hand over Sewal's. "Let's stay a little longer."

"What about James Ruell?" Sewal asked pointedly.

"I fed him a half hour ago, and Pole has taken him home already."

Sewal sighed, and gave in. "I suppose I can endure another hour or so. But mind you, seven o'clock—"

"Mister Blackheath! Mister Blackheath!" Her stark, close-set features red with anger, Rose Johnstone ran up to the table. "You've got to *do* something!"

Sewal rose in alarm. "What on earth—"

"Oh, it's awful. And Mayor Castebury won't lift a finger to stop her."

"What are you talking about, Miss Johnstone?"

Rose Johnstone's mouth moved, but nothing came out. Speechless, she pointed a trembling finger toward the center of the green. There, parting a sea of villagers, the diminutive form of Demetrios could be seen riding atop a trunk placed upon a low-wheeled platform and pulled by two spectacularly dressed "doves" from Madame Laurier's coop. The madam herself, dressed in purple and black velvet and wearing a hat covered with exotic feathers, followed a short distance behind. Even the band quit playing as the colorful procession approached. The doves, Molly and Salome, pulled the trunk into line with the others.

Demetrios stood, whipped off his hat, and bowed grandly to the crowd. "Ladies and Gentlemen!" he exclaimed in a shrill, rasping voice. "My mistress wishes to make a contribution to the collection taken up by the New Forest Women's Committee." The dwarf grinned, danced a quick jig, and thumped the brim of his top hat. As the crowd applauded his antics he leaped down and hurried to Madame Laurier.

The madam had not moved. The applause died, became an embarrassed silence. Slowly, regally, Madame Laurier climbed the four steps to the bandstand, then turned and faced the respectable citizens of New Forest. Slowly, regally, she curtsied deeply. "You are all *too* kind," she said in a low and throaty voice that dripped with sarcasm. "Too, *too* kind."

Someone coughed. The embarrassment became more acute. Horrified mothers snatched children unfortunate enough to be close at hand and hid them behind their skirts. Reverend and Mrs. Waldrop swelled with mutual rage. Disdaining to so much as acknowledge the town's reactions, Madame Laurier strode haughtily down the steps, snapped her fingers at her retinue, and stalked out of the party the same way she'd come.

"Now there's one that can't wait for the soldier boys to come home!" a bold voice shouted.

The remark broke the tension. Embarrassment gave way to nervous laughter and ill-conceived jokes. Jim Espey, the lead fiddle player, jumped down from the bandstand and opened the trunk Madame Laurier had left. Inside was a mound of woolen underwear. The crowd quieted again as the fiddle player held up a sample. "Hey! This'un ain't new!" he chortled. The statement seemed immensely funny, and generated bawdy suggestions as to how the owner of the Land Lock had taken up her collection. "By Michael, Mark, and Luke, if these drawers on top don't belong to the Mayor," Espey shouted, to a new wave of laughter. Cold sweat broke out on the back of the Mayor's neck as, afraid not to play along with the gag, he joined in with a fainthearted bray.

"Miss Johnstone looks faint, Father," Eve said as the music started again and the shock of Madame Laurier's appearance dissipated. "Perhaps you'd better see her to her chair."

"Yes, I do feel lightheaded. What a dreadful intrusion. Oh, Mister Blackheath, if you would be so kind . . ." Rose said, all but falling against Sewal.

"Why, of course, Rose," Sewal said, supporting the middle-aged spinster and fixing Eve with an icy stare. Eyes wide with innocence, Eve smiled in return.

"That man gonna get you for that, young'un," Eustacia chuckled, sitting heavily in the chair vacated by Sewal.

"It will do him good to have a woman throw herself at him. And there can't be more than twenty-five years separating them."

"What you sayin', girl? Now, that ain't ladylike."

"No. But it's the truth," Eve said.

Maisie hesitated at the edge of the dance floor, stepped onto the grass, and strolled nonchalantly toward the schoolhouse. Arvid and a few of his friends were preparing to run a foot race around the green. There would never be a better opportunity. Gathering her courage, she stepped onto the schoolhouse porch, only to spin about as a cheer rose from the crowd. Her heart felt as though it was caught in her throat. She looked around. Jon Naslund had just skewered a water barrel with a harpoon hurled from a distance of fifty feet. He had a chance at first prize. The band was playing. Sweat-soaked but undaunted, the hardiest of New Forest's citizens kept the pace to a New Hampshire Highstep. Hoopskirts billowed and the slim legs of the young men lifted and fell in blurs. No one was paying Maisie any mind.

Pulse racing, she opened the door, quickly stepped inside, and closed the door again. The schoolhouse was a twenty-by-twenty-foot-square room filled with pinewood desks arranged in order of advancing grades. Windows lined the walls on either side. The shutters were open and sunlight warmed the ordinarily cool interior. Primers and history and arithmetic books sat neatly arranged on a rack in front of the teacher's desk. In one corner a glass-enclosed case held a collection of seagoing memorabilia from whales' teeth to shells to a small, intricately fashioned clipper ship encased in a bottle of milky green glass. A ship's bell rested on the teacher's desk, along with a globe and a jar of pencils. Crossed harpoons hung over the chalkboard on the rear wall.

Her breath ragged, Maisie stood with her back to the door. Hamlet stood behind the desk. He wore a homespun checkered shirt crisscrossed by suspenders that bunched the material at his shoulders. His trousers flared at the ankles and would have appeared too short but for the pair of scuffed, well-used high-top laced boots he wore. His face was in shadow, and seemed darker than usual. Maisie began to sweat. Rivulets of moisture funneled down her sides and between her breasts.

"I seen your face in the window," she said, her voice quivering. "I wasn't going to come in, at first, but I did."

Hamlet reached out and brushed two fingers over the globe, which creaked on its axis. ".Yes." His voice rumbled in his chest. "I'm right grateful."

"I thought . . ." Maisie swallowed, tried again. "I wanted you to understand."

A muffled cheer from outside filtered through the heavy stone walls. Hamlet looked out the window. "Naslund's boy more a man than me?" he asked.

"That has nothing to do with it."

Hamlet's palm hit the globe, kept it spinning. "You said things. You and me, we had plans."

"What plans?" Maisie asked.

"You had no call leavin'."

Maisie kept her eyes on the spinning globe. "You know my ma didn't have no one else. And once I was home regular, I couldn't exactly go sneakin' off to walk up the cliff roads by myself."

"Who said anything about sneakin'?" Hamlet demanded, his voice harsh.

"You." Maisie nervously licked her lips. The globe ground to a halt. "Those was your words once, Hamlet Peters."

"You could have tried! I waited. I come to town and looked for you. And when I finally see you, you're with that goddamn white boy!"

"I never meant that to be, Hamlet. But bein' cooped up indoors day after day watchin' and carin' for Ma, it was just natural that when Arvid showed up at the door with a pot roast his ma sent, we visited. When he left, he asked to come back and I said yes."

Hamlet turned away in disgust.

"I was lonely for a friend, Hamlet," she went on forcefully. "Don't you see that?"

"You think you the only lonely person in this world, woman?" Hamlet asked angrily.

Maisie shook her head slowly. "He brung me flowers, Hamlet. He visited every day. I swear I tried not to, but I began to care for him here in my heart." She paused, almost afraid to say the next words. "And then one day he said he loved me, I told him . . . I told him that I felt—"

The sound of his palm slapping the globe stopped her. "And you wonder 'cause I'm angry? It hurts, woman. I got a hurt that don't never quit."

"Well, so do I!" Maisie said, near tears. The globe fascinated her because it gave her something to concentrate on, so she didn't have to look Hamlet in the eye. "I hurt for a home and a husband, and for children and a life."

"We could have those things, woman."

"That's what I said once," Maisie said. "And you said there weren't no place to go."

Hamlet stared at the globe, then pressed his palm against it to stop it from spinning. "I was wrong. There is a place," he said, his eyes burning. "I heard Mister Knight talkin' about it with the mayor a few days ago. They didn't pay me no mind, so I hung around the back of the store and listened. You ever hear of Liberia?"

"No."

"Me neither, but there's a ship leavin' from Boston next week. Maybe the last one, 'cause of the war. For the capital city, which is Monrovia. It's a city of freed slaves. Mister Castebury said that some society been helpin' colored folks get there for forty years."

Maisie's shoulder hurt where it pressed against the door. "And you want me to go?" she asked.

Hamlet nodded emphatically. "With me."

"You don't have no money."

"I'd get it. Somehow, I'd get it. My daddy's got some saved. Or Mister Blackheath would borrow me some. Wouldn't cost—"

"I can't, Hamlet," Maisie said softly, interrupting him.

Hamlet's face knotted into a frown. "You mean you won't," he said thickly, his eyes guarded.

She was trying not to hurt him, but there was no other avenue open to her but the truth. "Yes," she said. "I'm going to marry Arvid and have me a family. You got to understand," she pleaded. "I loved you, but now I love someone else. You just *got* to understand."

"No." Hamlet's hands knotted into fists as he leaned on the desk. "I don't got to understand nothin'."

"Hamlet, I—"

"Get out of here, woman." His voice was low and dangerous. "Go on back to your white boy. And pray to God Almighty he never learns who done took you first!"

Maisie blushed furiously. "Please, Hamlet . . ."

His fist shot out. The globe popped off its stand and shot up the aisle like a ball kicked by a child. The response so frightened her Maisie almost ran, but sensing that would be the extent of his violence, she regained her composure. Unable to think of anything further to add, she opened the door and slipped out.

The bright glare of the late afternoon sun was a painful contrast to her own gloomy state. As if in a dream, she walked slowly off the porch. A crowd of young men were racing around the green for the second time. Leading the pack was her own husband-to-be. She smiled then, quickened her step. She loved Arvid Naslund. Of that she was as certain as she had ever been of anything. Sorry for Hamlet but happy for herself, she melted unobtrusively into the crowd and headed for the blanket where her mother and sister waited, and where Arvid would join her as soon as he won his race.

Alone in the schoolhouse, a decision formed in the cooling recesses of Hamlet's mind. He slipped out the door and, skirting the crowd, struck out along the familiar road to Dawn Wind. In the awful silence of the empty schoolhouse a chipped and dented world came to rest in a far and dusty corner of the room.

A little girl screamed and ran for the safety of her mother's skirt. Two boys, no more than ten years old, gawked unashamedly, their mumblety-peg game forgotten. Aaron Milhouse, the youngest member of the family that owned New Forest's bank, stared with saucer eyes and open mouth. The soldier leaned forward and repeated his question. "Can you tell me where I'll find the Blackheaths, lad?"

Aaron remained mute. He tried hard to look at the soldier's shiny black boots or his crisp blue uniform dotted with polished brass buttons as bright as the sun or the black gun belt and holstered revolver, but couldn't. His attention was riveted on the soldier's face, the left side of which was covered from forehead to neck by a large, black patch. The patch was of velvet, edged with a band of thick stitchery, and held in place much as a simple eyepatch with a tooled leather strap that circled the soldier's head. Major Jack Travis leaned closer. His voice was normal except for a slight slurring effect, which hinted at the awful mystery hidden under the patch. "Are the Blackheaths here, boy?"

Slowly, as if some force outside his body moved his hand, Aaron pointed toward the east side of the green and the crowd gathered there.

"Thank you," Travis said, reaching out to pat the boy on the shoulder. Everyone in New Forest said that Aaron was old and wise beyond his years. Quick of thought, they said. Smart as a whip. His ability to manipulate his peers, and anyone else with whom he came in contact, marked him as one destined to surpass his father and go on to become a great financier. At the moment Travis reached for him, though, his courage collapsed. Suddenly, he was just a twelve-year-old boy who was quite unaccustomed to the peculiar horrors of war. He ran.

Travis had forgotten again. As if to remind himself, he touched the velvet patch. A wan smile—I'm sorry, it seemed to say, I didn't ask to look this way, you see—lifted the visible side of his face. I can live with it, he repeated for the thousandth time. I am no less a man. Shoulders straight, he started across the green.

He heard cheering to his left, his blind side, but could not see the group of sturdy young men bearing down on him as he crossed the path of the footrace. Suddenly, he was surrounded. One of the runners shouted for him to move. A pair of dockworkers, too drunk to notice much else about him other than that he was in the way, yelled and hooted. Running men darted past him. "Damn it, man!" one of them shouted as he swerved to avoid a collision. Another grabbed his shoulder and gasping for breath, spun him half around.

"Why don't you watch . . ." The words trailed off. The young man stared at Jack. His mouth worked as if he wanted to say something, but nothing came out. Even the drunken dockworkers grew silent. One woman inhaled sharply. Jack could hear another one to his left gasp, "Oh, my!" The young man still grasped his shoulder. Slowly, Jack turned his head, looked down at the offending hand. The young man jerked his hand away as if it had been burned. "I . . . That is," he stammered. "I didn't . . ."

"You don't have to say it, friend," Jack said, his voice soft and even. "All apologies accepted."

Unable to bear their scrutiny, doing his best to ignore the silence and blatantly curious stares, Jack moved through the crowd. He should have written first, he thought. Or never come at all. Of all the options, he had chosen the most painful. But he owed it to Eve and to her father. They deservd to hear the story firsthand. He moved more quickly, searching the faces of those he passed. Men puffed cigars, drank beer, talked of war or commerce. Women with parasols or broad, squarish fans chatted about dresses and children. Wherever Jack passed activity withered like corn in a drought. When it resumed in his wake the topic had invariably changed: Who is he? What happened? Why is he here?

He had stopped, and was scanning the crowd when Eve saw him. "Oh, my God! Jack! Jack Travis!" she exclaimed, running toward him. For a second he forgot again, and turned to face her.

Eve stopped an arm's length away. The blood drained from her face and her hand went to her mouth, stifling the scream before it came out. Not Jack! Not him. Not handsome Jack Travis.

They stood in the center of a silent circle. Jack stared at Eve, forced himself to remain motionless. This is why I'm here, he thought, quite clearly. Not for them, but for me. To see with my own eyes—*eye,* he corrected himself savagely—what she says and how she says it. Eve had not moved. Jack's heart sank. So now I know, he thought. Now I know.

"Oh, Jack," Eve whispered. Tears welling in her eyes, she stepped toward him. "Jack." Her hands touched his sides. She looked up at him and then, lips trembling, laid her cheek against his chest.

His throat burned and he thought his heart would burst with joy. Dazed, he felt his arms go around her, let his right cheek touch her hair. "Hello, Eve," he said, the words barely audible.

"You should have written. You should have come sooner. You should have let me know you were alive and well."

"I know." He cleared his throat, dared to say what he had not admitted to himself earlier. "I was afraid."

"No." He could feel her head shake sideways. "You needn't have been." Suddenly, Eve pushed herself away from him. Her eyes were bright, but with joy, as she took his hands. "Look at you!" she said, the laughter bubbling from her. "They've made you a lieutenant colonel! Come. Father will be happy to see you. Father?"

Eve led him through the crowd. "Charity Walker, meet Jack Travis. Elton Hubbard, Lieutenant Colonel Travis. Duty Meredith, Celia Castebury, this is Lieutenant Colonel Travis, a dear friend. He has so much to tell us, we'll simply have to have another party. Mr. Knight, Lieutenant Colonel Jack Travis. Isn't this exciting?"

And suddenly, it was. Eve's enthusiasm spread. Within minutes Jack had ceased to be a mysterious, scarred intruder, and became a wounded Union hero home from the war. Men rushed to shake his hand. Everyone remembered seeing him at Michael's wedding. He was a splendid chap. Awful that he'd been wounded, of course, but if there were more brave men like him the war would be over, and could he come to talk to the schoolchildren or the Men's Bible Class? The mayor wanted to make another speech, but had to settle for inviting the war hero to dinner at an unspecified date in the future. Even Alice and Rose Johnstone overcame their initial revulsion and concurred that the arrival of an actual hero had insured the day's success. The New Forest Women's Committee for the Preservation of the Union could not have planned it better.

The windows had been thrown open. A light breeze billowed the curtains, and the night music of a restless sea filled the room. Hanson Pole brought a bottle of brandy and three snifters. The butler looked haggard from an afternoon spent fussing over James Ruell, who had refused to go to sleep once he had been brought home.

"I want to thank you," Jack said once they were alone again. He placed his hand over Eve's. "For today. You are the supreme diplomat."

"I don't have the slightest notion of what you are talking about," Eve protested.

Jack smiled. "Of course you do." He held up his glass. "And you, too, Mr. Blackheath, for your hospitality."

Sewal waved away the gratitude. "The least we can do. And happy to have you, Colonel."

Jack stared at the wine glass, wondered how he could possibly break the news he carried. "I wish I could repay your kindness with something equally . . . of equal . . ." He paused, nervously touched the velvet patch. Tragedy announced itself in slight gestures, in broken, dangling sentences and awkward silences. He looked at Eve, standing near the window, silhouetted against the Moroccan tapestry. She was watching him closely. God, he thought. Anyone else but him. "I have yet to tell you how I received this . . . No. That isn't the way to begin. Damn!"

Sewal tensed in his Spanish governor's chair. "Say it, whatever it is," he rasped. "The best way to say something is to just say it."

Jack nodded. His fingers tugged absently at the half mask. He looked at Eve, shook his head. "Michael is dead."

The tension in the room tingled the skin. Sewal started to rise, then forced himself to sit back. "That's absurd," he said. "Michael's in California by now. San Francisco, I suspect, and doing quite well."

Eve sat. "I'm sorry, sir," Jack said. "It is absurd, but he is dead nonetheless."

Sewal's face had turned ashen. He shot from the chair. "Now, see here! By what right do you have to enter my house and speak to me of my son? I don't know what you've heard, or from whom, but I will not have you . . . have you . . ." He glanced at Eve for help.

"I was there, sir. I was with him." Travis spoke quietly, his voice unemotional, almost clinical. "He joined my command in late February as a scout. I had been ordered to find and eliminate Confederate raiders in eastern Kentucky. We caught up with them—because of Michael—in early June, and trapped them. In the ensuing battle, I received my wound, and though we carried the day, Michael was killed."

"Why?" Eve asked in the silence that followed. "You never mentioned him in your letters. You didn't tell us. Why?"

"I wanted to, but he wouldn't let me." Jack rose, paced nervously. "He had assumed an identity, and was traveling under the name James Black. He spoke of heading for California. I tried to talk him into doing just that once we knew exactly where the raiders were, but he wouldn't leave until we had actually caught McKenna."

"McKenna!" Sewal staggered as if struck, supported himself by grabbing onto the chair, and stared malevolently at Eve.

Eve paled, and her mouth hung open in disbelief. "Yes, sir," Jack said, thinking that he would at last learn why Michael had so hated the man. "The same McKenna I met here at Michael's wedding, later a captain and a raider in the Confederate Army. One of my men saw the two of them riding off locked in mortal combat. Later they found Michael dead." Eve's whole body felt cold, as if she had walked unclothed into a December night. She was unable to speak.

"Where is he?" Sewal's voice was sepulchral. "What have you done with my son?" he demanded.

"I was told he was buried with the rest of the dead of my command," Travis answered, shaken by Sewal's wrath. "I would have brought him back myself, but I. . . . During the battle, a wagon exploded. I was nearby, and—" As if reliving the horrible memory, Jack's hand went to his face, felt all over the black velvet patch. When he continued, it was in a barely audible whisper. "I . . . was . . . incapacitated. Not in my right mind. The pain was . . ." He drew himself up with a shudder, and went on. "A Lieutenant Schuler found his body and had him buried with the others. His grave is on a hillside overlooking a stream and a valley in a place called Printer's Gap in southeastern Kentucky. It's a rather lovely valley, really." He stopped, at a loss for more to add. "I'm sorry, Mr. Blackheath."

Age shrouded Sewal, came upon him without warning. Eyes blank, as if he were listening to something neither Eve nor Jack could hear, he nodded once, and slowly walked out of the room.

Travis glanced at Eve, who sat almost primly on the edge of her chair. Her head was cocked slightly to one side, her hands folded in her lap. Strangely, almost unnaturally composed, she looked up at Jack. "I think I knew this was going to happen. I read it in his eyes the day he left. Perhaps he suspected as much too. You do know the way to the guest room, do you not?"

"Yes. Of course."

"I think I'll go to mine, then, if you don't mind." She rose, sucked in a deep breath, and started for the door. "Good night, Jack. It was good of you—"

"Eve." His voice stopped her in the doorway. "If there's anything I can do," he said, lamely.

"We Blackheaths are a proud lot, Jack," she said quietly, but purposefully. "We must be allowed our private grief."

The doorway where she had stood was empty. The mystery remained. Perhaps he would never know. Alone, Jack picked up his glass and refilled it, then walked to the window. The moon had passed over the house, and cast a long, rectangular shadow over the east lawn. Beyond, the Atlantic was a gray smudge that rose and met the horizon. The wind was damp, as if the world were weeping.

Dawn Wind was dying. First Jennifer, Sewal thought, then Michael. What had once been a vital, living home had been reduced to ghostlike memories and empty rooms. Too goddamned empty. His footsteps were all but soundless on the stairway as he brooded. The clock in the lower hall chimed a quarter after three. Restless sorrow had driven him from his bedroom with its paintings and memories. His firstborn was dead. Michael lay in distant, unfriendly soil. And with him in the grave lay Sewal's dreams and hopes and aspirations for the future of Dawn Wind. Strange, how when a man grew old his knees hurt and his breath was hard to catch. Michael, Michael, Michael, Michael.

A floorboard creaked. A book fell in the study. Alerted, Sewal held onto the newel post and listened, then walked stealthily down the hall. The study door was open. A furtive shape darted past the moonlit window. A prowler at Dawn Wind? There was money in the desk.

"Who's in there?" Sewal asked, straining to see as he entered the library. He did not bother to look for a lamp. He'd been up for hours and was accustomed to the dark. He stood in the middle of the room. His heart pressed against his chest. "Who's in here, I said!" Footsteps, soft on the carpet. Movement in the corner. Sewal tried to follow the sound, but wasn't quick enough. "Show yourself, damn you!"

"Be quiet, Mister Blackheath."

"Hamlet!" He recognized the voice, tried to turn but found himself grasped from behind. A hand groped for his mouth. Sewal planted his feet and struck out to the rear with his elbows, but could not break loose. "What in the name of the devil? . . ."

"Don't fight me, Mister Blackheath," Hamlet grunted. "You an old man." His arms slipped under Sewal's and his hands clasped behind his neck.

Sewal gasped in pain. "Let go, damn you!" he wheezed.

"Only you don't try to fight me." Hamlet's voice was tense with fear. "I don't want to hurt you, Mister Blackheath, but if I got to, I got to." His grip tightened. "Say you won't try to fight me, an' I'll let you go."

"All right! All right!" The grip relaxed. Sewal stumbled forward a step, caught himself on the desk. When he turned to face Hamlet the black man stepped toward him menacingly. A sharp pain in the back of Sewal's neck made him wince, but he shook it off. "What's this all about, Hamlet? You, a common thief!"

"I'm sorry, Mister Blackheath." There was anguish in Hamlet's voice, but determination too. "I need the money. I'm leavin' here, an' you ain't never gonna see me again."

"But I pay you, damn it, man!"

"Not enough," Hamlet hissed. "Not never enough. I need more."

Coins clinked as a leather pouch of gold was deposited in one of Hamlet's pockets. The sound unleashed a fury in Sewal. The veins in his neck swelled with rage, not so much at Hamlet as at the whole world. "I'll see you in hell first," he roared, lunging across the narrow space separating them.

"Please, Mister Blackheath." Hamlet was younger, and stronger, than Sewal. He tried to shove the older man away. "I don't want to hurt you . . . I don't."

Sewal charged again. Grunting, panting, the two men struggled, collided with the desk, reeled into a chair and slammed into a bookshelf. Suddenly, Sewal cried out in pain. His grip loosened. Hamlet found himself supporting the older man rather than fighting him. "Sweet Jesus!" he groaned, lowering Sewal to the floor. He didn't have any time. The household was alert. He could hear footsteps on the stairway, approaching from the back of the house. The money was in his pocket.

"I'm sorry," he whimpered. "I'm sorry." Then, taking up a heavy walnut chair, he hurled it through the closest window and, leaping over the sill, disappeared into the sorrows of a waning September moon.

Chapter 30

Eustacia pulled the clay cooking pot out of the oven and placed it on the work counter. When she lifted the lid a cloud of steam rose to the ceiling. Working quickly, she stuffed potatoes and onions around the partially cooked roast and wedged chunks of carrots into the remaining crevices. Humming with satisfaction, she replaced the lid and slid the entire affair over the bed of coals inside the oven. Jubb watched her from the table. He ignored the piece of mincemeat pie before him, an action that revealed the depth of his depression. Now and then he ran calloused, wrinkled fingers through the snowy cap of hair crowning his head. His sulphurous eyes were crisscrossed with tiny red veins and dull from lack of sleep.

Hanson Pole entered from the stairway. He too, looked tired and drawn. He had neglected his hair, sandy filaments of which lay in disarray, leaving his growing bald spot exposed. He looked far less the Caesar, and more the hounded and beleaguered Brutus. His usually efficient demeanor had been sorely tested in the week since the house had heard the news of Michael's death and the ensuing but unconnected attack on Sewal. "Mrs. Sarandon is leaving shortly for the station," he announced, nodding his thanks as he took the cup of coffee Eustacia handed him. "She wants to know if everything will be ready."

Eustacia nodded. "There's coffee and pie, should folks be hungry early. I just put the vegetables in with the roast. It'll be ready by suppertime."

"Very well." Pole sat wearily across from Jubb.

"How's Mister Blackheath?" Jubb asked.

"As well as can be expected," the butler replied. "A stroke is something from which one recovers through one's own merit and efforts, and God's will. There is little a physician can do."

"One this an' one that," Jubb said derisively. "It's Mister Sewal Blackheath you're talkin' about."

Pole sighed. "Believe me, I am aware of that. But one *must* retain one's objectivity, especially at a time like this. Hysteria does no one, Mr. Blackheath included, any good. Besides, tragedy does not necessarily require one to abandon one's education or standards of grammar."

"Well, I'll watch Mister Blackheath tonight, 'cause if'n all your airy ways makes me sick, it prob'ly makes him sicker."

Hanson Pole did not deign to respond to such impertinence. He merely announced he was retiring to his room.

Eustacia shook her head in dismay. "There's trouble enough around here without you carryin' on so an' making more, Jubb Peters," she said, whisking away Pole's coffee cup.

Jubb lowered his head. "Can't help it, woman. It just comes natural, 'specially when Mister Pole comes along."

"Least you can do durin' tryin' times is to *try,* old man. Most 'specially when Mister Pole comes along. We all got to stick together. It's the only way." She wiped clean Pole's cup and set it on the rack to dry, looked around the kitchen with a practiced eye. Everything was spic and span, as usual. Moving ponderously, she walked to Jubb and rested her hands on his shoulders. "Don't seem right, somehow. Both them boys gone."

She could picture them. Hamlet as a tiny, squirming, happy, wild-eyed child; Michael quieter, lying in his crib and staring at things like he was memorizing them. They'd changed right under her nose. All the happiness had gone out of them both. Hamlet's eyes had gone suspicious and hard; his ways had grown devious. Michael had become morose, took to drink, then disappeared. With a pang she remembered the last time she'd seen him. He'd looked stronger then.

More like the man his mama, bless her soul, would have wanted him to be.

Jubb stirred, touched her left hand with his right. "Reckon I'd better help with them horses," he said.

Eustacia sighed. "I reckon." She moved heavily toward the door. "I'll be upstairs, to see if there's anything Miss Eve needs." The stairs creaked beneath her weight.

She found Eve in the formal parlor, waiting for Travis to bring the carriage and team around. She wore a deep blue riding gown trimmed with somber black lace at the cuffs and around the neck. Posed amid the stern, uncomfortable chairs and end tables in that little-used room, she seemed stiff and unemotional. The leatherbound family Bible on its pedestal by the window looked more at home, as did the Reverend Elkahan Waldrop. One hand resting on the back of a spartan horsehair cushion, the Congregational minister stood at the end of the sofa. Black eyebrows beetling above a beaked nose and thin, pressed lips left the impression of an utterly humorless, stern disciplinarian. That impression was close to the truth, but by no means the whole truth: there was far more to the man than met the eye.

Elkahan Waldrop, at age fifty-five, perceived himself as a man of God. His faith, forged in the harsh light of a vengeful Father and tempered by the blood of a forgiving Son, was as solid as Maine granite. If he was often overly righteous he also gave unstintingly of himself. He had no more use for weakness than he had for sin. He likewise abhorred bigotry: if all God's children were sinners, they were equal as well. Eustacia liked him not only because he was an Abolitionist, but because she bore him a debt of gratitude for finding her and Jubb and the baby Hamlet a place at Dawn Wind when they came North those many years ago. Above all Elkahan Waldrop was a decent man who expected no less of himself than he did of any man, and practiced what he preached. Eustacia found no discomfort in his angry profile, as did many of New Forest's townsfolk, nor could she discern the dust of brimstone settling from his coat to the floor, as she'd heard some say. She saw past the visage to the reality of a kind heart. The reverend seemed relieved to see Eustacia and greeted her warmly.

"Eustacia, my dear woman," he said, frock coat flapping as he walked toward her. He put his hand on her arm. "God is testing your courage and your faith."

Eustacia attempted a brave smile. "I'm keepin' an eye to the Lord. I only hope He's doin' the same for Hamlet, and will help that boy turn around from what he's done."

"He will. He will," the minister said. "Eve. I'll be upstairs with your father if you need me."

"Thank you, Reverend Waldrop," Eve said politely, but distantly.

"I'll try not to wake James Ruell," he added.

"He's a sound sleeper. You needn't worry about that."

"Yes, sir," Eustacia chimed in hurriedly, made nervous by the coolness between Eve and the minister.

"When that young'un wants to sleep, ain't nothin' gonna wake him up. And when he don't want to sleep, oo'weee!" The Reverend was starting out of the room. "He's a real little doozie," she added lamely, thinking at least there was Doozie. Out of all this, at least there was him.

Eve hadn't moved. The silence was unnerving. "Is there anything I can bring you, honey?" Eustacia asked.

"No, thank you, Eustacia. Colonel Travis and I will be leaving to pick up Justin at the station. We'll be home a little after noon, I expect."

"It will be good to see that boy again. You figure he'll be stayin'?"

"Who can tell? Father wants him to. I think." She shook her head. "I just hope they don't argue. Dr. Cutcheon said that would be the worst thing possible."

Eustacia's head bobbed up and down confidently. "He'll stay. I just know he will, when he sees Mister Blackheath lyin' there." Her hand shot to her mouth. "Oh, Miss Eve, I didn't mean . . . I'm so sorry."

Eve hugged the black woman. "I understand, Eustacia. There's nothing anyone can do."

"I jus' wonder how a little girl can be so strong."

"I'm not little anymore. And even if the days ahead promise worse, I just can't allow myself the luxury of fear," Eve said, more to herself than to Eustacia. "Maybe when Justin arrives. Maybe then."

"Lordy, Lordy," Eustacia sniffed. "You know what, Miss Eve? Awhile ago, all I could think of, with all that's happened, all I could think of was how Mister Michael forgot that packet of food I packed away for him the last time he was here. There was two chicken san'wiches, a hunk a'beef big as his two fists, a loaf o' my fresh bread, three apples— I figured to feed that boy at least half way to California. An' he lef' it behind. Oh, I reckon he thought about it, but he jus' couldn't bring himself to come back for it. Some folks is like that, I know, but I never even got to say good-bye to him. Hamlet neither. Seems like the sorrows some folks bear . . ." Eustacia broke down, rubbed a forearm across her eyes.

Eve was near tears herself. "I . . . I'd better wait on the porch," she said, kissing Eustacia on the cheek and letting her go. "Colonel Travis will be along."

Eustacia nodded and Eve left, her throat tight. If shock and sorrow weighted her footsteps, panic hurried them. Preoccupied by her father's illness, Eve had managed to force Michael from her mind, but now that Eustacia had mentioned his name, his face returned to haunt her. And with it, Lion McKenna's, but in a way far different from the musing of a lonely woman. Lion had killed Michael. She had often wondered if she would ever meet the Southerner again, whether passion and love would return to heal the wounds his departure had left. The question had been answered with Michael's death. Dull, cold ash filled the space in her heart once occupied by Lion McKenna: she cursed the day he set foot in Dawn Wind, and wept for cursing that same day.

Think of something else, a voice in her mind cried. Think of anything but what has happened. Think of anything but Michael or Hamlet or Lion or Father. A chilly breeze cut across the front porch. Eve breathed deeply, sucked in great gulps of fresh air in an attempt to calm herself. By the time Jack drove the carriage around to the front, she was able to concentrate on the task at hand: meeting Justin's train, and handling the tension that would surely accompany him during his first visit to Dawn Wind in nearly two years.

"I'm not certain I'll recognize him," Jack said, enjoying the feeling of Eve's arm in his as they scrutinized the passengers of the train through the drifting steam of the locomotive. "The last time I saw Justin was at Michael's wedding. About all I remember of him is a rather mysterious figure with a camera."

"That was Justin, all right," Eve laughed.

"Besides, I was preoccupied."

"I noticed," Eve said drily. At his surprised glance, she added, "You caused quite a stir. 'Isn't he *pretty!*' they said. I, of course, paid no attention."

"Of course," Jack said, disguising the lurking bitterness with a wan grin. The shielded side of his face began to ache. He touched the patch, adjusted it slightly. Sometimes just the weight of the fabric was almost unbearable. Pretty, he thought sourly. Those days were gone. Forever. Eve was standing on tiptoe, searching for Justin, completely unaware of what she had just said. He watched her out of the corner of his good eye, and his heart leaped. He had yet to approach her with his intentions. The terrible events of the last week had been too disturbing. Once the situation at Dawn Wind stabilized and Eve's mind was clear of worries, he would ask her to marry him. He was on leave until the fifteenth of October. There would be ample time.

Eve stiffened at his side. Travis followed her line of sight. A young gentleman and his lady were causing a sensation among those waiting on the platform. The man, in his early twenties, wore a broad-brimmed flat-crowned black beaver hat set at a rakish angle above a thin bony face and eyes that hid from the world behind wire-rimmed glasses. A dark blue knee-length cloak was draped across his almost pointed shoulders. He wore a black frock coat and white ruffled shirt with a narrow cravat, black trousers, and patent leather boots. He wasn't a big man, scarcely Eve's height, but his traveling companion was even smaller. Barely five feet tall, her skin was the color of coffee heavily laced with sweet cream. Straight midnight-black hair hung to her waist and framed a face that was at once beautiful and sensually mysterious. Her garb was spectacular. A baggy overgarment of silk embroidered with multicolored peacocks strutting and preening themselves on a russet background concealed her torso and hips. Much to the shock of everyone present, the remainder of her costume consisted of slippers and silk trousers of the same hue as her coat.

The man's hand fluttered at the hem of his cloak as he searched the platform. Unlike Travis and everyone else in sight, who wore sideburns, this fellow was totally clean-shaven and the lack of facial hair added to his look of debilitating undernourishment. "Who on earth is that?" Jack asked, nudging Eve.

"My brother," Eve answered. "Justin. I don't believe it."

The girl a pace behind him, Justin hurried across the platform. "Dear sister," he said, taking Eve's hands.

"Justin," Eve whispered, brushing a kiss against his cheek. Impulsively, the distance between them giving way to desperate closeness, she embraced him closely. "Justin. I'm glad you're here. Thank you for being here."

"Did you think I wouldn't come?" he asked, his voice trembling. He stroked the thick-coiled riches of her hair. In that moment they were brother and sister communing in the quiet, unspoken sorrow of a brother dead and a father grievously ill. Finally, eyes misty and red, they parted.

"How silly you look," Eve laughed, holding him at arm's length.

Justin grinned self-consciously. "Thanks," he sniffed. "I thought—"

"And utterly charming as well," Eve added good-naturedly. "Oh, Justin!" She hugged him quickly again, let him go and turned to Jack. "But we're not alone. This is my friend, Lieutenant Colonel Travis."

Travis held out his hand. "Eve insists on formality. My name is Jack."

"Yes, I remember. You were Michael's best man." Justin reached behind him, took the girl by one elbow. "Come," he said gently. The girl with the secretive, almond eyes hung back shyly as she studied Justin's sister and the man with the masked face. "It's all right. Really. Selene, this is my sister, Eve, and her friend Jack Travis." The self-conscious smile returned. "Selene is a . . . uh . . . special friend. I use her in much of my work."

The faintest trace of a smile touched the corners of Eve's mouth. No wonder the flow of Justin's letters had dried to a mere trickle. And Justin had always been so shy and self-effacing. "I'm very pleased to meet you, Selene," she said. Oh, my God, she thought frantically, her eyes unseen by the others as she embraced Selene. What will I do if they want to sleep together at Dawn Wind? If Father finds out . . .

"Justin has told me all about you," Selene said, warming to Eve. "You're every bit as beautiful as he said."

"Selene was a bit apprehensive about coming with me," Justin said. He coughed nervously. "I told her it would be perfectly fine."

"Of course it's perfectly fine," Eve said, knowing full well that Justin and his exotic woman friend would be the topic of a thousand rumors all over New Forest for the next two months. Every article of clothing they wore, every word they spoke, every gesture they made would be discussed and analyzed and dissected and assigned meaning beyond any semblance of truth or reason. But that didn't matter. People could say and think what they wished: Justin was home. "Father will be anxious to see you," she said, taking Justin's arm and leading him toward the carriage.

"How is he?"

"Weak. Tired and rambling. Sometimes confused."

"That must be an ill-fitting coat for him to wear."

"You won't be cruel to him, Justin, will you?"

Justin's look was grim, the tone of his voice flat and noncommittal. "I'm here, aren't I?" he asked by way of an answer.

Somehow, Eve was not reassured.

"My legs may be dead, but the rest of me isn't." Sewal enunciated each word with care. The effort brought beads of sweat to his forehead and stirred the sleeping anger. A stroke, he remembered them saying. Sewal Blackheath, a stroke. He'd never spent a sick day in his life. Try as he might, he had yet to fully comprehend his condition. Things were fuzzy, hazy. He couldn't think of words he'd used all his life. They'd gone somewhere, along with the sentences that, once begun, more often than not trailed off into oblivion. "Your praying woke me up. I thought . . ."

Elkahan Waldrop opened his eyes and leaned over slightly in order to see a little better in the dim light. "I'm sorry," he said.

"Ssss . . . All right," Sewal said, fighting the words. Willing each muscle into action, he turned his head and stared at the long, thin slat of sunshine streaming through the crack between the curtain and the window. In a moment it, too, would be gone as the sun shifted across the sky. He wished someone would open the curtains.

"Is there anything I can bring you?" Waldrop asked.

"Yes." Sewal could hear the unaccustomed sibilance, and hated the sound of it. "Michael. Bring me . . . my . . . son," he mumbled as his eyes closed and consciousness slowly began to slip away again.

"Justin will be here soon," Waldrop said, bending low over the sick man.

"Justin . . ." Even Sewal didn't know whether he'd asked a question or repeated the word, or merely thought it. The name clung to the receding fabric of his consciousness, followed him down into the confused semisleep of the seriously ill.

Justin, Justin, Justin. If only he had turned, looked over his shoulder to see Justin following him. The boy was twelve and frightened by the awful thing that was happening to his mother. Sewal had seen the question—Will she die, Father? Will she?—in his haunted eyes, but had evaded answering, as if refusing to say the word negated its possibility.

The past unfolded in meticulous detail. Midnight, black as Sewal's soul. Nothing else existed but the pent-up anger at the injustice of a world that was conspiring to take the woman he loved, and the unbearable frustration of being powerless to do anything for Jennifer. Driven from the house by weary longing and by the unbearable sorrow that stemmed from watching a wife too delirious even to recognize him, Sewal walked across the empty grounds to the stable. The creak of saddle leather and his horse's hooves, now clicking on stone, now drumming on packed snow, filled the emptiness. Sewal rode past the shipyards. He chose dimly lit alleys and narrow courses between buildings and, at last, came to the Land Lock. Quietly, he tethered the horse and stood outside the door. His face was drawn and pinched, every muscle in his body tense. It was a Sunday, and Madame Laurier, careful not to arouse the ire of a puritanical town that barely tolerated her in any case, was closed for the night. Sewal saw himself pound at the door, saw Demetrios brushed aside as the shipbuilder stormed into the anteroom.

It was all highly irregular. Unsure what to do about the intrusion of one of New Forest's leading citizens, Demetrios ran to summon his mistress. Seconds later, Madame Laurier appeared. The year had been 1853. Marie Laurier was in her late twenties then. Her waist was trim, her breasts swelled beneath her chemise. In the dim light she was beautiful. Torrents of soft hair covered her shoulders. Her cheekbones were high, her chin strong, her lips full, and her eyes a burning, crackling mystery that sent Sewal's blood racing.

"Get rid of him," Sewal rasped, nodding in the direction of Demetrios.

Laurier's head moved slightly. The dwarf disappeared behind a curtain.

"You must have something to drink here."

"Come."

Madame Laurier watched as Sewal downed three glasses of her very best Scotch, neat. She asked no questions. Everyone knew Jennifer Blackheath's condition, and Madame Laurier, more than most women, knew what living with a dying wife could do to a man. Patiently, she waited for the alcohol to dull the edge of the shipbuilder's anger. She had known men like him before; stern, stubborn men who would defy heaven and hell should they prove obstructions to a dream. And then she took him by the hand, and led him to her private chambers.

Painfully vivid scenes that he had worked too hard to forget flashed through his mind. Sewal could not help watching the final act of the drama that had stolen the affection of his son. Marie Laurier kissed him on the lips. She unfastened his shirt, knelt to slide his breeches down his muscular thighs, remained kneeling before him until he could bear her enticements no longer and, with a roar of anguish and desire, picked her up and flung her backward onto her canopied bed.

Shameful! Onerous! He did not want to watch. The harshest of penalties were well deserved for such behavior. No wonder Justin . . . No! Sewal's pain had been too great. He had been foolish, but not evil. There was a difference. There had to be!

She was naked, her flesh hot underneath him as he plunged between her thighs with deep, punishing thrusts. It had not lasted long, as a battle does not last long. An explosive skirmish, a violent torrent of energy culminating in an orgasmic shriek.

And then exhausted stillness. Sewal rolled from Marie Laurier's still eager warmth. He could taste the rouge from her lips. The inner joining of her thighs was flecked with his seed. Revolted, he glanced away from her and saw, in the firelight, Justin standing in the doorway. Horror welled in him. Stunned, Sewal covered himself. The boy must have awakened and followed him. How—and how he had entered the Land Lock unseen—did not matter. Only the stricken look on his face, the look of intense disillusionment and unutterable pain. And then Justin ran, bolted down the hall and into the night.

"Justin!" Sewal gasped, unsure if the name was uttered in the past or present.

There was no point trying to catch him. With Madame Laurier reclining upon the pillows, Sewal wept for one of the few times in his life. Body wracked with muscle-tearing sobs, he cupped his face in his hands, and wept.

"Father . . . Father?"

The dream blurred, broke apart into pieces. Light entered, and Sewal woke to see a figure standing by his bed. He squinted, blinked his eyes as he tried to separate reality from memory. Justin was in the dream, but a different Justin. Now he was older, and dressed in a loose white shirt, unbuttoned vest, and black wool trousers. Sewal's head hurt. If he could just sort things out . . . A hand floated toward him, rested on his shoulder. This Justin was real, then. Real! Elated, Sewal tried to speak, but words failed. He couldn't remember them, couldn't remember how they went. And there was so much to say!

Justin shook his head. "No need. I can tell what you're thinking." He sat on the edge of the bed. His gaze drifted up to the portrait of his mother. "She was beautiful, wasn't she," he said sadly. "A beautiful woman. I remember that much." He sighed, looked back to Sewal. "I guess I'd better say it now before you get your hopes up. I won't be staying."

Sewal's spirits sagged. Why couldn't Justin understand? Why? Exerting every ounce of strength he could muster, he made his hand move, and clutched Justin's leg.

"You fought me every inch of the way, Father. You refused me an allowance, did everything in your power to drive me back here and make me relinquish the one dream I had. Oddly enough, I find myself almost grateful, because the harder things became, the more stubborn I grew. In the process, I was forced to question whether or not I really wanted the life I was experiencing. The answer was yes."

Timidly, he took Sewal's hand, held it in his own. "To make matters worse, for you at least, I'm becoming successful. Every piece of equipment, every jar of chemicals, every square inch of my studio and gallery has been—" he smiled faintly "—is being earned with my sweat and blood and talent. I won't give that up, Father. I couldn't if I wanted to. Not anymore."

Justin cleared his throat. His voice was husky, but powerful. "That's why I came. To tell you in person that I have no other reason for not staying. I wanted you to know that, to hear it from me. And I wanted to say one thing more, for your ears alone. I never told anyone. Never. Do you understand what I'm saying?"

Sewal concentrated, focused his eyes again. "Yes," he said.

"I'm sorry for the past, sorry for what was between us. For a long time, I hated you." Justin removed his glasses, rubbed the bridge of his nose. "You see, I'd never loved anyone the way you loved Mother. Now, I think I understand. I guess that means I've grown up, even if not in the way you wanted." He placed Sewal's hand on the bed, tenderly arranged the covers.

"Going?" Sewal asked, confused again. Justin was going? He'd just arrived. Too many words. He couldn't be going so soon.

"I have an exhibition opening in Boston tomorrow, so I'll need to catch the Portland train south. Eve thinks I ought to stay, of course, but I'd be no good with ships. We both know that." He sounded too hearty, too hurried, even to himself. His eyes closed and the muscles in his jaws clenched. "I . . . Take care of yourself, Father," he whispered.

Justin moved toward the door, then paused. "Sell the damn yards," he said hoarsely, not daring to turn around and look at Sewal again. "Sell them before they break your heart. Before they kill you." His shoulders sagged. He was drained, more drained than he thought possible from his brief speech. "Eve will keep me informed. Good-bye, Father. Try to rest."

The door closed quietly. Sewal's throat felt swollen. Helpless against an old man's tears, he shut his eyes.

Eve blew out the lantern and settled back in the chair—her father's chair at her father's desk in her father's office. It was after nine o'clock, and she had been there since leaving Justin and Selene at the train station. Eliot, Sewal's head clerk, had left at six. Before he left, he had showed her Sewal's books and files, explained how they were arranged, and stoked the fire. Now the fire was dead and the desk was covered with piles of paper. The most important pile was directly in front of her. The result of two initial hours of scanning and winnowing, and a third of intense study, it held the essential facts of the Blackheath yards.

To Eve's dismay, the financial condition of the company was worse than she thought. There had been small contracts, to be sure, but not a single substantial government job had gone through the yards since the beginning of the war. This she had known, of course, just as she had known that there was plenty of work available. The yards in Bath were booming, as were others up and down the coast from Connecticut to Maine. What she hadn't known was how many of her father's bids had been rejected. Bid after bid—some of which must have been low considering the desperate need for work and the hair-thin profit margin her father worked on—had been returned. Not a single one had been accepted. And clipped to each bid was a letter —usually perfunctory at best—of explanation signed by, of all people, Admiral Dayton Cabell.

At first she had been shocked, but shock quickly grew into rage, and rage to cold-blooded anger: Cabell had to be taking revenge for Michael's desertion of Rosamond. Sewal's accusation, made months earlier, that he was in all probability accepting bribes for favoritism shown the other shipyards, and in the process costing the United States War Department a pretty penny as well, had to be true. The notion was at the same time infuriating and depressing, and drove her out of the office into the clear night air.

There was a light burning in the main workshed. Curious, Eve walked that way, only to stop abruptly as a low, throaty growl followed by a loud bark came from a stack of lumber to her right. A second later a ghostly gray shape detached itself from the shadows. The watchdog, Eve realized, with a start. "Down, boy. Down."

"Valky! What you see?" A door in the huge shed opened. Light spilled out into the yards. An adze in his hand, a man stood silhouetted against the amber glow. "Valky! What is it, girl? Who's there?"

"It's me, Mr. Naslund," Eve called, relief flooding through her.

"Who?"

"Eve."

"My God! Down, Valky. Come." Jon Naslund strode out of the shed, took Eve by the arm. "What you doin' here, Miss Eve? No place for a girl to be at night. Valky tear you up, I don't stop her."

"I needed some fresh air. I . . ." She paused. She needed to talk to someone, but wasn't sure what to say, or if Naslund was the one to talk to. "I've been going through Father's papers."

The Swede looked away, embarrassed. "*Ya,*" he said quietly. "Dot's a bad thing for your father. And all of us." He felt Eve shiver, and guided her toward the shed. "Come. We have hot coffee. Stay, Valky! Watch!"

Protected from the bay breeze, the interior of the shed was relatively warm. Naslund led Eve to the corner by the stove where he and his oldest son, Gunter, were completing an order for a dozen lobster traps. Eve did not begrudge the Swedes making a few extra dollars using Blackheath space for a private job. Her father had allowed them to do so, she knew, because the big, boisterous Naslund and his son were among the most loyal of Blackheath employees. Building ships for Sewal was not just a job for them, but a tradition.

The coffee was hot and sweet, the conversation revealing. Naslund was a very perceptive man, Eve learned, a craftsman who knew a great deal about the business itself simply from working with Sewal for so many years. One question followed another and, though he was reticent at first, the Swede was soon answering quickly and decisively. By the time a half hour had passed, Eve had learned more about the shipbuilding business than she had learned in the preceding three hours, including the startling revelation that every man in the place either knew or sensed that there was skulduggery somewhere in high places, and that there wasn't one of them there who wouldn't do whatever was necessary to solve the problem. "We can build their damned ships," Naslund said, pounding his huge fist against an eight by eight timber. "Good ships. Strong to take the wind and white water. Your father know that. I know that. The men know that. Why don't they give us a chance?"

The question pursued her as Eve, outside again, wandered absent-mindedly through the yards. Her buttoned boots beat a dull tattoo on the salt-encrusted planks. Waves lapped at the base of the pier. Valky, toenails clicking in time with Eve's footsteps, accompanied her. When Eve reached the end of the pier she stopped and stood staring over the moonlit bay. The lighthouse stabbed at the darkness, swept its golden rapier across the shoals to guide a single merchant ship to safe harbor. The ghostly patches of silver floating above the ship disappeared one by one as the unseen men in the rigging reefed the sails. Stately, serene, the merchantman drifted past the yards and headed for the docks near the center of town.

The mate's voice, in contrast to her own thoughts, was strong and confident across the bay. Troubled, Eve turned to face the silent yards. Valky, teeth white in the scant moonlight, nudged her hand. Eve patted the weimaraner's head. Her eyes wandered from the yards to the shoreline where it rose from gentle, level beach to the saw-toothed precipice and Dawn Wind. She could not see the house itself, only imagine it. Each stone, each board, each year she had lived there, was etched vividly in her mind. Dawn Wind was a place alive, a place she would not allow to die.

Resolution did not come with cataclysmic realization. There was no clap of thunder, no burst of lightning to accompany her insight. Eve loved the yards and Dawn Wind with a fierceness that had been ingrained in her since childhood. And simply put, she was damned if she was going to lose either of them. Michael was dead. He had been mourned; there was nothing else she could do. Justin was lost to her of his own free will; she was powerless to bring him back. Her father was bedridden, weak and helpless; his life was out of her hands. There was only one Blackheath left. But that Blackheath had a desperate idea. And if she was daring enough, it would work.

Chapter 31

"It's time," Jack Travis said, checking his watch and slipping it beneath the heavy coat he wore.

Eve acted as if she had not heard him. She continued to stare at the town house. Lights brightened the windows of this and a score of other Georgetown buildings. The incessant drizzle hardly diminished the call to entertain, the need for dress balls and less formal gatherings to offset the grimmer realities of a wartorn nation. In truth, there was much to be thankful for. Europe had turned its collective back on the struggling Confederacy. The nation's economy was stronger than ever before, and in this September of 1862, many thought the war was being won, if not always on the battlefields, in a thousand shops and factories.

Beads of moisture captured the distant party glow to form an amber rosary along the top edge of the coach window. "I wonder who lives there now," Eve said, a note of earnest pain in her voice.

Travis stared uncomprehendingly at the building. It looked no different from any of the others on this fashionable block. His military training left him with an intense dislike of the unexpected, and this journey to the hilltop had not been included in the plans formulated in Maine. "Eve? It's time we get started," he repeated nervously. "He's expecting you at nine. It's almost that now."

Eve released the curtain flap and sat back, her eyes closed. "Yes," she said simply. "I suppose so."

Travis reached across her and fastened the leather tie to keep out the moisture. He drew his Colt revolver and tapped the barrel against the roof of the cab, signaling Jon and Gunter Naslund, who sat outside on the driver's bench. The coach pulled away from the curbstone and moved smartly into the night. In her mind's eye Eve watched the cheerful home she had shared with Clifford Sarandon recede into the mist.

Jon Naslund pulled gently on the reins, pushed his foot against the brake handle and brought the rented coach to a halt a block away from their destination. The only sound to be heard was the rain.

Eve lifted the flap and glanced outside. Rainwater glistened in the narrow gulley along the curb. Tiny cataracts coursed among the cobblestones. In the distance sudden thunder heaved the clouds about and bludgeoned the air with basso profundo grumblings. Eve shuddered, touched Travis's arm for strength. The Lieutenant Colonel was out of uniform, dressed in faded homespun garments and a kerchief that he had wrapped pirate fashion around his head. Only the facial patch differentiated him from Jon and Gunter. "Are you sure you want to go through with this?" Eve asked, a variation of a question she had asked him a half-dozen times in the past hour.

"If we find what you think we'll find, of course," Travis said grimly. "It's worth the chance. People like him deserve what they get."

"Be careful he doesn't see you. It wouldn't be hard to find out who you are," Eve said, referring obliquely to the patch on Jack's face. "He won't be able to do anything to me, but you? He has many friends."

"I'll be careful."

Eve leaned forward and pushed aside the canvas shade. "We're ready, Jon. Time to shutter the coach lights, Gunter. Remember, just as we practiced it last night. Third door on the left, and then to the park to wait for our signal." The coach started rolling forward. "And if the ladder isn't there?" she asked Travis.

"It will be."

"You're sure you can find his apartment from the back?"

"Stop worrying, Eve. We'll be there," Travis said, squeezing her arm comfortingly.

The carriage stopped again. Eve looked out, took a deep breath and exhaled slowly, then opened the door.

"We'll give you fifteen minutes," Jack said, helping her from the coach. "Don't take any unnecessary chances."

"I won't." Eve looked up at Jon and smiled wanly. "You be careful too," she said. Jon nodded as the door closed behind her and the coach started forward. Her heart beating wildly, Eve started up the slate walk alone.

Admiral Dayton Cabell stepped out of the bathtub, dried himself carefully, and rubbed scented water across his flabby chest and generously into his groin. A light dusting of talc completed his toilet, and he moved to the dressing room. His valet, a burly Irishman who doubled as a bodyguard, was waiting to help the admiral struggle into a dress uniform that had, in the last months, become distressingly tight. Dayton grumbled and twisted his neck, trying to get comfortable in the starched collar. It felt as though it was choking him. The valet gave his uniform and shoes a final brush. "That should do it, sir," the valet said, stepping back.

Cabell inspected himself in the mirror, and was pleased. "Very well, MaGahan," he said, flipping the epaulette on his left shoulder so it hung perfectly straight. "My watch, please."

MaGahan removed a gold watch and fob from the dresser top, polished it with a soft cloth. Cabell watched him idly, his mind elsewhere. He hadn't seen Eve Blackheath since Rosamond and Michael's wedding, but she was, as he remembered, as lovely a woman as could be found. A widow, too, he recalled, and no doubt inured to requests such as he planned to make. He'd waited a long time to bring the Blackheaths to their knees, he thought, as MaGahan tucked the watch in his pocket. But if they wanted a naval contract or two, she'd have to do more than just kneel.

Downstairs, the doorbell chimed. "Ah! See her in, MaGahan, and leave her in the side parlor. I'll be down in a few minutes."

A moment later Eve followed the Irishman into the parlor. The apartment was much as she remembered it from the engagement party almost three years earlier, with one exception. The furniture and decorations had all been replaced with others far beyond the means of an admiral with no independent source of wealth. Eve was not surprised. Trying not to fidget, she reviewed the information she and Jack Travis had gleaned in the last few days. When not visiting his ailing wife in New York, a task the admiral avoided with singular ardor, Dayton Cabell resided in his town house on State Street, a discreet distance from the Capitol. Cabell liked his political and military colleagues well enough, but there were times he preferred—required, might have been a better word—a certain degree of privacy unavailable in the more busily traveled residential sections of Washington. Eve was grateful for this penchant for privacy.

"Eve Sarandon! What a delight!"

Startled, Eve rose and whirled about. Admiral Cabell, his rounded face and bushy sideburns making him look like a bear cub, had entered silently and was walking toward her with his pink manicured hands extended.

"Good evening, Admiral," Eve said, inclining her head demurely. It took no Madame Laurier to ascertain his intentions, she thought, hiding her anger. "I'm so glad you could find time to see me. I know you're very busy." Her mind raced. Had she heard a noise? Jack and Gunter should have been, at that moment, up the ladder and prying their way into one of the library windows.

"Nonsense. I'm never that busy," the admiral said, leading her to a plushly cushioned divan. He stepped back in order to better appreciate the full effect of her gown; the bodice, he observed, was cut daringly low and tight. "You look ravishing, my dear. Will you think me unbearably crass if I say that widowhood becomes you?"

Eve lowered her eyes. "You are flattering, sir," she whispered huskily, hoping she sounded as frightened and malleable as he wanted her to be.

Cabell laughed, sat next to her. He leaned forward and poured brandy into two snifters of French crystal that caught the glow of gaslights and imprisoned the images like miniature suns. "You said you would have had dinner earlier. I can have MaGahan prepare us a little something, if you didn't."

"No. Brandy will be fine," Eve said, her eyes wide now, looking directly and invitingly into his. She leaned back, sipped the brandy, and looked around. "Expensive books. Expensive furniture . . ."

"And expensive brandy to pour into expensive crystal," Cabell finished. He peered over the snifter. His eyebrows rose suggestively. "You will also find expensive paintings on the walls, and upstairs, a magnificent and very expensive four-poster bed that once belonged, I am told, to Marie Antoinette, and of which many fascinating tales have been told."

Eve smiled shyly. "You are very forward, sir."

The admiral shrugged. "You say you are returning to Maine tomorrow. There is little time for banter."

"Or bargaining," Eve said, a hint of sarcasm creeping into her voice. "But then—" She glanced around the room. "—I somehow doubt you are required to bargain very often."

"Come, come. An admiral's pay is simply insufficient." His eyes feasted on her. "Surely as the daughter of a businessman as shrewd as Sewal Blackheath, you can appreciate my trifling ploy."

"Of course," Eve said, her mind on Jack and Gunter. Where were they? Had something gone wrong? She rose, walked to the fireplace, and turned to face him. "For my own edification, Admiral. And so we understand each other. You receive . . . a gift, shall we call it?—from a shipyard, in return for which you manipulate the figures and your superiors in order to assure that yard a contract, whether or not the fortunate yard's bid was the lowest submitted."

"You are a clever girl." Cabell beamed. "I liken the situation to a deep well full to the brim with clear, cool spring water. And I am the owner of the only bucket. Sewal sent you, did he?"

"No. I came of my own volition."

"And he doesn't know—"

"I told you," her voice suddenly harsh, "I came of my own volition."

"I am touched. Deeply." Cabell sipped his brandy. The girl was frightened, but still tried to put up a fight. He liked that, would like it even better when the deal was finally struck. "Your presence softens my heart. Perhaps the Blackheaths have suffered enough for the shame that traitorous brother of yours brought to my family."

Eve managed to control herself. A minute more, she told herself. Only a minute more. "My brother was—is—not a traitor, sir." She was determined not to give Cabell the satisfaction of knowing that Michael was dead.

"But it doesn't matter, does it?" Cabell said, placing the snifter on the table in front of him. "Because our little discussion concerns only the two of us." He rose, started toward her. "You have mentioned a gift. Let me see. What have I to offer in return?" Her humiliation was not complete. Not quite. He reached out, fingered one of the ribbons on her bodice, let his hand brush against her breast. "A woman's breasts are a most remarkable portion of her anatomy. They feed our bodies when we are babes, and our passion when we are—"

Glass shattered in one of the rooms above. Someone shouted. The noise of a struggle filtered downstairs. Cabell leaped away from Eve. "Damn!" he muttered. Eve forgotten, he charged across the room and flung open the door. Eve caught a glimpse of a hellish countenance, a fleeting vision of ridged and furrowed flesh, of a sightless, milky eye set in pink melted wax. Cabell shrieked and fainted dead away.

Cold water splashed on his face. Admiral Dayton Cabell shuddered, shook his head, and woke up. Water stung his eyes. He blinked, shook his head again, and stiffened in alarm. The bookcase behind his desk had been swung away from the wall, and there for all the world to see was his wall safe. And if all the world had been watching, it would have seen that the safe was opened.

"What the devil—" The admiral tried to rise, found himself tied hand and foot to the chair. His face flushing a bright pink, he fought the ropes, felt them bite into his wrists. "Just what the hell do you—"

"If you struggle, you'll hurt yourself."

Cabell sputtered in rage. Eve Sarandon was sitting at his desk, going through a stack of papers. He could not help but think of a schoolmarm in Maryland who had sorted through papers as efficiently and coldly. But that was years ago, and the papers the Blackheath woman held were not spelling tests, but his personal records of contracts issued and the quantities of money he had received in return. Most damning, they were written in his own hand. He kept a different, less revealing set at the War Office.

"Your valet knew of the safe. The two keys required to open it were easy enough to find," Eve said laconically, not even looking up.

Cabell began to sweat in spite of the chill. Not only was he tied to the chair, but he had been stripped half-naked. The pair of keys that he always wore on a thong around his neck were in the open door of the safe. The safe itself was empty, and its contents scattered all over the desk. A badly battered MaGahan—both eyes were blacked and his lips were puffed and bleeding—was propped against the front of the desk. It was too much! One Blackheath had sullied his daughter's name, another was a common thief! He tested the ropes that bound his hands, felt them bite into his wrists again. The pain was excruciating. "Now see here—" He tried to rise again, but a pair of hands pushed against his shoulders and slammed him back into the chair. Cabel swiveled his head, caught a glimpse of a bulky blond man before turning back to Eve. "You and your accomplice will rot in jail for this!" he bellowed. "MaGahan! Wake up, damn you!"

"Be quiet," Eve snapped.

Cabell swallowed, felt the pressure of a hand on his neck. Maybe she failed to understand what she held.

"Here is what you are going to do," Eve began. The admiral's spirits sank to a new low. "The Blackheath Shipyards will be awarded the next three contracts. I see the Navy has ordered an ironclad frigate. That will do for starters."

"Sewal Blackheath builds wooden ships," Cabell protested. "Clippers."

"*I* don't," Eve retorted. "Unless there is money in it." She waved a piece of paper. "This is a requisition for repairs for two gunships currently on blockade duty. When they are relieved, next week, you will order them to New Forest. The Blackheath yards will effect those repairs."

"You can't. *I* can't."

"We can, and you'd better. I will not argue with you, Admiral. There is enough here to see you courtmartialed, broken to an ensign, and sent to ferry a mortar barge up and down the Mississippi." The admiral paled, wet his lips, as she continued, "We do not expect every contract, of course. Only enough to keep the yards open and operating at full capacity."

"You . . ." This couldn't be happening, Cabell thought as he searched for words. He'd have to revoke his word on the frigate, and the contracts for the repairs on the gunships had already been signed. Breaking them would be a nightmare. If he could save the frigate . . . "I've been watching you, you know," he said, trying to sound reasonable. "Tooling up for such a job will take more than you have. The sub-contracts alone will eat up every cent available, and you'll end up losing what little your father has. You simply don't have enough operating capital for such a venture."

Eve stuffed the papers taken from his safe into a leather valise. "You worry about getting that contract to me within the next ten days, Admiral. Let me worry about the capital. I assure you, I'll get it."

Cabell watched her round the desk. She'd get it? What the devil did that mean? "I pity the man and the bank," he said.

Eve stopped in front of him. The valise she held contained his life's blood. Her eyes glittered with excitement, but her smile was as cold as ice. "Pity yourself. You won't have time for anyone else." She jerked her head toward the still unconscious MaGahan. "I'm sure he'll untie you when he wakes up. Good night, Admiral. I'm so glad we've met again."

Gunter sported bruised knuckles and a cut above his eye, evidence that MaGahan had put up a good show before succumbing to the Swede's powerful fists. He cradled a shotgun while his proud father held the reins of the impatient team. Jack Travis, his face patch in place, helped Eve into the coach and climbed in beside her. Eve clutched the valise and sank back in the seat.

"We did it!" she whispered, her voice hoarse with tension. "We did it, Jack."

"Yes. *You* did it."

Gunter called down that the way was clear. The hired coach lurched forward. By morning they'd be in Baltimore and on the train north. "We did it," she repeated. "Everything we needed, everything we—" She stopped, looked up at Jack. "Oh, my God. They didn't see you, did they?"

"Cabell won't recognize me as long as I wear this." Jack touched his patch. "And with that ammunition you have, who cares." He put his arm around her, pulled her close to him. Outside, the rain increased. Inside, it was warm and snug. "Well?" Jack asked. "Do you feel like a pirate?"

"No." The rush of excitement was gradually subsiding. She held tight to the valise, let her head rest against Jack's shoulder. A new sense of self, and of strength, washed over her. She smiled wickedly. "Like a Blackheath."

Part IV

Chapter 32

" 'Now Negress night came solemn down upon the city and as the flames spread from the public buildings and the depot that had been fired, the whole heaven became illuminated by the lurid glare, while unexploded shells in the dwellings and storehouses became heated and exploded!' "

A sharp report issued from the fireplace as a bubble of trapped water turned into steam and burst through a log. Sewal glanced up from the two-day-old account of Sherman's entry into Atlanta as witnessed by a reporter for the New York *Herald*. Across from him, Pole jerked upright at the same time and twisted halfway around, his eyes widened with momentary fear. Realizing it was only the fire, he turned toward Sewal again, his dignity and station slowly returning. "Your pardon, sir," he managed.

Sewal resumed reading aloud, a daily ritual he had first begun some three months earlier as a means of regaining his speech. Christmas Eve morning was no exception. " 'Standing upon an eminence overlooking the doomed city, I had an excellent view of the conflagration.' " Sewal cleared his throat, paused to relish the fact he had made it without stumbling through a complicated word like conflagration and went on.

" 'Never had I beheld so grand a sight. As night waned, the gentle breezes carried the destroying element from house to house and block to block until one half of the Rebel city was in flames, the glare of which was so bright that the soldiers a mile distant read their last letters from home by the light. Next morning I rode over the city among the ruins, where nothing remained to tell the tale but tottering walls and blackened chimneys that, like gravestones, stood there as monuments of departed glory.' "

Sewal's voice trailed off. Seated in the warm quiet of the downstairs parlor, now converted to his bedroom, he envisioned the utter devastation depicted by the writer's graphic description.

"A tremendous victory," Pole said, beaming. "They can't hold out much longer, sir."

"Yes. Victory," Sewal repeated, folding the paper and laying it on his lap. "Well, well." He hadn't done badly at all that morning. The words had been crisp and clear, his voice self-assured and strong. "I believe that's enough for today, Mr. Pole. I expect, being Christmas Eve and all, there are a number of preparations still to be made. Is that daughter of mine back from the yards yet?"

"No, sir," Pole said, rising and squinting at the clock through the spectacles Eve had virtually demanded he buy. "But shortly. I should like to have everything ready by then, if I can," he went on, reverting to his most officious tone. "Will that be all, then?"

"Yes." Sewal nodded, wheeled himself closer to the hearth. Behind him the door closed as Pole left. The wind wailed outside the window, blew its wintry breath in vain against the stone walls. Alone, Sewal stared at the newspaper account, and beyond it to the flames. In them he was sure he could see tottering walls, blackened chimneys that looked like gravestones, and the ghosts of glory defeated. Christmas Eve, he thought sadly, would not be merry for everyone. Not that year.

The kitchen door blew open and a lanky, scruffily bearded man with an armload of kindling staggered through a cloud of snow. "Good God, man," Eustacia gasped, hurrying to slam the door. The man was named Vernon Allison. A veteran of two years' service in the Army of the Potomac, he had survived a serious head wound received at Gettysburg and mustered out with little hope of employment until Eve had hired him to fill the void left by the long departed Hamlet.

Vernon dropped his load into the woodbox with a thunderous clatter loud enough to wake James Ruell, two floors above.

"Land's sake, man, can't you be a little quiet?" Eustacia scolded. Vernon sniffed, wiped his coat sleeve across his mouth, and glared at the cook. "Wood's heavy," he grumbled by way of explanation, and started out again.

"Wait!" Eustacia called, too late, and grabbed her broom.

The dour veteran had already opened the door and, impervious to the snow, stepped into the gray daylight. Snow once more swirled over the floor. Eustacia sighed, swept the melting flakes into the corner. It was enough for a woman to run a kitchen and cook, she thought, without having to watch Vernon. She hated keeping tabs on the man, informing Eve when the veteran was drunk. At least today he had been sober. Eve would be satisfied, and there would be no guilt on the cook's part.

Eustacia poured herself a cup of coffee and, dabbing a molasses cookie in the cup, began to eat. Everything was done as could be, she thought, ticking off a mental list. The ham was ready to go in the oven. So was the turkey. The stuffing was fixed, needed only the bacon grease she'd mix with it before she went to bed that night. Potatoes were peeled and sitting in water. Carrots too. Pie crusts made. Mincemeat cooking. Special Christmas cookies for Doozie glazed. Oh, it was going to be a Christmas to end all Christmases!

"Oh, Lord," she muttered, her appetite suddenly gone. "Oh, Lord, Lord."

Twenty-one years ago, she thought, her eyes brimming with unaccustomed tears, the night before Christmas, the Lord had brought her her own baby. She'd loved that little boy, loved taking care of him, washing him, feeding him, watching him play and grow. And then the anger had come to him. He'd been gone for a year and a half, and still the ache was there. Who knew where Hamlet was? With such goings on, anything could have happened to him. The Reverend Waldrop said Hamlet's running away was her cross and that the Lord expected her to carry it bravely, but sometimes that cross was too much to bear.

The door at the top of the stairs slammed. Eustacia wiped her eyes on the hem of her apron so Maisie wouldn't see her crying. A year ago Maisie had come back to Dawn Wind as James's nanny after Arvid, her husband, had enlisted in the army. Though the girl was usually cheerful, Eustacia had noticed that worries beset her whenever she saw a paper containing war news. Not that Eustacia could blame her. Two of Jon Naslund's sons had already been killed in battle, Thorsen at Antietam and Swen at Gettysburg. Burl Naslund was reported to be aboard a gunboat on the Mississippi, and Arvid was with the Twenty-third Corps under Sherman in Georgia. Only Gunter, the oldest, remained at the shops, and that because Eve had insisted on buying his way out of the draft out of affection and gratitude for his past services. It also kept the craftsman where he was needed most. Arvid had been offered a similar opportunity to stay, but had refused to listen to his new bride's entreaties and enlisted before his father could plot to stop him.

"The table's all set, Mr. Pole. Oh." Maisie came through the door, stopped, and looked around. "Where's Mr. Pole?"

"Upstairs, I expect. Doozie asleep?"

"Mm-hmm. Like a rock. Did Vernon come in yet?"

"Come and gone. Why?" Eustacia asked, busying herself at the sink.

"Said he'd take me home on the way to meet the train. I guess I oughta go see." She crossed the room to her coat, took it off the wall peg, and checked inside the pockets. "Ah, Eustacia?"

"Yes, honey."

Maisie held two plainly wrapped gifts behind her back. "Close your eyes and hold out your hands." Eustacia did as she was told, and Maisie placed a gift in each of the black woman's hands. "Merry Christmas!"

Eustacia opened her eyes and beamed with pleasure. "Lordy me, girl! You shouldn't a—"

"You can open yours now, if you want," Maisie said shyly, pointing to the smaller of the packages. Eustacia set down Jubb's gift and carefully started to peel away the wrapping on hers. Maisie watched her closely, seeing Hamlet's face reflected in his mother's smile. Still, she felt occasional pangs of guilt about her part in the madness that had come upon him. For that reason she had refused at first to return to Dawn Wind, afraid that Eustacia and Jubb were aware of what had happened between her and their son. Times had been hard, though. Her mother had never fully regained her health. The money Arvid sent home was scant, and his enlistment bonus was soon exhausted. The only employment offered her had come on a blustery February morning when Demetrios the dwarf approached her in one of the back aisles of Knight's General Merchandise and told her that Madame Laurier was interested in her and would pay her handsomely to come to work at the Land Lock. Looking down on the diminutive figure, Maisie had felt only revulsion. A week later she talked to Eve, and was immediately rehired. The next day, grateful but wholly unnerved, she had arrived at Dawn Wind. If Eustacia and Jubb questioned the tears she shed they never said so, rather welcomed her back to the family with kindness that had never diminished.

"Lordy, a lavender sachet!" Eustacia held the little silk bag to her nose and inhaled deeply. "Just *smell* that, would you. Honey, how'd you know my weakness for lavender?"

"It's not much. Just a little—"

"Nonsense!" Eustacia gave Maisie a quick hug. Eyes twinkling, she held her at arm's length. "You know what I'm gonna do? I'm gonna take that old pine sachet out of my drawer and put this lavender one right in with my pretties." She glanced down at the table and Jubb's present. "What'd you get Jubb?" she asked in a conspiratorial whisper.

"Promise you won't tell?"

"Cross my heart."

"A jar of Mama's pickled Seckle pears."

"That man *love* your mama's Seckle pears," Eustacia said. "He gonna be in hog heaven. You wait here." She hurried into the pantry and emerged a moment later with a box wrapped in red tissue paper. "This is for you and your mother."

"Oh, Eustacia!" Maisie laughed, hefted the box. "One of your rum cakes?"

"Made in October, when the moon was full, so it wouldn't go bad. You give your mama a piece of that tonight. It'll perk her up for tomorrow. Now, you better run, child. Merry Christmas!"

Maisie bussed Eustacia's cheek, turned, and grabbed her coat. "Merry Christmas to you too, Eustacia," she said, and hurried out the back door.

Eustacia watched Maisie go and, alone again, sat heavily at the table. Poor little girl, she thought sadly. If only her and Hamlet could have worked things out. But it was a hard world for black and white to live in together. Maybe things was best the way they was. At least Maisie had found one of her own kind. She could only pray that her own Christmas baby had too. Pray, and hope, and maybe never know.

The clock in the corner chimed noon. The weight per square foot of the cast-iron plating shipped from Portland multiplied by the square footage of the platform under the forward gun was underlined in red on the last page of the weekly report. The plating was overdue, as were the specially ordered brackets for the engine. Meanwhile, the rifled Parrot gun, a pivoted cannon capable of hurling a two-hundred-pound ball through the side of anything the Confederate Navy had afloat, waited to be installed. Like dominoes falling, one problem caused another, and carefully devised schedules were left in shambles. Beckham, the bald, burly foundryman shifted his stance and glanced at Eliot, who avoided his gaze. Jon Naslund, a knit hat wadded in one fist, perched on the edge of the desk. He stared at the clock and thought of eggnog laced with whiskey. Finally, Eve finished studying the figures and looked up at the three men, her most trusted employees. "Larry?" she asked as Beckham nodded. "Last but not least. What about the mounts?"

"Wire came late yesterday," Beckham reported flatly. "Mahon Arms never shipped them, so they aren't going to get here. One of their clerks entered them as 'shipped,' which wasn't the case, and which caused the whole mess."

"Which means—"

"I started the men making them here yesterday."

"When will they be finished?"

Beckham squinted at his knuckles, as if the answer was written there. "The molds'll be finished and poured next week, but metal that heavy won't cool enough to be worked for a couple of days. It'll be week before Wednesday we can even start to install them."

"So the engine doesn't go in until . . ."

"The middle of January at the earliest," Naslund said. "And the deck don't go on until the engine is in, and the plates don't go on until the deck is on. We'll be two weeks behind, at least."

"All right." Eve glanced at her chief clerk. "Eliot, check our accounts with Mahon Arms and make sure we don't pay for those brackets. Jon—"

"*Ja?*"

"What can we do to hurry it up?"

Naslund scratched his head. "Get ready to install the engine and mount the guns, but I don't think nothing else. It's not all lost, though. We build our own brackets on the next ship, we'll cut three days off the schedule and save Mahon's markup." He shrugged. "Lose three days on this ship, gain three on them that come later. Maybe not so bad, eh?"

"Maybe." She initialed the page, set it aside. The center of the desk was clean. "Well, gentlemen? I think that's it for today. Any questions?"

"You still haven't said what you want to do about Monday," Eliot said.

"So I haven't." Eve made a tent of her fingers, gazed blankly at the opposite wall. The men were being given Christmas Day off, of course, along with Monday the twenty-sixth. They were to be paid for the Saturday, but no decision had yet been made about Monday. Briefly, she ran over the ledgers in her mind. December had been the eleventh month the yards had made a profit since she had taken over after Sewal's stroke. Not a fat profit, but a profit nonetheless. On consideration, she decided a day's wages were a fair bonus for the year past, and would keep the men's interest up for the next few months at least. "Pay them," she said abruptly. "We can afford it. Anything else?" No one moved. "Very well, then. It's Christmas Eve. We have families that I'm certain are impatiently waiting for us. Thank you for coming in today, and Merry Christmas."

Beckham gathered his papers and carried them to his desk in the front part of the office. Eliot picked up the company ledgers and started to stow them in the safe. Jon rose and stretched. "Well, we see you tomorrow," he said. "Two o'clock, eh?"

"Any time after church," Eve answered, tired now that the long planning session was over. "Jon?" She beckoned to him, and spoke softly. "Has Shropten given you any more trouble?"

The smile left Naslund's face. "A little," he said uneasily.

"Let him go."

"He's trying. The bottle is a hard friend to lose."

"I'm certain it is. However, we are here to build ships. Not counsel the problems of others."

"Just felt sorry for him," Naslund said.

"Pity is one task I leave to the Reverend Waldrop. It's in his contract. Let Shropten stay on until January second, then let him go with a half-month's extra pay. I'm sorry."

"*Ja.*" Naslund pulled his cap tightly about his ears. "So am I. Merry Christmas."

Eve tensed, but didn't say anything as her foreman walked out. Drained, she rested her elbows on the desk, pressed her middle fingers against her eyes, and propped her chin on her palms. Does he think I like it? she asked silently. A sour feeling washed over her. Maybe Jon has been right. New Year's was a terrible time to fire a man.

"I'll lock up if you want," Eliot said, breaking into her thoughts.

Eve moved her right hand, looked at the bookkeeper with one eye. "No, that's all right, Eliot. I'll see to it. Is the carriage where I can get at it easily?"

"Yes, ma'am. Right below."

"Good." She smiled. "Merry Christmas, Eliot."

"And to you, Mrs. Sarandon." The head clerk nodded, and stepped into the cold afternoon.

She was alone at last. Eve eased back into her chair. A wayward curl tickled her left ear. Unconsciously, she tucked it back into the knot of hair gathered at the nape of her neck. Embers popped and snapped in the iron stove. A bay breeze lifted a patch of snow from the roof of the building next door and splattered it against one of the front windows. Fire a man on Christmas Eve. What a Christmas present. The thought, and the unspoken accusation of coldness and cruelty, nagged at her.

Sighing, she opened the desk drawer and pulled out her own present, the latest letter from Hébert Sarandon. "My dear Miss Blackheath," the salutation read. Sarandon had refused, since learning that James Ruell's father had not been Clifford, to think of Eve as a Sarandon. It didn't really matter, Eve thought bitterly. Though everyone called her Mrs. Sarandon she too thought of herself as a Blackheath.

"Enclosed please find my check for fifty thousand dollars, the final payment in the arrangement agreed upon by us as a result of your visit two years ago." Had it been that long? Eve closed her eyes, counted back, to November 1862. Two months after the trip to Washington and Cabell's capitulation work was underway on the first Navy contract when the yards ran into trouble. The payroll had been tripled, and another fifty men were needed. A foundry had been built and equipped with a forge and metal-working machinery. Vast amounts of supplies had been ordered, and were arriving every day, and the initial payments from the government were too slim to cover the bills that littered her desk, as thick as a January snowstorm. Credit outside of New Forest, due to Aldrin's influence, had dried up. The Blackheath Shipyards were facing a crisis. Cabell had been right: The contracts were meaningless without working capital.

Desperate, Eve traveled to New York to see her father-in-law, Hébert Sarandon. The meeting was strained. Sarandon had aged drastically since Clifford's death, and his bitterness toward Eve had increased. "I had hoped never to see you again," he had said by way of greeting. "Please be so kind as to conduct your business as expeditiously as possible. I do not enjoy your company."

And she did. Eve was Clifford Sarandon's widow, and in the absence of a will she and James Ruell Sarandon were his rightful heirs. She knew Hébert would contest her every inch of the way, though. A trial would create a sensation that neither of them wanted. Not only she, but Clifford's memory, Hébert, and James Ruell would be sullied in the process. She had suggested, therefore, a lump sum settlement of two hundred thousand dollars, the amount she needed to keep the shipyards solvent until the crisis passed. Hébert bridled, hesitated, and finally offered to agree to such a settlement if Eve accepted an annulment—he was confident of arranging one, even at that late date—of her marriage to Clifford. Eve refused. Whether or not Hébert believed her she had loved Clifford, and an annulment betrayed his memory as well as jeopardized her son's legitimacy. In any case she was giving her word that no other claims against any Sarandon would ever be made, and the word of a Blackheath was beyond reproach. In the end a compromise was reached. Eve retained her composure until she reached the privacy of her hotel. Then, though she had saved the Blackheath Shipyards, she wept for shame, for her sole weapon had been a dead man who had loved her beyond measure.

"With these monies," she read, now, "the final quarter of the two hundred thousand dollars you have accepted as your share of my deceased son's estate, and with your signed and notarized statement of complete disassociation with the Sarandon family, the terms of our agreement are fulfilled. I abstain from further comment out of deference to your father, for whom I have had great respect in the past." He had signed the letter, "Yr. Ob'd't Servant, Hébert Sarandon, Esq."

"I don't care!" Eve said aloud, and angrily, the sharp sound of her voice surprising her in the empty office. She had been right. Strength was the only answer, whether facing Hébert Sarandon or firing a man. The four fifty-thousand-dollar payments over the past two years had made the difference between staying in business and losing everything. As for Shropten, he was a drunk, and a drunk on the job endangered other men's lives. One man dragging slowed down the other two hundred whose families depended on the Blackheath Shipyards for a living. There was work to be done, and done rapidly. Two heavily armed cutters and three turreted ironclads had arrived for refurbishing a week earlier. Every man in the yard would have to work doubly hard to finish the work on schedule.

Suddenly, the front door flew open. Eve jumped in alarm, looked in time to see a swirl of snow cut off by the closing door. "Justin!" she cried. "What in heaven's name . . ."

He cut a dashing figure in his ever-present broad-brimmed black hat and cloak draped over a heavy woolen coat. "Saw the carriage from the road and thought I'd surprise you." He dusted snow from his shoulders with the gold-embossed grip of his hickory cane. Snow clung to his long, drooping moustache and meticulously groomed goatee. The wire-rim glasses were the same. "Chastity is exhausted, so I sent her on to the house." He walked across the office, stopped in front of the desk, and peered closely at Eve. "I don't know whether to bow or shake hands," he said with a wry smile.

"Don't be silly," Eve said, rising and coming around the desk to hug him. "Or should I take offense at such a witty remark?" she asked.

"Neither, neither. Heed is what you should take, dear sister. Working?"

"Not really. We just finished. I was getting ready to leave."

"A little early, isn't it?" Justin glanced at the clock. "Quitting at two in the afternoon. For shame."

"It *is* Christmas Eve. Justin! You used to at least begin cordially before switching to sarcasm." Eve strode to the coatrack and pulled on a wool-lined hooded cape trimmed with rabbit fur. "Of course, without the calming influence of Selene . . ." She raised a questioning eyebrow as she moved across the room to blow out the lantern behind her desk. "Or is it Demelya? . . ."

"Chastity," Justin corrected.

"Oh, that *is* amusing. Without the calming influence of Chastity do you revert to your far less likeable self?"

"My truthful self, I like to say."

"Not only is it Christmas Eve, but we haven't seen each other since your August trip. I fail to understand why you must treat me so unkindly."

"Unkindly? My sister is aging before my very eyes. Shipyards are not a place for a woman, but you've made them your whole life. Look at you. You've become like . . . your hair, of all things. Drawn back, constricted." Eve's face was flushed, but Justin went on. "And that dress! My God, Eve. It's *gray!* I never in my life saw you wear a gray dress. Responsibility does not become you, damn it."

Eve glared at Justin, pulled the cloak around herself, and jammed her hands into a fur-lined muff. "Really? Then what do you suggest,

Justin?" she said, her voice snapping. "Shall I braid ribbons into my hair? Wear summer dresses? Play the coquette and spend my time giving at-homes?" She slammed and locked the desk drawer, dropped the key into her pocket. "Or perhaps I should change my name once or twice a month to let everyone know how gay and frivolous and carefree I am."

"That is unkind," Justin replied evenly.

"No. I'm only trying to be truthful."

"Touché, Eve." Justin bowed slightly, mockingly.

Eve moved across the room, stood in front of the lamp on the table next to the stove. The light flooded her from below, softened the hard lines that two years of work and worry and decision-making had etched into her face. "I'm sorry, Justin," she finally said softly. "I know you love me and I appreciate your concern. But I can't let everything Father worked and fought for wash out to sea. I can't. Not while he sits day after day, watching and . . . and . . ."

"I only want you to be happy, Eve." Justin stood behind her. "You don't owe Dawn Wind your life. As harsh as it may sound, you owe Father no more than you are willing to give. Nowhere is it written that this or any venture must continue until the end of time." He squeezed her shoulders gently. "All I ask is that you think on it. And that's all I have to say on the matter."

Neither moved for a long moment. At last Eve leaned forward and blew out the lamp. "They'll be waiting for us," she said. "Would you mind getting the other lamp?"

Justin blew out the remaining lamp and opened the door for her. Eve locked the door, then held Justin's arm as they descended the steps. Their breath billowed on the air, and the harsh words that had come between them died in the face of the brusque wind that hurried them to the covered sleigh. "Is that the *Andrew Jackson?*" Justin asked, pointing across the yard to the new shed Eve had had built the year before. It was only partially roofed, but the walls kept out the wind and allowed almost continual work even in the worst weather.

"Yes. Let's walk over and I'll show it to you," Eve said.

Valky came out of the doghouse Jon had built for her and accompanied them to the shed. With no work in process, the quiet was unnerving. Towering against the gray afternoon sky, a behemoth of iron and wood loomed like a giant slug surrounded by ice-covered scaffolding. The unplated framework of the ship's cruel prow, a

snout designed for ramming and fitted to ravage any vessel it chose
to strike, jutted toward them. Snow swirled around the stern where it
stuck out over the bay. "Ships," Justin said in a hushed voice, as if
accusing the monstrous shape of unspeakable future deeds.

"They float, nothing more," Eve countered. "Men do the rest.
Men make war, fight, slaughter one another."

"Amazing." Justin shook his head. "Not only have you assumed
control of the yards, but Father's ethics as well."

Contracts, gunboats, square feet of iron plate, cannons, never-ending news of victories and defeat, men dead, wounded and captured.
God, she hated it, sometimes wished she could flee from it all and
never have to think again. But the ships meant too many other things
as well: continuation of a tradition, a means of survival. Perhaps
even a quicker end to the war. Eve had lived with all this for the last
two years. Justin could say what he wanted. The extra burden was
nothing in comparison to what she already bore. "I am Sewal Blackheath's daughter," she said. "Shall we?"

They walked back to the sleigh without speaking, climbed in, and
pulled the rug over their laps. Justin slapped the reins. The horse
turned in the narrow space and started toward the main gate. Eve
closed her eyes and brooded silently at Justin's side. The runners beneath them scraped on the ice. The harness jingled merrily. Even in
its silence the shipyard felt alive. The foundry, a large pine-and-oak
building that still retained the shine of newness, slid by on their right.
Justin wrinkled his nose, sniffed to show his distaste for the heavy
odor that the snow could not hide. "I know," Eve said. "It's the
ironworks. The vapors permeate everything. It's worse in summer-
time."

"I was trying to smell the ocean. Or wood or wet canvas," Justin
explained, as he stopped the carriage and jumped out to close the
main gate.

"Wet canvas," Eve said, smiling secretly as Justin climbed back
into the sleigh. They lurched forward along the Bay Road to Dawn
Wind. "I'd almost forgotten." She sighed and pulled the rug tighter
against her. "Prosperity's price, I suppose."

Justin glanced at her, then back to the road. "Ah, prosperity," was
all he said.

"Silent night, holy night." Eve played, Justin and Chastity sang.
Eustacia hummed along in a rich, low alto. Across the parlor, James

Ruell sat in the middle of an army carved of wood. There were soldiers marching in a skirmish line, a drummer boy, and an officer on horseback who led his troops onward with a tiny saber that pointed toward the ceiling. Cannon pulled by mules brought up the rear and more soldiers, kneeling or charging with fixed bayonets, protected the flanks of the miniature command. His face fixed in a concentrated frown, James picked up a bugler and bowled over a company of infantry, then cut a swath through the remainder of the army with his foot.

"Hey, now! You goin' to break your Christmas toys before it's even Christmas!" Jubb said, reaching out to gather the devastated troops.

James Ruell, his black hair curling upward like the horns of a devilish sprite, grabbed Jubb's nose and twisted. The black man thumped his fist down on the boy's head and said "Bop!" James giggled and grabbed for Jubb's nose again, then tried to protect his head. But Jubb was too quick and bopped him again before straightening out of reach. "Pa-paw Jubb?" James said in a high, plaintive voice as he held out his chubby arms.

Jubb relented, bent and lifted the youngster into his bony arms. "Young'un, you gots the way about you," he said, setting the boy on the piano bench next to Eve. Justin and Chastity stood to the right of the piano, their backs to the frost-embossed windows. This was Chastity's fourth trip north to Dawn Wind with Justin. Eve had yet to summon the courage to ask Justin if they were married, and had long ago decided to pretend they were. She had grown accustomed to the girl's eccentricities and was determinedly friendly to the point of cheerfully accepting—and dutifully trying to remember—each change of name. After all, Justin had the look of a happy man about him, and if Chastity was in any way responsible, Eve was satisfied.

"Sle-ep in hea-venly peace."

Sewal listened and watched. The music rolled over him without effect. His wheelchair sat next to the end of the piano bench. Straight across Eve, he could see Chastity. She was dressed in a simple white crinoline covered with old ivory-colored lace, and her eyes shone brightly as she looked up at Justin. Troubled, Sewal let his focus shift back to Eve. The severe lines of her hair and the tired creases about her eyes made her look far older than she was. Closer still, James Ruell sat with his back to his mother and stared up at his grandfather. Sewal winked at him. James Ruell tried to wink back, but only succeeded in squinching up his whole face as both eyes closed. Sewal chuckled, imitated the boy. Before he could open his eyes, James was onto his knees and reaching for his grandfather's nose. "There now!" Sewal roared, his voice booming over "Adeste Fidelis."

James's clear laughter pealed through the song. "Got you nose, Grampa. Got you nose!"

Sewal put on his fiercest look, but James paid no attention. He grabbed for Sewal's nose again, tweaked it, and laughed uproariously. Sewal grimaced and reached for his grandson's nose, but the boy was too quick. Jumping from the piano bench, he raced across the room, only to run full tilt into the edge of the heavy mahogany table.

"Mommy!" he wailed, sitting down with a thud.

The music stopped abruptly amid startled cries. Eve looked in alarm over her shoulder. Justin started for the boy. Eustacia reached him first, and swept him into her arms much as she would have a bundle of newly dried wash from the line. "There, there, Doozie. There, there," she crooned, rocking him back and forth.

"He all right?" Justin asked, tentatively brushing away the hair from the rising lump on James's forehead.

"Mommy!"

Eve plucked him from Eustacia's arms. James flung his arms around her and buried his head in her neck. "There, there, honey. Mama's here," Eve said, tenderly stroking the back of his head. "You're all right. Everything's all right. Shh. Shh."

The wailing died down. Eve sat in an armchair, held her son away from her to inspect his forehead. "My goodness! You'll have a lump like an egg."

James Ruell snuffled and rubbed his eyes with his fists. "Hurts," he said. "I hate that table."

"I should think so. You hit it hard enough. Oh, my goodness!" Her eyes widened with mock alarm. James quit snuffling to look up at her. "I'll bet you broke it. Justin, take a look and see if this young man broke my good table."

Justin inspected the far side of the table, straightened up and shook his head. "Cracked it in two, I'm afraid."

James giggled in spite of himself. Eve wagged a finger in front of his face. "Now you see here, young man. I won't have you breaking my good tables, do you hear?"

"That'n's tired, Miss Eve. I think he's done had his fill of Christmas celebratin' for tonight."

"I'm afraid so. You sleepy, Doozie?"

The prospect of bed was worse than the lump on his head. "No!" James wailed. "Don't *want* bed."

"Give Mama a kiss." Eve pulled him to her, hugged him, and kissed the top of his head. "Off you go with Eustacia now. Mama'll come and tuck you in in a minute. Kiss Grampa good night."

Eustacia carried him around. James planted a wet kiss on Sewal, Justin, and Chastity's cheeks, and suffered Eustacia to carry him off upstairs.

"Well," Sewal grumped, clearing his throat. "Guess it's time for an old man to quit for the night," he said, blaming himself for the mishap.

"It's been a long day for us too," Justin said, taking Chastity's hand and starting across the room. "I talked to Eustacia. She's going to leave out the presents for the stockings."

Chastity smiled warmly. "And you thought he'd grown up. He's just a little boy. I think it's an excuse to be the first one downstairs in the morning."

"Which will be enough out of *you,* my lady," Justin said with a grin. "Good night, Eve. Father."

"Good night, Justin," Eve said, embracing him.

"Good night, Eve. Good night, Mr. Blackheath," Chastity said.

The room emptied quickly. Hanson Pole appeared out of nowhere to begin dimming the coal oil lamps. He had not been able to bring himself to join the family sing, but waited by a far wall casting disapproving looks at Eustacia and Jubb for associating so freely.

"You never know," Eve said, wheeling Sewal through the hall and into the front parlor they had remade into his room. Everything in the upstairs bedroom had been moved down, from the large portrait of Jennifer to the two watches and chains resting undisturbed on the bedside table. "It happens so quickly," Eve said.

"Bah! The boy's strong. If that's the worst that happens to him, consider yourself lucky."

"I suppose so. Still . . ."

"He'll be good as new tomorrow," Sewal said, not letting her finish. The wooden wheels creaked as Eve maneuvered the chair next to the bed. Sewal started the awkward process of getting out of his robe. "What about Hank Shropten?" he asked.

Eve sighed. "I'm sorry I ever mentioned him. You promised me—"

"Did you take my advice?"

"Yes. There. You were right. I should have had Jon release him weeks ago."

Sewal grumped. "I told you."

"And I listened, Father."

"Eventually." Sewal handed his robe to Eve, lifted the arm of the chair so he could get into bed. "Takes a damned stroke before my children will listen to me."

"And if you don't want another one—"

"All right. All right. I'm calm." He accepted Eve's hand, hitched himself with effort into the bed. "See? Tranquil as a Caribbean lagoon." He slipped under the covers. A single lamp burned next to the bed. "I don't suppose Justin said anything about what's-her-name."

"Chastity."

"It's easier to remember what's-her-name. Well?"

"If they're not married they act as if they were. In any case she's taken to wearing a ring," Eve said. "If you want to know for sure you'll have to ask him yourself."

"Humph. And likely have another stroke if he said they weren't. I prefer not knowing." He raised his head, peered across the room. "What's that?"

Eve followed his gaze, stepped to the dresser and retrieved a slim rectangular package wrapped in cloth and tied with a ribbon. "It says, 'Merry Christmas to Father, from Justin,' " she said, handing it to him.

Sewal tore away the wrapping and held up a remarkably detailed photograph of Dawn Wind. Taken from somewhere—high in a tree, Sewal wondered?—beyond the land bridge, the panorama included portions of the cliffs and all of the house. A white-capped Atlantic and a cumulus-filled sky surrounded Dawn Wind, held the family home in the eternal embrace of the elements that had nurtured the Blackheaths for generations. Sewal stared at the picture, found himself dabbing at his eyes. "Strange," he said, really to himself. "I never saw it from there."

"Justin did," Eve said quietly.

"Yes," Sewal whispered. "A different vision. Perhaps, after all . . ." His voice trailed off, lost in images evoked by a son he had never understood.

Eve left him, careful to close the door silently in order not to mar the moment of Sewal's discovery. Pensive, filled with warm feelings, she wandered through the house and finally up the stairs. The hall was dark, but the candle she held illuminated the way. James Ruell was fast asleep on his tummy, one hand formed into a tiny fist over his head. Eve brushed a kiss across his temple, tucked him in, and slipped out the door.

The house settled into sleep around her. In the morning, all would be brightness and laughter and the smell of holiday food. Eve leaned against the closed door to her son's room, rested her head against the center panel, and closed her eyes. Dawn Wind at peace soaked into her and drained the tension out of her bones. Justin's gift, his gesture of love, had meant as much to her as it did to Sewal.

A soft sound, different from those of the house cooling as the night deepened, caught her attention. Alert, Eve walked down the hall until a faint rustling sound stopped her. She heard a whisper, and only then realized she was opposite Justin's room. The wooden slats of a bed protested. Chastity moaned softly, her voice rising and then cut short as if she had realized the sound might carry.

Eve's face burned with embarrassment. The brief mystery solved all too clearly, she hurried to her room. Breathing was difficult, thinking impossible. She blew out the candle, set it on the night table, and walked to the window. The room was cold. Shuddering, Eve turned to the fire and mindlessly began undressing for the night. Blouse, skirt, shoes, and undergarments dropped to the floor, and the warmth of the flames washed over her. Entranced, she stared into the fire, saw there in its radiance the intimate communion her brother and his lover shared.

It was too much to bear. Eve had known such wholeness once upon a time, but the war and circumstances had shredded it. Lion, Clifford, Jack. . . . Suddenly, she was glad Jack hadn't been able to come to Dawn Wind for Christmas. The nearness of a man with whom she had once been intimate might have been unendurable. There was no time in her life for love. Too many other things took precedence.

Emptiness bore down upon Eve, fed in its negative manner the cold stoicism she must practice through the difficult days ahead. Calculation. There was the key. A son, a father, a household. Two hundred men and their families depended on her. Ships waited to be built, to be repaired, and fitted out for war and commerce. Deliberately, Eve walked away from the fire and stood naked in front of the window. Goose bumps rose on her arms, but she did not move. Outside, snow blew across the grounds. The Atlantic tossed and heaved, ice cold and brutally unreasoning. A freezing wind pressed against the house and leaked through the casement. These were her symbols: This was how she must learn to exist and stand against the world.

The compartment in her mind that had been opened by the soft sounds from Justin's room closed. The barricades in place, Eve strode to the fireplace, added a log against the night, and set the screen. The sheets on her bed were frigid, but she did not mind. They would warm to her body soon enough. Curling into a tight ball, she pulled the blanket and quilt over her. Sleep came slowly, filled with haunting dreams of a presuming stranger, of a deceived and deceiving heart, and of warm days spun upon the timeless wheel of September twilights.

Chapter 33

Two and a half years since Michael's death, Lion McKenna thought, as he watched the flames catch the dead grass and lick against the twigs he'd piled on the coals left from last night's fire. Two and a half years. He'd wakened moments earlier, stiff with cold and terror. He'd seen a lot of death in those war-ridden years, but somehow Michael's had come to symbolize all of them. The dream did not come frequently, but often enough to make him dread sleep. It was always the same: Michael, dark and brooding upon a shadow horse; Michael screaming in mortal agony, falling earthward, and dying there in the mountain glade.

The fire was burning steadily, would not go out. Lion rose wearily, crossed to a corner where the snow was clean, and filled his canteen. He had been transferred to Virginia after the defeat at Printer's Gap, placed in command of a new band of raiders under Jeb Stuart, and given instructions to reconnoiter and disrupt Union supply lines. More recently, with the fortunes of war turning sharply against the South, he had been assigned to Jubal Early, whose paltry army was expected to inflict losses on Sheridan's Union troops and drive them out of the already twice-scourged Shenandoah valley. Three times before he had stopped at the house he had one time called home. Each time he had hoped would be the last before the war ended. This visit was the most painful. Christmas was not a good time to be home.

Voices hung like daggers in the frozen air, disillusioned voices that complained about the marrow-chilling cold, about the hard ground, about ragged clothes, and boots with soles no thicker than paper. Caustic voices commented on Jefferson Davis's ravaged leadership. Joking voices marveled at the toughness of the breakfast steaks hewed from the two-day-old carcass of a cavalry mount that had broken a leg and had to be destroyed. Worried voices rang through the emptiness of the gutted house as they called to the unanswering men outside who had been on guard during the early hours of the morning.

"Burton, Gibson, and Ritz is dead, Colonel," the sergeant said through chattering teeth as he slipped through the blasted doorway. "Let their damn fire go out. I told 'em. Tired and hungry as they was, they was only alive as their fire. Now they're froze stiff as boards."

Lion ran a gloved hand over his beard. Icicles, minute and prickly, dusted down the front of his faded gray tunic. "More food for everyone else," he said dryly. He did not smile. A smile required thought and energy. He had neither to spare. The gloves lacked four fingers between them. He held his hands to the fire. The warmth felt good. "Assign new men to their posts, Sergeant . . . uh . . ."

"Groesbeck, Colonel."

"Groesbeck. Sorry." Lion turned his hands so the backs would warm. "Been a good many sergeants come and gone over the past few years."

"Yes, sir. Seen a good many colonels too." Groesbeck grinned apologetically. "No offense, sir. What about the bodies?"

"Leave them be for now. We might be grateful for the meat if the Yanks don't come along and kill us."

"You mean *us* eat 'em?" the sergeant asked in alarm.

"That's a joke, Groesbeck," Lion said tiredly.

"It's not that, sir." Groesbeck cackled, even if it was an old joke that had been told many times during the war. "It's that I didn't relish sinkin' my teeth into old Burton. He ain't taken a bath since Chickamauga." Grizzled, tougher than what little was left of the soles of his boots, Groesbeck left to roust out a perimeter watch, and to make certain the men apportioned the horsemeat equitably.

Lion turned his back to the fire and stared through the door at the pitiful remnants of his command. They ranged from sixteen on up to a corporal who was fifty-three, but deprivation and exhaustion had aged them all prematurely. There were no fuzzy-faced boys left in the Confederate Army. At least not that he had seen. A hissing noise brought him back to the fire. His canteen had a pinhole in it, and as the ice and snow melted, the water dripped onto the coals. Lion squatted and stirred the mixture of slush and water with his finger. There would be enough left to drink. The warmth would feel good in his belly.

Food, real food—potatoes, beef, vegetables, fruit—would feel better. My God, he thought wistfully, how long had it been since he'd eaten a normal meal, since he'd lived anything even closely approximating a normal life? He looked around at the stone walls. They were still black from the blaze that had consumed the upper story of the house sometime during the two years since he had last seen it. He was sitting in what had been the conservatory. There had been a piano there in the corner. And two settees. And hand-hewn chairs left over from his grandfather's day. When they were in season his aunt had kept a bowl of freshly picked flowers on a table by the window that looked out onto the main paddock. He had learned to dance in that room, had been groomed to be a gentleman.

The whole house was filled with trampled, maimed memories. Upstairs, right above his head, had been his sisters' bedroom. One room away to the rear, the kitchen had stood. It was demolished now, unusable. He could remember himself at eleven, being the first one there in the morning to make coffee and cook the meat that would carry him through another hard day of labor. The living room, now little more than four walls and a dirt floor littered with the meager belongings of his men, was but a half-dozen paces to his left. There his father had been laid out in his good suit, and there Lion had stood and mourned and become a man. There too, his mother had laid in rest before being carried to the family graveyard halfway up the slope on the far side of the paddock. What had happened to his aunt and uncle he didn't know—didn't even want to know at that point.

The water was hot. He took it from the fire, poured it into a battered tin cup, back into the canteen and the cup again before sipping it slowly to stretch out the minutes. That done, he checked the two Colt revolvers belted at his waist. One of the firing caps looked defective. He replaced it.

The waiting was the worst part. Lion stood, groaned, rubbed a cramp from his leg.

"Here's yours, Colonel."

Lion turned, watched Groesbeck enter with a steaming chunk of horsemeat impaled on a stick.

"Used the last of the salt yesterday," he said. "Still, it's better'n nothin'. Merry Christmas."

Lion accepted the meat, squatted in front of the fire again, and motioned for Groesbeck to join him if he wished. The meat was tough, but Lion had long since ceased to be particular. Food was food. If a man wanted to survive he ate what came his way, and didn't ask too many questions.

"Wonder if that sombitch Sherman done taken Atlanta yet?" Groesbeck asked around a mouthful of horsemeat.

"Sherman isn't our problem, Sergeant. Sheridan is."

Groesbeck ground on a piece of gristle a moment before giving up and swallowing it. "Hell, Sheridan already done burned the Shenandoah twice over," he said. "Ain't nothin' left to burn, being as snow don't make no kind a good kindlin'. What's the sense? Let 'em have it, I say."

Lion had lost the urge to confide in the soldiers beneath him. What was he supposed to tell them? Surely they suspected. The sixteen of them, seventeen counting Lion, had arrived the day before with orders to buy time for Jubal Early's battered retreating troops. The Yankee armies were not known for their initiative, and had a habit of bogging down when their advance elements were attacked. It took time for information to pass along the chain of command and orders to flow back. An hour's skirmish might hold up Sheridan for as much as a whole day, enough time for Early to escape and regroup in order to fight another time. Lion gnawed on his breakfast.

"Wonder who lived hereabouts?" Groesbeck said, taking the hint of silence and changing the subject.

Lion shrugged. In the same instant, the first shot sounded.

Groesbeck dove for the next room and his rifle. Lion tossed aside the horsemeat, rolled away from the open door as minié balls and bullets dug new holes in the already pockmarked walls. Close to the ground, he could feel the earth tremble beneath the onslaught of thundering, iron-shod hooves. Union cavalry, he thought with a curse, riding down from the wooded hillsides. "Groesbeck!" Lion shouted above the increasing pandemonium. "Groesbeck!"

There was no answer. Scrambling on hands and knees, he made his way to a window, dared to peer over the edge. Groesbeck lay crumpled by the campfire. There was no visible wound, but the man was obviously dead. Diving for cover, then rolling to the rear door, he reached it in time to see the last of his men, the sixteen year old, leap from behind a blackened wall and race to the nearby horses. Halfway across the yard the youth stopped suddenly and, spurting blood from his chest and throat, flew backward head over heels. The rest of the men wheeled their horses away from the line of charging Union cavalry. Gunsmoke sprouting like black blossoms from a hundred rifles followed them. Rebel soldiers tumbled from horseback. Mounts skidded on patches of ice, fell and screamed in pain until merciful shots put them out of their misery. Lion watched until the gunfire ceased, until the four remaining Rebel soldiers galloped out of sight. Resigned, he lay back and listened as the Union soldiers returned to circle the barren, broken walls of the house.

There would be no escape. Not this time, Lion thought. Funny thing was, he didn't care. Not any longer. He was too tired. The war was over. Ready for whatever came next, he walked openly across what once had been the ballroom. His journal was in his saddlebag. He took it out, tucked it under his belt at the small of his back. His revolvers lay where he had left them by the fire. He drank the last of his water, picked up the revolvers, cocked both, and stood with his shoulders against the stone wall. Waiting calmly, he faced the main doorway and the smashed wall to its left. Half a dozen men could enter at once if they wished.

Only one did. A Union officer stepped through the door, stopped, and stared in surprise at Lion. "I am Captain William Greer," he finally said slowly, taking care to keep his hand far away from his holstered pistol.

"And I, Colonel Lion McKenna, at your service, Captain."

Greer inclined his head. "I've heard of you," he said, paling. He was young and frightened, but controlled an impulse to run for safety. "Begging your pardon, sir," he went on bravely, "but your men are gone. Mostly dead. You are alone. Will you surrender to me, sir?"

At that moment, six carbines poked over and through the crumbled walls. The sound of rifles being cocked rang in the cold, clear air. Lion looked at them, weighed their power against his own weariness. He glanced at the dead boy lying on the ground outside the back door, then at the young Union officer, and eased down the hammers on his revolvers.

"Your lucky day, Captain," he said hollowly. He turned the revolvers in his hands, held them out to Greer. "Merry Christmas."

The train cried out as if in agony, mirroring the restless longing of the imprisoned men it carried. Through Virginia, through Maryland, through Pennsylvania and New Jersey. Time had lost all meaning. Only day, only night. Only bitter cold, and scraps of dried bread and greasy bowls half filled with almost frozen, thin gruel. The iron wail preceded them through a myriad of snowbound towns. Their destination was a prison scow anchored in Boston Harbor. For them the war was over.

"No one expected Yanks that early," Lion said in a low voice. "The men had just finished eating. I rousted them out. There were only seventeen of us left. Each had extra weapons." He paused. The tale seemed useless in the telling, but all the others had spoken, and there was nothing else to pass the time. "Well, we took our toll," he went on, embellishing the tale for the sake of his listeners, "but instead of hightailing it to the far trees, as I was sure they would, damn my eyes if the bastards didn't regroup and thunder down on me with ten times the men I had."

"A startling turn of events," said Miles Ryan, a captain whose troopers rode two cars behind in far more cramped quarters than were allotted the officers. Ryan had joined the train in New Jersey where, for reasons of hygiene—soap and razor blades were not issued to prisoners—his head had been shaved for the trip North. He was possessed of an aquiline nose and beetled brows, made more prominent by his high, hairless forehead. The flesh of his cheeks creased as he talked, as if he were constantly trying to smile and cry at the same time. Sometimes he simply looked deranged. But then, so did most of his fellow prisoners. "It appears you figured Sheridan wrong."

Lion groaned as the train ran over a loose rail and swayed sickeningly, jolting him forward and back to thump his skull against the wooden side of the boxcar. "Damn!" he cursed, feeling utterly powerless. "You're right, of course."

"So you made a valiant stand and died to a man. Yourself ex-

Christina Savage
434

cepted, of course," Ryan hurried to add. He fished a much-chewed cigar stub from his shirt pocket.

"No. My whole command took to their heels."

"But not their gallant colonel," Miles said, picking a bit of tobacco from his lower lip. The strange grin made his face into a chilling mask. "You stayed behind."

"Because my horse died two days before, and we'd just finished eating him that morning," Lion explained.

Miles Ryan chuckled, snorted, and wiped his running nose on his sleeve. "Admirable," he laughed. "Admirable." He held up the remains of his cigar. "I can break this in half if you want a chew." Lion passed, and Ryan nodded, happy to have the tobacco to himself. "Wonder what day it is?"

"I was taken Christmas morning. Kept me in a regimental camp until the end of January. They put us on this train, when? . . . three —four weeks ago."

Miles nodded again. "Something like that. It all runs together. Lose time like that—I don't know . . ." He rubbed his temple. "Damn head hurts. Been hurting since . . ." His voice trailed off. The pain and confusion that roiled through his brain and curled his thoughts inside themselves were something he wanted to keep private. The captain dug at his skull, winced, then looked around as if waking up. "That major over there?" he said, pointing. "He doesn't look like much now, but he was a budding genius on the battlefield not too long ago. The day before we were captured he told me the war was over. That it was lost for us and we might as well spend our time in the prisons until the final collapse comes."

"And what do you say?" Lion asked.

The grimace came and went. "The war isn't finished until I am," Ryan said slowly. "Of course, victory is out of the question. Always was, if you stop to think about it."

Lion's eyebrows raised. "Now, wait a minute . . ."

"Oh, come on, Colonel. It's too late to play the romantic. You're an intelligent man. You ought to know better. Right or wrong, the South didn't have a chance of a snowball in hell."

"If that's so," Lion said, his voice as cold as the wind that whistled through the cracks in the side of the car, "just why the hell did you fight, Captain?"

Miles shrugged. "We were right. Why else? Now the way I see it," he went on as if he had a choice in the matter, "if we were to fall

back into the hills, into the heart of the South and show Lincoln and
the rest of them a determination to fight until an equitable armistice
could be arranged, then we'd have something to show for all this."
Miles began to rub his head again. "Bloody though we'd be, bloody
and maimed, we'd not fall to our knees! Our honor—our honor, I
say, would be intact!"

"A fair speech," Lion said sarcastically. "You sure you were
never a politician?"

"I taught school in Winchester. All levels." The strange grimace
came and went and came again. "Speaking extempore was my forte."

"You don't look like a teacher," Lion said.

Miles laughed outright, as if Lion had told an immensely funny
joke. The sound, like a man being throttled, raised the hairs on the
back of Lion's neck.

"I did," Miles finally wheezed, wiping his cheek with the back of
his hand. "I wore shirts, and ties, and a suit. My boots were shined,
and I shaved every day. Once upon a time, I did."

They had stopped. It was night. Jerking awake, Lion pushed himself into a sitting position. The train wasn't moving. Christ, where
were they? That was the worst part. Waking up and not knowing.
Not knowing anything. Where, when, and how long? Lion's heart
leaped and a sour taste of fear came into his mouth. "Boston," he
whispered to himself. Boston, where a prison scow waited. He scrambled to his knees, pressed one eye to a crack. Barely visible in the
gloom another boxcar only feet away blocked his view.

Suddenly, they were moving again. Lion shifted to his left, found a
dry spot. The signal lamp, hung from the roof of the car to give them
a little light, swayed faster as they picked up speed. Lion looked out
the crack again. Each space between the stationary cars on the next
track let through a driving wind and freezing rain mixed with snow.
The rhythm of relative calm alternating with short spurts of wind and
rain increased. Suddenly, the adjacent track was clear. The wind
burned his eye but Lion didn't dare stop looking. At last, in the distance, lantern light spilled across a half-dozen tracks and down the
face of the sign. Lion ducked his head, wiped his eye, and peered out
the crack in time to see the sign flash by.

Christ! Providence, Rhode Island. How far was it from Providence
to Boston? Fifty miles? Less? Night wind buffeted the slow-moving
train. Rain and sleet scoured the boxcars, leaked through the cracks,

and puddled the floor. The lantern swayed like a metronome, ticking away the feet and yards and miles. Around him, sleeping prisoners sprawled in various states of discomfort and exhaustion. Emaciated and ill, most of them came from beleaguered Richmond, or had been sent north from Georgia when Sherman carved his path of infamy to the sea. A few, like Miles and himself, had somehow managed to maintain the ability to function. But that wouldn't last. He'd heard horror stories aplenty. Once locked aboard a prison scow the strongest men deteriorated rapidly. Somehow he had to escape before they reached Boston.

A wildness came on him. Rising, he stepped over sleeping bodies as he felt along the entire side of the car, then along the end and other side and other end. Nothing. The boxcar was old, but tight. He looked up. The ceiling was too far to reach. Somewhere. Somewhere there had to be a weak spot. Frantic, he dropped to his knees and began to crawl over bodies, feeling his way along the floor.

"Ryan, wake up!" Lion crawled back to his starting place, nudged the teacher turned warrior, shook him until he groaned and sat up.

"What the hell?"

"Listen. We just left Providence, Rhode Island."

"So?"

"Less than fifty miles to Boston. I think I've found a way to get us out of here. With your help."

Totally awake, Ryan got to his knees. In the dim red light the two men looked like animals facing each other. "How?"

"Follow me," he said, leading the way to the partially rotten plank he had found. "Here. Pull off my boot." Ryan complied, watched wide-eyed as Lion fumbled inside the boot and drew out a makeshift knife crafted from a filed-down bayonet fitted into a wooden grip. "With this," Lion said, plunging the point down between the planks. "Lift."

The crack widened enough for Miles to get a grip on the plank. Lion slid the knife deeper, levered again. Miles jerked and the plank broke in half. Several of the sleeping men stirred. A few woke to watch, but made no effort to help or hinder. For them there was no hope. Lion and Miles pried loose the remainder of the rotten plank and went to work on the next one just as the train creaked to a stop. Lion looked out the crack. "We're on a siding," he whispered, scuttling back to the narrow hole. "If we hurry maybe we can get out before they start up again." The plank was sound, but splinter by splinter it gave way. Sweat poured down their faces as they worked. Suddenly another train was passing them. As the last car went by the prisoner-of-war train jerked into motion.

"Damn!" Ryan spat. "Damn it to hell . . ."

"Keep working!" Lion snapped. "We just got the time we needed. One more board to go."

The third board resisted their efforts for half an hour, but at last the two prisoners succeeded. A hole two feet wide and half again as long gaped in the floor. "Nice of the Yanks not to station a guard in here," Lion said, sitting back and smiling grimly.

Miles nodded. "The doors are padlocked," he said, the grimace flitting across his face. "And what kind of fool would drop beneath a moving train?"

"I would." Lion wrapped the knife, put it back in his boot. "When it slows. How fast do you suppose we're going now?"

The two hunched over the jagged edge of wood and watched the ties flip past. The noise in the boxcar was a constant roar, but no one seemed to notice or care. Ryan considered. "The way this thing lurches about, and with the weather, no more than twenty miles an hour, if that," he said, finally. "Fast enough, though."

"Can I go with you, Colonel?" A spare, homely-looking brevet lieutenant in a uniform that may have fit at one time but now hung in baggy folds, climbed over two unconscious men who smelled of dysentery and diarrhea. "I've been watching. The name is Lieutenant Harold Larrott, of Birmingham, and I want to go home." From his voice, he wasn't even twenty, but malnutrition and dysentery had made him look middle-aged. "Take me with you."

"Let me see your hands," Lion said.

Larrott held out his right hand. It shook like a leaf. Lion glanced at Miles. "Yanks will be down on us like Valkyries on a Viking's corpse," Miles said.

Lion nodded. "You'd never make it, son," he said as gently as possible. "Believe me. Don't try. I'm sorry."

The lieutenant squatted on the filth-encrusted floor, fumbled at his crotch, and directed a stream of urine through the hole in the floor. Finished, he buttoned his fly. "That's for luck, you bastards," he said, near tears, and sat down to watch.

"I'm sorry," Lion repeated. "The war will be over soon. They'll send you home before you know it."

Larrott glared in return, jerking his head toward the hole. "It's slowing."

It was. Not enough for Lion's taste, but the best he could hope for, and he didn't dare wait. Ryan was looking out a crack in the side of the boxcar. "A grade, I think," he said, scurrying back to join Lion. "We're on a hillside." A madman's face leered in the dim red light. "Well, Colonel, who's to go first?"

Lion checked his journal to make sure it was tucked firmly under his belt, grabbed his cloak, and dropped it through the hole. Not waiting, he stuck his legs through the opening and, propped on his elbows, lowered himself into the void. The roar of the train was awesome. His boot heels struck a cross tie. He winced and raised his legs against the underside of the car as best he could, then shut his eyes and grabbed the edges of the opening with his hands and dropped.

Sharp gravel dug into his back. His momentum dragged him forward in a slide that almost carried him beneath the wheels. "God!" he screamed as the immense weight of iron and steel and wood roared over him. Grit and sparks flew into his face. Low-hanging supports under each car tugged at the buttons on his chest. Lion pressed his feet against one tie, his hands against another. He felt himself sucked toward the belly of the train. Sound attacked him. Wheels clattered across rail joints, axles squealed in their housings. His arms and legs were numb. He willed himself a piece of the railbed, and when his will failed he simply held on, because to loose his grip was to die.

When it came the silence was as awesome as the hellish din. Muscle by cramped muscle, Lion eased his grip on the ties and peeled himself away from the gravel. Stunned, acting on little more than instinct, he rolled off the tracks and landed in a puddle of frigid slush that jolted him back to consciousness. He blew muddy ice water from his nose and mouth. He stood, fell sideways, and settled for crawling until strength returned to his legs and he stopped shaking. He still had his journal. His cloak was fifty yards down the track. Wrapping it around him, he staggered forward until he found Miles Ryan. Somehow, the teacher had managed to land face down. Lion dragged him from the tracks and heaved a sigh of relief when Ryan sat up by himself. "Made it," Ryan gasped.

Too tired and shaken to get out of the wind and rain, the pair sat quaking on one of the rails. At last Ryan hauled himself to his feet and gave Lion a hand up. He jerked his head in the direction from which they'd come. "That way's south, I suspect. Best move," he said, his teeth chattering.

"No," Lion put a hand on Miles and turned him around. "They'll be looking for us that way."

"So?"

"We head north. For Canada."

"The hell you say. You're mad!"

"That may be. You coming or not?"

Fifty yards up the tracks, they found the first grisly chunk of Lieutenant Larrott.

Chapter 34

March 24, 1865, dawned bright and clear. The *Andrew Jackson* was finished. By ten in the morning, by sleigh and by carriage and on foot, the vast majority of New Forest was gathering at the mammoth open-roofed shed at the Blackheath Shipyards for the launching of the new ship. Inside the scene was one of patriotic gaiety. Bunting hung from the walls, the speaker's platform, and the rails and masts of the *Andrew Jackson*. The stern of the *Jackson* perched over the waters of the bay. A wisp of steam spewed from its stack and disappeared into the bright blue sky. The bow jutted far into the shed and towered twenty feet above the speaker's platform set immediately in front of it. A military band imported from Boston tootled on their instruments to keep them warm.

The ceremony itself began precisely at eleven with the arrival of the Blackheaths, the distinguished speaker, and the guests of honor, all of whom took their places on the platform. A hush spread through the shed as the band began the proceedings with "John Brown's Body" and "When Johnny Comes Marchin' Home."

Seward had been too busy, Fessenden ill with the grippe, Stanton occupied with strategic-planning sessions, and Welles, Secretary of the Navy, out of town on an inspection tour of the naval blockade that was bottling up what was left of Southern shipping in North and South Carolina. Not even Postmaster General William Dennison could attend. Speechmaker, then, for the launching was, irony of ironies, Admiral Dayton Cabell.

Eve had not known who the Navy Department had sent to New Forest until that morning, had known even less how to break the news to her father. Sewal had taken the admiral's presence in stride, though, and controlled his temper by the simple expedient of ignoring him.

The Navy man accepted the cheers of the crowd and, hiding his resentment and animosity toward the Blackheaths, launched himself into a windy speech complete with painful metaphors, turgid imagery, and flamboyant gestures for the reporters sent up from New York, Washington, Portland, Boston, and a number of smaller towns along the coast. Sitting next to her father's wheelchair, Eve applauded and smiled or laughed at the appropriate places, and with surreptitious nudges and frowns, admonished a glowering Sewal to do the same.

The moment they had all been waiting for arrived with the end of the speech. A half-dozen men with mallets took their places in front of the remaining oak supports that held the ship off the ways. Another dozen pushed back the crowd. A small walnut case held tightly under his arm, Eliot climbed onto the platform. "Here it is, Mrs. Sarandon," he said.

Eve opened the case. Inside lay a bottle of champagne encased in a mesh bag. "Thank you, Eliot. Father?" One hand on Sewal's arm, she crouched at his side. "I know you didn't want to build it, build any of them, but I couldn't let the yards die." She held out the champagne bottle. "I—we all—would be pleased if you—"

"No." Sewal patted her hand, looked directly into her eyes, and jerked his head toward the new ship. "She's yours. You deserve the honor. Just give me a kiss before you smack her, and we'll be even. I'm proud of you."

Her eyes bright, Eve kissed her father on the cheek, then strode to the edge of the platform directly under the bow of the *Andrew Jackson*. The crowd cheered, and quieted when she raised her hand for silence. "Jon! Gunter! We're ready."

An anticipatory silence filled the shed. "One, two, whoop!" called Jon. A half-dozen mallets struck their respective supports. "One, two, whoop!" Again, they struck. Eve stood poised and waiting. "One, two, whoop!"

The ship groaned, settled onto the runners that would carry it into the water, and slowly started to move. Eve's voice rang out loud and clear as she held the champagne bottle high over her head. "I christen thee *Andrew Jackson!*" she cried, and in the same instant smashed the bottle against the bow.

The newly named ship picked up speed. The crowd roared its approval. The band struck up "The Battle Hymn of the Republic." Magnificent in its mass, the *Andrew Jackson*'s stern dug into the water with a great splash. The ship settled momentarily, then rose to her proper level and floated free, held close to shore by arm-thick hawsers. A pair of tugs standing by saluted with their whistles. The *Andrew Jackson* answered with a deep, booming horn that echoed over the entire bay and could be heard a mile inland.

With the ship launched Sewal insisted on going home. Travis helped wheel him down the ramp from the platform and passed him to Gunter, who wheeled him to the carriage and helped him in. "I'll ride along and help you off, Mr. Blackheath," Gunter offered, after lashing the chair behind the seat.

"No need," Sewal said, unwrapping the reins. "Pole and Vernon are there for that. You go on and have a good time. Drink some cider."

"Ha! But not too much. We move Maisie into her new house today. Maybe you come by and see what we build for her and Arvid one day, eh?"

"It will be my pleasure. Arvid still improves?"

Gunter nodded. "Dr. Cutcheon says he won't win any more foot races, but he can come back to work soon. Plenty boys come home with worse than a bad leg."

"Yes, indeed." And some do not come home at all, Sewal thought.

Gunter shoved his gloved hands under his armpits. "I'll go, Mr. Blackheath. It is good to see you in the yards."

"Thank you, Gunter. I appreciate that." Forced by Eve to attend the launching, Sewal had found himself looking around at the new sheds, the familiar sail loft and rope walk—the whole yard—with renewed affection. "Yes" he said, shaking his head slowly. "I'll come down again."

Gunter's teeth flashed as he smiled. "That will be a good day, Mr. Blackheath."

Sewal watched the Swede trudge toward the shed from which the *Andrew Jackson* had been launched and then clucked to the horse. Feet, hooves, carriage wheels, and the sun had made a soupy mess of the snow. By the time the day was finished the cobblestoned yards would be one big puddle which, with nightfall, would freeze again. For a moment he considered taking the bay road, but changed his mind. It had been a while since he had driven through New Forest's streets, and with almost everyone at the post-launching party there would be few souls about to gawk at him. A man needed a little time to himself. He guided the horse onto the avenue that followed the shore. Waupinau Bay was fleeced with white caps whipped by a brisk breeze that whistled through the gaps between the shingled buildings separating the road from the shore. He cut inland, crossed the bridge into town, drove through the deserted streets, and finally turned into the public docks. The horse stopped, nervous at being on the wooden planking over the water. Sewal set the brake and leaned back.

The harbor was empty save for the usual workboats and a sole clipper that flew a Black Line flag. From where he sat Sewal could see down the shoreline to the Blackheath Shipyards. There, a black hulk against the buildings, the *Andrew Jackson* rode at anchor. Within another week or two the final fittings would be installed and the warship would go to sea for its trial run. Sewal found himself comparing the two vessels, clipper and warship. Ships had been his life. Wooden ships, crafted with loving care and driven by the wind under clouds of canvas. There was a naturalness about them that pleased him. They *belonged* on the sea, lived and breathed in their natural elements of salt water and wind. He could remember the first iron ship he had seen; squat and ugly with awkward lines, side paddles jutting up like great bulbous tumors, the stench of woodsmoke and hot metal. No. It was obvious to the rankest amateur that ships made of iron were monstrous, barbaric creations. He had sworn never to build one.

But times changed. Sewal might have been a romantic idealist, but he was no fool. He could read newspapers and journals and the handwriting on the wall, when it came down to it. Clipper and warship. There was no doubt which of the two was the more beautiful. Neither was there any doubt which was the more durable and the more terrible. Iron warships with their hidden underwater prows of reinforced steel could split a wooden ship apart and were immune to all but the heaviest armament. Driven by steam, independent of

God's wind, they were able to sail in the calmest sea as well as fight their way around cape or horn in the face of a direct gale. And under the circumstances they could keep a shipyard alive, as well as win a war.

The war, Sewal thought bitterly. More than anything else, war hastened change. Iron ships might have been inevitable in the long run, but not so quickly that he had to witness the death of his beloved clippers. Had it not been for the war it would have been Michael who watched the new era arrive, long after Sewal had passed away. Justin might have come back to him, had not the war fostered an era of immortality and created gods of new technologies like photography. Even Eve. The war had thrown Lion McKenna at her, then killed Clifford. The war had turned her into what amounted to a man. And left him a cripple in a wheelchair. It was as though the war had converted time itself to steam. Driven faster than it was meant to go, time whirled faster and faster, and old men tagging along behind were spun out on obsolete tangents and relegated to the role of spectators.

A sea gull dropped from the top of a rotting beam upended in the water. The gull glided over the chop, decided whatever it had seen was inedible and, wings flapping, pushed itself high into the air where it soared, angelic, across a golden sun. Sewal's leathery skin crinkled as he tracked the sea bird's flight. Calmed, he smiled to himself. Time could be a friend as well as an enemy. Time and strokes and obsolete tangents, from which vantage points a man could gain a degree of equanimity and objectivity.

"What do you see?"

Sewal started, looked down to his left. Madame Laurier gazed up at him, her face framed in fox fur. A moment passed; he considered not answering. Then he shrugged. "A ship, a bay. A sea gull, a dock. What do you see?" he asked in return.

Madame Laurier smiled. A breeze ruffled the hem of her gown, caught at the chocolate brown cape hanging from her shoulders.

"There was a time when I refrained from climbing down to offer you the services of my carriage," Sewal said. "Now, when I would, I cannot. I hope this time you'll forgive me."

Madame Laurier studied him. Except for the drawn tightness of his features and the wheelchair behind the carriage, he looked much the same as he had the night he came to her bed. "You were younger then, and your hair was darker," she said.

Sewal's anger changed to wry amusement as he realized she was being neither sarcastic nor vindictive. Perhaps even whores, he thought wryly, are doomed to view the world from strange and unsettling angles. "And more abundant, too, though I had hoped no one would notice," he said with a laugh.

"I'm sorry about your son. A little late to say so, perhaps, but then we haven't kept the closest company down the years." Marie Laurier's breath clouded the air, and she actually blushed. "You see, even the madam of a brothel is given to moments of introspection. Does that surprise you?"

"No," Sewal replied. "Not very much surprises me these days. You see, I did a great deal of thinking, lying in bed for weeks without the strength or coordination to make my way about. A great deal of thinking."

"Good. Men should think from time to time," Madame Laurier said. "A pity they rarely do. Perhaps the world would be better off if they did."

Sewal shook his head. "My apologies, Madame Laurier. I won't participate. You see, I've devised a treatment for myself. Whenever I feel bitterness well up inside me, I soothe it with imaginary poultice concocted of equal parts of time and optimism and objectivity. I will never approve of your profession, as I will never condone the weakness that overcame me that one terrible night. But I know now, perhaps too late, that none of us—with the possible exception of certain lawyers and a greedy admiral or two—deserves to be condemned too quickly."

"How sweet of you," Madame Laurier purred, the bile rising in her throat. Only through the greatest effort did she refrain from lashing out at him. "How touchingly forgiving. How condescending."

Sewal was confused, unable to understand how he had offended her. "I . . . that is, I was offering an apology," he stammered. "I thought . . ." Words fled him. For a moment he feared the return of the aphasia that had tormented him for the first months after his stroke, but he focused his thoughts. "If I may—" He mustered all the dignity left him. "—Offer you transportation to your door?"

"No. You may not!" Laurier's eyes narrowed with fury. One gloved hand reached out and, fingers splayed, beat dully on the carriage wheel. "I've been the town whore for too long. Stood up to too many of your insults. I don't mind not being invited to parties or the launching of ships, but I *do* mind being forgiven and condescended to by a self-serving, sanctimonious hypocrite. So, you may *not* offer me transportation to my door. Believe it or not, Mister Sewal Blackheath, I have my pride after all!" Her head high, her shoulders straight, Madame Marie Laurier stalked away from the carriage, across the dock, and disappeared in the alley that led to the Land Lock.

A shaken Sewal sat motionless, his eyes closed, his hands clenched like claws on the reins. Only gradually, slow as the tide that rose around the piers, did he regain full control of his senses. When he did he opened his eyes and looked about as if awaking from a dream. The sun was still high in the sky. The gull had returned to the rotting beam. "Your pride," he said to himself. "Yes. Useless as it is, I believe you have your pride." He clucked to the mare and resumed his solitary drive through New Forest.

Rosebud's neck and flanks steamed after the climb up the Whale's Hump. Her long gray mane was warm to the touch as Eve stroked the mare's neck and allowed the animal to lip a carrot from her hand while she rested. The day was beautiful, a false spring, sunshiny Sunday every bit as comfortable as Saturday had been. Church had been mercifully short. James Ruell was spending the day with "Aunt Maisie and uncles Gunter, Jon, and Arvid," along with an assortment of other Naslund nephews and nieces. Jack Travis, who had been the commanding officer of the supply depot in Portland for the past year, had come to visit for the launching the day before. He and Eve had stopped at Dawn Wind after church to collect a picnic lunch Eustacia had made for them and then, keeping the sleigh to the side of the road and in the snow, headed for the Whale's Hump. Each had a purpose for wanting to be alone with the other.

The night before had been a strange mixture of tension and relaxation. The *Andrew Jackson* was launched. The party had been a success. For Eve, a goal had been reached. The *Jackson* had been designed to contend with the fastest, most powerful ships of the Confederacy. Eve knew in her bones that it would succeed. At the same time she was troubled. Jack had first proposed to her over a year earlier, and she had rejected his suit. The first ironclad to come out of the Blackheath Shipyards was on the verge of completion. They had just begun work on the new shed. Painfully aware that she was missing those special moments a mother experiences but once with her first child, she spent every spare minute with her son. James

Ruell was three and a half now, and needed her. Every second of every day was full. There was not room or time in her life for Jack. Over the past months his letters had become more and more aggressive. It was clear he had grown to expect more of their relationship than she was willing to give. Eve realized what had happened. He had misconstrued her every move, beginning with their intimacy in New York. It was all her fault. Needing a friend, concerned first with her father's illness, later with the well-being of the shipyard, she had encouraged his affection and support. Last night had been his preamble. Today, she knew, he would propose to her again. She also knew her answer.

Rosebud whinnied and tossed her head. Eve dug a second carrot from her pocket and gave it to the mare. Jack was on the Atlantic side of the Hump, reading the inscriptions on the gravestones. Pensive, Eve wandered in the opposite direction, took the familiar path through the towering, ancient white pines. The stillness was complete, save for the soughing of the wind in the trees. A moment later she emerged in the small lookout clearing. The bay was a sheet of flat metal. New Forest was a patchwork quilt of roofs and open spaces. The huge double sheds in the shipyards stood out. Behind the largest one she could see the bow of the *Andrew Jackson*.

Two years and—she counted on her fingers—four months. Had it really been that long? Jack had returned in September of 1862. Her father had had his stroke then. Within the month she had taken over the yards and forced Cabell's cooperation. Two years and four months. A great deal had been accomplished. The shed built, two ironclads, followed by the *Andrew Jackson*. All debts paid off, inventories replenished, and the yard was making a profit. In the process, the town had grown and become prosperous. And within the next month they would begin construction on a trio of shallow draught ironclads designed to run coastal defenses and work the South's rivers. Sometime after work on the ironclads began the first of a half-dozen whalers they had contracted to refurbish would arrive.

"You broke your promise." Jack's voice startled her. "Sorry," he added, setting down the picnic basket, "but you did promise."

"What on earth do you mean?" Eve asked, a little too brightly.

"The expression on your face. The intensity of your stare. You were thinking of ships."

Eve blushed, forced a laugh. "Am I so obvious?" she asked, suppressing a touch of guilt.

"To one who cares, yes."

"I don't know whether I'm freezing or quite comfortable," Eve said with a shiver. She knew she was putting off the inevitable, but couldn't help it. "I was just thinking, here it is March already," she added lamely, pulling her long riding cape tighter about the forest-green gown she wore.

"Stay out of the shade. As long as we stay in the sunlight, we'll be warm." Jack stood behind her, let his hands rest on her waist. "I'm sorry about the holidays, but the war office is indefatigable," he said, a tinge of sarcasm coloring his voice. "Every time I try to get away, my sergeant brings me another stack of pages and forms from Washington that need initialing. I go out and meet people because my face makes me look like a hero. And I sit in an office for eight hours a day in order to do ten minutes' work. The galling thing is that that's all they think I'm good for. Worse, none of it matters. The war will be over soon, no matter what I do."

"Do you think so?"

"I'm certain of it. So certain I've even given up trying to get a transfer." He paused. Eve closed her eyes against what was coming. "June 25, 1861," Jack said, his voice low and soft. "Do you remember?"

"Yes," Eve said, at last. "Jack—"

"New York was beautiful that day, but no more beautiful than you. Did I ever tell you what I did after you left my hotel? I walked. I had never been so alive, so filled with energy, so aware. In those few hours I saw every flower, looked at every person I passed. I remember passing a bakery and smelling the fresh bread. I remember stopping in front of a coffee warehouse and soaking in the aroma of the roasting beans. Once I looked up as a fire engine company rounded a corner. To this day, the image of plunging horses and running men and careening pumper is indelibly etched on my mind like one of Justin's photographs. When I got back to the hotel I slept like a baby. That was three and a half years ago, Eve. Three and a half years."

Jack's hand left her waist. She could feel him touch her hair. "I know," she whispered.

He turned her toward him. Sunlight reflected off the shiny texture of the patch covering the left side of his face. "The war will end soon, and we'll all be able to resume our normal lives again. I'll resign my commission, and—" Jack drew himself up, wet his lips. "I'd like to come here to Dawn Wind, then, Eve. I'd like you to marry me."

Myriad images came and went through Eve's mind, none long enough to be focused on. Sewal in his wheelchair. Dueling pistols raised. A gray dog bounding toward her out of the night. Clifford slumped against her. A cove and a man with steel gray eyes. Oh, God! Not that, not him! Pain and birth. James Ruell. A cloud of smoke, a frightened team. A sleigh filled with Christmas presents. A face appearing in the night-mirrored cupola glass. Her tongue felt swollen, large in her mouth.

"You are silent," Jack said, his voice flat. "You never have an answer for me, do you? Unless I carry the answer with me. Shall I show it to you?" He reached for the mask covering the left side of his face and began to pull it away.

"No!" Eve said, catching his hand. "Please, Jack." Eyes closed, she shook her head. "No," she repeated, barely audible.

Jack let the mask drop into place. He spun on his heels and walked to the picnic basket, pulled out a clay jug, and drank from it. Aged cider, potent as sin, flooded down his throat. He straightened, almost gagged, then hurled the jug against the trunk of a pine tree. Cider and fragments of clay exploded in a dozen directions. Jack brushed his hand across the stain where the cider had dribbled on his tunic, wiped his mouth with a kerchief. His face was red, a mask beside a mask.

Eve wanted to go to him, yet felt frozen in place. Ashamed, she wanted to apologize, to tell him he was wrong about the cause of her refusal. She wanted to tell him that she wasn't—perhaps had never been—the same woman he had spent the day with so long ago in New York. There was so much more! Son, father, shipyards, ambition. "I'm sorry, Jack," was all she could manage, and that in a voice both faltering and weak. "I'm sorry."

To her immense surprise, Jack looked at her and smiled. "I can be quite an ass when I really try."

"Jack?"

He waved her to silence, picked up the basket. "Come. We'll go back," he said, offering her his arm.

Eve took his hand instead, held it in both her own.

"Did you notice Cabell when you introduced him to me at the station?" he went on, forcedly cheerful. They walked along the path toward the other side of the Whale's Hump and the waiting sleigh. "I thought he would swallow his false teeth. I winked at him. That hurt, I think. You could tell he knows it's too late to do anything about it."

Rosebud greeted them with a nicker and a wave of her head. Eve paused at the side of the sleigh while Jack put the basket under the seat. When he turned to help her in she put her arms around him and held him close to her. "I don't want to lose your friendship, Jack. It means too much to me. You still mean . . . too much . . . I'm sorry, my dear friend."

"Yes," Jack said, wondering at his affection and restraint. He breathed deeply. Eve's hair smelled as fresh and clean as a spring morning. "Your friend."

"Do you want me to read to you?"

"No." Dwarfed by the massive highbacked wicker chair, James pouted and sulked. He had wanted to spend the night with "Aunt Maisie and Uncle Arvid," but had been brought home instead.

"You want to sleepy-bed?" Eve asked, knowing the answer before she asked.

"No." James climbed out of the chair and toddled over to his grandfather. "Boat. Boat," he shouted, tugging at Sewal's hand.

Eve looked at her father and began to fidget uncomfortably. Sewal cleared his throat. "Boat, eh? Ship. Say ship."

"Ship," James repeated dutifully.

"Good."

James ran around to the side of the chair, pushed against the arm until the chair pivoted, then ran around back. His legs strained as he pushed his grandfather to the glass-enclosed shelf.

"We told him he couldn't have another when he broke the one you carved him for Christmas," Eve said in a disapproving voice.

Sewal unlatched the door, reached in, and pulled out a partially rigged miniature whaling vessel only twelve inches long from bow to stern. "He's not yet four years old, for heaven's sake. Christmas was a long time ago."

"Boat! Boat!" James squealed, clapping his hands.

Eve folded her arms. "You were the one who said a man has to learn his values as a boy if he's to learn values at all."

Sewal glared at her, glanced sidelong at his grandson. "Values are values, damn it, but ships are ships."

"Father!" Eve warned. "I think I remember something about spoiling too."

Sewal tried to think of a better response, finally decided to ignore her. He leaned forward and held out the model. "What's this?" he asked, pointing to the mainmast.

James Ruell reached for the whaler but Sewal pulled it back. "No. I'll hold it, and you tell me what I point to. Now, what's this?" he asked again, pointing once more the mainmast. The boy stared, perplexed. His lower lip began to tremble and his face wrinkled. "Now, none of that," Sewal ordered. James swallowed a sob and turned to his mother for support.

"I think it's high time you went to bed, young man," she said.

James looked wistfully at the boat and changed tactics. "Cookie?" he asked, determined to get something for all this trouble.

"He can bargain," Sewal laughed. "Better give in before he raises the price."

Eve looked to the heavens for help. "You're incorrigible. Both of you. I suppose— Yes, Mr. Pole?"

Hanson Pole stood in the parlor doorway. He glanced around, hesitated, and decided to relay his information. "You wanted to know. Vernon has just now arrived."

Eve looked at the clock and frowned. "It's been four hours. He was supposed to leave Major Travis at the station and come right back. What took so long?"

"Ah, I suspect he . . . That is, there is a definite aroma of spirits about him."

"This is the third time in as many weeks, isn't it?" Sewal asked.

"Yes, sir."

"I'll discharge him," Eve said, starting from the room.

"It's after nine," Sewal protested. "Morning will be soon enough."

"That's what happened the last time," Eve said. "He's been warned often enough. Mr. Pole, please take James to the kitchen and tell Eustacia to give him a cookie and put him to bed. I'll be up to say good night in a few minutes."

"Yes, ma'am."

"James, you go with Mr. Pole. Mama will be back in a minute." Eve grabbed a cloak from a hall chair, flung it around her shoulders, and stalked out the back door.

The spring wind was strong and whipped the cloak about Eve's legs. A gust caught the hood and pushed it off her head. Eve's anger increased. She was weary of incompetent, irresponsible employees. Her emotions had been frayed enough by the afternoon spent with Jack. She was tired, and the stable keeper's repeated drinking bouts had driven her to the brink. Surprised at finding the stable in complete darkness, she shoved the heavy oak doors open. Small favors, she thought. If the man was inebriated at least he hadn't struck a match and set the stable afire. She groped for and found the lantern hung by the door and, on the shelf next to it, matches and a striker. She struck the match, touched fire to the wick, and lowered the glass into place.

"Vernon?" she called, stepping farther into the stable. "Vernon!"

A horse snorted. Leather creaked. Anger turned to fury. He hadn't even unhitched Rosebud from the carriage! Eve stood at the mare's side, held the lantern high. "Vernon! Where are you?" she called, checking the stalls on either side of the central aisle.

Her voice caught in her throat and her stomach twisted in fear. The stable keeper lay on his side in the stall to her right. Blood seeped from a cut on his skull and a man dressed in the worn winter clothes of a fisherman was crouched over him. When the man grinned shadow-black creases etched dark lines across his face.

Eve shrieked, backed into a post and, thinking it an unseen attacker, whirled about. She darted past Rosebud and the carriage and ran for the door just as a second man materialized out of the shadows and lunged at her. She swung the lantern at him, but his hand caught her wrist. Eve's heart skipped a beat. In the pallid glare of the uplifted lantern she found herself staring at Lion McKenna.

Chapter 35

"You!" Eve gasped.

"Yes." Lion's eyes glittered. He wiped his free hand across his forehead. "Hello, Eve." He watched her staring at him, glanced up at the lantern, and let go of her wrist. "Aren't you going to say hello?" Eve's mouth opened and closed, but no sound came out. "Can't blame you, I guess. I suspect we'd better go to the house." He glanced around her. "Tie him up and cover him up so he won't freeze. We're going inside," he called to the first man Eve had seen.

Eve tried to concentrate, tried to figure out what was happening, but her thoughts were too fragmented. Led outside the stable, she almost tripped on her cloak as Lion and the strange short-haired man accompanied her to the house. Within minutes the entire staff was gathered in the dining room. As if posed for a portrait of fear, Pole, Eustacia, and Jubb were standing with their backs to the wall. Eustacia's face glistened with a faint sheen of perspiration. Caught without his spectacles, Pole squinted at the fuzzy figures and tried to keep from trembling. Jubb kept one arm around Eustacia. Sewal had wheeled himself to the corner of the long dining table. Eve, unable to stand any longer, had taken a seat at her father's side. James, thank heavens, had been taken to his bedroom by Eustacia. Eve prayed he wouldn't make a sound. She prayed more fervently at that moment than at any time in her life; she didn't want either Lion or his friend to know about her son. She prayed, too, from shock: her mind still could not accept Lion's presence. It reeled from the task.

But he was real, irrevocably, ominously present. She studied him, comparing him to the man she had loved in the past. The elegant attire was gone, replaced by filthy work clothes that barely fit him. The creases in his cheeks were deeper, and the lines around his eyes more numerous. A streak of silver slashed across his moustache and deep into his beard. The painful crook in his nose was the same, but his eyes, alternately dull with fatigue or flashing with what Eve took for fever, held weariness. He was lean, hungry-looking. The hard edge of his personality Eve had seen prior to the duel with Michael had been honed during the intervening years of war. He had forgotten, she was sure, how to be gentle. His partner looked equally formidable. His hair and beard were of the same length, and his mouth was curved in a frightening grimace that was half smile and half frown. He brandished a dragoon Colt revolver with one hand and, with the other, scooped whole sections of an apple-cinnamon pie into his mouth.

Lion swallowed the last of the chicken breast he had been chewing, wiped his mouth with the back of his hand. "If you're lucky," he said, holstering his pistol and hitching up his trousers, "you'll never know how good that tasted. I trust there's more where it came from. So. This is how it will be." Pointedly averting his gaze from Eve, he fixed the servants with a stare. "No one will leave without my permission. There will be no visitors unless it can't be helped, and at such times Miles and I will be upstairs with one or more of you at gunpoint."

"I have to be at the shipyards every day," Eve broke in angrily.

"The little lady will have to learn not to speak unless spoken to," Miles said around a bite of pie.

"Go to hell!" Eve's eyes blazed. She rose halfway out of her chair. Miles crammed the last of the pie in his mouth and quite casually aimed his pistol at Eve's head. Eve paled and sat abruptly.

"No!" Sewal shouted.

"Put it away!" Lion said, striking the gun aside. Miles stared at him, shrugged, and finally dropped the weapon into his holster. Lion looked at Eve. "Why?" he asked.

"I . . . I've been running the shipyards," she faltered. "Ever since Father—"

"Until I can walk again," Sewal interrupted, more for pride than added information.

Lion looked at the wheelchair as if he hadn't noticed it before. "I see." He closed his eyes, pinched the bridge of his nose with his thumb and forefinger. "Very well," he said at last. "Business as usual then."

"How long do you plan to stay?" Sewal asked.

"Until we've eaten regularly enough to have the strength to make it the rest of the way to Canada," Lion answered.

Miles's laugh was an obscene cackle. "You needn't trouble yourself how many days that will take, old fellow. All you have to worry about is what we leave behind. Maybe things as they are, or maybe ashes, like I found the last time I saw my place." A macabre grin twisted his face. "What happens here is up to you," he added, gesturing to the servants, Eve, and Sewal.

"And you go along with what he says?" Sewal asked, riveting his attention on Lion.

Color crept up the Southerner's neck. "To a point, yes," Lion admitted. "I have to. I've been captured once. I won't be again. I won't surrender to anyone without a fight. We don't wish to bring violence into your house, Mr. Blackheath. If you cooperate—"

"All will be well?" Sewal leaned forward in his chair. His face and the bald part of his head was a bright red and his eyes were black with fury. "Damn you, Lion McKenna. Do you hear me?" His voice was a whip. "God damn you for what you have brought unto Dawn Wind and my family!"

Miles started toward Sewal but Lion motioned him back. "Curse me if you wish. I've done the same to many a Yankee, Mr. Black-heath," he said sadly. "You'd know why if you'd seen—" He stopped, looked around the room. Nothing was broken, nothing was burned. Not so much as a single dish or a chair. His head jerked, as if he had been dreaming and awakened. "Will you cooperate?"

Sewal seemed to wither in his chair. He did not look at either of the intruders, only nodded in affirmation. "Do as these people wish," he ordered the servants.

"Father!" Eve flared. "No!"

"Enough. I've said what will be done." He turned his head slowly until he was looking into Eve's eyes. "I am still master of Dawn Wind, and I'll have no more death here. Do you understand? No more death."

Eve's face was red with anger. For a moment it looked as if she would contest her father's injunction. Instead she rose abruptly, lifted the hem of her skirt, and stalked from the room.

"Hey!" Miles said, pulling his revolver. "Hey!"

"You stay downstairs," Lion said, preceding the teacher to the door. "Send them to their duties," he added, gesturing to the three servants. Before Miles could protest, Lion was out of the room and following Eve upstairs.

She was in front of her bedroom by the time Lion reached the landing. When she turned to him he paused, suddenly awkward in the face of her defiance. "Eve." He tried to sound gentle, but because he could not remember gentleness her name sounded like an accusation.

"Why?" Eve asked, her voice trembling in the shadow-draped hall. "Why this place of all places? Why did you come back here?"

"Not to torment you. We've been other places. Dawn Wind was on our way, though, and since I—" He stopped. His eyes ached and the fever was burning inside him. Suddenly he was angry at himself and her. "Yank patrols are always on the watch for escaped prisoners trying to sneak past the lines and reach home," he explained harshly. "Security will be lax at the Canadian border. What Reb in his right mind would head north? Eventually we'll book passage on a Canadian ship and return to the South. The war isn't over yet."

"Oh?" Eve said with icy sarcasm. "It seems to be. For you."

Lion glanced down at the ill-fitting farm clothes he had taken from a dairyman outside of Lewiston. "The clothes are temporary, I assure you," he said lamely. "Escaped prisoners can't be choosy."

"Not all the time, at least."

"I'm trying to make this as painless as possible, Eve."

"How decent of you. Tell me," Eve hissed, "did the man who owned those give them to you, or did you have to steal them?"

A scene flashed across Lion's mind. The image of a farmer reaching for a shotgun over his fireplace and Miles crashing a three-legged stool against the man's head. "Miles is an educated man," came the halting answer. "A man given to thought and consideration once upon a time. A scholar, even, from the way I have heard him talk. But reasonable men forced into unreasonable situations tend to become extremely dangerous." Cold sweat beaded on Lion's forehead. He blinked his eyes, forced them to remain open. "I suggest you do what he says."

"I see." Eve wet her lips nervously. "I needn't be afraid of you. Just this Miles person."

"Fear me too," Lion cautioned, his gray eyes darkening. Suddenly he started as a thump and a wail erupted from another bedroom. "You said there was no one else upstairs," he said, moving toward the door.

Eve moved to block his passage, but Lion brushed her aside and entered the room. There, rubbing his head where he had run into a nearby chair, a child sat on the carpet. Lion glanced accusingly at Eve, then walked across the room to James who quit crying now that he had attracted some attention. When Lion stopped in front of him he grinned at the stranger and held out a three-legged cow. "Play moo?" he said. "Play moo?"

Lion squatted, stared at the child. In the soft light of the fireplace the boy's black curls gleamed with a special luster. His slate eyes twinkled. He puffed out his cheeks and shook the cow, then reached behind him and picked up a carved wooden pig and handed it to Lion. "Hi," he said. "Play moo?"

"Hi." Lion looked down at the pig, back to the boy. "What's your name?"

"Doozie. Hi. You play moo?" He shoved the cow toward Lion's face and laughed. "Moo! Moo?"

Eve's gown rustled as she crossed the room and scooped up James Ruell. "You can tell your friend I will do as my father wishes," she

said, her right hand protectively covering the back of her son's head.
"I will dismiss his nanny and the cleaning woman for the time
being."

"Eve." Lion's voice was strained. "He's—"

"As for Vernon," Eve hurried on, interrupting him, "you had best
keep him locked in one of the servant's rooms. He drinks. I would
hate to trust him with instructions of any importance."

"Eve!" Lion rasped, standing and reaching for her.

"This is my son," Eve continued, her voice edging on hysteria.
"Clifford Sarandon and I were married shortly after you left, and
James Ruell was born . . . This is . . ." She stopped and, terrified,
stared at the doorway where Miles Ryan had appeared.

"My, my." The horrid grin disappeared as Miles worked a piece of
gristle out of the meat he was chewing and spit it on the floor.
"Man, woman, and child standing before a blazing hearth. How picturesque."

"Get the hell out of here," Lion growled without looking back.

Miles refused to be cowed. "So you can have your way with the
Yankee lady? Now, Colonel McKenna? When the nigger is loading
the table with food?" There was no humor in his laughter. "I want
someone to watch my back while I eat."

"I'll be along."

"I'll wait."

Lion's hand fell toward the revolver holstered at his waist as he
spun.

Miles's hand dropped to the dragoon, stopped and waited. "No
sense in it, McKenna." His eyes flicked toward Eve and the boy in a
silent threat. "We are linked by necessity. Think. How tragic, after
four long years of war, to die by the hand of a fellow countryman."
The same flat laughter spread over the room. "Certainly you share
my sentiment."

"Boom!" James said, making his fist into a gun. He pointed at
Lion. "Boom!" he giggled. "Mama. Will you tell a story, Mama?"

"Hush, son," Eve said quickly, pressing him to her.

The look Miles gave the boy made Lion shiver. "Very well," he
said, shaken. He placed himself between Miles and James as he
walked toward the door. "By the way," he said, turning to Eve.
"Where is Clifford?"

"He was killed at Bull Run in the summer of sixty-one."

"I'm sorry. What regiment was he with?"

"Soldiers always ask that question right after they've said, 'I'm sorry.'" Eve sighed. "He wasn't in the army. He was a civilian, there to watch. I was with him. He was shot in the thigh and bled to death on the way back to Washington. James Ruell is all I have left of him."

Lion studied her. "The summer of sixty-one, eh?"

"Coming?" Miles called from the stairwell.

"Yes, damn it!" Lion blinked, squeezed his eyes closed, then opened them. "I may be a bastard, Eve," he said quietly. "But I'm not a blind bastard."

The door closed gently behind him. Eve held her son in a tight embrace and rocked him back and forth. When the tears began to form in the corners of her eyes she fought for control of her emotions. It was a minor victory at best.

The dream returned to plague him now. The fever he had carried for the past week raging inside him, Lion woke. The night was filled with the banshee warning of the wind. Miles slept in a lounge chair, one of Sewal Blackheath's fowling guns cradled across his lap. Lion stole soundlessly past him and into the hall, glanced at the shadowy staircase, then crept down the hall to the front door. His eyes burned. Rubbing them did not help. He clutched his woolen coat about his body and listened. Outside, he was sure he could hear music, a wedding song of long ago.

The music faded when he opened the door and stepped onto the porch. The cold pressed against the furnace of his cheeks, froze the sweat on his forehead. Lion walked down the steps, onto the firm, unyielding ground, where the night waited to embrace him. The wind howled, punished him with its wild turbulence. He pressed on, moving away from the house. Something was there, waiting. Lion blinked. The shape of a man—was he dreaming?—glided ahead of him, leading him toward the cliff's edge. High above, clouds scudded across the sky and dappled the ground with clumps of shadows.

Equally restless, Eve watched from her window as Lion ambled alone toward the cliffs. The moaning currents of darkness made her shiver. Why this night foray? she wondered. Lion paused and she held her breath. When he continued she breathed again. A gray, ghostly figure in the shadowed moonlight, he moved with disconcerting purpose, as if summoned. Long ago, her heart raging with love, she had watched for him from another window. She saw him now, but a lifetime separated them. Michael's lifetime. Lion had killed Michael. Twice.

Behind her, James Ruell stirred. Frightened, she had brought him into her room for the night. She glanced at him asleep in her bed, then back to his father on the heights. What did he seek? What drove him forth? What kept her at the window, sentinel for him?

She could not tell, at a distance, that he was trembling, that the dream image he so feared was speaking to him, calling his name.

"Lion?" The voice in his head was sharp, peremptory.

Lion swung around. The wind slapped his shoulders, bore into his spine like a hurled javelin of carved ice. The darkness shimmered, dissolved in bone-pale light. The shrieking wind—was it the wind that called his name?—curled around him. Sweat stung his eyes. He brushed a sleeve across his face before the moisture froze. He was freezing. He burned.

"Lionnnn . . ."

Did a shape move, there in the trees? For a moment he thought he saw a monstrous horseman bearing down on him, but the apparition dissipated, dissolved. A trick. Nothing but sculpted moonlight, shadowy stubstance.

"Lioooonnnnn!"

The wind buffeted his chest now, whirled, and surrounded him. A cold energy engulfed him, sucked the heat from him. The dream that had chased him from sleep and driven him from the house called him yet.

"What?" he screamed. "Who is it? Damn you! Who are you?"

The dream came to life. A hallucination so real as to appear lifelike stood in front of him: Michael, as he had on the day of the duel, only bloodless, translucent, at the edge of the cliff and eternity. Lion squinted, felt his heart thud inside his breast, as Michael raised his flintlock and counted. "One. Two. Three."

"You aren't real!" Lion cried, stumbling backward. "Please. Not again!" Lion threw aside his pistol. "I never wanted this," he shouted. "It was honor. War. Both, neither. What is a man without honor?"

Again the horrid laughter, cold as wind, mirthless as death. Michael's eyes blazed like live coals. His hair rose and streaked away from him like flashes made by guns fired in the night. His flesh followed, spectral streams of cells and sinew. Only the skeleton remained, stripped of clothes by the wind. "Kill me. Kill me. Kill me!" came the cry.

"No!" Lion howled, kicking the pistol away from him. The wind plucked at his voice, eroded the terrible skeleton now astride the spectral horse, until only the feet, resting in the stirrups, and the grinning skull remained. "What more do you want of me?" Lion whispered.

"Ten!" the gaping jaws mouthed, followed by the sound of a wracking groan as the spirit horse reared and bolted across the lawn and into the woods. In its wake, the wind eddied and moaned. "Father!" The word ballooned through his mind and collapsed, victim of the wind and the night. "Eve!"

Lion staggered back from the precipice and the froth-capped tumult below. He echoed the dream ghost, and his voice was kin to the suffering dead who want desperately to reach for life, to return from the stygian stillness that is neither life nor death, but loneliness and emptiness and incompleteness.

"Eve!" Lion called, his voice ransomed by the storm, lost to the gale as he collapsed.

Chapter 36

Lieutenant Colonel Jack Travis propped his boots on his desk, teetered backward in his chair, and laced his fingers together behind his head. It was just past ten o'clock and he'd finished the day's work. The next order of business was to figure out how to spend the rest of the day. His good right eye inspected the shine on his boots, traveled around the room searching for something that needed being done. Nothing, he thought sourly. Only an hour earlier he'd read the message sent to all local commanders informing them that Grant had broken Petersburg's defenses and was advancing on Richmond. As he had predicted the war would be over for everyone before too much longer. There was nothing of importance left for a man with one half of his face gone. Until two o'clock, at least, when he was supposed to catch the train for Boston in order to have dinner that night with his commanding general. Bored, he scratched underneath his patch, nearly lost his balance, and swung his feet to the floor in time to save himself from a spill at the same moment that an overweight second lieutenant knocked and entered. "Two men here to see you, sir," Lieutenant Broudette said, saluting with a broad plump hand.

"Who?"

"I can't say, sir. Never seen them before."

"Soldiers?"

"No, sir."

"Ship captains?"

"Civilians, sir. A Mister Harold Eliot and a Mister Jon Naslund."

"Jon Naslund?" Jack pushed his chair back from the desk. "Show them in."

Eliot entered first, followed by Jon. The clerk wore an immaculately tailored coat and matching pale green trousers. Jon stood uncomfortably in a black frock coat borrowed from his oldest son. "Lieutenant Colonel Travis?" Eliot asked, nervously looking around the office.

"Yes, yes. Welcome, both of you." Jack shook Eliot's hand, moved to Jon. "Jon and I are old campaigners together, eh, Jon?"

"*Ja,*" Jon answered, relaxing visibly as he pumped Jack's hand. "That was some fun, Colonel."

"Battle of Washington. Caught them by surprise from the rear. Jon here constituted our reserves." Jack laughed as he showed his visitors to seats in front of his desk. "Cigar?" he asked, opening a box on his desk and shoving it toward them.

Eliot, who knew of course about the Admiral Cabell incident shook his head no. Jon helped himself to three, and slid two of them into his coat pocket before accepting a light from Jack.

"Thank you, sir," the Swede said, crossing his beamthick legs. He folded his arms and puffed contentedly at the cigar.

Curious, Jack thought, taking his place behind the desk and assessing his visitors as he lit his cigar. He glanced at his calendar. Nine days earlier Eve had rejected his proposal, and now she had sent her clerk and foreman to see him. Interesting. Very interesting. "So!" he finally said, shaking out his match. "How may I help you?"

"Mrs. Sarandon sent us to handle certain problems involving a shipment of four boilers we've bought from the Newsome Foundry," Eliot said.

Jack leaned back in his chair. "Boilers hardly concern me, gentlemen."

"No. Of course. Uh . . ." Eliot coughed nervously. "This is rather out of line for us, Colonel," he blurted out, looking to Jon for support.

"Come on, man. Out with it. This is a military office, and I do have other pressing matters." Travis chuckled inwardly. The most pressing business he could think of was how to word the draft of his letter of resignation.

"Yes, sir." Eliot took a deep breath. "We're here on a matter concerning Mrs. Sarandon."

Who with some finality informed me I could go on my way, Jack thought, with a touch of bitterness. "Is something the matter with Eve?" he asked, almost clinically. "Is she ill?"

"No, sir."

"Then what, man? Be quick about it."

"What Eliot is trying to say, Colonel Travis, is that Miss Eve is not ill, but more peculiar like," Jon said, taking over. "I've been around the girl since she was but a plump babe, and can read her many moods like I read the weather."

"Peculiar?" Jack asked.

"For the past week and a half. Two days after we launched the *Andrew Jackson* she told Maisie not to come to the house until further notice. Same with the other maid. Since then, except for Miss Eve and her driver, old Jubb, no one sees any of the household."

"It's more than that," Eliot chimed in. "From that same time, she's taken almost no interest in the yards. It's as if something weighed heavily on her mind. Doctor Cutcheon drove up to Dawn Wind from town three days ago, but was told that Mr. Blackheath and Miss Eve were busy and couldn't be bothered. He never got past the front door. I myself tried to talk to her Saturday, but got no farther than the amenities before she sent me and Jon here to Portland." The clerk fidgeted anxiously. "Don't you see, sir? I know nothing about boilers and neither does Jon. If anyone was going to come it should have been Beckham. He's the one—"

Travis waved the man silent. "Mrs. Sarandon is a friend of mine, gentlemen, but friendship does not grant me permission to interfere in her affairs." He held up his hand as Eliot's mouth opened. "No, no. Let me finish. I know Mrs. Sarandon as a very strong-willed woman. You've described her as nervous and agitated, perhaps a bit absentminded. But both Jon and I have seen her that way before, haven't we, Jon?"

"You mean in Washington?" Jon asked.

"Of course."

Jon's hands knotted together. *"Ja,"* he said. "Maybe. But maybe not. That was different."

"Nonsense. I'm sure she has a reason for her actions. Some good reason, no doubt."

The Swede shook his head slowly. His bright blue eyes never left Travis's. "No. I think you are wrong, Colonel Travis. Miss Eve is frightened."

"Naslund!" Eliot snapped.

Travis straightened in his seat. His brows furrowed in concern. "What?"

Eliot glared at Jon, who paid him no attention. "She is," Jon continued. "By God, I tell you I know this girl from a pup. I know when she is frightened."

"Have you told anyone else about this?" Travis asked.

"Really, Colonel," Eliot protested. "I don't think—"

"Be quiet. Have you, Mr. Naslund?"

"Only Eliot. We both see it, but don't talk about it until Doctor Cutcheon say something first."

"Very well." Jack leaned back and closed his eyes. His hand toyed with the black velvet mask that hid the left side of his face. Perhaps Eve was in trouble. But more than likely she wasn't. She had been extremely nervous and secretive prior to the raid on Admiral Cabell's office. In all likelihood she was planning a new venture. One that Jack Travis, he thought bitterly, would be excluded from. Still . . . "When are you returning to New Forest?" he asked abruptly.

"Tomorrow morning," Eliot answered.

"Good." Jack stood, ready to bring the interview to an end. "I suggest you return as soon as your business here is concluded, and keep an eye on her."

"And you will come to see her yourself?" Naslund asked.

"I'll have to check my schedule," Jack said, shaking hands with Eliot. He grasped Jon's calloused hand. The two men's eyes locked. Naslund wanted a definite answer. Jack smiled reassuringly. "Yes," he said, compelled by the Swede's solid grip and troubled expression. "I will come to see her myself."

"Good." Relieved, Naslund led the way out.

Alone, Travis removed a pint of Scotch whiskey from the bottom drawer of his desk and poured a double shot into his coffee cup. What Eve did was none of his business anymore, he thought, swirling the Scotch around in the cup before drinking half of it. Ten days earlier he would have been on the next train, but now he had to consider the very real possibility that she didn't want him interfering with her life under any circumstances. Still, if she were frightened by something . . . But what? Or perhaps, more properly, who? "Broudette!"

The corpulent lieutenant bulged in the doorway. "Yes, sir?"

"What's my schedule for the week?"

"One moment, sir." Broudette disappeared a moment, reentered the room carrying an appointment calendar. "Here you are, Colonel. Tomorrow's the fourth. You have lunch with the mayor's council. Thursday is General Tomlinson's inspection tour. Friday the seventh you have dinner with Miss Amelia Goff and her father. Saturday the eighth is the all-day meeting with the Canadian Commission on Navigation for the provinces, and Sunday afternoon Mr. William Howze and the Board of Directors is hoping you'll join them for the opening of the Militaria Exhibit."

"Hmmm. Trapped. And next week?"

"Nothing until Thursday, sir."

"Good," he said, taking out his wallet and extracting a bill. If Eve was in trouble perhaps he would be able to help. As he had once before. "Have one of the corporals book me a seat on the Boston Flyer for Monday afternoon, please. I'll be getting off in New Forest."

Miles Ryan stood in the doorway of the barn and looked toward the house. Monday the third. Damn. If McKenna hadn't caved in they would have been in Canada by now. Miles rubbed his forehead, considered the possibilities. McKenna had looked strong enough that morning. A day or two more, maybe three, and they could be on their way. They were so close to Canada and freedom that it made him nervous. The last thing he wanted was to jeopardize his chances. Nothing to do now but see that the horses were fat and healthy. They were good stock. Shouldn't be much trouble . . . He heard movement behind him, turned, and in a fluid motion leveled the shotgun at Vernon, who was attacking a pile of hay with his pitchfork. "You wishing that hay was me, Bluebelly?"

Vernon paused, scratched his Adam's apple. His flesh looked pale beneath the stubble of a week-old beard. His cheeks were discolored by tiny explosions of blood vessels. He had not had a drink in too damned long. "Just pitchin' hay, Johnny Reb," Vernon said, licking his lips. "Like I was ordered."

Ryan's grimace wracked his face. His teeth flashed. "It's not over yet," he said. "Long as I am standing here and you are standing there, the war continues. The struggle endures . . ." His eyes dulled. What was the point of wasting rhetoric on this human relic? Killing him would be easier than talking to him. Ryan walked the length of the stable and, satisfied the horses were in excellent condition, took up his position in the front doorway and waited for Vernon to finish his chores.

Spring was definitely on its way. Patches of snow still lurked in low, shady spots, but most of it had melted off. Crocuses and daffodils were beginning to peek out of the ground. The lilacs were trying to bud, and the moss on the trees was turning a bright green. Miles led Vernon back to the house and locked the back door behind him, then wandered around to the front where Sewal was sitting on the porch taking the sun.

"Nice day, isn't it?" Miles grinned, leaning the shotgun within Sewal's grasp before lighting a cigar. Sewal stared at the shotgun, one of the two that remained. Miles had smashed the others. "Cigar?" Miles asked, offering Sewal one of the Havanas he'd taken from the humidor on Sewal's desk. "No? Too bad. Nice cigar. Best I've had in a long time. Hard to get tobacco during a war, don't you know?"

Sewal grunted, wheeled his chair a foot or two farther away from the shotgun. Miles laughed. "Very smart, Mister Blackheath. Very smart." He leaned against the porch railing and puffed on his cigar. "Magnificent, isn't it? My compliments to you, again. You've created a remarkable Olympus here."

"There were others before me," Sewal said, his voice rasping through the anger that almost choked him. "All Blackheaths. I added on some, kept the rest from washing into the ocean."

Miles shook his head. "I never had a home this nice. My wife and I lived above her brother's tavern. Not a boisterous place, mind you. Gentlemen came there to wager in quiet dignity and drink fine liquor and keep discreet company. Oh, we were comfortable. I taught school. My wife, too, until the diphtheria took her in fifty-eight. I kept the place with our son, Augustine."

"Named for the saint, no doubt," Sewal said, the sarcasm in his voice barely concealed.

"You are an educated man, sir. But of course you would be. You see, I wanted my son to be a thinker, a man of speculation, a philosopher among warriors. Saint Augustine by all means. And tell me, Mister Blackheath, are you a believer in free will?"

"Every man makes himself what he is," Sewal replied testily. "Take you, for example. You have the demeanor of a man of breeding, yet you obviously have chosen a different course." He paused for emphasis. "That of a vicious animal who enjoys bullying women and harmless alcoholics like Vernon."

"Don't forget crippled old men," Miles added, blowing a blue cloud of smoke that the wind whipped away. "Tell me, Mister Blackheath. Think carefully. Does a boy of eight have free will?"

"He does if he looks for it. My children had it to spare." Weary of the strange Southerner's company, Sewal wheeled himself along the porch.

Miles followed him. "What if the child is trampled into muddy rags beneath the horses of mounted Yankee troops?" he asked, pulling Sewal around to face him. "What then, Mister Blackheath?"

Sewal's eyes closed briefly. "Then he is dead, Mister Ryan," he answered at last, his voice softened by a note of sympathy. "Dead like my own son. Dead and far beyond this or any other conversation, petty or well meaning."

Creases spread over Miles's face. Grinning, crying, emotions indistinguishable. "But not beyond revenge. Revenge reaches past the grave. It soothes and frees."

"No!" Sewal shook his head, looked into the blazing eyes no farther than a foot from his own. "You are mad to say that."

"You've read Shakespeare?"

"I have."

"Then you know madmen often make the most sense." As if the strange spell that held him had been broken, Miles straightened and walked to the edge of the porch. "Well, well, well." He shielded his eyes and looked down the drive toward the land bridge connecting Dawn Wind to the mainland. "Your remarkable daughter is on her way home. I always feel better when we're gathered together." He walked to the front door and paused to glance at Sewal. "War is an amazing phenomenon, Mister Blackheath. It strips away all our noblest, useless philosophies, and leaves us with but one, indisputable ideology."

A band seemed to tighten around Sewal's chest. "And that is?" he asked, knowing full well he'd be told anyway.

"An eye for an eye, Mister Blackheath." Miles opened the door and stepped inside. Before it swung shut, Sewal heard James Ruell Sarandon calling for his grandpa to come play with him. Suddenly, Sewal Blackheath no longer felt warm in the spring sun.

Lion woke from a frozen circle of ashes that splotched the snow-covered ground of a field he could not name. He had been surrounded by nameless men, and though he had ordered them to move away from him, they had remained, motionless statues of flesh.

Thump . . .

A ball bounced off the foot of the bed and rolled across the floor where Eve's son scooped it up and held it out for Lion's examination. "Grampa won't play. See. You want to play?"

The heaving turbulence in his head was gone. Lion smiled and held out his hand as the boy approached and handed him a gaily painted wooden ball. "That's a very pretty ball," Lion said. "Is it yours?"

"Yes, sir." James Ruell shook his head and smiled. His gray eyes twinkled with a merriment Lion thought no longer existed in the world. Surprised to find some of it still in himself, Lion smiled back. James laughed and clapped his hands. He crawled onto the bed next to Lion. "Why are you in bed?"

Lion sat up and punched the pillows into a wad behind his back. "I've been sick," he said, mentally ticking off the days. It was close to a week since the night he had fallen unconscious on the bluff. Eustacia had brought him his food, he remembered, and had fed him, spooning soup into his mouth and forcing him to drink gallons of hot tea. Eve had come, too, and sat with him, he was sure. Dimly, he recalled her hand reaching out to touch his brow and change the cool, wet cloth, or to bathe his face and arms during the height of the fever. Once he thought he had seen her lean toward him and felt her press her cheek against the fevered flesh of his jaw. Or had he dreamed that?

"You're funny lookin'," James said, leaning against Lion's outstretched legs.

"So are you."

"Am not."

" 'Fraid so. You look like this." Lion screwed up his face, pulled the corners of his mouth wide with his thumbs, pushed his ears forward with his forefingers, and stuck out his tongue.

The boy squealed with delight. "Well, you look like this," he retorted, trying to match Lion's creation and managing to get his fingers all mixed up.

"Good gosh, we both look pretty funny, don't we?"

"Yeah," James giggled. He pointed toward the light-filled window. "Wanna go outside?"

"I don't think I'd better."

"How come?"

"Not allowed," Lion said seriously. "I'm still weak from being sick."

"Will you when you're better?" James asked anxiously.

"Sure." Lion grinned. God, he felt marvelous, all of a sudden. It wasn't just the waning fever, either. Something more positive. A child's ingenuous smile, his natural warmth, his sweetness, and untarnished sense of humor. Above all, the war had passed by him and left him unharmed. There had been too much of death, of pain, of carnage, of destruction. But there was this dark-haired, gray-eyed boy too. And if his existence didn't balance the grief and sadness, at least it offered hope. "You bet I will," Lion said around the ache in his throat. "I'd like that."

The boy brightened, squirmed into a newer, more comfortable position. "Did you know my daddy?" he asked, off on a completely different subject.

"Once," Lion answered softly. He tousled James's head. "A long time ago." He looked up and saw Eve standing in the doorway.

"Mommy!" James yelled. He rolled off the bed, hit the floor at a dead run, and crashed into Eve.

"Mama told you not to come in this room," Eve gently scolded, hugging him.

"But we were just playing," he said, as if that were explanation enough.

"You must mind Mama, and not bother Mister McKenna. He's been sick, and probably doesn't want—"

"But we're friends!"

Eve grasped him by the shoulders. "James Ruell, are you going to mind your mama?"

"Yes, ma'am," James mumbled, his face long. He glanced back wistfully at Lion.

"Now, why don't you see if Pa-paw Jubb has a present," Eve went on in a conciliatory tone. "He's in the kitchen with Eustacia, and I *think* he brought you something from town."

"Yeah?" James asked, brightening. "What?"

Eve laughed. "*That* you'll have to see for yourself, young man. Now run along," she said, steering him out the door. "And be careful on the stairs!" She closed the door behind her and walked to the bed. "I'm sorry. I told him not to bother you."

"My God, do you really think I minded?" Lion asked. "What did Jubb bring him?"

Eve shrugged. "He'll think of something. Your color is better."

"I didn't think you cared that much," Lion said, concentrating on the ball James had left behind.

"The sooner well, the sooner departed," Eve said.

"A well-deserved retort, no doubt," Lion said sourly. "Still, it was good of you to nurse me."

Eve's eyes left his and she moved toward the foot of the bed. "Eustacia did most of the work," she said, bending to pick up some of Michael's old clothes that had fallen to the floor. They'd fit loosely but were an improvement over the farmer's rags Lion had arrived in. Her stiff, pale-blue gown rustled whispers as she sat on a plushly upholstered Sleepy Hollow armchair near the window. The late afternoon glow illuminated her prominent cheekbones and pale-blue eyes.

Lion was still unused to her tightly drawn chignon. He remembered a cascade of soft, golden curls. And the fragile, splendid moments they had shared. "Very well, Eve," he said softly. "I give Eustacia her due."

"She'd appreciate it if you told her yourself."

"I will."

They'd run out of conversation. The silence between them was measured by the loud ticking of the clock on the dresser. "Well!" Lion said, startling her. "So how long have I been in bed?"

"You asked me that once before," Eve said.

"I don't recall the answer. My brain feels like an old, cobweb-lined hallway. Each day sheds a ltitle more brightness and sweeps away a little more dust."

"Ten days. Today is the third."

Lion nodded. "Of April."

Eve didn't react. He leaned back against the headboard. The lean muscles of his chest and shoulders and arms, though weakened by the fever, still looked as if they possessed the wiry strength of ash or hickory.

Eve took a deep breath. "I want you to tell me about Michael," she said suddenly. "You killed him, didn't you?"

"Yes." Lion wondered how she knew. He had dreaded this moment, but once it was upon him, experienced a sense of relief. "There was a battle. Nothing major, just a bloody . . ." He paused. That hadn't been how he'd meant to start. In the hundred times he'd imagined this conversation, he had begun with—what? Only the image of the afternoon was left him, and that was mixed in with uncounted other afternoons when men had met and blood had been spilled. "The Yanks trapped us. You may remember the man who led them. A fellow by the name of Travis, Michael's best man. At any rate, the Federals took us by surprise. Men died. Quite a few of them. We were outnumbered, beaten really. My command scattered. Michael pursued me into the hills. When my horse went down he caught me—" The memory was so painfully vivid. Michael had called Eve's name as he fell. Lion forced himself to go on. "I didn't know it was him. Not until after," he finished in a low voice.

"Would it have made any difference?" Eve asked faintly.

"I'd like to think so, but probably not. I'm not sure whether it was accident or fate or Michael's planning that brought us together that day, but I'm convinced that he wanted me dead, that he was consumed with the thought. There was no way for me to avoid it. Oh, hell—" Lion stopped, rubbed his forehead. "One of us had to die, Eve. If he had shouted his name to the heavens, I would still have fought to stay alive. I did go back that evening to bury him, but his body had been taken away. I suppose by the Yankees he'd been riding with. I did go back, believe it or not."

"Why shouldn't I?" Eve asked. "Thank you."

Lion sat quietly, waiting for more. Eve hadn't moved, simply stared out the window. "And that's all?" Lion finally asked. "Thank you?"

Eve's voice was low, barely audible. "I wanted to hear how my brother died. Now I have."

"Yes." Lion thought of all the details he'd omitted, considered them best left that way. Again he waited, again was compelled to break the silence. "You intrigue me, Eve."

"Oh?"

"This veneer, this lack of passion. I expected more. You are so grave."

"These are grave days."

"I know. Still, I wonder. The Eve I remember wasn't a woman to hide her feelings behind veils of self-control. The Eve I remember never pretended to be so coldly unemotional."

"Did you expect me to rant and rave?" Eve snapped. "Is strength in a woman that difficult for you to accept?" Her eyes glittered brightly, and she leaned toward him. "I assure you, sir, you misunderstand me."

"Ah, I detect an ember of the fire that was." Lion's gray eyes flashed, a storm flecked with lightning. Finished with the conversation, Eve stood and stalked toward the door.

"I love you, Eve."

Eve stopped, her back to him. Pages of Lion's journal, found in his clothes, flashed through her mind. *Is there not one tiny, dusty corner of your heart left for the Rebel who loved you?* "Don't," she whispered.

"I've loved you all along. I never stopped. Why didn't you come with me, that day?"

"Please!"

"You can't imagine what it was like. Death, disease, hunger, thirst, heat to boil the blood and cold to freeze it. Sometimes I think loving you was the only thing that kept me sane through the past four years, Eve. God knows, there wasn't much else to sustain me."

Eve rested her head against the door. She heard him slide from the bed. His bare feet scuffed against the hardwood floor. "Eve . . ."

"No!" She threw open the door and plunged down the hall into her room.

"Aha! Intercourse with the enemy is a crime punishable by a firing squad," Miles said from the stairway. Disembodied, his head rose, grew torso and legs as he loomed in the hall, his size increased by the dim light and the power of holding a house at bay. "I'm going to have to keep a closer watch on you."

Lion held onto the side of the door, stared at the bolts that had been attached to Eve's bedroom door. Miles read his mind. "A precaution. I had the butler and the old nigger install them downstairs too. And nail shut the windows for good measure. You weren't up to your share of sentry duty." He followed Lion into his room. "Looks to me like you're well enough," he added, watching critically as Lion tottered to his bed.

"Nearly," Lion said, sitting heavily before he fell. "I'm still weak."

"Of course. But not for long." He checked the room, found everything to his liking. "I'd leave a gun up here, but that nigger cook might take it from you."

"I'll be up and about pretty soon," Lion grunted, stretching out on the bed. His legs were trembling from the short walk across the room and back again. "A few days' exercise ought to do it."

"It won't be an easy trip. You'll need all the strength you can get. We've pressed our luck for this long. A few more days won't hurt."

"You sound pretty confident," Lion sighed, glad to be off his feet. He felt lightheaded, but at least the room had quit spinning.

"Why shouldn't I?" Miles laughed. "The Blackheaths are on our side. Long as that boy's around, anyways."

Lion propped himself on his elbows. "And just what the hell's that supposed to mean?" he asked.

The grimace transformed Miles's face. "Nothing, I guess. Only that this family is extra careful where he's concerned. They don't want him getting hurt. Natural enough. They don't know what suffering is. The only way they even know there's a war being fought is when money pours in for a new gunboat." He shook his head, squinted. His eyes were red and vague with distress. "It isn't fair, you know. We have suffered loss. Strife has scarred our souls. And these . . . this household turns healthy and proud bodies to the sun. They ought to experience what we have. They ought to learn pain, I say. They deserve—"

"That's enough!" Lion snapped. He stared intently at Miles. "No harm shall come to this house, do you hear?"

Miles chuckled, backed a step. "I was not speaking of the house, Colonel, sir," he said, mockingly. "Though it's an intriguing notion."

"And none to the Blackheaths—any of them—or their servants."

"The boy—"

"Especially the boy. Leave him out of this, Miles."

Ryan's eyes closed and he swayed back and forth. When he finally spoke his voice came from far away, as if he was in another world or time. "Augustine was a boy too, Colonel. Just a boy." His head shook slowly from side to side and his face contorted in pain. "Just a boy. And now he's gone."

"Miles! Listen to me, Miles!" Ryan jerked as if slapped. His eyes opened and he looked around to get his bearings. "No harm will come to the boy," Lion insisted gently. "Especially the boy. Do you understand?"

"Yes. Of course." Miles smiled. "But it is an effective threat. We certainly didn't come this far to make war on children. Still, as Shakespeare put it, there is a special providence in the fall of a sparrow." He nodded at his own wisdom. "Every educated man should have at his command a few memorable lines of Shakespeare. I'll send up one of the niggers with your supper. Afternoon, Colonel."

Lion lay back, folded his hands on his stomach, and stared at the ceiling. He looked to be daydreaming, but in truth his mind was racing through a thousand scenarios, each of which led to an intolerable conclusion. In succumbing to an overwhelming desire to see Eve again he had brought the stark possibility of tragedy to Dawn Wind. His threats of violence had been an act to insure himself a safe retreat, but Miles Ryan was capable of carrying out not only Lion's false threats but a deadly vengeance of his own creation. Speaking softly to himself, Lion concluded the passage Miles had begun. "If it be now, 'tis not to come; if it be not to come, it will be now; if it be not now, yet it will come; the readiness is all." Whatever else happened, it was plain he would have to keep a watchful eye on Miles Ryan until they were able to leave.

The curtains shimmered from a rising breeze. Gulls called and cried and circled in their endless wind dance. Lion listened to his heart beating. At last he rolled onto his side, swung his legs over the edge of the bed, and made himself stand. The Sleepy Hollow armchair by the window was his first goal. Letting go the bed, he took one step, then another. His knees threatened to give out and his legs trembled. The room spun, and he weaved like a drunken man. But he walked.

Chapter 37

Eve couldn't remember a more harrowing, disquieting week. All rules, all conventions, reality itself had been suspended from that moment she had seen Lion's face in the stables. At first she was merely stunned, but as the hours passed she found herself experiencing a bewildering array of emotions. Anger was one of the first. As anger faded there was confusion and fear and even terror. Why had he come? Who was the strange, evil man who accompanied him? What was Lion going to do? At one moment he was gentle and seemed glad to see her. The next he was harsh and threatening. Late that night, as she watched from the window and saw him fall to the frozen ground, a whole new set of emotions raged through her. And for better or worse, she ran downstairs, waked Captain Ryan, and helped carry the unconscious Lion back into the house.

The next days passed as if in a dream. Quickly, she told Maisie she wouldn't be needed for the next week, perhaps two. The yards lost all interest for her, and she found herself fighting to keep her mind on the simplest matters. At home or away she worried herself almost to illness about her son. Away, she fought to retain a semblance of normalcy. At home, she made herself walk and talk as if nothing out of the ordinary were happening. Somehow she managed. She kept Sewal from antagonizing Captain Ryan. She calmed Eustacia. She joked with Pole. She played more than ever with James Ruell, and tried to keep him always out of sight of Ryan. And in between, she found herself drawn more and more often to the guest bedroom. There, for the first four days, Lion tossed and turned and burned. There, against her will, Eustacia nursed him. There, uncertain, fearful, tender, Eve bathed Lion with cool cloths, sat for midnight hours at his side and tried, without success, to look into herself.

At last he rallied. Wednesday night he broke into a profuse sweat. By morning the fever was gone. Thursday and Friday he could barely move. By Saturday he was holding a cup by himself, and on Monday morning he stood for the first time. From that moment on his strength increased daily until he was walking up and down stairs and, indeed, all over the grounds. By Saturday, April 8, he announced that he was well. That evening, with everyone locked inside the house, he and Miles had sat on the front porch and discussed the next stage of their escape. And Eve, her eyes red with barely controlled tears, retired to her room with James for the night.

Sunday promised to be a quiet day. Shortly after dawn, when Vernon was left out to take care of the horses, Eve received permission to take a walk. With James still asleep in her bed, she wrapped a cloak about her and left the house. A mackerel sky and northeast winds were sure signs of a coming storm. Still the morning was bright as Eve walked down the front drive to the stairs overlooking the boat house, and began to wander along the edge of the cliff.

Lion had never been far from her thoughts. In the months after he left Dawn Wind, and all during her marriage to Clifford, he was a constant presence. After Clifford's death, when Eve returned to Dawn Wind, his memory had haunted her, for he lurked in every room, behind every tree, and always in James's eyes, which looked so much like his. Only after she took over the shipyards had she been busy enough to put him aside, and even then, fleeting images and brief whispers, heard because she had never truly stopped listening, intruded at odd moments. Rarely, during lonely hours when she was weary of the responsibilities of the ships and the yard, almost palpable memories of his touch tormented her. And always she wondered if he lived, and if he thought of her.

The morning winds swirled the thick folds of her skirt and whipped her cloak. Eve rounded the point, paused in her walk to stare out over the Atlantic, where lowering clouds rose from the horizon. Here she and Lion had walked the night of Michael's wedding. Here, early one September morning, they had shared a sunrise whose dazzling beauty mirrored their love. Eve reached inside her cloak, removed Lion's journal, and opened it at random.

FRIDAY, October 14, 1864. Hiding in Virginia.
Trees like corpses, limbs dismembered, trunks charred and splintered. Smoke impales itself on shattered branches. There is no beauty here. I hunger for beauty, for simple things. I have drunk from too many bloody creeks. The salt taste cannot be washed away. I have tried. I do not think trees will bloom again in this gap.
Madness grows. Beauty withers on the vines of war.

Eve. I have written another letter. Another after another after another, all unsent. What has honor and pride left us? For me, loneliness. And for you, Eve? In whose arms do you dance? Did we ever dance? Yes. At the wedding. Poor Michael. His death has sealed the last of my hopes in the sepulchre of despair. Were I to find you again, never could you love your brother's killer. And I would have to tell you. That is the horrible reality for me. Like a fool, I cling to memories of you. To lose them is to drown in the hopeless debauchery of death that surrounds me.

Are you married? Is there not one tiny, dusty corner of your heart left for the Rebel who loved you, who was driven from your arms by honor and duty? Centuries lie between us. Still, I reach. And my heart reaches . . .

Eve closed the journal for a moment and gazed down at the sea ledge draped in a mantle of olive rockweed flourishing amid bone-white striations of stone. A moment later, she opened it again and let the wind flip through pages.

FRIDAY, July 3, 1863. Virginia.
Sanders dead. Concussion. Bastard bluebellies! Robbed potato patch.

WEDNESDAY, November 4, 1863. ??
Have ridden for three nights. Circled Yankee lines. Everyone has a full belly for the first time in a month. No dead, except one Yank killed by my own hands.

THURSDAY, November 26, 1863.
Southern Tennessee.
Fought a holding action. Thanksgiving.

WEDNESDAY, February 10, 1864. Hiding.
Took a Yank patrol by surprise this morning. They broke. We lost two men. The Yanks will be back with ten men for the five they left behind. There are none to replace the men I lost. I fear the end has begun. I don't know this place. We may be in Virginia, maybe Tennessee, or even Kentucky again. Tired. So very tired, and hungry. To eat a full meal a day is to be lucky beyond belief. Dreamed of Eve last night. We were in a restaurant in New York City, I think. A

*waiter kept bringing in plates of food, which I devoured indis-
criminately, all the while staring at Eve, who sat across the table
from me and took nothing but a glass of water."*

And finally, the most poignant and painful of them all, the one to
which she had found herself returning over and over during the past
week.

THURSDAY, May 5, 1864. Hiding.
  Eve.

Suddenly cold, Eve tucked the journal inside her cloak and returned to the house. Ryan had ordered that the rear door be kept
barred from the outside, but feeling sure that Lion wouldn't allow him
to do anything to her, Eve removed the bar and entered the kitchen.
Hanson Pole stood in front of the stove and sipped at a cup of
coffee. Jubb and Vernon sat at the table, finishing theirs. None of the
men met her eyes, but studied the porcelain mugs they held. They
were arranged in a conspiracy, caught and held by Eve's accusatory
stare. "Where is Eustacia?" Eve asked, breaking the awkward silence.

"Upstairs with Master James," Pole finally answered after no one
spoke for a moment. "As you requested. She said . . . ah . . ."
Pole's face reddened as Eustacia entered and proved him a liar.

"I'm sorry, Miss Eve, but that man come and said he wanted to
take Doozie for a walk, and just up and took him before I could
make a move to stop him," Eustacia blurted, dabbing at her round,
ebony cheeks with her white apron.

The taste of fear spilled into Eve's mouth. "What man?" she
asked.

"Mister McKenna. I don't know where they went, or when they's
coming back. I told him—"

Eustacia went on, but Eve's relief that James wasn't with Ryan
was so great that she paid no attention to the actual words. No harm
would come to her son if he was with Lion, of that she felt sure.
"That's all right, Eustacia," she finally said, cutting the black woman
off. "James is safe enough."

"I don't like it," Eustacia harrumphed, eyeing the meager remains
of a meat pie that had been whole when she left the room.

"Going somewhere, Mr. Pole?" Eve asked. The butler had been

working himself toward the door. Eve's voice stopped him in his tracks, and her eyes held him riveted to the spot. "Well?" No one moved, no one spoke. Eve was even more sure that the men had been discussing something they didn't think she'd approve. "Is there something you want to say?"

Pole winced, avoided looking at Jubb and Vernon. "Ahh . . ." He sucked in a great breath. "Vernon plans to make a try for Miles Ryan. Jubb has agreed that something must be done, and has been talked into attacking Mr. McKenna. As neither of them would listen to reason, I resolved to help them in order to avert a catastrophe. I believe Jubb and I together can handle Mr. McKenna, if we act before he regains his full strength."

"No," Eve said without hesitation. "Ryan is constantly on his guard, and Mr. McKenna is stronger than you suspect. I won't have it. It's too dangerous."

Vernon snorted in disgust. "I told you," he said. "Women just ain't got the stomach for bloodshed."

Eve's face darkened. She leaned forward over the table, casting a shadow on the stable keeper. "While you are in this house," she said slowly, emphasizing each word, "you will do as I and my father order. Aggression toward these men might very well endanger my son, and I won't allow it. So help me God, I'll have you locked in the barn if you so much as talk of this again. Do you understand me?" She swung on Jubb, who withered beneath her stare. "Jubb. Don't listen to him."

"I only wanted to help, Miss Eve," the old man explained plaintively.

"I know." Eve's look softened, and she smiled warmly. "Thank you. I love you, Pa-paw Jubb," she said, patting his hand. "Mr. Pole?"

"Yes, ma'am."

"Please. Let's keep everything as close to normal as possible. They'll be gone soon, and then we can all relax. Eustacia?"

"Yes'm." Eustacia's tears mixed with the perspiration running down her cheeks.

Eve hugged her. "Don't worry. Everything will be all right," she said. The words sounded hollow, and false. "I promise you."

"Yes'm. I hope so."

Calm on the outside, but trembling inside, Eve left the room and climbed the stairs to the main floor. Thankful to find the hall empty, she closed the door and sagged against it, spent. She was not at all sure that everything would be all right. One hurdle after another, she thought, shuddering. If Vernon had tried to attack Miles Ryan, God only knew . . . She pushed the thought from her mind, took a deep breath, and stood straight. There was no time for weakness. Not on her part.

Miles's flat, tuneless whistle drifted in through the open front door. Eve stopped at the foot of the stairs and listened. The sound was without melody or rhythm, rather the discordant drone of a man who was lost in his own labyrinth of thoughts. Careful not to make a noise and attract his attention, she slipped into her father's room and closed the door behind her. "Did I disturb you?" she asked, as Sewal turned from the window.

"No. I'm grateful for the company. Far more enjoyable than my other visitors," he said.

"Captain Ryan?"

Sewal chuckled wryly. "Your mother and Michael, and all the many errors in judgment a man makes in his life. McKenna too."

"Lion?" Eve asked, astonished.

"Do we know any other McKennas?" Sewal said waspishly. He twisted the wheels on his chair so that he faced the window again. "I'm sorry. I find it as difficult to accept my own errors as I do those of others."

"We're all guilty at one time or another," Eve said, kneeling at Sewal's side and resting her arms and head on his lap.

"We talked some last night, McKenna and I. I told him the truth about the duel, that I could have stopped it, but didn't. Instead, I told Michael to fire early. Dr. Cutcheon wouldn't have stopped him. I wanted McKenna dead. It was one of those things that seemed right at the time, but later on . . ." His voice faded.

Eve looked up at her father. "What did he say?"

"Nothing. He stood here and looked out this window. There wasn't anything to see, except the lighthouse light. I was lying in the bed. Must've taken him a full minute before he even moved, and then he just stared at me like he'd never seen me before."

"And?" Eve prompted.

"And then he left. Never said a word. A strange thing, though. All the while we talked, he kept turning something in his hand. I kept trying to see what it was, but couldn't, except that it was brightly colored. Just before he left, I caught a glimpse of it as he slipped it in his pocket. I think it was that little wooden ball of James's. He knows the boy is his?"

"Yes," Eve replied in a voice that was barely audible.

"I thought so. You know that he's out with him now?"

"Yes," Eve repeated.

Sewal nodded. "A man should be allowed some time with his son. Especially if he is leaving."

A shudder passed through Eve. "That's why I came to talk to you," she said.

Sewal stroked her hair while Eve clung to him. "I have never seen you . . . vulnerable . . . since you were a little girl. But then, I tried to teach my children not to be vulnerable. Another mistake. Thank heavens, I failed." Sewal leaned forward and embraced Eve. They remained close, father and daughter, in the checkered sunlight.

Lion urged the horse to greater speed. "Sure you aren't afraid?" he said to the boy sharing the saddle with him.

"No. No. Run the horse!" James squealed. "Faster. Faster!"

The mare plunged forward as Lion's boot heels prodded her. Brown mane flying backward to sting the boy's face as he leaned forward, the horse thundered across the land bridge and toward the house. Trees blurred, gravel flew out behind them. James laughed uproariously. And so did Lion.

The Southerner reined in before the porch. Rosebud pawed the ground, snorted and blew, and appeared eager for more exercise. "We gonna ride some more?" James asked, not wanting to go in.

"Not today," Lion said. "Horse has had about enough, I'm afraid."

"Awww."

"You fit to ride like that, you're fit to ride to Canada," Miles said from the porch. He was leaning backward in his chair with his boots against the rail. His face crinkled in a humorless grin that exposed his stained, even teeth. An empty jar of canned plums sat on the railing. The rim of the jar was ringed with a half-dozen industrious, early bees exploring for sugar. "I read that men are taking to the hills. Let the god-damn railsplitter have Richmond for all the good it will do him. One more city isn't the war."

James shook the reins. "C'mon. Let's ride again."

Lion plucked him out of the saddle, and held him in front of him. "Nope. Horse is tired, James Ruell, and you are too. That's when accidents happen. Time to go inside. Eustacia has something good to drink and eat, I'll bet."

"But I wanna race. Please?"

"Down you go. Maybe later."

"Promise?"

"Yes."

James nodded and slid down, holding onto Lion until his feet touched the ground. He ran up the steps, stopped to stare at Miles a moment. Miles reached out and tousled the boy's black hair. "Something about that boy," he mused aloud, turning to Lion as James ran inside. "What do you suppose—" But Lion had already turned the mare away from the porch and was riding toward the corner of the house on his way to the stable. "Talkative, aren't you, Colonel," the Captain said, letting the chair drop forward and picking up the shotgun he'd left leaning against the post. "Not sure I like that a'tall, a'tall," he muttered, as he headed inside.

The door to Sewal's bedroom opened, and Eve exited as Miles came in through the front door. She glanced contemptuously at him and moved toward the stairs. Miles caught her by the arm.

"Your hand is on my arm," she said quietly.

Miles matched her stare. "Tomorrow's Monday. In the morning you will draw ten thousand dollars from the bank. Colonel McKenna and I will leave as soon as you return. I don't suppose I have to tell you, but maybe I'd better just to be on the safe side. You'll return alone, or there will be hell to pay."

"Your hand is on my arm," Eve repeated coldly. Miles grinned and released her. His hand settled on the butt of his revolver. "You'll have your money, Captain," Eve hissed. "And good riddance," she said over her shoulder as she started up the stairs. She meant what she said. Good riddance to that frightening and disturbed man. But what of Lion? He would leave too. Did she *want* him to leave?

The journal burned against her breast.

A hell of a way to spend a Sunday afternoon, Travis grumbled to himself, stepping out of his carriage in front of his office. The wind kicked up, spat dust into his face and over his dress uniform. He swore at the wind, at the Board of Directors of the Militaria Exhibit that was opening in less than an hour, and at himself. If he hadn't been so all-fired anxious to impress Harold Day he wouldn't have gone to the trouble to get the letter from Secretary of War Edwin M.

Stanton. And if he hadn't left it behind Saturday when he went home, he wouldn't have had to make the extra trip at the last moment on Sunday. Still, the war would be over before long, and Day had already hinted that a job offer might come soon after Travis's resignation. Jobs were going to be hard to find.

Travis banged through the front door, startling Corporal O'Hearn on the duty desk. The corporal jumped to attention and saluted. "Afternoon, Colonel. A wire just—"

"As you were, Corporal. Relax. I just need to pick up something." The whole place was quiet as a tomb. Jack's feet sounded unnaturally loud on the bare wooden floor. The door squeaked more than he remembered. The letter wasn't on his desk where he thought it was. "Broudette," he mumbled, going into the lieutenant's office. "Where the hell—" the desk was clean "—would he put it?"

The top drawer was empty. At last Jack found a box full of unfinished work on top of Broudette's filing cabinet, moved it to an empty table, and started rummaging through it. Requisitions, requests for orders, resignations, lists of deserters, and assorted malefactors complete with descriptions of the men and the crimes they had purportedly committed, another list of escaped prisoners of war.

A name leaped from the page. Travis stared. "My God," he whispered, shocked. "McKenna, Lion Burleson, Colonel, CSA. Escaped from prisoner-of-war train in company with Ryan, Miles H. (see Ryan, Miles H., Captain, CSA) night of 12/13 February, 1865. Location, twenty miles southwest of Boston. Probably armed, as a farmhouse three miles north of escape point was robbed that night. Escapees believed heading north, probably for Canadian border."

"Damn. Damn, damn, damn," Jack whispered, remembering the visit from Eve's clerk and Naslund. "Miss Eve is frightened," Jack said to himself, repeating Naslund's words. Good Christ, but it made frightening sense. McKenna had known the Blackheaths, had been at the wedding. Michael had hated him enough to chase him across the country and through a war. Whatever the reason, that hatred had been deadly. And the death might not stop with Michael. A cold chill swept through Travis. "O'Hearn!"

"Sir!" O'Hearn burst into the room, a startled expression on his face. "Yes, sir!"

"What time is it?"

The Corporal ducked into the duty room, reappeared immediately. "Five forty, sir!"

"How many men can you locate?"

O'Hearn winced. "Not sure, sir. It's Sunday afternoon. Most everybody has off. Might be one or two in the enlisted men's quarters. Another three or four live within a few blocks. But it'll be hard to find them. The war—"

Travis stood, advanced on Corporal O'Hearn. "You listen, Corporal, and listen well. I want at least six armed soldiers in civilian clothes ready to take the evening train to Boston with me, and I want them fast, do you hear? I don't care where you have to go to find them and I don't care what you tell them, but I want them here within fifty minutes. Not a minute less. Am I understood?"

O'Hearn thought his back would break, he was braced so tightly. "Yes, sir, Colonel. I think—"

"Don't think, Corporal. Move!"

O'Hearn spun and tore out the door. Jack stalked into his office and pulled down the map of Maine, checked reference numbers, and pulled out the folder with local maps, then the book of train schedules his predecessor had left him. The train for Boston left at six forty-five. And stopped, damn it, at every hamlet along the way. He could not hope to get to New Forest before nearly eight. Then they'd have to round up horses. A three-mile ride, more or less. Damn! He'd have to figure nine o'clock. An ungodly hour.

He had forgotten the museum and the opening of the exhibit and the pending job with Day. Jack sat at his desk and drew up maps of Dawn Wind from memory. His men would need them. Once on the train they'd review the situation, make what plans they could under the circumstances. By the time he finished it was six twenty. He folded the maps, went back into Broudette's office, and found a heavy cloak. Still no O'Hearn. Anxious, he paced the duty office and watched the clock.

At six twenty-eight O'Hearn burst through the door. "Five, sir," he announced, barely able to speak. "Two in the barracks, and I found three more at home." He winced as if expecting to be struck. "No one told them they were supposed to be available until tomorrow morning, sir. Besides, everyone's celebrating—"

"Good work," Travis said. "Let's go."

O'Hearn paled. "Sir?"

"You heard me. Let's go. I said six men. You're it," he said, starting down the stairs.

"But, sir!" O'Hearn wailed, hanging back in the doorway. "The duty. I have the duty. I can't—"

"Move, O'Hearn! Now!"

The men were waiting below. Jack told them briefly that a dangerous situation had developed in New Forest, that he would explain on the way. They all piled in the carriage, leaving O'Hearn to hang on as best he could, and started off the base. "What the hell?" Jack began, as the carriage slowed.

The streets of Portland were full. People shouted, shot off firecrackers, actually danced in the middle of the street. Travis whipped the horse, cursed at the crowds to get out of his way. The station was still a quarter mile away. "What the hell is happening?" he shouted to O'Hearn.

"I tried to tell you, sir. The news came over the wire just before you got to the office. General Grant has beaten General Lee at Appomattox, and Lee has surrendered all his forces. Unconditionally. Their back's broke, sir!"

Lee surrendered! For all intents and purposes the war was won. The South couldn't go on without the Army of Virginia. And yet . . . Jack whipped the horse again, cursed at a dancing couple blocking his way. New Forest might not have heard yet. And McKenna might not give a damn about the war. Michael certainly hadn't. The war might be over for General Lee, but it wasn't for Jack Travis. Not yet.

A rocket went up to his right. The horse shied, and kept on going. Ten blocks away Jack heard the Boston train whistle. Sweating, frantic, he laid the whip to the horse and maneuvered through the crowd. Eve was still in danger. That above all else he had to assume. Beneath the black velvet mask his ravaged face began to ache.

Chapter 38

THE HORSTMANN STANDARD UNIFORMS
Wm. H. Horstmann Co.
Philadelphia
Fifth and Cherry streets

YOUR MONEY BACK
without a word, for any
and all articles not
exactly right

THE CARE OF THE UNIFORM
When not in use every part of the uniform should be kept in the
proper compartment of this valise, and those articles that contain
gold or silver embroidery, laces, or metal mountings should be
thoroughly wrapped in tissue paper . . .

Most uniforms become shabby more from the way they are kept
than from any actual wear they get.

Once a customer always a customer.

Alone in the cupola, Lion closed the cedar chest that still contained Michael's dress uniform. As suggested by the manufacturer's
warning on the inside of the lid, those articles that contained metal
had been thoroughly wrapped in tissue paper. The uniform was almost new. It had been worn only three times. Lion sighed, pushed
the chest back under the window seat from where he had taken it.
Fancy uniforms, gloriously accoutred, for a shabby, bloody, dirty
war. Wear had turned his own uniform into a bunch of rags that had
been discarded long ago.

The rain, dumped in driving sheets from a line squall that had
swept in from the northwest, was stopping now. Lion stood, gazed
out through the windows as thunder rolled around him. Uniforms.

Thunder. Cannons. For all the months of war he had fought through, he had participated in only one major battle. The notion amused him grimly. The rest had been running and hiding and killing and butcher's work in a hundred unnamed glens or villages, gruesome skirmishes all, like the trial at Printer's Gap. And still he couldn't stop. Not with honor.

James Ruell slept. Eve tucked his arm under the covers and bent down to kiss his forehead. The grandfather clock in the hall struck eight thirty. Too early to go to bed, but nothing to do if she stayed up. At least, she thought, sitting at her dressing table, the next day would see the end to their trial. Ten thousand dollars was a reasonable price to be left alone. She entertained no delusions about getting through the morning without trouble of some sort, but was counting on Lion to see that his mad companion caused no real harm. Not yet tired, she undid her hair, shook it out, and began to brush it until it flowed about her shoulders like a golden mantle.

Each stroke of the brush gently tugged her head back. Each stroke became the mindless tick of a clock she lived, through which time funneled at varying and confusing rates. The next morning was an eternity away. The day Clifford died was lost in the dim past. By some quirk of mind, James Ruell appeared later on the scene. She had had him such a short while. And Lion? Lion ran through time, always there, never there. The moments he inhabited seemed, whenever she thought about them, to be just around the corner in the past where she could reach out and almost touch them. If only she had gone to him then, rather than listen to the hurt and angry pride that had kept her from him, the love they had found would have survived the war.

Their love? Did time recognize that love? Did it still exist? She had read his journal. He spoke of her often. But he spoke too of killing and hatred, and the unfortunate fact was that while his love was an important dream for him, killing and hatred were the realities that had determined his life four long years. War had leached the last vestiges of goodness from too many men, and there was no concrete reason to believe that Lion McKenna was different. Eve had loved him once, but the Lion McKenna she had loved laughed and danced and courted her.

Quietly, Eve rose and pulled her dressing gown about her. James hadn't stirred. Leaving him, she padded into the hall and started for the stairs, stopping only when she heard the measured tread of boots above her. She turned and went down the hall. Light spilled from the open door to the cupola. The footsteps stopped as she began to climb.

He was surrounded by mirrors, each one of which threw him back at himself in all his muddled confusion. Lion stood in the dead center of the cupola and stared at himself and the night beyond. His clothes, taken from Michael's wardrobe, hung on him like rags on a scarecrow. His face looked drawn and tight. In his mind's eye he saw himself as a warrior and then, after ocean lightning erased him, created him anew as a plain man with Eve at his side. He blinked, shook his head. She was still there. "We have to talk," he heard her say.

Lion spun, stared at her. Her long white silk dressing gown rustled as she stepped toward him. "Once, long ago," she said, "you found me here. As I have found you."

"You hadn't expected me to come upon you," Lion said. "I frightened you."

"No. I don't remember being frightened of you. Of what I felt, yes, but not of you. I wasn't frightened of you until later, when we made love for the first time. Even then—"

"Why did you come up here, Eve?"

Eve cocked her head to one side, looked quizzically at him. "I read your journal, you know."

"I guessed when I discovered it was gone. It wasn't written with that in mind."

"I know." The lantern lit one side of her face, left the other in darkness. "There were two Lion McKennas there. The one I loved, and still love, I think; and a stranger who spent his days killing and thinking of killing."

"That one—"

"I need to know, Lion," Eve interrupted before he could go on. "Which one survived? Is the Lion I loved still alive or should I bury his memory, in spite of all the ache and longing he still evokes in me?"

A smile touched the corners of Lion's mouth. The jagged line of silver hairs cutting across his black beard crinkled. "I've been asking myself that very same question," he said. "Standing here alone, wondering—"

"I need to know!" Eve insisted, steadying herself on the compass stand at her side. "Which one, Lion? What was your answer?"

"I don't know," he finally said. His neck felt stiff, his hands awkward. Standing still was an effort. "I like to think the first one, but I simply don't know. I'm too close to myself, too close to the war and everything that's happened during the past four years. I just don't know."

Eve inhaled deeply, tried to look into his eyes and found she couldn't. "I see," she whispered, turning to leave.

"Nothing is ever simple, Eve," Lion said quickly, stopping her. "I do know that I love you, never stopped and never will stop. The war will end one day, you know. But not my love."

Incredibly lovely in the soft light, Eve turned to face him. There was a heady sensuality in the lean, hard length of Lion's body that weakened her knees and made her want to go to him. But desire alone was a fragile bridge at best, easily swept away when its foundations were not firmly set. "And tomorrow?" she asked faintly. "Are you still leaving . . . tomorrow?"

"Only if you want me to," Lion answered. "If you ask, I will stay."

Eve shook her head no. "You—"

An explosion, followed by muted cries and more gunshots interrupted her. "Damn!" Lion moved around her without thinking and took the stairs at a run. Halfway down he caught a glimpse of Miles starting down the main stairs to the front hall. Eve close behind, Lion tore across the upstairs hall, plunged down the front stairs, and caught up with Miles. "What the hell's going on?" he shouted.

"Riders," Miles snapped. "I saw them from the front window upstairs."

Hanson Pole and Vernon came running up behind them. Lion shouted for them to get back, and in the same motion pushed Eve to the floor. "Where are the shotguns?"

"You!" Miles said, grabbing Sewal's chair and pulling it into the hall when Sewal's door opened. "Who the hell is it?"

"I don't have the slightest idea," Sewal growled.

"Miles!" Lion shouted. "Where the hell are the shotguns?"

"No time," Ryan shouted back, waving Lion off. "We find out now." His revolver dug into Sewal's back as he threw wide the doors and wheeled Sewal onto the porch.

Lion hesitated, followed Miles onto the porch. Men, apparently drunk, were circling their horses in front of the house and waving clay jugs in the air. "What's going on?" Sewal shouted, prodded by the gun in his back.

"Lee's surrendered, Mister Blackheath!" a cloaked figure yelled back as his horse reared. "Unconditional surrender!"

"The war's over! The war's over!" a second man whooped.

"We're spreading the news," the first man shouted. "The war's ended. Lee's thrown in his hand!"

Lion paled. He knew that surrender was inevitable, but that it had come so quickly was a shock that struck him in the pit of the stomach. Eve was beside him. She started to reach for him when a blaze of lightning illuminated the rider who had first spoken, revealing the black mask that covered half his face.

"Travis!" Eve exclaimed, caught off guard.

Hearing his commanding officer identified, the horseman nearest him threw away his jug and his pretended drunkenness, tossed aside the cloak that covered the weapons he carried, and leveled a revolver at Miles. "No!" Travis shouted, but at the same moment the soldier fired.

Lion shoved Eve toward the door, dived off the porch and onto the ground. Orange flame blossomed out of the darkness as other night-obscured soldiers joined the attack. Sewal threw himself back against Miles, knocking off his aim, then pushed forward and sent his wheelchair off the edge of the porch. Slugs raked the air, chipped wood from the front door as Eve stumbled against the sill. Lion hit the ground rolling, sprang to his feet and dodged Travis's charging mount. As the horse reared and struck at him, Lion dodged to the side, grabbed Travis's boot, and heaved upward, dislodging the man and sending him flying head over heels. Eve grabbed for Lion's shoulder, caught his shirt, and spun him off balance at the same moment a bullet glanced off Travis's saddle.

"For Chris'sake, stay down!" Lion yelled, pushing Eve away and grabbing for the horse's reins. Helpless, Eve watched him swing onto the horse. One boot dug into the panicked animal's side, the other clipped the jaw of a Yankee soldier as he raced forward brandishing a Spencer carbine. The soldier threw his arms wide and fell backward, flat in the dirt. Lion caught a glimpse of Eve. Their eyes met for a fraction of a second, and then he was gone, crouched low over the horse and charging into the night.

Travis rose from the ground, wiped mud from his good eye. Eve screamed as he raised his pistol and fired at Lion as he disappeared around the corner of the house. Evidently he was safe, for a dark form appeared a moment later and, riding fast, made for the land bridge. Lion was safe, Eve exulted—gone from her life again, but for the moment, safe.

"Are you all right?" Travis shouted, running to her and grabbing her by the arms.

"Yes. I think so," Eve said.

"That was McKenna, right?" Eve nodded. "They'll catch him when he tries to go through town. Don't worry. Where's James?"

The blood drained from Eve's face. "Oh, my God," she breathed, turning and starting to run up the drive. "He's in the house!" And then she saw the flames.

Miles Ryan had dodged the searching carbine fire. A lead slug peeled a strip of skin from his thigh, but other than that he was unhurt. He hurtled through the front door and collided with Hanson Pole, who had run from the dining room with the shotgun Miles had left behind. The shotgun flew across the foyer. Miles caught his balance, grabbed Pole by the back of his coat, and hurled the butler into a soldier who had just appeared in the doorway. No sooner had he slammed the door after them and retreated down the hall than the glass window in the door shattered, followed by a soft explosion as a coal oil lantern on the wall over his head burst.

Burning oil leaped from the wall and spewed onto his coat. Miles howled, twisted to free himself of the flames, then forgot them as Vernon, an iron poker raised over his head, emerged from the dining room. Miles shot him in the chest. The stable keeper was blown back inside the dining room. His body swept crystal from the tabletop, splintered china as his arm jerked convulsively. He died with the back of his head resting in a porcelain tureen shaped like a hen. On fire, Miles stripped off his coat, picked up the shotgun from where Pole had dropped it, loaded it, and stood in the doorway to the dining room.

"You had a good idea, stable keeper," he shouted at the corpse. "An eye for an eye and a tooth for a tooth. You damn Yankees left us nothing but burned homes and fields and the graves of our children. And now you think it's over, right?" His face was red and he was screaming, his voice a nearly unintelligible shriek of fury. "Right?" he howled to the four walls. "Right? Well, wrong! The war has come North! It's come North at last!"

The shotgun bellowed smoke and flame. The chandelier over the dining room table came crashing down from the ceiling, its ornate miniature lamps spewing oil over the table and floor. Miles kicked his burning coat into the room, and watched with maniacal glee as first one then another puddle of coal oil burst into flame.

"How do you like that, Mister Blackheath?" he screamed, moving across the hall into Sewal's room. Bullets from outside shattered the window, but none hit him. Miles raced across the room, picked up the lantern from Sewal's bedside table. "And this? How do you like this?" Oblivious to the rifle fire directed against him, he dashed around the room throwing oil on the drapes and furniture. "The war has come to the North! The war has come to the North!" he cried over and over again, finishing by smashing the lantern against the wall.

Fire raced around Sewal's room. Miles backed into the hall, stepped away from the flames that licked out of the dining room. None of the servants was in sight. He guessed rightly that the ones left downstairs had broken out the back way. He was alone. A smile-grimace enveloped his face as he whirled and danced between the flames. And then stopped. He was not alone after all. A small boy stood at the top of the stairs.

Jubb and Eustacia, their nightclothes flapping around them, stopped at the corner of the house when they saw the strange men lined up across the drive. "It's all right!" Eve called to them, waving them on. Terrified, they ran past the flames shooting out of Sewal's window and stopped at Eve's side. "Where's James?" she asked. The look on their faces drove like a thorn into her heart. Eve spun around and ran toward Travis, who caught her as she tripped over her torn gown. "James is in there!" she gasped. "Jack, my God, do something!"

Flames leaped from the dining room windows. A tinkle of glass followed by a soft *whoosh* sounded, and more flames erupted from the windows on either side of the hall.

A soldier had helped Sewal to his wheelchair. The older man worked himself closer. "What is it?" he yelled, over the crackling of the fire.

"The boy's inside," Travis snapped. Sewal slammed his fists against the armrests of the chair, and looked helplessly at the blaze. "O'Hearn, Abberly!" Travis called. He jerked his head toward the house. "Get in there. See what you can do!" The men handed their rifles to two of their fellows, and ran up the drive toward the house. He had four men left. "Baker and Oliver! Get around back and keep an eye peeled! Sergeant Banks and you, private, stay here with me."

O'Hearn and Abberly reached the front porch, kicked open the door and, shielding their faces, darted inside. Eve held her breath. Suddenly, gunfire sounded. A second later O'Hearn, one of the sleeves of his coat on fire, came flying back out and rolled across the porch. The unnamed private was at his side in a moment, beating out the flames on O'Hearn's arm and dragging him away from the house. Travis and Eve ran to his side.

"Abberly's dead, sir," O'Hearn gasped, wincing with pain as Travis pulled the still smoldering coat off him. "That Reb in there's crazy. He's up at the top of the stairs throwin' lanterns. He's got the boy, I'm pretty sure. Abberly tried to make it up the stairs for the boy, but the Reb shot him outright, and then tried for me."

"What about the back way?" Travis asked, forcing himself to remain cool.

"Don't know. Flames all along the hall. And smoke. Couldn't see too good, especially not knowin' the house and all. Ma'am? I wouldn't go in there."

"Eve!" Jack shouted, jumping up and grabbing her by the arm. "Where do you think you're going?"

"Inside. My son—"

"No, damn it!"

"Let me go," Eve shrieked, twisting free of him.

Jack lunged for her, caught her again and pulled her back from the house. "He'll kill you! Sergeant Banks!"

"Sir!"

"Hold this woman," he ordered, pushing Eve into the sergeant's arms.

"Travis, please! For the love of God!"

Banks's arm held Eve's waist. His free hand grabbed for her wrists as he tried to keep her from scratching his face and eyes. "Sorry, ma'am. Come on, now! Oww!"

"For the love of God, Travis! For the love of God!"

"There's nothing you can do, Eve!"

Eve tried to break free. Suddenly, sobs convulsed her and she collapsed in Banks's arms, weeping as the man pulled her away from the rising heat of the conflagration.

"Maybe there's something I can do," a voice said.

Adrenalin coursed through Eve's veins. She twisted free of the sergeant's hold. "Lion! James is in there!"

"You're under arrest," Travis snapped, reaching for his horse's reins.

"He's in there with Ryan."

"I know," Lion said. His hand touched Eve's cheek. Her fingers gripped his wrist. "Let go!" he ordered Travis, at the same time jerking free the reins. "Stay here! I'll try the back!"

"Hold, I say!" Travis shouted, raising his revolver.

"No!" Eve shrieked. Her arm slashed across Travis's. The gun blasted out a chunk of dirt three feet in front of them. His expression furious, Travis shoved Eve aside and brought up the revolver again. "He isn't escaping," Eve cried. "He's going after his son!"

The boy was Lion McKenna's! And the woman too. The barrel wavered. Travis studied Eve for a long second as he nodded, and lowered the pistol. Drained, Eve slumped to her knees and buried her face in her hands. Beside her, Travis and Sewal watched helplessly as the windows in her room exploded outward, and let loose a great gout of flames.

Glass from the explosion rained on Lion as he rounded the side of the house. The back was not yet fully involved in the fire. Lion brought the horse to the kitchen door, leaped off, and charged inside. The kitchen was clear of flames, as were the stairs to the main floor. The hall was another matter altogether. Shielding his face, Lion plunged through the dense smoke. Flames licking out of the dining room and Sewal's room had enveloped the bottom of the main stairs. Lion leaped, caught hold of the bannister, and hauled himself onto the smoldering carpet. He tensed for the bullet that would send him rolling down into the blaze. His throat filled with thick mucus and his lungs felt seared. He tried to keep his head low, but the stairway acted as a huge chimney that sucked smoke up and past him.

"North! North! How do you like it? Child-killers! Plunderers!" Miles's screams cut through the crackle of burning drapes and walls and furniture. A tinkle of glass, followed by another.

Lion reached the top of the stairs, fell to his hands and knees, gasping. The air was hot but there was little smoke. Miles had been diabolically thorough. All the doors were open, and Lion could see into Justin's room where the windows had been smashed out in order to feed the fire with fresh air. Ahead of him, dragging a burning drape, Miles emerged from the guest room, turned, and dancing wildly, tossed the drape back through the door. He carried James under one arm. His arms and legs dangling limply, the boy appeared to be unconscious.

Lion dared not risk a shot. Ducking low, he ran. Miles turned and saw him, grabbed the Colt revolver from his belt and fired. Lion's side felt as though he had been hit with a club. Spinning with the blow, he dove for Miles's legs. Miles dropped James and fell. Lion scrambled onto the man's chest, grabbed Miles's hair and slammed the crazed man's head against the floor until he stopped moving.

His side was numb, but pain knifed through his chest. Breathing raggedly, Lion sagged forward, shook his head to rid himself of the pain. Flames from the guest room reached for him. Willing his arms and legs to work, he crawled to James. The little boy was conscious. He raised his chubby arms and circled Lion's neck as Lion lifted him.

"I'm not scared," James whimpered, fighting back tears and digging his head into Lion's neck. "I'm not scared."

"Good boy," Lion said, his mind racing. "Now let's get out of here, all right? You just hold on, do what I tell you . . ."

Both front and rear stairs were out of the question. The bedrooms were so filled with flames that reaching the escape ropes in them was impossible. The only hope was the cupola, and the knotted rope that was coiled out of the weather in a box on the widow's walk. Lion stood, fought the pain in his chest, and rushed up the stairs into the cupola. A combination of night and heavy smoke trapped by the closed windows made it impossible to see. Lion coughed, groped his way toward where he thought the door was. The floor was hot beneath his boots and would soon burst into flame. If he could get out and shut the door behind him without venting the fire, and if the roof next to the cupola stayed whole long enough, they could get down safely.

He found the handle, opened the door. A billow of smoke followed him onto the widow's walk. He closed the door quickly, but even that little venting had given the flames a chance. At least there was fresh air outside. Balancing the pain of his broken rib against the necessity for oxygen, Lion gulped in huge lungsful as he made for the escape rope on the far side of the cupola. Below, he could see Eve shouting and pointing toward him. Sewal was next to her, and two other men. There was nothing any of them could do but watch, and pray.

The latch on the box was rusted shut. Lion set James down and kicked at it, finally smashed it with his heel. Suddenly, the glass behind him shattered. Lion tried to turn, but an arm locked around his throat and bent him backward.

"A son for a son!" Miles cackled in his ear. "An eye for an eye!" Lion's windpipe was being crushed relentlessly. "He's mine, McKenna! Mine!"

One window gone, the others exploded outward and the cupola, waiting only for fresh air, burst into flames like a torch. Lion drove his elbow back once, twice, a third time. Ryan grunted. Again and again. Ribs cracked and pain at last exploded through Miles's unbalanced mind. Choking, Miles let go and clawed at Lion's face as Lion whirled around and drove his shoulder into the madman's chest. Miles tripped over the sill and fell into the fire. Lion grabbed at his belt, but his gun was gone. Streaming ribbons of blood, his trousers catching fire, Miles rose to his knees. The dragoon Colt revolver he had snatched from Lion's belt was in his fist, and pointed at his son.

Lion stepped in front of the boy.

"Suit yourself!" Miles croaked, and thumbed back the hammer. At the same moment the floor of the cupola collapsed, and Miles plunged down into the horrid hellfire he had created. One final, tormented scream rent the air before it too was consumed by the roaring flames.

Lion tore off his coat and ripped open the collar on a piece of broken glass. "Get on my back!" he shouted to James. "Put your arms around my neck and hold on!" As soon as the boy was in place, Lion pulled on his coat again and fastened his belt on the outside of it. Even if James lost his grip, he wouldn't fall.

Lion threw the rope across the roof and climbed over the railing after it. "You ready?" he asked, checking the knot.

"I'm not scared," James Ruell repeated, his eyes clenched closed as Lion passed the rope in a loop around his waist.

"Me neither," Lion grunted, and started a slow, controlled backward fall down the steeply pitched roof.

The roof was easy enough. Loping, he hopped backward until he reached the edge. Lion stopped, leaned back as far as he could, and looked down. The windows in Eve's bedroom were directly below him and alive with fire. Slowly, he worked his way to his right, and paused again. Above him, no more than a quarter way up the roof, a tiny spot under the rope glowed red and then burst into flame.

Worried that the rope wouldn't reach to the ground if he went farther right, he quickly moved left, past the deadly window below.

"Here comes the hard part. Hold on tight." There was no way he could go down the side of the house with the rope looped around him. Swiftly, he let go with his right hand, felt the end of the rope fall free, and grabbed it again just below his left hand. Dropping to his knees then to his belly, he let himself slide over the edge and started down, hand over fist.

Fire surrounded them. Flames shot from windows, licked through the walls. Flames burned the hair from the back of Lion's hands and blistered the bloodied skin. "I'm not scared," James repeated over and over in Lion's ear, until his voice was all that existed, save the pain.

Lion had begun to cry. The rope above them was on fire. His face tucked inside the crook of his arm, he lowered himself inch by excruciating inch. Somewhere nearby, part of a wall collapsed. Lost in a shower of sparks, he almost let go his grip, but held on for dear life.

"Lion!"

The voice broke through the flames. He'd almost blacked out. Vast clouds of darkness closed in around him. He forced them back. Why aren't I climbing, he wondered numbly. What's happening here? Let go. Let go.

"I'm not scared."

"Lion!"

He hurt. Let go! Let go!

"Lion!" Eve's voice. Where was she? "Climb down! Climb down!"

I hear you, he thought to himself. *I* hear. Her voice pushed back the darkness and he began to move again, his poor burned hands leaving a bloody trail along the knotted rope. And then his fingers simply would not hold him any longer. Wide-eyed, he stared at his useless hands and felt himself slide through the air and into darkness.

The soldiers broke his fall. Helpless, only half conscious, Lion felt them carrying him away from the fire, felt the cool ocean breeze on his face, felt the boy squirming inside his coat. At last they lay him down and helped James out. Eve sank to the ground next to him and cradled his head in her lap, at the same time held her son pressed against her breast.

"I helped him, Mama."

"I know you did," Eve replied, unable to take her eyes off Lion.

"I wasn't scared, neither."

"I know, I know." Her face wet with tears, she pulled him forward, and together they hugged Lion.

Lion opened his eyes. Breathing was difficult. He felt as though someone had driven a red-hot poker through his chest. The light from the fire glowed like gold, instead of flames. It was Eve's hair, spilling across his face. His hands burned terribly. A voice was whispering in his ear. "Stay," it sounded like. "Oh, Lion, stay. Stay, stay, stay . . ."

He groaned, twisted his head in order to get fresh air. Eve lifted her head. In the light of the fire, he could see her. Her hair fell around her soot-smudged, tear-streaked face. Next to her, his eyes serious, James looked down at him. Lion licked his lips with his tongue, tried to clear his throat. "You . . . want . . . me . . . to?" he croaked. Eve's hand was cool on his forehead. Her head nodded up and down. "And . . . your . . . son?"

"Your son too," Eve whispered. "Our son. We want you to stay. Forever."

Lion's eyes closed. The pain in his hands and side was a distant, throbbing entity that existed in a world different from the one in which he found himself. He could feel Eve's hand on his forehead, his son's on his arm. He could feel the back of his head resting on Eve's thigh. He could smell the ocean freshness, hear the far-off crackling of the flames that ate away at the remains of Dawn Wind. He could feel each cell of his face and cracked lips as they bent into a slow smile that he couldn't have stopped for all the pain in the world.

"I . . . will, then," he said. "Forever . . ."

Epilogue

Ambrose Duquesne escaped the fall of Richmond carrying little but the clothes on his back. Later, his name surfaced alongside that of the ill-fated Maximilian. With the collapse of French influence in Mexico, Duquesne disappeared into Central America with a substantial portion of the Mexican treasury.

Hanson Pole and Jubb and Eustacia Peters continued in their

ways of mutual harassment and affection. Pole never learned to swallow coffee, and Jubb never lost his taste for hard cider. Eustacia never stopped complaining about stolen pies, but to the end she was secretly pleased.

Hamlet Peters, having been robbed of his ill-gotten gain during his first night in New York City, took odd jobs and slept where he could, all the while trying to earn passage money to Monrovia. During the Draft Riot that ravaged New York City in 1863, the unfortunate young man was hanged. Blamed for a war that was none of their doing, nearly a thousand black men, women, and children were beaten and lynched during those tragic days.

Jack Travis resigned his commission within a month of the events at Dawn Wind and headed west. There, in spite of the enigmatic mask he wore, he disappeared in the vast horde of pioneers seeking new homes and new lives.

Rosamond sought and received an annulment of her marriage to Michael on grounds of desertion. She later married the stockbroker, who financed, in part, her father's unsuccessful bid for the Republican nomination for President at the convention in 1868. On his death, in 1873, she inherited the wealth and security she had wanted so badly from the time she was a little girl.

Justin did not become the foremost photographer of his day, but did succeed in capturing a unique view of his world. His fame spread, and by 1868 he owned his own studio in New York and shared another studio in San Francisco with Menschell Trullion. Justin's lifelong affair with a certain celebrated actress, Amanda Tracy, was one of the scandals of their day. He and Amanda—Tiara had at last chosen a name to live with—enjoyed their notoriety to the hilt.

Sewal Blackheath returned to his beloved shipyards and oversaw the design and construction of a new generation of smaller, sleek sailing vessels. He maintained a vigorous pace until suffering a second stroke in the spring of 1870. Sawdust and shavings at his feet, a half model in his hands, and the smell of wood in his nostrils, he died at his workbench in his shop. He was buried next to Jennifer Blackheath on the high hill where there was always a wind in the pines and the echo of the sea for company.

The cornerstone for a new Dawn Wind was laid on May 26, 1865. That same day Eve Blackheath Sarandon and Lion McKenna were married on the stone porch, all that remained of the old Dawn Wind. Two months later, after handing over the reins of the Blackheath

Shipyards to Sewal, the newlyweds traveled to Virginia. There, with considerable labor, they resurrected the McKenna family farm and, with Blackheath dollars, turned it into a vast estate that Eve named Blue Valley. In the years that followed, Lion and Eve divided their efforts between their two homes. Though the wounds of war were slow to heal for some, Eve and Lion were happy in their love. The joy of their life together was their two new sons and twin daughters—and James Ruell Blackheath Sarandon McKenna, who grew strong and honest and true, and lived his own story.

One final act remained, and that took place more than a hundred years later when a crew of laborers connecting outlying Kentucky farm roads to Interstate 75 uncovered a mass grave near a place called Printer's Gap. Highway workers gathered what few rusted memorabilia they could find among the bones, and paved over the rest.